THAT FAR LAND WE

DREAM ABOUT.

THAT FAR LAND WE DREAM ABOUT

Paul Irion

Trafford Publishing
Bloomington, Indiana

Order this book online at www.trafford.com
or email orders@trafford.com

Most Trafford titles are also available at major online book retailers.

Printed in the United States of America.

ISBN: 978-1-4269-4504-5 (sc)
ISBN: 978-1-4269-4505-2 (e)

*Our mission is to efficiently provide the world's finest, most comprehensive book publishing
service, enabling every author to experience success. To find out how to publish your book,
your way, and have it available worldwide, visit us online at www.trafford.com*

Trafford rev. 10/26/2010

 www.trafford.com

North America & international
toll-free: 1 888 232 4444 (USA & Canada)
phone: 250 383 6864 ♦ fax: 812 355 4082

Dedicated to

All the brave immigrants who came before us

That far land we dream about,

Where every man can be his own architect.

Robert Browning
Red Cotton Night-Cap Country

PREFACE

Immigration, whether it be from one continent to another or from one stage of life to another, is a universal experience. We dream of the liberating changes our immigrations will bring, and at the same time we find that we continue to be bound by the threads of our past

CHAPTER 1

Johann paced restlessly, back and forth across the empty attic room where he slept with his five brothers. Alone, he marched from wall to wall in a narrow path between the three large beds under the steep sloping roof, stepping around the railing that marked the stairs to the floors below. His breakfast churned in his stomach. Passing the mirror over the wash stand he saw the tears of anger that were running down his cheeks. A twenty-three year-old man, crying! He banged his fist against a beam of the half-timbered wall. The rough wood drew blood on his knuckles.

"I can't take much more of this...," he muttered and punched the beam again, adding a kick for emphasis. Flinging himself across the end bed he rehearsed in his mind the conversation at the kitchen table that morning, when his father had been talking with the older brothers, Karl and Julius. It was as if the rest of the family were not even there. A very every-day conversation, to be sure, but it relit the fuse of an accumulating resentment.

"The weavers say they want more money," Father had begun, his voice deep and solemn, "but if we pay any more, we'll have to push our prices up--our business could dry up!" He punctuated his sentences with chewing the dark hard crusts of the bread, "People will pay just so much for linen!"

Karl immediately had taken up the same tone, "*Ja*, you are right, *Vater*. Last time Wagner was here he complained about prices. He was trying to claim that he could buy the same quality goods cheaper in Neuhaus. He's wrong, but if he believes it, it could affect his trade with us." Karl massaged his clean-shaven chin. He had adopted this portion of Father's mannerism of stroking his beard as he talked. It seemed intended to give a certain authority to his words.

"Pompous ass," Johann muttered under his breath.

Mother cut more thick pieces from the big round, brown loaf, cradling it against her body, slicing with a deftness born of years of experience, stopping the blade just before it cut into her apron. "Who wants more bread?"

"I'll have some more...." Father reached for the butter. "Wagner's bluffing. We're asking a fair price. The weavers, *nicht wahr*, don't get very much for their goods. I'm sorry for them. I'd like to pay them more for the linen they bring in, but don't they know that it's only a matter of time until the steam looms put them all out of business? Then what will happen to their families?"

Johann had dipped his coarse, crusty bread into his bowl of buttered warm milk and tried to join the conversation, "I think that....."

Julius, always soft-spoken, had broken in without even noticing that he was interrupting, "God willing, the price of the cloth will go up and we will be able to pass some of the increase along to the weavers. I feel so sorry for them. They hardly make enough to feed their families. Two or three *Taler* a week sure isn't much. But what can we do?" He folded his pudgy hands across his ample waistline. Julius was his mother's son: soft of voice and body.

Johann began to walk back and forth again as he relived that breakfast conversation. "Just like always," Johann muttered to himself. "I've got as much right to an opinion as Karl or Julius." His gut twisted with the tension of anger and envy pulling against the family solidarity that he had been taught all his life. "For years I just kept my mouth shut... the nice obedient son. If I am to feel like a man, you've got to start treating me like one." His mind recoiled against the bars of his life like a caged animal

He threw himself across Karl's bed. There was just no place for him in the family linen business...no steady job. It wasn't easy to work only three months in Krämer's store, only six months in the gristmill. Steady jobs were scarce. The wheat crop failures of the past two years had put pressure on everyone. Only Karl and Julius could work with Father. There was no room for him and his younger brothers. It was bad enough not to have a decent job, but to listen to the talk about the business at every meal and to be constantly reminded that he didn't have any part in the family linen trade was bitter medicine. How could he ever find a woman and get married? How could he ever think about living under his own roof?

The dividing line between the men and the boys in the family seemed to fall in the sibling hierarchy between Julius and Johann. The elder brothers, Karl and Julius, together with Father, looked and acted like men. They spoke deliberately, and wisdom somehow seemed to attach to their words. Johann, the next oldest, was the shortest of the six sons, slightly built but wiry. His mother often told Johann that he reminded her of her schoolmaster father. Small comfort when he wanted to be accepted into the men's world.

The bedroom for six sons was in the loft of the old house Father had bought in 1820, shortly after he married. Around the railed opening in the center of the room where the steep narrow stair from below opened into the loft, three big beds with their straw-filled mattresses and snowy feather beds dominated the crowded room. Karl now claimed the right to sleep alone in his bed. When Gustav left home nearly a year ago, Julius had moved down to his place in the bed with Johann. Gotthelf and Hermann slept in the third big bed. The only other furniture in the room was a couple of chairs, a washstand and the big wardrobe which held their Sunday suits. Their everyday working clothes hung on two long rows of pegs on the end walls. The rafters over-head sloped steeply and four low windows under the eaves gave light to the room. Johann had to bend down to look out a small window near the floor along the front wall.

Endigen wasn't much of a town. Nestled among the green wooded hills of Lower Silesia, a few dozen houses stretched along both sides of the main road curving through the long, narrow town. Johann could see the towers of the two churches, a cross on one and a rooster on the other. Near them were the handful of stores and shops. On a rise in the land at the far end of the town stood the three windmills, their sails slowly turning on this day. At the bottom of the hill were the watermills, their wheels turning by the dammed-up waters of *das Goldener Bach*. Farm wagons and ox carts passed along the road every now and then.

Johann walked over to the back wall. Looking through the window under the edge of the steep roof, he could see his mother stooping over the rows in the garden pulling beets for their next meal. The clothes she had washed just after sunrise were hanging on the line across the yard and draped over the bushes behind the garden. A short, plump woman, she stood up, stretched to straighten her back, then bent to pick up the basket of beets, stopping at the root cellar to fill the basket with potatoes. She slowly walked toward the kitchen door. Although younger sister Luisa was old enough to be some help, every day for *Mutti* it was wash--cook--clean--

3

garden; wash--cook--clean--garden; wash--cook.... She's as trapped as I am. I wonder if she feels it, Johann thought. His eyes filled with tears again, but he didn't know whether they were for his mother or himself.

He was well aware that in many ways they were really a fortunate family. They did not have to endure the grinding poverty of so many of the families in the town and surrounding valley. The linen trade provided a modest but steady income. They were certainly not rich, but Father managed to save some each year, even after caring for the needs of the family. He sent an occasional few *Taler* to his married daughter Mathilda in Lehmwasser. The six sons, all but Gotthelf and Hermann now in their twenties, contributed their earnings to the family income: Karl and Julius, contributed a portion of their "wages" from the linen shop for their board and lodging; Johann the little he earned in his jobs. Gotthelf, his younger brother, added what he could. Gustav had left home the year before to travel about as a dyer and had to use his sparse earnings to live now in Lübeck. Hermann wasn't old enough to earn much. Father took care of all their needs, as he always had done, and managed the family savings. A family business, indeed!

Johann, still wound tight with frustration, went down the steep stairs and out onto the road that passed in front of the house. He heard his mother in the kitchen but decided that it was best not to talk with anyone in his present state.

All his life he'd walked this road that ran down the center of the narrow village. He'd gone down this road hundreds of times to Hartmann's farm with the family milk pail. With the whole family he'd made the pilgrimage every Sunday to the large half-timbered church and its stone bell tower topped by its rooster weather-vane.

As a schoolboy for seven years he'd strode along this road; dusty one day, muddy the next. He usually walked alone rather than with the swirl of lads that bounded along and over the fences. On the way home from school he customarily made a few stops along the way, not only to postpone the chores that awaited him, but because he liked to talk to some of the folks who lived along the road.

There was old man Scharf, sitting under the tree in front of his house. Johann liked him. His bright eyes peered out between a shock of snow-white hair and his long grey beard, stained at the corners of his mouth. Old Scharf was filled with stories of things that had happened in the village during his boyhood and before. Johann stood with his slate and school book, leaning on the low, weathered picket fence that bordered the road, waiting for their daily visit to begin.

Old man Scharf held out an apple he had picked up from under the tree along the road, shining it on his shirtsleeve. "Hello, Johann. *Wie geht's?* What did old Radecke manage to teach you today?"

Johann fumbled with his book and walked slowly through the gate, accepting the apple. "We had a history lesson today. I knew my dates: when Luther put up the Ninety-five Theses and when the Thirty Year's War began. I knew them both," he said proudly, recalling Herr Radecke's praise.

Reinhold Scharf smiled, "Good for you, boy." He squinted into the sun. "Wittenburg may be all right in school." His lips smacked as he chewed his apple. "But let me tell you some history you can tell Radecke about this town, right here. Did you ever hear about the battle?

"No; a battle?" Johann, excited, sensed the beginning of a story.

"Well, about eighty years ago, just before my father was born, there was a battle right here outside of Endigen. I'll bet you didn't know that?"

Johann smiled, "I'll bet Herr Radecke doesn't know that either."

Old Scharf turned slowly to look up and down the valley. "The Prussians and them Austrians fought right here. My grandfather told me about it when I was a little shaver."

"Right here? Did a lot of people get killed?"

"Not in the village. But it was a real battle. Them Austrians come marching up from the south. The Prussians was up on the hill where the windmills are. They'd dragged a couple of big cannons up there. The Austrians marched toward the village from Wüstegiersdorf. They thought that they had the whole valley to themselves. As they was comin' marchin' up toward the village, all of a sudden the Prussians began to shoot over the roofs of the houses, right into them Austrians. Their cannons drove 'em back real fast into the fields and the Prussian soldiers come marchin' down the road toward the center of the village and right through, even though the Austrians were takin' some shots at 'em." Old man Scharf acted out his tale, marching, sighting his cannon, firing his imaginary musket. "They kept right on marchin' toward them Austrians, stopped ever' now and then to fire a volley. The Austrian soldiers saw that they was outnumbered and really moved outa here fast."

"How long did the battle last?" Johann asked, amazed at how many stories old man Scharf had stored up in his head.

"My grandfather told me 'twas all over in an hour. All the people of the village hid in their cellars. With all them cannon balls and bullets flying around, I tell you, it musta been mighty scary. Nobody in the town got shot but a few soldiers on each side was hit."

Johann gasped, "I hope I never see anything like that. That would be awful!"

"I think three Austrians and one Prussian soldier got killed, and a bunch of 'em was wounded. I tell you, it was quite a battle." Old man Scharf, animated by the drama of his own story, took another big bite out of his apple. "I bet you never heard of that before."

"A big battle, right here in Endigen?" Johann said, impressed.

Old man Scharf squinted at his young pupil and said, "Next time you're down by the church on a bright day, you stand on the shady side of the church and look up at the cock on the tower. You can see two bullet holes in it. They're from that battle. I bet you never knew that."

Wide-eyed, Johann thought about how he'd impress his buddies on the next sunny day. The schoolyard was right next to the church so they'd be able to see the bullet holes. None of the boys had ever noticed them, and, even if they had, nobody would know that they came from a real battle, right here in Endigen; not until he told them old man Scharf's story.

Interrupting Johann's childhood memories, the clock in the church tower struck eleven. He glanced up at the tower with its riddled rooster. His destination was Father's linen shop down the main road a little distance beyond the church. As he walked he kicked a stone along the road. He couldn't cover up his feelings any longer. He had to find out if he would ever have any future in Endigen.

Under his breath he said, "I hope Karl and Julius aren't right there. I need to talk to Father alone."

As he approached the shop, he saw that two weavers from the little farms along the Seitendorf Road sat on their barrows in the shade behind the shop, waiting for Julius to measure the goods they had brought in. Johann thought of the hours of work that the weavers had carried into the warehouse, the labor of wives and children working with the flax, spinning the threads. Only their hands knew the countless throws of the shuttle back and forth on the looms which dominated their one-room cottages. On most days they worked from dawn until there was not enough evening light coming through the window by the loom.

Johann saw Karl come to the door of the warehouse. The weavers held out their calloused hands for the coins Karl paid them. Then they pushed their empty barrows along the road past the graveyard between the two churches. Johann knew that they would go next to Krämer's store to buy a little sugar or salt and then to the mill for a sack of flour. He had seen the process dozens of times when he worked there.

He felt the weight of his own frustration when he thought of them making the long trudge home, the coins passed through, the week's flour bought. With the potatoes and cabbages from the root cellars, this would sustain them for spinning and weaving yet another week. Then it would be time for another walk with the barrows to Weber and Sons.

Standing at the corner of the shop Johann heard voices from the dimness of the warehouse. "*Es tut mir leid.*" Julius was saying to Karl. "They have to work so hard and get so little for it. I feel sorry for them. I don't see how they manage to live; God help them."

Johann could not hear all of Karl's response, but he was sure it was stern. Karl shared his brother's concern for the weavers, but he had little of the softness of Julius. Not unlike his father, he was a practical man, not swayed much by sentiment. His world was ordered by Providence, and piety required that one faithfully submit to that order. "Life is hard for them, *Ja wohl.* They've never known anything but poverty. One can only believe that God will reward their faithfulness and hard work in the world to come."

"I always worry that we could end up the same way. What if the spinners and weavers had to give up working. We wouldn't have any linen to sell. We'd be wiped out," Julius answered.

Johann thought of the bolts of cloth on the shelves, representing so many hours of toil at the nearly 300 looms in the cottages in and around Endigen.

Again Karl's voice came out of the warehouse, "*Ja*, it could all pass away. Nothing on this earth endures. 'What profit hath a man of all his labor which he taketh under the sun.' We do what we can in the time the Lord gives us."

Johann muttered, "Not me, brother. I won't just be piously satisfied with the trap I'm in. Something has to change."

Still unobserved, he slipped around to the front of the shop, relieved to know that the brothers were back in the warehouse. Father was standing at his desk in the corner. He looked up to see who was coming through the door. "Why Johann, I wasn't expecting to see you here. Karl and Julius are out in back if you're looking for them."

"No," Johann said, "I need to talk to you, *Vater.*" His voice sounded odd in his tight throat. It was as if he were hearing his words coming out of a long tunnel.

Gottlieb Weber stood erect, ran his hand over his curly beard in puzzlement. "*Was ist los?* Is something wrong at home?"

"No. It's nothing like that. I...I don't know how to say it...Father," Johann swallowed hard, "...I am really grateful for everything you do for us....I don't know what is going on in me. Can I talk to you about it? Now?"

Gottlieb nodded, not knowing quite what to expect. He put down his pen on the open ledger.

"What bothers me, Father, is....I'm old enough to start thinking about being on my own. I should be getting into a business like Karl and Julius...."

"That would be pretty hard to do," Gottlieb said, "You can't expect me to make miracles. You know that there isn't enough business to...."

"I don't really feel like a man, Father, just working for a few *Taler* at one job after another. I know that there are men in the village who live all their years like that, but I'd go crazy if I had to live without a steady job. I've got to do something!" Johann paced back and forth in front of his father, and then banged his fist on the desk.

Surprised by the uncharacteristic display of anger, Gottlieb asked, "What is it you want? You've got to be more patient... Look, it took me a long time to build up this business. My father didn't just hand it to me." His voice became deeper and stronger as he sensed what Johann was asking. "We just do not have enough business to keep all my sons busy. I know that life is painful for.... "

Johann persisted. "What kind future do I have here?" Johann banged down his fist again. "I feel like a little boy putting my few *Kreuzer* on the table every Saturday, and, even worse, having no *Kreuzer* on some Saturdays. I just drift around. Gustav felt the same way. That's why he is traveling around on his own. He doesn't make enough money to send home, I know, but at least he isn't just standing around Endigen waiting for work..... Can't I do anything?"

Stroking his beard, as if thinking out loud, Gottlieb said, "You are serious,..aren't you?" He paused, "You know...Wagner...who comes in here every two-three weeks from Neuhaus to buy linen to dye....He was saying that he was looking for an apprentice. I don't know if he has found anybody. Do you want me to talk to him next time he comes in? That would be one way to learn a trade."

Having asked his father for help, Johann hardly felt able to refuse. Apprentices were lads, not men in their twenties. It wasn't really what he had had in mind. He wanted to be treated like a man...responsible...taking care of himself...making his own decisions....But being an apprentice could hardly be worse than his present situation. Several years with Wagner wouldn't offer him any independence. Still, if he could become a master dyer, maybe have his own business, he could tie into the family business. Instead of just buying and selling the linen from the weavers, Weber & Sons could offer a finished product. If that ever could happen, it was years away.

"All right. See what Wagner says when he comes in next time. I've got to do something. I can't go on this way."

"I'll ask him," Gottlieb said and picked up a sheaf of orders from the desk, a clear signal that the conversation was over and it was time to go back to business. Johann turned to leave, just as Karl and Julius came through the door from the warehouse, surprised by their younger brother's presence.

Julius chuckled, "What brings you down to the shop--looking for work?"

Johann winced inwardly but kept up the humor. "Just taking a leisurely walk around town to see that all the boys here are earning their pay." He ducked out the front door as Julius laughingly threw a wad of paper at him.

Standing outside the door, Johann heard Gottlieb saying to his sons, "Johann was talking about finding new work. We just don't have enough business for him to work here, too. I mentioned to him that last week Wagner said he was looking for an apprentice. He may have found somebody, but if he hasn't, do you think Johann would work out?"

Karl, as always, spoke first, "It'd be a good chance for that young fellow to learn a trade. It would also give him some discipline...make him more responsible. I'm not at all sure he'd stick with the three years of apprenticeship. If he walked away from the apprenticeship, Wagner might get angry with us for talking him into it."

Gottlieb thought for a moment, "I doubt that. He has always been a fair man around here."

Karl went on, "Wagner could teach him a lot...he's a pretty stiff sort of fellow...no nonsense, lots of hard work." He paused, stroking his chin, "*Ja*, it might do Johann good."

Julius didn't seem so sure. "I'm afraid he would grind Johann down. Johann has an independent streak that would fight back against a hard-driver like Wagner. God be with him."

"He's got to find something more permanent soon," Gottlieb answered. "He's right when he says that the jobs around here don't have any future."

Julius went on, "*Ja*, when he was working at the mill, it looked good for a while. But then two years with very little grain raised, the job just dried up like the fields. There's barely enough grain to grind for the local folks. I felt sorry for him. That's the second or third time he has lost a job. No fault of his own; he can do the work. But he really seems to be plagued by bad luck."

Father Gottlieb ended the conversation. "I'll talk to Wagner. Now let's get to work on that order for the outfit in Waldenburg." He picked up the ledger from his desk and said, "How many bolts do we have in stock?"

Johann slowly retraced his steps down the road. For the first time he was faced with the possibility of leaving Endigen. One part of him rejoiced: freedom, opportunity, a future...if he could just get through the apprenticeship. But at the same time, what would it be like not to see all these familiar sights every day: the church, the schoolhouse, the gnarled apple tree in front of old man Scharf's house? What would it be like...not to sit at the table in the kitchen three times a day with the family? Suppose he ended up worse off than in Endigen?

Johann went through the door and started for the steps upstairs.

His mother called from the kitchen, "Johann, *kommst du hier.* I want to talk with you."

"I was...."

"Something's wrong with you, boy," she said as she wiped her hands on the apron tied around her ample waist and ran the back of her hand over her brow. "I watched you coming up the path like I did when you came home from school or from working. There was no spring in your step. It reminded me of the few times when you got in trouble at school with Herr Radecke. You look like you've lost your best friend. What's the matter?"

"I was just at the shop talking with Father. I'm just so discouraged because there isn't any work in town. I thought maybe Father could give me work like he does for Karl and Julius, but he said that there wasn't enough business to do that."

Christiana put down the bowl of peeled potatoes, wiped her hands on her apron and said, "I know he worries about the business. Sometimes he gets up at night and just sits by the window. These are hard times all over the country. Gustav's last letter from Lübeck said that it was hard there too."

"I know, but it bothers me not to have a job, a steady job."

"It's not your fault. You were a good pupil in school; you know how to work hard. Reis said you did a good job at the mill. It's just the hard times...."

"Father is going to talk with Wagner from Neuhaus. Last time he was here he said he was looking for an apprentice. Father thought that maybe he'd take me, if he hasn't already found someone. Then I could learn the dyer's trade. It would mean leaving here and living with Wagner."

"Neuhaus isn't that far away. Wagner comes every couple of weeks to buy linen. You could come with him on his wagon and have a little visit."

"Once I learned the trade, I might be able to come back here and work with Father and the boys. We could sell finished goods."

"Learn the trade first! You may find that you want to work somewhere else. Gustav has worked in three or four cities since he started traveling last summer. So there would be chances to go a number of places."

Johann chilled a little at her words. He thought, Why do I always have to be compared to another brother. I even start thinking myself that I ought to be like Karl or Julius or Gustav.

Gustav, even though he was two years younger that Johann, had already begun to stand on his own. Last summer when he had protested that he wanted to leave Endigen and try his fortune in some other places, Gottlieb had resisted at first. The thought of his son starting out without a having a job waiting somewhere offended his sense of order. He had tried to talk Gustav out of his plan, claiming that he would be no better off in some strange town. Father Gottlieb felt a strong sense of responsibility for his sons. It pained him that his business was not big enough to put all his boys to work there. He realized that Endigen could not support them all. But he had always taken satisfaction in seeing all his young men around the family table. He liked to look along the family pew at the church and see his sons: Karl and Julius with their serious faces paying close attention to the pastor's sermon, Johann slowly turning the pages of his hymnbook, Gustav looking very thoughtful, Gotthelf and Hermann waiting for the service to end so that they could run home ahead of the rest of the family. Luisa sat by her mother. Gottlieb pondered the breaking of the family circle. First Mathilda married and left for Lehmwasser with August. Now Gustav would be absent, too.

At the beginning of his *Wanderjahr* Gustav had worked a short time as a dyer in Waldenburg and thought he might be able to find jobs dyeing cloth in some other places. It didn't seem to bother him that he spent only a few months in any place. His letters came from one town after another: Waldenburg, Breslau, Potsdam, Hameln, Lübeck. He usually was able to find lodging with his employer. His letters would tell of this or that fellow-worker with whom he had become friendly. He described beautiful churches, town halls, parks. He told about his journey from one place to another, often on foot, but sometimes invited to ride on a farmer's cart or a teamster's wagon.

The whole family listened with great interest when Gustav's letters would be read at the supper table. Father sat at the end of the long kitchen table with his back against the wall. Mother sat at the other end, closest to the cookstove, while the rest of the family sat on the long benches beside the table.

Johann was touched by the way Father always mentioned Gustav and Mathilda in the family prayers he led every evening around the table. He would take down the big family Bible from the shelf by the clock, open it carefully to the crochetted marker and read the chapter for the day. Then he would fold his hands and pray fervently for all the family, present and absent.

Johann occasionally opened his eyes to look over the bowed heads of the family. Karl's hands were tightly folded in front of him on the table, as he sat at attention. Julius' body was relaxed in pious devotion, his face serene. Gotthelf looked up, caught Johann's eye and gave a small, secretive wink.

After *Mittagessen* Johann helped his mother by filling the woodbox for the kitchen stove. Then he went out to sit on the front step. Just down the road he could see Dr. Felsman's house. The doctor's buggy, with his brown mare between the shafts, was tied to the rail in the shade of the large chestnut trees that overhung the front of the house. The doctor must be about ready to go out into the countryside to visit a few people who were sick. Johann waved as the white-haired doctor in his long black coat came out of the front door. The big house didn't look as nice as it used to. The flower gardens, once neat when Frau Felsman was alive, were becoming overgrown. A few pickets had come loose from the fence along the road. Johann guessed that the poverty of so many of his patients meant that there was no money to pay the doctor.

Dr. Felsman had cared for the villagers and farmers for nearly thirty years, and his father before him. Johann grimaced when he thought of the miserably bitter potions the doctor had mixed and given to his mother when he had the fever. No wonder he got well; anything to stop having to swallow that awful stuff. Now the doctor was on his way to another patient with his little black satchel full of bitter medicines and his bleeding bowl. There was probably more healing in his smooth, ruddy face and twinkling eyes, than in the little black satchel.

The buggy pulled up in front of the Weber house and Dr. Felsman in his deep voice said, "How are you, Johann?"

"*Ziemlich gut, Herr Doktor.*"

"Want to ride along...We'll be back in a couple of hours or less."

The chance for an activity which would turn him away from his preoccupation with his problem was inviting. Johann said, "Let me tell Mother that I am going with you."

Then he climbed into the doctor's buggy. He always enjoyed talking with the wise physician. The mare walked slowly, switching her tail. The wheels of the buggy squeaked as they turned and crunched on the stones of the road, nearly drowning out the deep voice of Dr. Felsman.

"I'm on my way out to old Mother Pröhlig's house. You know...the little cottage near the bridge on the Waldenburg Road."

"We always call it Hansel and Gretel's house." Johann thought of the bent, toothless old woman who could be seen walking slowly around the house. He didn't mention that the schoolboys all called her "The Witch."

"Poor old soul. She's had a hard life. When her husband died, she had four little children. She raised all but the one who died of diphtheria. Her eyesight isn't good any more, so she had to give up working her loom. She takes care of her little garden to keep herself alive. Her children have all moved away because they couldn't find work here. I don't know if they ever see her. I look in on her about once a month. She's all crippled up with rheumatism. My medicine doesn't do much good for her, but at least she has somebody to talk with for a little while."

"She must be very old."

"Not really so old. I don't think she's much older than your mother. She's just had a very hard life. Where are you working these days?" the physician asked.

"Not much work around town, *Herr Doktor.* I was working in Reis' mill but there wasn't enough grain coming in to keep us all busy. The dry weather kept the crop small. So I'm just helping around at home right now."

"I am sure your father is glad for that. He works too hard, every day from sun-up to sun-down at the shop. I'm glad he has taken the older boys in with him. He'll live longer if he doesn't have to work all the time."

Johann felt the tugs of gratitude and of envy pulling at his gut.

Doctor Felsman's buggy pulled up beside the little, run-down cottage. He climbed down slowly, took his satchel from the seat and walked toward the door. Johann stood at his side. There was no answer to the doctor's knocks.

13

"She must be taking a nap," Dr. Felsman said as he opened the door and poked his head in.

"*Mutter Pröhlig*," he called, but there was no answer. "Come along in, Johann."

The little house had only two rooms. In the front room there was her table and two chairs. There was a dry sink in the corner but it was empty. Her few dishes were on the shelf. There was no fire in her iron cookstove; no pot was on the stove. Her old loom stood in another corner, long unused. Some of the warp was still in place. The only thing that seemed out of place was her big bread knife which was lying next to the shuttle on the loom.

The doctor went to the door of the bedroom in the rear. Sometimes she sat in there. He knocked on the bedroom door but, again, no answer. He looked into the room. The bed was made and the chair was empty.

He turned to Johann, "She must be outside...probably in the little garden she keeps out back of that shed."

"I didn't see anyone as we drove up," Johann said.

As they walked out back, he continued to call, "*Mutter Pröhlig*!" He didn't want to frighten the old woman by catching her unawares.

When they came around the shed, there she was.

Her small body was hanging from her crabapple tree. Johann stopped in his tracks, an icy tremor running down his back. The doctor ran to her but realized at once that her body was stiff and cold.

"Johann, run back in the house and get that carving knife that was lying on the loom."

When Johann came back, breathless, Dr. Felsman said, "Here, help me get her down. Lift her up a little."

As they cut her down, he said, "Look, she cut warp from her old loom to make the noose. She must have pushed her old wheelbarrow out to the tree and climbed up to put the cords around her neck and then just stepped off. It must have been so hard for her with her rheumatic legs to get up on the barrow."

Johann wiped his hands on his pants after touching the dead woman. "How terrible it must be for life to become so hard that you don't want to live any more. Poor woman!"

As Dr. Felsman's buggy came slowly down the road into Endigen, the doctor's face was tired and drawn as he reined in his horse in front of the Weber house. Mother and Father stood in the doorway. Pointing to

14

a blanket wrapped bundle on the second seat, the doctor solemnly shook his head.

"Poor old soul," the doctor intoned. "We found old Mother Pröhlig hanging from the crabapple tree behind her house. I brought her body back to town."

Mother, wiping her hands on her apron, walked the few steps to the road. Looking at the small bundle in the buggy, she shook her head slowly, wiped her eyes with her apron. "I knew her since we were both girls. We went to school during the same time. How sad to take your own life. She had such a hard time after her husband died."

"She must have done it very early this morning," Dr. Felsman said. "Her neighbors said they saw her in her house just before dark last night. But when we went into her cottage, there was no fire in the stove. She hadn't cooked anything today. I guess nobody saw her hanging from the tree. Poor old soul."

Gottlieb bowed his head. "God have mercy on her. She was such a little woman. But she was a good weaver while she could still work. She worked hard to raise her children after Peter died. She'd come with cloth every two weeks. I always paid her a little extra money for her goods because I knew how hard life was for her."

The doctor said, "I brought her body back to town. She doesn't have any family around here any more. Her neighbors said they don't even know where her children live now. Her sight was so bad that she couldn't read, so I don't imagine that there are any letters around the cottage. We looked but didn't see anything. In fact, there wasn't much there at all."

Johann climbed down from the buggy.

"Where are you going to take her?" Christiana asked Dr. Felsman.

"I guess I'll take her to my house. They I'll go talk to the pastor and have Adolph Meier make a coffin for tomorrow."

"Suppose I get Hannah Scharf and we can come over in about an hour to lay her out. I'll watch for your buggy to come back."

"That'll be very good. Many thanks for your help." The doctor clucked his tongue and the mare moved slowly on toward home. They watched as he got slowly down from the buggy, picked up the old woman's body, wrapped in a blanket like a child, and carried her through the dusk into his house.

15

CHAPTER 2

Looking out his garret window over the rooftops of Lübeck, Gustav could see the tall tower and the heavy brick walls of the *Marienkirche* dominating the city's skyline, playing off against the solid ornate buildings which had headquartered the Hanseatic traders. Finished with his day's work in the small factory where he dyed wool for heavy winter coats, he reread the letter from his brother Karl. It was the first word from home he had had in more than a month.

Sitting on his bed, with the fading evening light coming into the small dormer window by his head, Gustav reached for the letter and read it for the third time. Karl, as usual, painted a dismal picture. His letters, although filled with strong, pious affection for his distant brother, were gray descriptions of the pale world of Endigen. Crops were poor, business was bad. In his words, "Only trust in the Lord's overarching goodness sustains this troubled world."

But this letter had turned from gray to black with Karl's solemn announcement that a letter from Berlin to Gustav had arrived, instructing him to report to Charlottenburg for service in the Prussian Army on August 4th. Gustav felt a chill of excitement with this word. Even though he had left Endigen for his *Wanderjahr* with an expectancy that only partially tempered his sadness over being parted from his family, he was thrilled by the thought of being on his own. For twenty-one years he had lived in the warm circle of the family. It was time to stand on his own feet, to get his own job, to support himself. He still remembered his feeling riding on Krämer's wagon to Waldenburg, looking back again and again over his shoulder until the two church towers of Endigen were hidden by the hills. Then, looking ahead, he sat tall on the wagon seat; he felt like a man.

Now he would have to give up his job and start the journey back to Endigen. He had only a little more than a month until August 4th. As he thought about the next three years in the army he could feel freedom slipping away. He had reveled in the independence of traveling about, making his own decisions, moving on to another job and another city when he felt ready.

It hadn't been an easy year. There were times when he was homesick and lonely. He had to be careful to make his money stretch until the next pay day. Wages for a traveling dyer were small, but he managed to pay the weekly rent for his little garret. He stopped on his way home from work to buy several *Brötchen* and an occasional *Wurst* at the little shop on the corner. When he could, he tried to put a *Kreuzer* or two into the little leather pouch at the bottom of his carpetbag. He didn't want to go back to Endigen, as he knew he would someday, with empty pockets. He was determined that he would show the family that he had been successful, no matter how small the scale of his success.

The army was going to be different. He had heard the stories from the young fellows in Endigen who returned from their service. Independence had no place in their description of army life. It was not an easy life in spite of the excitement of walking around in a uniform. He didn't have any choice in the matter, after all. He would be the only one of the six Weber brothers to go to the army, at least up until now.

The next day during the lunch time he drew his employer, Rudi Schmidt, aside. "Can I talk to you for a minute."

They took off the heavy leather aprons which protected them from the gray and brown dyes. Sitting on bolts of thick woolen cloth, tearing off pieces of long loaves of bread, Gustav began, "I got a letter from my brother yesterday. I am going to have to go home to *Schlesien*."

"Somebody sick?"

"No." Gustav looked at his stained hands. "It's the army! Karl said that I got the letter from Berlin. I've been drafted and have to report on August 4th. So I'd better get home. I won't be able to afford the train... have to allow plenty of time. I've always been able to find rides, but sometimes you have to wait to find somebody going the right direction."

Schmidt said, "Going to hate to lose you. You been a mighty good worker...Think I can line up a ride for you...far as Berlin. You know my cousin Hans? He was telling me that he was hauling a load of furniture to Berlin...Think he said the first of next week. He'd be glad for the company. You could help 'im load and unload in exchange for the ride."

17

"I could be ready whenever he wants to go. I really hate to leave here. You've been mighty good to me...giving me work when I just wandered into your place. I wouldn't have minded staying here for a while."

"Good luck to you. Hans'll fill your head with army stories. He was in for three years. He can show you the ropes." Schmidt clapped his young worker on the shoulder, chomped his final morsel of crusty bread, and reached for his apron. "Time to get back to work. If you're going to leave in a few days,..might as well get all the work I can out of you," he laughed.

Thick gray clouds wreathed the hills above Endigen. The air was still and the leaves hung limply from the trees. The windmills on the hill were not turning. There was the promise of rain.

It was time for one of Wagner's linen-buying visits to Endigen. On his last visit he had agreed with Gottlieb that Johann should become his new apprentice. Now he was coming for more bolts of linen and for Johann.

At breakfast Gottlieb had prayed fervently for God's blessing on the family, now adding the departing Johann to the absent company of Mathilda and Gustav. Even though he expressed the comfort of his unswerving confidence that the loving God would watch over them all, Gottlieb's voice wavered at the thought of a family dispersed. Johann knew that his father's joy was never as great as it was when everyone was gathered under the family roof.

Johann felt the family warmth and was grateful. But he also felt the relief of getting away from the town which held so little promise for his future. His conscience was wrenched by his envy of Karl and Julius for their favored positions

Father took out his watch, wound it, and announced, "Time to go to work." With his older sons he liked to be at the shop well before any of the weavers began to arrive with their goods.

"Wagner usually comes around ten. Why don't you bring your bag to the shop about then. It will take him an hour or so to get his order sorted out and loaded. I wouldn't want him to have to wait for you. You could help load his order. He should know he is getting a good worker."

Christiana touched Johann's arm. "I am making a lunch for you. I'll put in enough for Herr Wagner too." There was the hint of a forced smile on her round smooth face.

Johann lingered at the table when the others left the kitchen. He wanted a few moments more of this pleasant place: its comfortable warmth, its tantalizing smells of food, the ticking of the clock, the morning sun angling across of floorboards white with years of scrubbing. There were things here he would miss.

He would miss the people too. Mother's and Father's love were without question, but how little they knew him. They saw the quiet, dutiful son. On the surface they knew that he was frustrated with life in Endigen. But they couldn't know how worthless he felt, the depth of his self-doubt. Nor could they be aware of the deeper doubts he had about the world they shared. In spite of more than two decades of Sundays in the family pew he could not share their faith which promised that everything would work out for the best.

His parents saw all their children modeled after Karl and Julius: pious, hardworking, loyal, patient, devoted to family. It was simply assumed that in time everyone would surely grow into such solid, admirable adulthood. Johann knew deep inside that he was not cut from the same cloth. He was not sure that he had the courage of a true rebel, but the impulse was there. He knew that even if he had his wish of being in the family business, he would soon have chafed under the authority of the elders. Deep within he wanted to soar to freedom, but the crushing reality of hard times in a backwater village bound him to the earth.

He wondered if Gustav's wanderlust was a symptom of the same frustration. Gustav was so excited the day he left home. It seemed like a wonderful adventure opening in front of him. His letters described the excitement of the new places he saw. Even though he seemed to have barely enough money to live, he sounded content and happy.

And now Gustav would have to become a soldier. He would be coming home soon, in time to report at Charlottenburg. Johann was sorry that he wouldn't be able to see his brother before he left for the army. By the time Gustav returned to Endigen, he would be working at Wagner's. I wonder, Johann thought, if I should put off going to Neuhaus until after Gustav goes into the army....Still, he could hardly expect Wagner to hold the apprenticeship for him for another fortnight. He'd lose his chance altogether, if he asked to wait for Gustav.

Johann pushed the bench back from the table and walked up the two flights of stairs to the loft bedroom. He had put his belongings on the bed: his suit and Sunday shoes, his extra work clothes, his razor. He saw that his mother, without saying a word, had added a small Bible and a new shirt. He put everything in the old carpetbag. Looking once more around the room with its three beds, he turned to go down the steps.

Christiana was waiting in the kitchen. She held out a package tied in one of her best towels. "Here is the lunch for your trip to Neuhaus. It's just bread and cheese and some apples. I hope you and Wagner enjoy it." Her eyes filled with tears.

"I know it will be good. I'm going to miss the good meals you make for us. It's going to be strange not eating with the family."

"I'll think about you and pray for you every day. Be a good boy, do what Wagner tells you to do. You can learn a lot from him." Christiana held out her arms and hugged Johann as she had not done in many years. "It's time for you to go. You want to be at the shop when Wagner gets there."

"Auf wiedersehen, Mutti," Johann turned quickly from his mother's hug and walked out of the front door with the carpetbag and the parcel of lunch. He hated goodbyes. Without looking back he knew that his mother would be wiping her eyes on her apron.

Walking down the road, just as he reached the Scharf place, Johann was startled when a figure jumped out from behind the apple tree. It was Gotthelf. Tall and handsome, just turned nineteen, he strode along with Johann.

"I'll carry your bag," he said. In spite of the fact that Johann was four years older and half a head shorter, Gotthelf sensed that he and Johann shared more in common than the other brothers. They rarely spoke in the pietistic formulas of the rest of the family; neither of them could find a steady job. Johann had managed to hide his frustration more successfully than Gotthelf, who made no secret of his disdain for Endigen.

Gotthelf proudly marched along beside his older brother who was striking out on his own. He had done the same thing when Gustav began his journey last year. He spoke haltingly to Johann, "You know, you are getting out of here because you can't find work; Gustav too. When I go, it is because I hate the place. I can't wait to shake its dust, or its mud, off my boots." He spat into the dust.

When they passed the church and neared the linen shop, Gotthelf put down the bag and threw his arms around Johann. Johann suspected that he didn't want this show of affection to be seen by Father or the elder brothers. He looked into Johann's face and said, "I'll be with you before long." Then he ran around behind the church so that no one would see tears in his eyes.

Johann put his carpetbag and lunch bundle behind the front door of the shop. His father was hunched over his desk writing.

"Sit down over here, Johann. Wagner will be coming along soon. Do you have all your things ready?"

"*Ja,* I think I have everything." Johann took the tall stool against the wall.

"I hope that this works out for you. Wagner is a strictly business sort of fellow, but he is one of the best dyers I know. He's got a good business, even sends some of his material to Berlin. If you listen to him, you'll learn the trade well. He knows good quality, always buys the best linen we have in stock." He put down his pen.

"Karl says that Wagner won't be easy to get along with, that he expects an awful lot of his workers. I don't know how that will be. I don't know anything about dyeing,..but I can learn."

"Just do your work and do the best job you can. If you show that you are really trying, he'll be fair." Gottlieb reached into his pocket and held out several bills to Johann. "Here, put these in your pocket. Once you get to Neuhaus and your room at Wagner's, hide them in a safe place. This is only for an emergency. Three *Taler* can help you if you have trouble or have to come home. Don't use this unless you absolutely have to. You won't be earning much as an apprentice and won't have any extra spending money, but don't make the mistake of using these *Taler* just to have a good time or to buy foolish things."

Johann nodded agreement and put the money in his pocket. He knew that Father always wanted the best for his children and tried to take care of them. Even when they were no longer under his roof, his concern stayed with them.

The clock in the church tower had just struck ten when Wagner's wagon drove past the shop window and pulled around to the warehouse. It was quite different from the farm wagons that usually creaked down the road through Endigen. This was a big, totally enclosed wagon with doors at the back for the loading of the bolts of linen. "Wagner--Fine Linen" had been painted years ago in elegant gold letters across the black sides. The wheels looked much newer than the rest of the wagon.

Heinrich Wagner heaved himself down from the wagon's high seat and snapped two nosebags onto the horses' bridles. A man of considerable proportions, he walked slowly into the shop. Wheezing from the exertion, his hearty voice rumbled, "...*Morgen.* Time for another shipment. How many bolts can you let me have today?"

Gottlieb got off his stool and shook Wagner's hand. "We've got some good material for you. I told Karl to put aside the goods that come from our best weavers."

Wagner laughed loudly, "So now, because I'm going to have your son as an apprentice, I can get the best goods. I don't suppose you'd want to give me the best price too."

Gottlieb smiled, "I'm sending with you a good son, so don't push your luck too far." He reached for his ledger and began to count up the available bolts.

Brushing some of the road dust off his dark coat, Wagner hoisted his heavy body onto one of the stools along the wall. "So this is the young man. You're Johann, are you? We're going to make a good dyer out of you." He poked at Johann's arm with a large dye-stained finger.

"Yes, sir. I'm really glad that you had a place for me."

"I got the papers with me. After you get the goods loaded, we'll sign the papers and put everything in order."

"I'll go help Karl and Julius put the linen in the wagon."

Gottlieb nodded. "They know which bolts to load." Turning to Wagner after Johann had gone to the warehouse, he said, "Johann is a good boy. He worked hard at the mill and got along with people when he was at Krämer's store. He's got an independent streak, but he'll give you an honest day's work."

Wagner's booming voice filled the room. "You know and I know that being an apprentice isn't easy. He's going to have to work long and hard, but in the end he's going have a good trade. I hope he's patient enough to wait for the reward. Jobs are hard to find, but a good dyer who knows his trade won't have trouble finding work."

Wagner moved over to the window to watch the men loading his wagon. He ran his fingers through his gray beard and said, "Through the years I've had quite a few apprentices. Some worked out well, others left after only a few months. Johann is the oldest I've taken as an apprentice. Usually they are young fellows of fifteen or sixteen. But, I promise you, my old friend Weber, that I'll give him good training."

Karl came into the shop with his tally of the bolts of linen which had been put in the wagon. Wagner counted out the money due Weber and Sons from the big wallet he took from his inner coat pocket. Then he took out the contract for Johann's apprenticeship and spread it out on Gottlieb's desk. "You sign it here, Johann, and I'll sign there. Your father can sign as the witness," he said in an official-sounding voice.

Johann looked at the paper that would regulate the next three years of his life. He didn't bother to read it through, but he knew that in exchange for being taught the dyeing trade, he would promise to work three years for a few *Taler* a month and his room and board. Taking his father's pen from the desk, he signed where Wagner's greenish-yellow finger pointed: Johann Adolph Weber.

He didn't like the feeling of being locked in, even by paper and ink. As much as he wanted to learn a trade and have steady work, making a binding commitment of three years was an inwardly painful reality. Outwardly he signed resolutely, but on the inside he wondered if he was striking a devil's bargain he would regret.

Wagner and Father sealed his fate with their signatures. The agreement was accomplished. Wagner folded the paper carefully and returned it officiously to his wallet pocket.

Wagner ceremoniously wiped his balding head and his neck, thick as a tree trunk.

"Time to be on our way. Put your stuff in the wagon with the goods, Johann, and we'll get started."

"I'll do that. Mother sent us some food to eat on the way." He loaded his bag and put the parcel of food on the seat. Wagner took off the nosebags, put them back under the seat, pulled himself laboriously up, and grasped the reins.

"All set!"

Johann turned to Gottlieb and his elder brothers and solemnly shook hands with each. Then, putting his foot on the hub, he climbed up beside Wagner. The wagon lurched onto the road and Johann gave a quick farewell salute as he heard Julius say, "God be with you."

Before leaving the village Wagner pulled the team up to the stone watering trough between the two churches. Then they moved slowly down the main road, past old Scharf's place, Dr. Felsman's, and the house which Johann had never left before. He looked to see if his mother was outside, but there was no sign of her in the garden. She was probably in the kitchen cooking the noon meal. Had Johann raised his eyes to the window of the attic room he had shared with his brothers, he might have seen his mother watching, wiping her eyes with her apron, as Wagner's wagon moved down the road toward Waldenburg and Neuhaus.

Neuhaus was twenty times the size of Endigen. Like his home town there were two churches with their tall towers. Here and there a smokestack marked the location of a factory. In the town center was a paved market square in front of the Rathaus. A large ornate fountain provided water for the round trough where the horses of the farmers and tradesmen could drink.

On a narrow little street just off the square, Marta bent over her work table in the back of the millinery shop. Her fingers gathered the delicate veil as she stitched it into place. For the past year she had been helping to make the hats she later saw as ladies strolled down the street or sat in the church pews. She had learned quickly under Fräulein Krause who owned the little shop. At first she was terrified of the tall spinster in her sober gray dress. In time she learned that in spite of the stern expression on her face and the posture as straight as a needle, Fräulein was not to be feared.

"You're a bright girl, Marta," Fräulein had said once. "You can work on the finest details because your hands are so small." That one bit of praise was spoken months ago, but still remembered for its extravagance. The milliner was a distant and reserved woman, living an unshared life. Her days and years were circumscribed by her little shop, its workroom in back, and her tiny apartment on the upper floor. Her major link with the world beyond the town was the small, but growing, collection of booklets from Berlin which showed the latest fashion in hats and inspired the creations of Fräulein Krause for the ladies of Neuhaus. She had quickly learned, somewhat to her dismay, that although high fashion was hardly the mode of Neuhaus, only a few of the younger women aspired to imitate in a modest way the pictures in the booklets from Berlin. However, the majority of the trade in the shop was for a standard hat for *die Hausfrauen* of Neuhaus, one for winter, one for summer. These understated "masterpieces" had only limited adornment and were more noteworthy for their durability than their artistry. Marta turned them out a dozen at a time.

The real joy came when the wife of the banker or of one of the richer merchants came to the shop. A high level consultation then took place between the customer, Fräulein, and the little books. Marta hovered around the edges of these conversations, instructed to bring this or that feather or veil or flower from the workroom to contribute to the creative process. After she had worked in the shop for some months she began to offer little suggestions about trying this ornament or placing it in this way. Marta sensed that Fräulein stiffened a bit at first at these initiatives. It seemed she was tempted to ignore the girl until several of the customers responded very positively to the suggestions. Fräulein nodded approvingly that Marta's notions had merit. Although it was never acknowledged in words, they began to work as a team.

Occasionally, when Marta was alone in the shop, she dared to try on some of the very beautiful hats that she had helped to make. She was a small young woman with shining dark eyes. Her brown hair was pulled back tightly into a bun. Sometimes she dissolved into laughter when she put on some of the larger creations. They totally overwhelmed her small face. In the mirror she looked like a turtle or a pixy peeking out from beneath a toadstool. But some of the hats gave her the feeling of being beautiful. She would put them on and for minute upon minute, turning this way and that, revel in the image in the mirror. It was the first and only touch with finery she had ever experienced.

The Wiesner home was modest, at best. Marta's mother had died when her younger sister was born. After a year of struggling alone to raise his two little girls, August Wiesner married Katerina Münsch. She did her best to fit into the household and tried to mother her small step-daughters. She was a good woman but cool and reserved. It was as if she lived in an invisible shell which inhibited any close relationship. She rarely held Marta on her lap when she was small, never hugged or kissed her.

Marta, deprived of a mother when she was only five, felt the distance. There was no unkindness in it. Her new mother rarely raised her voice to the children and never her hand. She provided, as best she could with the money the family had, an ordered but spartan household: scrubbed floors, simple food, clean, sturdy clothing.

There was no unhappiness in the family; each member had learned to accommodate to the lack of warmth. Marta, even as a little girl, began to comprehend that she had to make her own life, her own simple pleasure, her own advancement. When she started attending the school, she was the achiever. The schoolmaster smiled when he saw the determination with which she approached every task, head down showing only tightly braided hair, jaw set in concentration, hands working with no random motion, her tongue flicking at the corner of her mouth. She never smiled until she knew that she had mastered the lesson. When she found it difficult, she would start again and again until she knew she had it right--then the smile. She was smiling for herself, not for others to see. She was saying to herself, I did it!

After she had finished six years of school, Marta helped her step-mother at home until she was asked to work as hired girl in the Bauer household. Frau Bauer was overwhelmed by trying to care for her five small children, the youngest twins. Marta started her day by preparing breakfast for the Bauer family, helping to feed the smaller children. Laundry was a daily activity, except for Sunday, washing, wringing, hanging, ironing the countless children's garments. Then, if there was time, she helped Frau Bauer with the cleaning, an unending task with the accumulating clutter of children's play. This was followed by preparation of dinner, served promptly at noon when Herr Bauer came home from the Rathaus. After the naps for the children, there was mending and helping with supper preparation. After she had eaten her own supper, she washed the dishes and walked to her home a few streets away. For five years she had put in long days in the Bauer house. Every Saturday she took home the money she had been paid and gave it to her father. She knew that she was a help to her family. Not only did she bring home two *Taler*, she ate all her meals at the Bauer family table.

When the children were all old enough for school, Frau Bauer one day had told Marta that the work of the household no longer required two women. "You have been a wonderful help. I do not know how we could have done without you." She always spoke with a quiet lady-like voice

Marta had already seen that her work with the Bauers was not as needed as it has been. Frau Bauer was taking over more and more of the responsibilities of the household. Marta had thought about what she would do when it was time to leave. She was going to miss the *gemütlich* family, which contrasted so dramatically with the cool reserve of her own home. She was going to miss the pride of doing a good job, being a necessary helper to make the household run smoothly. She had never really minded the long hours or the tasks repeated a thousand times. It was a job to do, and she would do the absolutely best she could.

Before she had a chance to worry about finding another job, Frau Bauer suggested, "I have talked with my sister Berta about you. She has been wanting to have a helper in her millinery. She could pay you a bit more than we have been giving you, but you would have your meals at home. Do you think you might like to work with her?"

Marta's mind raced through pictures of working on pretty hats, handling finery she'd only seen from a distance in church. It would be a change from the endless cleaning and washing and cooking. "Oh, that would be wonderful. *Danke schön, Frau Bauer, Danke!*"

"You are a good girl, Marta, a dependable worker. I told my sister she could not find a better worker. You could start with her next Monday."

Marta hesitated, "I don't know anything about making hats. I've only had one in all my nineteen years. It would be fun to learn to do it." What a wonderful change from dishwater and scrub boards to ribbons and flowers and ostrich plumes! She could hardly wait.

Wagner's house was part of a tall half-timbered tenement only a short distance from the center square in Neuhaus. It had three storeys with small shuttered windows. On the steep roof, tiers of tiny gables showed that the attic also contained two additional storeys of rooms. At the east end of the building the ground-floor had a small shop. The sign above the shop window announced that here Wagner sold fine linens.

They drove around to the back of the building into a maze of stables and small buildings. "This is where we work," Wagner said as he heaved himself down from the driver's seat. He pointed to the door in the back of the big house. "That's the wareroom for the finished goods. It's right back of the shop. That building there with the chimney is where we do the dyeing. The wagon and the horse go into the stable there. We live in this end of the building. Let's put the wagon away and then we'll go in to meet the family and I'll show you where you'll sleep."

There was a back stairway from the rear of the shop to the Wagner apartment. With his carpetbag Johann followed Wagner up the creaky steps. When the door opened into the second floor kitchen, he saw Frau Wagner sitting at the table peeling potatoes. "Hilda, here's our new boy."

"What's your name, young man?" she asked with no smile.

"I'm Johann, Frau Wagner. I'm glad to meet you."

"Glad you got here 'fore it rains. I got only two more potatoes to peel. Then I'll take you to your room. You're up above."

She was of the same proportions as her husband, a large woman. Her apron was spotted with the signatures of the day's cooking and cleaning. The peelings flew from her knife, and the job was soon done. Wiping her reddened hands, she tried to fasten her hair which was pulled back into an untidy knot. "Come 'long then."

Johann followed her up the stairs which got steeper and more narrow as they reached each floor. At the fifth level she walked down a small dim hallway and opened a door. "This is where you'll stay, Johann. Gets the morning sun, so you won't have any trouble waking up," she laughed heartily.

Frau Wagner stood aside to let him in. Johann squeezed past her ample figure. Looking around the small room he saw that it was sparsely furnished.

"Come on down when you get your stuff put away. That shouldn't take you very long…Supper'll be ready 'fore long. We're going to have to fatten you up a little." She poked his ribs and gave a hearty laugh.

Slowly Johann unpacked the carpetbag on the bed. He hung up his good suit and his extra work pants on a peg on the wall. There was a small chest of drawers for his few shirts and other items. There was a small table which also served as a wash stand. Walking over to the small dormer window, Johann looked out over the lot behind the house with its numerous outbuildings. As he pushed the curtain to the side to get a better view, a cloud of dust made him sneeze.

Neuhaus seemed like a city compared with Endigen. From his window high up in the attic he could see row upon row of rooftops before there were fields and trees. No shady road here, no apple tree and weathered picket fences.

Putting his hand into his pocket, Johann felt the three *Taler* his father had given him. He looked around the little room for a place of safekeeping, as Father had instructed. Johann quickly discarded the obvious spots: in the bottom of one of his drawers, under the bed. There was a small framed mirror over the wash stand. A generous coating of dust on the top of the frame suggested that it was not handled often. Taking it from the nail on which it hung, he saw that the thin wood backing was held loosely in place by two small nails. It was easy to slide it out. The three *Taler* fit very nicely between the glass and the wood backing. That was done.

"*Johann, kommst du!*" Frau Wagner's voice wound up the flights of stairs. "Supper's ready."

Combing through his hair with his fingers, Johann followed the smell of food down the steps to the kitchen. He stepped into the room and saw the Wagner family. The parents had seated themselves at either end of the large table. Their five children, arranged in the pecking order of age, stood by their chairs, the smallest closest to their mother.

Standing beside the stove with a large ladle in her hand was a young woman. "This is Christiane, our hired girl," Frau Wagner announced. Johann nodded and the girl smiled shyly, as she began to ladle soup into bowls. "You can sit there with Christiane," Frau Wagner said, pointing to a small table against the wall.

The Wagner family ate a noisy supper: spoons drumming against bowls, soup consumed with grunts and wheezes. There was very little talking, Johann noted, remembering the conversations around the table in Endigen.

Apart from a quiet "*danke*" to Christiane when she offered him more bread, he, too, ate in silence. There was no lingering at the table when supper was finished. Frau Wagner herded the two youngest children to their room on the floor above, and the older ones thundered down the back steps to the courtyard behind the house to play while there was still daylight.

"Come with me," Wagner said and took Johann down the steps. He opened the door to the wareroom on the ground floor behind the shop. Pointing to the shelves that went from ceiling to floor, he said, "Here is where we keep the finished goods." The bolts were arranged by color. Even in the dim light from two small windows, Johann could see the rainbow of tinted linen.

They walked to the large unpainted sheds behind the house. "This is the one where we keep the undyed linen," Wagner said as he unlocked the padlock on the large double doors through which they had pulled the wagon before putting the horse in the stable.. The shed had two small windows high in the peak of the end walls. Johann could see racks of smooth, deep shelves along the side walls. Wagner's voice echoed through the large shed. "The undyed stuff goes on this side. With the wagon in here we can load and unload without getting the material wet when it rains. Now you can unload the bolts we brought in today. You surely know from home that you have to handle it carefully. Snag it on a nail or a sliver and you've ruined part of the goods. I'll tally the bolts for the inventory."

When Johann was finished, Wagner locked the door and walked with Johann to another shed. Behind it was a lean-to with a chimney over two large iron caldrons set in a brick platform where the dyeing was done. Pointing to the big woodpile along the wall, Wagner boomed, "This is where you'll start in the morning. You fill the caldrons up to this mark with water from the cistern and get the fire started under them. Now come over here."

They went into the shed and Johann saw the place where the dyes were mixed. Jars of various colored dyes were arrayed on shelves against the wall. Leaves and plants soaking in water in the jars creating a rainbow of color. A collection of graduated measures and mixing bowls stood on the table next to them for measuring the dyes. "Here is where the secret of the trade is. Anybody can put goods in a kettle and color them. But the dye you put in, that's where you make your money. If you can mix the tints people like, you more than double the value of the linen."

Johann nodded. Wagner proclaimed, "It'll be a year before you get into the mixing shed. You've got a lot to learn first. Come on, there's one more shed."

They went into a long low building where Johann saw long pieces of linen and cotton hanging from the many long clotheslines that went from end to end of the shed. "Here is where the material is dried, either here or on the clotheslines behind. Then we press and reroll the finished material on these long tables. From here it goes back to the wareroom. *Versteh'?*"

Johann wondered why it would take three years to learn this trade. It didn't seem that complicated. With the exception of the dye mixing, anybody with common brains ought to be able to do it right away. How long does it take to learn to fill a cauldron or hang up a long piece of material? Oh well!

"Better get to bed. We got a lot to do tomorrow. I'll call you just before sun-up. Those kettles have to be boiling by the time the other workers get here. I hope you're not a sleepyhead like the last kid I tried to train. We lost more time because he didn't have the kettles ready in time."

During the weeks and months that followed, life for Johann seemed to center on those cauldrons. He emptied the used dye in the sluice and filled the kettles with clear rainwater from the cistern. Hundreds of times he raked out the ashes and put them in the leaching barrel and built the wood fire. Wagner did the dye mixing and added it carefully to the kettles to begin each job. Hans, a burly fellow in his thirties, put the cloth into the cauldrons, stirred it with a large paddle, then, closely supervised by Wagner, took it out again at the proper moment, pushed it in a wheeled tub to the clotheslines. The other worker was Minnie, a large woman with bulging forearms. She spread the nearly dried material from the lines on the long table and with one flatiron after another from her small charcoal stove pressed the finished linen until it was smooth as glass.

Johann had resolved that he would try to be patient and content. He tried his best to do what he was told. For many months, it seemed an eternity, he had been assigned tasks that any handyman could have done. "Put this basket over there!" "Unload the bolts from the wagon and put them on the shelves!" "Go to the cellar and bring another cask of the indigo dye to the mixing room!"

It was a great relief when he was put to work actually handling the cloth in the dyeing process. He had helped Hans put the long pieces of linen into the dye cauldrons. After a carefully timed intervals, measured by a set of small hourglasses, they took short, smooth poles to lift the dripping linen from the dye. In a tub it was taken to the drying shed. As soon as it was cool enough to handle, Johann and Hans stretched it along the parallel clotheslines that ran the length of the drying shed. As it dried, they would periodically walk along, tugging at the edges to straighten the material.

The only breaks in the routine were mealtimes when Johann shared the small table with Christiane Köhler. Even though they did not talk much during the family meals, Johann sometimes lingered in the kitchen after supper to get better acquainted. Christiane, who was several years younger than he, relieved the isolation Johann felt so keenly. She was as tall as he was. Her blond hair was coiled in a braid around her head.

The Wagners were busy with their own family. After initially getting Johann settled in, they focused again on their own living. The only two other people with whom Johann had regular contact, Hans and Minnie, had their own families to whom they returned after the long work day. At first Johann had just gone to his room after supper and read until the light failed and it was time for bed. Occasionally he had walked around the town on Sunday afternoon. Once he realized it was not an obligation, he no longer went with the Wagners to church.

One evening as Christiane was clearing off the dishes from supper, Johann screwed up his courage to ask, "Herr Wagner told me he is going to give us the late afternoon off from work during the fair. Would go with me?"

"You've never seen anything like it. The whole square is so full of people you can hardly move. My girl friends and I go every year," she fairly bubbled.

"Will you go with me?"

"I can ask my mother," she smiled faintly.

A gypsy stood on the platform in front of the Rathaus, eating fire from a small torch. A band played in a corner of the square, while a few people in their Sunday clothes tried to do their clumping dance on the cobbles. Wagons and canopied booths lined the four sides of the square and spilled onto some of the side streets. Johann was relieved to see that things cost very little. He had managed to save a few *Kreuzer* from his tiny wage, possible only because he had come with fairly new sturdy clothing and had not yet had to buy any replacements.

Indeed, he had never seen anything like this in Endigen. The closest thing that village had, a pale replica indeed, was the annual Ascension Day celebration. After church people gathered in a meadow on the outskirts of the town to eat a meal, sitting in the shade of the old trees. The young people had races and games, while the older folks gossiped or napped. No booths, no gypsies, no band, no dancers.

Christiane looked so different, dressed for the fair. She had put flowers in her blonde braid and wore an embroidered white apron over her dress. She and Johann looked wide-eyed at all the wares being offered in the booths. For a while they watched the good burghers losing their money at simple games of chance. The smell of the food cooking in the stands drifted around them. They tapped their feet to the martial rhythms of the band. To get away from the crowded square for a little time, they strolled down a side street.

Christiane, knowing the small wage Johann received from Wagner as well as her own, didn't expect to be spending money at the fair. It was pleasure enough just to be part of the jostling crowd in which currents of people seemed to move like small rivers. Large women, wielding sharp elbows, moved like ships' figureheads, through the sea of people. Christiane's girl-friends, having heard daily bulletins on her plans for the fair, giggled and nudged as they watched for her and Johann in the square. When they finally spotted them in the crowd, they kept them under surveillance, moving with them. keeping just enough distance between them not to be seen.

Naturally, there was great interest in Johann. Elsbeth grinned when she said, "Why he's not much taller than Christiane."

"But look at those gray eyes. He's real nice looking, I think," Maria giggled.

"Christiane said he's strong, a good worker. He has a nice smile," Marta added.

The cat-and-mouse game with the chums lasted into the evening. Once in a while Christiane spotted her friends and knew from other years what was going on. She didn't say anything to Johann but tossed off an occasional self-satisfied smile to her spying sorority.

Johann and Christiane had eaten sweet buns from one of the stands for their supper. As it got darker, big torchiers were lighted around the square, throwing a reddish golden light over the crowd and making grotesque shadows on some of the walls surrounding the square. The festivities went on and the crowd became even larger. Progress through the square was even more difficult. Then, unexpectedly, the couple came face to face with the gaggle of young women who had been stalking them from time to time. They giggled nervously as Christiane introduced them to Johann.

The noise of the crowd was so loud that Johann could hardly hear the names: Maria, Elsbeth, Marta.

CHAPTER 3

It was almost a year into the apprenticeship before Wagner announced, as if awarding a prize, "Johann, I think you are about ready to begin learning to mix the dyes."

It's about time, Johann thought, but he said, "*Ganz gut.*" He noticed out of the corner of his eye the look of disappointment that passed like a cloud over Hans' face. Hans knew that his job was, and would always be, to put the linen into the cauldrons and take it out again. Johann realized, not without a twinge of pain, that his advancement toward becoming a dyer resulted in Hans becoming even more locked into his routine.

Wagner hooked his thumbs in his suspenders and began to expand on his decision, "We'll start you out with simple colors. After you master that I can show you how to get all the different shades we use." It was obvious that Wagner was proud of his accomplishments as a master dyer.

"I'll do the best I can. I know I can learn it."

"Patience! Patience, young man! There's a lot to learn and you have to learn it well," Wagner poked his finger into Johann's chest. "I don't write down any of the formulas. No use letting everyone know how to get the tints that the women want to buy. I keep it all between my ears. That's why I have to teach it to you one step at a time. *Langsam und deutlich.*"

Johann began to realize that, like all of his prior experience as Wagner's apprentice, this was going to take a lot of time. He could envision spending weeks with each tint. Even though he recognized Wagner's skill as a dyer, he sensed that there was more than a little self-importance attached to the snail's pace with which knowledge was shared. He realized that he would be told the secret colors only at the pace set by the Master..

After their supper of brown bread and potato soup, the Wagners and their children walked to a neighbor's house, Johann sat at the small table while Christiane cleaned up after the meal.

"Wagner told me today that I was ready to start in the dye mixing room. I wondered how long it would be before I got that far."

Christiane said, "That's good. That will be a lot better than wrestling around wet linen all day."

"*Ja*, but he already warned me that it will be very slow. I sometimes think he makes it go so slow because he gets a lot of cheap labor out of me while I'm an apprentice. If he teaches me all I need to know in a year, I'm out of here and he has to get somebody else."

"You're not very patient, are you?" Christiane smiled indulgently, as a mother would smile, building the character of her child.

"Right! I'm not a kid. I want to learn the trade so I can be on my own. He kept me hanging up wet linen for months. What was I supposed to be learning during all that time? I learned that job in an hour. I can just see it coming. One week to learn how to put plain blue dye in the water. One week to learn the fine art of putting green dye in. It'll be months before I even get to mix any colors."

Christiane, in a mood she rarely exhibited, joined herself to Johann's feelings. She said with uncharacteristic boldness, "I've worked here longer than you have. It didn't take me long to figure out that both the Wagners have their own way of doing things. That's the way it is going to be done. I got sat down real hard the first time I tried to tell Frau Wagner the way my mother did some things. So I just shut up. I do what she tells me, the way she tells me." She began putting away the dishes.

"I can tell you, I'm not going to stay one hour longer than I have to. I signed that paper and gave him three years. Even if he hasn't taught me everything he knows by then, I'm leaving. I hope I can stick it out that long."

Christiane reacted immediately, "That makes me sad. I won't have anybody to talk to here if you leave." She blushed and turned to the kitchen cabinet with a stack of clean plates.

Johann paid no more attention to the rising color in her cheeks than he would have paid to his sister's.. His daily contact with Christiane in the Wagner kitchen made them seem extensions of the Wagner family. Even in their infrequent excursions together out into the town, like the day at the fair, Johann felt like he was spending time with his younger sister.

35

Wagner continued to make his visits to Endigen every few weeks. "I saw your father and brothers today. They keep thinking that you will come along with me one day. It's been a long while since that one time you went with me. For your father's sake, I could afford to give you one day off to see your folks. You could work a few extra hours after supper that week."

Johann replied, "Maybe someday, but things are too busy around here." He didn't really understand himself why he was so reluctant to visit. Once in a great while he sent a note to his family along with Wagner. He felt guilty for ignoring them, but he remembered that the one time he went with Wagner had only rekindled the old resentments. Karl was still as stuffy as ever, posturing as an authority figure whenever Father was not around. And Julius continued to exude his pious passivity.

On the way out of town they had stopped at the house long enough for Johann to have a brief visit with his mother. She insisted that Wagner come in for a cool glass of milk and some *Stollen*. She had a small lunch packed for them, just as she had when Johann left for Neuhaus.

She pinched Johann's waist. "It feels like Frau Wagner is feeding you good," she joked, winking at Wagner. "I hope he's being a good worker for you. He's not much of a letter writer," she made a face at Johann, "but he's always has been a good hard worker."

On that one trip with Wagner Johann had been very quiet on the return leg of their journey. Wagner tried to draw him into conversation. "It must have been good to see all your folks."

Johann was a bit slow to respond. "Yes, things haven't changed very much. Karl and Julius seemed very busy."

"I thought your father looked tired. He didn't move around very fast."

"He doesn't have to work so hard, now that Karl and Julius are in the business."

Wagner didn't pick up the emotion beneath Johann's words.

Now, when the time came for his buying trips, he asked Johann if he had any messages for home. But Johann usually just said, "Tell them I'm all right." He never bothered to write a letter for Wagner to take. What did he have to tell them? That he had learned how to hang cloth on long clotheslines? What use was there in reporting his snail-like progress through the apprenticeship?

This particular evening Wagner had said, "I saw your father and brothers today. They asked about you. I told them that you'd moved up to learning to mix the colors."

Johann could picture Karl celebrating this "huge accomplishment": brother on his way to earning his own living. He probably quoted some pious text to Wagner to show that God could snatch success from the jaws of failure by inspiring patience and industry in the willing worker. Although he never put it into words, Johann simply could not rid himself of the feeling that Karl was always standing in judgment over him.

"Here," Wagner said reaching for the large wallet in his inner pocket, "they wanted me to give you this letter from your brother in the army." He passed over the letter, well-worn from many readings. Johann could picture Father reading it aloud to the family at the supper table.

"I'll read it after supper. Thanks for bringing it."

"They would like you to write to your brother. You know, every time I'm in their shop, they ask why you don't send a letter to them. I tell them that you are all right, but they always say to tell you to write to them."

"I'll try to do that next time," Johann responded, knowing that he wouldn't. He was glad that his parents knew that he was all right. He didn't want them to worry about him. But a letter from him being read at the supper table would just stir a judgmental response from Karl, and maybe Julius too, pontificating about how good it was that Johann was getting his life sorted out, even though he was still a lowly apprentice.

Wagner reached into his wallet again and handed a *Taler* to Johann. "Your father wanted me to give you this. He said you could use a little of it to post a letter to your brother Gustav."

"All right. *Danke schön.*" Johann put the letter in his pocket and dipped his bread into the potato soup before him.

Johann hurried to his room after supper, instead of his usual habit of talking to Christiane while she washed the dishes. He wanted to read Gustav's letter while there was still daylight coming through his window.

He had not heard anything of Gustav since he left Endigen to work for Wagner. He knew then that Gustav was coming home from Lübeck and that he had to report to Charlottenburg in August. He often had wondered how army life was for Gustav.

He unfolded the well-thumbed letter. It was written from Mainz in late December. His family must have had it for quite a while before they sent it on to him.

Paul Irion

Dear Family,

I was so happy to get your letter because there is no joy here. The drill is very hard. We get up in the morning and start to clean until 8:00 a.m.; then drill until 12:00 and again from 1:30 until 4:30 p.m. and cleaning again. From 5 to 6 p.m. instruction and cleaning again until the retreat. A person could get fed up with life here. The military service is much too hard....and in addition we got a new major who is finding fault with everything. From now on I will stand guard at the first shift on Wednesdays. The weather very nice, no frost till Nov. 18. Only heavy fog a few times. For the last few days we had snow and further up the Rhine there must be heavy frost because huge pieces of ice are floating down the river. Already the pontoon bridge had to be pulled away. I wish you could see this bridge. It takes about 5 minutes to walk across. The bridge is made out of 50 barges, with big spaces in between. Mainz is generally a big fortress. There is a rumor that the 38th Regt. will be moved to Frankfurt am Main on April 1. That will be four miles closer to home. In general it is supposed to be better there, only the barracks are not as good as here and the food even more expensive. One pound of *Kommiss* costs 17 *Kreuzer*, that is a lot, but it is good dark bread. You asked how much postage I had to pay for the letter. It was 13 *Kreuzer*. This Christmas I will not be able to celebrate as I used to do at home. Heartfelt thanks for the 3 *Taler*. Otherwise I wouldn't have a thing and would starve because my pay, 43 1/2 *Kreuzer* every 10 days, doesn't go very far. We have to buy so much cleaning stuff these days. I miss everybody. I really will be glad when the army is finished with me and I can be free once again.

Your son and brother,
Gustav

Johann reread the letter and tried to picture Gustav in his uniform. That part of it would be exciting. A uniform would be an improvement over a dyer's apron. But that's where the excitement would end. Johann was very grateful that he had never gotten the letter from Berlin. He had heard the fellows in Endigen talking about their army time. Some of them had actually been in battles, but most had stories only of being pushed around by officers and boring hours of endless drill. Johann had no desire for that. He only got pushed around by Wagner and was bored doing the same jobs over and over again. At least he didn't have to buy food to supplement the meals Frau Wagner and Christiane put on the table three times a day. He would write to Gustav.

Life for Johann did not assume the many colors with which he worked every day. Although he mixed beautiful pastel shades or vibrant blues and yellows under Wagner's careful tutelage, his days were mainly monochromatic. The work was hard, the hours long. His little attic room seemed smaller than it had when he first arrived, as if the walls were slowly closing in on him.

The leaves were beginning to come out on warm spring days. Johann came out of the mixing room with the dye batch for the cauldrons. A familiar figure stood by one of the poles supporting the leanto roof over the dye kettles. It was Gotthelf.

"Can I believe my eyes?" Johann rushed to his brother. "What are you doing here?"

Gotthelf put his arm around Johann's shoulders. "I finally decided to get the hell out of Endigen. Father wasn't very happy about it. Sunday after church I told him that I was going to leave. He said that he had helped you find a job and that he'd try to do the same thing for me, if I would only wait. But I've had it right up to here. When Karl started in on me, telling me to be patient, not to do anything foolish, I blew."

"What happened?"

"That big bag of wind. I get so sick of that pious stuff he keeps pumping out. I suppose Father told him I was talking about leaving Endigen. Karl always makes the most of a situation like that--acts like he's the father of the family. I'll take it from Father but not from that pompous ass."

"He rubbed me the wrong way time after time."

Gotthelf was so angry when he recalled the scene that he paid no attention to what Johann was saying. "We really got into a yelling match after supper on Sunday. I was standing out behind the house and Karl came out to talk to me. He started preaching at me. I told him to shut up. He kept right on, so I hit him. I knocked him down."

"I felt like doing that a dozen times, but I never had the nerve. Did he fight back?"

"No. He got up, brushed himself off, and kept right on preaching at me: how ungrateful I was, how I would hurt Father, how I'd be sorry."

"He never could understand either of us."

Gotthelf's voice conveyed his sadness, "I knew right then that I had to leave. If I put it off, things would just get worse between us. I didn't know where to go, so I headed for you here."

"How did you get here, to Neuhaus?"

"I walked most of the way. I thought once that maybe I'd ask Wagner for a ride, but I figured he'd have to say no if he knew Father didn't want me to leave now. So I just told mother that I was leaving. She cried a little but said she understood."

"What are you going to do?" Johann asked.

"I'm not sure. I walked first to Waldenburg and asked around for jobs. Nobody there had anything to offer. So I thought I'd try Neuhaus. Here I am!"

Johann thought fast. Did he dare ask Wagner if Gotthelf could work for him? Would Frau Wagner allow Gotthelf to stay with him in his room for a few days? "Do you want me to talk to Wagner about a job?"

Gotthelf said, "If Wagner found out that I left home over Father's objections, he wouldn't want to get in bad with him. I'd better look for something else in town. Besides, I'm not sure I want to settle down for a long time. I'd kinda like to move around the way Gustav did."

As they were talking, Christiane came around the corner of the building on her way to market. She blushed when Johann introduced her to Gotthelf. "This is my brother Gotthelf. He just came from Endigen to look for work. This is Christiane Köhler who works for Frau Wagner."

She smiled shyly. Gotthelf was taller than Johann and slender, with smooth dark hair and a fine mustache. He looked at her with his dark eyes. "*Guten Tag, Christiane.*" he smiled back as she walked by with her basket.

When she had passed down the alley, he said to Johann, "Do you mean to tell me that you've had that pretty girl right under your nose for over a year. What's wrong with you, man? All work and no play...."

"*Ja*, what could I do on one *Taler* a month and practically no time off. We went to the fair last fall and once in a while we go for a little walk around town."

"If I can find a job around here, I'll take her walking. You can bet on that! I'd better start asking around town if there is any work. I'll come back this evening and let you know if I found anything."

Marta shut the door of the millinery and turned the key in the lock. Fräulein now trusted her to close up the shop on those days when she had to go out on errands. It felt good to walk after the long hours hunched over her work table. After she helped her step-mother clean up the supper dishes, she'd go for a walk.

Elsbeth and Christiane walked around the square as they often did in the evening. Marta knew how they looked forward to an hour away from the houses and families in which they worked. She hurried to catch up with them, ready to join in their recreational gossip. They giggled over the contributions each could make from the day's activities. Elsbeth could regale them with tales of the intrigues of the master of her house, who regularly visited the widow Blasberg for an hour on his way home from his office in the Rathaus. Christiane amused them with her stories of the eccentricities of the Wagner household. But most of all Marta looked forward to Christiane's reports of her conversations with Johann. Although she and the other girls could make Christiane blush by implying that the apprentice was her boyfriend, Marta secretly wished that she could play that role. She remembered his shy smile, his warm gray eyes. She had talked with him only a few times since Christiane first introduced them at the fair last year. Fantasies of walking and talking with him filled her mind during the hours of stitching at the millinery. Only loyalty to Christiane kept her from trying to arrange some meetings with him.

This evening Christiane was filled with excitement over her brief meeting with Johann's brother. Her eyes glistened and high color came to her cheeks as she described Gotthelf in glowing words. "He is tall and dark. His eyes are almost black. He has brown hair with just a little wave in it. He looks like he ought to be in a uniform, like a young prince. You should see his smile!"

As Christiane babbled on about this new find, Marta's mind started to contrive ways in which she might get to know Johann better. Marta paid little attention to the excited accounts of the young "prince" from Endigen. All she was hearing was a tacit permission to pursue Johann herself.

Most of Marta's work was fairly mindless. For every lovely hat she and Fräulein made for the ladies of the town, there were dozens of the kinds of bonnets they sold to the other women. Marta could make them in her sleep. Johann's face came up again and again in her mind's eye as she stitched and turned, turned and stitched. She could picture him smiling at her. She imagined the touch of his hand on hers. She thought about the way she would tell her girl-friends as they walked in the evenings about the conversations she had with Johann. He would fall in love with her, returning the love she was already feeling. She had never been loved as she now was in her imagination. How wonderful to have somebody really love you. Her flights of fancy took her to a house of her own, children playing, a family laughing and talking around the kitchen table.

Marta was not an idle, but an active, dreamer. Since the time she was a little girl, she had worked to make her dreams come true. She was not often disappointed, because she had developed the art of tailoring her dreams to the real world in which she lived. She quickly sorted out unrealistic fantasies from those dreams which she felt she could make happen. She knew that the dreams of a cottage on the edge of town were not realizable, but she did understand that once she was no longer constrained by her loyalty to Christiane, she'd capture Johann's interest. This was more than simple girlish daydreaming. This was a pathway to adulthood and freedom and love.

Marta knew that she had to arrange to talk with Johann by herself. Nothing would happen if he saw her only with all the other girls walking around the square. Just trying to stand out in the group was not enough. If she just talked louder than the rest, or laughed more, or tried to walk next to him, it would be too obvious. She had to find a way to see him when she was by herself.

In her mind she tried to reconstruct what she knew of his daily routine. He would be working at Wagner's from early morning until suppertime. During those hours she was busy at the millinery. Besides, she wouldn't know where to find him in the various buildings behind Wagner's shop.

Through Christiane she knew that some evenings he would go for a short walk after supper. She had seen him at church, sitting with the Wagners and Christiane, but lately she noticed he was absent. Perhaps Christiane could tell her what he did on Sunday afternoons. But that was pretty obvious; besides she really didn't want Christiane to know that she was interested in Johann.

Good luck fell to Marta one day when, on one of the evening strolls, Christiane started talking to Elsbeth about Johann. She said, "He is so quiet. He spends a lot of time in his room. Once in a while he goes walking. He doesn't have enough money to spend much time in the *Biergarten*."

Marta was relieved when Elsbeth began to ask questions, questions that were on the tip of her own tongue. "Doesn't he have friends? I never see him with the other fellows."

"Once and a while he talks about one of the guys he met. He sings with the *Männerchor* sometimes and goes to their practices. Wagner doesn't give him much time off and I don't know...."

Elsbeth jumped in, "I saw him walking last Sunday afternoon, when my mother and I were out on the Waldenburg Road. He was all by himself. I don't think he was going anywhere in particular, because he wasn't walking very fast."

Christiane added, "I don't know what he does on Sunday afternoons. That is my time off and I usually go home for a few hours."

Elsbeth said, "I've never seen him with a girl, other than the times we've walked with him in the square. Doesn't he ever take a girl out?"

"Once or twice, when we've been talking after supper, he's sounded like he'd really like to go out. He says he just doesn't make enough money to ask anyone."

Marta finally joined the conversation. "It sounds to me that he must be awfully lonely. Poor fellow!"

Elsbeth purred, "Well, if you're so sorry for him, why don't you go walking with him some Sunday? I'll bet you don't have the nerve."

"Oh, don't I? I may just take you up on that. I'll find a chance to ask...."

Christiane said, "I'll ask him for you. Want me to tell him you'd like to go walking? Don't say I never did anything for you."

Marta, torn between not wanting to appear too enthusiastic and being excited by the possibility, nodded. "Why not? I wouldn't mind keeping him company, poor lonely man."

Elsbeth and Christiane smiled knowingly at this show of compassion. "Sure you would." Christiane said, "I'll make a deal: I'll arrange for him to go walking with you, if you'll set it up for me to walk with that good-looking brother of his. Alright?" She blushed as she asked.

"One thing at a time," Marta cautioned. Her mind was racing through all sorts of possibilities. She and Johann could go walking with Christiane and his brother. That might be one way to overcome his shyness. But, on the other hand, she really didn't want to set up a permanent foursome. That would keep things casual rather than opening up the possibilities of a deeper relationship.

Johann looked out the small window of his room as the daylight faded. He was tired; he was always tired. It wasn't just that his work was physically exhausting. Since he had started in the mixing room, the only times he had to exert himself at all was when he carried the small casks of dye. He was tired with the heavy burden of frustration.

As he had guessed, Wagner guided him through the steps of dye mixing with exquisite tedium. Every new lesson had to be repeated again and again until the master was certain that it was engraved on Johann's mind. Even when they were not actually mixing, Wagner would fix his eyes on Johann and make him repeat the formulas for mixing the whole palette of common and unusual tints. It was no different than school, with old Radecke drilling them over and over with multiplication tables. Johann learned fast and, once the lesson was learned, impatience begat annoyance, which quickly turned into anger.

Johann banged the wall beside his bed, wondering what had really changed in his life. True, he was learning a trade, but his frustration continued to overwhelm him. Instead of chafing under Karl's pomposity, he had to endure the control Wagner exercised over every working hour. Johann had to remind himself that most of Wagner's apprentices in the past had been boys; he was a man, twenty-five years old. He was halfway through his life, marking time while that fat-necked Wagner droned on and on about this color and that.

He unfolded one of the pieces of paper he had bought, took his ink and pen from the table drawer and began to write a letter.

> August 4, 1855
> Dear Gustav,
>
> Your time in the army is more than half over. I was glad to hear that you have been moved to Potsdam. I suppose that you turn the heads of all the girls as you walk down the streets in your uniform. I am more than halfway through my service to Wagner. I feel about the same way you do. I can't wait for it to be over. You say that you do nothing but drill. I do nothing but mix the same colors over and over. The man doesn't think that I can learn anything new in less than two weeks. I just wish I could yell at him, "Come on. Let's get on to something new." I don't mean that I am not learning. I am, and I'll be a good dyer. But this slowness just kills me. I sometimes think it is because he wants to save money by having me work for my *Taler* a month. Even as an apprentice, I'm worth a lot a more than that. So you dream of marching out of the army and back home. I'll dream of casting off the shackles of apprenticeship and being

on my own. If I didn't think Father would feel disgraced, I'd tell Wagner to forget his apprenticeship and walk away.

Dear brother, hope that I will have the patience to last another sixteen months.

Your brother,
Johann

CHAPTER 4

"We should turn back toward town," Marta said. "I'm supposed to be home by supper time." The bell of the Catholic Church in Neuhaus was tolling the angelus. Although neither Marta nor Johann knew what the bell meant, they were well aware that it signaled the same evening hour every day. They quickened their pace along the country lane.

"It's been nice talking. I really enjoy our walks in the country. I get so sick of the same walls every day," Johann said.

"You really don't like it at Wagners, do you?"

"I can hardly wait for my term to end. I always seem to be backed up against a wall. I'd like, just once, to feel like I was free to decide my own life. I'm always caught between somebody telling me what I have to do or having nothing to do."

Marta shook her head. "One of these days you're going to have to just start being your own master. I kind of know what you feel. When I first started learning to make hats with Fräulein, I was really excited. Then I had to make those plain hats, a dozen at a time. After a couple months I could have made them without even thinking. I thought about quitting but didn't know what I could do to make money."

"*Ja*."

"Then one day I figured out that I could walk away if I really wanted to. True, it wouldn't be easy, but I could do it. I could find another job. I've never let anything get me down."

Johann answered, "When I was young, I used to feel that way. But then I learned the hard way that we get ourselves trapped in situations. I felt trapped in Endigen where there weren't any jobs. I feel trapped now mixing Wagner's colors. I...."

Marta gave his arm a tug and smiled, "Quit talking that way! You're going to be a good dyer. You'll have people wanting to give you work."

Johann turned to Marta, looking into her eyes. "You've got more faith in me than I have."

She smiled, "I know a good man when I see one. I do believe in you. You can do it." She took his hand and began walking toward town.

The same ringing of the bell signaled Gotthelf and Christiane that it was time to walk back toward Neuhaus. She held his arm as they strolled, looking up at him from time to time. He was so handsome.

"Do you know that you were the only member of your family Johann ever really talked about before you came to Neuhaus? I guess that's why I felt I already knew you that day you turned up."

Gotthelf smiled. "Then I owe him a lot. I'll have to give him the next *Taler* I earn, because he certainly introduced me to the prettiest girl in Neuhaus."

Christiane felt her cheeks burning. "Why doesn't he make visits back to Endigen when Wagner goes to buy linen. I never could understand that. I'd want to go home every chance I got, if I were in his place."

"I suppose he'd like to see Father and Mother, but neither of us get along with our oldest brother. He's so damn smug and pompous. He throws his weight around more like he's our father than our brother. He's just standing there waiting to take over everything from Father."

"Is that why you left home?"

"Both Johann and I left because there weren't any jobs there. But Karl is the reason I'll never go back. Johann may go back some day, but I won't. Johann may send a letter once in a while, but I won't."

"I don't like to hear you talk like that," Christiane said. "I couldn't think of cutting myself off from my family."

"I'm going to make my own way. I can get along without them, you watch me."

They turned into the square. Gotthelf took Christiane's hand when they got to the door to Wagner's building. He smiled and said, "I haven't wanted to spoil the afternoon, but I wanted to tell you that I'm going to be leaving Neuhaus this week. I heard about a job in the *Altmarkt* in Stendal."

Christiane's eye filled with tears. "Do you have to go?" She buried her head on his shoulder.

Gotthelf put his arms around her. "I know it's pretty far away. It's a better job than anything I could find here in Neuhaus. I'll miss you so much. Can I write to you?

Christiane wiped her eyes. "I'll miss you too. Our walks have been the happiest times of my life." She tried to smile without much success.

"Me, too." He kissed her blonde hair lightly and turned away. He walked slowly down the street toward the little room he had rented. When he reached the corner, he waved once more and disappeared from her sight.

Sunday afternoon in the Weber house in Endigen had not changed as the family circle became smaller. Gottlieb gathered everyone for devotions as they sat around the supper table. In this setting Gottlieb still felt like all the family members were gathered around the table. His prayers each Sunday mentioned each one by name, calling the gathered to think about those who were no longer at home. He tried to picture them: Mathilda with her husband and baby, Johann at Wagner's, Gustav at the army *Kaserne*, Gotthelf wherever he might be.

He missed them all, but he was especially saddened by the absence of Johann and Gotthelf. They didn't seem to do anything to keep contact with their family. Johann sent a little note once in a while with Wagner. There was never a word from Gotthelf. Several months ago Johann had mentioned that his younger brother had been in Neuhaus. These thoughts caused a pain in his heart as sharp as the pain he often felt when he walked back and forth to the shop.

As he put the Bible back on the shelf, Karl said, "I'm going to write to Gustav and Johann to tell them that I'd like them to be here for my wedding. They both know the date, but I want to persuade them to come."

Mother added, "You could ask them to let Gotthelf know too, if they know where he is. Why doesn't that boy write to his mother!"

Gottlieb saw the look that came over Karl's face when Christina spoke. His eldest son turned his eyes to the floor and did not look up for a long time.

Julius broke the silence. "Do you think that Gustav can come?"

"I'll write this evening."

After the whole family had gone to bed, Karl sat at the kitchen table. He lit the lamp and its light cast long shadows on the wall. He arranged the ink bottle, the pen, and a sheet of paper on the table. Slowly he began to write:

Lieber Gustav,

It was good to hear from you, in particular because you had sent me a watch as a wedding present. Many thanks. I used the watch right away and it works fine. I appreciate very much that it has an alarm. We are pretty well. Mother is doing all right, but Father complains of bad pains in his chest and shortness of breath. The ground still has some snow. It has been very cold since Easter; little wheat can be planted. Prospects are bleak because the winter crop is meager and inflation goes higher. We can only trust in God to bring something good from all this difficulty. We have no news of Gotthelf. We assume he is still working at the same place where he started last fall. Please send the enclosed envelope for him soon, because Stendal cannot be far from Potsdam. You wanted to know more about my intended. The loving God has given me a very good girl, the daughter of a factory owner from Seittendorf, near Reichenbach. Her name is Emilie Diepolt. Her parents died very young, she lost her mother when she was only two and her father when she was four. She lives with her oldest brother at her parents' house and is only 19 years old. The good Lord led me to her when she visited her cousin, one of the Krämers. She was here for a month and we have been exchanging many letters since she went home. The wedding date is set for September 24. We would be happy if you could come. Since you are so close by, it would be convenient if you were to remain in Potsdam and go on leave for the wedding. I would gladly send money for your train trip from Potsdam. It would be mighty nice if you could wear your uniform. If you have to buy a pair of extra pants, it would not be a loss; you could always wear them. However, a uniform jacket is more expensive and cannot be worn after your time in the army. Well, we'll decide what is best. Please write to Gotthelf and tell him to write to you so that you can send us his letter. Father sends you two *Taler*, and one *Taler* is from me.

Your brother,
Karl

He addressed two envelopes to Musketeer Gustav Weber, 2nd Company, 34th Infantry Regiment, Potsdam. Carefully he folded the one envelope to be sent on to Gotthelf and the *Taler* notes for Gustav.

He took another sheet of paper to write a similar note to Johann. He would give it to Wagner on his next trip. Karl believed it was important for the whole family to be together once again. The up-coming wedding might be such an opportunity.

Johann told Marta about Karl's letter when they were sitting on a bench in the *Stadtpark*. "I wondered if he would ever get married. He's 33 years old and he's marrying a girl 19."

Marta laughed playfully, "The Weber men take a good while to make up their minds, don't they?"

"Karl has had a good job with Father for years. He could afford to get married. The rest of us aren't that lucky. He'll have Father's business one day. Then he'll be sitting pretty."

"Your eyes are turning green," Marta joked.

"He wants me to come to the wedding at the end of September. I don't know if I want to go. My brother, Gustav, is supposed to be there in his uniform. I suppose I'd better show up."

"Don't you want to see your parents?"

"Sure. But I hate to go home just as an apprentice. I was going to wait until I had a steady job and could take care of myself."

Gottlieb walked slowly as he returned home from the shop. Near Scharf's house he stopped to steady himself against the picket fence. He took a few deep breaths, then resumed his slow walk.

He sat in his chair at the table while Christina finished preparing supper. He said with a sigh, "I just don't feel good. When I think how I used to work all day and not even be tired... Now I can hardly drag myself home."

Christina walked over to the table and put her hand on his shoulder. "You shouldn't work so much. Let the boys take over. You don't have to go to the shop every day."

"I need to see how things are being handled. But I do worry. Sometimes when I go to bed at night, I wonder if I'll see the next morning."

"Stop talking nonsense," Christina scolded. "You'll make yourself sick, if you don't quit talking that way."

"I tell you, I've lived for 35 of my 59 years in this village, but I cannot remember so many deaths in all that time as we have had from Michaelmas until today. I don't know if it's sickness, or if people are just being worn down by the hard times. The inflation gets worse and worse; people work so hard but don't get ahead. I'm just so tired."

"Let the boys do the work."

"I keep getting this sharp pain in my chest."

Christina patted his shoulder. "Go in and lie down on the bed until supper is ready. Get a little rest."

When Karl and Julius arrived a few minutes later, she told them that Father wasn't feeling well and was resting. Karl said immediately, "I doubt if he is as bad off as he thinks. I suspect that most of his problem is boredom. Since Julius and I are taking more and more responsibility at the shop, he doesn't have as much to do. He's just bored."

Christina sighed, "Well, maybe so. His appetite doesn't seem to suffer, so I'd better get back to the soup for tonight. Supper will be ready soon."

The following Sunday afternoon, the family devotions were held right after dinner because Karl had arranged to take his mother for a short visit with Mathilda and her family. As soon as the dishes were all washed and put away on the shelves, the family sat at the table.

Gottlieb read from the big family Bible and offered his prayers for all the family near and far. Then he said, "Today we should sing a hymn." His booming bass voice began *Ein feste Burg ist unser Gott...*, drowning out the rest of the family. When they had finished, he said, "That was wonderful... even if you don't sing out with all your hearts."

Karl went after the horse and buggy he was renting from the grocer, Krämer. When he pulled up in front of the house, Father walked with Christina, Hermann, and Luisa. As he helped them into the buggy. Karl asked, "Are you sure you don't want to come along? It's only a half hour ride."

Gottlieb shook his head. "I'll just have a nap. You won't be back before dark."

"There's bread and milk for you and Julius at suppertime. Don't make too bad a mess," Christina said.

Karl clucked at the horses and turned the buggy toward Lehmwasser.

Although they had started their homeward trip as the sun was setting, it was dark before they got to Endigen. As they neared the town, at the place where the stone bridge crossed the *Goldener Bach*, Karl saw someone ahead on horseback, carrying a lantern. He pulled back on the reins. It was Krämer's young son astride their broad draft horse. He called breathlessly, "Julius sent me to find you. You have to come quick. Herr Weber is sick."

Karl flicked the reins and the horse broke into a trot. "Hurry! Drive as fast as you can!" Christina said as she twisted the corners of her shawl.

They went through the town with the horse's hooves pounding. Many of the houses were already dark. They passed the churches and could see light coming from their house. Karl helped his mother down from the buggy as Julius came running from the front door. "Father is very sick. Dr. Felsman is with him."

"What happened?" Christina asked, throwing off her shawl. "I never should have left him when he wasn't feeling good."

Julius put his arm around her. "Just before sundown he went out the back door and collapsed. I saw him fall. When I got to him, he just looked at me. He couldn't say anything....He just stared at me with eyes that didn't see anything." Together they went into the bedroom.

Dr. Felsman looked up and shook his head. They could see from the paraphernalia on the table that Dr. Felsman had bled the patient. Gottlieb's face was very white and waxen. His eyes were open but he gave no sign of recognition.

Christina moved to the chair from which the doctor had arisen. She sat and held Gottlieb's hand. With her other hand she smoothed his hair. Karl walked in and stood behind her with his hand on her shoulder.

Julius brought other chairs and they sat around the bed, not speaking. Dr. Felsman packed up his black bag. He motioned to Karl to follow him into the hallway. "I'll come again in the morning if he is still with us then. Call me if there is any change. I'm sorry."

Karl shook the doctor's hand and said, "Are you saying that there isn't any hope? I had no idea he was that sick."

"He's not been a well man for months. His heart just isn't strong enough."

"Well, thank you, doctor. I'm very grateful you were close by."

"Be sure your mother gets some rest. It won't do any good for her to get sick too. Don't bother coming to the door with me. Go to your mother." He walked slowly out the front door.

Karl went back into the bedroom. Mother was still sitting by the bed. She hadn't even taken off her bonnet. Julius sat with his head bowed and his lips moving in silent prayer. Luisa and Hermann sat quietly in the corner of the room, frightened by the nearness of death.

Summoning all the authority of his years as second-in-command, Karl broke the silence. "Mother, why don't you take off your Sunday clothes and make yourself comfortable. We'll stay with Father." Christina slowly got to her feet, went to the wardrobe for a clean work dress and apron. Then she walked across the hall to Luisa's room to change her clothes.

"Luisa, go down to the kitchen and lay out a little bread and butter and some milk. Hermann can help you."

Karl looked at Julius, when they had all left the room. "We've got a hard night ahead of us. Dr. Felsman doesn't hold out any hope. We'll send word to Mathilda. We've got to get in touch with Gustav and Johann, and Gotthelf, if we can find him. They have to come as soon as they can. As soon as Mother comes back, I'll get started writing the letters to Gustav and Johann. We'll post them first thing in the morning."

Gottlieb lay quietly, propped up on several pillows. His breathing became more and more ragged. The single candle on the nightstand had burned itself out. Christina sat beside the bed watching Gottlieb's face in the pale light of dawn. She sent Julius to call Luisa and Hermann, who were napping. Karl paced slowly back and forth as he had for the last hour. Gottlieb gave a deep sigh. There was no further sound of his breathing.

"He's at peace," Christina said. Luisa began to cry and ran out of the room. "Hermann, run over and tell Dr. Felsman!"

Julius said, "May his Saviour give him eternal peace and remain with us as our only Lord and Provider."

"If only the whole family could have been here," Karl added. "Father was always happiest when we were all together. It is a pity that the next time we are together, it will be for his funeral. I'll finish the letters I started last night."

> Dear Gustav,
>
> My hand is shaking because I have to give you bad news; sadness has fallen on us all. Yesterday evening Father suddenly took ill. Dr. Felsman did what he could but he was without hope. Our dear, good father fought all night but early this morning he died quietly, with all of us standing around his bed. He is now with the Lord. The funeral will be next Thursday. We send you ten *Taler*, money for you and Gotthelf, if you know where he is. Should you be able to come, you will have to go to Breslau Wednesday night so you can catch the train to Altwasser Thursday morning. This is the last train to get you here in time. I'll send a letter to the last address we had for Gotthelf in Stendal, telling him to get in touch with you at once. Should Gotthelf not arrive on Wednesday, we ask you

to come alone. Please leave five *Taler* with a friend as travel money for Gotthelf.

Your brother, Karl, in the name of all the others

It was less complicated to send word to Johann and Mathilda. Tradesmen going to Lehmwasser and to Neuhaus could carry the notes faster than the *Post*.

Johann, still dressed in his Sunday suit, drove the small buggy Wagner had lent to him. Only yesterday morning he had been driving down this same road toward Endigen. Now, the funeral over, he was returning to Neuhaus. He was glad in a way that Wagner, always the taskmaster, had insisted that he come back in time for Friday's work.

He felt so torn apart. He missed his father. When he had arrived in Endigen yesterday, the deep bass voice was not heard, the chair at the end of the table was empty. Father was in the coffin on the trestles in the parlor. Without anyone saying a word, Johann knew that he had caused his father pain by not coming back to Endigen on Wagner's trips. He knew how important the family circle was to his father, but he had willfully resisted contact with that circle after he moved to Neuhaus. The only thing that made him different from Gotthelf was the fact that Wagner kept his family informed about his life.

Talking with Gustav, who had arrived for the funeral alone, he learned of the regular exchange of letters. Gustav had written to Father and Mother; they had written to him. Letters came to and from Karl or Julius. Through the *Wanderjahr*, through the two years in the army, Gustav had not really left the family circle. He continued to feel the warmth of the family.

Now, as the buggy jerked along the road, Johann reflected on the lack of warmth he felt for the family. He had held his mother close when he arrived yesterday. She cried on his shoulder. Then Karl had come along with a question and she had gone into the parlor with him. That was the only moment during his day in Endigen that they had really been close.

Last night, Johann lay awake in his bed up in the loft, like all the other nights before he had left home. Only Gotthelf was not there. The brothers had not talked much after Karl blew out the candle. Soon he was snoring regularly in his bed. When Julius crawled into bed beside Johann, he quickly fell asleep. Gustav and Hermann talked quietly for a few minutes in the other bed, then fell silent. Johann lay as quiet as possible, but he could not sleep. He could hear branches from the big tree in front of the house rubbing on the roof. A dog barked somewhere in the village.

Johann had dreaded the funeral because the people of the town, his school friends, the neighbors who had watched him grow up, would all be there. They would ask, "What are you doing now, Johann?" "Where are you working now, Johann?" To answer them was a painful prospect. "I'm still an apprentice..." "I work for Wagner in Neuhaus for a *Taler* a month..." He imagined them thinking: why aren't you like your older brothers...? Why can't you stand on your own feet...? Don't you have a steady job yet...?

Fortunately, Gustav in his uniform had proved to be the center of attention. Old soldiers asked to find out how the army had changed. Others talked about when he would be discharged and come home.

As they had left the cemetery old man Scharf fell in step with Johann. As a member of the church choir which had sung in church and at the gravesite, he had his worn hymnal under his arm. "Well, Johann, this is a sad day for me. Your father was my good neighbor for—it must have been—35 years. He was a good man—solid—honest as the day is long."

Johann had replied, "Yes, he was. I haven't seen him for over a year. I didn't realize he was that sick."

"He'd stop at the house every so often on his way home from the shop. He usually talked about what Wagner told him about you and your work. You should come oftener. Your mama is gonna need to see you oftener now that he's gone."

"It's hard for me to come. I have to keep up with all the dye orders, mixing the colors, overseeing the dyeing. I can't just take a lot of time off."

"Can you stop at the house for a little visit before you go back?"

Johann shook his head. "I wish I could. I still remember all the stories you told me when we'd talk after school. But I have to drive back to Neuhaus tonight, so I can work tomorrow. I'm going to leave as soon as we have a little chance to visit at home."

"I notice Gotthelf wasn't here."

"Gustav tried to get in touch with him, but I guess he didn't get word in time to come."

"Too bad! He should have made more of an effort. Well, stop by next time you get to town."

Johann waved and walked to his front door. Several women from the neighborhood were putting bread and butter, pies, fruit, and coffee on the table in the kitchen. Luisa was showing them where dishes were in the cabinet. As he went up the stairway Johann could hear Karl talking to the people gathered in the parlor. "He was a fine man. The business will miss him. I will do my best to keep everything going the same way as when he was managing. Julius will help me."

He found his mother in the bedroom, her cheeks crossed by tears. She had taken off her hat and was tying on an apron, even though the neighbors were taking care of the food. She felt more comfortable in the uniform of keeper of the house. "*Mutti*, I have to go soon. Wagner wants me to work tomorrow, so I don't want to get back to Neuhaus too late at night. I'm so sorry Father died before I had a chance to tell him that I am grateful for all that he gave me."

"He always asks Wagner every two weeks how you are getting along. At least you haven't dropped out of sight like Gotthelf. It wouldn't hurt to write once in a while."

"I guess I never think I have anything to write about. It's just the same old business every day. Wagner teaches me the trade very slowly and thoroughly. I learn it about three times faster than he teaches. It gets awfully boring."

"Just be patient. You won't be sorry." She had put her hand on his arm as they walked toward the kitchen. Then she was engaged by several of the women for last minute instructions.

Johann shivered. A chill of loneliness passed through him as the buggy rolled toward Neuhaus. Not only did he feel the loss of his father deeply, he also felt in new ways the depth of his estrangement from the family. Spending a day in the familiar setting; seeing the house, the church, the cemetery, the shop, failed to produce any longing to be back there. More and more he felt himself pulling away from the past. His father's death would only hasten that process.

Outside of a concern for his mother, there was very little drawing him back toward Endigen. The other boys and Luisa would care for her. There was no need for him to be there, other than a very occasional visit or letter. Feeling free from responsibility did little to ease his loneliness.

Johann poured out many of these feelings to Marta on Sunday afternoon. During the first part of their walk, he was very quiet. Marta did not fill the time with the friendly chatter that usually went along with their weekly strolls. She sensed that he was in some pain and simply took his hand and walked beside him in silence. Finally she said, "I remember how it was when my mother died. I never felt so alone."

After another long silence Johann answered, "I guess I feel bad because I didn't go home more often to see my father. Wagner did say something once about Father not feeling well. He was always so strong; I didn't give it a second thought."

"Tell me a little about him."

"Well, he was a big man, quite a bit taller than I am. He had dark hair and a full, wavy beard that was turning gray. He talked with a deep voice. He used to be quite a bass singer in the *Männerchor*."

"How old was he?"

"I think Mother said he was 59. He took good care of us, as good as he could afford. I know that he worried a lot about how we would all get along. He wanted us to have it better than he did when he was a child. His parents were quite old when he was born and his mother died not long afterward. He was raised by a step-mother."

"I know all about that. Even if a step-mother takes good care of you, you are never really her child. You never quite feel that you belong."

"I feel so very alone. I still have a mother and brothers and sisters; but I feel alone."

Since they were walking along a country lane with no one to see, Marta put her arm around his waist and looked up at him. "Do you really feel alone when you are with me?" She leaned her head against his shoulder. She drew him to a large linden tree beside the lane and sat down.

"No. I don't feel alone with you. You are the only real friend I have." He suspected that Marta would have preferred to be regarded as more than a friend.

"I really care about you...a lot." She returned her head to his shoulder and drew his arm around her.

Johann did not reply. He just tightened his embrace and kissed her lightly as she nestled against him. They sat for a long time in silence.

"Still feel alone?" she asked after some minutes.

"No. I like being with you." Then thoughts of Wagner, the remaining year of his apprenticeship, the lack of a job crowded into his mind, chilling any further expression.

During the week Marta did a lot of thinking at the millinery. She knew that she was feeling more and more love for Johann. She was aware that he had not professed anything more than friendship for her. She had to persuade him to love her too. Once he was free from that miserable apprenticeship, he could get a job and make enough money that they could get married. Then she could move out of her father's house; she could get away from the endless days of turning out simple hats. If only Johann could realize how happy they could be. She'd been wishing and dreaming for months that they could somehow get married and start living their own lives.

What had started months ago as flirtatious chatter shared with Elsbeth and Christiane became for her serious dreaming and planning. Every week of boring hat-making provided time to think of a dozen ways to get him to fall in love with her, to start him thinking of getting married.

Johann, feeling some guilt over his very sporadic contact with his family before his father's death, resolved to be more dutiful. Each time Wagner made his trip to Endigen, Johann gave him a short letter to his mother. They were boring little notes but at least he was in touch with them. Wagner would bring return correspondence from Mother, or from Karl.

Karl wrote that Mother wanted his wedding plans to go ahead in spite of Father's death. He urged that Johann make plans to come to the wedding because it was more important than ever that the family be together. Gustav would not be able to come because he had used his leave time when Father died. Mathilda would not be able to attend because her new baby was due just at that time and it would not be safe for her to travel.

Johann thought, Isn't that just like Karl. He's playing the father now, instructing me to come to his wedding as if I were a little kid.

Expecting Wagner to insist that he was needed at work, Johann felt safe in making the request. He wouldn't have to turn down Karl's request; Wagner would say no and do it for him.

He did not know that Karl had already talked with Wagner. Karl pointed out that the family felt somewhat offended when their long-time business associate had insisted that Johann return to Neuhaus immediately after the funeral. He talked of the pain Mother felt in having to part with her son after such a short visit. Wagner, knowing that work was slowing down a little, had promised Karl that he would give Johann several days off for the wedding and lend him the buggy as well.

Johann made his request after supper that evening. "I know it was only three months ago that you gave me time to go to Father's funeral. Karl is asking me to come to his wedding in Seittendorf on the 24th.

Do you think I could have two days off?" He was prepared to look very disappointed when Wagner refused his request.

Wagner thought for a moment. "I guess we could work that out. I think I could spare you for three days. You could work a couple extra hours on the days before you go and when you get back to make up for it. I'll postpone one of my buying trips and do the mixing while you are away. You can have the buggy for the trip."

"Well, I don't want to take the time off if it is going to be a hardship for you."

"No, you go. It will give you a little time to be with your mother."

When Johann told Marta about that conversation, he was still puzzled. "I don't know what was going on there. That old slave-driver was all smiles. He purred like a cat and told me to take three days off and to use his buggy. Now I'll have to go to..."

Marta interrupted, "I know you get cross-ways with Karl, but why don't you just make up your mind to enjoy yourself. Weddings can be a lot of fun. I wish Fräulein would give me three days off and lend me a buggy on top of it. I'd go in a flash—anywhere."

Johann smiled, "Sure you would. I wouldn't mind, except Karl will be running around like king of the roost and expect everyone to fall all over him in his moment of glory. It would be nice to have a little time with Mother, though. I know these are hard times for her, so at least I can have a nice visit with her."

"I wish I could know her," Marta said. "I always picture her as if she looked like my mother."

"I've mentioned you in the little letters I've been sending to her through Wagner. She asked me to describe you in a letter."

"Why didn't you tell me that you wrote about me? I hope you said nice things."

"Sure I did. Mother said she thought you sounded like a nice young woman and she was happy that I knew someone so nice. I told her I'd buy for her a hat you had made."

"I wish I could meet her."

Johann smiled as an inspiration came over him. "Why don't you go to the wedding with me. You could stay with Luisa while we are in Seittendorf. That way you'd get to meet Mother and some of the family. I'd like the chance to show old Karl that he's not the only one with a pretty girlfriend," he laughed.

"If you're serious, I could ask my father and Fräulein." The very thought of such a trip brought a sparkle of excitement to her eyes. "They might even say yes if I put it to them just right."

"All right, ask them. We could have a good time, our first real outing."

As Johann was writing his next letter to his mother, telling her of the possibility that Marta would come along with him to the wedding, it began to dawn on him that this was going to send several signals. Marta might see the invitation as a confirmation that she was becoming part of the Weber family. His family would interpret her presence at the wedding as evidence that he was seriously interested in her as a wife. Although Johann thought often about the possibility of getting married, there was still nothing specific in his thinking about who his wife might be. It would be several years before he would dare to get serious about anybody. He enjoyed his walks with Marta, but he was far from certain that she was anything more than a friend. The whole notion of getting married to anyone was fogged over by the fact that he was without the means to support a household. Apprentices didn't marry.

Surely, he thought, everyone will realize that marriage isn't in the picture. They'll realize that this is just friendship.

Three buggies filled with Webers had converged on Seittendorf that morning. Karl and Mother were driven by Julius. Hermann drove with Luisa. Johann and Marta arrived shortly after, ending their three hour drive from Neuhaus. When they had entered the Diepolt parlor, Johann introduced Marta to his family. She was strangely shy. Christina hugged her and Luisa, only two years older than Marta, greeted her warmly. Even Karl expressed his joy that she had come to help celebrate this big event. Johann winced when Hermann blurted with a giggle, "This'll give you two a chance to practice."

Julius gave Hermann an unseen pinch of caution. "It was good of you to come, Marta. I'm sure you'll have a good time. Wait till you see the dining room."

Karl rejoined them and said that he and Emilie were going now to the Rathaus for the civil ceremony and that it would soon be time for them all to go to the church, which was only a short walk down the street.

Following the marriage service the bride and groom rode in an ornate carriage to the Diepolt house, while the rest of the families and friends walked. The wedding party, by Endigen standards, was extraordinarily splendid. Emilie's brother and guardian, Klaus, had spared little expense. He had taken over the family factory when their father had died more than a decade before. He was a respected member of the community.

The whole house was decorated with flowers and branches of small shrubs. In the dining room a long, large table was covered with food. Several farm girls, scrubbed until they glowed in their white aprons, carried platters and tureens back and forth from the kitchen. Karl, with Emilie on his arm, circulated among all the guests; she introducing him to her Seittendorf friends and he introducing her to the family members whom she had not met on her one visit to Endigen. Emilie directed them to their chairs at the dining tables.

Karl and Mother, sensing that the rest of the family was not familiar with these styles, quietly modeled the correct ways to eat the meal. Afterward as Marta stood with Johann and Luisa in the corner of the parlor, she confessed her uneasiness. "I was so afraid I'd make a terrible mistake in front of everybody."

"This is all new to me too, " Johann laughed. "I hardly knew what to do with my hands. Somehow my blue fingernails just didn't seem to fit in. No matter how hard I scrubbed, I couldn't get the dye off."

Luisa said, "Karl told us that Emilie's brother was spending more than 35 *Reichstaler* on the wedding. I've never seen anything this fancy."

"Imagine Karl finding a girl only a little more than half as old as he is, very nice looking, and, on top of it all, well-to-do," Johann added.

Marta was quick to say, "I think she's lovely. She reminds me of some of the young ladies Fräulein and I make hats for in Neuhaus. I wish I were beautiful like that...."

"I'd settle for a big house like this," Luisa added. "I wonder how she's going to like living with us in Endigen. Our house is nice, but nothing like this."

"With a husband she loves," Marta put in, "she'll be happy wherever she is."

Johann thought it best to change the subject. "Let's go outside and walk around a little. I've got to shake all that food down."

Marta took his arm and they strolled back down the street toward the church. She said, "It's been so nice. Thank you for bringing me along."

"I'm sorry for all the comments about other people getting married."

"It's all in fun. I think it's great when people have a good time."

They crisscrossed the streets of Seittendorf for an hour and then came back to the Diepolt house. Emilie's friends had departed, and she was directing the various Webers to the rooms where they would spend the night. Christina would have the guest bedroom. Johann, Julius and Hermann were to share a room on the third floor. Luisa and Marta were placed in a room normally occupied by the two hired girls, who had been sent to their homes in the country for the night.

The next day Klaus had organized a tour to Bad Salzbrunn about an hour's drive away. Still in their fanciest clothes they strolled through the gardens of the spa. There were gravel paths between carefully trimmed hedges and through groves of trees. Ornate buildings marked the location of various mineral springs. Several cups were chained to each fountain. Marta faced Johann and laughed, "Here you are, sir. Drink this, and you'll feel like a new man."

Johann laughed back, "I dare you to go first. If you drink a cup, I will too."

She took the cup, dipped into the flowing basin and raised it quickly to her lips. The smell of sulphur made her hesitate for a moment. She grinned mischievously at Johann and drank the cup down, handing the cup to him, "Here, your turn."

Not to be outdone, he drank deeply and made sounds as if he has just enjoyed a cool glass of beer. "*Wunderbar*! I've never had anything so good. I feel healthy already."

"You just wait," Marta promised. They laughed and joked as they saw the little outhouses that were placed strategically throughout the woods to minister to those who were taking the waters.

Walking through the surrounding village, Johann, Marta, and Luisa went, wide-eyed, from one shop window to another. Never had they seen such finery: gowns, hats, shoes, jewelry. Luisa said, "If I had something like that, I would never have any place to wear it. Can't you picture me, Johann, trudging through the dust to church in a gown like that? Endigen would never be the same. I'll bet they wouldn't even let me into the church."

Marta answered, "I'd like to take a couple of those hats back to show Fräulein. Her magazines don't have anything that fancy."

"There must be some people with enough money to buy those things," Johann added. "I can't imagine anybody with that kind of money. It would take me a year to earn enough to buy a dress like that, and I'd have to give up eating for a year to do it."

"Please buy it for me," Marta teased. "I'd like to show those ladies in Neuhaus that I could wear fancy clothes too."

Johann's smile disappeared. To see such fine things only reminded him how terribly poor he was. It was no longer a joke. Working for his room and board and a little bit of spending money was painful for a man his age. "Let's go. We should meet the others back at the livery stable where we left the horses and buggies."

Emilie and her sister-in-law unpacked the two baskets they had brought along for lunch. Some of the food from the wedding supper was spread on the cloth beneath the tree in the park. Klaus brought several bottles of cool wine from a straw-filled box in his buggy. Karl and Emilie were toasted again as the wedding feast resumed. Christina said, "Such wonderful food. I hope, Emilie, that this isn't all you are used to eating. Things are a lot more plain at our kitchen table."

Emilie smiled, "Don't worry. We really live a fairly simple life. Klaus just wanted to make our wedding special. He's always been so good to me since our parents died."

Karl put his hand on Klaus' shoulder, "You've done a good job, being both brother and father. We really thank you for all your kindness."

Johann thought, Why don't you say it? Tell him how impressed you are by his success, his money, his fancy house. You'd give your right arm to live like that.

The following morning on the long buggy ride back to Neuhaus, Marta was still filled with the excitement of the past two days. Her dark eyes flashed as she chattered on about Emilie's house, Emilie's clothes, Emilie's wedding. "This was just the nicest time I've ever had. Thank you so much for bringing me." She gave Johann's arm a squeeze.

"Don't get too impressed," he said. "No use filling your mind with dreams of things you can never have."

"I've always dreamed about marrying and having a nice house and lovely clothes. I know that it's a dream, but it doesn't do any harm, does it?"

"Dream on, but never forget that a dream ends with waking up."

"What do you dream about?" Marta asked, turning her head to look him full in the face.

Johann was taken aback by the suddenness of her question. "About all I can dream of now is finishing up at Wagner's and getting my own job. To dream about anything else just makes me frustrated. I'm stuck, so why dream? I've been stuck for what seems all my life."

Marta showed her growing impatience, "Listen, I've had much less in my life than you have, but no one stops me from dreaming! I'd go crazy making all those dumb hats if I couldn't dream while I was turning them out." With a sudden coyness she said quietly, "You know, you're even in some of my dreams."

"The monster who jumps out from behind a tree and chases you home?" Johann joked, trying to put a little distance between himself and the implied intimacy of her conversation.

"You're laughing at me. I'm serious. You'll go crazy if you don't have a dream. I'll be happy to be in your dreams."

"I'll see if I can arrange it....I'd better speed this nag up or Wagner will be waiting for us at the door with his face a mile long. Giddap!"

CHAPTER 5

"I love the beginning of fall. Look at the green trees on that hillside, just starting to turn color. I've never seen anything so beautiful." Marta squeezed Johann's hand as they walked through the dusty grass along their favorite lanes. "It's such a mild afternoon; I can hardly believe that soon it will be winter."

"*Ja.* We won't be taking many more long walks."

"You can come to my house. The folks won't mind. Father likes you, you know." Marta grinned, "He told me to hang on to you."

Johann answered with the same light humor, at least on the surface of things. "Aha! Spinning your web for me, is that it? I'd better watch my step with you."

Marta's smile faded. "Are you afraid of me, afraid I'll tie you down?"

"Who would be afraid of a little thing like you.?" Johann began to pick up the new seriousness. "I like to be with you. You know that. I wouldn't go walking Sunday after Sunday if I didn't."

Marta pulled on Johann's arm. "I'm getting tired. Let's rest a little while. We'll still get back to town before dark."

"I guess we have time to sit for a little while." They walked through a narrow gap in the roadside hedge. A small stack of hay offered a soft seat. Johann took off his coat and with show of gallantry spread it on the hay for Marta to sit upon. They leaned back on the sunny side of the stack, facing away from the road.

"It smells so good. I love to smell hay, don't you? Ouch! My shoe hurts." Marta untied her right shoe and slipped it off before she lay back against the sunwarmed hay.

Johann sat beside her. She took his hand. "Lie back and watch those clouds. Don't they look like horses galloping across the sky?" She leaned her head against his shoulder.

He said, "The sun feels so warm. You'd better keep talking to me or I'll doze off."

"Go ahead. I'll just watch the clouds." She moved a little closer to him. She slowly rubbed her stocking foot against his ankle.

Johann had never experienced this kind of closeness to a woman. He could feel the softness of Marta's hair against his cheek. He was very much aware of the stroking of her foot. Somewhat awkwardly he moved to put his arm around her and began to draw her closer. Closing her eyes, she snuggled against him, her hands smoothing the shirt on his back. Timidly he kissed her cheek, her closed eyes...her mouth. She pressed against him as they lay in the fragrant hay. For a long time their embrace was motionless. Johann was aware of stirrings which had always accompanied the world of fantasy but now were a response to the softness of Marta's body. Finally, he sighed deeply and began to twist from their embrace. Marta kissed him once again and whispered in his ear, "*Ich liebe dich.*"

Johann was speechless but for a moment longer turned and held her close. He didn't know what to say. Marta's words of love, words never said to him before, sent warmth coursing through him. He reached down and put her shoe on her small foot, lacing it quickly. Helping her up, he shook out the hay from his coat and said rather huskily, "We're not going to get back to town before dark, if we don't leave."

Marta could hardly wait to talk with Christiane. She had to tell someone that she was in love, that she had found someone she would some day marry. For the next few evenings she sat by the front window of her father's house, remembering that Christiane sometimes walked to her family's house for a few minutes after supper, while the Wagner children were being put to bed. She rushed out when she saw her friend, strolling along with her.

Christiane was wide-eyed when she heard the full account of Sunday afternoon's walk. "He actually kissed you?"

"I don't know how long we were there, but I felt like I was flying through the sky. I love him so much. If he were only finished with his apprenticeship, I'm sure he would ask me to marry him right away. He can't say anything until he's not tied to Wagner any more. How did he act at supper, after he got back from the walk?"

"Of course, I wasn't looking for anything, so it seemed just like always. He sure didn't say anything about it. He just mentioned something about the two of you walking in the country. Come to think of it, he did have a kind of silly smile, but I didn't...."

"What do you mean, silly? You mean he was making fun of what happened?"

"*Ach*, no; that's not what I meant. He just seemed a little more shy than usual, kind of sheepish. I never thought of him as a kisser. Our time in Wagner's kitchen is just sister and brother stuff."

"Well, I can tell you he was no brother on Sunday," Marta grinned. "He is so nice looking. When he looks at me, I just turn to custard. He's strong and gentle at the same time. I just know he cares about me. He wouldn't keep going for these long walks with me if he weren't interested."

Christiane put her hand on Marta's arm. "Don't get your hopes too high. It's going to be a while before he can think about getting married. He'll have to find a job when he's finished at Wagner's. He'd have to save some money before he could ask you to marry him. He might even have to go to some other town to find work, like Gotthelf. Did I tell you that Gotthelf is coming back to Neuhaus?"

Marta's eyes filled with tears. "I'd die without him. He can't possibly know how much I love him. We could be so happy together."

"Well, have sweet dreams about your Prince Charming....Listen, if I don't get back soon, I'll catch it from Frau Wagner."

The weeks of autumn spread out. There were more Sunday walks in the country, all of which seemed to stop at the haystack. Each week small new intimacies were added: a hand here, a caress there, more kisses, an opened shirt, a loosened bodice, more kisses, embracing in fragrant, prickly hay.

Johann was puzzled at first by Marta's eagerness. The pleasure of these weekly encounters was very real, but he sensed that it meant something different to him than to Marta. There was something wifely about the way she looked at him, or held his arm while they walked. If he told her how he felt, he would hurt her, and the weekly lovemaking would end.

When Gotthelf came back to Neuhaus, Johann mentioned his return to Wagner. He was surprised when Wagner volunteered to give him work as a helper for Hans. Frau Wagner cleaned out another small room near Johann's and Gotthelf moved in with the family.

Gotthelf told Johann, "This is the first good luck I've had in a long time....I walk right into a job, not much money but I get a roof over my head and food on my plate....But, best of all, I get to look at that pretty Christiane three times every day."

"'Count your blessings,' as good old Karl would say."

"Christiane said that you and Marta are getting pretty thick. Not bad for an old man." he joked.

"We only see each other once a week. We go for long walks every Sunday. That's the only time we both have time off from work. She's a nice little thing. But she's a lot more serious about this than I am."

"Don't tell me that after all these years you're not the marrying kind."

"How am I going to get married when I still have time to go on my apprenticeship? Then I'll have to find a job. It'll be a couple of years before getting married is in the cards for me."

"If what Christiane says is right, Marta'll wait for you."

"That's part of the problem. She's the first girl I ever really got close to. I'm not sure that I plan on getting married to Marta. By the time I'm ready, I might be miles away, and I might meet somebody I like better."

"Does Marta know you're thinking like that? If you ask me, when she looks at you, it's like a wife looking at her husband."

"She's fun to be with, but I'm not ready to be tied down."

Wagner sat on the stool in his little salesroom, puffing on his pipe. Johann had brought in several bolts of new material. In an uncharacteristically expansive mood, Wagner said, "Johann, sit down over here. We ought to talk a little."

Johann sat on the other stool, wondering what was coming now.

"You'll be finishing your time as an apprentice in another year. You've worked hard and 've been a good pupil. In your final year I'm going to teach you not only dyeing, but also I can show you how to run a successful business."

Inwardly Johann grimaced at the thought of yet another year as an apprentice, but he smiled and said, "I'll do my best."

Wagner went on, "You'll be able to use that when you go back to Endigen. Since your father died, Karl and Julius are doing all right running the business. They'll be glad to have you come back to join them in the business, I'm sure. You might even be able to teach them some of the things I'll show you."

"*Ja*," Johann said. But he was thinking: It would never work to be under Karl. Now that Father's dead, Karl will have the business. I couldn't stand to have him bossing me around all the time. He'd treat me like a little kid, even if I was pulling my own weight.

"You know, Johann, you are very lucky. You've got a good strong family, soon you'll have an honorable trade. Your father wasn't a poor man. You'll do all right."

"It has been very slow. I think it will be years before I can be on my own."

"Listen," Wagner stood up to shelve the new material. "You've got it good. Just today I was at the Rathaus. The burghers were trying to work out something for that poor widow who lives with her brood in the little cottage on the alley behind the dye house. Her husband never was good for much. Even while he was alive, every once in a while the town would have to help them get food and give them money for the rent."

"Yes, Marta was telling me about them. They really have had an awful time."

"The burghers are getting smart. Do you know what they're doing? They could see that the town would have to lay out money, lots of money, for a good many years until all those kids can start earning their own way. So they're going to buy the good woman and her kids a ticket."

"A ticket...?"

"To America. Her brother went there a couple of years ago. The burghers figured that it would be a lot cheaper to send her to America so her brother can look after her and that bunch of kids. So they came up with 60 *Taler* to buy passage for all of them. Her brother would have to look after her if he were still here, so he'll be in a better position to take care of them over there. He probably has a good-paying job."

"Does she want to go?"

"I suppose she'd like to be with her brother. But she isn't being given a hell of a lot of choice in the matter. It's either take the 60 *Taler* for the ticket or do without the money the town has been giving her. Lots of towns are doing that. Good business, I say," Wagner's voice boomed.

"*Ja.*"

"Some people might think that is kind of heartless. But what kind of future does she have here?"

"Some people would find it very exciting to set sail for a new country, a new world. But it would be an awfully shaky step. Who knows what you'd find once you got over there? You could be worse off than here."

Wagner tapped out his pipe. "I've never really had the desire to go, but you hear a lot of folk who'd like nothing better. Besides, the town isn't going to give me a ticket," he chuckled.

It was the day the first snow fell that Johann received a letter from Julius. He reported that Father's estate had now been settled. Instead of leaving everything to Mother, his will had directed that his estate of 13,598 *Reichstaler* be divided among his wife and children, with each receiving an equal share. Julius reported that the money would be put in bonds for each of the children.

Johann ran to Gotthelf's room. He read Julius' letter aloud again. Gotthelf sat with his head in his hands.

Johann said, "This means that each of us has over 1500 *Reichstaler*. I can hardly believe it."

"I don't have any sense of how much that is. My pockets have never known more than two or three *Taler* at a time. I know that you can buy a house for five hundred. Hey, I'm a rich man! Come on down to the Ratskeller. The drinks are on me."

"Maybe not rich. But you and I have got enough now to have a little independence. It's going to take me a while to get used to the idea."

"Come on, let's celebrate."

"Wait a minute. All your money is back in Endigen. What are you going to spend in the Ratskeller?"

"I'll tell 'em run a tab for me. I can pay it off when I get the money."

"If I were you, I'd just keep quiet about the whole thing for now."

"You mean you're not going to tell Marta? or Wagner?"

"Not right away. I want to think about it a little. I've got to figure out what this is going to do to my life. Help me out, will you, by not saying anything about the inheritance for the present."

"Well, all right. I'll do it to humor you, but I'm going to have a hard time. I'll bet if I told Christiane, she'd be ready to head for the church right now. She'd be ready to marry a rich man on a moment's notice. Can't say I'd mind that at all."

"I guess that's part of the reason I don't want to say anything right now. Marta would think that this opens the door for getting married right away. I don't want to get pushed into getting married. A few months waiting to tell won't hurt."

"If you don't want to marry her, why don't you just stop seeing her? What do you think is going to change?"

"I like her, but I'm not sure that I want to marry her. She's going to box me in. The door is just opening for the first real freedom I've had in twenty-six years. For the first time in my life I won't have to be dependent on someone else. I don't have anyone who ties me down, keeps me from doing what I want to do. I need a little time to feel that pleasure."

When he got back to his room, Johann took the old mirror down from the wall. Using his pocket knife he pried the thin board back off and took out the three *Taler* he had put there on his first evening in Neuhaus two years ago, the money his father had given him for emergencies. With many more *Taler* waiting for him in Endigen, he put these in his pocket.

"But what will I do with it?" he muttered. If he bought something for himself, Marta was sure to notice and ask how he had been able to afford it. If he bought something for her, it would only cement the relationship over which he had so many questions.

He took the mirror down and pried off the back again.

The winter months had brought an end to the long country walks and the haystack. Marta invited Johann to call at her house on Sundays. Sometimes they would sit with the family around the kitchen stove which gave off both heat and fragrance. It was fun to see Marta playing her part in the Wiesner family. She was clearly the liveliest of the bunch. Her father and step-mother welcomed Johann almost as if he were one of the family. There was always coffee and *Stollen*.

There was very little time for Marta and Johann to be alone. As he was getting ready to return to his room at Wagner's, Marta would walk with him to the front door while the rest of the family remained in the kitchen. In the gathering darkness they would embrace. As she kissed him she would often hold his hand against her breast. She would whisper, "*Ich liebe dich*," and wait for his response. Johann had grown accustomed to murmuring the words too, but he knew inwardly that he did not have the same fervor as Marta. If she suspected, she gave no sign.

"Let's find another haystack," Marta giggled.

"More likely a snowdrift right now."

"Couldn't I come to your room when Wagners and Christiane are all in church on Sunday morning?"

"Gotthelf would be in his room."

"Can't you get rid of him for an hour? You could send him on an errand or something. I'm just dying to be alone with you for a little while.

Maybe we could get Christiane to talk him into going to church with her some Sunday. She wouldn't have to know why."

"Gotthelf isn't much for church, but he's goofy about Christiane. That might be enough to convert him for at least one Sunday."

"I'm going to tell her to ask him to sit in church with her. She won't mind that at all."

"Bet it won't work."

"Listen, if she looks at him with those blue eyes, he'll tag along."

"You're quite a little schemer."

"If you want something bad enough, you can make things work out. You just watch me."

Marta turned her head on the pillow of Johann's narrow bed. She smiled contentedly and stroked Johann's hair on the pillow beside her. "You see, dreams can come true! I have never been so happy."

Johann drew her close once again, moving his hands over the hills and valleys of her body. "You are purring like a kitten," he murmured into her soft hair.

"Isn't it the most wonderful thing in the world to be so close?"

"*Ja,* it was wonderful." Johann stared at the cracked plaster of the ceiling of his room. His mind was tied in knots. He was excited and pleasured by their lovemaking, but he also was fearful of the attachment it implied. He was finding being her lover enjoyable, but he was not ready to be taken for a husband. It was not fair to her to hold back the mixture of feelings that consumed him.

Marta kissed him again and again. "It's like having our own house, our own bedroom; even if only for a couple hours."

They heard the church bell toll three times. "They're saying the *Unser Vater* after the sermon; that means they'll be coming home soon." Marta reached for her dress and began to arrange her hair. Johann quickly pulled on his clothes.

"We'd better be out of the house before they get here," he said.

Looking into Johann's mirror Marta satisfied herself that everything was in place. "Kiss me again," she whispered, "Oh, I love you so much."

Johann held her close for a moment, then handed her her coat and pushed her gently toward the door. "Come on. We'll slip out the back of the shop."

Although Gotthelf could not be persuaded to go to church every week, there were other Sundays when Marta and Johann could share an intimate hour in his garret room. The strangeness of these stolen moments diminished and even Johann began to feel some of the domestic contentment that Marta expressed.

Marta was both troubled and excited when she became aware of the changes that were taking place in her body. She really had not thought much about the possibility of becoming pregnant in the excitement of being with Johann. The thought of having Johann's baby more and more thrilled her. They could get married and have their own home. Her dream was coming true, although much sooner than she had anticipated.

She could hardly wait to tell the news to Johann. She thought: he always talks about how much he needs to feel like he is a man. Now he will know he is a man. He'll be a husband and a father.

One evening in early spring Johann drew Gotthelf by the arm into his room after supper. "I've got something I need to talk to you about."

"Sure. Did you hear from Karl? more about the money?"

"No, I need to talk to you about Marta. I have to tell you something you'll be surprised about."

"*Ja.*"

"Well, we've been seeing each other for more than a year and it's gotten pretty heavy. We kind of got carried away. We got to hugging and kissing and one thing led to another. She kept calling me a bull, so I pushed her. Now she's getting a little swelling in her stomach. We've talked it over with her folks and it seems like I'll have to marry her right after Easter."

"Eiii! Well. That settles that. You old rascal."

"*Ja.* It's not really what I had in mind. But she's a good girl and I guess she'll be a good wife. I wasn't ready for this. I should have kept my pants on. Then I'd have a little different future."

"Kinda locks you in, doesn't it."

"For sure. I thought maybe I could use Father's money to get started in a business. Now some of it is going to have to go to setting up a house somewhere. I'm not sure I want to stay in Neuhaus."

"What do you think Mother will say?"

"I'm going to write and tell her. They all liked Marta when she was at Karl's wedding. She'll understand."

"Old Karl will be crossways for a while, I'll bet. But he's got this thing about being Head of The Family, so he'll come through in the end."

"I want you to promise me something."

"What is it?"

"I don't want you ever to tell anyone: Mother, Karl, Christiane, anybody that I had all these questions about being tied down with Marta. That's in the past. I owe it to her to make the best of it. So, forget I ever told you about how I really felt."

"I'm sorry things are turning out this way. Sure. I promise never to say anything about it to anyone. You can trust that."

"What's done is done. *So geht's!*"

"What are you going to say to Wagner?"

"This is going to tear up the apprenticeship. He's supposed to have full control of me for the whole three years. I doubt if he is going to want to go on. My room and board are practically my total pay. If I have a wife and child and a home of my own, room and board won't be in the picture. He's not going to want to give me money instead. I think it will probably be easier if I just quit."

"What will you do for a job? You'll have to make some money with a family."

"I'll have to start looking right away. I won't be sad to leave Wagner. He's not a bad guy, but so pompous and tedious. He bores me to death, going over the same stuff again and again."

"I suppose Wagner will sack me too when you leave."

"I don't see why he should. You're doing a good job. I don't want to get you in any trouble. I'll talk to him about that when I tell him that I'll be leaving."

"I don't give a damn about the work, but I sure like being around Christiane. I'd like to hang on till I start making some real progress there."

"You really like her, don't you?"

"Sure do. She gets prettier all the time. I may even ask her to marry me, now that I have some money."

"So Father's money sets up two new homes."

"So you're going to get married," Frau Wagner said when Johann came into the kitchen the following evening. "My husband told me after you talked to him this morning. He's having a hard time understanding why you won't finish out your apprenticeship."

"*Ja.* I know. I could tell he was angry when I explained to him this morning that I would be leaving. He just walked away at first."

"He takes it as a serious responsibility to train young men for the trade. He thinks you are a good dyer. He likes you. I guess he feels you are abandoning him just when you really know enough to work without much supervision. We tried to be like a Papa and Mama to you."

"And I thank you. I don't like to be a quitter, but...well... you know that I couldn't support a wife on my little apprentice pay. I don't mean to be ungrateful."

"He thinks you're throwing away a big opportunity."

"I don't have much choice, do I? I'll have a wife, and after a little while, a baby to support."

"You should have thought of that." There was a reproachful note in Frau Wagner's voice. "You should have thought of that!"

"I know, but this is the way it is. So I'm going to leave."

"Wagner will get over it, but he's not going to be easy to live with for a while. He gives up hard."

"I'm sorry. You've been good to me. I really don't have a home any more. My brother Karl and his wife moved in with Mother after my father died. I'll never go back to Endigen. So I guess it's time for me to have my own home."

"Where will you and Marta live?"

"We'll find a couple of rooms somewhere here in Neuhaus for now. It has to be some place that doesn't cost too much. I'm going to have to spend the time between when I leave here and the wedding to find another job."

"Do you have any ideas?"

"Marta's father is going to ask where he works. He thought they might have something soon. I'll have to take anything I can get for the present. Do you think your husband will give me a character?"

"Right now, I'm not sure he would. Right now he thinks you let him down. When he cools off a few days, I'll try to tell him to give you a good character to help you find another job. You've worked hard and he owes you that much."

"I don't like it when people are mad at me. I really can't do anything else. I hope he realizes that. I'm just caught and have to do the best I can."

"I found it. I found it!" Marta greeted Johann when he stopped at her house on Sunday afternoon.

"Found what?"

75

"I found a place to live. It's a nice room at Ziebig's house. You know, the furrier...It's at the front of the house and has three nice windows. It's light and airy. I can hardly wait to show it to you."

"How did you find it?"

"I was walking past and saw a little sign in their window. I asked to see the room and liked it right away."

"Can we afford it?"

"It's only five *Reichstaler*. As soon as you get a paying job, we can handle that. It has just about everything we need. It goes across the whole front of the house. It has a big bed, a wardrobe, a table and chairs, a little stove where I can cook."

"It sounds nice."

"There's even enough room for a cradle by the bed." Marta's eyes sparkled and her cheeks flushed with excitement. "I can hardly wait. It will be wonderful to have a place all our own."

"I'm glad you're happy with it."

"Don't you want to go over and see it? I told Frau Ziebig that we might come to look at the room. She said that would be all right." Marta pulled on his arm. "Come on, let's go see it."

"Sure. That would be good."

As they walked along the streets filled with strollers, Marta continued her sales talk.

"It's got nice curtains and a carpet and a big feather bed. I didn't look to see what was there by way of dishes, *und so weiter*, but I can bring a few things from home if we need them.... Here it is..."

It was a tall three storey brick house, nicely kept. It was much nicer than Wagner's huge building. Frau Ziebig met them at the front door and took them up the stair to the second floor. Marta was two steps ahead of Johann. She ran ahead of Frau Ziebig and threw open the door.

"It is a nice room, " Johann said, walking slowly around. He pulled a curtain aside and looked out at the street below.

Frau Ziebig, puffed like a pigeon, smiled with pride. "It's as clean as any place in town. I try to keep my room just as if I were going to live in it myself. You'll find that it has everything you need. Do you like it, my dear?"

Marta responded immediately, "I simply love it. I love it."

"It's very nice," Johann added. "We'll take it."

"Good. I'll take down my sign. When do you want to move in?"

"Well, that's a little problem," Johann said, feeling that somebody had to snap things back to reality. "Right now I'm looking for a job and the wedding is still a couple of weeks away. Could you just hold the apartment until we are ready to move in?"

"Weeell," Frau Ziebig said. "I'd like to do that, but we count on the rent as part of our income. I'm not sure we can wait two weeks before there is any rent."

"Oh, please," Marta pled. "Can't we work out something? Oh, I want this room so much. It would be so nice. We don't have much money. Could we just give you part of the rent to hold the room until we move in?"

"Weeell....I'd like to have you. Tell you what....I'll split the difference. You give me three *Taler* and I'll hold the room until you move in right after the wedding.."

Johann thought of the three *Taler* behind the mirror in his room at Wagner's. "All right. I will come by after supper tonight and bring you the *Taler* to hold the apartment."

Marta held tight to his arm as they went down the stairs and out into the street. "I'm so happy. Having my own home makes me feel as free as that bird flying up around the church steeple. Don't you just love the room? It may be a little crowded, but it will be our home. I can hardly wait to move in."

"It looks like a good place to live." But on the inside Johann was feeling walls closing in on him: rent, money to buy food and clothes, responsibility. He had to find a job soon. He'd told Wagner he would leave at the end of this week. That gave him a week before the wedding to look for another job. Things were moving much faster that he would have liked. He had never felt that he could provide adequately for himself, now he was going to have to provide for two more.

It was pouring rain when Johann and Marta were married in church in Neuhaus. Only the front pews of the big church were occupied. Johann was pleased that his mother, Karl, Emilie, and Julius had arrived the day before. They had stayed at a boarding house near the Wiesner's home. Johann had been surprised when he got Mother's letter saying that they were coming to the wedding. He had wondered how they would react to his news. When he and Marta had greeted them last evening, Mother had without hesitation hugged Marta. Emilie did the same. Julius had greeted her with a warm handshake. Even Karl had a thin smile, playing his part as the father-figure of the family. Gotthelf and Christiane were standing up with the bride and groom.

Marta's father, step-mother, and sister, dressed in their Sunday best, smiled proudly as the young couple stood before Pastor Resdel. Behind them sat the Wagners. He had gotten over his peevishness and warmly accepted Johann's invitation to the wedding. Beside them sat Hans and Minnie, looking uncomfortable in ill-fitting suit and dress. In the third pew sat Fräulein Krause, next to Marta's girl friends, Maria and Elsbeth.

Marta wore a tan dress her step-mother had made for the occasion. On her brown hair rested a small, stylish hat (a gift from Fräulein) which matched the color of her dress. Her eyes sparkled as she looked up at Johann. Pastor Resdel's deep voice droned on as he read the words of the marriage service. Johann noticed that the pastor's vest was missing a button. He felt Marta's warm hand pressing his. The pastor sounded just like Karl, speaking slowly and impressively with a great air of godly authority. The voice sounded like it was coming from a long tunnel into which Johann was walking. The dimly lit tunnel got smaller and smaller, walls and ceiling closing in on him. A squeeze from Marta's hand brought him back to the church.

He put on her finger his grandmother's wedding ring, which Mother had brought from Endigen. She knew Johann would not have the money to buy a ring so she had written that she would bring a ring when she came to the wedding.

When Johann had told Marta of his mother's offer, she was pleased. "That makes me feel that she really wants me to be part of your family."

Johann said, "She's very kind. Of course, she is glad to have you for a daughter. She liked you when we went to Karl's wedding."

"I feel funny, not really knowing your family. I've only seen them for a couple days. Now I'll be part of them. What if they don't like me?"

"They'll like you. Even if they don't, it doesn't matter. I hardly have any contact with them any more. I'll never go back to Endigen, except maybe to visit once in a while. There's nothing for me there."

"Don't Julius and Karl want you in the business? You could be a lot of help them."

"It would never work. I wouldn't last an hour. The first time Karl ordered me around like a little kid, I'd either hit him or walk out...or both." Johann's voice raised.

"Why can't you like him? He is your brother."

"He's a pious snob. He makes me feel like I have to toe the line all the time. There's no freedom around him. He'd tie me down so I couldn't move."

Marta heard the anger in his voice. "What can you do?"

"I wish I knew. I've got to do something. Right now, I've just got to find a job to be able to pay the rent and buy food. That's going to be hard enough."

"You'll find something. How could anybody turn down my man?" She pecked him on the cheek.

"I heard that they were looking for somebody down at Müller's store. I was hoping for something better than that. With a wife I need more than a store clerk would make. I suppose I could buy food cheaper. I guess I'd better talk to Müller tomorrow. It's better than nothing."

"Cheer up. I can keep working for Fräulein for a while longer. I could keep working just about up to the time for the baby."

"I don't like to ask you to do that. But for a time both of us will probably have to work."

"I'll help all I can."

"I know you will." Without thinking Johann blurted, "Why can't I ever have a break? I get so afraid of having responsibility when for my whole life I have had to depend on someone else."

Marta was silent. Her eyes filled with tears, "Do you mean that I'm a responsibility that scares you?"

Johann felt trapped by the truth. He put his arm around her shoulders. "No. Not you. Don't worry about it. Things will work out. We just have to give things a little time."

"I love you. I want to be your wife more than anything. I'll try not to be too much of a burden. I promise you that."

Johann smiled, "You're too little to be a burden. Don't worry."

Pastor Resdel put his hand on their clasped hands in blessing. As they turned to face the small congregation Johann saw his mother wiping tears from her eyes. Were her tears the tears of joy and sentiment, or did she guess his thoughts, his self-doubt?

CHAPTER 6

As Johann went up the stairs at Ziebig's after work, he could smell his supper cooking. Marta was standing by the little stove stirring the pot. "Did you remember to bring the bread? We're having lentil soup. Get washed and I'll put it on the table."

Johann put his coat in the wardrobe. He watched Marta slicing from the big loaf of bread. He sat down while she ladled the thick brown soup into their bowls.

"I wish I had a regular kitchen. Then I could cook real meals for you. With just this tiny stove I can only use one pot. But if you can put up with such simple meals, I can put up with not having a kitchen. On these summer days, it gets pretty hot in here when I have to make a fire in the stove to cook."

"Maybe some day we'll have a bigger place. You do all right with the cooking."

"I love having our own place, even if it's small. It's our home. We don't need much to be happy. It's warm and it's clean." She looked around at the simple furnishings: table, chairs, wardrobe, washstand, and the big bed with its snowy featherbed. This had been her step-mother's wedding present to her.

"We're lucky to have this place. Do you think we can stay here after the baby is born?

Will there be enough room?"

"It'll do us for a year or so. We'll put the baby in a cradle over there in the corner."

"Where are we going to get a cradle?"

"Don't worry about it. I'll work something out."

After supper Marta washed the few dishes and put everything away. They sat at the table talking until the sun set to end the July day. Marta lit the candle. "We'd better go to bed. It's dark."

Johann folded the paper he had been reading and began to take off his shoes. Marta quickly slipped out of her clothes and into her night dress. She blew out the candle and giggled, "Come to the haystack."

Johann got into bed. Marta reached over and took his hand, placing it on her swollen belly. "Just another month and we'll have our baby."

At the urging of her step-mother and father, Marta had decided to have her baby in the Wiesner house when the time came. Johann could see the wisdom of that plan. There was much more room. Marta's step-mother could help her for a time until she got her strength back.

Marta's younger sister, Gertrude, came running through the front door of Müller's store. "Johann, come right away. She is at our house and the baby is coming. It's early."

Müller, with the experience of the births of seven children, overheard the conversation and waved Johann to run with Gertrude. "On your way, then, 'Papa'. Take the rest of the day off. You let me know if it is a boy or a girl."

As he came breathless through the front door, Johann saw old Frau Hafer, the midwife standing by the kettles of water on the stove. "Go on in and see her. It's going to be a little while."

Marta was in her parents' bed, her step-mother standing beside her, brushing back her hair. She was pale and there was fear in her eyes. "I'm glad you got here in time. Mutter Hafer says that I..." She winced as another contraction gripped her. Sweat stood on her lip and forehead.

Johann took her hand. "You'll be fine. Soon it will all be over." He tried to conceal the fact that his hand was shaking. Suppose things didn't go well? Suppose something happened to Marta? He recalled how Marta had talked about her mother dying when Gertrude was born and her fear that that might happen to her. He tried to push fears aside, but they would not stay away. He held her hand tightly.

Frau Hafer officiously nudged him away and said, "Let me see how things are coming." She slipped her gnarled hands under the covers. "It's going faster than I thought. Get out to the kitchen and keep Marta's father company. We'll take care of things in here. You men can keep the stove going."

The waiting was not over quickly. Hour dragged after hour. The long afternoon shadows fell across the kitchen. The sun went down. Candles were lit. There were moans and cries coming from the bedroom. Frau Hafer came to the kitchen for water or towels. She had little to say but her wrinkled face was grave. "It's going slower than I like to see. I think the baby is turned."

The vigil continued all through the night. Marta's cries became fainter, then stronger. In spite of his father-in-law's efforts at conversation, Johann grew increasingly silent. He rose every so often from his chair and paced back and forth across the kitchen.

The first rays of dawn were ending the darkness when Frau Wiesner came from the bedroom. She took more sheets from beside the stove. All she said was, "It's not an easy birth." Her husband put his arm around her shoulders as she stood for a moment beside the stove. Marta cried out again and they could hear Frau Hafer saying, "Now. Now." Then there was quiet.

The door to the bedroom opened and the midwife in her bloodstained apron said, "It's a little boy. But she is a very sick young woman."

Johann's heart sank, imagining the worst. He started toward the bedroom. Marta's step-mother said, "Just wait a little longer. Let me get things cleaned up."

Frau Hafer came out holding a small white bundle. A tiny dark red face shown out from the big white towel. "Here," she said thrusting the baby at Johann, "Hold him while we get Marta fixed up a little."

Johann hesitated to take the bundle, not knowing quite what to do. This seemed like a foreign body, something very apart from him. Wiesner, seeing that Johann was reluctant, said, "Here, gimme that baby. I ain't forgotten how to do this." He cradled the baby in his arms. "You'll have to get used to this. They won't break."

Marta was not a pretty picture when Johann went into the room. Her lips and eyes were swollen, her hair was still in disarray in spite of attempts to comb it. She moaned softly again and again. "Is he a beautiful baby?" she whispered.

"*Ja. Sehr schön.* Your father has him. We'll bring him in soon. You rest now."

The difficult birth left Marta very weak. Rather than come back to their room where she would have to go up and down stairs, it was decided that she would stay for a while at her parents' house, where her step-mother and Gertrude could care for her and the baby.

Days dragged to weeks and Marta recovered very slowly. She spent many hours in bed or sitting in a chair by the window. She was pathetically thin. She had barely the strength to nurse the baby. Johann came daily after work, bringing food from the store to supplement the Wiesner family's evening meal.

Marta would sit at the table with the family for supper. Then she and Johann would visit, while she held the baby in the rocking chair. "Don't you want to hold him?" she asked.

"He's happy with you. I don't want to get him crying."

"I think we'll be able to come home soon. Then we'll be our own little family again. My folks have been very good to me, but I want to be with my husband. Won't that be wonderful?"

"It has been terribly lonely at Ziebig's. I'll be happy when we're together."

"It's been a long time. I'm feeling so much better now. I'll be fine once we're all at home. As soon as I'm home we'll have to make arrangements with Pastor Resdel to have him baptized.

"What do you want to be the baby's name? We can't go on calling him 'baby' or 'little fellow' forever. I think since it's a boy, you should pick his name," Marta said after their first supper back at Ziebig's.

"I don't know. I really haven't thought about it. I guess I assumed you'd come up with a name for the baby."

"Don't you even have any suggestions? I thought that since the boys in your family all had the first name of Karl, even though they are called by their second names, you'd want to name him Karl. After all, you are Karl Johann.""

Johann's first, silent reaction was negative. Even though Karl was part of his name, he was always called Johann. Every time he heard the name he would think of the brother who for years had been the one who put him down.

"Karl. Karl. *Ja*, that name has been in the Weber family for generations," Johann said slowly, as if thinking out loud.

"All right, then. We'll call him Karl. You'd better stop to see Pastor Resdel tomorrow after work and set a time for the baptism. We've waited too long already."

Later, Johann sat quietly at the table while Marta rocked the baby in the chair she had brought from her parents'. He looked at the tableau of the madonna and thought: I'm a lousy son-of-a-bitch. I've got a wife and baby that I really wasn't ready for. Sometimes I feel like I'm swimming with people hanging on to me, pulling me under the water. It's not their fault, but they make me feel so trapped. I've got to find some way to get over these feelings before they destroy us all.

Müller's store was a neighborhood gathering place. There were a few chairs in the back around the stove, where some of the older men sat for hours exchanging stories. They joked with Johann, poking friendly fun at the new husband and father. They told tales about the days of their youth. They talked about their families, sons in the army, daughters with expanding broods. Once in a while they even made a purchase, which delighted Müller. He tolerated and encouraged their residency, feeling them to be old friends.

One of the gray-beards was Albert Hanke. He was full of stories from his years as a sailor. He had traveled the world over and could spin yarns describing graphically the beauties of foreign ports he had visited. His son, Adolph, had gone to America several years before. Occasionally he would bring a letter from his son and tell of his experiences in a town along the Mississippi River.

"I tell ya, he says he never had it so good. He's making real money. He's only been in that town for a year and he's got a job in a brick yard," Hanke reported.

His stoveside buddy, Schwartz, said, "Brickyard? I thought he was a weaver."

"He says lot'sa people don't work at the same jobs they had here in *Schlesien*. If they can't find work in their trade, they can find another kind of job."

"Is he married yet?"

"He's been writin' to that Schneider girl. He'd like to send the money for her to go over. I was talkin' to her the other day and she said her folks ain't happy about her goin' so far away."

"She'd better take the chance."

"Adolph told her that women have it better in America than they do in Germany. They don't have t'work so hard; they have fancier clothes; they have more money to spend. That's what he said."

"Sounds like a bunch of spoiled babydolls," Schwartz growled.

"That's why Adolph wants t'find a wife from here rather than marryin' an American girl."

"That Annie Schneider she is a good worker. She'd make him a good wife. I'm surprised she ain't jumping at the chance."

"I think she's willin' enough. It's her mama. She wants to keep her close. It ain't easy thinkin' you'll probably never see your daughter again."

Johann listened from his place at the little partitioned-off desk, where he was entering some purchases of the day in Müller's ledger. He had heard a number of customers talking about letters they had gotten from relatives in America. They all told tales of this distant, wonderful land.

Johann came out from the desk and asked Hanke. "Where does your son live?"

"..A place called Davenport, along the Mississippi River."

"Never heard of it," said Schwartz.

"He said it's a nice town. There's lotsa Germans livin' there. They got a couple of German churches, even a German newspaper."

Johann said, "That would be a lot easier than being all by yourself. If you've got some people around that can talk German...I suppose they work with other Germans and can talk to them."

"*Ja*," Hanke replied, "The guy Adolph works for is a German, so they don't have no problems. When Adolph first went over, he was in a little town outside Chicago. He and a young fellow he met on the ship heard about a grain mill there and thought they could get work. The big trouble was, everybody else only spoke English. They had a hell of a time gettin' along. They couldn't talk to nobody. Their boss would want them to do somethin' and they didn't know what the hell he wanted. Adolph got outa there after about two weeks. He said he just got on a train and rode west. He'd get off every time the train stopped for a few minutes and stand around the station. He said he went until he heard people talkin' German."

"Did he have trouble finding a job?" Johann asked.

"*Nein.* He says it's a lot better than here. He's never been without a job for more than a week or so. He's a hard worker, so they are glad to get him."

"It must be great to be in a place where there are plenty of good jobs."

"That's why there's a steady stream of folks heading for the boat. I'd go myself if I was twenty years younger," old Hanke put in.

A few months later Hanke came in with another letter from his son. "Adolph sent me a draft for ninety *Taler* which I am to give to Schneider for his daughter's ticket to America. They finally said she could go. They'll get married as soon as she gets to Davenport."

Müller came from behind the counter, "How soon's she go'n' to leave?"

"As soon as Schneider and I can make the arrangements. He likes Adolph fine, but he didn't like the idea of Annie goin' so far away. He was pretty impressed that Adolph could come up with the money for Annie's ticket. I guess he thought that was a pretty good sign that she'd be taken care of."

That evening at supper Johann told Marta about Adolph Hanke in America and about the plan to marry Annie Schneider.

"I know her," Marta said. "We were in school together. She is a maid for the Berger's--you know, the ones that live in the big house across from the church. In fact, I used to make hats for Frau Berger and Anna would pick them up at the shop. We used to have some good talks."

"Why don't you ask her about her trip to America? Hanke says she is going to leaving fairly soon."

"She knows Adolph from here, but to leave everything you know and go all by yourself to a strange country..."

"Hanke says that living is so much better there than here."

"I've heard some of those letters. I'm not sure I believe them all. They can write just about anything, and who's to know that they're lying. It would sure be a mean trick if Annie got over there and found that things weren't so rosy."

"If you know her, why don't you ask her about her plans? Hanke says Adolph is making enough money in a brick yard that he plans to buy a house in a year or so."

Marta smiled. "I'll bet. Promise her anything to get her over there. Then it's too late to turn around and come home. I sure wouldn't want to take a chance like that."

"Suppose I wanted to go to America, would you come?" Johann walked to the window.

"Go to America? What ever gave you that kind of a wild idea?"

"They say that there are plenty of jobs. That's certainly not the way it is here. I've looked for a decent job for ten years and the best I can do is stand around in a grocery store."

"That's not so bad. We could sure use more money, but it's a decent job."

"The great thing about it is that in twenty years I'll be in exactly the same place, doing the same thing, making the same pay," Johann paced across the room, resisting the urge to hit the wall.

"You aren't serious, are you? America?"

"What's so bad about that?"

"Well, we've got a baby to consider, for one thing."

"There are babies growing up in America too!"

"*Ja*, but the trip..."

"What about you?"

"I never thought about leaving Neuhaus. I just never considered it. I suppose that I could get used to the notion, if I took some time--like ten years," she laughed.

"Come on; be serious! Why don't you talk to Annie?"

Conversation around the stove at Müller's store never slowed. Johann waited for a chance to talk to Hanke about Adolph in America. One day he asked, "How are the plans coming for Annie Schneider to go to Adolph in America?"

"We just about got it all set. Her old man and I spent an afternoon up in Waldenburg talkin' to an agent who helps people make their arrangements."

"Can you trust him?

"Sure. I was on the same ship with him when I was a sailor. He's honest enough. Adolph said you have to be careful of these guys. There is plenty of folks who've gotten to the boat and found that no real arrangements were made. The agent just pocketed their money."

"Who is this agent in Waldenburg?" Johann asked.

"His name is Obermann. He lives next to the Rathaus. He's takin' care of everything for Annie."

"My wife has been talking with her. They were school girls together. She said Annie is really excited about going."

"Obermann has a ticket for her in about two weeks, from Bremerhaven. So she'll be on her way in no time."

"Marta says she is getting all her boxes packed. Her mother is giving her a lot of kitchen stuff to take."

"Adolph sent a little list of stuff for her t'bring along. I think he just wants to see somethin' from home. You can't tell me they don't have all that stuff in America."

"Marta says Annie is so excited about going that she doesn't even think about the people she is leaving. She doesn't think about never seeing her family again.... At least, she doesn't talk about it, Marta says."

"If you want a new life, you gotta give up the old. That's what I always say."

"Marta thinks that is a lot to give up," Johann said. "You know, I sometimes think I'd like to go....But I don't think I'd ever be able to talk Marta into it."

"You could go over and find a job and then send for her and your baby in a year or two, after you're settled."

"I don't think she'd go for that."

"Well, then, her choice would have to be to go along with you, wouldn't it?" Hanke smiled. "....More'n one way to get her to go along with your idea."

Johann said, "Tell me more about this fellow in Waldenburg who makes the arrangements."

Hanke settled back on his chair. "Like I say, he's honest and knows his stuff. He can tell you what you need to do to get outa the country and tell you about what some of his customers have done. If you had to figure it all out for yourself, you'd probably do the wrong things or forget somethin' important. Obermann--that's his name--can tell you all about gettin' trains to Bremen. He'd put you in touch with a passenger agent there who knows when the ships are leaving and will get you a ticket for a good ship. He'd show you what to take along, what you'd need on the way and what you'd want when you get there."

"I'd need somebody like that. I've never been more than half a day's buggy ride from home. My brother, the one who was in the army, would be better at this sort of thing. He lived in half a dozen different cities and travelled all over the place. I'd need somebody who knows the ropes."

"Obermann's your man, then. It's only costing about 40 *Taler* for Annie, plus a little extra in case she had a problem. Adolph sent 90 *Taler* for her to come."

Johann thought: The money I have from father would get us over there and be enough to get started, with some to spare. We could do it! If we decide to go, we can do it!" For the first time in his life he dared to have a dream.

"I don't want to go! I won't go!" Kurt yelled.

"Oh, yes you will, Kurt Nauman. You can't stay here any longer. I've had enough of your rottenness," his stepmother shouted back.

The fourteen-year-old shrank back, wiping his runny nose with the back of his hand. "If you were my real mother you wouldn't treat me like this."

"Listen, young man! I've been better to you than most would be. For ten years I've put up with all your mischief. I can't help it that your mother died. I did the best I could to take care of you after I married your father."

"You never liked me. You fall all over Katie and Maria because they're yours, and me you slap."

"I wish your father was still here. He'd knock some sense into you."

Kurt remembered his father. Before he got pneumonia just after Christmas, Kurt found life easier than now. Since his father died, Emma, his step-mother, had really turned against him. There was never a kind word.

She had really hit the roof that time last summer when he got in trouble for breaking into the bakery down the street. He climbed through the back window after the shop was closed. He figured they'd never miss a pie. How could he know that just when he was climbing in the window, he'd be spotted. When he went back out the window with the pie, the baker was standing right there with a rolling pin. He grabbed Kurt by the ear. "Aren't you that Nauman kid? We'll see what your mother has to say about this."

As they marched along the street toward his house, the baker muttered, "What is Korntal coming to? I ought to march you right down to the *Polizei*. I'll give you a break 'cause I knew your papa, God rest his soul. Ain't you ashamed, you little rascal?"

Kurt tried to squirm away but the baker's hold on his ear was vise-like. He'd catch hell now. The baker pounded on the door with his rolling pin.

His step-mother took in the whole scene at a glance. "*Du Teufel*. Now, you've done it."

"I caught him coming out my back window with a pie," the baker complained, twisting Kurt's ear harder.

Emma Nauman reached for the switch she kept behind the door. "I'll teach him a lesson he won't forget. You leave him to me!" She took over the baker's hold on Kurt's ear.

"Just be sure that he knows that if it ever happens again he'll be getting his punishment from the *Polizei* not from his mother."

"I'm really sorry that happened," she said to the baker. "He's just getting to be such a problem. Ever since his pa died, he's just wild. It's almost more than I can handle."

"He'd better learn that if he's going to make it here in Korntal, he's going to have to behave."

That was only the first of a dozen scrapes during the past year. Kurt's next antagonist was the schoolmaster. Kurt never was a good student. He read very slowly and his writing was miserable. He fell further and further behind in his class. When the schoolmaster questioned him in class, he would respond sullenly, if at all.

All the standard disciplinary steps had little effect. Scoldings, ridicule before the class, standing in the corner, switching--nothing seemed to break the pattern of sullen defiance. In exasperation the schoolmaster took him by the arm as school was being dismissed and said, "I'm going to take you to your mother and we're going to get things straight. I won't put up with this one more day."

The walk to the "gallows" was as terror-filled as his earlier marches down the street to his step-mother.

"What is it this time?" she sighed, glaring at the boy, then facing the schoolmaster.

"This boy is ruining my class. He just sits. He won't do any work. I've tried to help him with his work; I've coaxed him to try; I've punished him. I give up! I won't have it! I'm not going to let one rotten apple ruin the whole class. So, as far as I'm concerned, he's finished. I don't want him in school any more."

"Now you've done it," Emma complained. "I told you you'd get thrown out of school."

"He might as well try to find a job, although I don't know who'd want him the way he acts. He's never going to amount to anything until he learns how to behave."

Kurt had learned that it was better to stay silent at times like these. To offer an alibi only made it worse; to argue back really brought the walls down. He hung his head and tried to appear sorry for his misdeeds. Maybe that would take a little of the heat off.

His step-mother said to the schoolmaster, "I know what you're saying. It's the same around here. I really had it with this kid. I'm going to let his uncle try to deal with him. Maybe he can whip him into shape."

Kurt had lasted only two months at the home of his father's brother and his family. He was younger and smaller than his three cousins. They tolerated very little misbehavior. Kurt felt like he was the only prisoner in a jail filled with wardens. He was given a list of household chores that had to be carried out every day. He was severely punished if he did not have them all finished by the time Uncle Klaus came home. His uncle's whippings were much more to be feared than the switch wielded by his step-mother.

Obedience and compliance were only surface responses. Kurt had learned to play the game, but inside he hated the whole bunch. He turned his defiance to small acts which were not easily traced to him. He rubbed the rope of the bucket at the well on the stone curbing around the well until it was worn nearly through. It broke and dropped the bucket into the well while his aunt was drawing water. When no one was in the house, he reached in the back of the clock and bent one of the parts. He loosened the stake to which the family cow was tethered. The poor beast wandered off and was lost for hours.

Cleaning out the ashes from the kitchen cook stove was an early morning chore, before Aunt Frieda began to prepare breakfast. Kurt was to take the ashes out to the pile behind the outhouse and bring wood in to the kitchen woodbox. Then he was to start the fire for breakfast.

Kurt failed to notice that the fire had been so well banked the night before that there were still a few live embers among the ashes he hauled out behind the shed. It was not unusual for the ashes still to have a little heat from the previous night. While they were finishing breakfast, Uncle Klaus looked out the window and saw smoke pouring from the outhouse. He ran to the door, shouting orders for the boys to bring buckets. They took water from the trough beside the little stable and drew it from the well. In a few minutes they had put out the fire. It was very clear to Uncle Klaus what had happened.

His angry silence was more potent than vehement tirade. He said, "...All right, *du Kerl*. You're going back to your mother. I thought things were improving but you're more stupid than you were when you came. I gave you a chance. I tried my damnedest but there's no help for you. You're never going to amount to anything."

Kurt didn't know how to respond. Staying on in his uncle's house wasn't a happy prospect, especially after the fire; going back to his step-mother was no better. Uncle Klaus gave him no choice.

"Pack up your stuff. We'll see what your mother wants to do with you. Poor woman was at her wit's end when she sent you here. You ruin things wherever you are."

His step-mother leaned across the kitchen table and snatched him by the hair. "You don't belong here any more. Your uncle and I have talked it over. He's going to help with the money and we are sending you to *Amerika*. I'm going to get you as far away from here as I can. We'll give you enough money to get to America and then you're on your own."

"I don't want to go! I won't go!" Kurt screamed.

"Oh, yes you will. You can't stay here any longer. I've had enough of your rottenness," his stepmother shouted back.

The fourteen-year-old shrank back. "If you were my real mother you wouldn't treat me like this."

It was after supper that Johann resumed his periodic effort to persuade Marta to go to America. "I was talking to Hanke this afternoon and he told me that Annie had arrived safely in Davenport. She and Adolph got married right away."

Marta, holding the baby, stopped rocking in her chair, "I hope she likes it because she can't come running home. She's really burnt her bridges."

"Hanke says they are very happy. They have rented a nice little house and are all set up. I'll bet they have it a lot better than we do here in our room at Ziebig's."

Marta sighed, "Everybody says it's better in America. Maybe we could make a better start there."

Johann seized on this first sign that Marta was weakening. "I know it would be better. I could get a decent job. We could have a real house."

"Are you ready to say farewell to your family forever, like Annie had to do?"

"I've hardly had any contact with them in the last four years. You know, Marta, that doesn't break my heart. It would be a wrench to know that I'd never see Mother again, but the rest will get along fine without me. I wouldn't be missing a thing."

"Well, I'd miss my people, and my friends, miss them a lot. But I've got you and little...."

Johann seized the moment, "You mean you'd really be willing to go?"

"I never thought at all about ever leaving Neuhaus. But it would be exciting to see a new land. Once I got over being scared, I might even like it."

"Let me see what I can find out from this agent, Obermann, in Waldenburg. I asked Müller if I can take the wagon next week and pick up the goods for the store that we get from Waldenburg. I'll talk to Obermann and see what I can find out. Hanke swears he's an honest fellow."

Obermann turned out to be a short, portly man with thick spectacles. He puffed on his pipe as he talked with Johann, leaning back in his chair.

"So you've been talking with Hanke, eh? I fixed things for his new daughter-in-law to get to America. I suppose she is all settled there now."

"*Ja*. Hanke says they are married and have their own house in a town called Davenport. I was wondering if you could tell me a little about how arrangements can be made to go."

"Giving it some thought, are you?"

"I've been trying to persuade my wife to come with me to America. What would we have to do?"

"First we'd have to get you papers from the burghers in Neuhaus swearing that you weren't running away from debts you owe. We'd have to have a paper showing that you weren't being called up for the draft. Then you'd have to get a passport. That's no problem. It takes a couple of weeks but I doubt if you'd have any problems. You say you have a wife too."

"*Ja*. And a baby son. He'll be a year old in a few months."

"Traveling with a baby isn't easy, but lots of folks do it. You'd take a train to Berlin and then one to Bremen. I'd put you in touch with an agent in Bremen who'd help you get your ticket for the ship. He'd help you buy the stuff you'd need for the journey--food, simple utensils, bedding. He'd also tell you what to do when you get to New York or Baltimore."

"How much does this all cost?" Johann asked, not suggesting that he had an inheritance which he knew would more than cover the costs.

"For you, your wife and baby, you ought to be able to do it for less than 120 *Taler*. Of course, you'd have to have some more to get you to where you wanted to go in America. The arrangements I made for Hanke's daughter-in-law cost her about 65 *Taler*."

"We'd probably head for Davenport too. Hanke says his son Adolph would help us to get started."

"You need somebody like that, at least for a little while."

"How long does the trip take?"

"Figure on about a week to get to Bremen on the train and get set up for the sailing. If you get a good ship, one with both a steam engine and sails, you can figure on about three to four weeks minimum to get across the ocean. Then it will probably take you another week or two to get to Davenport. Maybe you could do it in less time, but with a wife and baby, you're going to want to take a little time in some of the cities to catch your breath."

"How much time do we need to plan for the trip."

"Ships are sailing from Bremen every day; a bunch of them. As soon as you know about when you'd be able to get to Bremen, my friend there would get you on one of them."

"If we go, we could get under way in the spring, say in *Mai*."

"When you're ready, give me about a month's notice and I can have everything arranged for you. I envy you. I travelled a lot when I was young. I was a sailor with Hanke. That's how we got to know each other. I've seen New York. Never seen anything like it. But I'm too old for pulling up stakes here and going to a new country. I envy you young fellows."

"Obermann told me all about it. He said it wasn't hard at all to make arrangements. We could go in the springtime. It's not as expensive as I thought, about 120 *Taler* for the three of us. We'd still have plenty to make a good start in America. What do you think?"

Marta caught the enthusiasm. "Springtime, you say. That would give us about five months to get ready."

"I'm not going to tell the folks in Endigen until we've got all the arrangements made. I want to make it very clear that I'm not asking their permission to go. I'm telling them that we are going. We'd have to go up there for a couple of days to say goodbye to Mother. I know it will make her sad, but I have to live my life. I'll have to make arrangements with Karl to get my share of the money. We'd take enough for the trip and to get us started. Karl could send the rest later when we need it. I wonder how he'll react when he gets the word."

"I told my folks that we were thinking about this. At first they were sad about us going so far away. But my father said that it might be our only chance to get ahead. He said he'd go too if he could."

"Old Karl will think I'm crazy, I suppose. But he can't offer me anything to keep me here, even if he wanted too."

"He has to give you your money, doesn't he?"

"I think he has to give it to me if I want it. I tell you, Marta, for the first time in my life I feel like Karl isn't in control of my life. If I want to go to America, he can't stop me. Once it's all set, I'll send them a letter about our plan, and then we'll find a time to go for a little visit before we leave."

"Have you told Gotthelf?"

"I haven't seen him for a while. He was going to get his money from Karl and get his own place in Waldenburg. I think when he's in Neuhaus, he is spending most of his time with Christiane. You told me that she said they were going to get married. I know he left Wagner's but I don't know where he is working, if he has a job."

"Christiane said he comes to see her on Sundays."

"Maybe we could get to see them next Sunday and tell them what's going on."

Under Obermann's guidance Johann took the train from Waldenburg to visit the passport office in Breslau. Visiting a strange city, much larger than any place he had ever been, standing across the counter from formidable Prussian officials made Johann realize how he was emerging very quickly from the cocoon of his country life. The twelve foot high ceilings of the passport office, the polished panelling, the windows looking out on the crowds of people hurrying up and down the avenue, all conspired to make Johann feel very small.

Finally his turn came. The clerk, with his black sleeve protectors, stiff collar, silky cravat, picked up his pen and spread the *Reisepass* form on the counter. I suppose he's done this a thousand times, Johann thought, feeling awkward and rustic. Even though he was wearing his wedding suit and would have been judged well-dressed in Neuhaus, to Breslau eyes he must appear to be a bumpkin. He had to clear his throat several times before he could begin to answer the questions the official matter-of-factly posed.

Finally the form was completed, officially stamped in several places. In the eyes of the Prussian government Karl Johann Weber, his wife Marta nee Wiesner, and their son Karl Johann were now permitted to go to *Nord Amerika*. Their emigration took on a new reality in Johann's thinking and feeling. Folding the document carefully and putting it in his inner pocket, Johann paid the fee to the official sitting at the till by the door to the office. He could hardly wait to get back to Neuhaus and show Marta this evidence of their new freedom.

She held the paper carefully and read every word. "Well, we've started our journey, haven't we?"

"*Ja*. We have six months to use this pass to leave the country. I got the *Reisepass* for all three of us, but on the way home I got to thinking about everything Obermann told me about the trip. It is hard to think of a little child making a long, hard journey like that. Then the idea hit me; maybe we could leave him here with your folks and send for him in a few years. Other people we know in Neuhaus will be coming to America and they could bring him along when he is a little older."

Marta's eyes filled with tears and her voice quavered. After a long silence she said, "I just don't know if I could leave him, even with my family." She put her arms around Johann and cried quietly on his shoulder.

"You're not backing out now, are you? It's getting a little late for that now that I've started making the arrangements."

Another long silence. "Even though I hate the thought of leaving Karl, you are probably right. Today I stopped to see Fräulein and tell her we were going to America. She scared me. She told me about her cousin who went with a baby and the poor little thing died on the ship. At first I felt angry at her for frightening me so, but now it makes me worry that the trip, especially on the ship, may be too much for little Karl. I would never forgive myself if something bad happened to him on the trip. Maybe we should wait until he is older."

Johann reacted firmly. "If we put it off, we'll never go. There will always be something to hold us back."

Marta took his hand, "No, that's not what I meant…. Fräulein told me about a couple families that brought children over later. My parents would take good care of him. It would be so hard not to see him, not to hold him in my arms for a couple years. That breaks my heart."

Johann wasn't really looking forward to all the responsibility of traveling with such a young child. There still was a feeling of distance between him and his son. Sometimes Johann dared to admit that he saw this baby as one of the chains of responsibility which constrained him. At first he had attributed his remoteness from the baby to sheer lack of experience. In his adult life he had never been around babies.

Weeks before, Marta had commented, just once, "I don't know what's the matter, but you never seem to pay much attention to little Karl. You hold him only when you have to help me. You never really play with him. What's the matter.?."

"I just don't know how to handle little babies. I'm tired when I come home in the evening. There's nothing wrong."

But Marta didn't seem satisfied with that answer.

Marta sat in the rocker, wiping her eyes.

Putting his hand on her shoulder, Johann tried to comfort her. "I know it is going to be very hard to leave little Karl, but it seems the only sensible thing to do. If we're going to America, we can't put it off for years." Then he added, "If we didn't have a good place to leave him, we couldn't even think about it."

Marta didn't tell Johann that the thought had crossed her mind that one advantage of leaving the baby here was that she would have an excuse to come back home if she didn't like America. She resolved that she would always keep secretly in a safe place enough money for a ticket to come back home.

Johann's misgivings about leaving the baby were of a different order. In the Breslau office he had had to swear that he was not leaving any dependent persons behind.... But surely, if they had to, they could explain that this was only temporary, the baby would join them later. It would sure be easier to travel without a little baby. Johann couldn't really picture what it would be like on the ship, or what living conditions would be once they got to America, but he knew it would not be easy with a baby..

"Well, if you think it wouldn't be too hard for you to leave him.it might be easiest that way. It would certainly be better for him not to have to make that hard trip....We could leave a little money behind for him. In time he could come over."

"I guess you're right that it's best that way. I'll miss him.... I can't imagine how it will be without him...I know they'll take good care of him, but I will miss him so." Marta cried quietly.

Now that he had taken steps that committed them to their journey, Johann wrote to Endigen telling them of their plans and promising to visit before they left. His mother would be saddened by his news, but he had been away from home long enough that it would not be a great wrench for him to leave. Karl probably would think it was a waste of money, that Johann should use his inheritance to establish himself here in *Schlesien*. Johann was careful in what he wrote. He would need some of his money right away to pay for their tickets. He knew that he had every legal right to the money, but a fight with Karl would create delays. Now that the decision was made and the details were working out, Johann wanted to be under way as soon as possible.

Johann and Marta decided that they needed to go to the photographer to have a portrait made to give to their families. The new art was very popular with people who were going to America. It had become part of the ritual of emigration. So, dressed in their very best clothes, they were posed by the photographer. They sat side-by-side in front of a canvas on which a palatial room was painted, with stately columns framing tapestries. It was a bit of contrast with their rented room at Ziebig's. Marta smoothed her hair, parted in the middle. Metal stands, unseen by the camera, were behind them holding their heads steady while the picture was taken. The photographer told Johann to put his arm around Marta's waist and asked Marta to hold Johann's left hand in her's. Now "Hold very still." He took the cap off his lens, counting "*Eins...zwei...drei....*"

Johann had the photographer mount their picture in a frame with small locks of their hair beneath the glass in the fashion of the day. It was as if they would be leaving a small part of themselves behind as a tangible presence in the family they would probably never see again. He had pictures made for his mother and for Marta's family.

Marta visited Fräulein and asked if she could make a hat to take as a gift to her mother-in-law. Fräulein was very supportive of their plan to go to America and was happy to have Marta in the workroom one more time. Marta knew that there was no point in making one of the fancy productions. What was needed was a very nice version of the standard town model. It would not be fancy but it would be exquisitely made. The materials were carefully chosen, the best black ribbons were used. The stitches were tiny and evenly spaced. Fräulein smiled as she saw Marta at work, her tongue at the corner of her mouth, her small fingers working her art. She remembered how Marta had come to work for her, basically unskilled. She had learned fast...and now she would be leaving....

Johann bundled Marta and baby Karl into the buggy Müller had lent to him for the trip to Endigen. A bag with small gifts for the family was on the floor behind the seat. They started early in the morning and arrived at the family home by mid-morning.

Johann's mother had been up since dawn, working in the kitchen. The house now was Emilie and Karl's home too, and she usually only helped

Emilie with the cooking and household tasks. But today she resumed her role of earlier years: mistress of the house. Fresh bread and *Stollen* stood warm behind the stove. Two of the chickens she tended in the pen behind the little barn were roasting in the oven, a treat reserved for very special occasions. She sat by the table peeling potatoes. It would be good to have Johann at the table once again. She wiped her eyes with the corner of her apron. She recalled the day she stood at the window in the loft and watched him drive off with Wagner to begin his apprenticeship. Now he would be leaving for always.

Emilie found her mother-in-law with her head down on the kitchen table, sobbing softly. She put her hand on the older woman's shoulder, "There. There. I know it hurts."

"*Ja*. First I lose Gottlieb, now I'll never see Johann again. *Ja*. It hurts." She put her hand over her heart and the tears ran down her wrinkled cheeks. "I'll shed my tears now. I don't want to spoil this day by blubbering."

Emilie nodded. "You'll be just fine. We all want this to be a nice day for everybody. Karl feels it is important that we send Johann off knowing that the family circle is not broken. He and Julius have the money Johann asked for. They got it all in gold coins like Johann suggested. Now you let me finish up here in the kitchen. You get yourself ready; they'll be here before you know it."

The clock in the church tower was striking eleven o'clock when the buggy pulled up to the front door. The new leaves on the trees cast their mottled shade over the small yard in front of the house.

CHAPTER 7

Marta had packed her kitchen utensils, dishes, bedding and the things they would need in their new home in two sturdy boxes Johann had had the carpenter make for them. It was hard to know what to take. Marta had visited Annie Schneider's mother to find out what her friend had taken along. Some people, who had had letters from emigrants, advised taking very little; just take money and buy what you need in America. Marta and Johann finally decided to take the necessities with them. They would be very practical and take only the things they knew they would need. There was something comforting in keeping these objects which were a tie to their lives in their homeland. The thought of going empty-handed into their new life was more than they could handle. At last all the decisions were made; the two wooden boxes and the trunk with their clothes were full and securely closed. They would not be opened until they got to America.

"Tomorrow--this time--you'll be on your way," Christiane shouted over the hubbub to Marta. "I wish we were going along."

Marta put her arm around her best friend. "Get packed. You've got fourteen hours to get ready," she laughed.

All the friends of Marta and Johann were milling about the kitchen of the Wiesner home. The table was piled with food. Young and old, the women had brought cakes and *Stollen*. The coffee pot steamed on the stove. Pitchers of beer were in the dry sink. The crowd spilled out of the kitchen into the back yard, where everyone seemed to be talking at once.

Wagner, the master dyer, by virtue of his standing in the community and his imposing size, spontaneously assumed the role of master of ceremonies. His deep voice boomed to quiet the crowd.

"*Meine Freunde*, we are here to wish godspeed to our young friends, Johann and Marta. We want them to know that they will always have a place in our thoughts. Herr Wiesner has asked me to tell you to eat as much as you can and enjoy yourselves.

"Johann has a little book over here on the table. We want each one of you to write a little sentiment in the book and sign your name. That way...on the journey...and when they get to wherever their new home will be...they'll be able to remember this evening and have fond memories of all their friends here in Neuhaus. So, don't anybody leave before you have written in their book. Johann, do you want to say anything?"

Johann began to speak. Several in the crowd yelled, "We can't hear you. Stand up on a chair."

Johann climbed onto a chair. "Now, can you see and hear me? We really thank you for coming tonight. We'll remember all of you always. That's why I want you to write in the little book my mother gave me. We have a long trip ahead of us. We don't know where we will be or what it will look like, but I have a dream that we're going to make into a new life. I've been reading the letters that Herr Hanke, over here, gets from Adolph. We're going to head for the town where he and Annie live. Just like him, I'm going to have a good job and a nice little house. Maybe some of you will decide to go to America and we'll have a chance to talk about Neuhaus and all our friends there. Marta and I thank you for all your good wishes."

Gotthelf shouldered to the front of the crowd and took Johann's place on the chair. "I just want to say a word. Johann has always been my favorite brother. I want him to know that I really admire his courage in striking out on a new life. I would like to be going too,.. but I'm not sure I've got the guts to head out like that into something I don't know anything about. I did want to say that I'm gonna miss him, and I wish him and Marta all the best."

Johann was pounded on the back by Wagner and Müller and Hanke. The men lifted their glasses of beer to salute him. Marta was surrounded by Christiane and all her other girlhood friends. Fräulein stood to one side talking with Marta's step-mother who was holding baby Karl. She jounced the wide-eyed baby up and down until he fell asleep, despite the hubbub.

People began to drift away, after embracing Marta and shaking Johann's hand. In time, only the remnants of the food and the used cups and plates filled the kitchen. Marta started to clear up the mess. Her step-mother said, "Just let that go. You go to bed. I'll clean this all up tomorrow, after you've gone. You'd better get your sleep. This may be the last chance you have for a good night's sleep for a while."

"I don't like to leave you with this mess, but I am tired. I hope I can sleep."

Johann and Marta had given up their room at Ziebig's two days before and had come to the Wiesner house for their last nights in Neuhaus. They stayed in the room Marta had had as a girl, the room where she had stayed during her recovery from Karl's birth. It was almost empty now that most of their belongings were packed in the two sturdy wooden boxes. Their clothes were in the small trunk Wagner had given them. They also had Edward's old carpet bag to carry the clothing they would need for the trip. The rest of their things had been given to family and friends.

Marta quietly put on her night shift and slid into the narrow bed. Johann climbed in beside her. Little Karl was in the cradle in the corner. Marta shivered as she lay close to her husband. Johann put his arm around her.

"Scared?"

"Aren't you? I hope everything will be all right."

"We'll get along just fine. Once we get settled...you'll see."

"That's not what I meant. I was thinking about the baby. I don't know if I can leave him!" She cried softly.

"He'll be all right here. Your folks will take good care of him. He'll be a lot better off than he would be on the journey. It would be awfully hard for him to make the trip. Look at it that way!"

"That's easy for you to say. I'm going to miss him so much."

"He'll be just fine. We'd better try to sleep."

Marta longed for one more time of closeness in the home they would be leaving forever. Both slept fitfully, but their times of waking and sleeping did not coincide, so there was no further conversation.

Morning came. As Johann shaved at the basin just outside the back door, he said softly to himself: "Finally, I'm able to break away from all the things that have held me down. I can't wait. Once I make good in America, they'll see that it wasn't me. I just needed a good break."

Breakfast was a sober meal. No one spoke very much. Marta's eyes were red. She held little Karl as she tried to force down her breakfast. The Wiesners sensed the power of the moment and said nothing. Johann was running down in his mind all the details that had to be taken care of before leaving.

As they were finishing, the carriage Johann had hired for the trip to Waldenburg pulled up to the door. Johann got up from the table and helped the driver load their baggage onto the rack at the back of the carriage. He put the carpet bag they had with the clothes they would need on the trip under the carriage seat. Then he went back into the kitchen.

"It's time. We have to meet Obermann at the station in Waldenburg. He's got some last minute instructions for meeting the agent in Bremen. Our train leaves Waldenburg at 11:15."

Marta, standing with her step-mother and father, sobbed, "Just one more minute." Then she handed the baby to her step-mother, kissed them all, squared her shoulders, took Johann's arm and walked to the carriage.

The same morning in Korntal another farewell was about to take place. Emma Nauman had packed a bag for her step-son Kurt. She unbuckled the old carpetbag that had belonged to Kurt's father. She folded, but not very carefully, the few clothes belonging to the boy. She had washed them because she was not going to send anything out of her house that wasn't clean. All was ready now.

Kurt sat sullenly at the kitchen table. Since his enforced return from his Uncle Georg's after the fire he had tried his best to behave. His step-mother's threat to send him to America had sobered him. He knew that she meant business, and he tried to be helpful around the house. He addressed her politely; he even called her "Mother" a few times, but nothing would change her course. She had visited the agent in Stuttgart and made arrangements for him to go to America.

"I've got everything ready for you. Hang this little bag around your neck. This is the money from your Uncle Georg for your ticket for the ship to America. I put in ten *Taler* to get you started in New York. If you get serious about working, you'll be able to earn enough to support yourself. If you keep on the way you've been around here, you'll starve and it will serve you right. Now you take care of this money"

Kurt argued, "It isn't fair. I'm trying to be good. Don't send me off. Please, don't."

"You brought it on yourself. This is the best thing for you. You need to be someplace where nobody knows you and the way you've done nothing but make trouble. I hope you can make a fresh start."

Frieda Nauman did not reveal how torn she was on the inside. She had tossed and turned in bed many nights worrying about what she was doing. Her anger and frustration struggled with her maternal feelings. She had loved Kurt's father and wanted to love his son. He was only fourteen; he'd lost both his mother and his father. But a woman by herself just couldn't deal with such a rowdy *Kerl*. If she tried to get him in line, she had to discipline him. If she did that, it only seemed to make him worse. Tears came to her eyes as she put his clothes in the carpet bag while he pled to stay. She turned her head so that he wouldn't see.

"What will I do in America? Where will I live?"

"You'll have to find a job right away. They say there are plenty jobs. You'll have to find one that gives you a place to stay.

"You won't be the only one. Other kids get sent over by themselves, the agent said, because there's a good chance to get a job and make money. Lots of them have already worked for a couple of years before they go. It's time you learned to do that too."

"But their families aren't sending them to punish them."

"That may be. But if they can make it, so can you."

"I'm scared to go," Kurt stammered, not really wanting to show how vulnerable he felt..

"I can't help it. This is the only thing I know to do. You'll just have to do the best you can. Uncle Georg is going to drive you to Stuttgart to catch the train for Bremen."

"When do I have to go?"

"Tomorrow morning early. There's no good putting it off. The agent has your ticket to Bremen. He'll give you the name of an agent to see there. He also wrote down the name of a society in New York that helps Germans. If you have trouble, you can see them. I put that name in your purse with the money we are giving you for the trip."

"So this is Berlin," Marta said as she turned wide-eyed from one side to the other of the broad avenue. "I can't get over it. In just one day I ride on a train for the first time in my life and see this beautiful, huge city."

Johann agreed. "Gustav always said it was a great city, when he was in the army in Potsdam. Let's walk down to that big monument and see what it is."

"I don't want to get too far from our rooming house. What would we do if we got lost? Do you remember the address?"

"*Ja. Invalidenstrasse 77.* We won't get lost. Just enjoy yourself."

"I wish that place where we are staying was a little cleaner. I don't know how people can be so careless. Dust everywhere."

"Well, it's not very expensive. I suppose they don't have any trouble filling it up, even if it is dusty. It was what Obermann recommended."

"Those windows haven't been washed in a year. The curtains looked pretty saggy too."

"You're going to have to get used to a little dirt for a while. I don't imagine the ships are very clean. Once we get our own place in America, you can scrub to your heart's content," he laughed.

"If I had a clean place to live, I wouldn't mind staying here for a while."

"You'll have to settle for a couple of days."

"Look at the size of that church. You could put all the churches in Neuhaus inside of it. Let's go in."

"We can go in tomorrow. I want to find the emigration agent, Eisenstein. The fellow in Waldenburg said we should talk to him. He knows ways to help us get on to Bremen."

"If he's the one that recommended that rooming house, I'm not sure I want to listen to him."

"The fellow I talked to in Waldenburg...Obermann...said that Eisenstein is the best in the business. Obermann has never made the trip as a passenger, so he can only go by what people have told him. But Eisenstein has gone to America and back a couple of times and knows the ropes."

Herr Eisenstein sat behind his large polished desk, looking at the couple sitting across from him. Johann could feel the agent's eyes examining them. They were dressed in their best traveling clothes. Johann felt a bit awkward. He thought: Here we are, a couple of country folk in the big city. Marta had already complained to him that her clothes stood out from the styles of the capital city.

"Well, now. Let's talk a little bit about what you can expect on the trip. I take it that you have trunks with your belongings."

"*Ja*," Johann answered. "Our boxes and trunk are at the station now. We just have our suitcase with our travel clothes."

"That's good. We'll see that the baggage goes on the train with you to Bremen. Now you'll have to decide what sort of space you want to get on the ship. I can tell you the kinds of accommodations most ships have. Then when you get to Bremen and see my colleague, Löwen, he'll know what ships are ready to sail and you can get your accommodations."

"We don't really know what we'll be able to afford. Obermann said that tickets are usually about 30 *Taler*."

"Well, that's right. But that's about the least you can expect to pay. If you want more comfort, it will cost you a bit more. Usually there are cabins and steerage. The sailing ships are older and slower and cost a little less. I'd advise you not to take a sailing ship. The newer ships have both sails and steam engines. They can cross the Atlantic is about three weeks if they don't have a lot of bad weather."

Marta said, "The less time we have on the ocean, the better I'll like it. I hear that the waves make some people real sick."

"Then you should take one of the newer ships. You'll have half a dozen or more to pick from when you get to Bremen. If you want to save money, you probably should get tickets in steerage. It'll be a little crowded. You'll share a kind of big hall with a group of other passengers. In steerage people get their own meals. In the cabins usually some of the meals are cooked for you."

"How will we know what food to take along?" Marta asked. "What will we need to cook it in?"

"Herr Löwen in Bremen will help you with that. No need to buy things until you get there. You won't have a whole lot of space, so you won't be able to take too many clothes to wear on the trip. I usually tell people to have two outfits, nothing too fancy...the sort of things you'd wear at work. Wear one and pack one. You won't be able to do much washing. so you'll want enough linen to see you through the trip."

"That's what Obermann told us too," Johann said. "In Bremen we'll put away the clothes we've been wearing here and pack our bag with the clothes for the ship. They're in the trunk."

Eisenstein continued, "I probably don't need to warn you, but you've got to be careful with your money. Keep it in a purse on your body at all times. There won't be any safe place in your baggage in steerage. In fact, I'd have two purses: one for your day-to-day expenses and one with your nestegg. Sometimes on the ship they sell some food in steerage from the kitchen where they cook for the cabin passengers; maybe a little meat, or some bread. So you may want a little money to buy something like that. You'll also want to be able to get at some money when you get to America. You'll have to have your trunks carried to a lodging."

Marta and Johann tried to take it all in. They nodded assent to all of Eisenstein's advice.

"And one more warning. You can't be too trusting of people. There are a lot of unscrupulous scoundrels who are out to cheat you. Watch out for some of these crooks in the harbor cities. There are going to be passengers who tell you hard luck stories and try to get money from you. It's easy to get taken in by some of these rascals. I know you want to be good people, but don't let folks take advantage of you....Now enough talking. You've got to see a little of Berlin while you have the chance."

"We already walked down *Unter den Linden*. Everything is so beautiful," Marta said.

On Sunday morning they decided to attend services at the huge church just a few blocks from their lodgings. They sat in the back and watched people in their Sunday finery walking down the aisle. Johann hadn't attended church for quite a while. Sitting through this service he thought of the many Sundays when the Weber family filled the pew in Endigen. A lump came into his throat as he remembered his father's booming voice singing out the hymns.

Walking back toward their boarding house after church service, Marta asked, "Do you think we could eat in a restaurant rather than going back to the house? What they were cooking for dinner didn't smell very good when we left."

"Sure. Why not? Let's look for a place." Johann took her arm as they promenaded down the avenues.

"These places look awfully expensive. We'd better look down some of the side streets where places aren't so fancy. I've never eaten in a restaurant."

"Outside of a *Wurst* or two at the Ratskeller, I haven't either."

"There's a nice little place. Look, you can eat at a table out on the sidewalk." Marta's voice rose with excitement.

"We ought to be able to afford that. Let's go."

They sat at a small table as close to the building as possible, so as not to stand out in the eyes of passers-by. A waiter in a black sateen jacket and white apron approached them. He smiled broadly under his flowing mustache, "*Speisekarte?*"

Walking down the avenue later, Marta held tightly on to Johann's arm. "That was so nice. I never had anything like that before. Oh, I feel like a fairy princess. Who would have thought I'd be eating in restaurants, walking the streets of Berlin, looking at the beautiful buildings."

"You looked like you were enjoying the dinner. You keep on eating like that and you'll fill out."

"This is all very wonderful, but I wonder if people are any happier here than in Neuhaus."

"It sure has a lot of bustle. Look, even on Sunday the streets are full of carriages, crowds of people on the sidewalks. It's exciting for a few days, but I'm not sure I'd like it all the time. There is so much luxury, I could never get used to that."

Marta pointed, "Let's go into that building where all the people are."

"It says it's the Museum of Art. Sure, let's go in."

Up the broad stairs, through the pillared portico, they entered to dusky, cool museum foyer. They wandered with crowds of people from one gallery to another. Everyone was talking is hushed tones. These were the first paintings they had seen, and they stood in awe before massive landscapes. Portraits of noble ladies in beautiful gowns attracted Marta's attention. Again and again they whispered to one another, "Look at that...."

As the afternoon waned, they strolled through a beautiful park. Vistas with green lawns and large beds of colorful tulips opened in every direction. Fountains and pools glistened in the sloping sunlight.

"I can't get over it," Marta said. "This is a day I'll never forget as long as I live. I've never seen such beautiful things. The pictures in the museum were simply wonderful, and now this park is the prettiest sight I've ever seen."

"We'd better head back to the boarding house before it gets dark. We'll want to get to bed early because we have to get to the station in the morning. I'm not sure I'll be able to sleep."

With a glint in her eye, Marta said, "Maybe we don't have to sleep for a while. We can add one more pleasure to the day.""

As they approached the Potsdam depot, Johann remembered Gustav telling about taking the train from there when he came home for Father's funeral. There was a huge clatter in the street behind them. A large state coach, surrounded by soldiers on horseback, drove by and stopped at the station. "*Der König*," Johann heard someone say.

A whole parade of carriages with uniformed coachmen pulled in behind the royal Victory Coach. There were many military officers in their colorful uniforms, golden epaulets and shining scabbards. People gathered on the sidewalk outside the station. Johann and Marta were caught in the thick of the mob. They couldn't see what was going on but they picked up snatches from others in the front rows. "There he is!" "Isn't he handsome!"

"Look at the gold braid on those uniforms!" "Have you ever seen such beautiful horses!"

Johann looked at Marta, "Well, even though we can't see him in this mob, at least we can say we stood within ten feet of the King."

"Wait until we write to the family about this. They'll think we're making it all up."

The crowd was breaking up as the empty carriages pulled away. The King and his entourage boarded their train quickly and steamed away. Johann and Marta made their way to the baggage room to reclaim their boxes and trunk from storage. Johann hired a porter to take them to the train for Bremen.

All day and all night they rocked back and forth on the train. The seats were hard. Soot and cinders blew through the windows as flat plains unrolled before them. They stopped often, briefly at towns and longer in cities. At Magdeburg, where the train stopped for an hour, Johann went into the station to buy a little food. When they had a longer stop at Braunschweig, Johann and Marta went into the station restaurant to have some soup and bread.

Every so often they came to a border of a neighboring state and had to show their *Reisepass* to the officials who went up and down the aisles examining papers. Although he knew their papers were in order, Johann always felt an uneasiness under the scrutiny of the officers. At one border point the official asked where the baby was. Johann remembered that baby Karl was listed on their passport. He quickly explained that they had left the baby temporarily with his wife's parents. He was sorry that Marta heard this interchange because he had seen her wiping tears from her eyes several times during the day.

All through the night the train stopped at station after station. Marta slept, but Johann was awake most of the time. When they stopped at Hannover in the middle of the night, Johann eased Marta's head from his shoulder and slipped out of the seat. In the cool night air he walked up and down the platform.

It was mid-morning when the train from Berlin pulled into the station at Bremen. Johann and Marta were tired and hungry. Marta said, "I feel like I'm covered with soot. How do I look?"

"Pretty...but a little grimy. You do have soot on the tip of your nose."

Marta tried to see her image reflected in the train window. "I don't see any soot..." Realizing that Johann was joking, she swatted playfully at him. "You don't look so good yourself."

"We'll find an inn where we can wash and get some real rest. We aren't going to have a whole lot of time. The first thing I have to do is find that agent, Löwen. We'll have to decide what ship to take and he'll help us get our tickets."

When they got off the train, a young man was on the platform. He held up a sign *"Göttinger Hof."* Johann looked at Marta. She shook her head affirmatively.

"He looks clean and dressed nice. That's a good sign."

Johann talked to him and found that rooms were available for one *Taler.* The young man helped him claim his boxes and trunk from the baggage car. He had a large handtruck on which he loaded half the baggage. "I'll come back for the rest. I know the baggage manager. He'll watch it for me. The inn is just a short walk."

Their room was large and airy. Marta made a quick inspection and pronounced it spotless. The innkeeper told them that they would be having dinner soon. After washing up and brushing their clothes, still wrinkled from the long train ride, they went into the small dining room. A few other guests were already eating heartily. The noon meal was soup, roasted pork, potatoes, and prunes.

"It tastes even better than that nice restaurant in Berlin," Marta said between mouthfuls.

"Eat it up. After tomorrow the meals are going to be pretty *schlimm.* From what Eisenstein said, we'll be eating only simple food on the ship."

"I'm so tired. I'll be lucky not to fall asleep before I finish eating."

"You rest a while after dinner. I'll go out and try to find Löwen's place. We need to talk with him yet today to pick the ship and get our tickets."

"I hope we won't have any trouble getting a ship."

"There are supposed to be a number of ships leaving every day."

"Yes, but look how many people there are. Just walking to the inn it seemed like there were hundreds of people loading up their baggage."

Johann got directions to Löwen's from the innkeeper. When he got there he presented the note of introduction Eisenstein had given him. Herr Löwen was a round little man with a shining bald head, fringed in white. He sat on a stool at a tall desk, like the one Johann's father used. There were large picture of ships and signs reading Hapag, Cunard, Lloyds, American Lines on the walls.

"Well, let's see what we can arrange. There are seven ships leaving the day after tomorrow. Several of them are old boats that I wouldn't particularly recommend. They are slow and pretty worn. You don't want a sailing ship anyway. It's a lot better to get one with a steam engine. They use the sails when the wind is right but can go with their engine when the wind isn't favorable. They make a much faster crossing because they don't have to go long distances out of their way because of the way the winds are blowing."

"I didn't see any big ships when we came into town."

Löwen smiled indulgently. "Well, you know, the ocean-going ships dock at Bremerhaven. That's a day's trip down the Weser River on a smaller ship. Then you get the big ships."

"I see. Do you have a particular ship that you'd recommend?"

Löwen looked at a slate on his wall which had a number of ships listed. "I'd say that of this bunch The *Indiana* would be best for you. It has sails and steam. It's not terribly old. It's an American ship. I've always heard good things about the captain. They come into Bremerhaven about six or eight times a year. I think they make a stop in England on the way over.... *Ja.* They stop at Southampton. So they'll have some German and some English passengers."

"That shouldn't be any problem."

Löwen made a tent of his hands and looked hard at Johann. "Now what kind of space did you have in mind. There are first and second cabins and steerage."

"Herr Eisenstein explained that to me in Berlin. Because I have to save my money, we thought steerage was probably best."

"That's all right. I can get whatever you want. Steerage is kind of rough, nothing fancy at all. It will cost you ten *Taler* less than a second cabin. Even in the cabins you'd be sharing the space with some other people. Steerage will cost you each thirty *Taler.* Is that agreeable?"

"I don't want to get to America with empty pockets. So I guess we'd better get steerage tickets."

"All right. We can take care of that right away. If you'll just give me sixty *Taler,* I'll send my clerk to American Line office to get the tickets. He'll have them in an hour. If they are sold out, we'll just look for another ship, so not to worry. They will also want another five *Taler* to take your baggage. You have to pay for everything over one hundredweight."

Johann counted out the gold coins from his purse. "That's fine."

"You're lucky you can pay that fare. Just the other day I had a family in here. In their town they were told that the fare would be 20 *Taler* each. That's all they had. By the time they got here to Bremen, the cheapest fare on a sailing ship had gone up to 25. They had to turn around and go back home. I felt very sorry for them."

Johann said, "It's hard to know. A fellow from our town just paid for a girl to come over to be his wife, so I thought I had a pretty good idea of what it cost."

"Yes, but even that isn't foolproof. Sometimes if there are way more passengers than there are places on the ships, the companies will raise the fare without notice. If you want to go, you have to be able to come up with the extra money on the spot. I've seen some heartbroken folks, I tell you."

"That would be a terrible disappointment...and the shame of having to go home again after all the farewells. I'm glad it's working out for us."

"Tomorrow you and your wife had better come back here. I'll have the tickets by then. We can go over what you have to take along and I'll help you find the things you need to buy for the voyage. Hopefully, by early afternoon we'll have you all outfitted."

"We'll be here at half eight. Is that all right?"

"*Ja, gut genug.* We'll also have to arrange to have your baggage sent to the ship. Where is it now?"

"At the *Göttinger Hof,* where we are staying."

"Good place! You ought to see some of the dumps people rent to the emigrants: filthy, broken down beds, torn linen, rotten food, bugs. You won't find that at the *Göttinger Hof.*"

"My wife was really happy with it. We were lucky to find such a nice place."

"Tell her to enjoy it. Things are pretty crowded on the ships. You won't have a lot of space and there'll be plenty of people around to keep you company. You'll have to make very simple meals. But its only for three weeks or so."

"Everybody seems to be going to America. This is a busy place."

"Somebody told me that on any day there are 6000 people in all the inns and emigrant houses waiting for ships. That's a lot of people. I know it keeps me good and busy."

After a breakfast of hard rolls and coffee Johann and Marta made their way to Löwen's.

"I like Bremen," she said. "People seem really friendly. In a way I like it better than Berlin. That was big and beautiful and fancy. But here you feel you really meet people. They seem to be more our kind of people... ordinary people."

"You'll like Herr Löwen. He's like a little *Grossvater*, very helpful. We'll see what he has for us to do today."

They entered the office and Marta was introduced to Löwen.

"I've got your tickets. *Alles ist in Ordnung.*"

"Oh, good."

"Now let's see about getting the rest of the things for your trip. There are shops right around here where you can pick up what you need. They outfit hundreds of travelers every day. Let's look at this list and see what you already have and what you need to get."

"We've got some things in our boxes at the inn," Johann said. We can get them out for the trip if we need to. But I have the boxes nicely nailed up"

"I suggest you buy a big wicker basket with a lid. Your boxes are going to be heavy and hard to open on the ship. Just plan to keep them nailed shut on the trip. Use the big hamper for the things you need from day to day: your food, the utensils. You can take enough clothes for the voyage in your bag."

Marta looked over the list. "We have a kettle and knives and spoons that we could take out of our box and pack in the hamper."

"If I may make a suggestion," Löwen continued, " Just buy cheap stuff for the trip. It's so easy to get it mixed up with other people's belongings, and, let's face it, there are some folks with sticky fingers. You can get the simple utensils for cooking and eating very cheap at some of the little shops along the river. You'll want to get a tin wash basin, and a chamber pot might be a good idea. You're probably going to want some kind of jug or pail with a lid for drinking water. They'll have fresh water on the ship, but you'll have to go to the water barrels for it. If you have a good container, you won't have to make so many trips.

"Here, I'll make you a little list. You're going to want: basin, chamber pot, water jug, a small cooking pot, some tin plates. knives and spoons. There will be a stove or two for cooking in steerage. Sometimes the ships have some utensils that have been left behind by other passengers, but you can't really count on that. You'll want to take a pretty good amount of potatoes. If you can get some dried fruit, that's good. You can't take fresh bread, but you could take *Zwiebach* or they sell a bread called hard tack. It's very dry and hard but it keeps long enough for the voyage.

"For food, I suggest you go to Textor's store near the docks for the river steamers. He's honest. Tell him I sent you. Just tell him you'll be on the ocean between three or four weeks and he can give you just what you need. Just be sure to take plenty of potatoes. He'll get you all set up. You can trust them... they won't sell you stuff you don't need. And he has fair prices, too."

"What else will we need?"

"Well, you'll need big straw mattress bags. They'll have straw on the dock at Bremerhaven. But you'll need to get the bags here. Be sure to get good big ones."

"One other thing....When you get on the ship, they may ask you if you have everything that you are supposed to have....Just tell them '*Ja.*' Sometimes they just want to sell you more stuff. And they've probably had bad experience with some people who brought too little food and then had a problem before the voyage was over....You'll have plenty....Don't bother giving them details. Just say you have everything."

The next morning early Johann and Marta went to the docks along the Weser. The boy from *Göttinger Hof* had their boxes and trunk, together with their clothes bag and their new wicker hamper on a pushcart.

"You need to find the steamer *Roland*," he said. "I think that's it...over there."

"It doesn't look very big." Marta looked at the compact river boat. It was, or had been, painted white but now was a sooty gray. Big red paddle wheels were on the sides. Already people were lining the rails on the two decks.

"I'll help you carry the stuff on board," the boy said. He and Johann wrestled the heavy boxes and the trunk onto the deck, adding it to piles of gear belonging to the other travelers. Johann tried to note carefully just where they had stowed their things, because there seemed to be no particular order to the way things were piled.

Then he and Marta climbed the steep stair to the upper deck. The ship was small and crowded. Men, women and children stood at the rails. There was a little cabin at the center of the ship, but it too was filled with passengers.

They stood and stood, but nothing much happened. A few more passengers straggled aboard. The time for sailing came and went. The river was full of ships, going in all directions. Johann heard from another passenger, who had heard it from a crew member, that they had to wait a couple of hours until the tide was in and they could move out to the middle of the river.

Finally the gangplank was pulled away. The little steamer's whistle split the air with a mighty blast. Marta laughed, "What a huge sound from such a little ship." They moved out into the channel and started down the Weser toward Bremerhaven. It was like a great water highway leading to the sea. Again and again they saw other steamers, like the *Roland*, filled with passengers going toward the port or coming from ships that had docked the day before.

Finally the Weser widened into a broad estuary and the port of Bremerhaven came into view. The harbor was crowded with large ships. Some were sailing ships with three and four tall masts, others had a smoke stack giving off black smoke between their masts. There were flags, totally unfamiliar to Johann and Marta, from all over the world. The *Roland* made its way between the anchored ships which were waiting to tie up at the docks. The piers reached almost as far as they could see.

"Can all these be going to America?" Marta asked. "It's a wonder there's anybody left here at home."

"I wonder which one is ours. I hope it's not too far. We've got to see that all our stuff gets on."

The *Roland* snugged up to a short wharf. Dozens of men with pushcarts dotted the pier. When they got off, Johann found one to help them with their baggage. One after the other they brought their things to the cart. Marta stood guard while Johann and the longshoreman went back for another load. The crowd milled around the pile of baggage, making it very difficult to move the heavy boxes. Finally, they had everything and set out looking for the *Indiana*. The longshoreman said he has seen it down along the waterfront where the American Lines docks were.

"You're lucky," he said. "Sometimes the big ships can't come in right away because of the winds or the tides. Then people have to go to a *Gasthof* for a day or two until their ship is ready to load."

They pushed their way through the crowd. Each pier had at least two huge ships tied up. Finally, "There it is," the porter announced.

The *Indiana* was not the largest ship in the harbor, but it wasn't the smallest either. It's black hull stretched along the dock for a more than a couple of hundred feet. There was a mast with big furled sails at the front of the ship and another at the back. In the center was a single smokestack. The dock beside the ship had piles of boxes, trunks, baskets, bags. Big nets were dropped from pulleys. The baggage was piled in these nets and swung up onto the ship. An officer in a blue uniform was supervising the loading. Johann asked where he should put their belongings. The officer did not speak German but looked at their tickets and pointed to the pile.

"I hope it doesn't get lost," Johann said to Marta. We'd better get on board as soon as we can so I can see where it goes when they haul it up."

"It looks like people are getting on down there," she said, pointing to the gangway ahead of them.

"I'll hang on to our bag with our clothes for the trip. They can haul the rest up. I guess they'll want our tickets down there where people are getting on."

"The sun is going to set in another hour. We'd better get on while it is still light and find out where we are supposed to stay."

At the foot of the gangway the German agent of the American Lines was taking tickets. He told them that steerage passengers were to go toward the back of the ship once they got to the deck. Their baggage would be coming up there. Somebody on deck would tell them where to go.

"Everything will be ready for you. Go to the steerage area and claim your baggage and set up your beds," he announced to the line of passengers at the foot of the gangway.

Once they reached the deck and walked toward the back of the ship, they found a milling crowd. Talking to the other emigrating passengers they were told that there was a stairway to the steerage area. "Just follow the crowd. All these folks are bound for steerage."

Johann guided Marta toward the railing near the stair. "We'll just stand here until we see our stuff get put in one of those nets. Then we'll go down and wait for it to be unloaded."

When they went down the stairs, they found themselves in a large space, more or less divided into areas by canvas curtains or crude wooden partitions which did not reach all the way to the ceiling. In each of the sections, some smaller than others, were stacks of four or more bunks. A large hatch opened to the deck in the center of this space. Every few minutes the net descended through the hatch with another load of boxes, trunks and baskets. These were added to the huge mound that was building up. No one could tell where his baggage was in the mound. It was fairly dark and it was hard to see the names inked onto the boxes.

"It's like being down in the cellar," Marta said.

A couple of hundred steerage passengers, at least a third of them children, pushed and shoved to get to their belongings. Elbowing their way into the melee, tempers flared. People yelled and cursed. Several women burst into tears. An older couple on the fringe of the mob were obviously praying in their distress. Children, frightened by the tumult, clung to their mothers and bawled loudly.

Johann told Marta, "Let's find a place where we'll stay. Then I can bring our boxes there."

They located one of the curtained areas where a family with two children were gathered.

"Is there more room here?" Johann asked.

"Come on ahead. Not much room anywhere. We put our bed sacks in the bunks along that wall. If you want, you could put yours over there in the bottom two bunks of that other stack.. We'll probably have somebody else coming in too."

The space was cramped: two stacks of narrow bunks, four high. A few square yards for their boxes and room enough to move about when they had their meals. The whole space for two or three families' sleeping and eating was not as large as the Weber kitchen in Endigen.

"*Danke*," Johann answered. "Marta, you keep this space for us. I'll try to find our big basket with the bed sacks. I'll be back as soon as I can." He plunged into the crowd.

Marta smiled at their new neighbors. To the children she said, "My name is Marta; what's yours?"

The little boy said, "My name is Wilhelm. They call me Willi. Hers is Katerina."

"We're Tilda and Klaus...Kümmel. We lived by Frankfurt," their mother added. "Where you from?"

"Johann and I come from *Schlesien*. We left our little boy there with my folks....Have you found all your baggage?"

Klaus spoke up, "We got here before most of this mob came, so we didn't have no trouble. I got our stuff stacked here. I figured we could make a kind of partition out of all our baggage. It won't take no more room between these two sets of bunks than against the wall."

"Sure, that's fine. I hope our stuff got on the ship all right."

"Maybe I can give your husband a hand. His name is Johann, you say?"

Several sorties into the mob brought out the boxes, trunk, and hamper. These were added to the piled-up partition.

"Where do you get the straw for the bed sacks?" Johann asked, pulling the bags from their hamper.

"There's a pile of straw on the deck back there. Just take your bags and stuff 'em."

Marta started unpacking the few things they would be needing. Tilda showed her a box where she could put their eating things.

People were settling to their spaces. A man complained to one of the sailors, "My water bottle and my chamber pot got stolen." The sailor, who didn't speak any German, just shrugged.

A voice came out of the crowd, joking, "Just find somebody else's to steal."

Marta whispered to Tilda, "I'm afraid of some of these people. Some of them look awfully tough."

"Guess we're stuck with 'em. We can just kinda stay outa their way."

A large woman holding a little girl by each hand came over to them. "Do those two bunks have anybody?"

"No."

"I wonder if the girls could stay there. There ain't enough room for our whole family in our place. We're just over there...in the corner. I wouldn't be far away. We just need a place for 'em to sleep. I'll keep 'em with me when they're up." The girls, probably seven and eight years old, held tightly to their mother's skirt.

Tilda responded at once, "Sure. We can keep an eye on 'em at night." She nudged one of the girls and laughed, "I'll bet you snore."

"Come on, girls. Let's bring your bed sacks over."

Tilda whispered to Marta. "They'll be all right. Better two little kids than a couple of these roughnecks in those bunks."

"You're right. Well, that fills up our little place."

When the woman came back, she said, "I'm Margareta Koch. This is Maria, and this is Lizzie." She stroked their tightly braided hair and gave them a broad smile.

"My children, Willi and Katerina, will be glad for some other kids to play with. They already got to know a little boy over on the other side."

"I'm sure glad the girls can sleep in your section. We were late getting here and there ain't many bunks left."

"We're pretty well packed in. It looks like they get everybody on that they can."

"Did you see the lines of people waiting to get tickets for just any ship. There must be hundreds leaving every day."

Tilda, on the basis of having been an early arrival on the ship, assumed the role of guide. "Come on, let me show you where some of the things are before it gets dark. I had a chance to look around a little before the mob came."

They walked through the steerage compartment toward the front of the ship. "There's a room here with cookstoves and a couple of tables for cuttin' stuff up for the pot. It's goin' to get pretty crowded when all them women wanna cook," she said as they poked their heads through the door to the cook room. "They got another kitchen somewhere, but I ain't seen it. I heard that the rich folks in cabins get some of their meals furnished with their ticket. Pretty nice, *nicht wahr*."

"Wait'll you see this," Tilda laughed. She led Marta to a row of little sheds built along the side of the ship. She opened a door and showed Marta one of the toilets. They peered down the hole in the seat to the sea many feet below.

"*Mein Gott*! I'm going to be afraid to go," Marta joked.

"Well, plenty o' fresh air anyway."

"No place to be in a storm, I'll bet."

Tilda's tour went on. "Over here's two washrooms; one for men and one for women. You can bring your basin up here. There's a pump that brings up water from the sea."

"All the comforts of home," Marta added with a note of sarcasm. "I'm sure glad that we've only got three weeks of it."

"Well, like I told Klaus, we might as well make the best of it. We never had much of a house in the country, so this ain't nothin' new. Did you live on a farm?"

"*Nein*, we lived in a town, Neuhaus. Our house was pretty ordinary. I used to work in a fine house, but I never really lived in one."

"They say it's pretty nice in America."

"I've seen a few letters from people who've gone over. I never quite believe them. I sometimes think they paint a pretty picture because they are trying to prove that they didn't make a dumb mistake."

"The men fall for all that stuff. Well. we'll see. We're supposed to go to Klaus's uncle in New York," Tilda sighed. "We better get back down below. Our men'll think we decided to get off the ship and run home."

It was getting quite dark. Sailors came through and hung a few lanterns here and there.

"Klaus, go find the kids, while I get out some bread for our supper."

Johann was lying in his bunk, second from the bottom. Marta nudged him.

"Want one of those rolls for supper? I'm too excited to be hungry."

"*Ja*. Some of the men said we aren't going to sail until morning.... Something about the tide." He chewed his *Brötchen* thoughtfully. "It hardly seems possible that we'll be on our way soon."

"I never thought I'd even see the ocean," Marta said.

"It smells like a barn in here with all the fresh straw in everybody's mattress."

"You can be sure it's not going to stay that way. Don't expect much..."

Johann rolled out of his bunk and took Marta's hand. "Let's go out on deck. This is our last chance to see land for a while."

Passengers lined the rail. The wharves were still bustling, even in the light of torches and lanterns. The windows of Bremerhaven had an amber glow. A wagon with huge casks was pulled up to the ship and two men were pumping their contents into the ship.

"That must be drinking water coming on."

"I hear a cow mooing," Marta said.

"Ja. When I was getting the straw, I saw a stall with a cow and a couple of goats. I suppose they are for milk."

"Look at those stars. Did you ever see so many? I hope it's a pretty day tomorrow."

"I wish we could stay out here all night. It's a lot nicer than being cooped up with all those people down below."

"It'll get pretty cool out here by morning. I feel it already," Marta shivered.

"Then we better go down and try to get some sleep."

"That's not going to be easy."

They climbed down the steep steps, down two decks to the steerage area. Only a few lanterns stilled burned.

"The little girls in the top bunks are asleep already. Be careful not to wake them," Marta whispered.

Before they climbed into their bunks, Marta kissed Johann lightly and whispered. "We're back in our haystack."

"*Ja*,..with 200 people in the hay with us," Johann chuckled.

They tossed and turned for an hour, recontouring their straw-filled bags. A choir of snorers provided a musical accompaniment. A baby cried, answered by another from the far side of the deck. Some older children giggled and were silenced in gutteral tones by their father.

Some daylight came through the grating that covered the big hatch in the center of the steerage section. People began returning to the waking world.

Lines of people began moving to the toilets and washing rooms. Maria and Lizzie were claimed by their mother for the day. Marta and Tilda brought bread for breakfast out of their baskets.

Tilda said, "You know. I been thinkin'. It's gonna be a madhouse up in that cooking room. What would you think of the two of us cookin' together. I'll put in more food because there are four of us. But we'd only hafta wait for one place on the stove."

"Well, that sounds like a good idea. We brought the kind of food the agent told us: potatoes, some beets, some onions. I did get a bottle of raspberry vinegar. The man at the store said you can cover up the taste a little when the food starts getting old. I have a little salt pork, but we didn't bring any other meat. They said it doesn't keep. We've got fresh bread for a while, some Zwiebach and a lot of that stuff they called hardtack. I've got some dried apples, and some prunes too."

"That's the same sorta stuff we got. I got a couple of kilos of rice too. We're not going to be able to cook much anyway. I was sort of figurin' on soup at noon. We'll just have bread in the morning and evening. The kids are going to miss havin' milk, but it's only for a few weeks."

"That'd be all right with us. Johann isn't a big eater anyway."

"I wish I could say that for Klaus. He eats ever'thing I put in front of him, and there'd better be a lot of it."

"Do you have a pot big enough to make soup for all six of us? I'm not sure my kettle's big enough."

"Let's see what the men think about us cookin' together."

May 9, 1857 was a beautiful clear day. All morning final preparations for sailing were being made. Johann and Klaus made frequent trips to the deck to watch; then back to steerage to report progress.

Just before eleven o'clock Klaus told the women and children to come on deck to watch. Passengers lined the railing, children in front, adults to the rear. Dark smoke poured from the stack, showering soot on those downwind. The whistle gave a mighty blast; the children covered their ears; babies cried. The big ropes holding them to the wharf were cast off one by one. The steam engine turned the propeller, churning the water white, and the ship backed away from the pier, turning slowly.

Once in the middle of the wide Weser estuary, the *Indiana* began to move downstream, picking up speed. Within a few minutes the wharf they had left appeared to be very small. The waterway was full of ships and small boats.

Johann said to Marta as the shoreline receded: "There goes my past. There goes the frustration of never being able to find a decent job. There goes Karl, old pompous Karl. There goes dear Mother ....."

Marta added softly, "And our little Karl...."

The estuary widened into the North Sea. In response to shouted orders from the officers, sailors began to climb the rigging of both masts like monkeys. Huge gray sails unfurled and filled with wind. The ship heeled over slightly as it sliced through the water.

"Time for *Mittagessen*. Let's see what we can do, Marta," Tilda broke the spell. "You men come down in 'bout an hour. Klaus, you keep your eye on Willi and Katerina."

Fortunately many of the women were still on deck watching the land fade into the distance. Marta and Tilda loaded potatoes and onions into the pot and made their way to the cooking room.

"I'll get water in the pot and get it boiling on the stove. You peel the potatoes. I think we can beat the crowd. Whew, it's hot around those stoves."

The men came down to eat. Johann got out their tin plates and spoons, tore off a couple of pieces of bread, and waited for the kettle to come from the stove. The rest of the Kümmel family lined up by their boxes, ready for their first real meal on the ship. The women arrived with the steaming pot.

After their plates were filled, Johann said to Marta, "Why don't we take it out on the deck to eat? We'll have plenty of days when we'll have to eat down here."

They sat on a chest, sheltered from the breeze, and slowly ate their potato soup. The sun was warm and the rolling movement of the ship was soothing.

"Look, the land has disappeared. You can't see anything but ocean."

Marta walked to the railing. "Look at all the ships. I can see...eight.. no, nine."

"I feel like I've thrown our ropes off the dock, just like the sailors did back there in Bremerhaven."

CHAPTER 8

The gentle roll of the ship made it a giant cradle. In spite of the many sounds: the creaking of the ship now added to the snores and infant cries, Johann and Marta slept soundly. Sunday morning dawned clear and beautiful. Under full sail the *Indiana* moved down the English Channel. Taking their breakfast *Brötchen*, they climbed the stairs to the deck. Some cabin passengers by the railing told them that the steerage passengers were to use the deck at the front of the ship. With their breakfast rolls that Marta had wrapped in a scarf, they went back down to the steerage deck and walked to the other stairway at the front of the ship. Climbing into the fresh air, they stood for an hour watching the prow of the ship cut through the waves.

"Look. You can see land again."

Johann said, "That must be France over there. And that will be England there."

"The shore looks so white. It couldn't be snow, could it? It isn't cold enough. Isn't it pretty?"

While they were still on deck, suddenly the wind blew harder. The sea became quite rough, causing the *Indiana* to begin to pitch and roll.

"I'm getting wet, like being in the rain," Marta shouted in Johann's ear.

"You go on down," Johann answered, watching the sailors scurrying up the rigging. "I'm going to stay out a little bit longer and watch those fellows climbing around up there with the sails."

The sails on the *Indiana's* spars were being reefed and the ship was moving ahead under steam power. The pitching became worse. As Johann went back down toward their bunks, he was passed by passengers hurrying to the rail. By the time he reached the steerage area passengers were retching into their chamberpots and basins. Children stood wide-eyed or whimpered as they were sick. Marta was in the lowest bunk. Johann climbed onto his straw sack.

"Are you feeling all right?" he asked.

"I was afraid I'd be sick...But I'm all right. It's sure turning some of them inside out. I feel sorry for those little kids."

"My guess is that this isn't the last time it's going to be rough sailing. We'd better get used to it."

"I sure hope they keep it cleaned up. It's going to be awful down here if they don't."

"There won't be much cookin' today," Tilda added from her bunk. "I ain't sick myself, but I sure don't have no appetite with all these folks pukin' all over the place. How about you?"

"I don't want to eat. How about you, Johann?" Marta asked.

"Maybe it'll be better later and we can get something to eat. I don't need food right now."

The rough seas lasted only a few hours. When they had passed through the Channel, the waves were lower and the sailing smoother.

By evening people were out on deck again. The ship was sailing along a few miles off the southern coast of England. Johann and Marta stood at the rail in the section kept for steerage passengers.

"It's pretty at sunset. Look how the light touches that town on the shore....over there...see it shine on that church tower," Marta pointed.

"I wonder how long it will take us to get to Southampton. I don't think they could go into a harbor at night."

"Are we going to get off the ship there?" Marta asked.

"I don't know. I suppose if we're there as long as the ship was tied up at Bremerhaven, they'll let us get off. We'll see."

"I hope they don't have too many more people to get on. I don't see where they would put more people down in our steerage compartment."

"Somebody told me that there are 350 people on the ship. It seems like more than that. I don't know how crowded it is up in the cabins."

"Look at those towns now that it's almost dark."

"Their lights look like fireworks floating on the water. That's real pretty. Are you going down to the bunks? I think I'll stay up here for a while."

The ship was entering a large bay when they got on deck on the next morning. There were green fields everywhere. In an hour they were approaching Southampton. Countless ships were tied up at the wharves. Slowly and carefully their captain maneuvered the *Indiana* into her berth. Lines were thrown and men on the dock pulled huge hawsers to the stanchions on the pier.

Johann watched from deck for a long time. The railroad came right down to the dock. Wagons were unloading coal from the railroad cars and carrying it to the ships. A line of wagons was pulled up beside the *Indiana*. For hours grimy men shoveled load after load through an opening in the side of the ship.

A few other wagons were loading what appeared to be provisions. Some people were going up the gangway with bags over their shoulders. They were dressed in working clothes. Johann assumed that they were sailors coming aboard. They didn't look like passengers and they didn't seem to have much baggage.

Later that day Johann saw some of these sailors on the foredeck with the steerage passengers. They were looking over the railing watching the activity on the dock. One of the sailors had a coal black face. Johann had never seen a Negro before. He studied the man from a distance and finally got enough nerve to walk over and stand beside him at the rail. Without staring he observed the man's shiny black skin, his short black hair in tiny tight curls, his large lips, the lightness of the palms of his hands. Wanting to be friendly, Johann reached into his pocket and offered the man a bite of his tobacco.

"*Danke schön*," the black man smiled.

"*Sprechen Sie Deutsch?*" Johann responded, amazed.

A lively conversation ensued. The man told Johann that his name was Alfred. He could speak German because he had been a slave for a diplomat, but had been given his freedom. He said that he could also speak French, and Italian, and, of course, English.

Later, back down in steerage for dinner, Johann was telling Marta and the Kümmels about the man.

"I heard that there were black people, but I never saw one before. I just about fell over when he talked to me in German."

"I want to see him too," Marta said.

"Sure, you'll have a chance because he'll be on the ship all the way over. He asked me if I wanted to go on shore with him while we're here. He said we weren't going to sail until sometime tomorrow."

"I'd like to get off and look around too. After you see how it is when you're on shore with this man, maybe we can go later."

"We can go this evening. All right?"

"I'll only go if Tilda or Klaus can watch our stuff. With the ship at the dock, somebody could just walk off with all of it."

"They may want to get off too. The mother of those two little girls would probably watch out for things. With all those kids, they won't be going ashore."

Johann was wide-eyed as he walked through the streets of Southampton near the harbor. Alfred pointed out various shops. He showed Johann how to exchange a little of his Prussian money for English money. Johann, feeling expansive with a handful of coins, bought cigars for both of them.

He said to Alfred, "You say these cost two pennies here, tuppence you said. At home they would be 20 *Pfennig*. Can we get a glass of beer somewhere?"

The streets near the docks were dotted with public houses. Alfred and Johann stood at the bar while the publican pulled down on the pump to fill their glasses.

"It tastes a little different; but good. We had good beer at home."

"And lots of it, I'll bet," Alfred joked.

"It fills you up as much as meat, and it's a lot cheaper. Things seem terribly expensive here. This glass of beer costs 20 Prussian *Silbergroschen*. That's about 4 times as much as at home."

"Wait till you get to America. Things aren't cheap there."

"That's one of the hard things about going to America. You don't have any way of knowing if you'll have enough money to get started there."

Alfred smiled, "I've never had a whole lot. I lived pretty good when I was working for the Count. But now I just live on ships. I work my way from one port to another. I figure that someday I'll find the right place. Then it'll be time to settle down."

As they walked back toward the ship Johann noticed other black men on the streets.

"I never thought there were black people in England."

"There aren't many. Rich English people, especially those who lived in other countries used to have black slaves. But we were given our freedom. So quite a few of these black people are still servants for the nobles; but now they are paid, and they can leave if they want. It's not a bad life."

That evening Johann, feeling himself now to be an experienced tourist, took Marta ashore. Since it was getting dark they didn't wander too far from the harbor. He had promised Marta dinner in a little restaurant he had seen not far from the ship. After strolling around peering into a few shop windows, looking at some of the larger buildings of the port city, they came to The Bull.

Marta held back. "Are you sure we can afford to eat here. We won't know how much things cost since the signs are all in English."

"Don't worry," Johann said. "Alfred showed me how to do it. I still have some of the English money we got this afternoon. We'll have enough for dinner."

"Well, if you think it will be all right. We never know how much we'll need in America."

"We've got enough gold pieces," he whispered, patting the pouch under his shirt, to see us through. If we get in a pinch, I can write Julius to send me more of my inheritance. I've got this purse around my neck under my shirt with the spending money we'll use on the trip."

Marta still held back as they stood in front of The Bull. "It looks nice. Are you sure it isn't too expensive?"

"Alfred said it was a nice place. He knows we don't have a lot of money."

"Well, all right then."

"Just enjoy it. This is going to be the last good meal we get for a while. I can see already that eating is going to be a mess on the ship: crowded, rough seas sometimes, only so much we can take along with us."

"I would like some good food. We won't eat much, but it will be nice."

The Bull was dimly lit with oil lamps swinging from the dark wood beams overhead and a few candles flickering on the tables. Feeling a little conspicuous in the crowd of English men and women laughing at the tables, they made their way to an empty table in the corner.

"How are we going to tell them what we want to eat?" Marta worried.

"We can always point to things on other tables, if we have to."

A large woman with a somewhat smudged towel wrapped around her waist approached them. *"Was wollen Sie?"*

Marta's jaw dropped and Johann said, "You speak German!"

The waitress said, "I heard you talking when you came in. My father was a German sailor who married my mother here in Southampton, so I learned it from him. I always wait on the Germans who come in here from the ships. It gives me a chance to practice."

Marta recovered from her surprise. "You can help us order. You know we don't have a lot of money, but we'd like one good meal before we sail away tomorrow."

The woman laughed. "Sure. Why don't you tell me how much you want to spend and I'll work it out."

Johann put the remainder of his English money on the table. "If that isn't enough, we could put one *Reichstaler* with it."

"That'll be enough for a nice plain meal and some beer."

She was back soon with a glass of beer for Johann and a smaller glass which she set before Marta. "Here you are, *Liebchen*, this is a nice lady's drink--it's a good cider. Try it!"

The dinner followed. "This is fish right out of the Channel, fresh this morning," she said as she put down two plates with a piece of a large flat fish on each. "Here are some potatoes and sprouts. That's about all that's left this time of year." Marta had never seen these little round green vegetables that looked like tiny cabbages. She popped one into her mouth and smiled at the waitress.

They ate slowly, enjoying every bite, mopping their plates with slices of bread.

After they had paid their waitress, she said, "I wouldn't mind going to America. One of these days I'm going to find a way to get on one of the ships as a cook and work my way over. So keep your eyes open for me after you are there. *Auf wiederseh'n.*"

When they left The Bull, Marta was glad they were not far from the ship. The streets were dark. Most of the buildings were big warehouses and had no lights in them.

"Walk faster," she said, hanging on to Johann's arm. "I don't like this. There aren't enough people around."

Thinking of the purses of gold they had tied around their necks, Johann stepped up the pace until they were almost trotting. Only a few drunks lurched along the little alley between two tall warehouses which led to the *Indiana.*

A blowsy woman stepped from a dark doorway and tried to take Johann's arm, until she saw Marta. Two archways further along the wall of the warehouse gave out the giggles and grunts of one of her colleague's coupling.

"Faster," Marta pled, starting to run.

"We're almost to the ship. See; there it is."

"Thank heaven. I've never been so scared. We could have been hit on the head and robbed...or worse."

They went quickly up the gangplank and were checked by the officer on guard. The ship was quiet as they made their way down the steps to the steerage deck and carefully walked among the sleeping people to their bunks.

The passengers were becoming restless and impatient on the following day. The feverish loading of coal and supplies seemed to be finished. But still they waited.

As they stood on the foredeck looking over the railing, Johann said, "I wonder if it wouldn't have been smarter to have gotten a ship that went straight from Bremerhaven to New York, rather than coming to England first. This just makes the trip longer. This waiting around seems kind of unnecessary."

"It's not too bad. We did see some pretty things sailing along the coast. And we did have that nice dinner last night."

"Don't tell me you've forgotten the lovely stroll back to the ship," Johann joked.

"I'll never forget that. That could have ended the whole journey right there."

"That's probably not the last adventure we'll have. You'll probably get chased by Indians," he laughed.

"Look! Here comes a train right down to all the ships."

A passenger train was disgorging a long line of men and women who moved toward the three ships tied up at the pier. Dockworkers pulled heavy wagons piled high with trunks and boxes.

"These must be our English passengers. That's probably what we have been waiting for."

Marta said, "I hope not many of them come down into steerage. We're just about as crowded as we can be right now."

Later Johann observed, "I think most of them must have gone into the cabins. I only saw a couple of people going into steerage."

"That's good."

"I sometimes wonder if we wouldn't have been smarter to have gotten a cabin. Sure, it costs a little more, but it has to be more comfortable than this steerage. Would you want me to ask if we could pay some more money and change to a cabin?"

"It would feel kind of funny to move our stuff out and leave Tilda and Klaus. They might get the idea that we think we're too good for them."

"We'll get used to it. It's only for three or four weeks. I guess we can stand that."

At about two o'clock the *Indiana* cast off and was warped out into the harbor. Black smoke poured from the funnel as the engines moved them away from the land.

Marta and Johann stood by the rail of their deck area and watched England fade into the distance.

"Well, the next land we'll see will be America. I hope we get there quickly. What day is it? I've lost track of time already."

Johann thought for a moment, "According to the dates I write in our *Tagebuch*, it must be the 13th of May. So much has happened in the past couple of weeks; I can't keep the days straight."

The first few days passed quickly. There wasn't much room to move about. The days were filled with the noise of dozens of family conversations, the occasional shouted orders to the crew coming from on deck. The ship creaked and snapped as it rolled with the waves.

Next to Johann and Marta, Tilda and Klaus' cramped living space and narrow bunks, there was a small alcove in which three crew members were berthed. It was obvious from the hammers and saws they carried that they were the ship's carpenters. They spoke a few words of German and Johann was impressed with their friendliness. They always smiled and said *"Guten Tag"* when they went past the crowded bunks and piles of boxes. Sometimes, when they returned to their cubbyhole after meals, they brought along part of a loaf of fresh bread which they smilingly gave to Tilda or Marta.

When they added the bread to their small stockpile of food, Marta said, "This will be so good. Our *Brötchen* are getting so stale you'd break your teeth without soaking them in coffee. And that awful hardtack..."

"We're lucky," Tilda said to Marta. "We brought the right stuff. I seen some people over on the other side that don't have nuthin' beside hardtack and apples."

"*Ja*, I noticed that too. I feel funny. It's not that we have so much, and it sure isn't fancy, but at least we've got food with some taste. If we just knew how long the trip was going to take, we could see if we had enough to share with some of those folks."

Tilda looked again into their hamper. "My daughter met some children over there by the far wall. Margaretta wanted to take them some of our food, because they don't have much. I hated to do it, but I had to tell her that we had to be careful to make our stuff last 'til New York. She had a hard time understandin' somethin' like that."

"Even though we don't have anything fancy, it's hard to enjoy a meal when you know that some families are running low already," Marta said, closing their wicker hamper.

"I heard that sometimes they's storms and ships take twice as long to get to America. We gotta be sure our food'll hold out through a long trip. It ain't our fault that those people didn't have enough sense to bring the right food."

After dark the sounds of the ship were exaggerated against the stillness of the night as Marta tried to fall asleep. Quiet conversation gave way to snores and sighs as people turned in their bunks. A few of the less modest steerage passengers provided the sounds of passionate encounters. Even in the dark Marta felt her cheeks turning hot with embarrassment. Every so often a little child cried, tired of confinement or frightened by the constant rolling and creaking of the ship.

Hearing the whimpering of the children, Marta whispered to Johann, "Even though it breaks my heart, I'm so glad we didn't try to bring little Karl along. This would be terrible for him. At least we know he's well-fed, dry, warm, with room to take his first steps at home."

"*Ja*, you're right. I told you that this is no place for a little child. You would worry yourself sick."

"But I miss him so much." Marta wiped her eyes on her sleeve. "Sometimes at night I think that the cries I hear are Karl crying for me. It hurts so bad."

Johann reached down and patted her arm.

The early morning sun came over the roofs of Neuhaus. Katerina Wiesner looked across the bedroom to see baby Karl in his crib. She quietly got out of bed and walked over to look at the sleeping child. Poor *Kindchen*, she thought, sleep peacefully.

August sensed her stirring around. "What's the matter? Is he all right?"

"Sound asleep. Poor little fellow must miss his mother. But he hasn't really cried since that morning they left."

August started pulling his clothes. "You always helped take care of him, so he probably don't miss them as bad as you think."

"Well, I miss them. They must be out on the ocean now. I worry about them. Ships sink…"

Just then Karl stirred and began to whimper. Katerina picked him up and gave him to August. "Here, hold him while I get my clothes on..Poor *Kindchen.*"

"They said they would write a letter when they got to America. Then you can stop worrying about them."

"I'll be glad when they get settled and can send for the baby. He belongs with them as soon as possible." She twisted her hair into a knot and pinned it in place.

"They're going to want to wait until he is a little older. But we'll keep our eyes open for somebody around here who is going to America. Can I put him in his crib while I go build a fire in the cook stove?""

The morning light was coming through the hatch. Johann said, as they were eating their stale bread and watery coffee, "I'm going to take a look around the ship."

"You'll get into some of those places we aren't supposed to be. Don't forget how that one fellow scolded us and said that steerage people weren't allowed on the main deck."

The embarrassment and resentment Johann had felt from that rebuke had cooled somewhat. He stood up and jammed his hat down on his head.

"I want to see what it's like in some of the other parts of the ship. You can't tell me that on a ship this big I can only go to one little deck way in front or down here in this barnyard. I'm going to look around until somebody tells me I can't."

"Just don't get in any trouble," Marta cautioned.

Johann knew that their deck was below the water line. Under them was the cargo hold. As he climbed the steps to the other decks Johann saw that there were portholes in the sides of the ship. He heard some of the cabin passengers talking German and began a conversation with one of them, a balding portly man standing by the rail.

Stung by the earlier reproof and the strong suggestion that he was inferior to cabin passengers, Johann tried to conceal that he was in steerage. Johann asked, "How are things in your cabin?"

"Pretty crowded. I am in a big cabin with four beds for twelve men. So we're three in a bed."

"*Ja*, we are jammed in pretty tightly," Johann added.

"They give us our meals but we have to line up two by two because it is so crowded. The food is not bad though."

"*Ja*, that is right," Johann answered, thinking that maybe the cabin passengers were not so much better off than those on the lower deck.

"In the morning it is bread and coffee. For lunch yesterday we had some soup, then meat, I guess it was beef, and potatoes, with some plums and dumplings for dessert. I do not know if it will be that way for the whole voyage, but it is not bad. You can have as much vinegar and salt and pepper as you want." He leaned back against the rail and lit a cigar.

Johann was mortified to realize that his companion must have guessed all along that he was not a cabin passenger, or he would not have shared all that information.

Deciding that it was less embarrassing to be truthful, Johann responded, "They sure pack everyone they can onto the ship, don't they? It's terribly crowded where we are staying on the lower deck. We cook our own food. We are lucky. We had good advice from the agent and brought along plenty of simple food."

The man looked out over the ocean as if he could see far over the horizon, "I have been looking forward to going to America for a long time. I suppose you have, too. My father did not want me to go. He wanted me to stay at home and help him run his apothecary. But I've had enough of that. I finally just bought my ticket and told him I was going. He really was very angry. He would not talk to me for a few days. But I am a grown man and make my own decisions." He thumped the rail.

"My family was not very happy about us going either."

Not hearing Johann the man pressed on, "But, you know, just before I left he took his watch out of his pocket and put it in my hand. He told me, 'Be a good man, be honest; don't bring any shame on our name!' It meant a lot to me that he did that."

A few days later the calm seas that had favored them since leaving Southampton changed suddenly. In the middle of the night Johann felt the ship begin to pitch and roll. There were loud bangs as the ship slammed into waves. Even down in steerage, he could hear the wind howling in the rigging. He heard thuds and scraping sounds as the crew dragged the heavy covers over the hatch above the center of the steerage quarters. It quickly became very stuffy.

"Johann, are you asleep?" Marta whispered. "What's happening?"

"It sounds like we're getting into a storm. It will be morning soon, I think. Then we can see what's happening."

"I'm scared. This is a lot worse than it was in the English Channel. My stomach is turning over and over."

In the morning it was foggy and cold. The *Indiana* continued to buck and heave. They could hear the engine throb as the ship seemed to move very slowly in the face of the storm. The steerage section was dark as night with the large hatch covered. Their only light came from several lanterns. People talked in low tones, even though everyone was now awake. Johann heard incessant sounds of retching and the air became fetid with the stench of vomit. Very few people got out of their bunks. No one even thought about eating.

When Johann heard Marta joining the multitude vomiting into their chamber pots, he, too, began to feel queasy. He heard the little Koch girls in the upper bunks whimpering. Finally, he got out of his bunk and began to move around, holding on to partitions and bunks. He took the girls and led them to their mother's cubicle.

In a corner of the steerage section a number of people were huddled around one of the bunks. Johann, with the deck heaving under him, tottered over to see what was happening. Two women were sobbing softly and a man held a lantern over the bunk. Johann could see a young woman, hardly more than a girl. Her cheeks were very flushed. She seemed to be struggling to breathe as she tossed on her straw pallet. One of the women, whom Johann gathered was her mother, kept wiping the girl's forehead with a cloth. Johann moved back into the dimly lighted area and wobbled back to their little enclosure.

Marta attempted a smile. "What's going on over there?"

"It looks like a girl is pretty sick."

"Most of us are pretty sick," Marta croaked as she reached for the pot again.

"No, this looks different to me. It's a lot worse than being seasick. It looks like she has a high fever and is delirious."

"God help them! Those poor people, having to worry about her in this terrible weather," Marta answered, then added, "I really didn't mean to joke about that kind of trouble."

The motion of the ship became more violent. Boxes that had been piled on top of each other toppled. Johann and Klaus, struggling to stand steady, tried to wedge their belongings in tightly to keep them in place. A couple of sailors came through with short pieces of old rope and helped people tie down their belongings. The activity provided distraction from the communal nausea, but it was temporary.

Johann wanted to go outside. When he reached the head of the stairs, a sailor stopped him and pointed to the little round window in the door. Johann could see why nobody was allowed on deck. Huge waves were pounding over the railings. Johann looked through the spray which dashed against the window at the men who climbed high in the rigging as the ship rolled and pitched. I could never be brave enough or crazy enough to do that, he thought. The few sailors who had to go across the deck after they had furled all the sails, held on to ropes that were stretched as lifelines. His ears rang with the deep growl of the fog horn which bellowed every few minutes.

As Johann passed the section where Marta and Tilda cooked their daily warm meal, he saw that none of the stoves were lit. The area was deserted, except for a slow procession of steerage passengers teetering from one hand-hold to another, making their way to the latrines.

The heavy weather continued through the whole day. People did not venture far from their bunks. It was dark with the hatch covered and a few lanterns swung back and forth on their hooks. Johann covered his eyes with his hat; the only time he felt seasick was when he looked at the swinging lights.

Finally, during the next night the ship stopped rolling, and Friday dawned clear and bright. Boxes, baskets, and bags that had fallen over and spilled onto the floor were stowed again. Johann and Klaus took more care to see that things were held firmly in place. The women all over the steerage section began to clean up the mess from the previous day. Tilda and Marta stood in line with their pail to get sea water from the pump and began to mop up the floor of their little cubicle where one of their basins had tipped over.

Marta told Tilda, "We're lucky. Did you see that mess over there. They'll have to scrub all day to mop up all the vomit. It's everywhere. Why weren't they more careful? Didn't they have any pots?"

Johann smiled to hear the always neat and clean Marta's protest.

Tilda grunted, "I hope we can get the stink out of this place. I see they took off that hatch cover again. At least we'll get some fresh air in here."

"The smell was enough to make me sick, even without the tossing of the ship."

Tilda turned to the men, "You fellows want some food? We prob'ly could go cook a little if you'll eat it. We can beat the crowd to the stoves if we cook now."

Klaus grinned, "I've got plenty of room for food, *nicht wahr?*"

Not to be outdone, Johann pushed back his hat, rubbed his stomach and said, "I've been ready to eat for hours."

Tossing a few potatoes and beets into their pot, Tilda and Marta headed for the cookstoves.

The small triangular deck area in the bow was jammed as steerage passengers sought fresh air. The sunshine almost erased memories of yesterday's nasty weather.

A sailor's voice rang out from the crows nest atop the tallest mast. Even though the German immigrants did not understand what he was calling, they could see his arm pointing. Marta and Johann saw other passengers pointing in the same direction and tried to see what everyone was watching.

"What is it?" Johann asked the man next to him at the rail.

"*Walfisch!* See...over there!"

Marta strained to see. Johann pointed, "See that black thing in the water. I can see three of them. There! One just blew his steam! Did you see it?"

"I see them now. Look at them dive with their big tails up in the air."

"Are those little ships trying to catch the whales?" Johann asked the man beside him.

"Those little boats are trying to harpoon the whales. See the guy with the spear up in the front of the boat."

As they were watching, one of the whales surfaced very close to the *Indiana* and blew his tall plume into the air. Some of the spray fell across the passengers.

Marta wiped her face, "Ugh. I don't like that."

Johann laughed. "He's just getting even for all the stuff we dumped off the ship yesterday into his ocean....Did you see the size of that thing?"

"Look! One of those little boats speared a whale. Look how it is dragging them through the water. It's a wonder they don't turn over."

"I'd rather fish with a pole the way we used to in Endigen. I don't see how they ever kill a big thing like that. Look at how those fellows have to hold on. They're lucky the waves are a lot smaller than yesterday."

The *Indiana*, under full sail, soon left the two whaling ships and their small boats to sink over the horizon.

During the night Johann felt the ship begin to roll once again. By the next morning the sailors had reefed the sails and the engine was pushing them through wave after tall wave. For several days the sailing was rough. Rain pelted on the decks and the hatch was once again covered tightly. A brief trip to the foredeck was wasted effort. There was nothing to see. Fog surrounded the *Indiana*. Johann could barely make out the tops of the masts.

The fog lifted the next day but the sea was still rough. Most of the passengers were getting used to the rolling of the ship. In mid-afternoon they heard shouts from the deck. Johann and Marta stood by the rail and watched as the *Indiana* passed through what seemed like hundreds of flying fish, jumping right out of the waves.

Klaus picked up through the grapevine that some sailors told passengers that flying fish were a bad omen. They meant that bad weather was coming.

Tilda chided, "That's sure good news. I thought they were pretty. Now you tell me they mean that we're headin' for another storm."

"I'm only saying what they told me. I'm sure not looking for another storm."

The omen proved accurate. The storm hit on Tuesday morning. The ship lurched and shivered as huge waves crashed across the deck. It was impossible to stand up without holding on to something. The forward motion of the ship was like going up and down steep hills. At the same time the deck rolled right, then left, then right again.

After one particularly violent roll Marta screamed, "We're going to turn over!"

Johann saw her pale, contorted face and reached out to her. He put his arm around her, wondering if he was trying to comfort her or to be

137

comforted. He had never been so frightened in his life. Nausea was being replaced by sheer terror.

The waves smashing into the hatch cover above the steerage area caused a steady stream of dripping water onto their deck. The poor folk who were quartered below the hatch scurried to protect their belongings from the shower of sea water. Rivulets ran across the deck through the cubicles. Klaus and Johann tried to rearrange their wall of boxes to withstand the pitching of the ship. They took down the trunks from their pile and put them into the foot end of their bunks. They pried a couple of boards off the top of the closest partition and slid them under the large boxes at the base of their wall of baggage. This might be enough to raise them above the trickle of water coming from the leaking hatch cover.

The cooking and eating utensils rolled around beneath the lower bunks, together with their chamber pots. They were surrounded by incessant noise: the ferocious howling of the wind, the explosion of the waves over the deck, the creaking and groaning of the ship as if it were in pain, the thump of falling boxes, the clatter of metal pots, the crying of frightened children, the sounds of people retching into their pails.

A man's voice called out, "Watch out. Our cooking pot is floating away."

Filled with despair his wife answered, "Let it go. We're lost. We won't need it any more."

The few people who tried to move around staggered like drunks. A few tried to get to the latrines or to find some place where there was a little fresh air. The stench became overpowering on the steerage deck, compounding the violent motions of the ship. There seemed to be no way for getting relief; standing up or lying down made little difference. The few brave souls who had ventured up to the door leading to the deck above reported that the waves were as tall as a house, that at times it seemed like the ship was between two tall gray walls.

Most of the people took off their shoes and stockings to keep them dry. Men rolled up their trousers and women hitched up their skirts, because rivulets of water sloshed to and fro across the deck as the ship rolled. A few took off almost all their clothes, thinking that in the dim light of a few lanterns on their hooks above their near-nudity was hardly observable. Their neighbors reproached them, saying, "Put on some clothes. You don't want to meet your Maker without any clothes on."

Johann tried to encourage Marta. "After that last storm I saw Alfred, that Negro sailor I met in Southampton. He said that that storm wasn't really a bad storm."

"I wonder what he thinks about this one. I'll bet he's as scared as we are. Sailors know that ships are wrecked and sink to the bottom of the ocean."

Johann tried to be reassuring. "Alfred told me that a well-built ship like the *Indiana* can make it through very big storms. He said that before a ship like this turned over the masts would snap off. That hasn't happened."

"But that could happen!"

"You remember in the English Channel, we saw how when it gets very windy, those sailors climb up in the rigging and take in all the sails. That's one advantage of being on a steam ship. They can tie down the sails and keep moving with the engine. We'll be all right."

"What would happen to little Karl if we were drowned?"

"Quit talking like that. We're not going to drown."

"I'm glad he isn't with us. Listen to those poor kids crying. They're so scared. I don't blame them one bit."

"Don't worry. We'll be all right. These storms can't last too long."

"How do you know? You're just talking."

"Well, I can't do anything about it. So I just have to think that the captain knows how to get the ship through the storm."

People in several of the cubicles had gotten their prayer books out of their baggage and were praying aloud. Some others were saying their rosaries. Voices called on the saints and the Virgin Mary to preserve them. People were repenting aloud for their sins. Others made vows to be fulfilled if they survived the storm.

Johann thought, if Karl and Julius were here, they'd be praying mightily. He thought about the many Sundays looking at the bowed heads along the family pew, knowing that the family piety was not part of his life.

It was so dark in the hold that night and day were pretty much the same. Mealtime was meaningless, since no one could bear the thought of eating. Johann looked at his watch in the dim light of the lantern that swung above them. "Do you know it's nearly nine o'clock? We've been in this storm all day."

Tilda said, "We might as well try to get some sleep."

Marta did not answer. Johann saw that she had already dozed off, exhausted by the stress of the day. Before long he, too, fell asleep.

The bad weather continued for another day. The terrible nausea subsided a little and they chewed on a few pieces of bread. A meal was out of the question. The fact that the ship had survived the pounding waves began to give them confidence. If they hadn't sunk by this time, they could weather the storm. So there was nothing to do but stay near their bunks and wait...and wait.

By Thursday the sea was calmer. There was still a fairly strong wind, which caused the ship to heel over to the right. But the terrible rolling and pitching had ended. As soon as they could, Marta and Johann made their way to the slanting deck. The sky was very blue and the sun warmed them.

"What a relief," Marta said. "Just to see the sun again, to breathe some fresh air."

"*Ja*, it is wonderful. My head was really pounding from all that stale air and the awful smells of the place."

"Somebody said it is Ascension Day."

"Is that right. That was always picnic day in Endigen. There would be no school; the children would play games and have races. Our mothers would pack a basket full of good food."

"Speaking of food, how would you like a good hot meal today. Tilda and I thought we'd use some of our beans make a pot of soup. We've got a little salt pork to give it some flavor."

"My appetite is coming back."

"Those two days saved us some food, for sure. We're going to come out all right. I was worried that we might run out before we got to New York."

"Is everything keeping all right?" Johann asked.

"*Ja*, we brought the right kind of things. Some of the women have had to throw meat that spoiled into the ocean. That's a shame. By doing what the agent told us, we've only got stuff that won't spoil, as long as we can keep it dry."

"I don't know why people would try to bring things that won't keep."

Marta said, "Some of the women said they put vinegar in with meat that is turning to cover up the taste."

"I suppose it's the water they give you to cook with, but some of the things have tasted a little funny."

"Sometimes I think there is some sea water mixed in with the water they give us in the cooking room."

"Is that what has been funny about the coffee? I didn't want to say anything, but sometimes it has been pretty awful."

"I suppose so. I never think coffee tastes good anyway. It must be the water."

Marta began walking toward the stairs down to steerage. "I'll find Tilda and we'll get that bean soup started."

As Johann stood at the railing a young fellow he'd seen in the steerage area came up beside him. The youth was perhaps 14 or 15 years old, his sallow complexion dotted with pimples. His clothing was several sizes too large for his skinny body. He stood quietly looking out at the horizon.

Johann struck up a conversation. "*Wie geht's?*"

"*Wie geht's bei Ihnen?*" the youth replied, his voice cracking between alto and tenor.

"How did you make it through that storm?"

"I thought I'd die. I puked for two days. I haven't had much to eat on the whole trip, so most of the time I was *kotzen* without anything coming up. It felt awful." He scratched hard at his tousled head.

Johann leaned against the rail. "Where do you come from?"

"*Korntal bei Stuttgart.*"

"What's your name?"

"Kurt. Kurt Nauman." He answered, spitting into the ocean.

"My name is Weber. Johann Weber. I come from *Schlesien*. Where is your family's place down in steerage?"

"I don't have no family." Kurt scratched again furiously.

"You mean you're traveling all by yourself!"

The lad looked down at the deck. "I have to. My stepmother, the old witch, threw me out and made me go to America. She's always hated me. After my papa died she made my life hell." He kicked the gunwale.

"How are you getting along on the ship, all by yourself?" Johann asked, feeling some pity for the young fellow.

"I don't have nobody to make me meals. I kind of hang around when people are eating. Sometimes they have more than they can eat and they give it me. I do have a sack of hardtack and some dried apples I brought along. I don't have no money, except for a few *Taler*. I'm gonna need them until I can find a place to work in New York."

"You mean they sent you off with only a few *Taler*?" Johann was touched by Kurt's hard luck story, but the sly grin that kept crossing the boy's face made Johann wonder if he was being tricked.

"Well, I had more, but I was robbed in *Köln* on my way to Bremen. I got off the train there and went with some other fellows I met on the train to a little inn to spend the night. While I was sleeping somebody went through my old carpet bag and stole the money my step-mother gave me for the trip. All I had left was the three *Taler* I had in my shoe."

Increasingly suspicious, Johann pressed, "How were you able to buy your ticket for the ship?"

"I already had that. They didn't steal that. But I didn't have nothing to buy food for the trip."

"Where did you stay in Bremen before the ship left?"

"I just hung around with some of the people from the train. They went to a God-awful *Gasthaus*. I went around the back and found that they had a little stable with a haymow. I climbed up there and found a place to sleep. The people told me we had to take a little boat to Bremerhaven to catch our ship. I didn't have no ticket for that so I just watched until nobody was looking and jumped onto the little boat. It was easy."

Johann's first impulse was to invite the young fellow to share some of their food. But his growing doubts caused him to hold back. It wasn't only his uncertainty about whether or not their supplies would last for the trip, but he vaguely sensed that it would be a mistake to rush into a friendship with Kurt.

When he told Marta about meeting young Kurt, she said that she had seen a number of young people who apparently were traveling alone to America.

"Tilda told me that she saw three young girls who had gotten together. They had joined up with two older boys who were also traveling alone. Tilda said that some of the women passengers were gossiping because all five had set up housekeeping in a far end of the steerage section."

"I wonder if the young fellow I met is one of that bunch."

"Might be. They sound like a wild gang. I suppose they figure nobody knows them, so they can do anything."

"They probably were shifting for themselves before they started the trip."

The beautiful weather continued for the next few days. Marta and Johann spent as much time as they could on deck, escaping the dark, crowded, foul-smelling steerage section. Even though there was no place to sit, they stayed on deck for hours at a time, walking back and forth or taking their turn standing at the rail.

It was pleasant to look out over the mirror-like sea. Twice on that day they saw other large sailing ships. Except for their brief encounter with the whaling fleet, this was the first time since leaving Southampton that they had seen other signs of human life. Both ships were heading toward Europe, probably to pick up other loads of immigrants.

"You can see how fast these ships go. It's only a couple of hours from the time we first see their sails until they vanish over the opposite horizon."

CHAPTER 9

It was another clear day but the breeze was cold. As Johann stood at the foredeck rail, he heard the voice of the lookout high on the main mast, "Iceberg! Iceberg!"

He looked up at the crows nest to see which way the sailor was pointing. There it was: a small mountain of glistening ice against the blue sky. Parts of it were white, parts were a dirty gray, parts shown with an ethereal blue as if illuminated from within. Johann ran down the steep stair to the steerage deck and called Marta, Klaus and Tilda. Together they went back on deck.

Now there were two bergs, one on either side of the ship. The ship seemed frail and tiny in comparison. The helmsman steered carefully between them and the dozens of much smaller icefloes which dotted the sea.

"They are ten times as high as the church at home," Johann said.

"Look how close we are to them," Klaus added. "I hope that fellow steering knows what he is doing."

"Isn't it cold! It feels like winter in May," Marta shivered. "It's so beautiful, but I'm not dressed for this kind of weather. Our heavy coats are at the bottom of our trunk."

"I think I'm goin' back down. I love watchin' this, but this wind goes right through my clothes," Tilda added

"What's that over there? On the other side of that iceberg?"

Johann strained his eyes. "I believe it's more whales. *Ja*, look at that. There is one blowing his steam."

Klaus put his arm around Tilda, "You women go back down if you're cold. I'm gonna stay up here with Johann for a while and watch."

More and more passengers came out of the deck. They were rewarded with the acrobatics of a school of porpoises. In twos and threes the glistening fish jumped in graceful arcs, swimming a parallel course with the *Indiana*. Each exhibition brought "ooohs" and "aaahs" from the audience along the rail. The show went on for almost an hour.

After their midday potato soup Johann and Klaus went on deck again. Around four o'clock they passed another huge iceberg.

"This is the biggest we've seen. Look at that!" Klaus said with amazement.

"The sun makes it look like crystal."

"It's like sailing past a big hill covered with snow."

"How are we going to make it through this stuff after dark?" Johann asked. "If we ran into one of these things, it would sink us in minutes."

"I suppose they know how to handle this. Do you think they just stop for the night and drift along with the ice?"

"I suppose if there was moonlight you could keep going, but plowing ahead in the dark would be crazy."

Just then another large sailing ship came from behind the berg and passed a few hundred yards away. It had three masts.

"Look at that. I count twenty sails on that boat," Johann said.

"He's really movin'."

The captain stood on the bridge with a big megaphone and hailed the other ship. Although Johann and Klaus could not understand the conversation because it was in English, they did hear the word "iceberg" several times. After the captains finished, the sailors on the two ships began to shout back and forth as they passed.

"You know, these are the first human beings we've met in nearly two weeks. The last ones were those fellows in the whale boats. I wonder if this means we're getting close to America," Johann said.

"I don' know. If the trip takes three weeks, we still have a week to go."

"I can't say I'll be sorry to get off the ship. I could use a little more space. I don't like being cooped up all the time."

"I wonder what it's gonna be like in New York."

"I've been thinking about that too. Tilda said you are staying in New York?" Johann said.

"My uncle's goin' to help us. We got to find a place to stay until I can find work. People say there's plenty of jobs. I'll take the first one that comes along. I got to get some money comin' in so we can find a place to live. Later I can look around for a better job if I need it. Are you stayin' in New York?"

"Just a few days; long enough to get our stuff together. We're going to go way to the middle of the country. A fellow I knew at home has a son who lives in a place called Davenport...in Iowa. I've never met him, but his father wrote to him about me. Marta knows his wife. I going to look him up when we get there and maybe he can help me find a job."

"Sometimes I think we're crazy to leave a place where we know the ropes and go into a country we don't know nothing about...can't even talk to nobody." Klaus spat over the railing.

"I was in a dead-end back home. I need some place where I have a chance to get ahead. I worked for a while in a mill, but then all I could get at home was a job working as a store clerk."

Klaus responded, "We was on a little farm but we worked from dawn to dark and couldn't hardly make a living. Sure, we could grow our own food, but ever' year we got a little fu'ther behind. I never could get outa debt."

"I was apprenticed to a linen dyer and learned that trade. I don't know if I can find that kind of work in America. I can't work in a store because I don't know English. I'll have to find something pretty quick after we get to Davenport."

Johann saw the shining black face of Alfred coming up the stairs to their deck

Johann held out his hand, "*Wie geht's?* Klaus, here, and I were just wondering...how many days do we still have?"

Alfred thought a moment and answered, "*Grüss Gott, Klaus.* We've had very good winds, except for those stormy days. I think we're making real good time."

"This good weather should help us."

"As long as the sea stays calm, and once we're away from the ice, the captain will move us along fast."

"Don't you get tired always bein' on a ship?" Klaus asked.

"It's not too bad. The pay is pretty good, and we don't have any place to spend it. We have plenty of food. Sure, it's crowded. We don't have as much living space as you have, but I don't mind it."

"Are you going to stay in New York?"

"I think I will, for a while anyway. If I can find a good job on land, I'll stay. I'd have a better chance in New York than most places. There aren't too many good places for a man with black skin."

"What do you mean?"

"Well, in many of the states black men are slaves. In the northern states we can live as free men, but there is always the danger someone will claim you are a run-away slave and try to take you down south to collect a reward. You have to be sure you're going where you are safe."

"Don't you have papers to prove you are not a slave?"

"Sure. But if someone makes trouble, they won't bother with papers. They'd just claim they are fake. I don't believe in taking chances."

It was warmer the next few days. The closer they got to America the more ships they saw. Johann watched as one ship after another passed them going toward Europe. It was amazing that way out here on the open sea there could be so many vessels. Sometimes it seemed like a road on which many wagons moved in either direction.

Johann saw young Nauman sitting beside the big capstan in the center of their deck. The youth ineffectively concealed a bottle under his coat. Looking around to see if anyone was watching, he would take out the bottle, pull the cork and take a quick swig.

Johann walked over to him. Kurt made an effort to push the bottle under his coat behind his back. Looking up with a silly smile on his pasty face, he said thickly, "*Gudden Daag.*"

Johann had little desire for a conversation with Nauman in this condition. "You're going to be worse than seasick, *Kerl.*"

"Whud of it!" Kurt answered, knowing that Johann saw the bottle. "Wanna swig?"

"*Danke, nein.* Where'd you get that stuff? I thought you were broke."

"I...found some...money. One of the shailors had some of zis for sale. Rum, he called it. Wanna swig?"

"Better not get into any trouble on the ship."

"Hell, nobody's gonna bother with me." His eyes glazed over and he leaned his head back against chipped paint of the capstan.

Johann turned away and walked toward the steep stair to the lower decks. As he came into the steerage section, picking his way around the flimsy partitions and the mounds of baggage, Johann heard a commotion on the far side of the deck. A small crowd was gathered. Several women were sobbing and holding each other.

"What's happening over there? he asked Marta who was lying in her bunk.

Her face was pale and drawn. "It's that young woman from Hannover. You know, the one who has been sick all along. I think she must have died."

"Oh, that's sad! It looks like their friends are helping them."

"Somebody said that she had some kind of fever. I hope it doesn't spread."

"I walked over there the other day and she sure didn't look good. She couldn't have been much more than seventeen or eighteen."

"*Ja*, I was talking to some of the other women. They said that she'd been sick ever since we left. I'm surprised they'd start the trip with a sick woman."

"They probably had everything planned and paid for and couldn't turn back."

"It must have been awful for them during that storm," she said as some ship's officers strode purposefully through the steerage section. The tangle of people parted before them. It was the first time they had seen officers down in steerage.

The two uniformed men, followed by a couple of sailors, walked over to the cluster of weeping women. After a brief conversation, mostly talking with their hands, it was clear that they wanted to remove the body of the dead woman. They wrapped her body in its blanket. One of the sailors, a large swarthy man, carried it like a baby. The other wadded the straw mattress on which she had been lying into a big roll and followed the officers back to the upper decks. The young woman's parents insisted on going along with her body.

The usual noises of the section were muted. People talked in hushed voices. Little groups stood here and there talking about what had happened. Children looked to their mothers for explanations.

Later in the afternoon Alfred was sent to the steerage section to inform the people in German that the young woman would be buried at sea at seven o'clock that evening. They could all go on the main deck for the burial service, if they wished.

Alfred stopped by the little cubicle where Johann stood with Marta. "Well now, so this is where you live," he smiled.

"Our castle," Johann laughed.

Marta looked embarrassed, as if a visitor had come to her house and found it in terrible disorder. "This is the first time we've lived like this. I'm really a pretty good housekeeper...I am."

Paul Irion*

"She really is," Johann quickly added.

A broad smile crossed Alfred's black face. "Listen, folks, I know how it is. When I was working for Count Woodford, I lived in nice big houses. Now I curl up in a hammock below decks. Listen, we all know that things won't always be like this. It's just something we put up with for a few weeks to get where we want to go."

"I hope we get there soon."

That evening as the sun hung low in the western sky, many of the passengers went on deck. Johann and Marta stood on one of the hatch covers. The mother and father of the young woman stood near the rail. Next to them stood a tall man.

"That must be *der Kapitan*," Johann said.

"What are they going to do?"

"I don't know. I've never seen anything like this before," Johann answered, thinking of the funerals he had attended in the churchyard at Endigen.

At right angles to the rail, on two wooden trestles, was a long plank. On top of it, covered with a dark blue blanket, was what they assumed to be the body of the young woman. Two sailors stood on either side of the plank.

The captain stepped forward and opened a book that looked like a Bible. He motioned to one of the passengers who stood nearby. This man, holding a prayerbook, read in German a prayer which many of the people recognized from their church services at home. He told them to join *"Unser Vater...."*

Then the captain, while reading in English from his book, nodded to the sailors. They pushed the plank out over the railing and began to tip it toward the sea. From beneath the blanket the woman's body, sewn into a shroud of rough canvas, slid out and fell into the sea. The low waves closed over it and the service ended. Passengers began to walk slowly back to their respective sections.

"I didn't like that," Marta said, quivering.

"It's not a very pretty sight. You'd think they could have made a coffin rather than just dumping her over the side."

"Poor girl. She'll never see America."

"I wonder where they are going to."

"Maybe she was going to marry someone in America. That would be hard. It's sad."

"At least it wasn't a stormy day, or pouring rain."

On the following day Johann and Klaus stood of the foredeck for a while. Johann counted, "I can see four ships. I'm amazed at how many ships there are out here on the wide ocean."

"We must be gettin' closer to New York, since there are all these ships. We didn't see hardly any sails out in the middle of the ocean."

Two men came up the stair from steerage, each with a pail which they quickly emptied over the side.

"Pi-ugh. That stuff sure stinks."

"Smells like rotten meat to me. I'm surprised they could stand it downstairs."

"The whole place stinks so bad, I didn't even notice if it was close to us."

"Who would want to bring fresh meat on a trip like this. They might eat it for the first couple of days, but any fool knows it would rot before long."

"Some of these people don't have a whole lot of common sense. They're gonna have a hard time making it in America."

"Saturday, May 30," Johann wrote in his *Tagebuch*, marking another day of their voyage. When he had gone on deck earlier, the sun was shining and the sea was calm. On the distant horizon he could see a blue, smokey line...or was it just a line of clouds? He wrote: We must be getting close to New York. The ship seems to be going slower. Only about half of the sails are up. There is hardly any rolling of the ship because the waves are very small.

"I think we'll be leaving the ship soon," he told Marta.

"Do I need to start packing things up?"

"It won't be that soon. But I thought I could see land."

"Where? I want to see land."

Quite a crowd had gathered on the foredeck. People were pointing to the west. Johann could see that it was indeed low flat land. Then someone saw land on the other side of the ship too.

"We must be coming into a harbor. There is America."

"I can't see. Help me get up to the railing."

"It would be easier if you could stand on this metal thing. Hold on to my shoulder."

Marta said with excitement in her voice, "Oh, I can see. There it is. But I don't see any city. I thought this was New York."

"Can you see any buildings?"

"Not yet. But it looks like there's a tiny little boat coming toward us."

Alfred came on deck. "So you're up here to get your first look at America."

"We can't see much yet. Where is the city?"

"You won't see that for a good while. We have a long bay to go through. I don't think we'll get to the city until tomorrow."

The *Indiana* moved slowly. The sailors had tied all the sails to the spars and the ship was moving forward powered by its steam engine. The little boat came alongside and a rope ladder was thrown down.

"That's the pilot coming aboard," Alfred told them. "He'll guide the ship through the harbor."

"Can't our *Kapitan* do that?"

"Even though he might have sailed into New York many times, the sandbars in the harbor are always changing. Sometimes they're here, sometimes over there. The pilot, because he is going in and out every few days, know where they are."

People were talking excitedly. There was great rejoicing that the voyage was almost over. A few folks bowed their heads, praying; a few others made the sign of the cross. Everyone watched the pilot, a tall, wiry man with a flowing beard as he came onto the main deck. He talked to the captain and a few of the ship's officers. Together they walked to the wheelhouse. The ship continued to move forward very slowly as the sun began to set.

Excitement filled the whole ship as night fell. On each deck people ate their supper.

While Tilda and Marta were in the cook room, they heard some of the women saying that they were eating up the last of their supplies, because they would soon be on land.

Tilda said, "I'm not going to do that kind of silly stuff. We're going to have to eat in New York, and so are they. Maybe they've got plenty of money to buy more food. But we're going to have to be as saving as we can."

"So are we," Marta answered. "I hate to think of dragging it along with us, but we'll need it I'm sure."

"I hope we can find a cheap place with a kitchen. It will be a relief not to have to cook with fifty other women."

"I don't have any idea how long it will take us to get to Iowa. Johann says we have to take a train."

"If you're not going to settle down in New York for a while, you'll want to have food that you can use without cooking while you travel--lots of bread, maybe some cheese and some dried fruit."

"Well, let's get that soup made."

There was more noise than usual in the steerage section that night. In one corner a small crowd of people were celebrating, passing a couple of wine bottles from person to person. There was laughing and shouting, hugs and back thumping.

A few others shouted for quiet so their children could get to sleep. It was a balmy evening and the large hatch cover had been left off. Johann could see a few stars high above the top of the mast that swayed gently back and forth. For the first time since leaving port there was no creaking from the ship's timbers.

"I'm so excited,' Marta said. "What's it going to be like?"

"*Es wundert mich.* The agent in Bremen told me that we wouldn't have any trouble. We'll see."

"I'm not sure I can sleep."

"Give it a try. We'll have a big day tomorrow."

"I'll be so happy to feel land under my feet and to have a little room to move around."

It was some hours before the raucous gatherings quieted down.

When they awoke after fitful sleep, the sky through the hatch opening was rosy with sunrise. Johann slipped away from his bed sack and made his way to the deck. The ship was still moving very slowly. The land on either side was now very visible. There were cultivated fields; here and there a farmhouse. Groves of trees dotted the landscape.

Then the *Indiana* stood still in the water. Sailors, Alfred among them, came onto the foredeck and motioned for the passengers to move away. They busied themselves with ropes and chains. Soon the huge anchor dropped into the water with a mighty splash.

Another passenger stood at the rail. He pointed to the land on their left. "One of the sailors told me that was *Steet-Neuland.* At least that's what it sounded like to me."

"It looks so beautiful and green. I wish the folks at home to could see how beautiful it is."

"Here comes another little boat toward us. I wonder what this is all about."

"It's pretty early in the morning for visitors."

There was a lot of activity on deck as several men boarded from the small boat. The little craft pulled away.

Officers motioned everyone to go below. Alfred explained that the sanitary police had come to inspect all the passengers to see if there were any sick folks among them. If there is sickness aboard, no one can leave the ship until everyone is well.

The word had reached the steerage hold by the time Johann got there. Passengers were clumped in their crowded areas. Two of the sanitary police in their dark blue uniforms came through looking carefully at each passenger. Occasionally one of them placed his hand on someone's forehead. They looked carefully to see that no face was broken out with pox. They made sure that no one was lying on any of the straw sacks.

Klaus said very softly between his teeth, "We're lucky that that girl died. If she was over there, we'd all be stuck on the ship for a long time."

Tilda chided him, "You oughtn't say we're lucky when that poor woman died. But, *Mein Gott*, sickness on the ship would be an awful thing. I sure hope everyone is all right."

The official looked carefully into the eyes of each one of them, not saying a word, listening for a cough or wheeze. There were no smiles, no effort to communicate. Finally he walked back to the stairway to the upper deck, looked back at the people and gave a weak smile.

"Does that mean we're all right? Johann whispered.

"God only knows. At least he didn't stop to examine anybody more closely. So we must have passed the inspection."

"They still have all those passengers on the upper deck."

"Yes, but they live better than we do. If there was a problem I'll bet it would be down here. It's a wonder we all didn't get sick cooped up here with that girl."

Johann did not think of himself as a religious man, but the pious home from which he came had left its marks. He told Marta, "My calendar, where I have been marking off the days, says that today is Holy Pentecost Sunday. It's May 31. That means that it has been 23 days since we left Bremerhaven and eighteen since we sailed from England."

"We must be half way around the world. I feel so far from everything." Marta's eyes filled with tears.

Johann put his arm around her shoulders. "*Ja*, but we wanted to be far away, to have a chance to get ahead."

"But to be in another world. I wonder if little Karl even remembers me."

"Don't worry. Your step-mother will take good care of him. He'll get along just fine."

"In a couple of years someone else will be coming over and can bring him along."

"*Ja.*"

"Why aren't we moving. You said we're still way out in the harbor. When will we get off?"

"They don't seem in any hurry. We'd better have some food. If we get to the dock there won't be any time to eat."

Marta looked around for Tilda and Klaus, but they had gone on deck. She opened their big basket. "We'll just have a bite. I'm too excited to eat." She shuffled the bags and small packages of food in the hamper. "The *Brötchen* the carpenters gave us are all gone. Here's some of that hardtack stuff. There's some cheese, if you want it."

"This stuff tastes awful; like chewing on sawdust. No wonder it never spoils. You could break your teeth on the stuff. I wish I had a loaf of *Mutti's* bread right now. Ummmm! Smell that fresh, warm bread; put butter all over it. Ummmm!"

"If you want more, we still have some things left. It's only the bread that's all gone."

Tilda and Klaus joined them and had a little breakfast.

Hours passed and the *Indiana* stayed at anchor in the outer harbor. It was time for *Mittagessen*. So Tilda and Marta took their pot of potatoes and turnips to the cooking room. Only a few women were preparing food.

"I don't know why they don't sail in to the dock and let us off. We're so close you can see the steeples of the city," Marta said, peeling potatoes quickly.

"I wonder if they found somebody sick somewhere on the boat and won't let us get off."

" I don't even want to think of that. What would they do with us?"

Tilda answered, "I suppose we'd just have to sit 'round 'til they got well...or died. *Mein Gott*, we'd be stuck for days...or weeks. Things'll get pretty nasty if that happens. Folks could put up with a lot while we were on the way. But with the dock right over there, they're not going to just sit quiet and wait. Mark my words, there'll be trouble...big trouble!" She banged the lid on the pot.

As they were eating their noon meal, there was a commotion at the far end of the steerage area. Alfred and another sailor carried in a small table and a chair. As soon as they had it set up under the open hatch, a ship's officer came in and sat at the table. Alfred shouted in German: "You are to line up as families and give this officer your name, your age, the country where you were born, and your occupation."

People started to line up in front of the table. There was room only for a short line, so people waited their turn to join the end of the line. The officer, who spoke no German, began to list every passenger. People simply gave the necessary information and the officer, frequently dipping his pen in an inkwell, wrote long columns on printed sheets of paper. The officer listened to the information and then wrote very fast. He never asked anyone to repeat the information, just wrote.

Alfred stood near Johann. "That fellow is making lots of mistakes. He just writes down what it sounds like to him. I offered to translate, but he told me to get on with my work."

Johann was concerned. "Suppose he gets it all wrong; will they let us off the ship."

"Don't worry. You'll get off all right. The officer said to me that the names and other information aren't important anyway. He said the authorities are only interested in the total number of people coming into the country."

Johann and Marta joined the line and waited their turn with Klaus and Tilda. Finally Johann stood in front of the officer:

"Name?"

"Johann Weber." The officer scrawled what looked like: John Vaber.

"Age?"

"*Sieben und zwanzig.*" The officer wrote down 23.

"Born?"

"*Schlesien.*" The officer put a check in the column headed Germany.

"Occupation?"

"*Färber,*" which was entered in the column headed: "laborer" on the passenger list.

Then the officer pointed his pen at Marta. "Name?"

Marta tried to speak up but her voice caught in her throat. "Marta Wiesner Weber," she stammered. The officer for some reason wrote down: Caroline.

"Age?"

"*Drei und zwanzig, Mein Herr.*" The officer put down what he thought he heard: 36.

He didn't even ask where she was born, just putting another check in the column headed Germany.

"Occupation?"

"*Putzmacherin.*" It was quickly translated in the "laborer" column.

The officer waved them aside and repeated the inquiries for Klaus and Tilda. As they walked back to their cubicle Johann whispered to Marta, "He didn't even want to see our passport. I was all ready to give it to him."

"I don't see how he could put anything down right without knowing any German and us not knowing any English."

"He put you down as being 36," Johann laughed. "I saw him write it down: 36."

"After three weeks without a chance to really wash at all, I probably look like an old crone."

"You look very nice to me. It will be good to get clean again and put on some clean clothes. Let's go up on the deck."

They made their way up the steep stair to the foredeck. Several couples stood along the rail looking at the city that spread before them across the harbor. They were all pointing and talking excitedly.

"Look at all those ships. Everywhere ships. All their masts look like a forest growing out of the water."

"You can make out the people on the shore. Look at the crowd all along the docks."

"Lot of those buildings look like they have four or five storeys. They're as big as they were in Berlin."

"Even then the church steeples stick out way above them," Johann said. "I'll bet they don't have bullet holes from battles in them like the steeple in Endigen."

"I can't wait to get on shore."

Marta took Johann's arm. "How are we going to be able to get along in America when we can't speak any English? You saw how it was with that officer. We won't be able to buy anything. I don't see how you'll be able to get a job. It's going to be hard!"

"Oh, not so bad. The other people who have come over have been able to make a go of it. I'm pretty sure we'll always be able to find some people who speak German."

"I hope so. When I see how hard it was to do anything right with that officer, I wonder how easy it will be."

All of Sunday passed with the ship swinging from its anchor in the harbor. On Monday morning, June 1, the *Indiana* began to move slowly toward the city and eased alongside one of the long piers. Many people, thinking that they were about to disembark started gathering their belongings.

Ship's officers raised their arms and pointed the passengers back to their quarters. Another group of uniformed officials came up the gangplank. These were customs officers who spread out over the ship to inspect all the passengers' baggage.

In steerage they went from cubicle to cubicle. Every basket and box and trunk and bundle had to be opened. This was not easy because things had been piled several boxes high in the confined space in steerage. Johann and Klaus had spread out their things as much as possible in the limited floor space. Johann and Marta watched as the tall man in his blue uniform pawed through their clothes and household goods. He didn't say anything, but put a big "X" with chalk on each box or trunk. Then he moved to Klaus and Tilda's belongings with a look of total boredom on his face.

Once the inspection was over, they were allowed to haul their baggage to the center of the area under the hatch.. The huge net was lowered, filled with belongings and hoisted up from the hold and swung out to be deposited on the dock.

Johann and Klaus tried to stack their belongings together in the net which was flat on the deck. They sent Marta, Tilda and the children to the deck with instructions not to take their eyes off their baggage on the dock when it was added to the pile. If possible, they were to get off and stand by their boxes on the dock. Johann and Klaus would wait below until their load was hoisted. Then, as quickly as they could, they would join the women on the dock to sort out all their boxes and bundles.

As they got off the ship, Johann could see a clock on a church steeple. It was one o'clock. It had taken half of the day to dock the ship and go through the customs inspection and unload their baggage.

A man in a uniform, standing on a box so everyone could see him, pointed them to a large round building near the piers where the ships were unloading. "All of you...over there...Castle Garden!" he shouted in English, his uniform and gestures speaking more clearly that his words, which fell on uncomprehending ears.

"*Kommen Sie*, Johann," Klaus shouted, "let's find the women."

"I don't see them. *Mein Gott*, what a mob. Marta! Marta!" he yelled.

They pushed their way through the crowd at the foot of the gangplank. Klaus, who was much taller than Johann, called, "There they are...Over there...Follow me."

Marta and Tilda and the children stood with some other passengers beside a mound of baggage that had been dumped out of the huge cargo net. Klaus, taking advantage of his size, said, "Here, let me drag our stuff out of the pile. You take it to one side and stack it up."

One by one he fought through the mob with their big wicker hampers, the trunks and boxes. Johann kept count as he moved them to their own stack. Finally everything was accounted for.

Johann wiped sweat from his face and sat on the edge of one of their boxes. "It looks like our boxes made it through all right. Everything is here and nothing is smashed. How is your stuff?"

"...all right. It's all here. Some of them poor folks are goin' to have an awful time. Did you see all them bundles busted open. There was clothes and kettles and food just flying around loose. How they'll ever get that sorted out I don't know. Some people are goin' to lose a lot of their stuff."

"That's a shame," Tilda said. "I feel sorry for 'em. I don't know if they weren't able to get solid boxes or if they were just plain dumb."

Marta added, "It would be terrible to come into a strange place, all this pushing crowd, and then find that half your things were lost. I'd just cry my eyes out if our stuff was gone."

Klaus grunted, "You shoulda seen people fightin' over all that stuff. Two people would grab a shirt and pull. Two owners for everything. One of the fellows got socked in the eye and some of them women; they started pulling hair."

"I'll bet most folks will only get half their things back."

"I saw that young rascal you was talking to on the ship...right in the thick of it...just stuffing things into a big feedsack. He hardly looked at what he was takin'. He just grabbed something and jammed it in his bag as if it was his. A few men ran him off, but he just went to another pile and started in there."

Johann looked around. "Well, what do we do now? They said that officer told us to go to this Castle Garden. I guess it is that big building over there."

Tilda said, "We ain't goin' to be able to stay together in all that mob. I am going to say goodbye to Marta here in case we get separated in that place."

Klaus held out his hand to Johann and Tilda enfolded Marta in a long embrace.

Klaus said, "As soon as we get out of this Castle Garden, we're pushin' off. I'm gonna to find a guy to haul our stuff to my uncle's house. He'll let us stay there a few days 'til I can find a job. Then we can get our own place right here in New York."

"Do you know where his house is?"

"Don't have the slightest idea...but I got his street and number on a letter. The teamster'll be able to find it. I want to get there before it is dark."

Tilda added, "They know we're comin' sometime but we didn't have a chance to tell 'em exactly when we'd get here. So we'll be quite a surprise. We ain't seen 'em in six years, when they came over."

Marta put her arms around Tilda once again. "I'm going to miss you. Do you know that you're the only friend I have in America!" she smiled.

"I'll miss you too. I never had no sister, so for a few weeks I did. I kinda like it."

"I hope Klaus finds work real soon and you get a nice place to live."

"You too," Mathilda said. "I'm sure glad I still don't have such a long trip aheada me. I've gone as far as I want to go...anywhere. Once we get our own place, I ain't never gonna walk more than little way from it in the rest of my days."

"You'll see."

"Well, maybe...But one thing I can tell you for sure, they'll never get me on a ship again. Well, goodbye." Tilda turned away quickly, took her children's hands, and walked as fast as she could toward the end of the pier, following Klaus and the stevedore's barrow with their boxes.

Marta gripped Johann's hand, lest he too slip away. "We are all alone now. We don't know a single soul in all this country. I'm scared to death."

Little knots of people many of whom they recognized as fellow-passengers from the *Indiana* were clumped around their piles of baggage. Another big ship was tied up on the other side of the pier, disgorging its passengers and their baggage onto the same dock. There was terrible confusion.

Johann heard from another German on the pier that nine immigrant ships were coming in that day. He walked in the direction Klaus and Tilda had gone to find someone to help them with their boxes and hamper. A couple of men pushing large wheelbarrows came toward him. One of them struck up a conversation in German with the new arrival.

"*Mein Herr*, looking for some help with your stuff?"

"*Ja wohl, Landsmann*."

"Where you going?"

"...don't know yet. We have to find a place."

"Well, this here's Castle Garden. It's the government immigration house. Ever'body has to go there to register. They'll help you find a good place to stay. I can take your baggage to Castle Garden for you and you can send it on from there."

"Our stuff is right over here," Johann said.

"With all these ships coming in today, there must be a thousand people standing around there. It will be a crazy house. I wouldn't stay there, if I were you...they tell me the dormitories are crawling with lice there."

"My wife wouldn't go for that. Do we have to go there?"

"You have to go through there, but you don't have to stay there. Let's load up your stuff and we'll go over there. It's going to be dark in a couple of hours. You're going to have to decide where to stay."

Marta helped to supervise the loading of their baggage on the long wheel barrow. Once piled high and tied in place, they began to weave their way through the crowds on the pier. In several languages men were shouting the names of hotels and boarding houses. Other men were shouting that they would change foreign money into American dollars.

The burly man with their baggage said, "These rascals along the street will cheat you out of every *Taler* you have. You better do all that inside Castle Garden."

Ahead of them they saw a tall wooden fence surrounding the large building. Inside the wooden fence there were what seemed to be hundreds of families, each clustered around the pile of their baggage. Ahead of them was a tremendous stone doorway with the name Castle Garden above it. The nail studded gates stood open. The lower storey of the circular building was made of huge blocks of brown stone, a wall with large portholes, a fortress but no cannons. Built on top of the fort was another storey covered with a large domed roof. A few outbuildings were arranged just inside the tall fence. Both outside and inside the fence the area was crawling with people.

Their porter, Max, told them that he would wait for them by a bench along the wall. "You have to go in that building over there, through the big door, so that you can be registered. Some official will probably make a little speech when a bunch of you have been signed in, then you can come back here and we'll figure out where you want to stay."

As they joined the nearby line, Marta whispered to Johann, "I hope he's honest. He's got everything we own piled on that wheelbarrow. What is to keep him from wandering off with our stuff while we're inside?"

"He seems honest enough. He told me he came from Potsdam two years ago. I guess we just have to trust him. I told him that my brother was in the army there."

"Maybe one of us can go to the door every now and then to see if he's still there."

"I guess so. But I don't know what we'd do if he walked off with our boxes."

"Probably the best thing would be to get through the line fast and get back to him."

"Right."

As they entered the building the first thing they saw were large washrooms; men on one side, women on the other. Marta poked her head into the one for women and quickly came back.

"There are big stone troughs for bathing," she reported. "They are handing out towels and soap to anybody who wants it. Folks can't wait to wash off the dirt after weeks on the ships. We can wait until we get to our lodgings. I want to put on clean clothes anyway."

Johann agreed, knowing that Marta would never be satisfied with such public facilities.

Inside Castle Garden was a huge room in the center of which was a large dome supported by eight tall pillars topped by ornate arches. Light streamed in from the skylights in the dome. The walls of the building had a sort of balcony, supported by more pillars, which reached to the curved ceiling high above them. The ceiling was painted with large circular designs, following the lines of the dome. A large clock on the front of balcony rail kept everyone aware of how slowly they were moving through the registration process. The balcony was filled with people sitting on long benches. The main floor was crowded. They were directed up one of the large staircases leading to the balcony and told to sit with several dozen others in one of the sections of balcony seats, waiting to be called to the main floor.

"Did you ever see such a big place, and so fancy?" Marta asked.

"It reminds me of the huge building we saw in Berlin. That's what it looks like."

The ornate building, filled with carved plaster cones where the pillars joined the rounded arches and blended into the ceiling with its intricate designs, was in stark contrast to the groups of waiting immigrants. They looked tired, disheveled from their long voyages. Only a very few were well-dressed. Little children whimpered, mothers tried to find ways to amuse them. Some of the adults pulled their hats or shawls over their faces and tried to nap. There were not enough benches, so some people sat on the floor along the outside wall. The air was heavy with the smells of camphor and the multitude of unwashed bodies. A tall man in a black coat and a high hat stood near the top of the stairway. He was passing out little booklets. Some were in German. He pushed one into Marta's hand. She looked at it carefully as they got to their bench and saw that it was a little book of Bible verses. The overwhelming size of the hall caused people to speak in hushed tones.

The main floor was filled with clusters of people lined up before desks beneath the central dome, like ants gathered about a piece of candy on the pavement. Finally a uniformed guard came and called out to their section of benches and motioned them toward the stairway. He led them to a large square of many desks with a line of clerks, each taking down information in large books. Johann and Marta moved up the line to the table and gave their names, ages, occupations, and showed their passport.

They were amazed when the registrar talked to them in German. "Where's your son? It says here you have a boy with you," the clerk objected, pointing to their passport.

Johann saw tears come into Marta's eyes as he told the clerk, "He's back in *Schlesien* with my wife's folks. When we got our passport, we thought he would come long with us."

The man shook his head. "*Ganz gut..* You are passed. Now go to that desk over there with all those people. You said you are going to Davenport in Iowa. If you are ready, you can buy your train ticket right there. Just tell him what day you want to start your journey. You have the money?"

Johann stammered, "I have *Reichstaler* in gold. I do not have American money yet."

"He'll take your Prussian dollars. Don't worry. The government makes sure it is honest and fair. After you get your railroad tickets, ask him to send you to *die Wechselstube* to change some into American money."

At the railroad desk, after another half hour of waiting, they told the clerk their travel plans and he began to make out a long string of tickets. He accepted Johann's gold and gave him some change in American paper bills and coins.

"Do you want to send your baggage to Davenport? They can take care of that right over there," the clerk said, pointing to the next desk.

Marta shook her head. "We are going to need things from our boxes. Our clothes are so dirty from the time on the ship."

"Would it work to take it with us to where we will stay?" Johann asked the clerk.

"Sure, if you want to. Since you are going to stay in New York for a few days, you can take it to the station the day before you leave. The address is there with your tickets. Be careful not to lose them. Or if you want, you can have your baggage brought back here to Castle Garden and we can send it from here."

Marta nodded and Johann told the clerk, "*Ja*, we will take it with us."

"Now, if you want, you can go to that office over there, where you see that big blackboard on the wall, and change some more of your gold into American dollars. It is better to do it here, where you will get fair value. That blackboard will show you how many dollars you get for a *Reichstaler*. Never change your *Reichstaler* except at a bank. People who want to change your money on the street or in little shops will cheat you," the clerk warned.

As they turned away they heard a commotion at another of the railroad clerk's desk. A woman was sobbing on her husband's shoulder while their two small children, crying, hung on to her skirts.

"*Was ist los?* Johann asks one of the men near him.

"They just found out that they did not have quite enough money to buy their railroad tickets. Some of us are giving them a little money so they can get their tickets to Cincinnati," one of the men said, holding out a handful of coins.

"I only have a little American money, a few coins, the clerk gave me when I bought our tickets. I am not even sure how much each is worth, but here, you can add this to your collection to help them."

The man turned to the clerk and put all the coins on the desk. "Is that enough?" he asked.

The clerk counted out the coins. "It is near enough. He was only a dollar short. I'll give them their tickets."

The young man reached out to shake hands with the strangers who had helped him. His young wife, wiped away her tears and tried to soothe the children. "*Gott sei ewig Lob und Dank'.*"

As they walked away Johann and Marta heard other immigrants, learning the cost of a ticket to their intended destination, who had to make difficult decisions. Should they stay in New York and look for work? Should they choose another city closer to New York, a ticket they afford. Profound sadness etched the faces of men and women as their dreams began to deflate.

Marta said to Johann as they walked away from crowd around the desks, "I worry about all these warnings about people cheating us. All the clerks have warned us, and they have signs every place in all kinds of languages saying that you should only do business in Castle Garden and not with people on the street."

"We will have to be careful. We can't afford to be cheated or robbed. They certainly do their best to scare us *Ausländer.*"

Walking through the crowd Johann said quietly to Marta, "I am glad I took some of the gold out of the money bag around my waist this morning. I will get enough dollars to get us to Davenport."

Marta whispered, "How do you know how much to get?"

"I'll just have to guess. We will have three days in New York, then four or five days for the trip to Davenport. If I get thirty dollars, that should be plenty. I'll put most of it in my money bag when I have a chance."

"You take care of getting the money," Marta said. "I am going back to see if our baggage is all right. I worry about trusting a stranger."

"You go and see. I'll come as soon as I finish with the money."

True to his word, Max was sitting on the handle of his barrow under a small tree. "All done? What have you decided about a place to stay? It won't cost you anything to stay here in one of the dormitories for a night or two, but it's not very nice, *meine Frau.*"

Johann had already reported on the lice, so Marta was more than ready to consider alternatives. "What do we do if we don't stay here?"

Max pointed to an area in front of the building inside the fence. "There'll be inn keepers here, looking for lodgers. The ones in here are more honest than the fellows out on the street. They know that if they cheat people they will be reported and won't be let back in here to get business."

"There's a fellow with a sign in German. It says there's a *Fremdenzimmer* nearby. Let's go over and talk with him."

Seeing potential customers, the man lowered his sign and began to talk with Max and the new arrivals. "It's not far, *ein hundert vierzehn Zederstrasse*. It's nice and clean and not crowded like this dump. It will cost you one American dollar a day for your room and meals. You'll see, that's a very fair price in New York."

Max said, "You will have to pay with American dollars. Do you have that?"

"*Ja*, I got some inside Castle Garden," Johann said, smiling inwardly at his efficiency.

Once outside Castle Garden Max pushed their way through the crowd of shouting men on the sidewalk. "Stay away from all these fellows. See how they go up to families and offer to be helpful. They take one of their little bags to carry, or sometimes they even pick up a little child of the family and carry it. The people don't have no choice but to go with him because he has their child. When they get to the rooming house where he has led them, they have to pay big rent and can't get away."

114 Cedar Street was a three storey brick building, part of a row of almost identical buildings which lined both sides of Cedar Street. Their guide led them through the front door. There they were met by John Staud, the innkeeper. Telling Max to wait with their baggage, he led them up the stairs to the third floor. He opened the door to a large room. There was a large bed covered with a quilt. Two simple wooden chairs, a small wardrobe and a washstand completed the furnishings. The floor was covered with a rag carpet. Herr Staud lit the lamp on the table.

He said, "Are you planning to stay long in New York?"

"Just a few days to rest from the voyage. Then we'll be on our way to the west."

"Then there's no need to drag all your stuff up here. Why don't you pick out what you'll need in your room. Your man can bring it up right away. You can store the rest in my cellar until you are ready to leave. It'll be safe there, you can be sure of that."

Marta sorted out the small trunk with most of their clothing in it. "Take that trunk and the carpet bag, up to the room. The wooden boxes can go into the cellar." Turning of the landlord she asked, "Can I get to it. I need to repack some things."

"*Ja.*, sure. I will give you the key any time you want to go down there."

As Max put the trunk on his shoulder to haul it to the third floor, Marta pulled Johann to one side. "You go along down to the cellar and see that our stuff doesn't get mixed up with somebody else's baggage. Other folks are going to have stuff down there too."

Max told Johann as they hauled the boxes to the cellar. "It's easier than having it all in your room. But the innkeeper also knows that you can't leave without paying him because he has all your boxes locked in his cellar. You don't have to worry about Staud. He's honest."

By the time Johann had paid off Max and climbed to the third floor, Marta was already unpacking some of their clothes from the trunk and putting them in the little wardrobe.

"What a relief after being cooped up in that little dark pen on the ship. I'm starting to feel human again."

"Staud said he'd send up two buckets of hot water right away so we can wash."

"That will be wonderful. I can hardly wait to get out of these filthy clothes. I wonder if I can wash them here before we have to leave. I'll ask Frau Staud."

"We were lucky to find a place as good as this, but it costs more than I thought."

Marta said, "It seems like a palace after that crowded ship. And it is nice and clean."

"So I guess it's worth the price. We're going to have to watch our money."

"Should I ask the innkeeper if we can have a little food, even though it's getting late?"

"If you want something. I'm too excited to eat anything."

"I'm the same way. Let's just wash and go to bed in our new homeland."

There was a knock on the door and Staud's son came in with two pails of water. "Father said you'd want water for washing. Everybody does after all that time on the ship. When you're done you can put the water in the pails and bring it down when you come down in the morning."

When he had left, Johann told Marta. "You can wash first."

She poured the warm water into the big pitcher and then into the bowl. "I want the water as hot as I can stand it. It will feel so good to be clean." She dropped her dress and petticoats to the floor and kicked them aside.

Pulling off his boots and hanging his coat and pants on a hook behind the door, Johann stretched out on the bed and watched Marta standing before the washstand. She bent over the basin to wash her long, dark hair. Her smooth back glistened as she bathed, modestly turned away from her husband. Again and again she soaped the washrag, washing and rinsing again. Finally she dried herself from head to toe and pulled a clean shift over her head.

"...Your turn," she smiled.

When Johann had finished and put on a clean suit of underwear, he looked over at the bed. Marta was lying with the quilt pulled up to her chin, her dark braid resting on the cover. Her face glowed from her bath.

She smiled, "It's like heaven, having a nice place to wash, a room with a little space. But the nicest thing is to be alone. These last weeks were like living your whole life right in the middle of the market square."

"Of course, most of my life I've been living in the same room with a bunch of brothers."

Marta smiled coyly, "Yes, but you didn't have a wife in your bed then, *nicht wahr*? Blow out the lamp."

"I haven't had a wife in my bed for almost a month." Johann slid beneath the quilt and put his arm around Marta.

"On the ship, tossing around on those straw mattress bags, I told you it was our old haystack. Remember? But with all those people around, it couldn't be our haystack, could it?"

Johann drew her closer. "Nobody around now.., and I turned the key in the door."

CHAPTER 10

The sun was filtering through the shutters of their window when Johann woke. Kicking off the quilt, he stretched and stretched. Marta stirred sleepily. A shy smile crossed her face as she looked out over the crumpled bedcovers. With the end of her long braid she playfully tickled Johann's mouth and eyes. Laughing, he put his arms around her as they rolled back and forth on the soft bed.

"I haven't slept that well since we left Neuhaus," he said.

"Isn't it wonderful to be alone; just the two of us? I'm sick of living in the middle of a crowd of people, all eyes and ears."

"*Ja*. There certainly wasn't any privacy on that ship."

"It didn't seem to bother some folks, all that thrashing around at night," Marta said, clicking her tongue.

"Having our own room is mighty nice," Johann chuckled.

"You better get up and get shaved."

Johann pushed the shutters open and put his arm around Marta as she stood beside him in her nightshift.

"Look at that sight. Over all those roofs that must be Castle Garden, the one with the dome. And look at all the masts of the ships behind it."

Marta stuck her head out of the window. "I've seen all I want of ships and Castle Gardens. I want to get my feet on Cedar Street and look around New York. It looks busy already. What time is it?"

Johann looked at his watch. "Half-eight. We really slept."

"*Ja*," Marta smiled and then broke into giggling.

"After breakfast we'll go out and look around."

Marta grabbed the bedpost as she started walking across the room. "I still feel like I'm on the ship. The whole floor is moving under me. It's as hard to get used to a solid floor as it was to get used to the rolling ship."

"We'd better put on our better clothes if we're going to walk through the city."

"I'll see if there is a place for me to do some washing. Our clothes are pretty dirty."

"Good idea. But once we leave New York, we'll be back on sooty trains. We won't try to get at the stuff in our boxes. Just wash out the few things we are carrying right with us in the carpet bag. "

Jostled by fast-walking pedestrians, dodging the steady procession of wagons and carriages and pushcarts as they crossed streets, Marta and Johann walked the busy streets of New York. Cedar Street was full of shops and boarding houses. They turned down Broadway, wide and bustling.

"What a beautiful main street, but did you ever hear such noise; I can hardly hear what you are saying. It's a lot busier than Berlin was," Johann said.

"This may be the land of milk and honey, but the streets are so dirty," Marta answered, walking carefully around piles of horse droppings on the cobblestones. The gutters were cluttered with splintered boxes which had been unpacked at the stores. Papers and bottles littered the sidewalks.

Stopping in front of a large stone church, Johann answered, "Yes. but the buildings are beautiful. Look, there's a cemetery here, right in the middle of the city."

"Lots of the buildings look so new."

Trying to sound out the unfamiliar English, Johann mouthed the words "*Vall Schtrayt*" from the sign. "What a huge city."

"Everybody seems to be in such a hurry. It makes me dizzy to see all these people almost running along the streets."

"It must mean that there are plenty of jobs. Everybody seems very busy."

"Everything is so big. I feel like a little ant."

As they walked past two men who were rolling large kegs of beer from a wagon onto a thick, round rope mat, Marta said, "Have you noticed that a few of the people are talking German?"

"That will make it a lot easier to find out how to send our stuff to Davenport."

"I suppose lot of people get off a ship and just stay here. Why go any further if you can find work here?"

"Well, they save the cost of more traveling."

Marta took Johann's arm. "I'm just as glad we aren't going to stay here more than a few days. I could never get used to such a big place. Give me a nice clean little town where people can know each other."

"Another week and we'll see what it's like in Davenport."

Back at the lodging house on Cedar Street, Marta smiled as Johann told the landlord of their successful morning ventures. He was so proud of himself for not getting lost.

"We just walked all over and saw the wonderful buildings. It looks very prosperous. You don't put up buildings that size unless you are making a lot of money."

The innkeeper had heard it all before, but he smiled indulgently.

"We leave on Thursday afternoon; day after tomorrow. That'll give us a couple of more days to rest and get organized," Johann went on.

Marta said, "I am glad we can stay a few days. I'd like to look around the city some more before we have to leave."

The innkeeper Staud said, "You're lucky it's in the middle of the week. The trains and the steamboats don't run on Sunday. That helps us innkeepers because folks have to stay until Monday."

Johann asked, "Do you think that's why they kept our ship out in the harbor until Monday?"

Staud responded, "Could be....You'll be wanting to get your baggage to the station the day before you go, that'll be tomorrow. You'll want to send it what they call freight. It might not get there as fast as you travel, but it won't cost near as much that way."

"Can I get your man to help me get our boxes to the station?"

"Sure. Just give him half a dollar and he'll be happy to help."

The trip to the freight station was made on Wednesday afternoon. Wagons full of trunks and boxes and hampers were everywhere. Johann wondered that anything got to its rightful destination. He stood by the counter making out the labels the agent had given him for each of their boxes, carefully printing Johann Weber, Davenport, Iowa. When he finished, he gave the labels to the agent, who took a pot of hot glue and plastered a label on each box, hamper and trunk.

Each box was weighed on the large scale on the platform, while the agent totalled the weight of their shipment. "I make it 189 pounds." He consulted his book, running his glue-stained finger down the columns. "That's going to cost you twenty dollars to get it to Davenport."

Johann counted out the unfamiliar money, recognize the dent being made in their funds. It had cost ten dollars to bring their baggage across the ocean. Now it was costing twice as much to get it to Davenport. Their tickets for a five day trip cost almost as much as their fares all the way across the ocean. He was worried. Once off the ship, their spending had increased dramatically, eroding their funds: lodging, meals, hauling baggage, railroad tickets, now the big amount to send their boxes.

He noticed several small groups of people clustered at the scales. He could hear them talking. "What are we going to do now? We don't have enough for our tickets and the baggage. The only thing we can do is try to sell some of our stuff, if anybody will buy it."

Apparently this happened fairly frequently because several fellows lounged around sitting on their wheelbarrows. Seeing the problem of the immigrants, they moved in like birds of prey. Holding a handful of coins, they began to bargain for items people were going to have to abandon: sometimes a coat, sometimes a whole box of utensils. Having sold off some of their boxes and bundles, the immigrants moved again to the scales, hoping that they had reduced the charges to fit their slim pocketbooks.

Back at the rooming house Johann leaned back in his chair, describing the experience to Marta. "Well, our stuff is on the way to Davenport. One thing I see now: we would have been wiser not to have brought so much with us. You saw from the stores this morning that the prices here, when you try to figure it in *Reichstaler*, are about the same as they are in Germany. We could have waited to buy things here rather than dragging them halfway around the world."

"I think you're right. But how can you know that before you get here? Because almost everything has been packed up from the time we left Neuhaus, I've lived with two dresses for more than a month. You've had on the same suit. That's enough for the trip if you bring some clean linen and undergarments. The rest is all in the boxes. You're right, we could have waited and bought a lot of it here....There's a little difference in the style of the clothes here, but not that much."

"We would have saved thirty dollars at least by not paying for all the shipping. We'd have had that much more for buying things here."

"*Ja*, and you wouldn't have had to break your back hauling all that stuff on and off ships, to and from stations."

"Well, we'll just have the carpet bag and food bag for the rest of the trip. It's going to take us five days, the railroad agent at Castle Garden said."

"Will we have time to look around New York some more before we leave?"

"We have to be on the steamer to start our trip at four o'clock tomorrow afternoon."

"Steamer? I thought you said we were going on a train."

"Our boxes are going all the way by train but we take a boat as far as Albany. There we get on the train. I don't know why. I suppose it's cheaper to ride ships up and down the river than to go on the railroad.

As they walked again down the broad streets of the city, Marta asked, "Do you have enough American money to get us to Iowa. It might be hard to use our gold along the way if we're always on the train."

"I've been wondering if it would be easier to exchange most of our gold here, where there are lots of banks and lots of immigrants coming through. I don't have any idea what Davenport will be like. It's supposed to be a good size city and there are lots of Germans there, at least that's what Hanke's son wrote in the letters I saw in Neuhaus."

"That sounds so strange. Everything that happened in Neuhaus feels like it was a hundred years ago. It hardly seems real. I don't like that feeling. We've got people we love over there; I don't want to feel that I'm forgetting them."

"We'll write them a letter before we leave New York. That way they'll know we got here all right. I'll write them some of the things I've been putting in the *Tagebuch*. We can tell them some of the things we have seen since we left home."

"Home...that sounds kind of funny. We don't really have a home. We've cut ourselves off from Neuhaus; we don't have any more than a little *Fremdenzimmer* right now; I can't even picture in my mind what Davenport must be like. I don't like this feeling. I've never lived without a place I could call home." Marta wiped her eyes.

"Now don't start crying, right here in the street. I know it all feels strange."

"I feel so alone. Of course, you're here with me, but we don't really have a single friend in New York. In this whole big city there isn't a soul who knows us or cares about us."

"You'll feel better once we get to Iowa. Hanke and Anna will introduce us to people there. There will be lots of folk who have had the same experiences we're having. They'll know how you feel. They'll help you to start feeling at home in America. You'll see."

On Thursday afternoon Johann and Marta took the little baggage they had left and went to the pier along the Hudson River, following Staud's directions. It was only a short walk from the boarding house. Once again they saw the dozens upon dozens of ships in the harbor.

Beside the pier stood a small steamer, *Mohawk*, loading passengers. Johann was overjoyed to hear many of them speaking German. Obviously they also were immigrants headed for new homes across the country.

Johann said to Marta, "It really is a lot easier to travel without having to take care of all that baggage."

"I'm not taking all the food we have left. I sorted out what will be best for the trip, what we can eat on the train. The rest I gave to Frau Staud

"There probably will be places when the train stops where we can buy some milk or some coffee."

"I'm really surprised that things kept as well as they did. We got most of this more than a month ago in Bremen. It's still good."

"It'll last us until we get to Iowa."

"Do you think our baggage is on the steamer?"

"I don't think so. The man at the station said that it would probably not be right with us, but it would go all the way by train and would get to Davenport a few days after we do. I put labels on all the boxes to get them to Davenport. He said I'll have to go to the station after we get there to claim it."

"It would be awful if things got stolen along the way."

"The agent said it would be all right. There's not much we can do about it."

"So now, not only don't we have a home, we don't have any belongings except the carpet bag, the food bag, and the two little bags around our waists. I'm scared. We really are helpless."

Johann put his arm around her shoulders. "Just five more days and things will settle down. Don't spoil your trip by worrying about it."

At six o'clock the steamboat gave a blast on its whistle and began to pull away from the pier, heading out into the middle of the broad river.

Johann and Marta stood at the rail with the several dozen other passengers and watched New York quickly fade into the distance.

The river was full of ships, large and small. On both sides of the wide river little towns could be seen. In some places there were steep hills and cliffs, little mountains coming right down to the water's edge. As the sun began to set they could see several large houses on the hillsides overlooking the river.

There were only a few cabins on the boat. Johann was sure that they would be very expensive. So they joined most of the other passengers on long benches which lined the railing and stood in rows in the deck house.

Thrown together in the confined space of the steamer, a number of German immigrants began to converse as they munched on bread and cheese. Almost all of them had gotten off ships from Germany in the last few days and were moving inland.

One man, a round, ruddy fellow with a heavy black beard, announced that he was on his way to join his brother Georg in Albany. "I haven't seen him in three years. He sent some money to help me to come over."

Johann didn't have to offer much encouragement to keep the story going. He was anxious to learn anything he could about life in America. "Does he have a good job in Albany?"

"*Ja*, he's been earning good money. He's learning to talk English; says you have to do that to get along."

"You're lucky to have someone to go to."

The man, lighting a cigar, asked, "How about you, where are you going?"

"Davenport, Iowa, out on the Mississippi River. I knew a man at home who has a son living there. I'm hoping he will help me find work and get settled."

"What sort of work do you do?"

"I apprenticed as a dyer, but I've worked in stores, too. I'd be willing to do about anything to have a steady job."

"I hope your friend can help you find a job. In his last letter Georg said that things were slowing down. He told me I wouldn't have a problem because his boss would put me to work. But he did say that there were a lot of people out of work all over the country."

That thought caused a chill to pass through Johann. He hoped Marta had not overheard that part of the conversation.

Fortunately it wasn't terribly crowded in the deck house. People began to settle in for the night. Johann found a bench on which they could rest. There was room for Marta to lie down with her head in his lap. It might even be possible to get a few hours of sleep.

It wasn't a very pleasant night. Try as he might, Johann found it hard to get comfortable. The hissing and thumping of the engine below decks kept him awake

At six o'clock Friday morning, just twelve hours after leaving New York, the *Mohawk* docked in Albany. Passengers were already moving about, collecting their belongings.

Three couples had told Johann that they were going to a city called Buffalo by canal boat. The pool where the canal ended was very near to their pier. Johann and Marta could watch them as they took their baggage and walked to one of the long boats waiting to move down the canal. Teams of horses waited on the tow-paths to pull the barges along.

"It's going to take them a long time to get to Buffalo; much longer than it will take us on the train, I think. It doesn't look like those canal boats move very fast," Johann said.

"I suppose it is a lot cheaper than going on the train."

"I suppose so, but we've already got our tickets. Some of the other folks said they are taking the train. We can all go together to the station."

At the depot they learned that the westbound train would leave at noon. Putting their bags in the baggage room, the passengers, most of whom were German immigrants, began walking around the town. It was so different from New York. Many of the smaller streets were not paved. There were a few sizable structures which looked like government buildings, but most of the stores in the center of town were only two or three storeys tall. Looking down the side streets they could see many modest houses. On other streets they could see, here and there, some large red brick mansions.

"I like it better here than in New York. It seems a lot more peaceful," Marta said.

"I wonder if this is what Davenport is like."

"I just can't picture it at all. I guess I always think of it like Neuhaus, but it will probably won't be anything like home."

"It may look different, but a lot will be the same. They'll have stores and churches and factories. They'll have houses and schools. Once we learn a little English or find a good German neighborhood, I'll bet you'll feel right at home."

"I hope so. I miss all my friends and Father and Mother…and little Karl. They are always in my mind." Marta wiped tears from her eyes. "Don't you miss your people too?"

"I suppose so, but I've been away from my family for quite a few years. I suppose I'm a little sad that I'll probably never see them again, unless some of them come over here. I think most about not being trapped the way I was at home: no good job, no future. That's going to change over here."

"Have you noticed how many men here are walking around the streets or sitting on benches? I wonder if they don't have jobs."

"Maybe it's some sort of holiday, or maybe they don't start their jobs until later in the day."

"You heard that man on the steamer who said that his brother told him jobs were getting harder to find."

Johann answered, "This is a big country. Things will be different in Davenport. You'll see."

"I wonder where they are now," Katrina Wiesner said to August across the supper table.

August chewed the hard bread crust. "It's over a month since they left. They should be getting to that town where they are going. Maybe there already."

"We should be getting a letter soon. I try not to worry."

"It probably takes a long time for a letter to come all that way."

"I keep showing little Karl that picture they had taken before they left. I don't want him to forget them. I point to Marta and say, '*Mutter, Mutter.*' And I point to Johann and say '*Papa, Papa.*'"

Johann and Marta settled into their seat in the long passenger car, a thick cushion covering the wooden seat and straight wooden back. The back could be moved so two seats could be facing each other. The seats had room for two large or three small people.

"*Schmutzig!*" Marta protested, running her hand along the window sill. She eyed with disgust the faded dusty velvet curtains at the top of the long narrow windows, each with a decorative tassel that swayed with the movement of the train.

Aboard their coach they spent the afternoon talking to other German passengers about the homes they had left, about their voyages across the Atlantic, about their impressions of New York. There was another family from Silesia who were going to settle in Buffalo. Johann had a long conversation with Otto Bauer, who sat with his family across the aisle.

"I heard you talking in the station. I thought that your dialect sounded familiar," Johann said.

"*Ja*, we come from near Breslau."

"We're from Neuhaus, about 80 kilometers to the southwest. It's not a very big town. You probably never heard of it."

"Did you just come over?"

"*Ja*, we got off the ship in New York on Monday. We stayed in New York until Thursday. We needed a few days to get over the voyage."

"We didn't think we'd have enough money to stay in New York, so we came right to Albany on a boat yesterday. We sat in the station all night so we could get on this train to Rochester. Then we have to get another train to Buffalo. The kids are pretty worn out."

"Are you going to join family members in Buffalo?"

"There are quite a few people from our church who already live in Buffalo. The government at home was making it so hard on us that we had to get away from Prussian control. Our pastor was in jail for two years before they kicked him out to go to America."

"I never heard of anything like that," Johann responded.

"What is your church at home?"

"*Evangelisch.*"

"You mean you don't know what happened after the Prussian king decreed that the Lutherans and the Reformed had to get together in one church. He got tired of their arguing with each other. It was when I was just a lad. Our Old Lutheran congregation just wouldn't go along with that. We kept our own faith, and the government started cracking down--hard. They seized our churches and locked us out; they put our pastors in prison."

"The government did that?"

"You bet. They let your churches alone, but they made life very hard for us. We wanted to get out of the country to America, but they wouldn't let us leave. Finally they said that groups could go but each group had to have a pastor to go with them. So whole congregations put together all their money and came with their pastor to America. Lot of them went to Buffalo. A lot went to Milwaukee. Others went to St. Louis."

"Did you come across with people from your congregation?"

"No. Most of our congregation came to America five years ago. The money ran out and we had to stay at home for a few years. There were so few of us left that they eased up on us. Now we're permitted to leave Prussia as families because most of our people have already left. But we'll be joining a lot of people from our town."

"You'll have lots of help finding a job. That's good. We're going to Davenport in Iowa."

"How far is it to Davenport?"

"I don't really know. It must be half way across the country. It takes five days to get there from New York."

The train puffed through the countryside. Cinders and soot rained down on the windows, filtering through the cracks. The seats were hard and the coaches rocked back and forth over the rough roadbed. They had run alongside the Mohawk River for a time after leaving Albany. This part of the river was also part of the canal that ran to Buffalo, so they could see many canal barges moving along the river's edge.

They chugged through small villages and stopped in every town and city. Passengers came and went at most of the stops. Freight was unloaded and loaded. The scenery was lovely as they rode up the Mohawk valley. There were low wooded hills, gray-green in the distance. Fields and farms stretched along the tracks where the valley widened.

A large red-faced man puffed down the aisle, holding on the seatbacks against the swaying of the moving train. He stopped beside Johann. "Didn't I hear you talking German when we got on the train in Albany?" he asked.

"*Ja*," Johann answered. "We only speak German."

"Where're ya from?"

"*Schlesien*, not too far from Breslau."

"I come from Braunschweig. I been here five years. Came over in '52; February."

"I'm Johann Weber and this is my wife, Marta."

"Oskar Braun," he said extending a ham-like hand.

"I heard you talking English to some of the other passengers."

"I'll tell ya, you gotta learn English as fast as you can. It's all right to stay in a little circle of Germans, but if you're going to get a decent job, ya gotta be able to talk to people."

"Did it take you long to learn?"

"I just listened real careful. My first boss, even though he was German, always made me try to talk English. You learn the words pretty quick. I taught myself a kind of game. Whenever I'd be sitting around, I'd try to think of the English name for every thing I could see: tree, sidewalk, store, girl, cat. If I didn't know, I'd ask."

"Everything goes so fast. In New York it wasn't so bad because we found people who talked German. But I'm sure we're going to be getting into places were nobody will."

"Just try to talk a little English to them. Learn a few words and let people see you're trying to learn. Where are you heading?"

"We're going to Davenport."

"I'm only going as far as Chicago. You'll be going through there too. I only got as far as Albany after I came to America. I always wanted to move on further. This is a great big country. It's always easy to move on."

"What is your work?" Marta asked.

"Butcher. That's why I'm not worried about finding a job in Chicago. There's always a spot for a good butcher. People have to eat."

"Do you think much about home?"

"Naw. I write my family a letter once in a while. I tried to talk my brother into coming over, but his wife wouldn't leave. So I gave up on that. They don't know what they're missing. I really like it here."

"It still seems pretty strange to us. We haven't been here for a week yet."

"You'll catch on fast. You were smart to move west rather than just sticking in New York. This is a growing country and you want to be where the new growth is happening. I don't know nuthin' about Davenport, except it's further west than Chicago."

At suppertime all the passengers brought out their food supplies. Johann and Marta had their supper of *Zwiebach* and cheese. After nightfall, Marta pillowed her head on the carpet bag and tried to sleep. Johann nodded in his seat. It promised to be second restless, sleepless night.

At five o'clock in the morning they reached a city the conductor called Rochester. "We get off here to change to the Buffalo train," said the father of the Lutheran family as they got together all their bundles, sleepy children in tow, and moved into the station.

Another man joined the conversation. "I wish I was going with them. When I had to buy my ticket in Albany day before yesterday, I thought I would head for Buffalo. But the ticket cost too much. I didn't have enough left to go very far. I can tell you, I never felt so alone in my life. I just stood in that depot like I was the last man left on earth. I thought maybe I'd just walk around Albany in the morning and try to find a job there. I sat in the station all night."

Johann asked, "Weren't you scared stiff, to be all alone in a strange country and out of money?"

"An old fellow sitting in the station waiting for a train in the morning started talking to me. He could talk some German because he said his father had come from Germany as a young man. He even took me to the cafe first thing in the morning and told them to give me a cup of coffee. I really thought I was at the end of my rope. Then all of a sudden I remembered Schantz, Adolph Schantz, from my home village. Last I heard he was in Albany. As soon as people started to move around on the streets, I started walking, listening for people who were talking German. Then I'd ask 'em if they knew Adolph Schantz. Finally somebody said that he was working in a tannery on the edge of town. After about three hours I found him; followed my nose for the last quarter mile."

"You were lucky."

"He was glad to see somebody from home. I could tell him all the news. I told him the trouble I was in. He said that jobs were not very plentiful in Albany and that I was smart going on to the west. He told me where to meet him at his boarding house after he was done work. He said he didn't have enough for me to get a ticket to Buffalo, but he could help me get as far as Rochester. So he gave me the two dollars I needed for my ticket as far as Rochester and another dollar for food until I get settled here."

Johann listened. "He must be doing all right if he had money to give you."

"I didn't really have any right to expect it. I've never had to be a beggar like that. I'll pay him back as soon as I get a job."

"Where are you going to in Rochester?"

"I don't have any idea. Maybe I can find work somewhere that will give me a room. I'll start looking as soon as things open up this morning. I'll just hang around until all you German folks leave, then start looking. It's going to be hard without anybody to talk to."

Johann's gut felt tied in knots. Every time he thought about arriving at their destination, the same worries kept burning through his mind, again and again. Suppose he couldn't find Hanke when they got to Davenport! Suppose Hanke wanted nothing to do with them! Suppose their money ran out before he could find work! He didn't want to worry Marta, but he was not as confident as his words sounded.

Johann and Marta watched the small cluster of immigrants who got off the train in Rochester. The people stood for a few minutes on the platform, looking all around as if in search of a familiar face. No one knew they were coming; no one was there to greet them. Slowly they moved toward the station.

Oskar looked at his ticket and at Johann's. "We go on together. We've got to change trains here too. I'll go in and find out where our depot is."

Johann answered, "Marta and I will walk with you to the next train"

"Next train?" Marta asked.

"*Ja*, Oskar told me that we have to change trains here. He's going along to Chicago on the same trains, so we'll go out and look for it together. You get off with us and wait on the platform."

"You stay here with me until Oskar comes back," Marta protested.

Johann and Marta walked back and forth on the platform to stretch their legs. As the sun was rising they could see many factory chimneys in the distance. The wide street in front of the depot opened into other avenues lined with what looked to be lovely large homes.

Oskar returned and announced, "The station for our train is just over there. It doesn't go for two hours yet."

In spite of the early hour the platform was busy as a beehive. Several wagonloads of crates and boxes were being loaded onto the baggage car. Soon the train upon which they had ridden would be heading back toward Albany.

Johann said. "Why don't you sit over here? You can get a couple of the *Brötchen* from our food bag. We can eat on the platform."

Other passengers were doing the same thing, sitting on some of the benches or boxes on the platform. The Germans gathered in a little cluster, homing in on the sound of familiar language. Oskar pointed out various signs along the platform and told them what they said in English.

Johann said to Oskar, "Tell me again what those signs say. Don't go too fast." He thought: I've got to start remembering these words. I'm going to start trying to use some of the English words I learn, even when Marta and I are talking.

Marta laughed when he first used an English word. "My, my, listen to the Herr Professor. Already he's talking English."

"We're going to have to learn. Once we learn enough English to get along, we can still keep talking German at home. We'll have German friends to talk to."

"I sure hope so."

"But if I'm going to get a good job, I'll have to know enough English to talk to Americans. I might not be able to find a good job with a German boss."

"Well, all right. I'll try."

"Look at Oskar. He can talk German with us but he can read all the signs and talk to the Americans. Listen, you'll pick it up faster than I do. You're quick at everything."

Carrying their bags, with Oskar in the lead, the small group of Germans straggled to the depot of the Rochester and Niagara Falls Railroad a block away.

The immigrants, their circle reduced by the folks who went on the other train to Buffalo, clustered on one end of the platform and talked about their plans: the only subject they could think about.

"We're going to Davenport," Johann said for the tenth time.

"We probably will get off in Detroit. We could only buy a ticket that far."

"Are you going to be with somebody there, a relative?"

"No. We just have to find a place to stay and start looking for work. I've got to earn some money right away. We only have a little money left."

Picking up their two bags, they walked along the platform.

Oskar puffed up to them and said, "Our train is the one over there."

"Well, we certainly didn't see anything of Rochester," Johann said as he heaved their bags onto the rack over the window. They settled into their seats.

"Where do we go now?" Marta asked.

"Oskar said that we are going into Canada for part of the journey."

A few hours after leaving Rochester they came to a huge bridge. The train moved very slowly and stopped just short of the bridge. Johann and Oskar leaned out the window.

Oskar said, "The sign says that it is the Clifton Suspension Bridge. It says it is 820 feet long. Imagine that."

"It's the biggest bridge I've ever seen. It reminds me of a bridge we have at home at Görlitz, but this one is ten times bigger. Look at those cables holding up the bridge. They are as thick as a big tree."

The bridge seemed quite new. On either side of the deep valley there was a tall steel tower, like a huge four legged stool. Long, thick cables starting in the earth far from the edge of the chasm, looped over the towers, reaching across the valley in a graceful curve. There were two cables on each side of the bridge. From them other smaller cables reached down to hold up the bridge. Dozens of steel girders, standing on end, looking like a parade of soldiers, supported the two decks of the bridge.

The train moved forward very slowly. Marta looked out the window. "Don't look down," she shuddered.

Oskar said, "They say that's the Niagara River down there. What a deep valley! Those cliffs on each side are straight up and down."

"And the river is just pouring through. Look at those waves."

The train reached the far side of the bridge and pulled into a station. Some officers came aboard and walked through the train. They stopped at each seat to ask where each person lived. They were very patient with the immigrants who explained in their own languages where they were from and where they were going.

Johann reached into his shirt for the bag around his neck. He took out their Prussian *Reisepasz*. The official barely glanced at the paper and went on to the next seat.

Oskar said, "They are telling us that we are going to stop here for three hours before we get our next train. We can leave our stuff in the station. It's 11:30 now. Our Great Western train will leave at 2:30. Check your watch. We don't want to miss the train."

Johann and Marta climbed off the train. With Oskar they started walking through the small town. Everyone was walking in the same direction from the train. Oskar asked, "Have you ever heard of Niagara Falls. It's one of the biggest waterfalls in the whole world. That's where all these folks are going.

A few minutes later they were standing on the edge of the cliff looking at the huge falls. The cloud of spray swirled around them and the roar of the water crashing on the rocks below drowned out their voices.

Marta shouted in Johann ear, "This reminds me of the storm when we were on the ship: the crashing of the waves, the water pouring in everywhere."

They moved away to a point where they could still see the falls but without the terrible roar of the water. "Isn't it beautiful? I've never seen anything at all like this," Marta said.

"It's two waterfalls, side-by-side. Just think how much water is pouring over."

"We should have brought our food bag. We could have our *Mittagessen* right here."

"Look at the way the water boils down over those huge rocks down below. I wonder how far that river runs."

"Look over this way at the bridge we just came over. It's huge."

"It looks like there are two bridges, one above the other. The railroad runs on the top bridge, and underneath it is another bridge for wagons and people walking."

Marta said, "I'm glad we went across it before I really saw how it hangs there high above that roaring river. We don't have to go back over it, do we?"

"I don't think so. You didn't have to worry; look at the size of those cables that hold up the bridge."

A couple of hours later the Great Western train slowed to a crawl as it neared Hamilton. The tracks ran near to a large lake. Oskar came down the aisle again, stopping to talk to all his newly-made friends. "You know that bridge we just went over just now, very slow? I was talking to one of the railroad men in the front of the car. He told me that a whole train had gone off the track and dropped off that bridge early this year."

"They must have all been killed, falling all that way down to the river." Johann gasped.

"Not that big bridge we went over this morning. This was a smaller bridge here, right outside of Hamilton. The fellow up ahead said that nobody got killed, but some folks were hurt. They have to build a new section of the bridge. Trains couldn't run on this line for a while, until they put up a temporary trestle. That's why we were going so slow."

Marta said, "I haven't been worried up until now, even going over that long bridge this morning. I wish you hadn't told me about that wreck."

"We're coming into Hamilton."

Only a few passengers got off, and a tall, thin boy got on the train with a basket of buns and a big pot of coffee. The train pulled away from the station after only a few minutes. Marta was concerned that the boy didn't get off. Then she saw what was happening. The lad walked through the train selling the food to passengers, pouring luke-warm coffee into the tin cups he took from his bread basket. Oskar appointed himself interpreter and walked with the boy and helped him negotiate with the German passengers. Several became customers.

Marta, standing on the seat, got their food bag down from the rack. She took out their hard rolls and a little cheese. Johann said, "Some coffee would taste good but I don't have any Canada money."

Oskar came to the rescue. "Here. I thought I might need some money before we get back into the United States so I exchanged a couple of dollars for schillings back at the waterfalls. You can buy me some coffee tomorrow."

Johann held on to the tin cups as the train rocked back and forth until Marta put the cheese on the bread, offering a piece to Oskar. They carefully balanced their supper, bread in one hand, coffee in the other. Rather than risk spilling as the coach bounced back and forth, they drank most of their coffee quickly.

As soon as his customers had finished their coffee, the boy collected their tin cups. The train slowed for a station, stopping just long enough for the young fellow and his wares to swing off. Johann said, "I suppose he gets on the next train going back to Hamilton."

All night they rode, passing through towns called London and Paris, even though they were in Canada. In the early morning the train stopped at a station beside a lake. Somebody said they thought it was called Lake Erie. Where the station stood the lake was very narrow, more like a river. They could see a city on the other side.

They had to board a small steamer with most of the other passengers. Baggage from the train was also loaded on the little ferry. Johann wondered if their trunk and boxes were being loaded, but didn't see any familiar baggage.

They crossed over to Detroit. "Now what do we do?" Johann asked Oskar.

"Well, we are back in the United States. Here we get another train that goes to Chicago. But today is Sunday and the trains won't be running. We'll have to find a hotel and get the train tomorrow. Do you want to look for a place together?"

There was a boarding house nearby the station. For seventy-five cents they could get a small room.

"Ugh! Soot everywhere," Marta protested when they came into the dinghy room.

"I guess it's the best we can do. No use getting far from the depot. We can get our meals here too," Johann answered.

"I'd like to get at this place with a broom and a scrub bucket. I don't see how people can let things get so dirty."

"Well, it's just for one day. After two nights trying to sleep on the train, it will be good to stretch out on a bed."

"I hope there aren't bugs," Marta said, lifting the corner of the blanket on the bed.

"Let's go out and walk around a while."

When they heard several people talking German, Johann asked, "Do you know anybody named Sandmann? He comes from our town."

"*Nein, Nein.*" was always the answer. It would have been nice to have seen a familiar face after all these weeks.

It was about nine o'clock Monday morning when their train left Detroit. The land was fairly flat, like yesterday. The track passed through forests and grassy plains that seemed to reach forever. Oskar called them prairies. Cattle dotted the pastures and green fields. Here and there were farmhouses and barns. It wasn't like Silesia where farmers lived in the villages and went every day to their fields here and there.

Late in the afternoon they arrived in Chicago. For an hour the train had run near a large lake, which Johann told Marta was Lake Erie. Coming into the city, the train moved slowly past row after row of wooden houses, crossing one street after another. Here and there a tall church steeple pushed out of the sea of roofs. Then they saw groups of large brick buildings and the train came into its station.

As they got off the train, Oskar held out his hand, "Well, *Landsmann*, this is where I leave you and your good wife."

"I hope you get settled real soon," Johann said.

"Say, why don't you folks stop off here for a couple of days. You could meet my friends, Karl and Lizzie. I'll bet they'd have a place for you to stay."

Marta smiled as she said, "That would be nice. I'm getting awfully tired of riding on trains."

Oskar, expansive as ever, added, "You might even like it enough to stay here."

Johann answered right away, "We're not really city people. I wouldn't know how to get along in a place this big."

"Well, if you won't stop off here, at least let me find out where the station is for your train to Iowa."

"We'd really appreciate that. I'd hate to get lost when we're getting this close to Iowa."

"You just wait here until I go into the station and find out where the Rock Island Railroad station is. I'll be right back."

A few minutes later he returned. "You've got a little walk ahead of you. They told me that your train doesn't leave until ten tonight. You can walk over there and then still have some time to look around a little if you want to." He gave them directions.

"How are you going to find your friends?"

"When I wrote them that I was coming, they wrote back and told me how to get a horse car to their part of the city. I'll find them....Sure you won't come along for a few days. I know it would be all right with Lizzie."

Even though he sensed that Marta would like to stay here for a few days, Johann shook his head. "We'd better push on. Thank you for the invitation. It's mighty tempting, but we just can't stop."

Oskar held out his hand again. "Well, good luck to you then." He turned and walked out into the street.

"We're on our own now," Johann said quietly, turning to Marta. "Let's go to that other station and find out about our train. Here, I'll carry the bags."

"Can't say I like the looks of this place. It seems terribly dirty," Marta said, trying to hold Johann's arm.

"It seems unhealthy, with that smelly river running right through."

"I liked New York a lot better. This doesn't look like the other nice cities we've passed through. So much of this place just seems to be tacked together."

They picked their way along the dusty streets following Oskar's directions until they saw the depot. Johann went to find out when their train left. It was impossible to speak to the man in English, so, after showing his ticket, Johann took out his watch and lifted his hands in a gesture of questioning. The man held up both hands with all ten fingers extended. Johann nodded and went back to where Marta was sitting on a bench.

"I'm pretty sure he was telling me that the train goes at ten o'clock. It's half six now so we have a few hours. Do you want to look around or stay here?"

Marta answered, "It's still light enough to walk around a little, then come back here and eat our bread. I surely don't want to be on the street after dark."

Just across from the station, as they walked along with Johann still carrying their bags, they heard an accordian playing from behind a fence. Then voices, men's and women's, broke into song, *"Ich weiss nicht was soll es bedeuten, dass ich so traurig bin...."*

Smiles broke across their faces as they walked to the doorway. Here was a small *Biergarten*, right in the middle of Chicago.

"Can we afford to go in?" Marta asked. "We were just going to eat our bread at the depot."

"Sure, let's go. A stein of good beer and a wurst would sure taste good. We haven't had any decent food since New York. Let's go in."

When they entered the fenced-in yard, they saw half a dozen tables. There were a couple of large trees and the garden was roofed with grape vines strung on wires. People were having a good time, laughing and singing. The man with the accordian was sitting on a barrel.

A very fat waiter in a shiny black coat, with a white apron tied around his waist, motioned Johann and Marta to a small table placed against the board fence which walled in the garden. He had a glistening bald dome and a spectacular drooping mustache. With his towel over his arm, he greeted them in German.

Having taken their order, which was small compared to the feasts displayed on the other tables, he was back very soon with two steins, one large, one small. Several minutes later he returned with a plate with four sausages and *Brötchen*.

Johann took a deep breath and closed his eyes in ecstacy. "That's the best thing I've smelled since we left Germany."

"It's good," Marta answered. Then speaking softly from behind her hand she added, "Did you ever see so much food. Look at some of those tables; they have three or four kinds of meat."

"*Ja*, at home we wouldn't see that much meat in a couple of months. They do eat good here."

"It must cost a fortune to eat like that. Are we going to have enough to pay for our wurst and beer?"

"Oh, sure. It can't be too expensive. It's not as if we'd bought a feast like some of those tables."

"I haven't seen food like that since Karl and Emilie's wedding; remember that?"

"It seems like a hundred years and a million miles away."

The singing at nearby tables grew louder. One of the men raised his stein in salute, inviting them to join in. Smiling and laughing like the others, Marta and Johann added their voices to the familiar songs.

"I haven't heard you sing like that since we left home. You've got such a nice voice," Marta said.

"A stein of good beer helps a lot."

During a lull in the singing the couple at the next table pulled their chairs around, smiling at the newcomers. The woman waved her hand at Marta.

Holding out his hand, the man said, "*Guten Abend.* You look like you're enjoying yourselves."

Johann smiled, "We've been traveling for a solid month. It's awfully nice just to sit peacefully for an hour and to feel so at home."

"Where'd you come from?"

"*Schlesien,*" Johann said. "You been in America long?"

The woman said, smiling at Marta, "We came last year. We're starting to feel at home. My brother and his wife are supposed to come soon. Do you have family members over here?"

"No. we're the first ones, maybe the only ones," Marta answered.

"How long have you been in Chicago?"

"We just got here this afternoon and we leave tonight."

"You mean, you're going further west," the man asked.

"*Ja,* we're going to Davenport in Iowa."

"Chicago is far enough west for me. We come from *München.* I like cities. There's lots of good German people here. We didn't know anybody when we came, but we've got lots of good friends now."

"We have three little girls," the woman smiled. "Do you have children?"

Marta swallowed hard, "We have a little boy, but he's still at home with my folks. We didn't think he was big enough to make such a long hard trip. He's not quite a year old."

The man put his hand on Johann's arm, "I hope you have good luck finding a job. Things haven't been so good this year. When we got here, I found a job as a teamster in about a week. Then my boss couldn't pay me any more. It took me about a month to find another job in a brewery. I probably had a hand in making that beer you're drinking."

"I'm going to find a job as soon as we get to Iowa. A fellow from our town lives in Davenport and he'll help me find work."

"Well, good luck. There are lots of people looking for work. I've seen fifty men lined up to get one job."

Johann tried to keep his voice strong. "I thought that there were plenty of jobs in America. That's why we came over here, because I couldn't find a decent job at home, at least not a job with any future."

Marta took his hand under the table. "We got this far and we'll make it the rest of the way too. You'll see!"

Her new acquaintance draped her arm over Marta's thin shoulders, giving a weak smile intended to reassure. "You'll be all right. Things won't stay this bad for long. Just get settled and live simply until a good job comes along."

"Living simply is something I'm pretty good at. We never had much at home. We'll get along, but it's hard not to worry. We're so far from everybody. We don't have anybody we can turn to. If we were at home, we'd have family close by."

"You'll make new friends here. You'll see." She laughed heartily, "Just find a nice *Biergarten*. Look at the nice people you meet. *Prosit!*" She tipped back her stein and wiped her chin with the back of her hand.

Johann pulled his watch from his pocket. "We've got to get to the depot. Our train leaves in less than an hour." He picked up their two bags. "It's been good talking with you."

"Now don't you worry. Once you get to where you're going, things will all work out." the woman said, patting Marta's arm. "Don't you worry."

"...*Wiedersehen*," "...*Wiederseh'n.*"

The Rock Island depot was quiet as passengers straggled along the platform. Johann and Marta boarded one of the coaches and walked down the aisle until they found a vacant seat. A lamp, swinging from the roof of the car, provided enough light to see their fellow passengers.

"One more night on these terrible seats," Marta grimaced. "I don't think I ever want to see another train."

"I can promise you this is the last one. We get to Davenport in the morning. Tomorrow night you'll have a bed to sleep in. As soon as we find Hanke, we'll get a place to stay."

"How will we find him?"

"I guess we'll just have to ask around. There are supposed to be lots of Germans living in Davenport. They'll know where to find him."

The train whistle gave several toots and the coach lurched ahead. The click of the wheels and the swaying from side to side soon had Marta and Johann nodding.

"Here, roll up my coat and use it for a pillow. You can lie on this seat. I'll go to that empty seat over there and stretch out too. I'll use the food bag for my pillow. Try to get a little sleep," Johann whispered.

"It isn't going to be easy. Listen to that fellow up there snoring. He makes as much noise as the engine," Marta laughed.

"Try to sleep anyway."

Johann could not get comfortable. The hard wooden slats of the seat punched hip-bone and shoulder. The night became a cycle of turn to the right, try to sleep, turn to the left, try to sleep, look out the window at the pitch dark landscape, try to sleep, turn to the right....

His mind would not shut down. The familiar parade of worries stood in line to torment him. Turn to the right, try to sleep, turn to the left.... He looked at Marta, curled up under her shawl on the hard seat across the aisle. She was sound asleep. He could see a little smile on her face. She must be dreaming of home. She looked so small and vulnerable. Things weren't going to be easy for her.

Johann realized that she was the only person in this whole country who had known him for more than a few hours, who had seen the home where he grew up, who knew his family, who was aware of his disappointments and his dreams. She was the only one who was not a total stranger. She alone was the antidote for the terrible loneliness that clawed at his heart. Of course, the same things were true for her. He was her only tie to her life in the past. He longed to reach out and hold her close, to embrace the one manifestation of reality as he had known it....Turn to the left, try to sleep, turn to the right....

The sky behind the train began to lighten ever so slowly along the horizon. The last day of their journey was dawning. Johann kept looking out the window as the train moved across the prairie. Soon it was light enough to see that the land was flat as a tabletop. Today's sunrise was not pink but shades of gray. Dark clouds scudded across the sky.

Marta stirred, rubbed her eyes and slowly drew herself to a sitting position. She pulled herself upright and stretched like a cat. Johann went to sit beside her.

"I'll never be able to stand up straight again," she whispered.

"You got some sleep, though. I think you even had some pleasant dreams."

"Did you sleep too?"

"Not much. I just couldn't get comfortable on that hard seat. I just kept thinking about all the things that will happen today."

"The last day of our journey. What day is it anyway?"

"If I'm right, it is June 9. Tuesday. The day we finally get to our new home."

"We left Neuhaus on the first of May. We've been traveling for more than five weeks. It seems longer than that. It's like it was years ago we said goodbye to everybody. Berlin and Bremerhaven seem like old history to me."

Johann nodded. "It was interesting to see all those places, but I'm awfully glad to get to a place where we'll stay."

"Want a little bread for breakfast? We've still got a few pieces of *Zwiebach* in our bag."

"Sure. Once we are settled, we can get some fresh food and throw away our little bag. Can't say I'll be sorry. I'll bet you've forgotten how to cook."

"Once I get my own pots, I'll know how to use them. You can be sure of that."

It was mid-morning when the train arrived in a place called Rock Island. A light rain was falling as they looked out the window of the coach. They watched as passengers got off the train for a few minutes while baggage was being unloaded.

"Do you want to get off too?" Marta asked.

"I suppose we could. We're almost to Davenport. It hardly seems worth getting off when we're almost there. Well, we can stretch a little. Come on."

They ran through the drizzle into the station.

"Johann, stand by the window here so you can see that nobody walks off the train with our stuff."

"They wouldn't get much. The food is just about gone. Our extra clothes are all dirty," Johann laughed.

"Did you say we're almost there?"

"I think I heard one of the men say that we just have to cross the river and we're in Davenport."

"I can hardly wait to see what it's like. Too bad it's raining like this. We can't walk around until it stops."

The conductor paced the platform looking at his watch while passengers boarded. Johann and Marta returned to their seats. Marta wiped the steam from the window so they could see as the train slowly moved out of the station. They could see a long wooden bridge sitting atop large stone piers rising from the wide river. The complex arches and trusses were painted white.

"It looks new," Marta said with excitement in her voice.

"That must be the Mississippi River." Johann looked out as the train started across the bridge. They could see a long stone levee for tying up the river boats and barges, but only two steamers were there. In a few minutes they puffed into the depot at Davenport. Brick-walled warehouses lined the river bank near the town center. Some factories with tall chimneys were mixed with the warehouses. Up and downstream they could see green fields. Gathering their bags, Johann and Marta moved quickly through the rain with the other passengers.

Johann wiped sweat from his forehead as they stood in the crowded depot. He said to Marta, "You sit on the bench here with our bags. I"m going to see if I can find somebody who speaks German and try to locate Hanke."

He walked around the station and out onto the street. Hearing two men talking German, he went up to them and asked if they knew Adolph Hanke.

One fellow said, "...don't know nobody called Hanke. There's two thousand Germans in this city. You're looking for a needle in a haystack."

The other told Johann, "I don't know him either, but why don't you go over there to the *Post Amt,*" pointing to a building across the street. "They may know the name and might be able to tell you where he lives. If that doesn't work, there's two German newspapers in town. They might know where he is."

"Hanke, you say? Adolph Hanke?" said the man at the window of the post office in German. He scratched his head, "*Ja,* I've heard that name. He picks up letters once in a while. I think he and his wife live out on Second Street, somewhere near the brick yard. The street runs right along the river, right down there." He pointed to the left. "If you walk out there and ask at one of the little stores in that neighborhood, they can probably tell you where they live."

Johann picked up their carpet bag and Marta their food bag, which was getting very light. They walked along the streets of Davenport under the gloomy skies. It had stopped raining for the moment, but water dripped from the eaves of buildings along the sidewalks and, later, from trees along the street. A few blocks away there were several large handsome houses on high ground. They passed a long line of two storey stone row houses. Along Second Street the houses became smaller and more humble, the street muddier. Johann spotted a store with a sign proclaiming *Lebensmittel*.

The shopkeeper was friendly. He thought he knew an Adolph Hanke but was not sure. "Is he a big fellow, red beard?"

"I don't know. I've never seen him. I know his father in *Schlesien*. I know he has been in Davenport for a few years. I think he works in a brickyard. My wife knew his wife back at home."

"Why don't you ask the *Pfarrer* over at the church down the street. He would know lots of the Germans around here."

The pastor thought a minute. "*Ja*, I know him and his wife. They live in a little brown-painted house down this street a little further. See that big tree down there. Their house is about across the road from that. You can't miss it."

Their pace quickened as they got closer to their destination. Marta's voice quavered with excitement. "I haven't seen Annie in more than a year, ever since she left to come over. She's going to be surprised. You did ask Adolph's father to tell them in a letter when we made up our minds to come, but she wouldn't know when to expect us, because we didn't know ourselves when we'd get here. "

Johann rapped on the door. They could hear a baby crying. Then the door opened a little.

"Annie, it's Marta, from home; Marta Wiesner."

The door swung open and Annie held out her arms. "Marta, *Liebchen*. How wonderful to see somebody from Neuhaus! And this must be your husband."

"This is Johann. I'm Marta Weber now."

"Come in, come in. The place isn't very big, but it's home." She picked up a baby from the little bed in the corner. "This is Gretel; she's four months old."

"What a pretty baby. It makes me long for our little son. We left him at home with my folks. I miss him so much, but I'm glad he didn't have to make that long trip with us," Marta blinked back her tears.

"Well, sit down and tell me all about Neuhaus. Better yet, just rest for a little while and wait until Adolph comes home for *Mittagessen*. He'll want to hear all about it too. He should come pretty soon. He doesn't stay long, but since we live so close to the brickyard he comes home for some soup at mid-day and then goes back to work. Marta, put a couple of more bowls on the table for you and Johann. There's plenty of soup."

"*Danke*," Marta laughed. "I've got some good stale bread in the bag here. We've even got a couple of pieces of *Zwiebach* all the way from Bremen. Your soup will soften it up."

"I'll get things ready to put on the table."

"Let me hold the baby while you work. I haven't held a little one for so long."

Adolph Hanke arrived, stomping the brick dust from his boots and brushing of his clothes outside the back door. Annie greeted him, "You'll never guess who's here: Marta, my old friend from Neuhaus, and Johann, her husband, who knows your father. They've just gotten to Davenport."

Adolph stretched out his huge, rough hand. "So you got here. We were kind of looking for you a couple of months ago. When you didn't come, we thought maybe you'd changed your minds. When you see how things are here now, you might wish you had."

Annie poked him, half in play, "Don't start talking all the gloom. Let's hear what's going on in Neuhaus. Sit down and let's have our soup while we get all caught up on how folks are."

As soon as his bowl was empty, Adolph pushed back his chair. "Have to get back as soon as I can. With jobs as hard to get as they are right now, I sure don't want to upset my boss."

"I heard that there were lots of jobs in America," Johann said.

"The last four or five months it has been bad. Nobody is hiring right now. You see lines of men looking for jobs everywhere."

Marta reached for Johann's hand. "What are we going to do? You were expecting to be able to find work right away."

Adolph stood up. "Things are bad here in Davenport. If I were you, I'd push on to Iowa City. I heard there's some work there. It's still the state capital. That's where the railroad ends now, so they tell me the town is building up. You're sure welcome to stay here for a few days, but I think you'd be smart to try Iowa City. I know Peter Braun; I worked with him when I first got to Davenport. He works now in Iowa City. He'd help you find whatever is there. He works in a lumber yard. If you tell him I sent you, he'll do what he can."

Annie asked, "Are you sure there isn't anything in Davenport? I hate to see them go on; it's so wonderful to see somebody from home."

"You can try here," Adolph said, "but there just aren't any jobs."

Marta shivered. "We were hoping to find a job right away and get a place to live and settle down after all these weeks on the way."

"You know what it's like here, Adolph," Johann said slowly. "If you think there's a better chance to getting a job in this place called Iowa City, we'd better go there. I suppose we can arrange to have our stuff that's coming by freight to be sent on to Iowa City."

"You could stay here until it comes to Davenport and take it on with you to Iowa City," Annie put her arm around Marta.

Marta looked at Johann, who shook his head slowly. "If jobs are so hard to find, we shouldn't wait. I think we should move on as soon as we can."

"Well, at least stay with us overnight. You can get on the train tomorrow. We've got to have some time to visit. I've made a few friends here in the neighborhood and at the church, but I miss all my family and friends at home," Annie held on to Marta's arm.

Marta put her head on her old friend's shoulder. "It seems so very far away."

CHAPTER 11

Annie walked with them to the depot the next morning. "I wish you could stay here instead of going to Iowa City. It was so wonderful to see somebody from home."

Marta laughed, "I haven't talked like that since I was a girl."

"The two of you twittered away half the night," Johann said with a yawn.

"I had to hear all the gossip. The only thing I hear from home is a letter from my mother at Christmastime. She never has any news about my friends. So Marta was my newspaper."

Marta took her friend's arm. "I haven't been this happy since we left Neuhaus. There was a nice woman we traveled with on the ship, but she wasn't really a friend. We helped each other and talked about what we could eat next. But she didn't have any way of knowing anything about my life before I got on the ship. And I didn't know anything about her. There wasn't anything to talk about except storms; or that crowded, filthy steerage place. We got along just fine, but it wasn't anything like the wonderful time we had last night."

Annie looked right at her. "That's the hardest thing about living over here. You'll find out, too. There are no 'old' friends. Everything starts all over. It's hard. Adolph is good to me and we talk about home a lot, but I miss talking to the people I knew all my life."

"*Ja*, I wish we could stay in Davenport, too. Johann and I feel so alone. You just listen all the time for somebody who is talking German. That's the only way you know what is going on. We've been pretty lucky so far. We've always been able to find a few people in the cities or on the train. I

196

dread the time we find ourselves in a place where we can't talk to anybody. I'm not sure I'll ever be able to learn to talk American."

Annie turned to Johann who was walking a pace behind them carrying their carpet bag. "Johann, do you have to go to Iowa City? Can't you just stay here in Davenport?"

"I wish we could. I've got to find a job so we have some money coming in soon. If there aren't jobs in Davenport, like Adolph says, we have to go on to a place where there is work. The sooner we get there, the better."

At the depot Johann bought tickets to Iowa City and tried to learn if their freight had arrived. It was hard to make the agent understand his question. Annie could not speak enough English to explain the problem. Finally the agent called a man from the loading platform. The fellow spoke German and enough English to be a translator.

After animated conversation with the agent and shuffling through some papers, he explained, "Nothing with your name has come in from New York. He wants to know when you sent it."

"About a week ago, 3, *Juni*."

"Freight moves slow. It could be a couple of more weeks before it comes."

Marta was distressed. "So long? We need the things that are in our boxes. Everything we own is in there."

Johann explained to the agent through their interpreter that they were going on to Iowa City. "Can the boxes be sent on to us there?"

"You'll have to pay a dollar more, but he says he can do it. Do you have the papers they gave you in New York?"

Johann completed the arrangements as the train came across the bridge from Rock Island. Marta gave Annie a quick embrace and climbed aboard before she broke into tears. Johann found her crying on the seat, waving through the window at Annie.

Marta wiped her eyes with her sleeve. "Maybe we can visit her once in a while, if it doesn't cost too much to come to Davenport."

"We'll see. First I have to find a job and you can look for a place to live."

"We'll have to find a room for a few nights while you look for a job. That's a nice little house Adolph and Annie have."

"You'll have your own place, too, as soon as we know how much money we have coming in. I'll have to find this Peter Braun right away."

Iowa City was much smaller than Davenport. Although the railroad was poised to push west, this was, for the time-being, the last stopping point for travelers. The depot was piled high with boxes and crates. Large bins for grain stood beside the tracks.

It seemed like a very new town. The streets were muddy from yesterday's rain. The downtown was a small collection of stores and businesses, overshadowed by a large yellow limestone building. Set in a large open square, it had huge white wooden columns on a front portico. It was crowned with a stepped tower supporting a pillared lantern with a rounded dome. Surrounding streets were lined with modest houses. There didn't seem to be many factories.

Once in the station Johann repeated the familiar pattern of trying to locate their contact, Peter Braun. Hearing a couple of men talking German on the platform, he made his inquiry.

"*Ja*, I know him. He lives in Frau Hausmann's boarding house, over there on the other side of the capitol building. Just ask people on Jefferson Street for Frau Hausmann and they'll show you."

Frau Hausmann was an expansive woman, busy scrubbing her front steps, when they approached. "*Guten Tag*, we're looking for Peter Braun. They told us at the depot that he lived here."

"You just missed him. He left yesterday with a couple of fellows, heading up to Grundy County. He packed up all his stuff and said he was going to try to find work on a farm up there. His job at the lumber yard folded up."

The disappointment was clear on Johann's face. "He's the only name we have in Iowa City. A friend in Davenport told us to see him. We're just coming from Europe and need to find a place to stay while I look for work."

"Well," Frau Hausmann smiled at Marta, "Braun's room is still empty. You can rent it if you want to. Come on in and have a cup of coffee and I'll show you the room."

Once settled into the boarding house, which would cost them seventy-five cents a day with their meals, Johann asked Frau Hausmann's advice about how to go about finding work.

"Well, you could ask some of the other boarders at supper tonight. They might know of places looking for laborers. Sometimes there are notices down at the depot. People looking for workers put up a paper. You could check there. I hate to tell you, but jobs are scarce. That's why Peter left. He was a good worker but the lumber yard just wasn't very busy. Since last year nobody has been building much. Ever since they moved the state capitol to Des Moines, Iowa City sort of quit growing. They didn't even finish the capital building. You probably saw it, the big building with the tower. Soon the trains will go on further west."

"I'll go out and see if I can find anything."

It was a dispirited Johann who returned late in the afternoon. He had gone back to the station to look for the papers Frau Hausmann had mentioned. There was only one notice written in German. It announced that Jakob Schwartz was looking for a man to help with the haying on his farm. The job would last for three or four days only. Johann saw no value in pursuing that. He wanted a steady job. There were three other job notices written in English. Johann kept walking up and down the station platform listening for someone talking German whom he could ask to translate them for him. He heard no familiar tongue.

He walked up and down the streets looking for signs in German in any of the store windows. Clusters of men were sitting on benches and curbs around a brick building with rounded arch windows and a sign on a small cupola: Holz and Geiger Brewery. Johann walked slowly past them. Finally he heard German. Moving close to three fellows dressed in worn work clothes, he said, *"Guten Tag.* It's good to hear somebody talking *auf Deutsch."*

They looked him up and down. One put out his hand and responded, "Sounds like you come from Silesia. Haven't heard that for a while. I used to live in Breslau."

"We just got here. We've been on the way for weeks. Now we want to settle down here. I'm looking for a job to get us started."

"Good luck. You're gonna to need it. Jobs is awful hard to find around here. I ain't worked in a month."

"I'm starting to wonder if it was smart to come," Johann muttered.

"When I got here...couple of years ago, there was plenty of work. Lots of places...being built and the carpenters and bricklayers was all looking for laborers. Well, you can see some of the big new houses. Never many factory jobs in Iowa City, but the railroad was hiring. Then about beginning of the year it just dried up. First no new jobs; then the bosses started laying people off. Got to work one Monday and the boss told us that our jobs were *kaputt."*

199

Johann said sadly, "Before we came everybody was writing home that there were plenty of good jobs. The ships are pouring into New York with hundreds of people expecting to find good jobs right away. Every place we've stopped on our way to Iowa it's the same story: there were jobs, but there aren't any now."

"What kind of work do you do?"

"I'd take any kind of job. I had an apprenticeship as a dyer. I know something about the linen business. I probably wouldn't find anything like that around here. But I've also worked in stores and gristmills."

One of the other men spoke up. "You've come to a dead town, *Mann*. If I was you, I'd get right back on the next train and head back to Davenport. It's a bigger place and you'll have a better chance there."

Johann answered, "I'm going to try one more day here. If I can't find anything, we'll have to go back."

"You're just wasting a day. If there was a job around, we'd all be standing in line for it. I'm getting so low on money I'll take any job."

When Johann trudged back to the boarding house, Marta agreed that it probably was best to think about going back to Davenport.

Johann kicked a chair. "Isn't that just our luck. I really thought it would be easy to find work. I knew that I might not find the job I'd want to stay with right away. I figured I'd get something to earn food for the table and then look around for a job that I could stay with."

"I was talking with Frau Hausmann some more and she tells the same story. Some of her boarders are still working but a number of them lost their jobs and left town. It doesn't sound good."

"Adolph wasn't very encouraging about finding work in Davenport either."

"I know, but at least we'll have somebody we know around. Here we don't have anybody."

"All right. No use wasting any more money staying here. We'll head back to Davenport tomorrow."

Standing on the platform they had left two days before, Johann said, "I'd better talk to the stationmaster and tell him not to send our boxes on to Iowa City. I hope he gives me the money back."

That done, Marta said, "I don't want to just walk in on Annie. I don't want them to think we're going to try to move in with them. We'll find a place to stay before we let them know we're back in Davenport."

"I saw a little hotel near the station. We can stay there for a night and look for a room to rent tomorrow."

"We've got to find our own place. I can't stand to keep moving day after day. We need to have some place that we can call home. It doesn't have to be anything fancy. But we've got to have a place to cook and wash and sleep."

"You're right. I'm sorry things aren't working out the way we dreamed. Just hold on. It's going to work out. This is just a bad time that won't last forever."

The baggage master at the station gave them the names of a couple of landladies. Marta and Johann went right from the depot to look at these places. They were greeted at the first house by a slatternly women who took them upstairs to a rear room. They had not even reached the room down the dark hallway when Marta caught Johann's eye and shook her head "No."

Minutes later they were walking along the street to the next house. Marta said, "I couldn't have stood that place for an hour. Everything was so dirty. You could tell as soon as you saw that woman that it wouldn't be much. I wouldn't have stayed there even if she offered it without any rent."

"Well, let's go and look at the other place."

The second house was clean enough and had a good sized room looking out over the back yard. There was a bed and chest of drawers, a table and two chairs, and a kind of kitchen cabinet containing a few utensils and dishes.

Frau Bach, the landlady, was as small as Marta. Her gray hair was covered with a straw hat. Gray eyes peered out from behind small wire rimmed glasses, which she kept pushing back up her nose. Her movements were quick and purposeful. Her gray checked dress was covered with a clean apron.

She proudly pointed to the room. "You'd like it here. It gets the morning sun. I run a quiet house. Another couple lives in a room in the attic. Me and my husband live downstairs. The rent is only four dollars a month. There ain't no stove but you can buy one for a little more than twenty dollars. You can see there is a flue in the corner. You can do simple cooking on it, and in the winter it will keep you warm. I know there isn't a whole lot of room for cooking, so I let the women do their baking once a week in my kitchen. There's a little wash house out back where we wash our clothes."

Johann and Marta looked at each other. When he saw her faint smile, he proceeded to negotiate. "It's a real nice room. We like it, but we don't have a whole lot of money left and I have to find a job."

Frau Bach smiled back, "*Ja*, I know. We all have the same problem when we get here. I can't make the rent any lower, because that's part of what we have to live on. You understand that. But I like you folks. I think I can save you a few dollars. My neighbor has a stove that I think she'd sell for six or eight dollars. That would save you some and help out 'til you have some pay coming in."

Marta smiled at Frau Bach. "Our boxes are on the way from New York. We only have a few clothes with us, and none of our cooking stuff. I see there are a couple of pans and a few dishes on the table. Can we use those until our boxes come?"

"Sure. The last folks left those here. You're welcome to use them once you get your stove set up."

"Good. We'll stay then. It will be so good to have the same place for more than a couple of days. If you'll tell me where to go, I'll go out and buy a little food for the next few days."

That evening they strolled down the streets to Hanke's house. They explained their futile trip to Iowa City. Annie and Marta sat at the kitchen table, overjoyed to be able to visit. Hanke and Johann walked around in their little back yard.

Adolph said, "I'm sorry I sent you on a wild goose chase. I heard things were better there. I guess that was wrong. Well, welcome back to Davenport. I hope you have better luck here, but it ain't going to be easy."

"I'll get out in the morning and see if I can find anything."

"If I hear of anything, I'll let you know right away. As soon as there is a job anywhere, there are six fellows standing there to take it. Your only chance is to be first in line."

Every evening for five days Johann came home with discouragement written all over his face. Marta could tell from his slow steps on the stairs that there was no good news.

Putting her arms around him, Marta would say, "Don't worry. Tomorrow you'll find something."

Johann shook his head slowly. "I don't know. I just don't know where to turn. I feel so alone walking up and down the streets. I keep looking for signs, even though I can't read them if they're in English. When I see a sign, I go in and try to ask for work. Sometimes somebody knows some German and can talk to me, but usually they just shake their heads as soon as they figure out why I'm there."

"Maybe Adolph..."

"He's busy with his own job at the brickyard. I can't expect him to be worrying about me finding work. I'm not going to hound him."

"Annie said he'll send word if he hears of any job."

"At least in Endigen or Neuhaus people knew who I was. They knew I could be counted on to do an honest day's work. Here in most of the places I'm nothing but a stranger who can't talk English."

"Well," Marta said with a wan smile, "have some supper. You must be hungry. I've got noodles and a little piece of ham."

"It's so good to be able to come home to you. I'm sad that I never have any good news, but just to be here with you is the best part of the day."

Johann's steps were quick coming up the stairs. Marta's heart beat faster. What was he doing coming back in the middle of the day? The door burst open.

"I found a job. I start tomorrow morning."

"*Gott sei ewig Lob und Dank!*" Marta ran to him and threw her arms around him.

"It's in a saw mill. I'll get paid $1.25 a day; that's $7.50 a week. It's not a lot, but it will be so good to have some money coming in rather than only going out."

"Did you say you start tomorrow morning?"

"I have to be there at six o'clock. The regular workmen start at seven, but new men have to work an extra hour because they don't know the job. I don't know how long that goes on. We work until six in the evening."

"I'm so happy. At last we can get settled and start having a good life."

"Don't start getting any big ideas. It's only a start, and like people have told us, jobs can dry up overnight."

"But now you'll be working regularly and there will be wages every week. Let's go and tell Annie and Adolph. I'll take some of the little *Stollen* I baked this morning in Frau Bach's kitchen and have them celebrate with us."

There were a couple of other men on the sawmill crew who spoke German although the boss didn't. Most of them were burly men who seemed huge standing next to Johann. The mill was powered by a noisy steam engine fueled with the bark covered slabs they cut from the logs. Wagons would come in piled high with logs several feet in diameter. These were unloaded in the lot beside the mill, stacked two and three high. The logs to be sawed were those which had been seasoning on the lot the longest. Johann's first job was to drive a team of horses, dragging the log to be sawed next from the lot to the mill. There was a tong-like device which clamped onto the end of the log and was tied with chains to the doubletree which was connected by long straps to the harness of the horses. The boss at the beginning of the day would point out to Johann the piles of logs to be dragged.

It was very hard work. The July days were very hot and steamy. Many of the men worked without their shirts. Those close to the huge circular saw were soon covered with sawdust sticking to their perspiring skin like white moss. There was a wooden bucket by the well with a long-handled dipper where the men could drink. Johann was instructed to water the horses at the trough several times a day, being careful that they didn't drink too much. At the end of the day the men took turns at the pump filling the bucket and pouring it over their heads to wash away the sawdust and grime of the day's work.

Suppertime of Johann's first day at work was filled with detailed description of the mill, his fellow workers, his duties for the day, the heat.

"It seems to me that they work a lot faster over here than they do at home. The boss is right in the middle of things working along with the crew and nobody loafs. He's friendly enough, but he's working hard and sweating like everybody else."

"You must be tired."

"I haven't worked like that for a long time. I used to work hard in the grist mill in Endigen, carrying the sacks and shoveling the grain into the mill. At Wagner's it was only hard work when we had big bolts of wet linen to carry. Working in stores like I have for the last couple of years only was hard work when you have to bring in shipments of goods. All this traveling has really made me soft."

"Eat your supper and you'll feel better."

"I keep real busy. When I get three logs hauled up to the mill, I tie the team under the tree and then go around to the other end of the mill and help to stack the lumber that has been sawed. When they get down to one log to be sawed, the boss gives a little toot on the whistle of the steam engine. I'd get the team and haul up three more logs."

"Did they say when you'd get paid? I'll be needing money for food in a few more days."

"The fellows told me that they pay us at the end of the day's work on Saturday. Of course, this week I'll have only four days, not six."

The boss gathered the men around him when they finished working on Saturday. "I've got some bad news. The company doesn't have enough money to pay you this week. We've got a big shipment going out on a keelboat next week and there will be money then. So you'll get paid for both weeks next Saturday. I'm sorry, there ain't nothing we can do. If anybody wants to quit, we'll see that you get this week's pay if you stop by next Saturday. I hope you'll all stay with us, but you have to make that choice." The other workmen told Johann what the boss had said.

A few of the men grumbled under their breath, but no one made a move to leave. One fellow said, "We may be lucky. One of my buddies had a job where there wasn't no money paid out for 3 months, now it's already the fourth month. They are still working with only promises for pay. These are bad times."

Johann went home with a heavy heart. He was so looking forward to taking his week's wages home and putting them on the table in front of Marta. She'd just have to wait for another week.

Over supper they consoled each other. "I believe the boss," Johann said. "He seems like an honest fellow. He sounded just as disappointed as we were that he couldn't pay us today."

"I hope you're right. But we don't have a lot of choice, do we? If you walked away, there would be no money coming in. At least here you have a promise."

"We'd better figure out how much money we have left and how we are going to make it last as long as we can."

Marta pulled out the little bag she kept tied around her waist and poured out a small pile of gold coins. This is what we have left of the money we brought along. You figure out what it will be in American money at the bank."

After counting and computing Johann announced, "As best I can reckon, we've got about enough to equal about two month's wages. If I'm right, we have about just under seventy American dollars."

"I'm starting to get an idea of what stuff costs here. I got half a bushel of potatoes for eighty cents. Butter is 25 cents. I found flour selling for $1.90 for a 50 pound sack. Beef is 16 cents a pound. But I can't buy big amounts because we don't have a kitchen to keep it in. I have to buy a little bit at a time and that costs more. We could get by easier if we had a little house rather than a rented room."

"You've always been a good manager. I know that you'll stretch the money as far as you can."

"And we'll have some money coming in every week."

"So far that hasn't brought in anything, but that will change. I suppose I could write to Julius and have him send over some more of my inheritance."

"Let's not do that unless we have to," Marta urged.

"I sure wouldn't like to ask him to send the money just for food and rent unless we are absolutely desperate. I don't want them to think we can't make it on our own over here, that I can't support us."

"I always thought that if we asked for that money it would be to buy a house when we were ready to settle down with a regular job."

"That's the way I figured too. So let's just keep trying to make it on what we have and what comes in."

"We can make it on your $7.50 a week. That would surely cover our rent here and food."

"Of course, if there are many weeks where the company doesn't have money to pay us, it's going to be a problem."

"Do you think that might happen?" Marta asked, looking hard at Johann.

"I don't know. I probably should keep my eyes open for another job, just in case it does. This job isn't bad. I don't mind working hard. It feels kind of good after all those weeks of just sitting around."

"I guess you were lucky to find it."

"It doesn't pay much. I hear that carpenters and masons can make two dollars a day. Cabinet makers too."

"*Ja*, but you don't know how to build or lay bricks. So that won't do us any good."

"What I've got is a job, at least. We've got some money coming in."

"Well, not really, if they can't pay you."

Johann was puzzled when on the following Friday all the men were paid, both for the current week and the past week. The men stood eagerly in line, smiling. The boss handed out the money, saying again that he was sorry that he hadn't been able to pay them on time last week. Johann wondered why they were getting paid a day early.

When the last man had been paid, the boss said, "Well, I'll see you all next Monday."

Johann said softly to a couple of the men who spoke German, standing nearby. "Don't we work tomorrow? Are we being laid off?"

"*Nein*. Tomorrow is the Fourth of July. Don't you know about that? It's a holiday; nobody works."

"I just got here. I don't know anything about holidays."

"You'll remember this one."

"What is it, a church festival?" Johann asked.

"Americans have this holiday all over the country to celebrate when they got free from the English king. Nobody works; everybody has a good time. You can do whatever you want to amuse yourself. Better give your pay to your wife when you get home, so you won't be tempted to spend it all for beer tomorrow."

Just after sun-up there was a huge bang, followed almost at once by a popping sound. Marta sat up in bed, eyes wide, and grabbed at the sleeping Johann's arm. "What's that? It sounds like a battle."

"I don't know. Do you suppose it has something to do with this holiday?"

"Are people shooting?"

"We'll ask Frau Bach when we get dressed."

"It's nice that you don't have to work today. We can walk down to Annie and Adolph's later on."

"I don't mind not working, but I'll miss a day's pay. Every dollar counts. But at least we've got the pay I brought home yesterday." The first money I've earned in America....It's a start anyway....thirteen dollars and some coins...."

The popping of guns and firecrackers continued all day in the streets. Even in the Hanke's kitchen where they sat around the table, they could hear the sporadic volleys, punctuated by an occasional deep boom of a cannon fired down along the river.

Adolph described last year's holiday. "When it gets dark, everybody goes down to the river and they have fireworks. You've never seen anything like this. The whole town lights up."

Annie said, "I don't like all this shooting. It makes me nervous."

"They're sort of reminding themselves how they fought a war to get free from *die Engländer*. When you stop to think of it, they've gotten a lot done in about 80 years."

"We haven't seen much, but we do know how big the place is. We spent days on the train and, I guess, we're less than half way across the country. It has to be many times bigger than all of *Europa*," Johann said.

Annie turned to Marta, "It's so big, I feel like a little ant in the middle of huge field."

Johann added, "There's plenty of land here. You saw it when you were coming to Davenport. We went mile after mile on the train coming across Michigan and Illinois; there'd be a farm here and there, then a little town. But you could look out over the flat land and see only a couple of barns."

Adolph tilted back in his chair, "I'll tell you what I like most...I can do pretty much what I want to do. In the old homeland I always felt that somebody was standing over me, some little pip-squeak official telling me what I could not do, some Prussian officer saying he wanted me for his army. My old man probably told you that I don't like to be fenced in."

"One of the first things I noticed in New York--that is, once we got off the boat with all those inspectors--is that you feel so free."

"I don't think there are as many officials in this whole country as there are in a little place like Silesia."

"Right away when I got to New York," Annie chipped in, "I noticed that there weren't uniforms every place, like at home."

"*Ja*, once in a while you see a policeman or the fellow on the railroad that takes the tickets. I don't think that I've seen the uniform of a single soldier on the street in the time we've been here," Johann said.

"Somebody told me," Adolph said, "that the whole country has an army of only 1800 men. That would turn the Prussians pale. It sure helps to keep taxes low here, instead of paying for thousands of soldiers."

"I guess they never heard of conscription. My brother had to spend three years in the Prussian army. I was lucky that I didn't get called before I came over."

"Listen, I came over here to get out of that mess, so did about half the German men who are here."

Annie added, "I think people live a lot better over here. Look at the houses most people have, even workers. They're bigger and nicer than we had at home. Even after only a few years here, Adolph is better off than most of his friends at home, even after they worked at a job for many years."

Johann said, "Well, it's not that way for us...yet...but it will be." Looking at Marta, he added, "You'll see."

Annie put in, "You've just arrived at a hard time, when there aren't many good jobs. It wasn't this way when I got here last year. You'll see; it will get better."

"Some people say that the hard times are because so many workers are coming into the country from Europe." Adolph said. "Well, you saw the boats unloading every day. But I think the hard times are because some people are doing a lot of shady business behind the scenes. I don't know exactly what they do, but they make a lot of money without really doing any work. All at once almost all the *Fabrik-arbeit* stopped. A lot of banks went broke, people lost their savings."

Marta responded, "Even after a little time I can see that people eat better here. Prices are high but people eat a lot more meat than we did at home."

"Yes, and lot more sugar, too. During the summer we have good vegetables. It's rich land and things grow good. I love the good fruit we have, wait till you see the apples this fall. They're this big..."

"It sounds like ordinary people live like the burghers here."

Adolph observed, "The way I figure it...when people get over here, unless it's hard times like right now, they use the extra money they earn to eat better and dress better and have nicer houses. I'm not sure they save a whole lot at first, until they start living better."

"Well," Johann said, "right now, until I get a good job that I know will last, we have to be pretty careful. Once we get on our feet, we'll be able to do some of those things. But right now we have to hang on to the few dollars we have left from the money we brought along."

Johann drank the beer Adolph had poured into his glass from the little metal pail he had carried from the saloon. "You know, the thing I've noticed is how you can travel thousands of miles and never have to show a pass; you just go wherever you please."

"Remember how it was in the old country? You had to get permission to move from one place to another. Here you just pick up and go. If you find a city where you want to stay, all you have to do is find a place to live and a job and everything is in order. You don't have to report to anybody. I tell you, I like that."

Annie smiled at her husband and winked at Marta, "He won't even listen to me, you know."

Marta laughed and Johann said, "The laws are very liberal here, and no official orders us around, but my little dove turns into an eagle if I don't do what she thinks I should."

"I'm an eagle now...We've got to get back to our room and unpack our boxes that you brought from the depot yesterday," Marta laughed. "I didn't know that your boss would give you a special holiday to help me unpack, or that the whole country would celebrate that at last we've got all our stuff."

"Was it all there?" Annie asked.

"*Ja*, I haven't seen any damage to the boxes," Marta said. "But I don't know what we're going to do with the stuff now that it's here. There's just that tiny cabinet in the corner of our room."

Annie turned to Adolph, "Would there be any room in that little shed out in back where they could leave a few things until they have a bigger place."

"We could probably fit the boxes in there, once you've taken out what you have room for. But we'll have to be careful. I'm afraid the roof leaks a little. I'll help you carry the stuff over when you get it sorted out."

Marta took Annie's arm, "I don't know what we'd do without you folks. I hope we'll be able to repay you someday for all the help you've been to us."

"Don't worry about it. It's just wonderful for me to have a friend from home to talk to."

"I'll come over after supper and help you move the boxes," Adolph promised. "Then we can all go down to the river for the fireworks."

A few weeks later Marta knocked on Annie's door. "Come in. Adolph just left for work. What brings you out so early."

Marta twisted the corner of her apron. "I'm worried about Johann. He's sick again this morning and couldn't go to work. He vomits up everything he eats and feels just terrible."

"Just give him custard and broth...a little at a time. He shouldn't try to eat a meal."

"He hates to miss work. He missed a day last week. Now he's sick again. He's afraid he'll lose his job by missing so many days. He just can't work when he feels so bad."

"That's a worry."

"We can't afford to lose too many days' pay. Everything costs so much; the wages cover our rent and food. I don't know what it will be when we need new clothes."

Annie put her hand on Marta's thin shoulder, "It was hard for us at first too. After Adolph was on his job for a while, they gave him more money. That made a big difference."

"Things are better than they are in Silesia, even with the high cost of things."

"Once people get set up, even the lowliest worker can earn enough to help them through the winter when lots of jobs peter out because of the cold weather. We have a little garden out back and can raise enough potatoes and beets to use all winter."

"I wish I could find a milliner, Marta said. "I was a hat maker in Neuhaus...a good one. Once we feel a little more settled, I may just look for a place."

"They're there," August Wiesner shouted to Katerina as he came through the kitchen door. Fritz told me there was a letter at the *Postamt*, so I picked it up on my way home from work.

"What do they say?" She sat at the table and picked up Karl as he toddled over to her.

"Johann says that they got to Davenport all right and found Hanke's son. They have a place to stay. He got a job working in a saw mill. Said the trip on the ocean was stormy but they had a good ship."

"Here you hold Karl while I read it all."

"Marta wrote some things at the end."

Katerina read through the letter. "She says how much she misses Karl....It's hard for her and hard for the *Kindchen*."

"They'll send for him in a year or so." August showed the letter to Karl, "*Mutter, Papa.*"

Karl snatched the paper from his hand and with childish glee ripped it in two.

The leaves were turning color on the trees, falling on the wooden sidewalks and paths. Marta walked slowly toward the little Hanke house. Annie answered her knock, giving her a little hug. "Where've you been keeping yourself. I haven't seen you in almost a week."

"I've been staying close to home. Johann is sick again. He has real bad pain in his back, right behind his right shoulder and can't hold any food down."

"How long has that been going on?"

"Almost a week. He's hardly been able to work since the beginning of September. He's going to have to quit, if they don't let him go first."

"He sure has had a lot of trouble."

"I think it's gall colic. I had an uncle in Neuhaus who was sick like that. Johann worries so about not being able to work...and that makes it all the worse." Marta began to cry.

Annie put her arms around her friend. Marta blubbered, "That's not all...I'm going to have another baby."

"Are you sure?"

"I haven't told Johann yet, but I haven't had my time ever since we've been here. I figure I must have gotten pregnant right after we got to New York. I'm going to have to tell him soon, but I just hate to add another worry to that poor man's life."

"Are you feeling all right?"

"Pretty good. I guess Johann thinks I'm not eating much because he doesn't feel like eating. I've covered it up so far, but I'm going to have to tell him."

"He'll probably be happy, even though it is a little problem now."

"Well, I don't know. He wasn't terribly happy when I was carrying little Karl. He didn't have nearly the problems then that he has now. I don't really know how he'll take the news. I guess that's why I haven't had the courage to tell him."

"You have to tell him. He needs to know."

"He's going to be so worried, not just because of the hard times. He'll worry about me. I had a very hard time when Karl was born. They tell me I almost died. It was weeks before I could take care of the baby. My step-mother helped to bring us through it. But she's on the other side of the ocean now." Marta burst into tears again.

Comforting her friend, Annie whispered, "You know, you're not the only one whose going to have a baby."

Marta looked at her friend, amazed. "You...you, too. I don't believe it. Both of us pregnant at the same time."

"When are you due?"

"March, as I figure it."

"I think I'll be having my baby in April. Adolph is really happy. That's why I think you should tell Johann. Adolph wants a son so bad. He loves Gretel, but he wants a boy."

"Won't it be nice for both of us to have little babies about the same time. When they get a little bigger, they can play together."

CHAPTER 12

Davenport was quiet. All the stores were closed, as they were every Sunday. Johann and Marta sat at the little table in the corner of their room.

"I wish you had as much color in your cheeks as the leaves of that tree," Marta said, pointing to the fall-colored maple tree behind the house. "You feeling any better?"

"A little. I've been able to keep my food down now for two days. If I can start eating again, my strength will come back; I know it will."

"You've gotten so thin. I worry about you."

"Don't worry. You think about yourself and being healthy for the baby."

"At least I'm not sick in the morning any more. That was a sight, each one of us with a bucket."

Johann laughed, "Maybe that's what's wrong with me; I'm having a baby too."

"That's the first laugh I've heard in weeks. You must be feeling better."

"Well, there hasn't been a lot to laugh about, has there? How many weeks of work have I missed? Four? I didn't work at all for the whole month of September."

"I just know that you're getting better now. You'll be able to get another job soon. Then things will start looking better," Marta smiled wanly.

"Tomorrow we'll have to go downtown to the post office to see if the letter from Julius has come. How long has it been since I wrote?" Johann asked.

"I know it was during the summer, around the time you got sick while you were working at the saw mill."

"That would have been late July. So we should be getting his letter soon. I hope it isn't too hard to get the money I asked him to send."

"He doesn't really know how bad we need the money,"

"I didn't want to tell him how little we had left and how hard it was to get work. Karl would just be sitting there with that smug 'I told you so' look on his face. I wasn't going to give him that satisfaction. So I only said that we needed more of our money to get set up here."

"We've got only one gold coin left. I've tried to be careful. Since we're not eating much, I've been able to save some on food. Milk soup and bread is good for us and keeps our stomachs settled."

"If I keep feeling better today, I'll go out and look for a job tomorrow. I've got to start getting pay again."

"I don't want you going if you don't feel good. You don't want to make yourself sick again."

"Let's walk over to Hanke's this afternoon and see if he has heard of any jobs."

A month later Johann walked slowly along the street, kicking at the leaves which had fallen from the now bare trees. His clothes were covered with red brick dust and white lime from the mortar he carried. He had been working for two weeks as a mason's helper. They were building a warehouse down along the river.

Marta heard his steps on the stairway. Opening the door to their room, she curtsied. "*Wilkommen, mein Herr.* How was work today?"

"Not bad, the walls are up shoulder high. So we've got scaffolding. You ought to see me scrambling up and down a ladder with bricks and mortar."

"Looks you brought a good bit of it home with you. Maybe you'd better go out back to the washhouse and brush that dust off your coat."

"I had my coat off for couple of hours after lunch, but it felt good early this morning and when the sun started going down before we quit. I don't think winter is far away. That wind cuts right through sometimes."

"I know. I just about froze my hands when I was hanging up our wash this morning."

"The boss told some of the men that he hoped we could get the walls all the way up so the carpenters could put on the roof before it got real cold."

"Does that mean the work will stop if it gets cold?"

"I suppose so. Some men were talking about not having work all through the winter. They try to save some of their wages every week to see them through until spring."

"We don't have anything to save. What will we do when it gets cold and you can't work."

"I don't suppose that there are jobs because a good many men won't be able to work in winter. Everyone will be looking for extra work."

The letter from Julius containing the long-awaited *Geldschein* came a week later. Marta burst into tears when she saw the bank draft.

"I've been so worried. We hardly had enough money for one more week. I still have a dollar left from your last wages but that's all."

"Not working this week because it's too cold for the masons to lay bricks was the last blow. Another week without any money."

Marta smiled. "This letter makes all the difference in the world. You get Adolph to go with you to the bank, so you can get the American money."

"I imagine with all these Germans here in Davenport, they handle these bank drafts from home all the time."

"We were so relieved to see that bank draft, we haven't even looked at Julius's letter. What does he say?"

Johann read the letter aloud. Marta listened intently as Julius told about each family member, even though she knew them only from spending a few days with the family.

Johann smiled, "It doesn't sound like much has changed in Endigen. Mother isn't working as hard as she used to. I'm glad for that."

"She probably doesn't have much to do since Karl moved into the house and Emilie is running the household."

"Old Karl is still ruling the roost. That's clear. Well, that's his right as the oldest son, but I'm sure glad to be out from under his thumb."

"Once we get settled, and you are able to find a steady job you can let him see what a good idea it was to come to America."

"I'll have to write Julius and let him know that the money got here safely. I'll just tell about the town and Hanke and things like that, without talking about how jobs are so hard to find."

"There's no point in worrying your mother."

"I'm not going to give Karl a chance to put me down either."

One November morning when Johann got out from under the featherbed, he exclaimed, "Eiiii! Marta, look at this! There's ice as thick as my finger in our water bucket."

Marta's response was to pull the featherbed over her head. Then she poked her face out, "You're joking."

"It must have turned very cold overnight. This means no work again for a while."

Fortunately the cold spell lasted only a few days and then there were several weeks when the nights were cool but the days were sunny and warmer. At suppertime every day Johann reported on the progress of the warehouse.

"The walls are up and the carpenters are putting the roof on. We only have a couple of small buildings behind the warehouse to finish. Because they want to get the building closed in before the really bad weather, the boss has us carrying lumber for the carpenters on the roof. I don't know if the boss has another job lined up. It may be getting too close to winter to start another building."

"So we might have quite a while before any money is coming in."

"Now that we have the money from Julius in the bank, it's not so desperate, but we'll have to be careful. We should only use what we absolutely have to from the bank."

By early December all work stopped. The days were cold and the nights colder. Gray clouds filled the sky day after day. Strong, wintry winds blew from the north, and snow covered the ground for several days at a time.

Johann and Adolph spent part of most days sitting near the stove in a little grocery store in the neighborhood.

"This reminds me of Müller's store where I used to work in Neuhaus. Your papa used to sit by the stove with his cronies. In fact, that's where I heard about you and about Davenport. Until I heard your father talking about your letters I really hadn't thought much about coming to America."

"Hey, you aren't blaming me for coming, are you?" Adolph laughed.

"*Nein*, I'll even give you part of my first million dollars."

One of the other men around the stove spoke up. "Did you see the notice about a meeting of an outfit called the Swiss Colonization Society tomorrow night down at the *Turnverein*."

"What's that?"

"I don't know much about it but a fellow who worked with me is a member. He's Prussian, not Swiss, but that doesn't seem to matter. He was telling me about it. I'm thinking of going to the meeting."

Adolph said, "Is it some kind of a club?"

"No. He told me that a bunch of Schweizers are getting together and buying land somewhere along the Ohio River down south to build a new town. He said there'd be a lot of building going on there, so there would be plenty of jobs."

Johann said, "When did you say that meeting is going to be. I might just go along with you to hear what it's all about."

About twenty men gathered at the *Turnhalle* for the meeting. Johann sat in the back row of chairs because he knew only the fellow he had come with. Many of the others seemed well-acquainted, laughing and slapping each other on the back. There seemed to be as many or more Germans than Swiss, judging from their accents. Clouds of smoke from cheap cigars fogged the room.

A big man stood up and got the group's attention. He was much better dressed than most of the others in the room: frock coat, shining white shirt, stiff collar and silken cravat. He was an imposing figure with wavy dark hair and neatly trimmed beard. He spoke German with the sibilant accent of the Swiss. His language suggested that he was well educated.

"*Meine Freunde*," he began. "My name, for those of you who don't know me, is Ferdinand Becker. I have Becker's Haberdashery down on Third Street. I come from Canton Glarus in Switzerland. I came to America in 1854 and settled first in Cincinnati. Then I came out here to Davenport about a year and a half ago.

"I called this meeting because I want to tell you about an organization I belong to and which might be of interest to you. It is called the Swiss Colonization Society. It was organized last year in Cincinnati. I am a close friend of one of the founders. I got to know him at the University in Zurich when we were both studying there. Swiss people in more than fifteen towns and cities along the Ohio and Mississippi Rivers have joined the organization and have formed local groups, like I'm proposing to do here in Davenport. That's why I called this meeting.

"The Society now has nearly 8000 members. This is not just a social club. The purpose of the society is to help Swiss immigrants...Germans too...to pool their money and buy a tract of land along the Ohio River where we plan to build a new city. Each member pays $15 into the land fund. For that you will get two lots in the new city.

"The latest report I had from the Society is that since June of this year they've had representatives out looking for a big enough tract along the Ohio River to start a good-sized city. They've been traveling in northern

Kentucky and in Indiana west of Louisville. The report says that they located several tracts around places called Rome and Coaltown and Hainesville, but the price was too high. They finally gave up looking in Kentucky because many of the members didn't think they wanted to build a new city in a state where they have slavery. We Swiss are a liberty-loving people and can't see ourselves living in a slaveholding state.

"As soon as they find the right place, they will let each branch know by telegraph. I thought that there might be some of you Swiss and Germans here in Davenport who might be interested in being part of this new town. Because we'll be starting fresh, there should be business opportunities and jobs for a lot of people. We'll have to build houses, stores, businesses, saw-mills, brick yards, everything a town needs. I would argue that rather than coming into a place like Davenport, which is pretty well established, it will be a great advantage to be part of the beginning of city. All the opportunities will be there. With all of us working together, everyone can get ahead, rather than trying to work your way into a place where people got in on the ground floor years ago."

Murmurs of approval were heard around the room. One man stood. "I like what you're saying, but I got a couple of questions."

"I'll try to answer them," Becker responded.

"If everybody puts in the same money, how do they decide who gets which lot? Some are bound to be better than others. How can you be fair?"

"I think they've thought of that. Every shareholder will get two lots. Once they buy the land and surveyors lay out the town, they will have a lottery. Each shareholder's name will be put in and there will be a drawing. That seems the fairest way to do it; just leave it to chance."

"Sounds fair. My other question is: how soon will this all get under way?"

"Well, as I told you, the representatives are searching for the land right now. Once they find the right place, there is already a fund of more than $40,000 dollars in the bank for buying the land. So they should be able to move right ahead with it. In my judgment the laying out of the town and the beginning of building should be able to start no later than a year from now."

Conversations broke out around the room. "Sounds like a good deal to me...." "I'd have to know a lot more than I do now to get involved...." "This idea sounds crazy to me. Some smart Schweizer is going to get the money

219

and run...." "Becker seems to be a good business man. If he's interested, it must be a good plan...."

Johann told his companion, "It's so hard to get steady work in Davenport. I could get interested in something like this if it gives a person a real chance to get established."

Becker stood once again. "Now, fellows, everybody have a glass of beer and think it over. As soon as I get any definite reports, I'll post another meeting. I'll try to have a map then to show you just what we're talking about. In the meantime, if any of you are interested, give me your name. You're not under any obligation, but I'd like to know who would consider becoming part of this plan. We'll meet again."

When Johann got home, he gave Marta a full report of the meeting. He asked, "What would you think of going to a place where they were building a new town?"

"Davenport hasn't been too good to us. I love Annie, but I don't feel tied at all to the city."

"What Becker said made sense to me. Here we came into a town where people got businesses started years ago. The early ones had the best chance of succeeding. Now we come in and all the good jobs are taken. We just get the little crumbs left over. In a town where the whole place is just beginning, there'd be a real chance to get a good job."

"Would we have to travel far again? I can't do much traveling with the baby coming."

"Becker said he'd have another meeting when he had more information. He asked for the names of those who might be interested. I told him I'd like to know more. It might be a chance for us."

The winter weeks passed slowly. Johann found a job of sorts splitting stove-wood for a man who sold it door-to-door from his wagon. It wasn't much of a job, but it brought in a few dollars from time to time. Things were not much better than they had been at home.

Johann and Marta were discouraged, but they talked more and more about going to the new city. Even though the Society meetings didn't have a lot more information about the plan, it seemed more and more promising.

Marta was standing at the door of their room when Johann came home for supper. "Look at the letter Annie brought for us from the post office."

"Letter; who sent us a letter?

"It's from Papa. Sit down and I'll read it to you," Marta said, barely able to contain her excitement. "His writing is hard to read."

> Dear Marta and Johann. I only wrote about three letters in my whole life. I hope this gets there all right. We was glad to hear you arrived safe in Iowa. I went to the schoolhouse and asked the schoolmaster, Reichart, to show me where it was on a map in one of his books. We found Iowa but didn't see any place called Davenport. We hope you soon have nice house and Johann can find a good job. Things are pretty much the same in Neuhaus. Little Karl is growing. He runs all over the house. Mama chases him so he doesn't fall down. I think he is going to be a tall boy. We taught him to call Katerina *Grossmutter.* I will say he is stubborn little *Kerl.* He knows what he wants and yells 'til he gets it. We do everything we can to keep him happy. Do not worry about him. I saw Hanke down at the store and told him I was going to write a letter. He said to tell Adolph and Annie hello. Write soon. Your Father August Wiesner.

Marta could picture him sitting at the kitchen table struggling to write even a short page. She wiped her eyes, "Oh, I miss Karl so much. We are missing all the joy of seeing him grow. He is even forgetting his mama. That is breaks my heart. As soon as we get settled, we have to find a way to bring him over.

"*Ja.*

Right after the new year a notice was posted announcing another meeting of the Society. Johann anxiously awaited the gathering. This plan, which was still quite vague, took on the proportions of a vision of the Promised Land.

Gathered again at the *Turnhalle* the men listened intently as Ferdinand Becker read a report from the Society's headquarters in Cincinnati. It was in a copy of their newspaper, *Die Zeitung.*

"The representatives of the Society have located a large tract of land along the Ohio River in southern Indiana. It's west of Louisville and east of Evansville. Here is a map of that section of the state." Becker pointed to a large map he had tacked to the wall. "The land is right about here.

"The report says that the land has small hills and is covered with forest. That means there will be plenty of wood for building. It is being bought

221

from a number of landowners, practically all of them English. A lot of
land in this area was bought years ago by wealthy people in the east as
an investment. I guess they think it is time to sell now that the Society is
interested in building a new city."

The men crowded around the map, locating some of the established
communities, pointing to the section being bought for the new city.

Becker continued, "The key part of the land is a 700 acre estate owned
by a Judge Huntington. It's called "Mistletoe Lodge.""

"What's a mistletoe?" one of the men asked.

"It's *Mistel*," Becker responded. "The report says that once they got that
big single tract right along the river, other owners of nearby tracts saw the
advantage of selling at the same time. So the representatives have options
to buy 4154 acres. The total price for all that land is a little more than
$85,000. I know that that sounds like a lot of money. But, as I told you at
our last meeting, there are about 8200 members and the Society plans to
assess every member $15. That will give more than enough to buy the land
and pay for surveying it into lots. Every member, as I told you, will get
two lots in the new city. So it's a real bargain, two lots for an investment
of only $15. You'll have to put some of your own sweat into clearing the
lots before you can build. But you'll have some logs for lumber too. The
Society has so much faith in this project that they are willing to make
three year loans for those members who might not have all the money in
hand to build a house."

Johann looked at the man next to him. "Compared to what lots cost
in places like Davenport, is that a good price?"

"Sounds like a good deal to me. My guess is that one lot in Davenport
would cost that much or more," the man sitting next to Johann
responded.

Becker continued, "Think of it this way. You can build a house on one
lot and sell the other one, or hold it for later as an investment. Or you could
build a house on the second lot to rent and have a nice income.

"Several of you have told me that you are seriously interested. I'm
planning to go to the place as soon as we can travel on the river in the
spring. If anybody wants to go along to look things over, I'll be happy to
have you join me."

Several men immediately jumped to their feet. "Count me in!" "Sounds
good, I'll go along." "Me too."

Johann looked around. Enthusiastic little conversations had broken
out all over the room. Turning to the man next to him, Johann said, "I'm

going to look into this. It sounds good to me." Then he stood up and called to Becker, "I'll go along too."

Becker held out his arms for quiet. "All right. Those of you who want to go to Indiana to have a look, put your names on this paper on the table. As soon as the river levels are high enough for the boats to start moving again, we'll make the trip. I'll get the information together as soon as I can and let you know. We'll have another meeting to make definite plans."

It was February when word came from Becker that the steamboats were starting to move. They would go from Davenport to St. Louis. There they would get a boat heading for Louisville which would drop them off at the site of the new city. The trip would cost them $5 each way. Becker thought that they could make the trip and be back in Davenport in about two weeks.

Johann discussed the plan with Marta. "This is really the best time to go. Work hasn't really started up yet, so I won't miss a lot of wages."

"*Ja*. That's so. "Can we afford the money for the trip?" she asked.

"I don't like to spend the money, but we've been paying a price for not having had the chance to look at America before we came. I want to have a look at this place before we decide to go. I think that would make the expense worthwhile."

The paddlewheel steamer *N.J. Taylor* cast off from the pier in Davenport. The decks were piled high with barrels and boxes of all description. River traffic was just beginning after the winter with its low water and ice.

Ferdinand Becker stood on the upper deck with Johann and Willi Egli. A number of other members of the Swiss Colonization Society had decided that, although they were interested, there was no point in everyone making the exploratory trip. Johann and Willi wanted to make the trip and promised to bring back a full report for all those who were interested. A number of the men contributed twenty-five cents each to help the travelers with their expenses.

Johann was surprised that so many of the other men had been willing for him to be their representative. He had only spoken in the meetings a couple of times. His enthusiasm for the project was clear from his words. He felt that the trip was a good investment. "We've got to know that this is a solid proposition. All of us left the homeland because of the promise of the New World. After we got here many of us found that things were not as good as we expected. This may be the next step in the journey of a lot of us, but we have to know that it's not going to be another dream that doesn't work out."

Others had murmured approval. Johann continued, "I think that if we go there, we'll be able to see what kind of place it is, learn if there will be work."

Becker had welcomed this willingness to explore the new settlement. "You're right, Weber. If a few of us look it over and report what we saw, the rest can make up their minds."

Already the steamboat had rounded a bend in the Mississippi and Davenport was no longer visible. Johann walked around the boat, comparing it to the *Indiana* which had brought them from Bremerhaven to New York and to the little steamer which had taken them to Albany. The *N.J. Taylor* was broad and sat low in the water. There were two iron smokestacks which belched soot and sparks whenever the boiler below decks was being fired. At the back of the boat was a huge paddle wheel which pushed them forward at good speed, assisted by the river current. The engine throbbed constantly and with every stroke of the large pistons which drove the shafts that turned the paddlewheel there was a burst of steam from a tall pipe and a gasp that sounded like a dying man. A deep-throated whistle sounded every time they approached another boat and when they were ready to dock.

The boat was even more crowded than the *Indiana* had been. The deck was piled with cargo, leaving only a narrow path along the railing for passengers to walk. To sit or stand on deck you had to go to the upper deck. In the center of the main deck was a large room with benches for passengers. The room was rather dim because the piles of deck cargo blocked off most of the windows. Some of the benches were occupied, a few by families. Personal baggage was piled in the corners, or under the benches. At each stop a few passengers left the boat and others boarded. Becker had suggested that they look at a cabin on the upper deck. These were crowded. Three-tiered bunks were on one wall and there was a small washstand with pitcher and basin.

"Well, what do you think?" Becker asked. "This isn't as nice as the boat I took to Davenport before."

Willi agreed, "I can't see that we'd be much better off in a cabin. They are about as crowded as the deck house below."

"The only difference I see is a straw mattress," Johann contributed. "We'd probably pick up lice from it. My Marta would have a fit. Even coming across the ocean on a very crowded ship, she kept our little corner as clean as could be."

"Let's just decide every time we get on a different boat," Becker said. "Some of them are a lot nicer. If the cabins aren't much better than the public rooms, we're just as well off on a bench. Even though they try to sell you a ticket for a cabin, I've noticed that a lot of folks wait until they're on the boat and then make up their minds."

During the day they made short stops in Burlington, Keokuk, and Quincy, where they tied up for the night. Some of the river towns looked very much like Davenport: wharves, a levee paved with stone blocks, some factories and warehouses, rows of modest wooden houses punctuated by an occasional church steeple. Other towns were located a distance from the river on the bluffs overlooking the broad bottom lands.

The trees were bare and one could see farms scattered here and there on high ground along the river. There were long stretches where there were flat bottom lands extending several miles back from the Mississippi. The river twisted and turned as the pilot guided them through the channels where the water moved more swiftly. Mudbanks and sandbars could be seen on both sides. Sometimes the boat slowed to a crawl and they steered down the unfamiliar channel.

Becker, who could speak English, was their interpreter. He told them that they would stay on the *N.J. Taylor* as far as Cairo. He estimated they would reach there by the end of the third day. Then they would get another steamboat going up the Ohio River. He pointed out their route on the map he had brought along.

There was a little dining room of sorts on the *N.J. Taylor* but, like most of the other passengers, the three from Davenport bought a little food at the various towns where they stopped and ate their bread and cheese and sausages. One could buy beer or coffee on the boat.

They stopped in St. Louis, the largest city Johann had seen since Chicago last spring. They docked along a broad sloping levee where many boats were tied to floating landings. Because a good bit of cargo was to be unloaded and loaded, passengers had several hours to explore the city. Becker was their guide.

"I passed through here on my way from Cincinnati to Davenport a couple of years ago. It's quite a place. We don't have much time but I'd like to show you the courthouse here. It's that building over there with the dome."

Cairo was a bustling river port, joining the traffic of the two great rivers. Becker made a few inquiries and quickly led them to another steamer, the *Queen of the South*. "This one is going to leave in a couple of hours. But before I get our tickets I want to be sure that they will put us ashore at the new settlement. Since it isn't a town yet, they might not want to stop there."

He was back in a few minutes. "I talked to the Captain. He knows where we're going. He said he's not sure he can get the boat right up to the riverbank, but if he can't, he'll put us ashore in a rowboat. He said that there is already some activity there. So we're on our way. He'll have us there by day after tomorrow morning. So let's get our stuff on board."

The engines labored to push the boat upstream. The trip up the Ohio River was a bit slower because they were moving against the current.

Standing at the rail as they pulled out of Paducah, Johann struck up a conversation with a man who had been on the boat when they boarded at Cairo. Venturing a "*Guten Tag*," Johann was pleasantly surprised when the man answered in German. He was a recent arrival in the United States.

"We came by sailing ship and landed in New Orleans." It took us almost seven weeks to cross the Atlantic. Because it was in the winter we had some terrible storms."

Johann recalled their voyage and the stormy days they had had. "That is no pleasure. We had some days like that."

"These storms lasted more than a week. I thought a couple of times that the ship would break in half and sink. I was mighty glad when we sailed into the mouth of the Mississippi River. Then we had to take a little steamer to New Orleans."

"Is that a nice city?"

"It's all right, but it's all French. There were a few Germans around, but not many. I looked for a job for a couple of days, but there wasn't anything."

"That seems to be the way it is everywhere," Johann added, giving a brief account of their experiences in Davenport.

"We decided to get a river boat to *Luis Will*. We know some people there who will help us get settled. I'm sure going to be glad to settle down someplace. We've been on the journey since way before Christmas. Are you going to *Luis Will*?"

"No, we're heading for someplace in Indiana where they are going to build a new city. We can buy land there and be in from the very beginning. There are three of us from a group in Davenport who are interested in this new city. We're going to see if it is on the up-and-up and report back to them."

Mist was rising from the river at first light of day when the *Queen of the South* moved slowly and carefully toward the northern bank. One of the crew leaned over the bow, dropping a lead-line to test the depth. A mate stood beside him with a megaphone, shouting instructions to the captain and the pilot at the helm.

Johann, Becker and Egli stood by the rail peering into the fog. There was a cleared place along the bank. Tall pilings had been driven into the earth along the water's edge. Other pilings stood out from shore. A short, crude wharf reached out into the river. Very slowly they moved toward the flimsy pier.

The Captain appeared at their sides. "I don't feel safe going any closer. I just don't want to get stuck on a sandbar for days. We'll put you fellows on the wharf with the skiff. You got your gear?"

"We're all ready," Becker responded.

"I'm not going to blow my whistle and wake up everybody for miles around, not to mention my other passengers. Once you get ashore, you'll be able to rouse somebody."

Picking up their carpet bags, the three scouts made their way to the gangway at the bow of the *Queen of the South.* A crew member was holding the small flat-bottomed boat for them at the end of the gangway which had been lowered almost to the water. Another man was at the oars. They cast off and slipped through the mist a dozen yards to the crude wooden dock.

Once ashore the trio made its way toward the little cluster of rude buildings. No smoke was coming out of their stove pipes. Everywhere were big piles of logs from the trees that were being felled to clear the site. Heaps of ashes dotted the land where the scrap limbs of the trees had been burned.

There was one large building at the edge of the cleared land. They headed toward it. It was the one building that appeared to be well-built, contrasted with the dozen or so crude shanties that were scattered across the clearing.

Becker surveyed the building. "This must be Mistletoe Lodge, the house of the judge from whom this land was bought." As he finished speaking a stocky young man with a close-clipped black beard stepped out of the door.

"You fellows are getting an early start today. My name is Steinauer, Charles Steinauer."

"Ferdinand Becker. And this is Johann Weber and Willi Egli. We're Society members from Davenport. I think I met you in Cincinnati when I lived there a few years ago. Aren't you the secretary of the Colonization Society?"

"Yes, I was. I lived in Cincinnati for about eight years. I think I remember you now. I know that your name is on the members' list. Come on in. We're just getting ready for breakfast. You might as well have some bread and coffee with us. Then you can look around. My brother and I bought the judge's house, and we're making it into a hotel." He gestured toward the sprawling frame building.

Becker spoke, "We're only here for a day or so. Members of the Society in Davenport sent us to look the place over and report back. There are, maybe, half a dozen families that are very interested."

Johann and Willi nodded their assent, looking around the land as the rising sun lit up the scene. A few men emerged from the shanties and began moving around.

Steinauer swept his arm in a half circle. "What you see here, gentlemen, is the only totally new city in the state of Indiana. Most places start with a handful of settlers and then grow gradually through the years. We're taking a forest and making it into a city all at one time. We've only been here a couple of months, but you can see how much land we have cleared. After this fog lifts, I'll show you around. You're going to be excited by what you see. Come on in and have some breakfast. My treat this morning."

Seated around the table in the large kitchen, the men listened as Steinauer told them. "I don't suppose you've heard that last month the Society officers decided to call this place Helvetia."

"Helvetia?" Johann queried.

"Yes, named for our home country. But it's for Germans too; for anybody who wants to be free. This town is going to give us all new freedom: freedom to work, freedom to build and own our own homes, freedom to vote, freedom to be good citizens in our new homeland! The greatest day of my life was the day we laid $20,000 in gold on this table to seal the deal and signed the papers for this land. I tell you, men, this is going to be the most exciting place to be."

"You're a pretty good salesman. Too bad you're not out talking to the societies in all the different cities. You'd have this Helvetia full in no time," Johann laughed.

By the time the sun was fully up, the sound of axes and saws came from every side. Large trees crashed to the ground. Crews of men swarmed over them to trim away the branches and hook up the teams to drag the logs to the timber piles.

Steinauer's voice was excited as he walked with them. "The surveyors are almost finished laying out the town. Here you can see the main street, 80 feet wide, running pretty much north and south parallel to the river. All the other streets will be 70 feet wide. We've got an experienced surveyor, a fellow named August Pfaefflin, working. You'll meet him when we get down to the south end. They're laying out city blocks. There are going to be several thousand city lots, and some blocks at the edge of town which will have more land for gardens and small fields. As you can see, most of the land we bought is covered with heavy forest. That means we have our own lumber supply right here. As soon as we get the main streets cleared and the stumps pulled or burned out, we're going to set up the saw mill and start turning these piles of logs into lumber. It will be up to the individual lot owners to clear their own land."

"There's going to be work here for years," Johann said with excitement in his voice. "I worked in a sawmill in Davenport last fall. I also worked for a while on a crew of bricklayers. Building a whole town is going to take an army of workmen."

"It's going to be a little primitive at first, but we're expecting the first families in a couple of months, as soon as we have enough lumber to start building houses and stores."

"When will they have the drawing for the lots?" Willi asked.

"As soon as the survey is finished and the plot of the whole town is on paper. I expect we'll be ready for that in a couple of weeks. August says he is almost done with the survey. You can see his stakes all over the place."

Becker asked, "You say you expect settlers to start getting here soon?"

Steinauer sat on a log and lit his pipe. "Well, as you can see, we've got this gang of men cutting logs and clearing the streets. Most of these fellows are members of the Society and will be wanting to start building their own places in a few months. We've got to get the streets laid out and cleared first, so people can get to their lots. I expect we'll be ready for that by Eastertime."

229

"So people had better get here soon to get the good lots."

"No," Steinauer argued, "people will know which lots are theirs before they get here. As soon as we have the survey map, we'll have the drawing in Cincinnati. Every member who has paid his assessment will get his two lots and be able to locate them on the map. We'll send the numbers from the drawing and a copy of the map to all of the branches of the Society. You should have that all in Davenport in less than six weeks. So your people who decide to come, ought to be able to get down here in the late spring."

Becker said, "My guess is that we'll have six or eight families from Davenport ready to come as soon as possible. Don"t you think so, Johann?"

"Once we tell them about the place, they'll get interested in a hurry. Just to be in a town where there are plenty of jobs is going to persuade a lot of them."

"There's going to be plenty of work. We've got about thirty men working now, clearing. August has about six more on his surveying crew. My brother and I have three carpenters and a bricklayer working down at the judge's house fixing it into our hotel. I want to have that done as soon as possible, so there is a place to stay when families start getting here. People will need a place for a few days until they get some shelter on their lots to use while they build their houses."

"And the saw-mill will need quite a few men. You'll probably need more than one mill." Becker said. "How are you going to get supplies and people into the town?"

Steinauer drew a crude map in the soft dirt with a stick. "We've got a rough road about half built to Coaltown; five miles up river. So in a few months we'll have a way to get wagons and livestock in here. But we're going to work next on a proper boat landing. Most of the people and supplies will come on the boats. The channel comes pretty close to our shore along here. So if we build a levee and wooden landing, the boats can get right in. We're just waiting for a man to come from Louisville to help us lay it out."

"There are plenty of boats passing. I've seen about three or four just this morning."

"That's what makes this such a good place for the town. We can get supplies, and once we build our factories we can ship our goods up and down the river. When I was one of the committee looking for the land to buy, I kept insisting that we had to be right on the river. We could have found cheaper land away from the river, but then you depend only on roads for transportation, and you know what that can be like in the winter and the spring."

Becker said, "Suppose we just walk around and look the land over. We need to get an idea of how far the town will extend. We're going to have to describe the place for the people back in Davenport. I'm going to make a few crude drawings to give them an idea of what it is like. Weber here is going to write about how the place looks. We want to be honest with our people, but I think we're going to have a lot of interest."

"You should know, too, that the Society plans to use the lots that are not drawn in the lottery and will build some houses on them to rent to people who want to live here but don't have enough money to build their own houses yet. You can tell your people that. It won't be this year, but next year for sure."

Becker and his companions walked through the cleared main street, lined with piled-up logs. Intersecting streets sloped up from the river to the higher land to the east. Drovers and their teams dragged the logs from where the trees were being felled. Sawyers were cutting the longer logs into lengths for the planned sawmill. Clouds of white smoke rose from the tree branches and brush, trimmed by a dozen axemen, which were piled over the stumps to burn them out for leveling of the streets. There were a few gullies where little streams ran down to the river.

Ahead they saw the surveying crew at work. A bulky man, roughly dressed with a wide-brimmed hat, bent over his transit, looking toward another fellow holding a tall white pole. With arms signalling, he directed the man with the pole to move to the right or the left. Two other men stretched a chain along the line he was sighting, driving stakes at regular intervals. Axemen stood ready to fell any tree that obscured the line being surveyed.

When the strangers walked up, the surveyor raised his head from his instrument. "... *Morgen*," he said, extending his hand. "My name is August Pfaefflin, what's yours?"

Johann held out his hand and introduced his companions, explaining that they had come from Iowa to look over the planned town. Pfaefflin pointed to the young man who stood nearby making frequent notations in a leatherbound book. "This here is Christopher Huntington. He's an *Englischer*, but a pretty good lad anyway," he joked. "His papa owned this land. Now he's helping me with the survey and the filing of all the paper-

231

work with the county. He's a good fellow, even if he knows only a little German. We get along real good, *nicht wahr, Kris?*"

The young man tucked his pencil into the band of his hat and reached out to shake hands with the newcomers. His close-fitting woolen breeches were tucked into knee high riding boots. He wore a tailored blue coat that looked like it was copied from a military uniform. He stood out from the rest of the surveying party. Carefully and slowly he ventured a greeting in *Hochdeutsch.*

Pfaefflin smiled. "Christopher has been a big help. He's been playing on this land as a boy. Now he is the keeper of the records and helps me every night when we draw on the map of the town. You here to work until folks get lots and start building?"

"We're here just for a day or two to look at the place for a group of members of the Society who are interested in coming," Becker explained.

"Like what you see?" Pfaefflin spat a stream of tobacco juice at a pile of brush.

Johann was the first to answer. "We are pretty excited about what is going on here. It's the first thing I've seen in America that is really lively. Everything else has seemed to be standing still: jobs hard to find, people running out of money."

Becker smiled at the enthusiasm of his fellow-traveler. "We think we can persuade a number of families from Davenport to come to Helvetia when we tell them what we've seen."

"Then we'll be seeing you in a few months. I'd like to talk more, but they're pushing me to get this survey finished so they can have the drawing for lots." He began to look through his transit and young Huntington started marking again in his book.

Back at Mistletoe Lodge Steinauer welcomed them. "It's pretty hard to picture a town here now, I know. But I can see stores and businesses, houses and churches here in less than a year."

Becker laughed, "If it wasn't for waiting for the lottery, I'd roll up my sleeves and grab an ax right now to start clearing a lot."

Johann added, "I feel the same way. My wife is going to have a baby soon. As soon as she is ready to travel after that, we're going to be on a boat heading for here."

"You won't regret it. The first few months won't be easy, until we get things organized. But after that it's going to be a great place to live."

"I don't know that there is a whole lot more for us to see," Becker said. "We wanted to be able to picture what the place was like and to get some idea of how plans would unfold. I don't think we'll learn any more by sticking around for several days. I think we might as well start heading back for Davenport as soon as we can."

"Come in and have some stew. We'll put up the red flag on the end of our little dock and one of the boats will stop for you. That's the signal we use for wanting to go downstream."

"We really appreciate your hospitality," said Egli, moving through the door.

"Some of our fellows like to hunt in the woods after work, so we have game to eat every day. It's *Hasenpfeffer* today."

They were barely finished with their meal when a blast from a boat whistle echoed across the Ohio valley. A steamer stood off the dock, and a skiff made its way to shore. Johann and his companions picked up their carpet bags from Steinauer's hallway and walked quickly down to the river bank. Steinauer shook hands with them all.

"Glad you could come. I hope you liked what you saw. As soon as you find out what lots were drawn for you, come back and help us get the city started. I'll see you in a few months."

Becker planned to call a meeting of the Society the day after their return to Davenport to hear their report. On the boat he had told Johann, "I get the feeling that some of the men in Davenport think I'm pushing this plan too hard because I'm going to get something out of it. It might be better at the meeting if you could do a lot of the talking, tell the fellows what we saw and what you think of it. Just tell them honestly what you think."

It was mid-afternoon when Johann came up the steps to their room at Frau Bach's. He poked his head around the door and said quietly, "Surprise. I'm home."

Marta was resting on the bed when he entered. She held out her arms to him. "I'm so glad to see you. It seemed like a year you were away."

"It was only ten days, but it seemed a lot longer for me too." He hugged her. "How are you feeling?"

"All right. I feel as big as a house. One more month and we'll have our baby and I can move around like I always did."

Johann told Marta in detail about their trip: the boats, the cities passed enroute, the landing in Helvetia in the fog, the forest being cleared, Steinauer, Mistletoe Lodge, Pfaefflin, Huntington, stumpy streets, log piles, dreams.

"You really think this is the place for us?" she asked.

"I do! It's not much now, just forest, but in a couple of years it is going to be a city. You'll see. It's the kind of place of opportunity I was expecting to find everywhere in America. This is what I was dreaming of, a place to make a new start, to get ahead in the world: where I can get a steady job, where we can have our own house, where there is a future! You'll see!"

"Tell me again what it looks like."

"Well, like I said, right now it is just long straight streets cut right through the woods, only one nice big house and a handful of rough shacks. There are logs everywhere that in a few months will be walls and roofs. There is smoke from piles of burning brush that will be replaced in a few months by smoke coming from chimneys and cookstoves. There's crude little dock reaching out into the big river that in a few months will look like the riverfront here in Davenport, with boats tied up loading and unloading. There will be warehouses and stores, factories and churches and a school. If you close your eyes and let your imagination run loose, you can see a new city coming right out of that forest."

"I wish Annie and Adolph could go along too. It would be so nice to have someone I know."

"We'll tell them about it, but I imagine Adolph wants to stay with his job here. He is lucky enough to have steady work and their own house."

"I'm going to miss Annie so much."

"There'll be lots of new people in Helvetia. Because everybody will be a newcomer, it'll be easy to make friends."

"How soon do you want to leave?"

"As soon as you feel ready to travel after the baby is born. I'll be able to find work here for a few months now that the weather is getting better. Then we'll pack up and take the boat down river. I'd like to get to Helvetia in time to get our house finished before next winter."

The Society responded to Becker's notice that the travelers had returned and were ready to report. Johann and Willi sat with him on the platform. The air was heavy with cigar and pipe smoke as the men talked and joked with one another.

Becker clapped his hands to get attention. "Men, you've heard a lot from me about the plans the Society has been making. But now it's time for you to hear from somebody else who has seen the place too. So I asked Willi and Johann to tell you about what we saw in Indiana."

Egli poked Johann on the arm, urging him to speak first. Johann stood and began to describe what they had seen in Helvetia: the lay of the land, the work of clearing and surveying, the river landing, Steinauer.

"I tell you, men, this is the most exciting place I've seen in America. I've seen big cities like New York and Chicago. I've seen factories and bridges and railroads. This town is practically nothing but woods right now, but everywhere is promise. Everybody there is excited. They are going to carve a big town right out of the forest. You can see already where the streets will be. I just closed my eyes and I could see houses, I could see businesses and factories. There are hundreds of people who will be heading for this place to build their homes in America. There will be plenty of jobs because we've got to build a city. I made up my mind as soon as I saw it and talked with Steinauer. This is where I'm going to live. I hope that a lot of you will be going too. Willi, tell them what you saw."

Egli put his cigar on the edge of the table and looked out at the crowd of men. "I ain't much for talking, but I stand by what Weber just told you. I probably won't be able to go right away because I don't have enough money yet to build, but I'm gonna get my lots and wait for the right time. I'll get there in a couple of years, as soon as I can save a little more money."

Johann stood up again. "The important thing, in my way of thinking, is that here you've got hundreds, thousands, of members of the Society working together toward one goal--to build a new town. It's not like Davenport, or any place else, where you're on your own, trying to make a place for yourself in a new country. In this new town everybody is starting together. The Society has things planned out in very orderly fashion. Well," he laughed, "you know how these *Schweizers* are."

Then Becker stood. "I'm glad you could hear it from Johann and Willi. I have to tell you, I was impressed with the men we talked to there, especially Steinauer. He has been the secretary of the Society since it started and really knows what is going on. He told me that because they had been able to buy more land than they had originally planned, they were going to add a five dollar assessment for each member. That means that for two lots you'll be paying a total of $20. In my judgment that's still a very good buy."

Some of the men began to murmur. One stood, "So the price is going up. That's what I figured would happen. As soon as they get your $15, they tack on another five. How do we know they won't keep adding assessments?"

Becker as quick to respond, "I can only go by what Steinauer told me. He impressed me as an honest man. They've been so thorough in their planning that I'm sure they have the costs all worked out. The extra assessment was because they were able to get another tract of land at such a good price they didn't want to turn it down. Once the town is built, the land around it will go up a lot in price. So it was smart to buy it now, while they had the chance at a good price."

"How do we know it's not just going into the pockets of this Steinauer you talk about and some of his buddies?"

Johann spoke up, "I trusted him. He was right in there working with all the men. He and his brother were making a big old house on the property into a hotel for people to stay in while they were putting up their houses. He struck me as being a good businessman, but not a shyster."

Egli added, "I'm willing to put in five dollars more because this place is going to go. Even though it's only a few shanties in the woods right now, everybody we talked to there could see it as a thriving town in just a couple years. I think they knew what they were talking about because they were all willing to pitch in to make the town. They weren't just waitin' for somebody else to do it."

A few men got up to leave but a dozen or more came up to the table to become part of the project. Becker listed their names. "I'm going to be heading down river as soon as I can make arrangements to close my store here. I'll be happy to have any of you come with me. Others can come as soon as they are ready."

Johann said, "We'll be on our way as soon as my wife can travel, probably in a couple of months."

Becker added, "In a couple of weeks we're supposed to get a map showing all the streets and lots and the numbers that were drawn for every member. So those who have already paid their $15 will be in the first drawing. They'll get title to their lots when they pay the other five dollars. Others who join later will be part of the next drawing. That's the way Steinauer explained it to me."

Johann turned to Marta across their supper table. "I told them at the meeting last night that we were going to move to the new town. I need to write to Julius asking for the rest of my money to pay for our house. Is it still all right with you to go?"

She hesitated. "I guess I have a hard time picturing what it will be like. I know you're excited about going. There's nothing holding me here, except Annie is my good friend. But we have to find some place where there are jobs and a chance to settle down. That's what we came across the ocean for."

"So it's all right with you if I write to Julius for the money?"

After the dishes were cleared away, Johann wrote a long letter describing his trip to Indiana and the new town that was being built there. He wrote enthusiastically about the wisdom of moving to a place filled with opportunity.

After reading the letter to Marta he said, "You know, when I hear that, I get kind of angry with myself. It's like I'm asking their permission to go to Indiana. We're free to do what we think is best. It's not their decision, sitting over there in Endigen. It's my own money that I'm asking for."

Marta answered, "They'll be interested in where we are going."

"*Ja*, but old Karl will be clucking about it not being a wise move, too risky, not sound business."

"Forget Karl! You're letting him control your life by always being afraid of what he will think. He's there; we're here....So just do what you think is best."

"You're right. Here, let me add just a little note about the new baby coming soon. Then we'll send this on its way tomorrow."

Marta stirred in the bed and groaned. Johann could hear the stove pipe in their room whining with the March wind. "What's the matter?"

"I think the baby is coming. I had a pain a little while ago, but this one was harder."

Johann lit the lamp and started to put on his clothes. "I'd better wake Frau Bach and go after the midwife. Will you be all right by yourself for a few minutes? I'll tell Frau Bach to come up and sit with you until I get back."

It was starting to get light when he got back to the house. Frau Bach was sitting by the bed holding Marta's hand. "I don't think there's a great hurry. Her pains aren't coming real close together yet."

"Well, Mutter Kurtz will be getting here soon. She said she'd come as soon as she got dressed."

As he spoke there was a thumping on the front door. The midwife hung her shawl over the stair railing and puffed up the steps to the back room. "Nothing to worry about, *Liebchen*. Mutter Kurtz is here now. We'll have your new little baby soon." She put a stack of bed sheets on one of the chairs.

Frau Bach busied herself with a large kettle on the stove. "I got the fire started. Johann, bring in another armload of wood from the shed. We want it nice and warm in here, and we'll need hot water."

Mutter Kurtz slid her hands beneath the blankets to make an examination. "Here, Frau Bach'll give me a hand and we'll get some of these sheets under you. I think we're goin' to wait for an hour or two."

Frau Bach said, "Here, let me rebraid your hair while we are waiting. I was there when both my grandchildren were born. You'll get along just fine."

"Sure you will," Mutter Kurtz added. "I've got a hundred or more children running around Davenport that I helped into the world. In the old country I got a couple hundred more."

Marta smiled wanly. "I had a hard time with my other baby."

"*Ja*, I know. But this will be different. You'll get along just fine. I can tell."

Johann, having delivered wood and carried buckets of water to the second floor, was sitting, under orders, in Frau Bach's kitchen downstairs drinking a cup of strong coffee and chewing the piece of *Stollen* she had set before him. Every few minutes he walked to the window, then back again to the table. He could hear steps from the room above.

The wall clock had just struck eight when Frau Bach came into the room, smiling. "You've got a daughter. Everything went just fine. It was a nice easy birth."

Johann rose but Frau Bach held out her hand. "Give us a few more minutes; then you can come up. We want Marta to look nice for you." she smiled.

"I want to name her Emma," Marta said. "That was my mother's name." She cradled the baby in her arms.

Johann looked at the tiny face. "I don't really remember what Karl looked like when he was born. She seems so tiny."

"He had dark hair just like she does. I think he was bigger."

Frau Bach stood at the door with a large wicker basket in her arms. "How do you think this would be for a crib. I have a nice soft blanket to cover the sides. She'll be snug in here."

Marta smiled, "You've been so good to us. It's hard when you don't have any family close by. My step-mother was with me when Karl was born. I really thank you for being with me."

"Why not? I got two daughters of my own. I'd want somebody to be with them if I couldn't be there when they have a baby. Mutter Kurtz said you got along just fine."

"I was so worried because the first time was so hard. Mutter Kurtz said not to be afraid, she'd help me, and she did. She just held my hand and smoothed my hair until it was time to push the baby out. I just knew it would be all right, and it was."

Johann smiled with relief. "So now we have an American baby."

Marta blinked a tear, "...And a baby in *Schlesien*. I think about little Karl every day. I miss him and wonder how he is. I doubt if he would even know me if he saw me. Maybe it won't hurt so bad now that I have Emma."

Johann took her hand again. "Things are going to start getting better, you'll see. Once we get to Indiana, it's going to be good. I'll have plenty of work; we'll have money coming in; we'll have a house of our own."

Frau Bach said, "I don't like to think about you leaving. You can't go right away with this new baby."

Marta struggled to sit up in bed. "We'll wait a month or two. I'm as anxious as Johann to get to our new home. You've been wonderful to me, but we have to have our own place. We've never had a house of our own, not since we've been married."

"Johann tells me that new town is going to be pretty rough living for a while. It's not like coming into a place that has all the houses built."

"He said we'd get started building our house right away. The baby and I can stay at a hotel until there's enough shelter to move in. We can finish the house after we're in it. It won't be a great big place anyway."

"Well," Frau Bach said, "You just get your strength back real soon, so you'll be able to make the trip."

As Johann arrived home from work a few weeks later the house was quiet. Coming into their room he looked in the basket and saw it was empty. The bed was made but there were no signs of preparations for supper. In the middle of the table was a scrap of paper.

239

Johann read, "Annie is very sick. Adolph sent for me. I have Emma with me. Come as soon as you get home."

Johann ran down the stairs and along the street. When he arrived at Hanke's door, Adolph met him. Tears were running down his cheeks into his red beard. Marta, holding Emma, stood just behind him. Her face was white and she had been crying.

She threw herself into Johann's arms. "It's terrible! Annie is dead!"

"What?" Johann exclaimed, his face turning pale.

"A neighbor saw her laying on the ground out in the back yard. Her baby started to come early. She was covered with blood; it wouldn't stop.. They sent for Adolph and he brought the doctor as fast as he could. I got here just after she died. I can't believe it. The woman next door is keeping Gretel at her house."

Adolph was inconsolable. Tears poured down his cheeks. He kept pounding one huge hand into the other. Softly, he kept saying, "Annie. Annie."

Johann looked at his friend as he held his wife and daughter close. "Marta, why don't you sit down with the baby. You still don't have all your strength. How can I help you, Adolph?"

"*Danke*, my friend. I was so glad Marta could come right away. Annie loved her so much....I can't believe she's gone....I don't know how I'll get along without her."

"I'm so sorry. I just can't say anything."

"She just brought so much into my life. Everything was so different after she came from Neuhaus. Life was good. We were so happy, waiting for the new baby. Now they're both gone. What will Gretel and I do?"

"Marta, maybe you could find things here and make a little supper for Adolph. I can go back to our room for some of our food if you need it. We'll have a little to eat and stay with Adolph for a while."

Marta found bread and milk and cheese in the kitchen and put it on the table, where Adolph was sitting.

"I'm glad I got home before she died. The neighbor women had her on the bed. The baby was born dead. Annie was so weak I could hardly hear her talk. She was such a good woman. I'm not much, but God will help us somehow."

Marta said quietly, "Eat a little bit now."

They had just finished when there was a knock at the door. Several women from the neighborhood came in to lay out Annie's body. Adolph sat with his head in his hands. "The doctor said he'd have Gus Weisz, the cabinet maker, come in to arrange for the coffin. We'll have the funeral day after tomorrow. I'll talk with the *Pfarrer* in the morning."

Emma began to cry as Marta walked her back and forth across the kitchen. "I'd better take her home and put her to bed. She's fussier than usual."

"All right. I'll walk home with you. Do you want me to come back and stay with you for a while, Adolph." Johann asked.

"I appreciate that. I'll have to write to Annie's family right away and tell them. That's going to be hard. I'm not much on that kind of letter-writing."

"After the women are finished and things quiet down, you just tell me what to write and I'll put it down?"

The lamplight cast long shadows on the wall as Johann and Adolph sat at the kitchen table. The house was quiet now. Johann had paper, ink bottle and pen in front of him. "What do you want me to say?"

"Dear mother- and father-in-law. I am very sorry to send you sad news. Annie and I were going to have our second child and were hoping for a son. Today, April 10, Annie had a bad fall out in our garden. The baby came early and was born dead. No one could help Annie, not even the doctor we called. They got me from work and I got home just before she died, shortly before six o'clock. I was so glad that I could be holding her hand when she died. We will have the funeral in a day or two and bury her behind the church here in Davenport. I know how you feel, because my sadness is almost more than I can bear. She was a wonderful woman and gave happiness to all the people who loved her."

Adolph sighed, "That's about all I can think to say right now. I'll sign my name."

When Johann crept into their room, not wanting to awaken Marta or the baby, he heard her soft sobbing. When he slipped into bed beside her, he put his arm around her.

"I'm so sad; so terribly, terribly sad. Annie was so good to me. I'll miss her."

"I know you will."

"Poor Adolph. All alone, and with little Gretel to take care of," she sobbed.

"He's a strong man. In time he'll be all right."

"I was worried that I might die when Emma was born. I was even more afraid of dying when Karl was born."

"I worried too, but somehow I knew you'd be all right."

"But suppose I hadn't," her tears fell on his shoulder.

"I'd have felt like my life had ended, like Adolph."

"When I worried about dying when Karl was born back in Neuhaus, I thought you might be relieved, that you'd feel free."

"Whatever made you think like that?" Johann asked, remembering his terrible ambivalence when they were married.

"Do you think I didn't realize how trapped you felt when you had to marry me? You never said anything, but somehow I knew that you weren't happy about losing the freedom you were hoping for."

"I wouldn't ever want to lose you. You know that I'd be completely destroyed if anything ever took you away."

"Next to you and our children, I loved Annie more than anyone I know. I was dreading leaving her when we go to Indiana. Now there will be nothing at all to hold me in Davenport."

A second release from Davenport arrived the following week when Julius' letter arrived with the bank draft. He expressed cautious support for their move to Indiana, wishing them well and asking that they keep the family informed of their whereabouts.

He concluded his letter:

> "I need to remind you, dear brother, that this bank draft represents the remainder of your inheritance from our beloved father. I have sent the entire amount as you requested. So this represents all of your money. The only other expectation you can have is for a modest inheritance of no more than several hundred *Taler* when Mother joins our Father in their heavenly home. So we all urge you to be very careful in taking care of the money I am sending."

CHAPTER 13

Johann pointed at the riverbank. "Look over there, Marta, right where I'm pointing. See that place where the trees are all cleared from the bank. That's where we'll land." The morning light made the forest look lush. "When I was here all the trees were bare. It looks so much better with leaves on the trees."

Marta shifted baby Emma to her other shoulder. Several families were lining the rail of the riverboat. They, too, were planning to land at Helvetia. The night before in the deck house Johann, the only one in the group who had actually been in the new town, was telling them all of his experiences. His excitement had not diminished in the three months since his visit.

The whole crowd on the deck jumped, startled when the boat's whistle gave a mighty blast as they neared the shore. There was now a wooden barge with a small hut in the center, a wharf boat, tied up at the shore, so the paddlewheeler was able to nose right up to the floating dock. After the passengers made their way onto the wharf boat and up the wide wooden ramp which bridged to the shore, roustabouts from the boat off-loaded their trunks and boxes and baskets from the piles on the deck. Each family tried to make sure that all its belongings were collected in one place on the landing.

A wagon pulled up to the landing. "Charlie Steinauer told me to come down and pick you folks up: second trip to the wharf boat today. We'll get all your stuff loaded on the wagon, then you can walk up to the hotel... right over there. Steinauer said he'd see you there. I'll bring the wagon to the hotel."

The air was full of sound as they walked together toward the hotel. There was the whine of the saw-mill punctuated by the puffing of its steam engine. The sound of hammering and sawing came from here and there in the wooded land. Johann saw that several new, substantial buildings were located along the main street. A few houses in various stages of construction showed through the trees.

Steinauer was waiting for them on the porch of the Mistletoe Lodge. "*Wilkommen, meine Freunde.* Welcome to Helvetia." Seeing Johann in the group, he held out his hand. "Well, you said you'd be back, and here you are. Is this the missus and your baby? *Guten Tag.*" Johann basked in the personal recognition.

Turning to the others, Steinauer continued. "We'll get you to your property as soon as we can. I suggest that the women and children just have chairs out here on the porch. You men come along with me to the office. We'll look at the map and show you where your lots are. To be perfectly legal, I'll have to see the deed that was sent to you last month. We've already learned the hard way that we need to have things all written out. A few of the early birds got into squabbles because two families would think that the same lot was theirs....Come on in."

Gathered around the surveyor's map of the town, Steinauer showed the new settlers which lots had been drawn for them. "When they had the lottery in Cincinnati, they would indicate two lots and then draw the name of a member. They started with the lots closest to Main Street and then moved out to other blocks. You have my word that it was very fair. Nobody got any special advantage.

"This is John Selbert. He's the agent for the Swiss Colonization Society. He's the one who signed your deeds, He'll show you how to get to your lots."

The men looked at the blocks that were laid out on the map. Steinauer continued, "Weber, since you have already visited here, let's take you first. You've got Block 60, Lot 21 and 22. That's over here on Twelfth Street." He pointed to a location on the map with a stick.

"Who's next? Reiff? Let's see. Here you are. You're on Eighth Street, down toward the south end." Each householder found out where he would be building. Selbert made out small certificates for each, verifying that they held the deed to those lots.

Steinauer talked to the families on the porch. "Just leave your stuff here. It'll be all right. You're going to want to see your lots right away. Then you can come back here and decide how you'll get started. Some families have pitched tents on their lots while they cut down the trees and get their houses started. Some have stayed here at the hotel for a couple of weeks until they had a building on the lot that they could stay in while the house is finished."

Johann carried baby Emma as he and Marta walked up the bumpy streets toward their lots. They were little more than rutted tracks through the woods, pocked by small craters where stumps had been burned out. The only mark that this was a laid out city was that the tracks ran straight, intersected by other tracks running a right angles. The land was rolling, small hills separated by little gullies. A creek, called Windy Creek, ran down to the river. Crude street signs were nailed to trees at each corner. "Here's Twelfth Street. Let's see what the numbers are on the stakes....This one is 46....Let's look at the next one to see which way the numbers are running. This one is 45, so our lots are down this way. This street coming up from the river has a sign Hermann Street."

Looking at the stake at Lot 22, Johann said, "*Zwei und zwanzig.* This is it! And that lot next to it. This will be our home." Marta took his hand as they stood before the lot.

"Will we put the house right here?"

Johann looked over the land carefully. "Lot 21 looks more level. There are good big trees that will give us lumber."

Marta said excitedly, "We haven't even talked about what kind of house we want."

"We'll have to find a carpenter to work with us. I can do a lot of the work, but we'll hire a few fellows to help us. I'll talk to Steinauer about how to get started. The first thing will be to cut these trees and get the stumps out."

"They're building two houses on the street behind us. We could talk with them."

"We'll find Becker first. He's been here for a couple of months and will know the people to talk to."

"Let's get back to the hotel now and get a room for a few weeks. Or maybe there's a rooming house. I can't come out here with the baby until we have part of the house closed in."

While they were still walking along the rough street, Marta asked, "Where are you going to keep our money to pay for the house. We can't keep carrying these little bags with gold coins around our waists."

"I heard Steinauer say something about a bank in this town called Coaltown. I want to ask him if it is a good safe place. We can't risk losing all our money. If he can vouch for the bankers, I think I'll see if I can get a ride over there and put the money in the bank. Julius was right; this is all we have, so I want it in a safe place."

"Do you think the house will use all the money?"

"It better not. I think we need to be sure that we still have some left in the bank when the house is done, so we have something to fall back on if we need it."

Becker explained to Johann that since all the new settlers were working hard to put up their own buildings, men had come in from the surrounding countryside to work. With Becker's help Johann was able to hire two of these men to help him clear their lot. They felled seven large trees and cut the logs in lengths, rolling them to the edge of the street to be dragged to the saw-mill. The smaller trees and brush were cleared, piled over the stumps to burn them out.

A carpenter from Coaltown had established a thriving business as an advisor, craftsman for particular tasks, and teacher. Working with half a dozen settlers, he helped to plan and lay out the houses, got the owners started on each stage of the construction, undertook the more technical tasks of setting the rafters and framing the windows and doors.

The carpenter, Ernst Fleischer, smiled when Marta listed all the things she had in mind for their house. "You'd better buy a couple more lots, Weber," he laughed. "This little lady has a mansion in mind."

Marta laughed too. "You men don't do all the dreaming. I know, really I do, that we can have only a small house. So let's get to work." Together they planned a simple three-room house, with a loft that could be a second bedroom.

The logs were dragged to the sawmill and added to the growing piles of timber that surrounded the mill. A large steam engine, belching smoke, was connected to the saw by a wide leather belt. Half a dozen men placed logs on the platform that moved back and forth as the saw cut off plank after plank from each log.

John Hermann, who with his brother Peter were the sawyers, explained to Johann that it was best if wood had a chance to dry before being used. He said, "Most of the wood here is green. So what I've been doing is sawing first the logs that were cleared from the streets last winter. It dries some in the stacks of planks and boards. The deal I've been making with the people is this: We'll measure the logs you bring in. I'll give you the same amount of lumber that will come out of those logs, charging you only for the sawing. You're not getting your own wood back because I'll let your logs dry as long as I can. But you won't be cheated. You probably will need to buy more lumber as your work goes on. We get some lumber from other towns along the river. It comes in by keelboat or steamer every couple of weeks. So you get Ernst to give you a list of what you're going to need and we'll get you the best wood possible."

Ernst said to Johann and Marta after they had finished driving stakes to show the boundaries of the house, "I've got a suggestion for you. You're going to need a shed behind the house anyway. Why don't we build the shed first. If you don't mind being cramped, you could live in the shed for a few weeks until the house is finished enough to move in."

"*Was denkst?*" Johann asked Marta.

She said, "It wouldn't be much more crowded than that little room at the hotel, and we'd save some money. If we can make it good enough for Emma, I'm willing." So the shed was built first.

A farmer with his team and a scraper began to dig out a small cellar and trenches were dug for the foundation of the house. Johann had learned enough as a mason's helper in Davenport to be able to put in the foundation walls. In the days that followed the house began to take shape.

Groups of families would gather in the evenings to talk about their progress. Wives and mothers began to help each other. The men also organized informal groups to help one another at particular stages of building requiring more than one man: raising rafters, putting on roofs. There now were close to a hundred buildings under construction. Steinauer announced that the population was now over 700.

The earliest buildings were very crude. Frank Herm's log cabin at the corner of Eighth and Tell was pointed to as the first house built in the new town. There were several more cabins made just of logs; others were shanties of rough-sawn planks. Most of the houses began as fairly crude buildings whose only purpose was shelter. Once erected, they could be lived in. Niceties like weatherboard siding, trimming, porch railings would be added as planed lumber became available. Windows and doors came by boat from mills in other towns.

In mid-summer a great celebration was held in the town. According to plans made months before, a steamer was coming from Cincinnati with a large group of Swiss and Germans, 600 members of the Society who were not yet residents of the new town. They came for a three day stay to celebrate progress and to visit their friends among the settlers. Their pilgrimage was designated the Second Convention of the Swiss Colonization Society.

Preparations were underway for days. Charles Steinauer had a large banner painted which was hung between two large trees above the landing. It announced to the world: "Helvetia: A City of the Future." A band from Coaltown was engaged to play. Scrap wood from the building and tree clearing was gathered for a huge bonfire along the riverfront. Crude tables and benches of slab wood were knocked together behind the saw-mill. A steamer brought in food Charles Steinauer had purchased with Society funds, to be prepared by all the Helvetia women for a great community picnic. All the families in town were persuaded to lay aside their work for a day or two to participate in the celebration.

The great day arrived and the paddle-wheeler *Prairie Rose* churned up to the landing in mid-afternoon. The band had been picked up by the boat in Coaltown an hour earlier and were playing mightily on the top deck.

The town was decorated with a number of Swiss and American flags. Many of the Helvetia settlers had come from Cincinnati and were shaking hands with old friends as they got off the boat. Others, like Johann and Marta, knew none of the visitors and hung back on the fringe of the crowd. Very soon it became evident that a common interest in Helvetia made everyone old friends. Perfect strangers began to converse about experiences in the new town. As the crowd began to spread out, people who had never met before were being given conducted tours through the newly built houses. Groups strolled the dusty streets with their wagon tracks down the middle.

In late afternoon the whistle of the *Prairie Rose* gave three sharp toots. This was the signal for everyone to gather for a picnic in a wooded section near the hotel where all the tables and benches had been assembled. Tables loaded with the bowls of food which the women had prepared were set out. Since early morning an ox had been roasting over a fire pit, with teams of men in successive shifts turning the spit. Men with long sharp knives cut legs off the ox carcass, put them on wide boards, and began carving them. Lines formed with people holding their plates to be served. A wagon pulled up with barrels of beer for all. For the next few hours they feasted and talked. Children played in the woods, running in and out among the trees to hide in the growing twilight.

Conversations were all about the new town. The folks from Cincinnati were full of questions about what life was like in Helvetia. Most of them hoped to move there within the next year or two. They had gone to locate the lots they had received in the drawing. Husbands and wives talked about the kind of houses they would build. They tried to find people who had built or would build on adjacent lots, their new neighbors.

When the sun had set, everyone gathered on the river bank and the huge bonfire was lit. The band played on. A few of the folks tried to dance on the boat landing. Others sat, looking into the fire, talking, dreaming of the future. Mothers took little ones off to bed. Many of the visitors stayed on the *Prairie Rose*. Settlers, carrying burning pine torches or lanterns, wound down the streets to their houses.

The *Prairie Rose* lay in port for two more days. Some passengers bought their meals at the hotel and boarding houses. The saloons put out tables of food for their patrons. Simple meals were also served on the boat. Some had brought their own food supplies in hampers. At night many of the visitors went back on the steamer and slept in cabins, the deck house, and on deck. A few stayed with friends in the new town. Others filled the hotel and rooming houses beyond capacity. Tents were pitched in the clearing along Main Street.

On the second day there was a great gathering in the large clearing in the center of town. There were many benches and stools from the picnic, but most of the crowd stood in the late afternoon sun. A wagon was the platform for the officers to conduct the business meeting of the Society. There were reports on membership, on the balance in the treasury, on plans for the future. The crowd wildly applauded every indication of success. The major item of business was the Treasurer's proposal that in order to build the economic foundation of the community, the Society should grant low interest loans up to $1000 to new businesses that would employ at least 12 persons. There was a loud shout of "*Ja!*" from the assembly when it was put to a vote.

Some of the visitors were so enthusiastic about the new town that they moved up their plans to come to Helvetia. A few single men even decided to stay and arranged for friends to pack their belongings and send them by steamer to Helvetia.

The last day of the visit Marta saw a young woman walking around in the trees next to their unfinished house. Wiping her hands on her apron and carrying Emma, she went out to talk with the visitor.

"*Ich bin Marta Weber.*"

"*Ich bin Sadie Ullrich.* My man and I have Lots 23 and 24, right next to your place."

"Would you like to come over and sit by our little shed?" Marta asked. "We're living in there until the house is finished enough to move in."

Marta motioned to the chairs in the shade in front of the shed. Sadie looked to be in her early twenties. She kept pushing her brown curls out of her eyes. She dabbed at the perspiration on her forehead and brushed the dust from her skirts as she rocked back and forth.

"Is it hard to get started? Compared to Cincinnati it all seems so wild and strange. Don't you miss living in a city?"

Marta answered, "The only place we lived in America before coming here was in Davenport. We only had a room there, not a house. I was pregnant most of the time we were there, so I didn't get out into the city much. In Silesia I lived most of my life in a nice old town, not a village, but not a city either. So this has all been new to me, but having my own place more than makes up for everything being rather rough. The people here are nice, and we're making friends."

"But so many things are missing. Is there a school? Where are the churches? What do you do for a doctor?"

"They say that we'll have all those things in the next year. Right now everything is going into building houses."

"I hope that by the time we get here it won't be quite so...wild." Sadie looked at the shed in which Marta and Johann were living until they could move into the house. "I've always lived in cities like Zurich and Cincinnati. I'm not sure I'm cut out to be a pioneer in the woods."

"Once you are actually part of the people here, it won't feel so strange. We all help each other."

They were interrupted by a long blast of the steamboat's whistle. "That is supposed to be our signal to go to the boat," Sadie said.

"It was good to get acquainted. We'll see you some time next year. Come on, little Emma, let's go down to the river and say goodbye to our friends."

The house of Twelfth Street took shape nicely, surrounded by several large shade trees. It was a storey and a half, with a porch across the front and a smaller porch at the kitchen door on the south side. The brick chimney Johann had built reached through the steeply pitched roof. After Johann finished putting on the siding in another month, he planned to paint it gray, with black trim.

When Johann and Marta were able to move from the shed to their partially completed house at the end of summer, they sat in their kitchen eating supper as twilight enveloped the town. The kitchen contained only their stove, a table and two chairs. The sturdy boxes they had brought across the ocean were stacked like shelves in the corner to form a primitive kitchen cabinet.

"This is the first time since we left home that some of these dishes have been out of the boxes. We never had room for them before. Now we've got our own house," Marta purred.

"You've waited a long time for this, haven't you?"

"For the first time, I feel like we're finally settled down. For more than a year the only thing we knew was that we would soon be moving on to someplace else. Now we are where we are going to live."

Johann looked around the unfinished room. "We'll probably be here longer than the house will. I tell you, these places are just thrown together. I've tried to see that we got a strong house, but there just isn't the good material. Most of the wood is so green that it bleeds when you pound in a nail. When I think of the house I grew up in Endigen, it had stood there for generations. It felt solid, like it was rooted right into the earth. These places feel like they would blow over in a strong wind."

Marta smiled, "Don't you talk that way about MY house."

"It does feel good to think that we are finally settled into America. Are you sorry we came?"

Marta thought for a moment before answering. "There have been plenty of days when I wished we were back in Neuhaus, but now that we're here in our own house, I'm glad we came. The only thing I really wish for is little Karl." She put her hand on Johann's arm, "But I'm glad we're here now."

Johann opened his *Tagebuch* on the table and added to the column of figures. Marta asked, "Do we still have enough money to finish the house?"

"So far we've spent nearly $200. Ernst thought that it would take about $50 more to finish it. So that won't take all our money. We should have at least a hundred dollars or more left when the house is all done."

"That we're going to have to save in case we have trouble."

"You bet. I should be able to start bringing in some wages as soon as I don't have to work on the house any more."

"You've been working so hard. It's saving us a lot, but it will be nice to have some money coming in again."

"Don't you worry. Things are going to start working out now that we're settled."

"I know. I just know that things are going to get better."

During the next months the town really began to take shape. As more and more families were able to occupy their houses, businesses began to spring up along Main Street. The saw-mill had been first, an obvious necessity. It wasn't long before Haussler established an adjacent lumber yard. Shipments of planed lumber and millwork arrived from Cincinnati and Louisville. There were at least four saloons, rough plank buildings put up along the riverfront. Signs proclaiming *"Lager Bier"* were hung on the front walls. Barrels of the promised nectar were stacked in cellars behind the saloons. Jacob Loew started a shingle factory, splitting and bundling cedar shingles for the roofs of Helvetia. Just downstream from the town, Heim's brickyard began to produce material for building chimneys. Wood was in such ample supply that brick buildings were a rarity at first. Two general stores began to supply food and clothing for the new residents.

Ferdinand Becker had the merchandise from the store he had had in Davenport shipped to Helvetia and soon opened his new store, full of men's work clothes and some Sunday suits. He was constantly talking to his customers about the excitement of the new town, a fact with which they were well acquainted. Each day saw new arrivals and houses were being started all over town. This rapid growth got attention in many other communities up and down the river. Becker had posted in his store window an article from the Coaltown *Reporter* about Helvetia.

> "Helvetia is a marvel. There is nothing like its history and progress, and it has no precedent. It now has over 11 miles of street, cut 70 feet wide through the forest, has 1500 people and 300 houses. All this has been done since April 15. The shareholders are coming in daily, and as soon as they can find their lots, commence the improvements....By this time next year we expect to see 5000 people here, and the establishment of sufficient branches of industry to give full employment. This union of German and Swiss, of energy and economy, of thrift and industry will accomplish wonders."

Knowing that few of his customers read English, he put a carefully written German translation beside the article. The next evening Johann took Marta to read the article.

Marta said, "You said you were going to write to your mother. You should tell them all this, to give them an idea of how Helvetia is growing."

The planners for the town, who were officers of the Colonization Society, were, for the most part, well-educated Swiss. They saw their new town as a focus of learning being carved from the forest. As they plotted the town, they had given the north-south streets numbers. But to the streets running in from the river they gave the names of great heroes. There were American heroes: Washington, Jefferson, Franklin. To this they added Europeans who had fought heroically for American independence: Lafayette, DeKalb, Steuben. To honor inventors they named a street for Watts and another for Fulton. Education, science, literature, art were valued with streets named for Pestalozzi, Humboldt, Schiller, Rubens, Mozart, and Gutenberg. While all the settlers mastered the names of the streets, the majority were completely unaware of the rich historical legacy being conveyed.

Not all the newcomers were as fortunate as Marta and Johann. Some weeks so many new settlers arrived that there was no place for them to stay. The Society had put up a few houses to be rented. They were in such short supply that most of these dwellings had two families living in them. A few recent arrivals became discouraged and went back to Cincinnati and Louisville without even taking their belongings off the wharf.

A few people found that their lots were on streets which had not yet been fully cleared. Only the surveyor's stakes showed where the streets would be. It was impossible to get wagons to their lots, so construction was out of the question for the present.

The Colonization Society had given Alois Frey responsibility for overseeing the development of the city. Except for Charles Steinauer, all the officers of the Society lived in Cincinnati or Louisville or St. Louis. Frey had many issues which had to be decided promptly, so he was unable to consult the officers. Men whose lots were clearly unbuildable because of gulleys or rock outcroppings demanded that they be exchanged for lots which had not yet been claimed by those who were assigned to them in the lottery. There was a lot of pounding on Frey's desk in his small office near the boat landing.

Frey confronted all the frustrations of day to day operations. He tried to deal with the shortage of materials which thwarted many who were ready to move ahead with building. He sent urgent letters to lumber yards and mills in other cities, begging that materials be sent as soon as possible. Sensing the shortages, the suppliers promptly raised their prices, which put an additional burden on the homebuilders in Helvetia, who took out their anger on Frey.

The visionaries of the Colonization Society had laid out their dream for a large, thriving city. They had unlimited confidence that settlers would rush to the site and that overnight there would be a finished community of homes. They believed that industries would spring up on the edge of the river to provide jobs and support the city's economy. They implemented schemes for subsidizing employers to get these businesses started. They sought investors up and down the Ohio and Mississippi valleys to respond to their dream.

Frey, on the other hand, faced the daunting responsibility of making that dream come true. For him it had the characteristics of a nightmare as he struggled with shortages of material, wide street right-of-ways still clogged with large trees or stumps in spite of their fancy names. He complained that the city plan was "*zu groszartig.*" The urgent reports he dispatched to the officers were filled with pleas for a more realistic approach. All the officers could think of was the enthusiasm and good feeling present at the time of Society's Convention visit. They tended to dismiss Frey's pessimism and began to think about getting a manager who could share their vision.

Once their house was finished, Johann found work on new houses being built for the steady stream of new settlers. The Society began in earnest to build more houses on a number of lots that had not been drawn in the lottery. These houses were to be rented by the Society to settlers who were not able to build their own dwellings.

On the strength of the work he had done in finishing his own house, Johann got work lathing and plastering the houses built by the Society. He already knew how to mix mortar, so mixing the plaster was not difficult. In a few days Fleischer had shown him how to lath and plaster his own walls. There was so much building that the work was steady. It was a relief to have some pay coming in regularly.

When Johann came home from work one September evening, he saw that Marta had put a letter in the supper table. Only a month before, the first post office had been opened in Helvetia. John Hermann, one of the saw-mill owners, was the first postmaster. Marta had formed the habit of stopping every few days at the little post office next to the mill, hoping for a letter from her parents or Johann's family. She usually came away empty handed, but this afternoon there had been a letter. It was an answer to a long letter she and Johann had written to Adolph Hanke in Davenport telling him about life in their new town and giving their new address: Helvetia, Indiana, and expressing the hope that Adolph might come to live there..

"Wait until you see Adolph's news," she said. "It's all in his letter."

Johann began to read:

> "You will be surprised that I just got married. When Annie died last winter, I was so alone. I couldn't take care of little Gretel because I had to go to work. A neighbor woman let me bring Gretel to her house when I worked but that couldn't last. I had to get married again to have somebody to look after Gretel. One of the fellows at work said that I should bring Gretel with me to *Mittagessen* at his house Sunday. His wife had a friend visiting her, woman called Marie. She comes from Saxony. After dinner she held Gretel on her lap and told her stories. Then my friend and his wife said they would take Gretel for a little walk. Marie and I talked about how we both came to America. She told me that she come here to marry a fellow from her home town, just like me and Annie. But while she was on the ocean, he got killed when his team ran away. So she needed somebody too. My friend had told her all about me and Gretel. He must have done a good job, because when I told her I wanted to get married, she said it was all right with her. I know that was moving very fast but we both saw that we needed each other. The next day we went to the *Pfarrer* and he married us in his front room. She's working hard to get our house in shape once again. I wasn't able to do much around here...working such long hours. I know this was all very fast, but both of us needed each other. I think you'd like Marie. She is a good worker. Gretel is right at home with her, but she still cries when anybody talks about Annie."

"I could still cry too when I think of Annie dying so young," Marta said. "I know it was very hard for Adolph to get along without a woman in the house. When you've got a whole ocean between you and your family, there just isn't anybody to help when trouble comes. I worry about that a lot."

"*Ja*, it isn't easy."

"If anything ever happened to me, you'd have to find another wife to take care of Emma."

"I don't even want to think about that," Johann answered.

"Well, it's one of those things that can happen when you're so far away from your family, like Adolph said."

"Some of the single fellows were talking about letters they were writing home to see if there were girls who would come over to marry them. They sit around and think about all the girls without husbands they knew at home. That tall fellow that works at the store, Ludwig, said he had sent letters to girls in his home village. He's willing to send money for their ticket. I think he has one in particular that he hopes will come, but he says he'll marry any girl who is willing to come. You probably see him when you go to the post office. He says he goes every time the mail comes."

"How can he have enough to support a wife?" Marta wondered.

"Most of these single fellows have to live in boarding houses. Ludwig told me that he pays so much for his room and meals and laundry that it will cost very little more to pay for two of them in their own place. He's probably right."

Just a few days later as Marta was approaching the little post office to see if there were letters from home, she heard a whoop. Ludwig was standing in the doorway waving a letter.

"She's willing to come!" he shouted over and over. Recognizing Marta from her visits to the store, he couldn't contain himself. "Sadie Zirbel said she'll come and be my wife. She's a good woman. My prayers are answered. She said I have to write to her parents and send her the money for the ship."

Marta looked at the happy face dancing before her eyes. "I'm happy for you. Did you know her well at home?"

"I wrote three girls I knew in my home town and I had my sister talk to them.. I would have been glad if any one said 'yes.' But deep down inside I was hoping Sadie would be willing to come. Wait till you meet her. She's such a nice girl, always a smile on her face. She's pretty--you'll see. I'm goin' to write to her father tonight to tell him about Helvetia and my job at the store. I hope he'll let her come. He knew me when I was growing up. He's knows I won't just get her over here and then leave her in the lurch."

"You tell her the truth, Ludwig. Don't get so carried away that you don't tell her that for a while this isn't an easy place to live."

"She'll like it here. I just know she will. Already Helvetia is bigger than our village. She'll have all the nice ladies like you to help her get acquainted."

"Do you have the money to send for her right away?"

"I've been saving from my pay ever since I got here. I ate a lot of dry bread and haven't bought a stitch of new clothes, but I've got enough. I'll send her 35 dollars for the ticket and another ten dollars for her trunk. If she comes on the boat to *Neuorliens*, she can come all the way up the river to here for only 2 1/2 dollars. I've been talking to the fellows on the boats that stop here."

"Are you going to send the money before her father gives permission?"

"I'll just tell them that if she can't come for any reason, they should just give the money to my family over there. I'd trust them to do that."

"Will you have enough money left to get set up in housekeeping?"

"We won't have a whole lot. We'll get one of those houses the Society is renting to people until they have enough to start buying it. We can live pretty plain for a while. Lot's of folks are doing that. You don't have everything you want in your house, but you're happy to have it, aren't you?"

"You young folks will do all right. You let me know when she is going to get here on the river boat. I'll get a few of the other women to help her feel welcome."

Telling Johann about her conversation with Ludwig, Marta said, "I hope he's honest with her. I worry about letters that say this is the Promised Land. These girls need to know that life is pretty hard in a town which a year ago was forest. They shouldn't think they are going to have an easy time."

"Is it that bad for you?"

"Well, I'm happy that we are finally getting our own house, but it's not a palace. I'd have to admit that I was a lot more comfortable in Neuhaus and I didn't feel so cut off from family."

"Give it some time. You'll see! I believe them when they say that Helvetia is going to be a fine place to live in a few years. It's very hard getting started, but it's going to get better."

"I'm not saying that I'd rather be back in Neuhaus, at least not all the time. But I do hope those fellows aren't telling the girls that they can just sit in the shade and enjoy the good life."

"You wait till you see this place in a few years. People will be so glad they came here. It's going to be a prosperous city. As soon as there are enough houses for people to live in, the factories will start going up along the river.. There will be jobs for everyone. You just watch."

"I still think that the men who try to talk girls into coming to live here ought to be honest."

"Haven't I been honest with you? I thought we both wanted to be here."

Marta's lip quivered. "Of course, I want to be with you. You never lied to me. But can you honestly say it has turned out to be as good as you thought it would be?"

"I didn't really know what to expect. I guess I did think that it would be plenty easy to make a good living. I didn't know that we'd arrive at a time when there weren't many jobs and money was short. I never imagined that we'd be living in a new city being cut out of the forest. It is more primitive than anything we've known before. But I have the feeling that the future is really starting to open for us. In a year or two things will be good for us. There will be money coming in regularly; we might even add onto our house."

"We've been lucky enough to have the money you inherited from your father to get us started. I've talked to some of the women who are really worried. They are running out of money or are already in debt."

"I know there are some that are close to the edge. But lots of people are coming with gold. They've been saving or have money they brought from the homeland. They've got enough to pay their bills."

"But some of the women say that because some people have enough money to pay for the lumber and bricks and hardware, when there isn't really enough here for everyone to buy, the prices keep going up."

"Don't you start losing sleep over other people's problems. We're going to get along fine," Johann reassured her.

"I feel sorry for some of the people. They said at the store that some families are giving up and moving back to where they came from. It's just getting too expensive here."

"They can't have planned very well. I feel sorry too, but there is work here, helping with the building."

"You are earning enough to buy our food and clothes, but if we didn't have the money from your inheritance to pay for the house, we'd be bad off too."

"That's true. But some folks thought they could just get along by magic. All they had to do was wish for a house and there'd be one."

The colorful leaves were falling from the trees. More lots were cleared along Twelfth Street and Eleventh Street behind them. The sounds of hammers and saws filled the shortening days from dawn to dusk as one house after another took shape. Johann often worked for new neighbors when they were putting up rafters or building chimneys in addition to his plastering jobs. The women gathered nearby and new friendships were begun.

"I've gotten to know the nicest woman," Marta told Johann. "They just started putting up that house on the corner. She's so friendly. Their name is Frantz. She is Matti and he is Paulus."

"*Ja*, I met him. He was helping with the logs over at Schneider's. Big fellow, strong as an ox, but he has a bad limp. He said he was hurt in Cincinnati and his leg never mended right."

"She's one of the friendliest people I've met here. She works hard too, but she's never too busy to visit a little. They come from near Stuttgart. She said they lived in Cincinnati for three years before they came here a couple of weeks ago."

"I can't keep all these women straight. I always see them in groups and don't know who is who."

"Matti is the one with the red hair. She has a little girl just a little older than Emma."

"All right. I know who you're talking about now. She always seems to be smiling or laughing."

"Nothing much bothers her. I guess that's why everybody likes her. Most of us stand around worrying about how things will turn out. She just says, 'Quit worrying about it. Things will turn out; you'll see.' She'd be good for us, because we seem to worry all the time."

"Her husband seems to have his feet on the ground. They tell me he's a school teacher. As soon as they get their house finished, he's going to start the school. The Society is hiring him to be the teacher. The teachers we had at home were smart men, but always seemed to be little shriveled up fellows. Paulus is a strong man, even if he has that bad leg. There won't be any nonsense in his classroom. One day he'll be Emma's teacher."

"He speaks good *Hochdeutsch*. With all these dialects around here-- Swiss, Swabian, Saxon, Bavarian--he'll have a job getting all the kids to talk good German."

"How about good English?"

"Most of the parents think German is enough, so all the teaching will be in German. There are a few people who can speak enough English to help us get along with the *Amerikaner.* We can get along fine as long as we're here in Helvetia."

Johann pondered, "I'm perfectly satisfied with them learning their lessons in German, but I wish they could learn some English too. Just remember all the problems we had coming across the country because we couldn't read or talk English. They won't need it here in Helvetia where everybody speaks German, but with all the river boats going up and down every day, some of the young people are going to want to go to other towns to work. They'll need to know some English."

"It would feel funny if Emma learned English and we couldn't talk or read a word of it. I don't know....."

"It's a few years before you have to worry about that."

Even when winter came, the building went on. Johann had found work laying brick to build a new factory along the riverfront. This was the beginning of the Colonization Society's ambitious scheme to develop industry in the new city. The Society had set aside land near the river for factories. Recognizing that as soon as the building of homes was completed there would need to be jobs in the city, they set about to encourage the development of factories. Lots along the river were sold for $1 a front foot. If a factory owner pledged to employ more than ten workers, he was given a lot with 100 feet frontage. Once the factories were built, the Society also offered loans of $500 to $1000 at only 6% interest to get the businesses going. Owners who had been given lots for factories would not receive the deed for the land until they had been in business for five years.

Johann was glad to see the furniture factory taking shape. The winter weather kept them from working some weeks, but Johann used the time to work on their own house, putting finishing touches here and there. The perennial problem of lost wages due to winter weather continued to plague them. He managed to make enough to cover their living expenses but the savings they had hoped for did not materialize.

In the fall Hans and Sadie Ullrich had come back from Cincinnati to build on the lot next to Johann and Marta. Now only the frame of their house stood silhouetted against the trees and the snow.

Marta looked sadly at the skeleton of a house. "It makes me sad to think that we've lost our neighbors," she said to Johann as they ate their supper.

"Hans said they will come back in the spring to finish," Johann answered.

"I think not. Sadie didn't do much except complain about all the hardship here. She hated this place. They weren't like some of the folks who just went away because their houses weren't finished enough to live in during the cold weather. Mark my words, the Ullrichs won't be back."

"Then they are better off back in Cincinnati. I could tell that something was wrong. Hans never had the excitement most of the men have when they are building. I offered to help him a number of time but he always turned me down. I remember thinking once: I don't think he really wants to finish the house."

"I suppose they'll be able to sell the lot and the frame of the house to someone who wants to live here."

"There have been so few new people showing up during the winter, the town seems to have stopped growing. It's so different than the last two years when there was a steady stream of families coming."

"The winter is a hard time. Maybe in the spring people will start coming."

Some dreams collapsed; some dreams went on the shelf for the time-being, some dreams persisted--with difficulty.

CHAPTER 14

The hills to the east of Helvetia were wreathed in fog. A light rain outlined the bare branches of the trees with diamond drops. Undergrowth in the wooded areas was beginning to show tinges of green as spring buds appeared. The town in its state of chronic incompletion looked shabby indeed. Unpainted wooden walls, up and down the street, took on variegated colors, ranging from dark gray to tawny yellow, depending on how long the boards had been exposed to the weather. The weather tempered the enthusiasm of the town visionaries and deepened the discouragement of those who were no longer sustained by the dream.

"Wipe that mud off your boots before you come in here!" Marta complained. "Better yet, take them off and leave them by the door! Did you ever see such a mess? Mud everywhere! I'm going crazy just trying to keep the floor wiped up."

"It's hard to move around town since winter turned to spring. Wagons are stuck up to their axles trying to bring materials to the buildings we're putting up. We spend more time digging and pushing and pulling than we do laying bricks. We'll never get that furniture factory finished at this rate."

"Hannah Leinig stopped in this morning. She said they can't get their furniture from the river to their house. It came down on the steamer from Louisville, but there it sits on the wharf boat. It's furniture that Kurt made with his own hands. It's been packed in crates for months and she misses it so much. Until they can get their own stuff, they've been living with straw mattresses on the floor and a few boxes and a table Kurt knocked together out of left-over lumber."

"He's supposed to be a good cabinet maker. I heard that he is going to be one of the foremen at the furniture factory. I never really talked to him, but I know him when I see him."

"She's real nice and friendly. Their house is over there on Rubens Street. They weren't able to get it finished enough to live in before the bad weather came. So they went back to Louisville for a couple of months. Hannah said that they have it good enough to live in now, while they finish it up. I'm sure glad we're past that point."

"This year the town will really get in shape. People will be able to build their houses a lot faster than we could because there are more workmen and a lot more material than when we got here."

"Hannah says she misses Louisville. I told her I didn't miss Davenport, but I do miss Neuhaus. I wish we'd get a letter soon. I miss Papa and Mutter Katerina, but most of all I'm dying to hear how little Karl is doing. Every night I think about him and wish I could see him." She turned her head so that Johann would not see the tears running down her cheeks. "Every time I see a lad about four years old I try to picture how he must look now."

"He's still not big enough to make the trip with some family from Neuhaus. Right now we wouldn't have enough room for him with Emma and the baby that is coming this summer."

Marta said quietly, "I'm not so sure you'll ever want him here."

Johann said nothing in response.

At that same time Charles Rabert was cursing the mud as he looked over the bare room of the frame building on Main Street where he was preparing to set up his newspaper office. A steamer from Cincinnati had the day before brought him, his wife, Gretchen, all their household belongings, and his precious printing press and type trays to Helvetia. *Die Zeitung* had been published in Cincinnati for two years under the sponsorship of the Society, after a few years as a struggling independent German newspaper. Now it was being moved to Helvetia which was destined to become a center for Swiss and German immigrants in the mid-west. The Society had erected a two-storey, rather crude, board and batten building in the center of the town. The first floor was to be the newspaper office and print shop, the second was a modest apartment for Rabert and his wife.

Rabert was an imposing figure, tall, broad shouldered, flowing hair which was beginning to gray at the temples, a scar on his left cheek. Unlike the other men in Helvetia he wore at the moment a well-worn black frock coat. But beneath this formal garment, his black trousers and boots were caked with mud.

The steep road down the river bank to the landing was so muddy that nothing was moving off the new wharf boat, a barge that had been floated down from Cincinnati and made fast to the shoreline with pilings. Two steamers could now tie up to unload cargo. There was a barnlike shed on the barge to shelter the cargo until it was hauled to its destination in the town. Due to the mud, the whole barge was piled high with boxes, barrels, and crates awaiting passable roads. The master of the wharf boat had at first tried to put the things that could be damaged by rain in the wareroom, putting the rest in high piles beside the building. Some of the piles had canvas tied over them. Owners or consignees of the freight paid anxious visits to the barge to see if their things were safe.

Charles Rabert ran his hands through his long hair impatiently. Gretchen was in their room at Mistletoe Lodge until their furniture could be brought ashore. He wished she were here. It was frustrating not to have anyone to listen to the eloquent tirade that was brewing inside his head. *Verdammten Wetter; Verdammten* mud; *Verdammten* delays.

It was critically important to get the weekly paper publishing regularly again. It was the only instrument for informing the Society's scattered members of progress in the new city. It was the main channel for encouraging people to join the growing number of families on the banks of the Ohio River as settlers in this new community. For two dollars a year people could learn about this wonderful new venture, as well as news of the larger world. But nothing was going to happen with the press probably getting rusty down on the wharfboat. No new settlers were going to be recruited until he was able to start setting type. *Verdammten* weather!

The front door swung open and Charles Steinauer stomped in. "Your missus was afraid you were stuck somewhere in the mud when you didn't come back to the hotel. I was on my way to the saw mill, so I said I'd stop in. Well, what do you think of this place?" He looked around at the unplaned board walls, beginning to turn gray instead of their former yellow hue. "It's pretty crude now, I know, but I see it as only temporary. Once we really get organized, we'll be able to put up a good substantial building for the newspaper, and you can get a decent house to live in. We'll soon have you as well situated as I remember you were in Cincinnati. We in the Society gave you a lot of support there...and we will here too."

"I'm about ready to explode," Rabert said. "It's so damned frustrating to want to get started and to have everything stuck down at the river." His dark eyes flashed, and he ran his finger along the dueling scar that crossed his left cheek, a mark of his student days at Heidelberg.

Steinauer walked to the window. "If we have a few days of sunshine and a little breeze, things will dry out and we can start moving things. I thought about planking the little stretch of road down to the wharf. But the planks would get so slick from all the mud that the horses couldn't make it anyway. I can promise you that we know how important the paper is, and we'll try to get your stuff moved up here on the first wagon."

"I'm desperately anxious to get publishing again. We have subscribers all up and down the Ohio and the Mississippi valley and they haven't had a paper in a month. I warned them in the last issue we put out from Cincinnati that we were moving to Helvetia and would start publishing as soon as possible. If I can just get the press up and set type for a one page edition, I could let them know that we're back in business. I hope we won't lose too many subscribers with their two dollars a year. That's what keeps us going."

"I don't think you have to worry. There's a big demand for a German newspaper, not just here in Helvetia but wherever there are groups of Germans and Swiss. People depend on it to know what is going on in the world outside their town, as well as the town news. You'll see. You're not going to be hurt by moving to Helvetia."

"I'll do the best I can. It will certainly be different from Cincinnati. They had the telegraph there, so we learned what was going on in the world. Here I'll have to wait until I get newspapers from Cincinnati or Louisville or St. Louis before I can report the news."

"Most of these folks get all their news through *Die Zeitung,* so they'll be glad for whatever you are able to print. Everyone is too busy putting up buildings to do a lot of reading, but they talk plenty while they work. So they'll be talking about what they saw in *Die Zeitung.*"

"That's what a newspaper should do: make people think. It was the good newspapers and the universities that got people at home thinking in forty-eight. They woke people up."

Steinauer smiled, "You Forty-eighters haven't lost your *Zeitgeist,* have you? Still want to shake things up! Half of me wants to spur you on, and half of me says, 'Go slow.'"

When Rabert got back to the hotel, Gretchen was lying on the bed. She opened her eyes as he came into the room carrying his muddy boots. She said, "You don't have to be quiet on my account. I wasn't really sleeping." She smoothed her soft dark brown hair.

"I didn't want to track up the hall with these things, although downstairs everything is muddy. Somebody is going to have a lot of cleaning to do."

Rabert washed his hands in the basin of the wash stand. Walking two steps toward the bed, he folded his large frame into the wooden rocker next to the bed. His wife turned to face him. The day was so gloomy that even with the curtains open, the room was in twilight.

With a wan smile Gretchen said, "It makes me long for Cincinnati. I feel like I'm in the wilderness. I expect to see Indians with feathers in their headbands jumping out from behind the trees. What did the newspaper office look like?"

"It's pretty crude right now. It's just rough wood, but they tell me it is only temporary. There is a big room, about 20 by 30, which is where we'll put the press and type bench. Upstairs there is a little apartment for us. It has a small parlor, a big kitchen and a bedroom. It's nothing fancy; you'll see. But it is only until we can find a nicer house to rent."

Gretchen forced a smile. "We'll make it do. It's good that there are only the two of us. We wouldn't have room for any children in a little place like that."

"Things would be so different if we just had the money that should be coming from Papa's estate."

"I wish we could count on that. Your father has been dead for almost three years, and Wilhelm hasn't sent you any money."

Rabert's scar turned darker as his face hardened. "Who would think that a brother would cheat you! Why isn't he man enough to send me the money that is rightfully mine? If I were still in Freiburg, he wouldn't be able to do that to me. But here I am, half-way around the world. He can just forget about me; act like I don't exist."

"It is sad to think that someone you ought to be able to trust would be so treacherous."

"I'm sure he's publishing father's newspaper now. He probably doesn't want to sell it so that I can get my inheritance."

"At least he ought to be sending you some of the income from the paper. And your father must have had other investments. He was a good business man."

"There's money there, I know it! But Wilhelm just ignores me. We've had one little letter since he wrote to tell us that father was dead. He didn't say a word about the estate. He must have a dozen letters from me he has never answered. He's afraid to write to me because he doesn't have any intention of sending me what is rightfully mine."

"Maybe you ought to write to Bauer, the lawyer in Freiburg, and have him try to get what should be coming to you."

Rabert turned his head away. "I've thought of that, but I'm not sure he wouldn't just play the game too. He'd charge me big fees and take the money from any inheritance he was able to get out of Wilhelm."

"That's the trouble with being the younger brother, especially since you had to leave Heidelberg to come to America. You didn't have time to get all those details settled with your father. I'm sure he wanted you to have your share of his newspaper. He was proud of you. Oh, if only you had your inheritance, you could buy *Die Zeitung* from the Society and be the publisher of your own newspaper like your father."

"It would be a real chance to start a good business. Now all we have is the salary the Society pays me as editor and printer....Oh, well. We can get along on that."

"Once we get acquainted with all the new people here in Helvetia, you'll be an important man in the community. I know you must be one of the best educated men here."

"The women will get acquainted with you too. There will be lots of things to do once the whole place gets over this frantic building. When people get their own houses in order, once the new factories have plenty of jobs, people are going to want some of the things that give pleasure to life. There will be music and organizations where people can improve themselves. You'll see."

"Well, I'm going to stay right here in the hotel, if you can really call it that, until this sea of mud dries up. I'd ruin all my clothes if I'd go walking around in this mess."

August Wiesner could hear little Karl wailing as he opened the kitchen door. "What's going on? I could hear that yelling all the way down to the corner. All of Neuhaus is going to think we're killing that child."

Katerina pushed her hair out of her eyes. "I've tried everything to get him to stop. He broke the head off that little wooden horse you made for him. He's been screaming for twenty minutes."

"Well, let's see." August picked up the broken horse and put Karl on his lap, fitting the head onto the body of the horse. "I'll heat up my glue pot and we'll see if we can fix him. Now you just quit crying."

Karl sobbed a few more times and put his head on his Grandpa's shoulder.

"You are spoiling that child. You give him his own way in everything. He's going to have to learn that he can't have *everything* his own way."

"*Ja.* I feel so sorry for the little fellow, with his folks way on the other side of the world."

"I know, but he has us. I doubt if he even remembers Marta and Johann. It's been three years since they left."

"He may not remember what they look like, but he knows something isn't right."

"I try to take care of him."

"Of course you do. You took good care of the girls after we were married. I am very thankful for that."

"I tried. It was easier when I was younger. I am not like you. My patience has limits."

"We're getting a lot done with the summer days so long. Here it is half eight and there's still light enough to work." Kurt Leinig sat down at the kitchen table. "Supper smells good. Let's eat."

Hannah put out a bowl of steaming potatoes which she had cooked with a ham bone. "Get the children in here for supper. They were playing out in back."

Soon the little ones were sitting in their tall chairs. Magdalena rubbed her eyes as soon as she had eaten a few bites. "She's so sleepy, she's going to fall off her chair," Hannah said. "Here, let me hold her." The little blond head nestled against her shoulder.

Kurt said, "You know, I'm sad that they'll never see their grandmother. When I got brother Hans' letter yesterday that Mama died, it twisted my heart. I guess I knew when we left home that we'd never see them again. It hurt then, but it hurts now 'cause our children can never know any family back home."

"I think about that often," Hannah answered, wiping tears from her round face with her apron. "When our two babies died at home, your mother was there to help me. She did see Peter before we left...a little baby, but she never saw Magdalena, the baby we named after her."

"I feel like part of me was cut off when we left home." Kurt smiled at Hannah, "I know; I have you and the children. That's important, but when I think about Father and Mother and my brothers and sisters. I keep wondering how it goes with them. Ever' letter we get is filled with sad news that somebody died. Martha last year...and now Mother. We don't even know if Martha's baby lived. When the post office has a letter, the first thing I think is: who died now?"

"Hans is good to write you every year," Hannah said, "even if most of the letters have sad news. He wants to keep in touch. You hear more from your family than I do from mine. Only Papa is left and he never was much for writing. I try not to think about it. I never get any answer to my letters. Since Grandma died, he's all by himself. I'm the only family he has left and we got an ocean between us. Sometimes during the night I worry about not hearing anything from him. If I was a good daughter, I would have stayed there."

"He could've come long with us. We asked him. You could look after him here....Probably can't work much any more, but he could have a little garden and do a few odd jobs around the town."

"He'd be too old to come now. I'm not sure he could have stood the trip, even when we came. Someday I'll get a letter from somebody, probably *der Pfarrer*, telling me that he's dead. Or maybe he's been dead for a couple of years and no one bothered to write to us. It breaks my heart," she wept softly.

Kurt put his hand on her arm, "*Ja, es tut mir leid*! I was relieved that Father wrote that Mama died peacefully. That's some comfort. Just think, she died at the end of April and we're just hearing it now. She's been dead and buried for three months and we only start grieving now. It's like for the family she died in April and for us in July."

"We got to try to write more often. I want them to know about the children and about our new house here in Helvetia. I guess we did tell Hans that we were leaving Louisville to come here...Of course he knows... his letter came here."

"*Ja*. Down at the post office they were saying that a lot of letters don't get to people 'cause folks at home don't know that they have to put the name of the state on the letter. They just write *Amerika* and expect the letter to go to the right place." Kurt rubbed his balding head. "They just don't know how big this country is and how people move around trying to find a new home. They still think it's like at home, where families live in the same place generation after generation and everybody knows where people are."

"There are times I think I'd like that again," Hannah said. "I suppose that Hans and his family will move onto the farm now and take care of your father."

"It makes good sense because Hans has been farming that ground for ten years. Someday it'll be his anyway."

The sun had set in Neuhaus and Katerina Wiesner lit the lamp on the kitchen table. She had just put little Karl to bed and sat down with her mending. Turning to her husband who dozed in the rocker beside the kitchen stove, she said, "August, you awake?"

"*Ja.* I am now. I guess I fell asleep." He stretched.

"August, we have to talk about the little boy."

"What's the matter? Is he sick?"

"No; not that. It's just that I think he needs his Mama and Papa. It is more than three years since they left for America."

August lit a splinter from the fire in the stove and touched it to his pipe. "Is it that long? The older I get, the faster time goes."

"Karl doesn't even remember them. I show him that picture they gave us and tell him they are his Mama and Papa, but it doesn't mean anything to him. He even said, 'You are mama.' That broke my heart, I tell you."

"As soon as they get set up in that new place, he can go to them."

"Frau Schade told me that her son and daughter-in-law are going to America in the spring…some place called Missouri. I don't know where that is, but it might be near this Helvetia. Johann could go after the boy and then he'd be with them."

August scratched his head. "Well, I can write a letter and tell them. We'd miss the little lad, but, *richtig*, he should be with his Mama and Papa."

The first major community building project in Helvetia was the new schoolhouse. Leaders of the Colonization Society had always had a concern for education and had recruited families with the promise that a school would be built as soon as possible. Charles Rabert had written in *Die Zeitung* that a school was the most important investment for the community to make. He read his article to Gretchen at the dinner table in the little apartment.

Rabert put down his paper next to his plate. "If the people of Helvetia are ever going to really take their place in America, these children need education. Most of the older folks will keep on pretty much as they are, but the children will have to know more than their parents if they are really going to get ahead."

"It's going to be hard to get that across. There aren't many educated people here. You and Becker and, I guess, Paulus Frantz, are the only men who have been near the university. Most of the folks have just gotten what they could from their village schools at home."

"Don't let that fool you. There are quite a few very bright people here. They may not know any philosophy or literature, but they have had very practical educations. They read the newspaper faithfully. They can write what they need to write. They can do the arithmetic it takes to handle their money. It's part of my job through the paper to keep them learning."

"Once things settle down, maybe we can get a few programs: some good music, maybe we could have a play like I used to be in at home."

"It seems almost impossible in these very crude circumstances. But once we get over this terrible period of just building the basic structure of the city, we'll see what we can do. But first we've got to get that school going."

Even more pressure for a school came from parents. There were now more than fifty children of school age in Helvetia. Paulus Frantz had already been enlisted as the teacher. He spoke to several informal gatherings of parents and promised that as soon as a schoolhouse was available, he would begin.

The Colonization Society's funds were more and more strained by the problems of beginning the new city, but they dedicated $300 to build the school. Paulus and Albrecht Weisz were appointed to plan the school and organize construction. They planned the building on Tenth Street. It had two storeys, each of which had a classroom and a small room for a teacher. Since Paulus and Matti had built their own house, the room intended for the teacher in the new schoolhouse could be rented for income for the school.

During the summer, men who had finished their own homes were hired by the Society to work on the school. The building took shape quickly and was finished in record time because the entire community was anxious to have a school. Founding the school and erecting the building within the first year of the new city was a mark of its seriousness and stability.

"Well, the first day of school is over," Paulus Frantz sighed as he dropped his big frame into a sturdy chair at the kitchen table. "I don't really know why I'm so tired. Teaching isn't as hard as putting up a wall and climbing up and down ladders to shingle a roof."

"You've been working very hard getting the schoolhouse ready," Matti said. "How many children were there when you got started?"

"There were forty-six, between the ages of five and thirteen. They're good kids but it was hard. Many of the younger ones have never been to school. Their families have been on the move, some for more than a year. The older ones probably went to school in Cincinnati or Louisville, but it's been the better part of a year since they were in a classroom. So I had to spend most of the day just getting them sorted out, but I got the job done."

"I'll bet you did," Matti chuckled. "I can picture you towering over that mob of kids, ordering them around like a Prussian sergeant."

"That's about the way it was. 'Five, six and seven year olds over in that corner. Eights and nines over there. The rest of you in the back of the room.' I tell you, it took about three minutes to work that out. Then I had to get the older boys to help move the desks and benches around. Finally, we had everybody sitting down. That was a real accomplishment."

"Were some of the mothers there?"

"Those with little ones brought their children up to the schoolhouse and then went home. That little Weigel girl cried and cried. I finally told her mother to just leave her with me. As soon as mama was out of sight, she quit crying."

"Have those folks who wanted the teaching in English quieted down?"

"*Ja.* We'll start all the lessons in German. In a couple of of years, we'll start putting in some English for the older ones. Since practically all of them speak German at home, it won't be easy to get them going on English. We were talking about that in one of those meetings we have down at the newspaper. Rabert is really strong on that. You'd think that since he runs a German newspaper, he'd want to keep German strong. I was surprised that Johann is strong for learning English too. They say that if you are ever going to get ahead, outside of Helvetia, you're going to have to know English."

Matti smiled at her husband. "I don't see how you can handle 47 kids."

"It's just a matter of time until we have a second teacher. The society is ready to hire one as soon as we find the right person. They say they have enough money for paying each one of us thirty dollars a month and a cord of fire wood and a little place to live."

"I hope it doesn't take too long to find the new teacher. With new families coming in regularly, you're going to have more children than you can manage by yourself."

"The Society would like to start a high school in a year or two, when they have the money. Then we could really educate the older children: history, geography, English, maybe even singing and drawing. It's not enough for these children to have only reading and writing and a little simple arithmetic. It's going to take money, but people have to see that it's a good investment.

Since moving into the newspaper office, setting up the type tables and the Franklin Press, Rabert had resumed weekly publication of *Die Zeitung*. Copies of the paper were distributed through the town and sent with the mail on steamers going up and down the Ohio and Mississippi linking members of the Colonization Society with the new city of Helvetia.

Once established in Helvetia, Charles had encouraged some of the men in the community to join him for occasional after-supper conversations about politics. He took his role as an educator seriously. He found a kindred spirit in Paulus Frantz, who welcomed the chance for intellectual stimulation. He had known Rabert during the three years he was in Cincinnati and was glad to renew their acquaintance. He had suggested that two of the men from his neighborhood might also be interested. Kurt Leinig had lived in Louisville and would bring a different perspective, and Johann Weber was a recent immigrant. Although his background was strictly small town and he had only common education, he possessed an inquiring mind and seemed anxious to learn all he could about America.

About once a week, usually on Monday evening, they gathered at the newspaper office. With no particular pattern they took turns bringing beer in a covered tin pail from one of the many little saloons along Main Street. Pouring the lager into glasses Rabert provided, their lamp-lit discussions ranged from raucous political arguments to the editor's "university" lectures.

"I was a political activist at the university. When the authorities started cracking down on the student radicals in forty-eight, I had to get out fast. My father gave me money for a ticket to America and a little to get started over here."

Paulus said, "You were lucky; some students ended up in jail."

"But a lot made it over to America too. I spent a year in Baltimore and then traveled west to Cincinnati; I saw an advertisement for a journalist. I had worked for my father's newspaper between university terms, so they hired me as writer for a struggling German language paper."

"You were lucky to find a job," Johann added.

"*Ja.* The best luck I had was meeting Gretchen. She and her family had emigrated from Berlin at about the same time I came from Freiburg. Her parents weren't very enthusiastic about their daughter's marriage to a poor newspaper writer. They were afraid we would not have enough income to live comfortably. When the Swiss Colonization Society took over *Die Zeitung* and hired me as editor, they gave their blessing, but I tell you they weren't happy at all when I told them that the paper was being moved to the new city down the river."

"Well, you're here now," Paulus said. "They should be proud of what you have accomplished."

"I am excited by the possibilities. The newspaper is important in a democracy," Rabert argued. "If people are going to vote, they have to know what is going on. They have to understand politics."

"But," Paulus said, "only a couple of hundred men in town have been in the country long enough to vote. I still have one more year to wait before I have my five. So most of the men can't vote. Lot of them won't have much interest in politics."

Johann, recognizing that he was not as well-educated as the others, was hesitant at first to speak. "I never gave much thought to voting until I got to America. At home, like your homes, we didn't have much choice in anything to do with government. We could just hope we had a wise king who didn't demand too much tax or kill us off in wars. So it's a new idea for me to think about voting for who you want to be king--or I guess you say here, 'president.'"

Kurt Leining jumped into the conversation. "There are plenty of folks here who don't want us to vote. A couple of years ago, when we were living in Louisville, there was an election. On the day of the election a gang of roughnecks came into the section of the city where us Germans lived and started tearing things up. They wanted to scare people away from going to vote. They threw stones through windows and even set a couple of places on fire. The trouble spread. Some of the gangs had guns, some of the Germans fought back. The ruffians would find a German store and carry off the stuff and set fire to the store. They beat people up and shot some. Later, folks called it Bloody Monday, because more than twenty people got killed and lots more were hurt. The next few weeks a good many families, especially those who were just renting rooms or houses, packed up their stuff and left Louisville. We didn't leave right then, but it sure did help us decide to come here."

Paulus spoke up, "We had the same thing in Cincinnati in '55. The Know- Nothings lost a close election for mayor and started trouble. A mob started to attack the German neighborhoods, what they called 'Over the Rhine.' When the police didn't stop them, the *Turnverein* and some of the Germans with military experience put up barricades on the bridges over a canal and held off the mob. There was a lot of shooting. It was a regular battle for a while. Several people were killed and quite a few wounded. That's where I got this bad leg. I was one of those shot. The Germans beat off the attack of the Know-Nothings with a volley of rifle fire in which two of them were killed and some wounded. These Know-Nothings can be pretty tough."

"I can't believe this could happen. Isn't it a free country?" Johann asked, a look of puzzlement on his face.

"You've got something to learn and you won't like this," Paulus said to Johann. "There is a big group of people, so big that they are a political party, who are against *die Ausländer*. They wish we'd all go back where we came from--especially Germans and Irish."

"How can they do that?" Johann asked.

Rabert jumped in, "They started as secret lodges. That's how they got their name; when members were asked about the lodges, they said 'I know nothing.' They've become so strong in the last few years that they have elected a number of people to Congress in Washington and the state houses, where they make the laws. They are trying to get laws that will keep people from coming into the country. They are *die Feinde der Ausländer*. They want those of us who are already here to have to wait for 21 years until we can become Americans and vote."

"But didn't they all come here from Europe, or their parents?" Johann asked.

Rabert leaned back in his chair. "They're only against immigrants now. A lot of it has to do with jobs. A few years ago they needed people to take jobs when they were building new factories everywhere. You remember how they used to send agents over to Europe to talk people into coming over. But then hard times came and jobs got scarce and the folks already here didn't want any more to come."

Paulus added, "And some of them believe that this is only a country for the English, since they started it. They are afraid that the Germans will take it over."

Kurt asked, "Are these English who live all around Helvetia part of the Know-Nothings?"

"I doubt it," Rabert responded. "In the first place, they sold the Society all this land. Some of them became well off through that deal. Probably a lot of them think that Helvetia is a good thing for them. This is the closest river port to them, and it's a place that buys some of their harvest and livestock."

275

"You know, it's hard to feel at home in a strange country. Everything is so different, sometimes not as good as you expected. It sure doesn't help you feel at home to know that some of *die Amerikaner* don't want us here at all," Johann said.

Rabert said, "I don't think there are Know-Nothings around here; at least I haven't heard of any. But the townships around Helvetia are mostly English. This county has a lot of old-time Whigs. That's a political party which believes the states have the right to make all their own laws. Right now that's a big issue because the states where they have slaves want to keep their laws and don't want the national government to pass laws that do not allow slave-owning."

"Yes, but not everyone here thinks that way." Kurt said. "I was talking to that fellow, Bradley, who runs the store in Coalville. He said that there are lot of people, especially those who came here from the east who think slavery is wrong and belong to this new Republican Party."

Paulus spoke up, "This fits in with the leaders of the Colonization Society. I remember when they were looking for land to buy, they gave up on Kentucky and Missouri because they didn't want to settle in states where people owned slaves. The Swiss have always felt the need to be independent. I guess that rubs off on us Germans too. That is why this new Republican Party sounds good to me."

"I want the readers of *Die Zeitung* to understand the politics of the country since they are going to be citizens. You know, in forty-eight we used the name Democrat to describe people who were for the new order. Some of our *Brüder* do not realize that it does not mean the same thing over here. They call themselves Democrats without realizing that the Democrats here are the ones favoring slavery, who are holding on to as much of the old order as they can. Some of the Germans, since they can't vote yet, don't have much interest in the issues. They just are willing to do as they're told and not think much about things. Other people want to get involved in politics and try to make a difference. It's not much different from what we found in forty-eight. Not enough good leaders and too many blind followers. That's why I want to help people know what the issues are."

Paulus pushed back his chair. "You'll have your chance with the election for president next year. Then folks will see how it works...*Brüder*, I've got to get home. Tomorrow comes soon."

It was just about mid-year when Marta delivered a second daughter, whom they named Anna. Matti and Hannah took turns helping her for a week, while she regained her strength.

"Every time gets easier," Marta laughed when her friends visited.. "I really am thankful to you for taking care of Emma and bringing in the food. Johann can help me now and we'll get along fine."

Johann's construction job had ended when the furniture factory was completed. The Helvetia Furniture Company was hiring men, and Johann found work as a varnisher. Kurt was in charge of a group of skilled cabinet makers and joiners. Soon they were turning out dozens of kitchen tables and chairs, beds and wardrobes. Some were sold to the new settlers in Helvetia, but much of their production was loaded on river boats to be sold in towns as far away as Pittsburgh and New Orleans.

Kurt and Hannah sat with Johann and Marta on their small porch. The sun had just set and the leaves in the tall trees rustled in the evening breeze. The children were all asleep. The women fanned themselves and Kurt waved mosquitoes away from his bald head, reaching for his hat which he had put down beside his chair. Conversation turned to the furniture factory.

Kurt asked Johann, "How are you liking your work?"

"It's not very heavy work. I keep busy because there are plenty of pieces to varnish. We give each one three coats. In good weather like this, it dries pretty fast."

"We're sure turning out a lot of stuff, about a boatload a week. That's making the owners a pretty penny. I get so bored, though, just turning out this plain stuff; everything the same.."

Hannah said, "Kurt likes to do beautiful carved pieces, like some of those he made for our place."

"That's what I really enjoy, making something truly beautiful," Kurt said, turning his gangly frame in the chair. "But as long as they want to put out a boatload a week with this ordinary stuff, there's no chance to do anything really artistic. It would take me at least a week to do the carving on a really fine piece, and we'd have to use a lot better wood."

Marta added, "*Ja*, I know how it was when I was a milliner. I loved to make beautiful hats, but most of the time I had to make one every-day bonnet after another. I'd get so excited when one of the ladies in town went through the style books and picked out a pretty hat. I knew I'd have a good time for a couple of days, even if Fräulein did some of it herself."

"I must say that I never have had a job I enjoyed like that," Johann said. "At one time I thought I might be a master linen dyer, but that didn't work out. It's been one job after another, all different; so I am always starting from the beginning."

"If things ever settle down around here, I can teach you a lot about cabinet making. Judging from the work you did yourself on this house, I'll bet you'd be pretty good at it."

Hannah laughed and said to Marta, "You and I ought to get together. I'm a good dressmaker. I could take orders for dresses and you could make the fancy hats. We'll get us a shop up on Main Street and go into business. These men aren't the only ones who can have dreams."

Kurt joined the fun, "Keep dreaming ladies. You'll make us all so rich that we can stop working and spend all day sitting in the shade talking politics with Rabert."

Marta was waiting at the kitchen door when Johann came home from work. She threw her arms around him, her face glowing with excitement.

Puzzled, Johann held her at arm's length.

"We got another letter from Father today. Karl can come." Words poured out as Marta pulled Johann over to the table. "Look! The Schade's son is coming to America in the spring and they can bring Karl. Oh, I'm so happy. I've been so excited, I even forgot to make supper."

Johann sat her at the table. "Just what did the letter say."

Marta took it from her apron pocket and smoothed it out before Johann. "See! It's not long, but it is the most wonderful letter in the world. I've waited three years to know that Karl can come."

"We'll have to do some figuring. I've just started getting paid. We'd have to send enough money for them to bring him along."

"We'll find the money. We can skimp on a few things and get along all right. We still have a little money in the bank."

"But that is for emergencies."

"We may not get another chance like this for someone to bring him over."

"*Ja*, I know. But you have your hands full with the new baby. Karl would be a handful now. You'd make yourself sick worrying that he'd wander off into the woods or fall into a ditch somewhere. This place is still pretty rough."

"He wouldn't be in any more danger than any of the other kids. He'd have playmates. Oh, I can hardly wait to see him. I'll bet he is this tall."

Johann spoke slowly in contrast to Marta's excited chatter. "I think we should wait until next year. By then we have enough money to get the ticket. Anna won't take so much of your time. A year will make a real difference. He'll be a little older and can stand the hardships of the trip better. Don 't forget how hard it was on the ship."

Marta broke into tears. "What in the world is wrong with you!' she yelled. "You don't want to be with your own son. That's wrong!"

Johann answered quietly, "I just don't think this is the right time. Next year will be better. Tell your father that there will be another family who can bring him next year."

It was Ferdinand Becker who first suggested that Helvetia needed a *Turnverein*. He reminded those families who had come from Cincinnati how the club had become a social center, as well as a place to learn the discipline of gymnastics. Other men picked up the refrain and soon the possibility of a *Turnverein* was a constant subject of conversations.

The Colonization Society agreed that it would add to the amenities of the new city and set aside a lot on Humboldt Street. They said that if a *Turnverein* were organized it could have a 99 year lease for the lot for one dollar a year. Families who wished to belong to the society were asked to contribute a dollar to a building fund. Some of the business men gave five dollars.

Becker called a public meeting to discuss building a hall. After a stirring speech extolling again the values of exercise, healthy disciplined bodies, team spirit, he urged building a hall. It would give the city a place for public gatherings, suppers, bazaars. Then he provided an additional incentive. He had corresponded with leaders of the *Turnverein* in Cincinnati, Louisville, and some smaller communities. If Helvetia could finish its hall by the end of September, the other clubs would gather there to help dedicate the new hall with a massive gymnastic exhibition.

"Ladies and gentlemen, in a little more than a year we have built up a growing city, carving it out of the forest. We've done most of it ourselves. We know how to build. Even people who had never done such work before are now experienced carpenters. A lot of us have pretty well finished our houses; some are still working hard on their places. But if we all work together, if every one of us gives a few hours a week, we can get the hall built in time for the exhibition. Those of us who have finished our houses might be able to give a little more time. We can do it, folks! We've got enough money to make a good start. The rest will come in when people see that this is a serious project. How about it? Are you with me?"

Becker, with his imposing size, was a natural leader. People recognized that his enthusiasm could create a real asset for the community. "We train the children's minds at the school, but we need 'Sound minds in sound bodies.' That's important for a healthy community."

Men stood and pledged their support. Hannah Leinig jumped up and said, "I'll make a couple of pies every week to sell to these bachelors around town who hanker for some good cooking." A chorus of women's voices joined in approval.

"Well, then," Becker announced, "we're on the way. We can have plans drawn by next Monday. We'll start digging for the foundation walls as soon as we know the dimensions of the building. So bring your shovels, men, and we'll get started. I'll have a load of stone here and we'll get that wall laid up as soon as possible. The saw mill can have the timbers ready for us. We've got enough people that, even working only in our spare time, we can get this hall finished by the end of September easily. I'm so confident in the strength of this new city that I'm going to write to the other societies tonight and tell them to be here on the last day of September."

A new spirit swept through Helvetia. Up until now almost all the feverish construction of houses and factories had been private; here was a second project, like the building of the schoolhouse, which pulled together the whole community.

Matti recruited her neighbors, Marta included, "Come along with me this evening. I'm going down to the Turners' Hall. Some of the men go at sun-up for a couple of hours before they go to work. Paulus has a gang that comes right after work and stays until dark. Then they go home to supper. I take along some butter bread to hold them over until suppertime."

Hannah said, "We could get a couple of little buckets of beer to pass around too."

"I'll come along," Marta added. "Johann has only worked one evening so far. I can't do much because of the babies. But I'd like to see how the hall is coming along."

The scene was one of frantic activity. Anxious to take full advantage of the short time before sundown, Paulus stood in the middle of the floor and directed small groups of workers. "You fellows pick out the straightest lumber for the rafters. Hans, you do the measuring and marking. Kurt, you and Johann can saw them to the right length."

The women stood to one side, watching. Matti called out, "Here's some bread and beer, if you can stop long enough."

Paulus was impatient. "Drink up fast, men. When we get the hall done, you can have a *Bierstube*, but first we've got to get it finished." He made a mental note to talk to Matti about the time lost through her warm-hearted contributions.

"Nails! Bring us some more nails!" the men putting up rafters shouted. Boys ran to the nail kegs and filled some small wooden boxes with nails and tried to clamber up the ladders. Mothers snatched some of the younger lads from their appointed rounds.

Each day saw more progress. Sturdy floor, walls with windows that could be opened wide to let in fresh air, roof took shape. At one end of the hall there was a small stage for programs.

Even before the hall was completed, the gymnastic practices began in the open air. Families paid dues of ten cents a month to enroll their children. Experienced Turners led groups of boys and girls in learning the various drills for the September competition. Mothers made the simple costumes that the children would wear for their exercises. Every participant had the goal of helping Helvetia to show that the new city could outdo even the established *Turnverein* from the big cities.

Completion of the *Turnhalle* spurred a series of new cultural developments. Now that the early settlers no longer worked on their houses with a sense of urgency, leisure time re-emerged in their lives. Evenings and Sundays offered a few hours for pleasure. A *Männerchor* was organized with twelve members. Not to be outdone a number of men unpacked trumpets, trombones, tubas, or had them sent from their former homes. The Helvetia Brass Band was organized. Every month one of these groups would present a concert in the Turners' Hall. The singers joined with choruses from Evansville, Henderson, Coaltown in a mass chorus called the *Schillersängerbund* for a song festival.

Gretchen Rabert cleared away the supper dishes. Charles lit the lamp and spread out newspapers he had received on the steamers from St. Louis and Louisville.

Gretchen sat down in her chair. "I've been thinking about a new project. Why don't I get together some of the people from town and start a *Theater-Sektion* in the *Turnverein?*"

"It's not Berlin, you know. But, why not? A little culture would do everyone good."

"I've talked to several folks already when I found that they had taken parts in plays in their former communities. I was surprised that there are at least six or eight who would be interested."

"Now that the Turners' Hall is finished, we might as well use it."

"We could start with some of those German farces that we used to do at home. Mother could send me some books from Cincinnati. Life gets dreary enough around here when the weather is bad. People could stand something to make them laugh a little."

"I know it gets pretty boring around here for you. You're used to city life. There aren't many here who come out of that sort of background. Even if they lived in a city in the old country, they were from working-class neighborhoods and lived pretty simple lives."

"The women here are nice," Gretchen said, "but we have so little in common. They are all 'cooking and children.' I doubt if they read anything other than *Die Zeitung*."

"*Gott sei ewig Lob und Dank*'," Rabert smiled. "You're right. They just haven't had your experiences of the finer things in life: music, literature."

"I feel sorry for them. They work so hard from sun-up to dark. Children, new babies, trying to make their houses livable, sewing, cooking, keeping their vegetable gardens in the summer. Sometimes I feel lazy when I sit down to read a book. I don't really know if I'm missing something in life, or they are."

"There's nothing wrong with living your life as it is. You aren't miserable here, are you?"

Gretchen thought for a moment. "No, not miserable. I've got a good husband, a comfortable little apartment, books Mother sends me. Without any children I have a lot more time than the women in Helvetia. If I were having a baby every year or two like most of these women, life would be very different."

"We've hoped for a baby for five years now. I guess it isn't our fate to be parents. So why not use the time to read, and to start your *Theater-Sektion*.

"I've already talked to the Dreylings and Peter Hermann. They're willing to get started right away. I think that Ferdinand Becker would be interested. He's very handsome. I wonder if he has had experience as an actor."

In spite of the excitement of the new school house, the *Turnhalle*, and the growing number of completed houses, construction of the new factories moved slowly. The grand plan called for the Helvetia Industrial Society to put up money for many factories along the riverfront. Society members as far away as St. Louis and Louisville, joined with those already living in Helvetia to buy stock for ten dollars a share which would finance the factory construction.

The whole community was abuzz with plans for new businesses. The instantaneous success of the earliest ventures; the sawmills, the shingle factory, the brick yard, the sash and door factory, the furniture factory had convinced everyone that prosperity would be easily achieved. Lots were procured and buildings erected for two foundries, the furniture factory, a flour mill, a brewery, and another sawmill. According to their agreement with the Colonization Society which gave them land and loans at very favorable rates, they had to have their businesses in operation within six months.

After the first few plants were built and production got under way, funds of some of the other business men began to run out. Clearly some of the owners were over-extended. They had assumed that profits would start rolling in as soon as they began to operate. Additional loans, after the Society's loan funds were exhausted, were difficult to get from banks in Coaltown or Louisville or had extremely high interest rates.

Johann and Marta were having one of their frequent discussions of their family economy. Johann ran his hand nervously through his hair. "Right now, we're pretty lucky. I'm making my dollar a day at the furniture factory, but some of the new places are closing down already."

"There's no chance that will happen at the furniture factory, is there? I worry about that." Marta said.

"I don't think so. They're selling a lot of stuff all along the river. But some of the businesses are really hurting. I heard that one of the saw mills and the weaving place were having a hard time. They are paying their men only a half-dollar a week in money. The rest of their pay they get in a paper that they can exchange for food. Because farmers don't have money to buy things, they trade flour and potatoes and vegetables and eggs to the company. The company has set up a kind of store where their workers can collect some of their pay in food."

"Well, at least they have food to eat."

"*Ja*, but there is no money for anything else. Some people owe on their houses. They can't pay that off with a paper for groceries."

"I suppose they are so thankful to have a job at all, that they have to take their pay in any form they can get it."

Johann added, "I heard that because there aren't enough jobs for the men in Helvetia, they've fired everyone who doesn't live in town. That's going to make some of the people from the other towns unhappy. I guess it can't be helped."

"I can't understand it. Back home all the letters from people who had come over here were full of stories about plenty of jobs, lots of money. I get pretty mad about them lying like that."

"They may have been telling the truth about the way things were then. Rabert says that it has only been since 1857 that there have been hard times." He added ironically, "We got here just in time."

"Would you have come if you really knew what it was like?"

Johann paused and furrowed his brow. "I have to admit that it isn't what I'd expected. I wasn't expecting hard times. But we have to remember, we didn't have everything so nice back home. I couldn't find a decent job there."

"I guess we have to be glad that you've got a steady job here and that the pay is enough to buy what we need, even if we can't save much. And now with another baby coming, we'll have another mouth to feed."

"Some days I think I'll never have a chance to be anything but a varnisher in the furniture factory. But on other days I still have hope that I'll get a good paying job and we'll be able to save enough to start our own business."

"But what could you start?"

"Well, I know a little about running a store. I might be able to buy in as a partner with somebody, like Becker or one of the grocers."

"Things will have to get a lot better before we can ever do anything like that."

"*Ja*. You're right. But we can't give up hope."

The whole city was shaken when one of the new furniture companies had to go out of business because the Coaltown bank which had been backing them went broke. People began to realize that the very optimistic dreams of the planners of Helvetia were beginning to fade into reality.

There was a spirited discussion in one of the sessions in Rabert's office.

Kurt Leinig pointed a finger at Charles Rabert, "You and your buddy Steinauer pulled the wool over the eyes of a lot of people."

"Just a minute," Rabert protested angrily, half rising from his chair. "I never lied to anybody."

Kurt argued, waving his finger at the editor, "You painted such a glowing picture: growing city, new factories, thriving businesses, plenty of work."

"I'll admit that things have not turned out quite the way I pictured them, but I wasn't lying."

"All right," Kurt lowered his voice, "I'm not saying that you are a liar. I just think that you fellows planned too big."

"It seemed reasonable to assume that people would keep coming the way they did at first. You remember how exciting it was when every steamboat brought a few more families, when several new houses were being started every day."

Paulus Frantz took Rabert's side. "This place has a lot of promise. It was reasonable to assume that it was going to become a prosperous city very fast. We've got the river, we've got boats to bring us materials and deliver our products. We were told that there were coal deposits just north of here, but they haven't developed. I don't think that it was wrong to expect this to be a thriving place."

"The Society did have dreams and laid out a city that reflected those dreams," Rabert said. "We cut this place right out of the forest. When you think of the progress that has been made in two years, I think it's still reasonable to believe it will prosper."

"It's not that way now," Kurt argued. "If they'd spent the money they put into laying out streets that are not used into investing in factories, we'd be a lot better off."

"We didn't having any trouble raising the money we needed to buy the land for the city and to get some of the things started here. But we are hurting because the whole country is going through a hard time. People just don't have the money to put into new businesses and factories. That's everywhere in the country. We thought we'd have plenty of investors to put up plants and make jobs for everybody. We thought that we'd be shipping boatload after boatload of our products all up and down the Ohio and Mississippi valleys. But lots of people don't have the money to buy, so the orders don't come in."

Paulus put his arm on Rabert's shoulder. "Look; nobody is to blame. We are all victims of hard times right now in the country. People just don't have money right now, or if they have it, they are hanging on to it."

"Who can blame them?" Johann added. "I'm hanging on to our little savings as hard as I can. We don't spend a penny we don't have to."

"That's the way it is. If a business has enough capital, it can hold on until times get better. It's not always going to be hard times. People will start of buy again; people with a little money will start investing. I hear that some of the new factories down by the river are trying to persuade

285

people to invest by promising that the children of shareholders will be guaranteed a job in the factory. But until there is more money around, companies without much backing aren't going to survive. Several of the local factories are paying their men with stock. But right now that stock can't be sold for much. So in the future they might have something, but right now it's not much more than a promise."

"That's where Johann and I are lucky, I guess," Kurt said. "The Helvetia Furniture Company has enough backing to keep us working and getting our money every week."

Marta's letter brought gloom to the Wiesner household. Katerina and August read it several times. Katerina was the first to speak, trying to hold back her tears, "Marta doesn't say it, but I am sure this waiting for a year is not her idea. It must be Johann dragging his feet."

"I wish I could talk some sense to that young man." August pounded the table. "That little boy needs his Mama and Papa; not a couple old folks."

"I wish I had kept my mouth shut. I told Karl that soon he would be going to his Mama. Now I have to tell him to wait. That isn't fair."

As Katerina sat on the edge of the bed, she stroked Karl's wavy brown hair.

Karl, who regularly resisted bedtime, said, "Why are you crying, *Grossmutter*?"

"We got some bad news today. You know, I told you that you would go with the Schade's on a boat and would go to your Mama and Papa. Well, we have to wait until next year. I'm sorry."

Karl responded defiantly, as he often did, "I don't care!"

Both relieved and troubled, Katerina continued to pat his hair, "You know that we'll always take good care of you. *Grossvater* said he is going to make a wagon for you. How about that!"

Charles Rabert finished rolling copies of this week's edition of *Die Zeitung* for mailing. Gretchen stood at the bottom of the stairs leading to their apartment. She smiled, "Well, that's done for another week. What are you printing this week?"

"I'm trying to help people understand how politics and government work in this country. Even if only about half of the men have been here long enough to vote, the rest need to know what's going on so that when they're able to vote, they'll be ready to make the right choices."

"You should be a university professor. Everything is getting people to think!"

"If I hadn't been so interested in politics in forty-eight, I'd quite possibly be a professor at Heidelberg or somewhere by now. I'd have liked that. But I'm here. So I have the same job to do. You're right. My mission is to make people think--and there's a lot to think about these days."

"You mean the fight in the government over slavery?"

"It's tearing the country apart. The southern states won't give an inch. Political leaders from the north are fighting to keep slavery from spreading into the new territories being opened up in the West. They try one compromise after another, but each one only moves the states further apart."

"Why can't people see that slavery isn't right?"

"Come look out the window. See the trees on the other side of the river over there. That's how close we are slavery. That river is the dividing line. *Die Zeitung* goes into slave states, cities like Louisville and St. Louis. Practically all our German readers are not for slavery but they live in the middle of it."

"How do the men in Helvetia feel about it?"

"I wish they thought more about it. I don't think there is any strong support for slavery. In principle they think that it is wrong for one person to own another like an animal. But they don't think it has a lot to do with their lives. They've never thought about owning a slave. Only a few of them who have traveled in the south have seen slave markets or fields full of slaves."

"I hear some of the women talk about *die Schwartze*. They don't think much of them. Some of the ones who lived in Louisville say that they are ignorant and crude."

"I suppose they are. One wonders what would happen if they were no longer slaves. They don't have any education and I'm not sure they can be educated. So you'd have a couple of million people to take care of. I suppose they could keep on doing the work they are doing but be paid for it."

"I read in one of your newspapers that there are some organizations working to make it possible for the slaves to be sent back to Africa and given their freedom there. That makes some sense."

Rabert ran his fingers through his hair. "Yes, but what would it do to the southern economy to send their whole labor force back to Africa. As long as cotton is king, that won't happen."

The editor continued to follow the developing political picture. He marked sections of the newspapers from Chicago, Cincinnati, Louisville, St. Louis to share with the men who gathered in the office to talk politics.

He said to Paulus, who was the most politically astute of the little group, "I have just about made up my mind to have *Die Zeitung* come out for the Republicans. The three other parties are all supporting slavery in one way or another." He did not say that he had had a letter from Caleb Smith, a major Republican leader in Indiana, who was building support for a man named Lincoln among the German immigrants. Rabert had heard a rumor that Smith believed that he had promises that he would be in Lincoln's cabinet, especially after he had been tapped to second Lincoln's nomination in the Wigwam in Chicago.

Paulus responded, "I heard that the Coaltown paper is favoring the Democrats. They say that the compromises Douglas is proposing are the only way to hold the country together."

"But how can you compromise with slavery. I believe with all my heart that it is wrong. It is against nature for one man to own another like an animal....Besides, I don't think Douglas could win an election. The Democrats have split, north and south, so they don't have the commanding majority they used to have. Douglas isn't going to get many votes in the south when there's another Democrat running who is four-square pro-slavery."

Johann joined the conversation. "I wish I knew more about these parties, even though I can't vote. Somebody said there are four different parties."

Paulus was quick to provide information. "Like Charles just said, there are two parties that call themselves Democrats. They used to be one strong party but they are divided now between those who want to keep slavery like it is and those who want to let slavery exist in just the southern states and in the some new states out west. There's another party called the Whigs. They used to be a strong party but they've been taken over by these Know-Nothings. Nobody who has come from another country is going to give them a vote. Then there's this new Republican party. It has come out strongly against letting slavery expand anywhere in the new states. Most of the Germans and Swiss seem to be leaning to the Republicans."

Rabert spread a newspaper on the table around which they were sitting. "This is from Chicago. It tells about the Republican convention where they picked their candidate for President. They had a real battle until somebody had enough votes to win, but finally chose a man from Illinois; a fellow named Lincoln."

Kurt Leinig broke into the conversation, "One of the bosses down at the factory told me that this Lincoln grew up just a few miles north of here."

"So that must make him a pretty good man," Johann grinned.

Rabert reached under his desk and spread out another newspaper. "Here's a paper from Cincinnati called *The Railsplitter* that is supporting Lincoln. They don't say a whole lot about him, but they sure don't have anything good to say about that Democrat Douglas. They are strong against slavery but they don't have much use for *die Schwartze.* They have a nice woodcut of Lincoln here."

"If he wins, it won't be because he is so handsome," Kurt laughed. "But he sure does look like a common man."

Johann spoke with conviction. "I wish I could vote. I never took much interest in politics at home, but I like this idea of electing your leader."

"But suppose your candidate doesn't win?" Paulus asked with a grin. "Then you have to live for four years with a President you didn't want."

"It's only for four years," Johann answered. "At home we had the king for life, whether we liked him or not."

"You've got the spirit." Rabert slapped Johann on the shoulder. "It's my job to get all the Germans and Swiss as excited as that. If we're going to make our mark on this country, we have to learn to vote."

The election campaign was described in every issue of *Die Zeitung.* Rabert was able to stir interest in both voters and non-voters because Indiana was playing a critical role in the fate of the Republicans.

Ferdinand Becker enjoyed stopping by the newspaper office for animated conversation with Rabert. They were both well-educated men. Becker was Helvetia's other subscriber to American newspapers from St. Louis, Louisville and Cincinnati. Of a somewhat more conservative bent than the editor, he still favored the Republican party's cause.

"You know," Becker said, "we are going to have a chance to see what Lincoln's chances are."

"If the Republican party can win the election for state officers in October, they should be able to win for Lincoln in November."

"The whole country is going to be watching Indiana, and I guess Pennsylvania too, in October. They are the only states with that unusual schedule of elections."

Rabert asked, "What do you make of all the tub thumping for Douglas in Coaltown. My colleague at *The Reporter* is certainly pushing him hard. I'm going to push as hard for Lincoln."

"I agree with you most of the way," Becker argued, "but I guess I worry most that this election will divide the country. That would ruin business. We are out of the panic that began in '57. I would hate to see hard times come again."

"Douglas's compromises are only going to prolong the struggle to deal with slavery. That means that Congress will continue to be tied in knots. Every effort to pass good laws gets sidetracked by the debate over extending slavery. Until that gets solved, no real progress is going to be made on anything."

"I can't argue with your point, but forcing a break up of the Union is bad too. I'm afraid the south will follow through on its threat to pull out of the Union if Lincoln gets elected. That will ruin commerce. My business depends a lot on cotton. If the south pulls out, we won't be able to get cotton easily, and our textile mills will be slowed to a trickle."

"That may be a risk we have to take. Don't forget. They need the money you pay for their cotton. That puts some pressure on them, too, to hold the Union together," the editor countered.

"I am all for holding the Union together but I hope the hotheads on both sides cool off a little."

Rabert pushed his graying hair back. "Yes, but I have to remember what I believed in forty-eight. There are some issues so important that you have to stand up for them, even at a price."

"Don't forget that my country idolizes William Tell.'

"Keep your bow and arrow handy," Rabert laughed.

On the day after the October election the Raberts entertained Becker for dinner. Gretchen set the table with her family china and silverware and spent the day cooking and baking. She was delighted to revive some of her former social activity, recalling the splendid dinner parties her mother used to have in Berlin.

"Since you are so happy about the election, I'll make dinner a celebration," she said to her husband that morning.

In her best gown she greeted their guest at the door, "Good evening, Ferdinand."

"You certainly are bringing beauty to our drab town. What a lovely gown."

"You are handsomely dressed yourself, sir," she smiled with a token curtsey.

"I have to show that my store does have more than work clothes and boots. I don't sell many suits like this, so I have to wear one." He smoothed his black hair and straightened his silk cravat.

"Come in. Come in and make Charles jealous."

Rabert, knowing that Gretchen was planning a special dinner, had put on his best frock coat. "Welcome, my friend. Come in, come in."

"You men talk for a few minutes while I finish in the kitchen."

Charles smiled, "Too bad we can't afford a maid. Gretchen is having a wonderful time making this festive dinner. She has been singing in the kitchen all day."

"Well, we do have reason to celebrate, don't we," Becker said, sitting on Gretchen's settee, running his finger along the sharp crease of his trousers.

"The Evansville paper said that the Republicans had 10,000 more votes than the Democrats for the legislature seats. That certainly must mean that the state will go for Lincoln next month."

"This should make your friend in Indianapolis, Caleb Smith, happy. Is he still thinking that he will be in Lincoln's cabinet?"

"I had a letter from him just before the election. He was full of confidence. He was particularly sure of the German voters."

"I always worry about ambitious men. Oh, I don't mean ambitious in the sense of hard-working. Some of these politicians are much too interested in power. They want to get to the top of the heap, no matter what they have to do."

"I agree Smith is ambitious, but I think he is sincere in his support of Lincoln and the desire to preserve the Union. I wouldn't have anything to do with him if I thought he was just after something for himself."

"Dinner is ready," Gretchen called from the kitchen.

When the men came into the kitchen, she laughed, "Sorry to have to serve you in the kitchen, but the dining room is being redecorated and the butler had to go to his sick mother. So we'll just pretend that we're in the dining room."

Becker bowed low. "Madam need not be concerned." he said as he surveyed the kitchen table, covered with a gleaming white tablecloth, with place settings of lovely china. "You've made a miracle."

"In another year we'll have a house of our own and Gretchen will have her dining room and can entertain as she was accustomed to do in her parents' home."

"This is the finest dinner I've seen since I left Europe. I am sure it will be the tastiest as well."

Gretchen blushed. "Flatterer!"

"I can't help myself," Becker with a courtly bow to kiss her hand, "I am overwhelmed by this little center of beauty and style. You, dear Gretchen, have to keep us civilized in this wilderness."

Rabert, not to be outdone, stood behind Gretchen's chair to seat her formally.

The editor was troubled by what he read in the newspapers in the next weeks. He brought it up in one of the evening discussions.

"You know, this is getting serious. The papers are reporting that southern politicians are saying publicly that if Lincoln is elected, the south will withdraw from the Union. That would be bad."

Paulus answered, "They're bluffing. How would they make it on their own? They're poor states, mainly farms and plantations."

Rabert said, "It shows that they think slavery is absolutely necessary to their survival. Unless they can keep slavery and expand it into the west so that there are always enough votes in Congress to defeat laws that would end slavery, they are willing to pull out of the Union."

"What would the north do if the southern states made their own country?" Johann asked.

Rabert responded, "I don't know. Some congressmen say that we should let them go. Others say that the union must be preserved at all costs, even if it means going to war."

"I doubt if it would ever come to that."

"I wish we could be sure of that."

On November 6 the nation voted. There was great excitement in Helvetia and Coaltown as the votes were being counted. In Helvetia 244 votes were cast; all but three were for Lincoln. Rabert was elated. It really demonstrated how convincing his arguments in *Die Zeitung* were. "We did it," he gloated to Gretchen. "We showed that if you give people good information and good reasoning, you can lead them.

In Coaltown the same lesson was being demonstrated. In the whole county Lincoln got 1026 votes and Douglas was supported by 947. The editor of *The Reporter*, the Democratic newspaper there, recognized that his English readers held firm but were edged out by the German and Swiss Republicans in Helvetia.

Ferdinand Becker walked into the newspaper office. No one was in sight. Walking to the foot of the stairs leading to the editor's apartment, he called, "Anyone home?"

Gretchen appeared at the top of the stair. "Oh, hello, Ferdinand. Charles drove to Coaltown this afternoon. He'll be sorry to have missed you."

When Becker did not turn to leave, she added, "Would you have time for a cup of tea?"

"Thank you. That would be a great pleasure."

"Come up, while I put on the pot."

He sat on the settee, while she busied herself in the kitchen. The apartment, in spite of its small rooms and somewhat crude workmanship, was decorated with taste. An oil painting in a wide gilded frame graced one wall. The afternoon sun filtered through the dark rose velvet drapes which bordered the windows. The furniture of this room reflected a gracious continental style.

He stood to attention when Gretchen re-entered the room bearing a tea tray which she placed on a table.

"Do sit. I haven't had such courtesy since Berlin," she smiled.

"And I haven't seen such loveliness since I came to America; at least not since the last time I had the pleasure of your company."

"Flatterer!" She paused..."Really, Ferdinand, you shouldn't speak like that."

"Dear lady, do not compel me into silence. It is not empty flattery; I speak the truth. You are so lovely." He reached out to put his hand lightly on her arm.

"You mustn't. I'm a married woman."

"I can't help it. I am completely enthralled by your beauty."

"Please don't talk like that. I know you are a gentleman. You must see that it is not right of you to put me in a compromising situation."

"Let me tell you a little about myself." He leaned back in the settee. "In Zurich I was very much in love with a beautiful young woman. Her name was Elise. She was tall and graceful, like you, and so lovely. We had hopes that we could marry as soon as I finished the university. Just before I received my degree, she fell suddenly ill with fever. After a week in a coma, she died. I was desolated. My whole future, all my dreams died with her."

"I'm so sorry," Gretchen murmured.

"It was then that I decided to come to America. I suppose I was looking for a new beginning, a new future. But it really has not worked. Oh, I have a future in business. Gradually, in Cincinnati, in Davenport, and now here in Helvetia I have managed to make a good living selling clothing. But life still seems empty. Except for putting money in the bank, I really do not feel that I have anything to live for. I have no beauty in my life, no graciousness, no gentleness. Please do not deny me that pleasure."

"I would not deny you, Ferdinand, but you must remember that I am married to Charles. I cannot be involved even in an innocent flirtation."

"I only ask your friendship, which I have come to treasure. My respect for you would not permit me to go beyond admiration from a distance."

"Very well. So long as we both understand. I do appreciate you as a friend. It is pleasure for Charles and me to be able to have conversation with a man of your education and sophistication and culture. Without making any judgment on the fine people of Helvetia, it is such a gift to be able to talk to someone about culture and art. Charles is able to fit in better than I, but we both love the opportunity to spend an occasional evening like we used to in the homeland."

"I would be delighted to be able to enjoy your hospitality occasionally. Forgive me for my boldness. I will try to dampen the pleasure I feel in your company."

"Good. Then we understand each other." Gretchen began to put the cups on the tray, turning her head to hide the blush in her cheeks.

Marta put her head in her hands as they sat at the table after supper. "Matti said today that there might be a war. Is she right? That would be terrible."

Johann put his hand on her shoulder and could feel her shaking. "Rabert said that the states down south, where they have slaves, are against the man who is the new president. They said if he was elected, they would pull out of the country and make their own. This man Lincoln, won't be president until March, but they may not wait that long."

"Would there be a war if they make their own country?"

"Nobody knows. Rabert thinks they'll work out some kind of an agreement to live in peace. He thinks that the states down south won't be able to stand on their own and will come back. Paulus thinks that the government will fight to keep those states from breaking up the country."

"Suppose there was a war, would it be around here?"

"I doubt it. But that state right across the river might be one of those that pulled out. They have slaves over there. We'd be living right on the border between two countries, one part of the United States and one which doesn't want to be; there'd be nothing but a river between us."

"I thought we'd get away from all that fighting business once we left Silesia and the Prussian army," Marta shook her head.

"It's been a relief not to have soldiers everywhere, making young men go into the army like Gustav had to. I was lucky to be missed. Wouldn't I have been something as a soldier?"

"It worries me when people talk about wars."

CHAPTER 15

In Coaltown *The Reporter* and in Helvetia *Die Zeitung* kept their readers informed as best they could of the storm clouds of secession and possible war. Their difference was not only the fact that one was published in English and the other in German, one was edited by a Douglas Democrat and the other by a Lincoln Republican. *The Reporter* was widely read by the English residents of Coaltown and the county. Some of their families had been in America since colonial times. *Die Zeitung* was read by the more recent German and Swiss immigrants in both Coaltown and Helvetia.

A variety of forces pulled on these diverse readers and their newspapers. The majority had in common their desire to preserve the Union.

There were lively discussions as the men ate their lunches at the factory.

Kurt Leinig argued, "If the country is cut in two, this river out here will have one country on the south bank and one on the north. If they can't get along, river traffic will slow or stop altogether. Then where will we be? Helvetia depends on that river, men."

Several of the men nodded, thinking about the furniture they were making, which would be shipped on the boats up and down the Ohio and Mississippi.

"You're right," Johann put in, "but Rabert says that lots of *Englischers* over in Coaltown have most of their relatives in the south and don't want to see them break away."

One of the other fellows spoke up, "*Die Zeitung* said that the south would not break away if the government just let them keep their slaves."

Johann added, "But the paper said that the south wanted all the states that are beginning out in the west to have slaves too."

"The whole thing is being stirred up by a bunch out in the east. They want the whole country to do away with slavery. They are willing to go to war over that," Kurt slammed shut his lunch pail.

A tall thin craftsman spoke up, "I'm glad we don't have none of them troublemakers around here." Most of men nodded assent.

"It's going to be trouble for a long time, I'm afraid," Johann added, getting up to go back to work.

The immigrants fell roughly into three groups, all supporting the Union. The small number of Forty-eighters held fast to their idealized view of American democracy and resisted any efforts to weaken it. Many of the newer arrivals were uninformed or indifferent, so caught up in the hard work of making a start in a new country that politics was not a priority. The majority of the Germans and Swiss were dedicated to the notion of freedom, which had attracted them to America, and were willing to defend against any forces which would threaten that freedom. While they opposed slavery in principle, shown in the choice of Indiana as the site for Helvetia, they certainly did not share the political assertiveness of the abolitionists.

Even before any states seceded there were local efforts to enlist support for the Union. A Colonel John Mansfield of the 55th Regiment of the Indiana Volunteers spoke at the court house in Coaltown just before Christmas. Because he was an officer of what was being called the Second German Regiment, many Germans and Swiss were in the audience. Charles Rabert and Alois Frey rode over from Helvetia out of interest in what would be said.

Rabert described the assembly to the group who gathered in his office the next evening. Drinking steaming coffee from the large pot on the pot-bellied stove in the center of the room, Paulus, Johann, and Kurt listened as the report was given.

"The courtroom was filled; some men even stood along the walls. August Krönlein, the banker in Coaltown who looks after your money, introduced the Colonel. He said that he had known him for ten years or more, had been in the Indiana legislature with him. He called Mansfield a brave and patriotic man, a good soldier, an honest man with extraordinary common sense; just the man to lead the Second German Regiment.

"The Colonel was pretty impressive in his blue uniform. His speech was not very long. He spoke in both English and German. He said that every citizen, everybody who lives here, has a duty to act in this time of crisis. He really appealed to all the Germans and Swiss to step forward and join his

regiment to suppress the rebellion if it came. Then he really made an appeal
to us immigrants. He said that we should show the native-born citizens that
we didn't come to this country just to better our situations in life but that
we are willing to sacrifice our life-blood on the altar of liberty."

Kurt shook his head. "That's strong stuff. How did people react?"

Rabert turned up the lamp a bit. "Lot of them were pretty impressed.
It was a stirring speech. Two or three men stood up and said that they were
going to enlist and take the boat this morning to Evansville and Camp
Vanderburgh."

Johann's eyes brightened. "I wish I'd gone over to the meeting. I don't
understand all the politics, but I think it would be terrible to break the
country in half...."

Kurt interrupted, "I'm not sure I really understand why us Germans
should get in this fight. Lot of us can't even be citizens. I have a hard time
forgetting those Know-Nothings who don't even want us in the country.
Why should we have German regiments in their army, when they don't
want us here."

Paulus took up the argument. "I can understand how you feel, but I'm
afraid you think all Americans are Know-Nothings. Most of our men will
be citizens as soon as they are here long enough; some of us already are. I
came over to make this my country." Johann nodded assent.

"That's the way I feel too," Rabert added. "They're planning another
public meeting on the first day of the year. I'm going to be there."

Before long, after every issue of *Die Zeitung*, conversations on the
streets, in the factories, at home were about the growing danger that the
United States was breaking in two. Even though most of the people had
little grasp of all the issues, they recognized that the country to which they
had come was in trouble. Rabert tried to explain the situation clearly so
that his readers could understand the growing crisis. He put a woodcut of
a map of the United States he had brought from Cincinnati in one issue
with the suggestion that people save it so they could locate the various
states that were talking about withdrawing from the United States.

The telegraph did not come into Perry County. Four weekly mails were
brought by the packet, *Gray Eagle*, between Louisville and Evansville. Six
weeks after Lincoln was elected, while James Buchanan was still President,
the city newspapers brought by the steamer had blazing headlines
announcing that the state of South Carolina had seceded. Charles Steinauer
ran to the newspaper office with the papers.

Waving them before Rabert's eyes, he shouted, "What do you make of that? Those fools.are going to send us right into war."

Rabert scanned the page quickly. "You're right! They are claiming that they are an independent country and that the United States has to turn over to them all the forts at the harbors along the coast."

Steinauer looked over Rabert's shoulder at the newspaper. "It says that some congressmen want to turn them over and others are calling for the President to send more troops to hold those forts. What a mess! But we've got to show those bastards that they can't break up the country without a fight."

"Sending the army is a pretty hollow threat. I read that there are only 16,000 men in the whole army. Probably more than half are from the southern states and wouldn't fight against their people, so Buchanan wouldn't have very many troops to send."

"They'd be crazy to give up those forts. If those damn stupid southerners want to have a fight, we're going to need those forts."

"I suppose they think that the forts belong to them as much as to Washington. They helped build them, pay for them. But I agree, to give them up now would be a mistake. I sure hope this one state will not lead all the southern states out of the Union."

Steinauer shooks his head. "This is not going to be a happy Christmas with war clouds coming up over the river."

The courthouse in Coaltown was crowded to overflowing on January 1, 1861. Rabert, Paulus Frantz and Steinauer had driven over, partly out of curiosity, but also as self-appointed representatives of Helvetia. The meeting was conducted in English in formal parliamentary style with resolutions drafted, debated, and voted upon.

Rabert said, "It reminds me of the debates we used to have at Heidelberg. Not a bad idea. It gives people a chance to speak up but keeps everything in order."

The main focus of the discussion was what would be the best course to follow if other southern states seceded. Almost all of the proposed resolutions pledged loyal support to the Union, moderated by a sympathetic understanding of the plight of the border states. They knew the Kentuckians across the river; some were even related to families in Kentucky. They had a brisk trade with the towns on the other side of the river and were reluctant to see that end.

Several speakers expressed their fear that the Ohio River would become the boundary between North and South. Some speakers even suggested that if a new national boundary were drawn, it should be north of them.

Steinauer rose to his feet speaking in heavily accented English. "I disagree with that proposition. It would mean that Helvetia, and Coaltown, too, would become part of Kentucky and the south. That would never work. When we came here and bought land for Helvetia, we deliberately turned down a plan for building our city in Kentucky because we didn't want to be part of a slave state." There were nods of agreement all over the room and the idea of moving the national boundary did not find a lot of support.

The basic resolutions affirming support for the Union and seeking some compromise to end the conflict passed without much opposition, but the resolution proposing putting the border far to the north of the Ohio River lost by a vote of 99 to 55. A great many abstained from the votes, reflecting their uncertainties. Two things were clear: the majority of the people in the meeting wanted the Union to remain intact and favored making the compromises on slavery necessary to satisfy the south and end the movement toward secession. Several speakers railed against the abolitionists, the radical easterners who were fanning the flames of secession by insisting that slavery be outlawed in the entire nation. There were boos and hisses when abolitionists were mentioned. *The Reporter* in Coaltown had printed an inflamatory editorial proposing that the leading Secessionists from the South and the leading Abolitionists from the North should be hanged in pairs from the same gallows, opening the way for peace. The meeting adjourned.

The next night in the newspaper office the three delegates reported on the meeting to a small group of men.

"It was a very interesting meeting," Steinauer said. "It was clear that almost everyone there wants the country to stay together. Nobody was calling for outright war."

Rabert added, "Since the meeting was in Coaltown there was pretty strong support for the Douglas plan to compromise on slavery and to hold the south in the Union. But there were also some Republican voices raised, saying that the Union had to be preserved, even if the cost is high."

"The meeting was pretty well dominated by the big men in Coaltown," Paulus said, "and they are all English. They organized the debate and presented the resolutions. There were a number of Germans from Coaltown there too, but only two Germans spoke, Steinauer, here, and a grocer in

Coaltown, a fellow named Pleisch. The rest didn't say anything, even though they could speak English."

Steinauer shifted in his chair. "I guess what troubled me was that on the one hand this Colonel Mansfield calls on us to form another German Regiment to fight to preserve the Union. On the other hand it was pretty clear that the debate was in the hands of the English, most of whom wanted to work out a compromise with the slave states. Kind of a mixed message, I think."

"Meanwhile," Rabert announced, "the word from Cincinnati is that President Buchanan has called for Friday, January 4, to be a national day of fasting and prayer for deliverance from national calamity."

"Not sure that will prevent it," Paulus said.

Marta questioned Johann every time he came home from Rabert's office. "What did Herr Rabert say tonight? Are they still talking about a war?"

Johann answered, "Rabert says that states in the south are still talking about pulling out of the United States."

"Does that mean they would fight?"

"Well, around here people are trying to keep away from that. Rabert said that several times lately a bunch of businessmen from Coaltown rowed across the river and met in friendly way with the store keepers and company owners on the Kentucky shore. They even had a dinner at the Old South Hotel in Hainesville."

"That doesn't sound like they want to fight," Marta replied, sounding relieved.

"Rabert says they want to get along. The owner of a coal mine in Hainesville wrote a paper which promised that if fighting broke out in other places, they would try to get along here. They were willing to promise that they would still do business across the river like always. They wouldn't fight each other. They all signed the paper."

"I don't care about all this politics. I don't understand any of it anyway. I just don't want fighting," Marta sighed.

"Let me see Marta's letter again," August Wiesner said to his wife. Putting on his spectacles, he scanned the two pages. "Do you think she sounds happy?"

"She sounds happy enough about her house and her daughters. But I can almost see her crying when she asked about how Karl is. She misses him, as any mother would."

301

"I don't know why they don't send for him. I have told them twice about people from Neuhaus going to America. But it never works out."

"She writes about all that war talk. I suppose they are afraid for him to come if there is going to be a war." Katerina got up from the table, poured a cup of coffee, and sat again.

"I thought it would be good for him to go to America before he started school next fall."

"I wonder how he will get along in school. Frau Bessel told me that he was fighting with her Georg. She was pretty unhappy about it."

"That's just kids. They fight one minute and are comrades the next." August smiled indulgently.

"Next time she comes to complain, I'll let you talk to her," Katerina snapped.

"He's not a bad boy: a little bull-headed and short-tempered."

"He's getting to be more of a handful. I'll be glad to have the teacher shape him up."

"Surely, once this war talk dies down, they'll send for him."

During the next weeks Rabert followed very closely what the Louisville papers were saying about the political situation in Kentucky, a quarter mile across the river. In *Die Zeitung* he tried to explain to his readers the issues that faced their neighboring state. The whole country was watching Kentucky. Although that state was not part of what was called the deep south, it did allow slavery. One political party in the state legislature favored the Union, the other the possibility of seceding; but the legislature was controlled by the party supporting the Union. So for the moment it appeared that Kentucky would not join the south in secession.

Johann listened carefully to the discussion around the stove in Rabert's office. He began to grasp the difference between Indiana and the state just across the river.

Rabert, usually so calm, was obviously troubled. "It gets worse every week. Now there are seven states seceding from the Union."

"When will it stop?" Paulus exclaimed. "Can't they see that this is madness?"

Rabert put the Louisville papers on the little table in front of them. "Look at this. They are trying hard to persuade Kentucky to secede too. It says that representatives from Tennessee and Georgia have come to talk to the Democrats in the Kentucky legislature.."

"Do you think Kentucky will pull out of the country," Johann asked.

"This paper says that the governor, Magoffin, told them that he believes Kentucky supports the south, they want to find some compromise to hold the union together."

"What are chances of that happening?" Johann inquired.

"I understand that they have been asking that a convention with representatives from all the states be called to work out ....."

Paulus interrupted, "Isn't that something Congress could do?"

Rabert ran his hand over his forehead, "Congress has been trying for years to find a compromise. Crittenden, one of the Kentucky senators, has proposed one amendment after another which would let the south keep slavery with some expansion in the west. The northern states will have no part of it."

"So nothing can be done?" Johann said, as much an expression of despair as a question.

"At least the Kentucky state legislature is refusing even to consider secession. They know how divided the state is."

Paulus reported, "Charles Steinauer told me that he went with a second group of business men from Coaltown over to Hainesville. Steinauer says that they all wanted to maintain friendly relations between the two sides of the river. Both sides promised that so long as Kentucky didn't secede they would continue to trade across the river."

Rabert observed, "We have to remember that all the people there have known each other for some years and are able to overlook political differences. If Kentucky secedes, it would be different, because then we would be in different countries, straddling the border. The whole thing is all mixed up. We've got some people living on this side of the river who favor the south, and Steinauer says that he met some strong Unionists in Hainesville who want to compromise on slavery. For the present we can make it work...but it might not last."

In Coaltown just after dark four men slipped, one-by-one, into a barn on the outskirts of the town. Their hats were pulled far down and their coat collars turned up. Once inside, they gathered around a lantern, sitting on sacks of grain piled along one wall. They spoke in hushed tones.

Matt Dowd drawled, "I'm glad you fellers could make it. I need some help in a scheme I been thinking about."

Arching tobacco juice across the barn floor, Jim Morrison asked, "Why all this sneakin' 'round, Matt?"

Dowd leaned forward. "Listen, you don't know who you can trust these days. I asked you lads to come 'cause I know what you think about all this northern war talk. These Yankees fireeaters ain't going to rest until the country is completely ruined. Mark my words, war is coming! And when it does, I am with the south, heart and body!"

A third man, older than the rest, "My daddy, and his daddy afore him, was Georgians. Us Burkes always thought Georgia was home and we was just kinda visitin' up here. I'll always be a southerner."

"That's what I thought, Otis. I knew you'd be with us." Dowd put his arm around Burke's shoulder. "How 'bout you, Mike?" he asked, looking at the fourth man.

Michael Smith smiled slyly. "I thought you was cooking up somethin', so I come prepared." He patted the bulge in his coat pocket. "I got my Daddy's old revolver here," he said, giving a mock salute. "I'm ready for to fight right now."

Dowd held up his hand. "Don't get out ahead of me." Then he added with determination in his voice, "But you might need that firearm!"

"What ya got in mind, Matt?" Morrison asked.

Dowd looked from face to face of the men gathered around him. "Well, I suppose you heard that the governor ordered the muskets that have been stored in the courthouse for the militia to be boxed up and shipped to Indianapolis."

The men nodded solemnly.

Matt Dowd continued. "There's supposed to be fifty muskets with ammunition at the courthouse. I got to thinking. I wager they could use those over in Kentucky when the trouble comes. They will be raising troops to support the south over there and they will be short of guns, if you get my meaning."

Jim Morrison launched another stream of tawny juice. "Think we can pull that off. Sounds a little risky to me."

"Not if we use our heads," Dowd reassured him. "I thought out a plan, if'n you lads are willing to help me."

Heads nodded, and mumbled approvals indicated that the conspiracy could go forward.

Dowd took a stick and drew on the barn floor. "I heard that they were moving the crates with those guns and the ammunition down to the wharf to wait for the next steamer going to New Albany, where they'll put the guns on the train for Indianapolis. Moving the crates to the wharf is supposed to happen tomorrow afternoon. The *Gray Eagle* comes the next morning. Here's what I think...."

The men moved even closer together as plans were laid for the next night.

It was a cloudy night with the wind blowing from the south. Dowd and his comrades moved slowly along the waterfront. They moved silently from building to building until they came to the gangway to the wharf. Looking around the corner of the shed which concealed them, Otis Burke said, "Do you think they have a watchman on the wharf?"

Dowd whispered, "Can't be sure...I walked around down here this afternoon when they carted those crates down here. There were three boxes, about the size of coffins. It shouldn't be too hard to find them on the wharf."

"You'd think they would have a guard on them," Smith said very softly.

"If they do, Mike, you've got your gun. Use it!" Otis Burke urged.

"You think I'm crazy? I'd use it if I had to, but we've gotta be a lot smarter than that. If there is a watchman, we've got to get him outa the way without raising the alarm."

Dowd took control. "Listen! This is the way we're going to do it. Otis, you're pretty well known around town. You've never shot your mouth off about politics. So we'll let you go out on the wharf. If there's a watchman, you talk him off the wharf anyway you can. The rest of us'll take care of the guns while you have him out of the way."

Burke started walking out the wharf, deliberately weaving ever so slightly. There were boxes and bales and barrels stacked high, leaving a walkway down the center of the wharf. As he got close to the end of the wharf, he heard Billy Barnes, the town constable, saying, "Who goes there?" Barnes' voice quavered as he raised his lantern to show the intruder. "Otie, what the hell you doin' out here?"

"Take it easy, Billy. I been down at Sully's and I'm just takin' a li'l walk to clear me head. What the hell you doin' out here at this hour of the night?"

"The boys at the court house wanted me down here tonight. Lot of nonsense, if you ask me. They're seein' seseches everywhere. Hell, I'm just wasting my time."

"Come on down to Sully's with me. I'll buy you a drink to warm your heart," Burke chuckled.

"Not sure I can do that, Otie. But it would sure hit the spot. I shoulda brought me a jug out here."

"Aw, come on. I'm buyin'"

"Naw, I cain't," Billy lamented. "They give me strict orders to stay here."

"What the hell, Billy. What harm can it do to come up to Sully's for a quick one. You'll be back in half an hour. It ain't gonna float away in that time. What you s'posed to be watchin' for anyway?"

"I don' know. They just told me to watch out on the wharf."

"Com'on, man. A shot of Sully's white lightnin'll make the night go faster for you."

"All right. You talked me into it. We'll make it a quick one."

Three pairs of eyes watched Burke weave down the wharf and onto the levee, his arm draped around Billy Barnes' shoulder. As soon as they were out of sight the conspirators walked quickly onto the wharf.

Dowd pointed to several crates. "There they are. Let's get them over to the edge."

Morrison grunted as he shoved one of the crates. "You were right when you said they were like coffins. This devil ain't light. How we goin' to get it out of here?"

Matt Dowd said to Smith, "Mike, get that long boat tied up over there."

Smith ran to untie the boat. "Can we get them all on without sinking?"

"If we keep them in the middle of the boat, we will be all right. Besides, there is a big skiff right beside it. As long as we are going to take one, we might as well take both," Dowd urged.

"We better hurry. If anybody came along, they're gonna see us."

They quickly loaded the crates, two in the large boat and one in the skiff.

Dowd said, "You two men take the long boat and I'll row the skiff. Try to stay together, and, for God's sake, be quiet about it." He pushed off.

The river was swollen with melting snow water from upstream and the swift current made it difficult to row the overloaded boats. The oarsmen puffed and groaned as they tried to get across the river, drifting downstream in their battle against the current. Smith grappled the gunwale of the skiff. They were only twenty yards from shore, but drifting rapidly downstream.

"We ain't gonna make it. I can't get this thing to go across," Morrison complained.

Dowd recognized the problem as real and said as loudly as he dared, "We are not going to make it to Kentucky tonight in this current, men."

"What do we do now, pitch the crates overboard?"

"Not on your life. These guns are important if we have to fight. We have drifted down from the town. Row back close to the bank."

"Then what?'

Smith chimed in, "I say let's get rid of the guns and get ourselves back to town."

Dowd answered cooly. "No. I have got a better idea. Chisholm's farm is just around the bend. We can pull right into Casselbury Creek beside his barnyard. I am sure he is on our side. We can land there and put the crates in his barn for the present. Some night soon, when the current is slower, we'll row them across to Kentucky."

Rousing Jefferson Chisholm from his bed, they explained their predicament. He dressed quickly and helped them carry the crates of muskets to his barn. They put them against the wall and forked hay on top of them.

"Now let's get rid of those boats," Dowd said.

"You just want to let them float downstream?" Chisholm asked.

"Maybe we ought to hole them a little so they sink after they float downstream a piece," Dowd said, picking up an axe as they went back to the riverbank.

Once finished with that task, Dowd proposed, "We got to get up on the road and walk back to town. We don't want to be seen tonight."

Morrison commented, "They're gonna be mad as hell when they find those guns are gone."

"We better split up. If somebody sees the three of us together, they might get ideas," Smith added.

Chisholm said, as the reached his house, "Listen, each one of you take a swig of my whiskey jug and splash a little on your coat. Then if anyone stops you, you can act like you've spent a night drinking."

"Good idea--in more ways than one," Morrison laughed. "Lead me to the jug and force me to drink, but I refuse to waste it pouring it on me coat."

"Go easy on the stuff," Dowd ordered. "You've got to have your wits about you. So just enough to smell like you have spent the evening with the bottle."

"As soon as we get to the edge of town," Smith said, "we'll go in different directions and fade into the background."

"Tomorrow we can all play dumb. Some of them Unionists will probably point the finger at us, so have a story for where you were tonight and be sure you can back it up."

Chisholm pledged, "I never saw you and you were never here. I want you to promise me that you'll get those guns out of here as soon as you can. I can't afford to get caught with that kind of stuff."

"We're all in this together," Dowd shook Chisholm's hand. "Come on, lads, back to Coaltown." The night folded around them.

News of the theft of the weapons spread quickly. When the mail packet docked the next afternoon in Helvetia, Rabert received a letter from August Krönlein, the Coaltown banker. He read it to Gretchen who had come down to the office when she heard him return from the Post Office, hoping for a letter from her parents.

"Listen to this! Krönlein writes: 'It is clear that the Indiana towns along the the river are in danger from Kentucky. We believe that somebody got word to Kentucky about the shipment of the muskets. A bunch from Kentucky must have rowed over in the middle of the night and stolen the guns from the wharf. They took a couple of boats from the wharf so nobody could go after them. The watchman swore he hadn't left the wharf all night. Unfortunately he did have a bottle with him. He wasn't drunk, but he probably fell asleep. He's a strong Union man, so he wouldn't have been part of a plan to steal the muskets.

'This does show that we must be vigilant in our river towns. This shows the danger of raids by southern sympathizers from Kentucky. We have enough of those in our own town. Somebody here unquestionably sent the message to friends in Kentucky about the shipment. I fear that this is only the first of many attacks to come.

'I know that the people of Helvetia are strong behind the Union. Will you warn them through *Die Zeitung* of the need to be vigilant, watching not only for raids across the river but also for traitors in our midst. Maybe you could print a few broadsides and post them around Helvetia to tell people of the danger which this raid demonstrates.'"

Gretchen asked, "What do you make of that?"

"We don't know where Kentucky is in this struggle. It seems pretty certain for the present that the state is not going to secede. But there are plenty of people who have sympathy for the south. They're going to be working, maybe even fighting, to take Kentucky out of the Union, no matter what the legislature does."

"Do you think there could be fighting around here?"

"I really doubt that there will. But Krönlein is right, we have to keep our eyes open. There are just enough hot-heads around to start something. I just don't want to see people get into a panic about it."

The newspapers which came from the big cities along the river were full of accounts and articles about the rising tensions in the seceding southern states. Most attention focused on forts in Charleston. South Carolina was claiming that the Union garrison in several forts in Charleston harbor were foreign troops violating the sovereignty of South Carolina. President Buchanan, with a couple of months remaining in his term, struggled with the question of whether to withdraw these forces or reenforce them so they could resist an assault from South Carolina forces, which had set up batteries of cannons in strategic locations along the shore, across from the forts. Finally Buchanan decided to reenforce the fort. This struggle dominated the night-time discussions in Rabert's office.

Ferdinand Becker had joined the group. He was a vocal supporter of the Union. Leaning back in his chair, he said, "I tell you Buchanan had to decide to hold Fort Sumter. It was bad enough that they pulled back from the other forts."

"If the Union has to put down this rebellion, they'll need those forts to bring troops into the harbors," Paulus Frantz said, walking to the coffee pot. "It would be a terrible mistake to pull out in the face of all this saber rattling."

"I think so too," Johann added, "I was looking at that map that Charles had in *Die Zeitung* and that harbor looks important."

"Johann, you and von Clausewitz. I didn't know you were a military strategist." Becker laughed.

Johann responded without smiling, "From what Charles has been printing it seems to me that there has to be a war. How can America let half the states pull away? The army will have to fight to show those states that they can't rebel against the government. If that's the way it will go, you don't give in right at the start."

Frantz clapped Johann on the shoulder. "You're right about the Union. If this country comes apart and is just two weak halves, all those countries in Europe which still suffer under kings will say, 'See, all this democracy stuff doesn't work. Give people the right to vote and they'll spoil everything.'"

Kurt Leinig broke in. "Johann and me aren't as educated as the rest of you, I know. But we know what we left at home and what we were coming half-way around the world to find. So we're starting to feel pretty strong about breaking up this country."

"I can't really explain it," Johann said. "I admit I've been disappointed that we haven't been able to get ahead the way I thought we would, but I like the freedom we have here. I felt completely locked-in back in *Schlesien*. Here, even though times have been hard, I have the feeling that things can get better. But if the country gets divided, that might not happen."

Rabert took a long drink of coffee. "That's the way everybody has to start thinking. Talking things over the way we do here, reading every newspaper you can get your hands on: will make men good citizens."

"*Ja.*," Frantz said. "Even though you haven't been here long enough yet to become a citizen legally, you can start thinking like one."

Marta looked hard at Johann when supper was finished and the girls put to bed. "I have something I want to talk over with you."

Picking up the resoluteness in her face and the authority in her voice, Johann responded cautiously, "Oh. What?"

"I have been thinking about this for weeks. We have our house finished as good as it is going to be. You are working every day. Things are not going to change." She paused, took a deep breath, "I think it is time we brought Karl over from Neuhaus....It has been more than four years. You said last year that we could bring him in a year."

Johann responded defensively, "I know, but he is still pretty small to make the trip."

"He is almost five years old. There were much younger children on our ship coming over," Marta insisted.

"But who would we get to bring him along?....He would have to come with another family."

Marta said loudly, "Last year we had a family willing to bring him along, and we threw that chance away. We had a chance..." She broke into tears.

"There will be others when we are ready to send for him."

"I have thought of that. When I wrote to Papa, I asked him if there were any of our friends who were coming to America soon. I got a letter from him today. The girls and I went to the Post Office while you were at work."

Johann's face reddened. "You wrote to them about Karl coming over without saying anything to me? I do not like that. In fact, it makes me very angry. You had no right to do that."

"You are never going to bring that up. You don't want him here."

"I just think it would be too hard right now."

"Papa says that the Wernecke's are coming next spring. He mentioned it to them and they said that could bring Karl with them. They would be good to him. They are going to Cincinnati. You could get Karl from there."

"It would make the house too crowded. You know that we hardly have enough room now."

Marta began to cry softly. "He is not going to remember us at all. If he doesn't come soon, it will be much harder for him to learn to know us as his mother and father. And I miss him so much. I think about him every day and wonder how he is and what he is doing. I just sit here at the table and cry while I am working."

"You have no right to be working behind my back to arrange all this. We need more time to get on our feet here."

"I will not rest until I have our son here with us. I have waited long enough. You know how much I miss him."

"We just can't do it now. You write to your father and tell him that it will have to wait."

"You are asking me to do something that tears the heart right out of me."

"You have plenty to do to take care of the girls."

"I try to be a good wife and mother. I have a right to have my son with me," Marta's voice grew louder.

"We just can't do it now," Johann shouted back. "Suppose he got half way across the ocean and a war broke out here. It would not be safe."

Marta covered her face with her hands and ran into the bedroom, throwing herself across the bed and pulling a pillow over her head, sobbing.

Johann went outside and walked up and down the street for an hour.

Conversation with Marta was very muted for the next few days, but the subject was not mentioned again.

News that South Carolina had begun bombarding Fort Sumter took two days to reach Helvetia. The captain of the *Gray Eagle* gave a long blast on his whistle as the packet pulled up to the wharfboat. Men on the dock, hearing the news that war had broken out, ran up the main street telling everyone they encountered. They went into stores and saloons, into the factories along the river. Someone started banging on the iron wagon wheel rim they had hung from a tree in the center of town as a fire alarm bell.

The quietness of the balmy April afternoon was broken by the tumult. Rabert put his head out of the front door of the newspaper office. "What's all the excitement?" he called to Konrad Buhl who was running by.

"The southerners...are f-f-firing on...that f-f-fort in...Charleston," Buhl gasped.

Rabert turned back into the office where Gretchen was sitting. "Well, I am afraid it is happening....War is starting. The southern states are starting to act as the enemy of the Union. They threatened to do this when Lincoln became president. He's been in office less than two months. What a tragedy!"

Gretchen ran her hand across her brow. "I thought when we left Prussia, I would never have to see armies marching. Do you really think there will be war, or is this just a little clash."

"I suppose it depends how resolute the southerners are. If they are just trying to make a point and then will settle down to negotiation, perhaps war can be avoided."

The next visit of the mail packet brought the news that Fort Sumter had been forced to surrender and that it was in the hands of South Carolina. The Union garrison was being sent back to the north. The Union was indeed torn in two. The debate which had taken place in Coaltown on New Year's Day was no longer academic. The Union had truly been broken and the sides were being drawn for conflict.

Both Rabert in *Die Zeitung* and the Coaltown *Reporter* pointed out that the attack on Fort Sumter was disastrous for the south, inflaming and enraging the north. Both newspapers called for calm in the face of the gathering storm. Both editors proclaimed that the Union must be preserved, even if a price had to be paid.

The next days were filled with news of one development after another. President Lincoln had called for 75,000 men from the militias of the various states in the Union to resist the rebellion. Lincoln's rival, the Democrat Stephen Douglas, who had long sought compromise with the south, published statements condemning the capture of Sumter and supporting Lincoln and the Union.

The gatherings in Rabert's office reflected the varied responses of the people of Helvetia. Every week new developments unfolded.

Schoolmaster Frantz reported, "I heard that over in Coaltown they have organized what they call a home guard. They have about fifty men who have guns. Charlie Mason, you know, the fellow who runs the brewery, is their captain. They have built a kind of watch tower so they can watch the river in case a gang tries to come over again from Kentucky. Charlie has them drilling in front of the courthouse a couple of times a week."

"We're going to have the same thing here," the editor added. "Jake Geyer stopped by the office this morning and told me that he is organizing a unit here to watch the river. He is going to call them the Helvetia *Förster*. He is announcing a meeting in *Die Zeitung* to sign up a bunch of men."

"I don't know if that is necessary, or if they just want to play soldiers," Frantz responded. "I suppose there could be a danger from Kentucky; they did steal those guns from the wharf in Coaltown."

"My guess is that Kentucky is going to be what they are calling a border state, still in the Union, but with a large number of citizens who favor the southern cause, maybe even fighting for the south. So it probably is not far-fetched to think that armed men might come across the river and raid our towns."

"But, Charles, what would they want with a furniture factory, a couple of sawmills, a brick works, and handful of little breweries? We are hardly an arsenal."

"To control a section on both sides of the river would be very valuable to an enemy. Some carefully placed cannons could shut down all the traffic on the river. That would be a disaster for the north. So, I say, let them play soldiers for now," Rabert answered.

The northern states, responding to the President's call for 75,000 militia from the states, began to recruit volunteers to be sent to the Union army. Rallies were held in Coaltown and Helvetia. *Die Zeitung* carried an announcement of a rally to be held on the land which had been set aside for a park on Ninth Street. The Helvetia Brass Band was to play and a Captain Mason was going to make a speech. The first men of the Helvetia *Förster* would parade briefly.

The Town Board of Helvetia ordered a quantity of gunpowder and lead for bullets for possible defense of the town. At the time members of the home guard were furnishing their own weapons. All available arms owned by the state were reserved for the militia. Indianapolis sent out promises that soon there would be muskets enough for the home guards and some of the companies along the river would receive a cannon.

Old differences between native-born sons of families who had been in America since colonial times and the recent immigrants, between Douglas Democrats and Lincoln Republicans, between readers of *The Reporter* and *Die Zeitung* faded away under the urgencies of the preparations for defense.

Within a few weeks after the surrender of Fort Sumter, stirred by the oratory of the public rallies, a group of men from Helvetia were organized by Aloys Frey and Ferdinand Becker to enlist as volunteers in the militia. Many of them had had military training in their native Switzerland. Their enlistment was to last for three months. They crowded onto the *Gray Eagle* and disembarked at New Albany. There they were put on a train for Indianapolis where the Indiana militia was gathering for outfitting.

In this time of rallies, home guards, militias, talk of raids across the river, Johann and Marta were preoccupied with the approaching birth of their new baby. As the time drew near Johann would hurry home from work every day. Matti Frantz had promised to stay with Marta during the day. Although she was not a mid-wife, she told Marta that she had assisted her mother, who was a midwife in Germany, many times.

As Johann turned onto Twelfth Street at the end of a balmy May afternoon, he saw Matti come out of the kitchen door and throw a large pan of water into the back yard. She saw him and ran toward him, brushing her bushy hair out of her eyes.

"Well, Papa, you've got another daughter," she called.

Johann ran to the house and into the bedroom. Marta was sitting up in bed, holding the baby. "It is easier every time. I am not even tired. Isn't she pretty?"

Johann put his finger out to touch the soft brown hair on the baby's head. "She looks like you. In a few years you are going to have a lot of help around the house. We are surely getting a lot of girls around here."

Marta said wistfully, "...And a son in *Schlesien*. How I wish little Karl could be here. Our family will never be complete until he is here too."

"She is a pretty little thing," Johann said, sitting on the edge of the bed.

Matti finished gathering up the sheets and towels from the corner of the room. "I'll take these home and wash them, Marta. Should I bring over something for supper?"

Marta smiled, "You've done enough already. You are a good friend. Hannah said she would bring supper. I can always have Johann make milk soup like his mother made. He is always bragging about that."

"Well, then, I'll get back home. What are you going to name your baby?"

"I'd like to call her Jenny. Is that all right with you?" Marta turned to Johann.

"*Ja.* That is fine with me."

"I'll come over in the morning and give you a hand. Got everything where you can get at it?" Matti bustled to the door.

"We will be fine. *Danke schön, Liebe 'Schwester.'*"

River traffic increased ten-fold as preparations for defense of the Union expanded. The normal passage of commercial river boats carrying passengers and freight was augmented by fleets of steamers leased by the government to transport troops and supplies up and down the river. Some gunboats appeared for the first time, hulking craft with a few cannons bristling from their sides.

Charles Steinauer had ridden to Coaltown one morning in mid-September to take care of some banking. He returned to Helvetia in the afternoon filled with stories of excitement in the county seat. He walked heavily into the newspaper office.

"Want to make me a writer for your paper, Charles?" he laughed. "I've got a story for you. I was sitting in the bank talking with Krönlein when there was a big row on the levee. A whole fleet of steamers and barges had pulled up to the Coaltown levee, all tooting like the world was coming to an end. I counted thirteen steamboats, led by the *N. W. Thomas.* There were a bunch of barges too. They stretched from one end of town to the other. They were all government boats. Folks stood along the levee to see this navy. Most of the stores closed. They even turned out the town band to play. Some fellow in a uniform with a lot of gold braid, they all called him "Commodore," went to the Cannel Coal Company. He told Newcomb, the manager, "I need to buy 25,000 bushels of coal to get me to the Mississippi.""

Newcomb started to hem and haw. Half the town was gathered around. They sort of followed this officer up to the coal company office.

Old Newcomb started to sweat. "I don't reckon I can give you that much," he says.

The officer looks him right in the eye, "I'll have 25,000 bushels and it will be loaded today."

"That would take my whole coal supply, all my reserves. I won't have enough for other ships that might stop. And I have factory orders to fill."

The officer sort of strutted around. "Sir, we need that coal today. You can get more for your reserve coal pile. Just get your men to dig it faster. I have to have this whole fleet into the Mississippi by day after tomorrow."

Newcomb didn't give in too easily. "I can't give you all of it."

"I am going to pay you for it. We are not stealing it from you. You wouldn't want people to think you were trying to help the south, now would you?"

Newcomb kept hemming and hawing. Finally this officer turned to some of his men and yells, "Bring that gunboat up here and set your aim on this fellow's house, the big one right over there. We may have to give him some encouragement to sell his coal to us."

Steinauer paused for effect, "I tell you, Charles, old Newcomb turned about six shades of purple then white. He didn't have much choice. He had half a dozen cannons pointed right at his place, Oak Hall. So he tells his men to pull up the wagons and start loading the coal on the steamboats and barges."

Rabert said, "Well, it was a good enough business deal for him. He got his whole coal supply sold in one afternoon. They can add some more miners and produce some more coal before long. He could send a barge over to Kentucky to bring in some more coal."

"You know," Steinauer leaned against the printing press, "I always hoped we could find that vein of coal near Helvetia. When we bought all this land, there was talk of coal deposits."

"I know," Rabert agreed. "But nobody has ever located the vein. It would surely be a boost to the town if we had a good coal mine here. We'd have lots of steamboats docking. Our factories would not have to bring coal in. It could be the bit of luck we need."

Steinauer pulled up a chair and straddled it. "Back to those boats in Coaltown; I guess they could not get any coal in Kentucky since they were under Union command and there is supposed to be an agreement that Union forces will stay out of Kentucky."

"I've been following the Louisville and Cincinnati papers to see what Kentucky is going to do. There is a lot of politics being played. Their two senators do not see eye to eye. Breckenridge is an old fire-eater. He would like to take them right into the Confederacy. Crittenden keeps promoting his compromise to try to negotiate the slavery question and hold on to the Union."

"*Ja*. I guess the people are divided. I heard that both sides were trying to recruit soldiers."

Rabert pointed to a Louisville paper on his desk. "They say that the Governor, Magoffin, favors the south but knows that the majority of people in the state legislature support the Union. So his straddles. He wouldn't answer Lincoln's call for militia."

"Doesn't that throw him in with the south?" Steinauer asked.

"He knows he cannot go that far. So he called a special session of the legislature and has proclaimed that Kentucky is neutral in the conflict. He said that neither side can send any troops onto Kentucky soil unless they were invited to come by the legislature and the governor. He told the people that they cannot show support for either side. Pretty smart, I say."

"And useless, I'd say." Steinauer shoved his hat back on his head and scratched his beard. "If there is serious troop movement, there is no chance that either side is going to stay out of Kentucky, even if it is neutral. The only way they could get at each other west of the Alleghenies is across Kentucky."

"You are right," Rabert answered. "They can say they are neutral; I suppose they have to because they have so many supporters of both sides. As a state they are still in the Union, but they are not going to send their militia to fight for the Union."

"You know, if Kentucky were to go with the south, our river would be between the two countries. In a war neither side could use the river. The Union would lose the river for moving armies and guns. Think of how it would be if all the steamboats that go by here every day stopped altogether because they could be shot at by cannons on either side of the river, depending on their flag."

"That's why Lincoln has to be so careful. He cannot push Kentucky very hard or he would drive them right into the arms of the south."

"*Ja*," Steinauer agreed, "and the south can't push hard either because there are lot of people who want to stay in the Union."

Rabert unfolded the Louisville newspaper again. "It says that both the north and the south have promised that they will not send armies into Kentucky. But this paper makes a strong case for staying in the Union. They are organizing Union clubs and rallies, just like we had around here a month ago. They are organizing home guards, just like here, but in the southern part of the state they are in favor of the south and in the east and north they are Unionists."

"How they going to keep them from fighting each other?" Steinauer wondered.

"We are living right across the river from a powder barrel," Rabert said. "The state of Kentucky may stay neutral, but there are going to be southern sympathizers with guns who can cross the river any night and make a lot of trouble over here. *Die Zeitung* is going to have to tell that story. I do not want to frighten people, but there is a danger which people need to know."

"Then you are saying that this home guard is necessary. I sort of had that figured out as a bunch of fellows who wanted to march around as if they were real soldiers."

Johann and Marta talked about the latest issue of *Die Zeitung* after supper when the girls had quietened down in their bed. Marta pulled her chair up to the kitchen table once the evening chores were done.

"I'm really getting worried with all this talk about Kentucky. Matti and Hannah were full of it today. Hannah said that while they lived in Louisville, there were a lot of people who thought the south was right. Do you think they would cross the river and fight over here?" Marta asked.

"Nobody knows. We were talking about it at the furniture factory while we ate our bread. Kurt said that it is hard to know what is involved because it is all under cover. If you face an army, you can see them, but we have no way of knowing how many people across the river want the south to win, or who they are."

"Could they really come and fight here in Helvetia?"

"That is why they have these Helvetia *Förster*. They have made a couple lookouts in that woods south of town. They say that they take turns watching the river. They would give a warning if men tried to cross at night." His mind went back years to old man Scharf's story of the bullet holes in the church weathervane from the battle between the Prussians and Austrians in Endigen.

"What would we do if they started shooting around here?" Marta shuddered.

Johann put his hand on her arm. "Try not to worry about it. Maybe the best thing is to see that it cannot happen. Some of the men at that factory are in the *Förster*. I have been thinking that maybe I ought to join with them."

"*Nein, Nein!*" Marta protested. "I don't want you to do that. Besides, you don't know anything about being a soldier."

"True. Outside of being with Gustav when he was in his uniform and reading his letters from the army, I don't know much. But maybe I ought to do something to help."

"That scares me."

"There is not a lot of worry about being a *Förster*. They just march around a little and stand guard along the river at night with a musket. I could do that. I used to hunt rabbits back in Endigen. I was a pretty good shot."

CHAPTER 16

As summer came the excitement faded into routine. Kentucky had an election in which the Unionists outvoted the states'-righters almost 3 to 1. The state sent eight strong pro-Union congressmen to Washington and only one who supported states' rights. It became clearer that Kentucky would not pull away from the Union due to a majority of Unionists, but at the same time, in spite of the considerable number of southern sympathizers, it would not become part of the Confederacy.

Rabert also had news from the St. Louis newspapers which he reprinted in detail in *Die Zeitung*. Missouri was another slave state where the sentiments of the population were deeply divided. Among those who supported the Union were the large numbers of recent German immigrants. Their German newspaper had little use for slavery and no old loyalties to draw them toward the south.

The story unfolded in *Die Zeitung* through several weekly editions. In St. Louis there was a large federal arsenal with enough weaponry to outfit an army. Southern sympathizers, who included the state's governor, planned to smuggle in enough guns from the Confederacy to arm the southern sympathizers and seize the arsenal. To counter this, a congressman named Blair, well-known among the German immigrants, hurriedly organized them into a kind of home guard, even though he had no authorization to do so. Then using his influence with the government in Washington, he got permission to reorganize and arm them as a militia made up largely of Germans. He also prevailed on Washington to put an officer, a General Nathaniel Lyon, known for his strong abolitionist sentiments, in command of the arsenal. Fearing a southern attack, plans were begun for temporarily shipping all the military supplies in the arsenal to Springfield, Illinois.

Governor Jackson started gathering southern sympathizers, also calling them a militia, just south of St. Louis. Arms for this informal army were shipped up the Mississippi from Baton Rouge. Soon nearly 12,000 men were gathered in a camp, preparing to capture the arsenal. Lyon watched these developments closely. One day he disguised himself in one of his wife's dresses, with a hat and veil, and rode in a buggy around the militia camp and back to the city. When he saw how lightly defended the encampment was, he called on his German militia and the regular army garrison of the arsenal and without hesitation surrounded the southern camp. With cannons from the arsenal pointing into their faces, the southerners quickly surrendered and gave up their muskets.

Lyon marched them all as his prisoners back into St. Louis. Southern sympathizers from the city gathered along the route. Two small contingents of regular army troops were at the front and the rear of the long column. The German militia marched on the outer edges of the straggling line, guarding the prisoners. The hostile crowd yelled derisively at the Germans, who were recognizable as troops only because they had guns. They had been given no other uniforms. Most had marched out in their work clothes, belted with a cartridge box.

"Look at them furriners holding guns on our good American boys!"

"Turn 'em loose, you foreign apes. Any one of them good southern gentlemen is worth a dozen of you."

Taunts were soon followed by rocks and bricks thrown from the back of the mob. Hearing the tumult the small contingent of regulars from the head of the column turned back to face the mob. They fixed bayonets and pushed their way through the crowd that was closing in on the militia and prisoners. Some of those who had been captured tried to break through the thin militia line to join the shouting mob, but fell back into line at the sight of the blue coats. As the regulars drew up, a shot rang out from the window of one of the buildings. The lieutenant leading the regulars fell to the pavement, holding his arm. The Germans, panicking at the first exposure to hostile fire, began to shoot back at the mob which was pressing in on them. Only after a number of civilians lay dead or wounded along the street did the crowd pull back and let the column through to the arsenal and its defenses.

For several days pockets of fighting broke out between armed southern sympathizers and the militia. Then the trouble died out, and St. Louis was firmly under Union control.

Reading about this fight in St. Louis in *Die Zeitung* stirred up many of the men in Helvetia. Here were immigrants like they were, from the homeland, who were now fighting for their new country. Some of the families in Helvetia had relatives in Missouri and wondered if they were part of this struggle.

War was also taking form in the East, far from Helvetia. The Union Army and the Confederate Army faced each other in northern Virginia. Washington was just across a river from a strong southern slave state. Thousands of militia from the northern states, including troops sent from Indiana, poured into the capital under three month enlistments. In July the newspaper told of a battle at Manassas, outside of Washington. The paper brought the sobering news that the large Union Army was forced to retreat in disorder to the capital city.

Even in remote towns like Helvetia the news was shocking. Everyone in the north had assumed that the gathering Union Army would quickly overwhelm the southern army in one decisive battle; the south would see that rebellion was impossible and rejoin the Union. The battle along Bull Run was seen across the country as a sign that the war would not end with one battle.

Because most of the troops in the Union Army were sent by the northern governors for only three months, President Lincoln immediately called for 300,000 volunteers to enlist for three years. It became increasingly clear that a large army would be needed for a considerable time to put down the rebellion. To make volunteer enlistments more attractive the federal government offered a bounty of $100 to be paid to the soldier when he was discharged.

The build-up for war was having an effect on production at the furniture factory. Much of their market had been in cities and towns along the Ohio and Mississippi. Many of these communities now were in the Confederacy. The steamers that had picked up loads of furniture from Helvetia were now being used to transport army goods and soldiers. The factory's warehouse was full to overflowing and new orders were not coming.

For the past several weeks nothing had been talked about but the war while the men at the furniture factory sat in the shade on the north side of the building as they ate their lunch. There had been a number of public meetings at the *Turnhalle,* encouraging men to volunteer for the army. Because those who had answered the first call for militia had enlisted only for ninety days, enlistments were running out. Many more men were needed, so political orators who were often former army officers eloquently called for men to serve their country.

Johann and Kurt often shared the things they had learned at the discussions of the latest news in Rabert's office. Johann became more and more vocal as a strong Union supporter, arguing with those who claimed that the Germans had no stake in the fight since they weren't even citizens. He talked about the need for the *Förster* as a defense against possible raids from Kentucky.

"*Ich bin ein Amerikaner,*" he proclaimed vehemently. "We came here to make a new life, to leave the old country. We all have traveled across the country since we got off the ships that brought us across the ocean. We've seen the cities and towns, we've known how free you feel when you don't have to be showing your papers all the time to some fellow in a uniform. We're learning about how people can vote for their leaders rather than having to bow to some king."

One of the other workmen, Jake Schmuck, countered at once, "They won't let you be *ein Amerikaner* until you are here a lot longer than it has been since you got off the boat."

Johann drew himself up to his full height. "I guess what I am trying to say is that this is more MY country than anything I knew in Europe. I don't want to see that destroyed. *Verstehst du?*"

"Don't get your steam up! You're starting to take all these speeches to heart."

Albrecht Geyer joined in. "I agree with you, Johann. I listened to that fellow Pleisch from Coaltown when he was over here on Saturday. He's trying to enlist men to form a company for the Second German Regiment."

"He's just a grocer over in Coaltown," Jake responded with a laugh.

Geyer insisted, "He's a *Schweizer* who was in the Swiss army. He sounds like he knows what he is doing. I'm thinking about joining up with him. I am going to Coaltown to talk to him. It's pretty clear to me that we're not going to be able to work much longer here, since we can't ship the furniture out any more."

On their way back into the factory, Johann said quietly to Geyer, "Let me know when you go to see Pleisch. I might want to talk to him too."

"I have a ride to Coaltown after work tomorrow on Schmuck's wagon. You can go along, if you want. We'll be back before dark."

Theodor Pleisch was an impressive figure: tall, broad-shouldered. He had gray eyes set off against his swarthy face. His dark hair and beard gave him a look of fierceness, although his speech was quiet and slow.

"So you men are thinking of becoming part of my regiment, *nicht wahr?*"

Johann quickly said, "I haven't really decided, but I am thinking about it. I have a wife and three daughters, so I can't do anything foolish. I have to think about them too."

"True, true," Pleisch drawled. "

"There is talk that the factory may have to close or cut down. I may not have the job that feeds my family. But ever since that fort had to surrender I have felt that I ought to do something to help bring the country back together."

"That's the way I feel too," Geyer said, "even though I have only one child."

"I can't promise you it will be easy. But you will have your pay from the army, thirteen dollars a month. You can send almost all of that home because everything you need is taken care of by the army--food, clothes."

"But it costs more than thirteen dollars a month to take care of the family," Johann said softly.

"*Ja.*" Pleisch sympathized, "but lot of towns are organizing Aid Societies which also give money every month to the families of soldiers. And the government will give you a hundred dollars when your three year enlistment is over. It is my guess that we will all be home in less than three years."

Geyer said, "I talked it over with my wife last week and I am ready to sign up. How soon will we have to leave?"

Pleisch put out the papers before Geyer and set an inkwell and pen on the counter. "My guess is that we'll leave around the end of October. I want to have at least a hundred men signed up by then. How about you, Weber?"

"Not till I have a chance to talk to my wife about it. If I think I can take care of my family's needs, I'd like to go, too."

It was a warm Sunday afternoon in early October when Johann broached the subject of enlistment to Marta. "I have been talking a lot with some of the men at the factory who are going to the army. There is a lot of talk about work being cut back and some of the fellows see being in the army as better than being out of work."

"Nonsense," Marta snapped.

"It might make some sense. The army pay can be sent home every month and the people of the town help too."

"Nonsense!"

"If I knew my family was taken care of, I'd go too. I've been thinking a lot about it."

Marta shouted at him, "You? You? You'd go off to the army and leave us here? *Nimmer.*"

"Now, just wait. Let's talk about it a little."

"I don't see how anything you could say would make me think it was a good idea," Marta protested, walking around behind his chair.

Johann turned, "Just listen to me for a few minutes. This is something I've thought about seriously. Even though we have been in this country for only four years, I really have come to believe in what it stands for. I think it is worth keeping."

"You never talked that way before. What has gotten into you?"

"You know, I've never before really stood up for anything, except maybe when we decided to come to America. I let Father and Karl and Gustav and Wagner tell me what to do. I never stood up, except that one time, for what I thought was best. The jobs I have had were always just ways of earning money to live on. I never had to take a stand. I think it is time I did."

"But going away in the army. What will become of us? How will we live?"

"You'll have my pay and help from the Aid Society. We still have almost $200 in the bank if you really needed money. I'll miss all of you, but so do the thousands of men who are going into the army. I really think I need to do this, Marta."

"I'll never think it is a good idea, but I can't stop you," Marta responded, turning away with a shiver.

"I know I wouldn't have to go, because we are not citizens yet, but I have started to think of myself as an American."

"I say it's their fight. No need for you to get involved."

"We've known since we left Silesia that we would never go back. This is where we are going to live the rest of our lives. Our girls will grow up here. Isn't that so?"

325

"But we still have a son in *Schlesien*. Have you forgotten that?" Marta protested, her voice rising. "We haven't talked for a year about bringing little Karl over here to be with his family."

"True. Maybe when this war is over, we can work something out. It would be too hard for travelers now," Johann replied. "I told Pleisch that I'd think about it for a week and then let him know if I want to enlist, so we'll think about it for a few days."

The following morning after Johann left for work, Marta walked to the Frantz house, carrying baby Jenny, with the two little girls trudging along beside her. Her face was tearstained beneath her sun bonnet.

Matti was already out in the garden. She looked up to see who was coming around the corner of the house. Seeing the tears, she ran to her friend.

"What is the matter. You look like you have had bad news from the homeland. Did somebody die?"

Marta began to sob. "I am so upset. Johann told me that he wants to join the army and go to the war. How can he even think that? Doesn't he know how awful that would be for all of us?"

Matti put her arm around Marta's quivering shoulders. "These men! Paulus has been making some of the same kinds of noises, but with his leg, he can't be a soldier. Come on in the kitchen. We'll give the girls a little milk. Then we can talk and have a good cry."

"How can he march away and leave me...and the girls?" she sobbed. "It is mean and hateful to desert us like that. I don't see why he wants to be a soldier. He always said he was so glad he never got called for the Prussian Army. And he had lots of stories about how much his brother, Gustav, hated being in the army. And now he wants to go...."

Matti shook her head. "Paulus talks about how important it is for our future that the country stay together, that those states come back into the country. He keeps pointing across the river and saying that it would be terrible to have that a foreign country."

"I knew all that talking at night down at Herr Rabert's office was going to lead to trouble. Johann never had any interest in politics before he started spending time there. He is a different man than he used to be."

"Paulus says that it is one of the few exciting things around town. He says it is the best way to really learn about this country. They are all good men and they want to do what is right. Herr Rabert is a very smart man."

"Why can't they leave well enough alone? Why get involved in somebody else's fight?"

"I guess they think it is their fight too, since we live in America."

"I wish we'd never come, if going to war is what comes of it!" Marta said vehemently, her eyes filling with tears.

"I know it is hard. I'd feel that way, too, if Paulus could go into the army. But if a man feels it is important to go to fight for the country, I guess we have to respect that feeling," Matti responded.

"I don't think I can do that. I hate the whole idea! How can he leave us? I feel so helpless. I have three little girls to think about."

"The men all say that the war will not last long, that the army will be so strong that the south will have to give in and come back into the country."

"I thought about writing to Johann's brothers to tell them about this crazy idea. They would tell him not to go."

"That would take months...and I am not sure Johann would listen to them if they told him not to go. When he talks about them, I always feel that he is glad to be free of their influence."

"I suppose you are right. If they told him not to go, he might just do it to show that he doesn't have to follow their orders. He had enough of that while they were growing up. You are right."

Two small groups of volunteers had left Helvetia and Coaltown during the summer. The communities turned out to honor those brave men who were marching off to defend the Union. But when Captain Pleisch's company was preparing to leave on Tuesday, November 12, Helvetia knew if was sending ninety of its men into the army. All along Main Street flags had been tacked to the fronts of the buildings. Boxes and crates on the wharf boat had been stacked into a makeshift bandstand, swathed in bunting. Paulus announced that school would be dismissed for the morning.

The excitement did not reach into the house on Twefth Street. Marta resolved to be brave, trying to keep back her tears. She had held Johann close before they got out of their bed. She put their best clothes on Emma and Anna, and a new cap she had knitted for baby Jenny. Johann had been told to wear his work clothes because uniforms would be given to them when they got to Camp Vanderburgh in Evansville. Marta determined that the rest of his family would be well-dressed for the farewell.

"You are not eating your breakfast," Johann observed.

"I'm not hungry. You eat. This will be the last home-cooked meal you will have for a while."

"I will miss that. I will miss talking with you while we eat supper. I will miss having you and the girls around."

Marta wiped a tear from her cheek with the back of her hand. "I promised myself I was not going to cry, but I can't help it."

"You will get along all right. I will send a letter every week and send money from my pay. All the fellows say we will be back home in a year or less. It seems a long time, but we will make the best of it."

Straightening her shoulders, Marta said, "We will have to. Matti said she would keep me from being lonely. She is such a good friend. I don't know what I would do without her."

Johann pushed back his chair. "We are supposed to meet at the *Turnhalle* at nine o'clock and march down to the steamer. You and the girls can go down by the wharf boat to see us off. We will say goodbye here."

He picked up each of the girls and held them close. "You take good care of Mama," he smiled.

Marta put her arms around him and buried her head in his chest. "*Ich liebe dich.*"

"*Ich liebe dich.* Don't cry. I will think of you every day." Johann held her close for a moment and then held her out at arm's length. Looking into her tear-filled eyes, he had to clear his throat as he said, "*Auf wiedersehen.*"

He picked up the small bundle in which he had his razor, a modest supply of writing paper and pencils, a little picture Marta had given him back in Neuhaus. He hugged her once more. "'*Wiedersehen.*" He walked out the front door and closed it quietly behind him.

Carrying Jenny on her hip, Marta had to allow time for the two little girls to walk with her to the river. They were excited to see the flags and the crowds of people gathering at the wharf. The steamer, *Eugene*, was pulled up to the wharf. A contingent of volunteers who had boarded at Coaltown already lined the rail on the top deck.

The crowd heard the parade approaching from the center of town. First came a small group of men from the Helvetia *Förster*. One carried a flag while the others marched along carrying their muskets. They did not have uniforms except for military caps and cartridge boxes belted around their ample stomachs. Then came the Helvetia Brass Band in their fancy red and black uniforms, purchased after an ox roast the previous summer.

Behind them marching, after a fashion, to the martial airs came the ninety volunteers, led by Capt. Pleisch who already had his uniform. They were in rows of six and stretched back down the street for a block. The crowd along the parade route shouted again and again *"Hoch," "Prosit," "Auf wiedersehen."* The men waved to their families as they marched out onto the wharf. Once on the *Eugene* they gathered at the rail along the lower deck and waved. The captain in his pilot house pulled on the whistle lanyard and drowned out the band for a moment. The side paddlewheels began to splash and the *Eugene* turned out into the channel, soon to disappear around the bend of the river below Helvetia.

Less than an hour from Helvetia small groups of men started playing cards on some of the crates on deck. Johann stood for a long time at the railing, looking back toward Helvetia. Then he slowly moved along the deck until he found a spot in the shade and sat on the deck with his back against the deckhouse wall. He pulled his hat over his eyes and tried to sleep, but sleep would not come.

What have I done? he thought. Have I made a terrible mistake? Have I hurt my family by leaving? Then arguments from the other side flooded in. This is now my country. I believe in a strong Union which gives people freedom and opportunity. I have to stand up for what I believe.

He looked out at the Indiana river bank, the low hills with their bare trees in the background, the little river towns which dotted the shore every few miles.

At noon a small crew of men moved along the deck with tin cups of strong coffee and hard *Brötchen*. It reminded Johann of their weeks crossing the ocean. It seemed a lifetime ago, but it was only a little more than four years.

The *Eugene* docked in Evansville in late afternoon. The men were told to get in rows of eight to march to Camp Vanderburgh. There they were assigned to tents and given sacks to fill with straw for mattresses and issued a blanket each. A bugle blew and they saw men pour out of other tents and line up. Johann and his tent mates did the same. A column formed for the march to the mess hall. It was a large frame building, somewhat rickety looking. Each man was given a metal plate and a knife. Moving through a line cooks dished a kind of stew onto the plates and the men sat down at the long tables. There were baskets of bread on the tables and tin cups with coffee pots. The men were hungry and fell to eating amidst the racket of knives clashing on plates as they speared the chunks of meat and potatoes. The several hundred voices got louder and louder, making conversation difficult. Johann realized that he was hungry and found the food reasonably tasty. His tentmates, Albrecht Geyer, Konrad Buhl, Jakob Stocker, and Fritz Bauer, wiped up their plates with bread.

Stocker patted his belly. "Just as good as the old woman makes back home. I bet we'll get a lot more meat than we ever got in Helvetia."

"I hear...they feed the army pretty g-g-good," Buhl added with a belch.

Johann looked up from his plate. "Here comes a fellow with a lot of stripes. Now what?"

"You, men," barked the sergeant, standing on a bench. Realizing that most of his troops spoke German rather than English, he motioned directions as he gave his orders. "Take your plates over there and wash them in the barrel. Then get to your tents and get ready to bed down. Better get a good night's sleep because tomorrow is going to be a busy day. When you hear the bugle in the morning, you pop out of those tents and line up. As soon as breakfast is over, we'll get you your uniforms and start making soldiers out of you."

Those in the ranks who knew some English quickly interpreted the main points of the sergeant's orders.

In a big tent the next morning the men lined up. A couple of doctors from Evansville thumped them a few times on the chest and back, took their pulse, watched them walk a few paces and quickly passed them through as physically fit. The line moved to long tables stacked with uniforms: union suit underwear, light blue pants, shirts, dark blue woolen jackets, caps with little round tops, belts, and shoes. Soldiers behind the tables sized up each volunteer quickly and picked items from specific piles: tall, medium, small. Because shoes needed to fit better to make marching possible, each man was able to hold the shoes up to his feet to get them close to the right size. The shoes were not in pairs because all were made to fit either foot. They became left or right shoes only after being thoroughly broken in by the wearer.

Back at their small tent Johann and his tentmates struggled into their new ill-fitting uniforms.

Bauer laughed, "Johann, here...trade coats with me. My sleeves come up about to my elbows and you look like you could turn around twice in yours. They sure picked 'em off the wrong piles when we came along."

"I am going to have to cut a few inches off these pants. I wish Marta could get her hands on them; she would make them fit," Johann answered.

Geyer waved his pants in the air. "Here, Johann, try these. I could stand a little more length."

They took turns sitting on the box in front of their tent to put on their new army shoes. They were intended to be a bit tight at first, so each hobbled and hopped a bit, getting used to the fit.

"These damned things are plenty tight. *Scheiß*! If I have to walk very far before I get 'em broke in, I'm gonna have a mess of blisters," Stocker groaned.

"I wonder how long they will last; not many weeks, I'll bet," Johann answered.

Geyer said, "I'm going to try wearing two pairs of socks until they fit better."

They inspected each other and joked about the hap-hazard fit of some of their uniforms. They laughingly practiced flowing salutes and bows.

The next morning the four hundred men were marched to the railroad and put on a train for Vincennes. When they got to the tent encampment on the outskirts of the town, they are again assigned to tents by the sergeants who were attached to the camp.

A bugle sounded and the sergeants yelled for them all to come to the parade ground in the center of the encampment. They were again arranged in ranks in front of a small platform on which a group of officers stood.

The sergeant growled, "You men are going to have to get into ranks by yourselves from now on. This is the last time I'm going to lead you around by the hand. And you better learn damned fast how to form ranks: straight lines, no gaps, units together."

The men from Helvetia were formed behind Captain Pleisch and Nicholas Steinauer, his first lieutenant. Just behind them, trying to look like experienced soldiers in their new uniforms were Ernst Kipp and August Cram, the second lieutenants. They had gotten their commissions because they worked hard during the recruiting in Helvetia. The men in the ranks knew them as neighbors or tradesmen or fellow-workers in Helvetia. To acknowledge their superior rank would take some time.

A redhaired officer in a dress uniform stepped to the front of the platform and raised his arms for quiet. The men stood roughly at attention.

"Men, I am Lt. Col. Robert Browning. I come from Perry County like many of you do. I want to introduce you to our commanding officer. He is Colonel Richard Owen. He has a distinguished army record. He served as a captain in the Mexican War and commanded a regiment of Indiana militia last spring which answered the President's first call for troops. They fought in western Virginia and chased a small army of Confederates out of that part of the state. He wants to say a few words to you." He paused long enough to allow the officers of the German companies to translate for their men.

Col. Owen was a middle-aged man, standing straight in his uniform. His dark eyes moved across the ranks in front of him. With his hand on the sword at his side, he began to address his troops. He spoke first in English and then to everyone's surprise summed up what he was saying in German.

"Men, you are the first part of the 60th Indiana Volunteers. During the next few weeks we are going to be joined by five hundred more men to fill out the regiment. We are going to become the Second German Regiment in Indiana, and I am resolved that we are going to be a crack regiment. We are going to be known for our discipline, for our courage, for our ability to fight for the Union.

"We are going to spend a few weeks here in Vincennes training, learning how to be good soldiers. The rest of the men will join us here. You will be ready to teach them what you have learned. So you are going to be the core of this regiment. Here in Vincennes we are going to be drilling with wooden guns. We'll get our muskets when we move to Indianapolis in a few weeks.

"I am asking you to work hard, harder than you have ever worked before. We want the 60th Indiana to be known across the state and the country as the very best. I will do my best and I know you will too. We are going to start drilling by squads this afternoon. Your sergeants will have you drilling as good as regular army before we leave Vincennes."

Captain Pleisch turned to the men of Company A. "You heard the Colonel. I want us to be the best company in the 60th. Let's show them what the men from Helvetia and Coaltown can do."

The next few weeks were an endless cycle of drilling, mess call, cleaning up the camp, drilling, cooking, mess call, washing, marching. When dusk came, the exhausted men were glad to get to their tents and fall into deep sleep. Morning came too soon; the daily cycle began all over again.

A few of the men had served in the Swiss or Prussian armies. Many others had left their homeland to evade the Prussian conscription. Johann was resting in front of his tent as the sun was setting. A man he had known slightly in Helvetia, Peter Schulz, sat in front of the next tent. He was telling the story of his coming to America. "You know, I had a lot of trouble when I came across in 1854. In our village we played a lot of games to get out of going to the army. We didn't like the Prussians. I kept telling people that I was younger than I really was. I moved into town from the country after my papa died, so nobody knew me as a little child. I didn't have trouble getting permission to emigrate. They didn't think I was old enough for the draft. After I left, somebody found out and told the authorities. They couldn't get me, because I was already on my way to America. But they did find out that I had a few *Taler* coming to me by inheritance from my uncle. So the state took that money, which my family was keeping for me. Oh well, I won't miss it, since I never had it. But isn't it funny that I went through all that business to stay out of the Prussian army and now I come over here and volunteer for this army."

Johann said, "It is the same for me. I didn't get called for the draft, but my brother had to go. I never wanted any part of the army, except maybe the uniform. But here I am, too. I got the uniform, but it doesn't even fit and itches something awful when we are drilling. I can remember my brother saying how boring it was to be drilling all the time."

"Maybe one of the good things that'll come out of it is that the country'll see that us Germans can be good Americans. I get mighty tired of some of those loudmouths who want to put us all back on a boat for Europe. We'll show them a thing or two."

The steady drilling of the troops and the discipline of camp life molded the men into soldiers. Conversations while they ate their meals usually focussed on their officers. Those with prior military experience in Europe made ready comparisons with officers under whom they had served. There was general high regard for Col. Owen. He was seen as a fair man, dedicated to turning his regiment into a well-trained and effective force. His willingness to speak some German bonded the men with him.

There was not the same high regard for the second in command, Lt. Col. Robert Browning. He had come to Perry County and had bought a large, tract north of Coaltown where there was a coal mine. He soon became one of the wealthier land-owners. Some of the soldiers had known him there.

Matthias Kunkel who lived between Coaltown and Helvetia, said he had done business with Browning. "He don't know nothing 'bout soldiering. Us fellows who were simple musketeers in the Prussian army know more than he does. He never spent a day in the army before he got his uniform."

"Then how did he become an officer?" Johann asked.

"Influence, man, that's how!" Kunkel said. "He was a big Democrat politician, making speeches for the men running for office. They returned his favor by arranging for him to be an officer. That's the way we got most of these officers."

"About the only thing I have seen him do is to make speeches," Geyer added. "And because he talks English we don't even know what he is yelling about."

Buhl put in, "He's a b-b-big mouth all right...One of the fellows who understands some English told me that B-B-Browning talks a good f-f-fight: all about marching right into the heart of Dixie and showing the rebels who is boss."

"We'll just have to listen to Pleisch and do what he tells us. I guess he knows what the big mouth orders."

Buhl laughed. "B-B-Browning struts around in that uniform. He's got more gold braid hanging on his soldier suit than Col. Owen, who is a real soldier. And that sword he wears...I'll b-b-bet there are jewels on the handle."

Geyer said, "Ja, fake jewels. Somebody told me that he writes letters back to be published in the Coaltown *Reporter*. He tells all about what the regiment is doing and how he is turning us into good brave soldiers. He even wrote about a ball the officers went to in one of the fine houses in Vincennes."

Kunkle arched a stream of tobacco juice, "Better if he would tell folks about our party, in our fine tents and our fancy dress uniforms. We dance with our wooden muskets in rows of eight; left, right, back and forth across the field."

Johann added with a touch of seriousness, "Maybe Rabert is able to put some of that in *Die Zeitung* so our wives could know a little about what we are doing. I have only sent one letter to Marta to let her know where we are."

Johann stood with the crowd every day as mail was distributed, waiting. A week later Marta's answering letter arrived.

Lieber Gatte,

I was so happy to get your letter from Vincennes. For a
moment you seemed close once again. I miss you so much. The
days go so slowly, and the nights never seem to end. The little
girls are all well. They had a hard time trying to understand
why you were not coming home every night. I tried to tell
them but they are too young. *Die Zeitung* said this week that
the county is selling bonds to get money to give to the families
of soldiers. They will pay the bonds back beginning next year
with tax money. I don't know how much they will give us or
when it will start, but it will be a help. The paper said that it is
for poor families whose husbands and fathers have gone into
the army. That sure sounds like us. Some of the women have
started what they call a Patriotic Aid Society. They heard about
a group in Coaltown and decided to start one here in Helvetia.
They are knitting socks and gloves. They are also going to send
shirts and underwear for you soldiers. I will try to find out if
some can be sent to you. Always tell me where you are so I can
write to you. Tell me about what you are doing. There is not
much new here. Paulus brought me a nice pile of stove wood.
He said he misses you. He said he wishes he could be with all
you men from Helvetia. Dear husband, I think often of you
and love you.

Your wife,
Marta

At the beginning of the new year, 1862,, after several hundred more
men arrived to fill out the ranks of the regiment, the officers began to
organize the troops more efficiently. The companies were divided into five
squads with a sergeant over each squad.

Captain Pleisch stopped in front of Johann's tent and called,
"Weber!"

Johann struggled out of the low tent flap and stood at attention.

"Weber, I have been watching you during the last week. You are not
a big strong hulk like some of these fellows, but you follow orders very
well in drill. I notice that the men respect you and your opinions. You are
serious about what is going on."

"*Danke schön, Herr Kapitan,*" Johann responded.

"We are getting the company organized and I want you to be one of
my sergeants. You will have about 20 men in your squad. It will be up to

you to see that they learn to follow orders and become good soldiers. Can you do that?"

"Yes, sir!" Johann answered, trying to sound resolute and self-assured.

"Tomorrow we start getting ready to move. So you'll get a good chance to lead your men right away. We leave on the train to the assembly camp in Indianapolis day after tomorrow. The sergeants will meet first thing in the morning to get orders for packing up what we are going to take along and organizing the move to the depot. We are going to march out of here like an army, not like the bunch of sheep that got herded in here two months ago."

Johann was taken aback by this offer. He had not thought of himself as a leader. "I will do my best," he stammered.

"You can do it. I think I know how to judge good men."

Johann wrote immediately to Marta to tell her about his promotion. He was especially proud to share the news that Capt. Pleisch had told him that his pay would now be fifteen dollars a month.

They loaded onto trains in Vincennes and rode all day to Indianapolis. Company A was ordered into one of four coaches but most of the men rode in box cars. They were being taken to the camp where most of the Indiana regiments gathered for final outfitting before being moved to join one of the Union armies in Virginia or along the Mississippi River. The mustering camp, named for the Indiana governor, Morton, was a large tract of 30 acres a mile or so north of the state capital. It had been the State Fair Grounds for several years before the war.

The 60th Indiana Volunteers marched from the railroad station to Camp Morton. Several months of drilling produced a column which marched smartly through the streets. The city had grown so accustomed to marching men that citizens barely looked up from their activities, in spite of a drum and bugle corps that marched at the head of the column.

On the fair grounds there were many buildings: barns and long rows of stalls roofed and walled on three sides, exhibition halls, a large dining hall, broad walkways, numerous shade trees. A creek ran through the grounds. Every hundred yards or so a small wooden bridge spanned the creek. There were benches and little pergolas from time to time along the quietly flowing waters. It had been a show place for the capital city.

Pressed into use by the regiments of volunteers who had responded to President Lincoln's call after the fall of Fort Sumter, the stalls had been converted to makeshift barracks and a ten foot high fence of oak planks was built around the entire camp. The 60th and a couple of other regiments were assigned to the long sheds along the west side of the grounds, six men to the tier of bunks in each stall. A number of large barracks were almost finished, built by carpenters in open spaces here and there in the camp. They would give more permanent shelter to the troops that would be coming later. With the new sheds and barns, the camp would soon be able to house 6000 men.

Camp routine here was not much different than Vincennes, except that the troops had now been supplied with muskets, bayonets and cartridge boxes. There were endless hours of drilling on a large field which had been leveled just to the south of the camp.

The newspapers they read told of some great victories in the south. Every few days there were new accounts of the major campaign led by a General Grant. A large Union army was moved by relays of steamboats from the Ohio River, up the Tennessee River from Paducah to attack Fort Henry. Seeing the massive federal force coming against them, most of the Confederate forces were withdrawn to nearby Fort Donelson on the Cumberland River. After heavy bombardment from Union gunboats and artillery the defending rear guard holding Fort Henry surrendered.

Grant had then sent his gunboats back down the Tennessee to the Ohio River and then up the Cumberland to Fort Donelson. He marched his army the twenty miles from Fort Henry and began an attack. Again the southerners, seeing that they could not win, tried to break out but a Confederate General Simon Bolivar Buckner and 15,000 troops had to surrender to Grant. It was the first great Union victory.

Lt. Col. Browning addressed the troops drawn up in formation on the Camp Morton drill field. He had added a long curling white plume to his hat. His oration went on and on. The German-speaking soldiers knew little of what was being said, but gathered from the dramatic pauses and extravagant gestures that he was describing the battles they had read about. Finally, he drew his sword, faced toward the south, whirled it around his head and slashed at the air as if leading a charge. The soldiers at parade rest smiled and then began to cheer.

The men talked about the battles as they ate their supper. Stocker proclaimed, "I wish they'd wait for us before they win this war. There ain't goin' to be any fightin' left by the time we get to shoot our new guns."

"Don't give up hope, Jakob," Bauer laughed. "Capturing two forts is not going to end this war. You'll have your chance."

Johann had talked with Capt. Pleisch after the oration. He reported, "Ja! These battles did drive the rebels further away from us, way down into southern Tennessee, but they still have a big army down there. The officers all think that there will be a lot more fighting."

"Everybody except that cockerel Browning," Bauer slapped his knee. "He acted like he had scattered the enemy all by himself, from a distance of 150 miles."

"Let him have his f-f-fun," Buhl chuckled. "He is harmless."

Bauer responded, "True enough. But if we ever get into the fight, I don't think I would follow him too closely."

Buhl joined the fun. "Listen, if there is a f-f-fight, I am going to stay as close to him as I can…You can be sure he is going to be in the safest p-p-place possible."

Charles Rabert mailed a dozen copies of each edition of *Die Zeitung* to Johann with instructions to pass them around the Helvetia volunteers. They were passed from tent to tent as the men devoured the news from home and the stories about the progress of the war.

"Listen to this," Johann said to the men around him. "Rabert writes that on Sunday, February 28, the steamer *Argonaut* stopped at Helvetia for a few hours. It had aboard the Confederate General Simon Bolivar Buckner who was captured at Fort Donelson on February 13. There were about 300 southern prisoners from the battle who were being sent to Indianapolis.

The paper says that several boatloads of wounded soldiers have passed through on their way to a military hospital in Jeffersonville. It says that some of our women in Helvetia took sheets and bandages to the wharf boat when these steamers come in. They told Rabert that if any of their men were ever wounded in fighting they would hope that women in some town would help to care for us."

When Johann passed the paper on to Capt. Pleisch, the officer said, "You are going to get to see those men on the boats. This camp is going to be made into a prison camp. We start getting it ready tomorrow morning."

Johann asked, "You mean we are being moved out tomorrow?"

"*Nein*," Pleisch answered. "The troops who are in camp now are staying right here. We are ordered to work with the carpenters for the next days to strengthen the stockade and to build a walkway for guards on the outside of the wall all around the camp. Lots of men from the city will be here to help us too. The prisoners are being held in New Albany, and a bigger bunch in St. Louis. So this wall has to be strengthened fast."

The next morning wagonload after wagonload of lumber came to the camp. Once the wall was braced from the outside, a walkway was built all the way around on the outside about four feet from the top of the high board fence. Here guards could walk their posts and watch over the prisoners. Three double gates with sally ports were built into the wall, two along the turnpike and one near the culvert where the creek flowed into the camp.

Outside each corner of the wall on small embankments two cannons were placed, pointing along each side. These were to deter any expectations that large groups of prisoners could rush the gates.

The soldiers of the 60th and companies from the 61st and 63rd regiments were moved out of the long buildings with stalls and pitched neat rows of tents outside the wall. The whole 30 acre camp was surrounded by encampments of companies. Johann and his men of Co. A were told to pitch their tents just to the east of the water gate. They had cots and new straw bags for their beds. Each of the Sibley tents was built on a wooden platform and had a small stove, which they used for cooking and heating. Wooden sidewalks were built connecting the tents and the gates, because the ground had become very muddy.

"You know," Geyer said, "even though these are tents, they are better than those three-walled stables we have been in."

"They smell better. That is for sure," Stocker added.

"At least we are not cooped up inside that high wall."

"We'll see how them rebs like that."

Col. Owen addressed his men, speaking both in English and in German. "We have our first assignment. The training is over. We are on active duty at last. It is our task to see that this camp is well-run, that the prison is secure. We have to guard the fence; we have to maintain order and discipline among the prisoners; we have to get them organized and see that they have food and water. We will be fair and just with them. I will not tolerate any meanness toward them. Your officers will explain to you how we are going to divide the duties. I want every man to do the job that is assigned to him. It will take a few days to get everything in place, but right now I want two squads from Co. A. to take positions with their muskets and cartridge boxes all around the wall. The first prisoners will be here by sun-down. So, Capt. Pleisch, post your men!"

Johann and his squad of twenty went up the eight wooden steps beside the main gate to the walkway which was built onto the high plank fence all around the camp. According to instructions he posted his men every twenty yards or so along the walkway. They overlooked the deserted camp. It looked so different from when the regiments were training there. Now only a few men were unloading piles of straw and firewood from wagons. Although the grass, browned by winter, had been worn off by the feet of the troops, there were clumps of trees reaching their bare branches to the gray wintry sky.

Soon they heard the sound of marching men. A column of several hundred men in ragged clothing, some of them barefooted, began to march through the main gate, guarded on each side by Union troops. Col. Browning, complete with white plume, was on horseback, his sword pointing the men to the low sheds with their stalls along the west wall of the camp. The prisoners, looking very tired, walked slowly toward their new quarters. Many had small bundles of their belongings. As each man passed through the gate his name, rank, and unit were recorded by clerks at a long table.

Johann watched this first contingent of many to come. Their orders were to watch for any prisoners who might try to scale the wall and to look for any disorder within the camp. They could be seen easily by the prisoners, a constant reminder that the wall was defended.

Within the next several days the ranks of prisoners swelled to more thirty-seven hundred. The crowds of captured southerners walked about slowly or stood or sat in small groups. Some were in recognizable uniforms, others looked like roughly dressed workmen or farmers. Many had blankets draped over their shoulders to warm them against the early March chill. The Quartermaster secured several wagon loads of Union uniforms which had been rejected by army inspectors as shoddy and distributed them to men without proper clothing.

On the far side of the creek that ran through the camp was a collection of long, white, wooden barracks with small windows high in the walls. Vent openings ran along the ridge of the roofs for the entire length of the buildings to provide some light and ventilation. There were washlines strung between the numerous trees, large and small, scattered inside the enclosure. Blankets, underwear, shirts and pants were flapping in the breeze. A grove of tall elms stood just outside the fence just beyond the guards' tents.

Johann, as sergeant, walked from man to man along the walkway overlooking the camp. He stopped to talk a little while with each of the guards as they looked out over the prison.

"They look like a pretty sad...sort of bunch," Buhl observed. "They look all worn out. See how slow they all move...The f-f-fight has gone out of them."

"A lot has happened to them. Less than a month ago they were fighting a couple hundred miles away. Then it was a week or more on steamboats and trains to be put behind the fence here. The captain said this first batch rode all the way from St. Louis in box cars

"They won't be here too long. The Colonel told us that we only keep them until the other side has a number of our men they have captured. Then each side sends back an equal number of men: a general for a general, a captain for a captain, a private for a private. He said that a general is exchanged for 30 privates, if the other side has not captured a general. He said they sometimes exchange them right on the spot after the battle if both armies have prisoners. But they captured so many southerners at those forts that they had to bring them here to wait until there are enough of our men to exchange. They will probably be out of here in a few months and go back home to fight again."

"Where is that g-g-general that was captured, the one that was on the boat that stopped in Helvetia?..I don't see anybody who looks like a general."

Johann responded, "They said that the general got here from New Albany a couple of days ago. The captain said that Buckner and his staff are in a building downtown. The other officers are in here with their men. They are probably the ones that have uniforms. Most of these fellows are just ordinary soldiers like us."

Buhl spat over the top of the fence. "I hope that never happens to me. I would go c-c-crazy being cooped up like that in a big pen with hundreds of other fellows. I don't blame them for wanting to try to escape."

The prisoners were so hungry that they devoured their rations in minutes. When this was reported to Governor Morton, he purchased four thousand extra rations from state funds to supplement the first days of army rations. Many citizens of Indianapolis, having seen the miserable condition of the prisoners marching from the railroad station to the camp, started bringing gifts of food, clothing, blankets from their own homes.

After a month on guard duty the 60th Indiana had settled into a well-organized routine. Two squads were always posted onto the walkway around the fence, relieved after four hours by the next watch. Other squads patrolled inside the camp and every morning required the prisoners to fall in by ranks to count the men.

The only trouble in the first week was an order to remove all the officers from the camp because it was rumored that they were organizing various escape plans. Col. Owen formally and courteously requested all Confederate commissioned officers to gather inside the main gate. A few of them had with them black servants who had accompanied them since they left their homes. Col. Owen and Governor Morton telegraphed Washington for instructions on what to do with these black slaves. Commanding General Halleck told them that any who wished, could be let go free. Those personal servants who did not wish to leave were assigned to the crude camp hospital as orderlies. The rest of the officers were marched to a *Turnhalle* downtown, where they were confined until they were moved to Johnson's Island in Ohio. General Buckner was sent to Fort Warren in Boston harbor.

Because this was the first time in the war that large numbers of enemy soldiers were imprisoned, there were no established procedures or regulations for prison camps. Col. Owen published a list of eleven rules for Camp Morton. It divided the prison population into thirty divisions, each with a number of companies. The chiefs of these divisions, selected from the sergeants of companies, were made responsible for keeping their areas clean and orderly. They were to judge and punish thievery, insubordination, fighting. There were arrangements for issuing tobacco, stationery, and reading material to the prisoners. Provision was made for bathing and for sports. Regulations for mail to and from families were set out. Tubs, soap and clotheslines were provided. Col. Owen told his officers that he wanted to treat prisoners in ways that would make them less restless and would encourage them, after they were exchanged, to tell neighbors and fellow soldiers that they were well-treated by the Union.

Once the officers were removed, Col. Owen had given the sergeants in each company of prisoners responsibility for organizing their men and getting the necessary food, blankets, and clothing for them. Some of the guards drove a wagon with food supplies daily to the prisoners' kitchens.

Another contingent was posted at the gate to admit the steady stream of patrols, as well as civilians from the community who had passes to enter the camp. They carefully checked everyone leaving through the gate.

In April a large bakehouse was built in the camp to provide bread for the 5000 prisoners. The quartermaster computed the savings from not having to buy the bread and a fund was established to buy equipment for the camp: brooms, buckets, tobacco, stationery, stamps, scissors for cutting hair.

The sutler of the 60th Regiment was W. P. Beacon. He came with his wagon daily to the guards' tents to sell his tobacco, food items, socks and gloves. The off-duty soldiers flocked around this little general store on wheels to make their purchases.

The enterprising sutler arranged with Col. Owen to enter the camp twice a week to sell to the prisoners. A few had money which had not been taken from them at the time of their capture. Others received federal greenbacks, now unpopular in the south, in letters from home. Prisoners were glad to buy tobacco, playing cards, harmonicas, pencils and paper, newspapers to make life behind the fence a bit more tolerable.

Col. Owen was faced with a problem when rival sutlers tried to enter the camp to sell their wares at inflated prices. He quickly issued orders that they were to be barred from the camp, but local citizens vehemently protested that the army was discriminating against local merchants.

The most popular activity was whittling. Prisoners had been allowed to keep their pocket knives. They carved wood and bones from their meat rations. They made pipe bowls, rings, puzzles, brooches. They were allowed to send many of these items home.

Regimental headquarters was set up in several of the buildings just outside the main gate. This street of buildings had been part of the turnpike approach to the fairgrounds before the war. Most were one storey frame cottage-like buildings which now housed the officers. The big bare-limbed trees lining the street in front of these buildings had trunks whitewashed to the height of a man. There was one larger two-storey building painted dark barn red. Its cornices and porches were decorated with intricate white-painted scroll work. This was Col. Owen's busy headquarters. A steady stream of officers and men went in and out, past the two sentries standing guard at the corners of the porch.

Johann led his squad, bayonets fixed to their muskets, through the gate into the camp. Every fourth day it was their turn to patrol inside the fence. Because they were outnumbered more than a hundred-to-one by the captives, they stayed together.

A small group of prisoners sat on the ground around a box playing cards. Some of the men had a ball and were throwing it back and forth across the creek, which some of the Union troops had named Potomac. A few were reading or writing letters. From one of the barracks came the sound of a fiddle, apparently sent from home, playing a plaintive melody. Because this was early afternoon, Johann and his men had a push cart with bags of letters from home and some packages for the southerners. All these had first been examined by a group of officers in the headquarters. A small group of prisoners who were sergeants or corporals came up to the cart and were given armloads of the mail. They walked back to the troops who gathered around anxiously hoping to get messages from home. The few packages containing food or clothing were greeted with joyful whoops. At the end of the exercise more men went sadly away than those who waved letters.

After one of these sorties, walking to their tents from the main gate, Albrecht Geyer said, "Their faces bother me. Sometimes it feels like they look right through us. They may be laughing with their buddies, but when they look at us, the smiles vanish. You can see in some of their eyes just plain hate."

Johann responded, "I see that too. We treat them well. They have clean barracks, sleep on cots or bunks; they get the same food we get. We do not mistreat them in any way. Col. Owen would have our hides if we did."

"Then why the hate on their faces," Geyer replied. "They are not in any danger here. They lived through the fight at the forts. If it was me, I would be glad that I was safe."

"But don't forget that they had to surrender their forts. They were beaten in the battle. Now they are prisoners many miles from their homes."

"But we did not defeat them or capture them. Why do they hate us?"

"We are here, close to them. So they hate us for their defeat."

"I guess that is why we stay together inside the fence," Geyer said.

"You are right. Our orders are to be careful and not let any fights get started," Johann answered.

The next time Johann's squad was on patrol inside the fence, they walked past a group of prisoners standing outside their kitchen. Stocker's attention was attracted to a small piece of bright red cloth hanging out below a soldier's cost. Approaching the tall, bearded man, Stocker asked to see what was under his coat. Other prisoners began to gather around and the squad, following Johann's order, with their bayonetted muskets motioned them back. Johann and Stocker, unable to talk with the prisoner, motioned him to unbutton his coat. When he did, they saw that he had wrapped around his body the colors of his unit. He had hidden them since his capture. Cursing under his breath, he handed over the flag he had carried into battle. Johann took it and marched his squad to the gate. Leaving his soldiers just inside the gate, he walked quickly to the headquarters with the flag he had confiscated.

He explained the situation to Capt. Pleisch and Col. Owen.

Pleisch ordered, "Get back to your squad right now and resume your patrol! Be extra careful! The southerners are not going to be happy about this. Do not let them get into groups of more than three or four."

Col. Owen added, "Well done, Sergeant." and to Capt. Pleisch he said, "Get another squad into the compound right now. We do not want to give any time for trouble to start. And double the guard around the fence."

One of the captains said, "Colonel, I am concerned about all those knives in there. I know they are just used for whittling, but if things got nasty we could face a couple of hundred men coming at a patrol with their knives. That worries me."

"You are probably right. I just wanted them to have a pastime, but when there is trouble, it is a real danger. Tomorrow we will go into the camp with the regiment and confiscate all the knives. We will have it planned so the whole camp is covered at once and there will not be time to hide the knives. We will put a tag with the owner's name on each knife and promise to give all of them back when they are exchanged."

That night in his cot, Johann could hear the cold rain pelting onto the canvas over his head. He gave silent thanks that they were not guarding the fence tonight in the downpour. Over the sound of the rain he heard what sounded like a tree branch snapping in the icy rain. Almost immediately he heard the clanging of the iron wagon wheel rim that hung from a tree outside the little guard house at the gate. The men jumped off their cots in response to the alarm. They put on their heavy coats and their oilskins, took their muskets from the rack beside the tent flap and formed up awaiting orders. Capt, Pleisch shouted for Johann and another sergeant and told them to spread their men through the grove outside the fence.

"Two or three prisoners have climbed over the wall and run into the woods. Get your men around to the far side of the grove and see if you can head them off. The guard took a shot at them but doesn't think he hit them. Get your men going!"

Pleisch called his other sergeants and sent additional squads inside the fence to keep any disorder from growing. All through the rest of the night the guards in the pouring rain scoured the woods and surrounding area without success.

The following morning when the rain had stopped and all the troops had returned to their tents, Col. Owen assembled the regiment. He stood on the porch of the headquarters. "Well, men, we failed to live up to our orders. Our first job is to keep this camp secure. We failed! Three prisoners are missing, including that fellow you took the flag from. They braided a rope from the clotheslines we gave them and scaled the wall. Many of the guards, instead of being doubly alert because of the rain, put their oilskins over their heads to stay dry. The prisoners were over the fence, off the walkway and into the woods before anybody saw them and fired on them. They are miles away by now. We failed!

"I recognize that you are green troops. I could have those guards court martialed for their failure to follow orders. I am not going to do that, but to make the point the squad that was on the fence last night will have hardtack and water for a week. That will remind us all that we have to be alert every minute we are on duty.

"First thing tomorrow we are going to take those knives out of the camp. Dismissed...."

On that sweep of the camp they found nearly fifty old pistols of a heirloom variety, which the men had been permitted to keep because they had no ammunition, and several hundred pocket and sheath knives. The southerners protested when these were taken but had little choice in the face of overwhelming force. They trusted Colonel Owen to keep his promise to return their property.

On one patrol in the camp, Johann noticed two prisoners standing near to the gate. He kept his eye on them while his squad went through the camp. They were still standing there when the squad was ready to leave the camp. Johann motioned them to get away from the gate, as his men got closer. One held up his hand and walked toward Johann.

"Take us to Col. Owen," he said in a low voice. "Take us to the colonel...please."

The name gave Johann a clue to what they wanted. He motioned his men to get on both sides of the two prisoners and marched them through the gate. Rather than going to their tents, now that their patrol was over, Johann marched his men with their two wards to the headquarters.

The officer of the day was summoned and talked with the prisoners.

"We wanna see Col. Owen. We wanna take the oath."

"Come with me," the captain said. "Come into my office. Sergeant, you come along."

Once inside the captain looked hard into the eyes of the two Confederates in their tattered clothes. "So you want to take the oath? Well, let's hear your story."

The two men looked at each other. Then one spoke up. "Sir, they calls me Jerry Swift. I was raised up in Grand Rapids, Michigan. Because there wer'n't no jobs at home, me folks sent me to me Aunt Betty, me mom's sister, on their farm down near Neshoba, Mississippi. I was workin' there for 'bout a year when the war broke out. We di'n't have no money and there wer'n't no way I could get back home. I wanted to be back in Michigan, but couldn't figger out any way to git there. I was stuck in Mississippi. A lot of the young fellows from the farms and towns around there went to the Confederate army right away. I di'n't want to do that. Then they started to draft all the young fellers into the army. My uncle told me not to say I was from the north. He said they might lynch me. So they put me in the army. We got sent up to Fort Henry right away. I was captured there. A little while back a feller in the camp said that one of the men went to the colonel and took the oath to be loyal to the Union. Ever'body was talking about him. They really hated him for doing that; said he was a traitor--that they'd git him someday. So I jess kep' quiet about being from Michigan. Then, Buddy, here, and me decided that we had enough and wanted to take the oath and git out. So we asked the sarge here to bring us to the colonel."

The captain looked at the other man. "And what about you. What is your story?"

The lanky redhead hitched up his pants and shifted from one foot to the other. "Well, sir. I ain't a Yank like Jerry here. My name is Buddy Simmons. I come from over in eastern Tennessee. Ya might not know it, but we got lotsa folks there that hold with the Union....And lots that believe in the South. I never really thought much about politics, even though I heard a lot of shoutin' about it. Some of the men went north to join the Union army and some went to the army in the south. My friends, Zeb and Pete Cahoon, was goin' south. So I went along."

The Captain interrupted. "How old are you, son?"

"Sixteen I guess. I tol' 'em I was 18 when I joined up. Zeb and Pete, they got killed at Fort Henry. I got captured and brought here. The more I thought about it, the more I figured that I was really a Union man. I really got mad at them officers of ours. They thought they was so much better than us. They treated us like dirt. I don't want no more of that. I got to thinkin' that when I was back in Tennessee I shoulda gone north to join up. Then Jerry and me got talkin' one day and found out neither of us wanted to be there. So when we heard you could take the oath, we thought about it a long time and decided to come talk to the colonel."

"I will talk to the colonel and tell him what you have told me. He will have to decide if you can take the oath of allegiance to the United States. Meanwhile, we can't send you back into the camp for your own safety. Sergeant, you take these men to the stable where the officer's horses are kept. Put them under guard and keep them there until I come back." Realizing that Johann did not understand much English, he made motions to convey his orders. Johann saluted, called four of his men and marched off to the stable.

The captain returned in less than an hour and took the men to the headquarters. Johann and his men went back to their tents. He never saw the men again and assumed that they had sworn their loyalty to the Union and been sent to some Union regiment in Indianapolis.

Johann received a letter from Marta with news from Helvetia, the first he had heard in several weeks. She told of a trip made by steamer by a number of citizens of Coaltown and Helvetia down the Ohio and up the Tennessee to a place called Pittsburg Landing, where they fought the battle of Shiloh. Two doctors and a number of women from Coaltown and Helvetia went with relief supplies to help the wounded. They took bandages and medicine, many parcels of food, blankets hastily collected from the two towns. When they returned nearly two weeks later, they told of working on steamboats that had been turned into improvised hospitals. The doctors had assisted the regimental surgeons who were still dealing with the badly wounded. Marta reported that Frau Rabert was one of the women from Helvetia. When she got back, she called a meeting at the *Turnhalle* and told of her experiences. She said there were still many wounded men on the hospital boats. Many had already been sent back north but the more seriously wounded were still on the boats. She said there were still scores of men who had lost arms or legs, who were blinded by head wounds. She told of visiting these men, writing letters to their wives and mothers. This was very difficult because she said the doctors told them that most of the men still on the boats there probably would not live. Marta also reported that one day a steamer had stopped for fuel at Coaltown. It was loaded with bodies of Union soldiers who had died at Fort Henry.

She added, "These things make me worry so much. I know that you are safe in Indianapolis, but what if you got sent to a battle. It must be terrible. All those men dead, all those men without legs or eyes. I can hardly sleep at night thinking about it. Keep yourself safe. The girls and I miss you. Love, Marta"

In late March Col. Owen received word that an exchange had been arranged with the Confederate States. He was to send one thousand prisoners by train to St. Louis from which they would be sent to the exchange point on the Mississippi River north of Vickburg.

Only a week later train after train began pulling into Indianapolis with prisoners from the battle of Shiloh. Long lines marched through the streets under guard to Camp Morton. Col. Wilder and his regiment were faced with the task of adding several thousand new prisoners to the camp.

The barracks were filled to overflowing. Tents were pitched wherever possible on the grassy areas in the northeast corner of the camp.. The masses of men overtaxed the creek which ran through the camp, providing water for washing clothing and bathing. The latrines along the north wall were no longer adequate. To prevent pollution of the creek and the springs from which they got drinking water, materials were supplied for the prisoners to build a large new latrine on a cleared area many yards from the creek. It was a large conical tent structure, surrounded by an area enclosed by canvas nailed to posts, forming a man-high curtain.

Once the spring weather came, because he wanted to prevent the men from bathing in the creek, Col. Owen had the prisoners taken in groups of 20 under armed guard to Fall Creek. There they could bathe in a swimming hole about a quarter mile away from the camp. This practice worked very well until one group coaxed the guards into examining their muskets. Two of the guard foolishly handed their guns to their wards. Immediately the guards were overpowered and the prisoners and muskets vanished into the woods. Only about half of them were recaptured and brought back to camp in the next few days.

With the rapid growth in the prison population, Col. Owen tried to do what he could to keep the captives comfortable and healthy. He arranged for local farmers to bring cartloads of vegetables to improve the camp diet and prevent scurvy. He got from somewhere a collection of baseballs and footballs which he gave to the prisoners. He invited some of the ministers and priests of Indianapolis to hold services of worship with the prisoners. The Masons and the Odd Fellows lodges from Indianapolis held occasional meetings in the camp. A local photographer was allowed in the camp and began a vigorous business taking pictures of the prisoners who could afford his nominal fee, pictures which they could send home to show that they were faring well. The colonel encouraged the prisoners to amuse themselves with glee club concerts and amateur dramas.

One day a delegation of men, led by the editor of an Indianapolis paper, called upon Col. Owen. They stated vehemently that they objected to the conditions at Camp Morton.

The editor, a large man with a bushy red beard, banged his fist on the colonel's desk. "I tell you, you're coddling these rebs. These are the fellows who mowed down our soldiers at Shiloh. They are the enemy."

"You, sir, are guilty of treason, giving aid and comfort to the enemy," shouted Silas Bennett, an Indianapolis councilman, his face turning beet red. "I am appalled at what I have seen in the prison. Those rebs have it as good as our own soldiers, maybe even better. You'd better get tough and show them that they are defeated."

Editor Branscomb kept up the verbal barrage. "I was in there yesterday and I was appalled. I was expecting to see a gang of whipped dogs, regretting that they had taken up arms against their country, repenting of their traitorous secession. And what did I see? A bunch of fellows laughing and having a good time playing football. I even heard a fiddle playing in one of the barracks."

A third man chimed in, "I have two sons in the army, fighting these scoundrels. What in heaven's name are you doing here, treating these enemy troops as if they had done nothing wrong? It's the like of these fellows who are shooting at my boys. That's wrong! They need to be taught a lesson."

Col. Owen listened patiently until the heat of their protest died down a little. Finally he said, "Men, I understand what you are saying. I want to tell you a true story of what happened here at Camp Morton just after we were posted here. A squad of guards was in with the prisoners as usual. A couple of the Confederates started getting nasty. They kept yelling insults at the sergeant. A crowd gathered. Some of them started to surround the squad. The sergeant sent a runner for the captain of the guard, but before he could get there a guard fired his musket and the prisoners started to rush the troops. They fired a volley and hit four prisoners. One of them was killed."

"I'd say it served 'em right," Bennett said.

"Look at it this way. That was when there were less than 2000 prisoners. Now we have nearly 5000, guarded by a few companies of green troops. Start a riot now and we'll have either a slaughterhouse or hundreds of men going over the walls. I would rather treat them like human beings and not have to worry about having to try to put down riots."

"I take your point," Branscomb responded. "But there must be something between a tough jailhouse and a summer resort."

"I have one more reason for wanting to be humane. Maybe it is my main reason," Col. Owen went on. "I have a son in the army too. Someday he may be captured and in a Confederate prison camp. If that ever happens, God forbid, I would want him treated like a man, a human being not an animal.

When no response came from the delegation, the colonel thanked them for their understanding.

The issue grew more acute in mid-April when a group of sergeants from the prisoner divisions had been given permission to go into Indianapolis on their honor to buy items for the patients in the prison hospital. They pledged not to engage any citizens in conversation. They made their purchases and then, contrary to their orders and good judgment, stopped in a saloon. Several of them drank too much and made the serious error of bringing several bottles of whiskey to the camp.

A couple of men in their company got drunk and began throwing stones and beef bones at the sergeant of the guard and his squad patrolling inside the camp. One hit the sergeant in the head and he fell. He gave the order for his squad to fire and four prisoners fell wounded, while the rest dove to the ground. At the sound of the volley, the gate swung open and the cannon just outside fired once into the camp, which no one knew was a blank powder charge. Col. Owen strode into the camp and the incident was over.

The sound of the gunfire called public attention to the events of April 15. Governor Morton immediately demanded that privileges of prisoners be severely curtailed and reprimanded Owen for his leniency. The colonel replied that if the Governor knew of someone who would be more satisfactory "the officers and men of the 60th would be grateful for the change." He pointed out that his men had not been paid for the past six months.

CHAPTER 17

"We are moving out," Capt. Pleisch shouted to the regiment in the mess tent

"What'd he say?" asked Stocker, through a huge mouthful of food.

Geyer responded, "You have so much in your mouth, it has plugged your ears. He said that we are moving out. That must mean we are finished being jail guards."

"*Ja*, but it also means we may be going into the f-f-fighting," added Buhl with his characteristic caution.

Stocker blustered, "Better tell them Rebs we are comin'. Get ready for a fight, boys."

Johann said, "I'll find out the particulars as soon as I can. I'll talk to the captain as soon as we're done eating."

Before long the entire regiment was abuzz with the details of their orders. They had three days to pack all their gear. Their replacements would arrive on Friday. Then the 60th was to board a train for Louisville.

General Halleck needed a much larger force to strengthen his thinly scattered troops to garrison towns in Kentucky and Tennessee, to build and rebuild railroads and bridges, to move supplies to the advancing armies of the North. Politically he needed troops to support Union sympathizers in Tennessee and Kentucky and hold down those who supported the south.

Excitement mounted as the day for moving south approached.

"I hear they are gettin' together a big army in Nashville. They are goin' to follow up on Shiloh and whip them rebels for one last time. We'll hit 'em so hard, they'll have to stay down," Stocker boasted.

Johann answered him, "Don't get too cocky. We don't know where we are heading: just south. The captain said that a lot of regiments are on the move."

Stocker kept it up, wiping his musket with an oily rag. "I can't wait to get into the fight. I am sick of drilling and standing guard, miles away from any action. I di'n't join up for that."

"Don't be in such a hurry to get into the fight. I will fight if I have to, but I have a wife and baby to be concerned about," Geyer put in.

Bauer spoke up. "Listen, Stocker! I'll bet you are the first to run when we see the elephant."

"You want to bet? Here, Sergeant, you hold the bet!" He fished into his pocket. "I'll give you a dollar. Let old Bauer give you his dollar. If I run, you can give them both to him. If I fight, I get both dollars. All right?" Stocker handed his dollar to Johann.

Bauer slowly handed a dollar to Johann. "I'll take his bet. But it seems foolish to me to look forward to a battle. We know that a lot of men do not come out alive. That scares me." He walked away and Johann followed.

Johann nodded, "I guess I feel that way too. It is too serious to be talking like it is just a game."

"Do you worry about it?" Bauer asked.

"I sure do. I come from a family of worriers back in Germany. Marta always writes about how worried she is. I can't answer back that I am worried too because I don't want to make it worse for her. But I toss and turn at night worrying that I will never get home again."

"Most of these fellows just bluster around, like Stocker. It is a relief to talk to somebody who will admit he's scared and worried. It is somethin' that's hard to talk about. We are supposed to be big, brave soldiers."

Johann replied, "You can be sure that far more men feel like we do, even if they don't say so."

"I worry that if we do get into a battle, I'll run and hide. I want to do my duty, but I am not sure that my fears will not get the best of me."

"You will be all right. You are a good man. You will be all right." Johann put his hand on Bauer's shoulder

"I wish I could sure of that. I guess you never know until you see the elephant."

Led by their modest regimental band on the 20th of June, the 60th marched through the streets of Indianapolis to the railroad depot. Their troop train had just delivered a contingent of new recruits.

A group of friendly Indianapolis women stood with baskets at the steps of the coaches passing out cheese sandwiches, cookies, and the wilting remains of last year's apple crop. They nudged each other when they heard these soldiers talking German, but offered their food with straight faces. Johann and his squad clambered aboard one of the coaches in the middle to the train.

The coaches were crowded with men standing in the aisles. There was a lot of laughing and banter. Soon the train clattered along the tracks, swaying from side to side, as it picked up speed.

Johann looked out the open window as they moved through southern Indiana. The light wind was moving the smoke from the locomotive and the shower of cinders away from his side of the train. When they approached the Ohio River, before moving slowly into the railroad tunnel into Louisville, Johann looked at the brownish water. In a few days this same water would be lapping up on the landing in Helvetia. A wave of homesickness swept through him. He thought of Marta and the little girls, of Rabert, of Paulus and Matti. How long would it be before he stood again in his own home? It could be years! An even more chilling thought struck him. It was possible that he would never return. Who knew what the next weeks and months would hold for him and the soldiers of the 60th Indiana?

Their train puffed slowly into the railroad yards in Louisville, where a dozen other trains were being loaded and unloaded. Capt. Pleisch told Johann to get his men off the coach. They were to pick up their packs and muskets from the freight car forward and form ranks beside the tracks. They marched to another of the trains and began the whole process again. Company A was put in the first two coaches and Company B in the next two. The sun was setting as they began to move south on the Louisville & Nashville Railroad toward Nashville.

Stocker was holding forth in their section of the crowded coach. "They're not wastin' any time. We are goin' to be pointing our guns at rebs in a couple of days. You just watch! We are on our way!"

"I bet they are s-s-scared to death,.. knowing that you are coming," Buhl laughed.

Johann finally broke into the conversation, "Better get some sleep. We may have a busy day in front of us."

Around midnight the train stopped and, jolting and clattering, was switched off the mainline to a siding. The men who were awake wondered why they had stopped. One or two tried to leave the train but were told by sentries along the track to get back inside.

When morning came, they were ordered to forms ranks alongside the train. Straining under their heavy packs and muskets the 60th was marched to a meadow within sight of the junction. Captains indicated where their companies were to pitch their two man tents. Farmers had unloaded several wagon loads of straw for bedding in the tents. Soon cook fires were burning and coffee was being boiled. The men breakfasted on hardtack and coffee.

Captain Pleisch walked along the row of tents and talked with the men of Company A. "They tell me we are going to camp here for a few days before moving on. We were headed for Nashville, but there are reports of a Confederate raiding party somewhere just south of here, so we are going to stay here to help fight them off if they show up around here. So keep your stuff together so we can move out on a moment's notice. *Versteh'?*"

"I suppose this is goin' to start all that drilling business again," grumbled Stocker. "They ain't going to let us sit around, you can bet on that."

"A little drilling will walk off some of that fat we put on at Camp M-M-Morton, standing around on the wall or patrolling inside the stockade," Buhl said.

Johann added, "If we are going to have to fight, we better know what we are doing. Stocker, you are going to become the best soldier in the squad. By the time we leave here, everyone will point to you and say, 'You ought to see him drill. Now that is a crack soldier!'"

"Then you are goin' to have to feed me more than these damn' shingles. I'll show you I can drill."

And so it continued as one week extended into two.

Twenty miles to the southeast Muldraugh Hill was a heavily forested ridge which extended more than a dozen miles, east to west. In this isolated area a group of southern loyalists had been gathering for the past several weeks. Farmers and workers had quietly left their homes and gathered on the hill. About half of the men brought their horses. At first they had thought of traveling south in small groups until they came to Confederate units in which they could enlist. Then, joined by Seth Smathers a country lawyer from Campbellsville, they talked more of organizing right here on the hill and fighting the enemy by burning bridges and tearing up rail tracks and capturing supply wagons and raiding towns where there were

Union sympathizers. There were always rumors that Confederate army columns would come. When they did, they would find fifty fighting men on the Hill, ready to open the way for them.

Those who lived nearby returned often to their homes for a few days. In two's or three's they stopped by farms of other southern sympathizers. They were given food and money to purchase supplies.

Smathers devised a plan to arm their unit. Gathering the men around their campfire, he explained, "What we need most are arms. This collection of squirrel guns we've got are not going to get us anywhere. We need army issue, and plenty of it. I've got a plan."

Two nights later, a dozen chosen men rode along the dirt road which stretched along the ridge, halfway down the slope, toward a place on the L & N line where the tracks wound by the western end of the ridge. Smathers rode in the lead with Magnus Culp and Angus MacDonald.

"You fellows know what you are supposed to do, " Smathers said.

"Sure and enough we do," MacDonald responded, speaking with his Scottish burr. "You just watch us."

Smathers went on, "This idea came to me when we were sitting around camp and Magnus, here, said that he worked on the railroad for ten years."

Culp nodded, holding up his hand with two fingers missing, barely visible in the darkness. "I lost those fingers uncoupling trains. We'll get that train stopped, just like you planned it. I can get those cars uncoupled. The train Scotty and me watched go up the grade last night slowed down to the point where a person could just walk alongside it, easy."

"And like you said, Seth, when it goes around the big curve, there's a time when the whole front of the train is out of sight," MacDonald added, "Magnus explained what to do to me and to Grogran and Marchbank. Each one of us has his job and we'll sure get it done. It's gonta work like a bonny clock. You'll see."

"Magnus explained his plan to me. I trust him to know enough about railroads to make it work," Smathers said.

"It'll work all right. But I am na gon' to be as fast as he is. I'd just as soon keep all my fingers."

Culp stood in this stirrups. "There's the track."

Smathers waited for the rest of their party to catch up. They were a rag-tag bunch with their assortment of hunting muskets and shotguns. They had to travel slower because they were being followed by a team-drawn farm wagon. "We'll just wait here out of sight until Cy comes with the word."

"What if he does na come," MacDonald asked.

Smathers answered, "Then we do it all over tomorrow night."

After an hour of waiting they heard a horse galloping along the road through the woods. Most of the men blended into the brush along the road.

A horseman came into view. Smathers stepped into the road.

"There is a train coming. It left the Junction about 10 o'clock. It is all freight cars, no coaches," the breathless rider reported. "I watched 'em load. They got a car with soldiers at the front and the back. Brownie, who was hanging around the rail yard, told me that this looked like the one for us. He said it looked like most of the cars toward the end of the train was loaded with boxes of muskets and ammunition. We are in luck."

"All right men, you've got your orders. If everybody does just what he is supposed to do, this is our night," Smathers said.

Four men rode off a hundred yards to the north parallel with the track. The others, with their wagon, went a short distance to the south where the track made a large curve. They pulled the wagon behind some evergreens and tied their horses in the trees. Smathers led them to the nearby track. Quietly they hid themselves on both sides of the the rail line. Smathers put his ear to the rail. "It's coming. Keep down when the engine and the first couple of cars go past. Then you know what to do."

They could see sparks coming from the funnel of the locomotive as the train labored slowly up the long grade. When only a few cars remained on this side of the curve, Culp stepped out and climbed between one of the cars. He pulled a heavy iron pin from the coupling link and the last four cars detached from the train which continued very slowly around the bend. Climbing quickly to the top of the car, he spun the brake wheel to keep the car from rolling back down the grade. At the same time, MacDonald following the instructions Culp had repeated over and over again, climbed onto the train two cars back. He pulled the pin as Culp had instructed and the last two cars disconnected and slowly rolled away from him back down the steep grade and began to pick up speed.

With the small detachment of Union troops who were guarding the train moving away from them in both directions, the rest of Smathers' men jumped from the brush to the doors of the stopped cars. As they broke the locks and pushed back the doors, the wagoneer quickly pulled his wagon near the train. The men loaded as many boxes as they could carry in the few minutes that they had. As soon as the wagon was full,

Smathers ordered them all to mount and start back to the Hill. Remaining behind for another minute or so, Smathers pulled a flask of lamp oil from his saddle bag, poured it on his neckerchief, struck a match and threw the burning cloth into the car. Straw and debris on the floor began to burn. He spurred his horse onto the road and followed his men at a gallop.

This raid brought an end to the drilling and boring camp life of the 60th Indiana. Companies were deployed every day in all directions to guard the tracks and to patrol the rail yard where the trains were switched.

Col. Owen was given reports from the telegraph. There were constant pleas for more supplies to be sent south from Louisville. General Buell's army in northern Alabama was suffering under short rations because not enough supplies were getting through. It was critical that the rail lines be kept open.

The Colonel assembled the garrison that afternoon on the pasture that substituted for a parade ground. He stood on a wagon to address his troops.

"Men. You have seen Confederate soldiers in Camp Morton, but they were prisoners. You may get a chance to see a lot more Confederates, and they will not be behind a prison wall. Our armies are deep in the south, but our forces are spread very thin across Kentucky. Our main army is scattered between Chattanooga and northern Mississippi, many miles away from us. But between that army and us Forrest and Morgan have a couple thousand Confederates on horseback. They can strike a town without warning, capture the garrison, take all the supplies they want, take the money from the bank if the banker is a Union sympathizer, and ride off to find another town to attack miles away. We never know where they are. There is very little warning when they attack, so you are going to have to be on your guard every minute of every day.

"We are going to strengthen the outposts at every road and bridge coming into the Junction. The railroad through here is filled with trains every day going from Louisville to Nashville. Our job is to see that this railroad stays open to keep the supplies flowing to our army in the south. That is the task we have been given, and we will guard those trains with our lives."

Day by day the telegraph reports held more and more bad news. In early July dispatches began to report that Morgan's cavalry was starting to move north. On July 9 his force of 900 men captured Thompkinsville in southern Kentucky. The next day he was reported 40 miles closer in Horse Cave. That meant that a major southern force was less than 30 miles to the south of the Junction.

Morgan's cavalry troop began to move north and east toward the town of Lebanon, which was a supply depot on the turnpike from Cincinnati to Nashville. Lebanon and Lexington were the two railheads from which operations in eastern Kentucky could be supplied. Materiel was brought that far by rail and from these supply depots sent by wagon to the garrisons in the southeastern part of the state. A small detachment of Union troops had been stationed in Lebanon since November 1861. They had been welcomed by the local population, many of whom were Unionists. The small advanced guard gathered there briefly in preparation for an action against a Confederate army in southern Kentucky. Not until Morgan's raid in July 1862 had the community been threatened.

When Morgan's raiders were sighted near Campbellsville, Union sympathizers sent out several riders to warn towns in the path of Morgan's force. As one of these horsemen neared Lebanon, he saw the cluster of army tents on a farm along the Campbellsville Pike. Galloping into the camp, he shouted to the small group of soldiers that Morgan was heading for Lebanon. The colonel in charge shouted orders at once to go the small earthworks they had built on both sides of the Campbellsville Pike. As they marched along the dusty road they could hear the court house bell ringing frantically, calling out the loyalist home guard. Before long men with their muskets ran down the road to join the troops in the earthworks.

Colonel Johnson sent one of his sergeants to the railroad depot with orders to telegraph Lebanon Junction that Morgan was advancing on the town and asking urgently for reinforcements to be sent.

As soon as the request for troops reached Col. Owen, he telegraphed Louisville and received orders to load his regiment on a train and go to Lebanon as quickly as possible. Bugle calls echoed through the camp. A locomotive and a half dozen empty freight cars pulled through the switches onto the line to Lebanon. Because the men of the 60th Indiana had been ordered to keep themselves in readiness to move, it took only an hour to get the regiment and their supplies on the train.

Sweating heavily from their exertions Johann and his men climbed aboard a freight car, and the train began to move. Snatches of information spread among the men.

"I thought we were supposed to go to Nashville...why are we p-p-puffing along this spur line to Lebanon?" Buhl asked.

"I heard some of the officers saying that Morgan was coming this way. It is up to us to stop him," Johann reported.

Stocker continued his wiping of his musket with his oiled flannel.

"You are going to wear that thing out before you get a chance to fire a shot," Bauer joked.

"Never mind. I am just bein' sure that it is ready for a fight. Man, we are goin' to see the elephant," Stocker replied. "Finally we get a chance for some action. I hear that that Morgan is tough."

"It's getting dark. How long is it going to take us to get there?"

Smathers and his Muldraugh Hill boys heard that Morgan was in the neighborhood of Campbellsville, heading north. This was the moment they had been waiting for. Smathers ordered his men to get ready to move into action, while he rode down to find the Confederate force. He encountered one of their scouting parties in less than an hour and asked to be taken to Gen. Morgan.

In his dusty civilian clothes he stood before Morgan. "I have nearly fifty men on that hill, loyal to the south. We have been arming ourselves and are ready to do whatever we can to help the cause. Do you have orders for us."

Morgan looked hard at the man. "Well, another surprise! We heard there were companies like yours all over Kentucky. So you want to fight? All right, you know this country better than I do. I want you to get your men behind the Federals in Lebanon. Do whatever you can to make mischief. Burn bridges, tear up a few rails of a train track, cut any telegraph lines you come across. I'll be in Lebanon before suppertime. My job will be easier if you are making a lot of confusion off to the side. We will be in your debt."

Smathers made an awkward salute, "You can count on us to do our best." He mounted his horse and galloped toward Muldraugh Hill to rejoin his men.

Morgan's horsemen rode through the late afternoon heat, raising a huge cloud of dust. Just before sunset they encountered the small force of Union troops and the Lebanon Home Guard behind their earthworks. The entrenched troops fired a volley and two of Morgan's men fell. Gathering the forward elements of his force, he ordered them to charge the crude fortification. The sight of several hundred cavalrymen galloping toward them showed the overwhelming odds. A few of the men fired again, but most turned and ran away from the road toward the woods. Some of the horsemen pursued them and captured a home guard lieutenant, but most of the troop rode steadily toward the defenseless town.

Morgan and his men fanned out through the town, encountering no resistance. The population either had fled or were huddled in their cellars. The Confederates quickly went through the piles of supplies at the end of the spur line. They started a huge bonfire, tossing on sacks and barrels of rations, bundles of uniforms, crates of muskets and ammunition, which exploded like fireworks. The raiders tossed some of their own weapons, old and obsolete, on the fire, replacing them with brand new rifled muskets from the federal stores. Individual troopers filled their saddle bags with sacks of coffee beans, dried beef and hardtack. The wagon yard, full of wagons and several ambulances, was also put to the torch.

Knowing that Lebanon had many Union sympathizers and had even mustered a regiment of Kentuckians for the Union army, Morgan ordered that the homes of several known Unionists be burned after making sure that no one was inside. A small army hospital at the camp on the edge of town was burned down. Squads were posted in the center of town and along the roads leading into Lebanon.

A volley of shots rang out from the darkness as the train neared the little town of New Hope Station, halfway between the Junction and Lebanon. The engine braked to a halt because a large tree lay across the track.

"Keep down," Johann ordered. He tried to look out the door of the freight car. He could not see the men who were shooting at them from positions well hidden by brush and rocks on both side of the track. A bullet came whistling through the partly opened door over their heads and drilled through the wall of their car in back of them.

The train began to back down the track a little way from the barrier. Everything was quiet for a minute or two. There was no gunfire. The full moon came out from behind the cloud that had covered it.

An officer came running along the track. "Everybody out! Form ranks beside the track!" he shouted. The men snatched their equipment and scrambled out of the train, anxiously waiting for shots to ring out in the night. But no shots came.

They heard Capt. Pleisch, "Company A, over here." They ran toward the sound of his voice. Several of the men stumbled and fell on the rough ground. Breathless, they gathered around the captain.

"We are to form a skirmish line and go down the track toward where we stopped. There can't be many of them. Probably just a bunch of farmers. Once they see how many men we have, they will head for the hills," Pleisch said. "There is another company doing the same thing down the other side of the track. *Mach' schnell!*"

Stocker was the only one to do much talking as the line advanced cautiously in the moonlight. "Watch out, you rebs..... We're goin' to show you a real fight.....We'll teach you a lesson you won't forget."

The other men just walked along in silence, peering ahead into the moonlit pastures along the track. On a low hill to their right a herd of cattle milled around. They could see other companies moving forward on both sides. Johann kept expecting gunfire to break the stillness as they came to the brushy place where the train had been stopped.

"They ran," Stocker exclaimed, "Those bastards ran away. We didn't even get a shot at them. We been in the army for eight months and I ain't shot a musket yet."

Bauer said quietly, "I wouldn't complain if I was you. One of them might have popped you."

"I'd run too...if I saw a whole regiment c-c-coming after me," Buhl added. "They are half way home by now."

Once they got to the edge of the little town of New Hope, they saw that not just one log, but five big trees had been felled across of the tracks.

The officers gathered. Col. Owen ordered one squad to repair the telegraph line beside the track, which had been pulled down by the falling trees.

Browning told one of the captains, "Go, see if there are any axes on the train." None were found.

Col. Owens sent squads to the few farm houses which could be seen in the light of dawn and ordered another squad into the little town in search of axes and cross-cut saws. Others were sent to get farmers and their teams with log chains to help pull the trees off the tracks.

Morgan and his telegrapher went into the empty Lebanon railroad depot. As he had done the night before in Horse Cave, the telegrapher sat before the clicking telegraph.

"Well, Ellsworth," Morgan said, "see what you can find out."

Listening for a minute to the morse code coming into the instrument, Ellsworth reported, "Somebody identifying himself as station Z is calling a station B.

"Can you find out where Z is?"

"Let me try something. Station B must be the operator here in Lebanon. Ah'll try something," Ellsworth replied as he began to tap the key:

Z: Just stepped out for a little while. Were you calling long?--B

B: Getting worried because I did not hear from you after your message from the captain--Z.

Z: A gentleman here in my office bet me a cigar you cannot spell the name of your station correctly--B

The answer came right back, with Ellsworth repeating the message to Morgan: Take the bet. L-e-b-a-n-o-n-J-u-n-c-t-i-o-n. How did he think I would spell it?--Z

Z: He gives up. He thought you would put two b's in Lebanon--B

B: Ha! Ha! Enjoy cigar...Have more serious news. Your message about possible attack from Morgan put 60th Indiana on train heading Lebanon.. Ran into trouble--Z

Ellsworth winked at Morgan, Z: What trouble?--B

B: Tracks blocked at New Hope Station. Fired on. Repelled attack. Now working to clear track. Likely not reach Lebanon before tomorrow--Z

Z: All right. We think Morgan heading east.--B. Ellsworth smiled, "That should throw them off the track."

"It does mean we have to be out of here before sun-up. We'll send out a few men to tear up a couple of rails about a mile down the line. That will give us plenty of time to move north," Morgan said. "Good work, Ellsworth. I don't think he has any idea what was happening."

"It wasn't as good as last night. That Louisville operator really fell for the story that we were federals in Bowling Green. He told us all about Forrest capturing Murfreesboro and how much they lost. Ah think he believed it when Ah told him Bragg was still in Chattanooga. Doesn't it ever occur to these bumpkins that someone can tap a key into their line anywhere and pick up all their traffic?" Ellsworth asked.

Morgan laughed, "Good thing they can't hear that Georgia drawl of yours over their wires. They wouldn't believe a thing you tap out. Let's get those men out to tear up a little track."

It was the next afternoon before the 60th Indiana marched into Lebanon. The men were weary from losing sleep all last night, working for hours to clear the track at New Hope Station and then marching to Lebanon from the place where the track had been torn up just west of Lebanon. The possibility of another attack from sharpshooters hiding in the woods kept their anxiety level high.

None of the houses along the road at the edge of town, where the column had stopped, showed any signs of life. They could make out the contour of the low hills surrounding the town. Several church steeples stood out over the roof lines of the town a short distance away.

"Well, there is Lebanon," Johann said.

"Never heard of it," Geyer added. "It must not be a very big place."

As they marched along the quiet street they could see the remains of Morgan's attack. The huge bonfires still were smouldering. A big warehouse by the station was gutted by fire, and another bonfire burned outside the courthouse. Several houses were in ruins, just chimneys standing amid the ashes, or smoking brick shells.

Taking in the situation quickly, Col. Owen assembled his officers. "It is clear that Morgan has gone. He did as much damage as he could and went on to some other town. He travels fast and travels light. He could not take all this with him so he burned it. Now it is up to us to see that this doesn't happen again. He got what he wanted here, so he will not be back right away. But once supplies come back in, he or some other raider will try again. It is our job to see that it does not happen again."

To Browning he said, "Get the leaders of the town together. We want to find out just what happened. Have the men fall out and get some food and rest. We have a lot to do in the morning."

As the companies looked for places to spend the night a small detachment of Union soldiers was discovered locked in a large unpainted board and batten warehouse near the tracks. After the lock was knocked off the large door, the unarmed men led by Col. Johnson were brought into the center of town and reported to Col. Owen's headquarters.

Johnson went inside to report. "We tried to defend the town. The Home Guard joined us in some earthworks we had made southwest of town, down toward New Market on the Campbellsville Road. We got off one or two volleys at the first riders who came down the road, but they were too many for us. A couple of the Home Guard were hit. I am not sure if they were killed or wounded. Morgan's main force was upon us on every side in a matter of minutes. I had less than fifty of my men against their hundreds. I had no choice but to surrender. Morgan put us in a warehouse near the depot, after he had emptied it out and was burning the supplies. He made out these parole papers and ordered me to turn our detachment in when the reinforcements arrived. Before he rode off, he came back and reminded us that we were parolees. So I turn myself and my men over to you."

Col. Owen nodded and said, "Right. You had no chance against such odds. I have been told that two of the Home Guard were killed. As you can see Morgan destroyed as much as he could. He even burned a few houses.

"I will send a telegraph to Louisville and ask instructions. Until we know what to do, go back to that warehouse and rest your men. I will have rations brought over to you. I think that it would be best if your men did not mix with our troops, because, after all, you are under parole."

Johnson saluted and marched with his men to the warehouse.

Formed into ranks the companies of the 60th began to march to the west, away from the town. Rounding a bend in the road the men saw a field with some gray tents stretched across a pasture. Behind the tents was a sloping hillside dotted with trees. Next to the road was a small farmhouse, unpainted clapboard. A short flag pole stood in the yard. A few chairs were strung along the porch. This must have been the headquarters for the garrison. A ramshackle barn stood behind the house. A bullet riddled sign bearing the words Camp Crittenden hung crookedly from a fence post. The sun began to dip behind the hills.

"There is home," Johann joked with the men as they marched through a gap in the fence, "at least for a while."

Companies gathered in the pasture and began to pitch their tents in rows. They found hay in the barn and carried armloads to put on the ground under their tents. Bauer went up the hill to the woods and returned with an armload of wood for their cook fire.

"You goin' to cook us a meal. I could sure use some decent food," Stocker complained.

"You will have hardtack from your pack until the supplies get here. They put us on that train so fast at the Junction that they didn't load any food," Bauer answered.

"Maybe the colonel'll get us some food from the town," Stocker insisted.

"It all depends what Morgan left in the town and how friendly the people are," Johann said.

The bugle called the regiment to assemble on the flat area beside the farmhouse. In company formation they waited for the colonel to come from the house. He stood on the porch to address them.

"Well, men, you have had your first contact with the enemy and you did very well. We have a lot of work ahead of us. We are now the garrison here in Lebanon. The handful of men who were stationed here in this camp, tried to fight off Morgan but were overwhelmed. They were captured and are waiting in the town to be paroled back to the north. We are now a strong force and will give this town the protection it needs.

"I have to warn you to be vigilant with the people of Lebanon and the countryside. You know that Lebanon, like the rest of Kentucky has a lot of people who support our side, but there are probably quite a few who sympathize with the south. They could do a lot of damage if they get together. We do not think that there are enough of them in this area to launch an attack, but they can steal our supplies or set them on fire, blow up bridges, even shoot at us on guard duty. So keep your eyes and ears open.

"But at the same time I am ordering you to treat all citizens and their property with full respect. Anyone who breaks that order will be reported to me and disciplined severely. We are a friendly force in this town and I intend to keep it that way. We are here to protect them from southern raiders. Since there probably are very few of the folks around here who speak German, most of you will not have too much contact with the people. But when you do, be friendly! And be careful!

"Your officers will give you your orders. We will have twenty men at each of the guard posts set up two miles from Lebanon on every road leading into the town. And fifty men will be at each of the two railroad bridges near Lebanon. There will be twenty men at the courthouse in the center of Lebanon. You will stand guard for twelve hours, then come back here to the camp. But first we are going to fortify the town in case raiders try again. Now let's do the job we were sent here to do. Dismissed!"

For two days the men worked to saw down trees and drag huge logs from the nearby woods to build barricades across the main roads into town. They dug a deep wide ditch across the street and piled the dirt against and on top of the logs, making a barrier at least six feet high. Three of these barricades were built across each road a few yards apart. The narrow openings in the barricades to allow normal traffic were staggered, so that a wagon or rider would have to go through slowly, twisting and turning, until past the obstructions.

On top of the Shuck's Hall, a large three storey brick building near the center of town, they built a watch tower, which was manned night and day.

After two days of feverish activity, working from dawn until dark, life settled into the more familiar camp routine: going on guard duty for twelve hours, then back to camp to sleep and get ready for the next day's guard duty.

Captain Pleisch stopped by their cook fire and said, "I just got in the mail a copy of *The Reporter* from Coaltown. I thought you might like to hear what it says about Lebanon. I'll translate it for you.

"The sea upon which we are sailing looks gloomy. The storm cloud of civil war is as angry as at any period since the evil spirit of rebellion let loose upon our once happy land its desolating and bloody furies. In our sister state, Kentucky, untold misery is being afflicted by her own people. Her towns are sacked and burned, her people murdered and plundered, the smoke of the rebel torch darkens the heavens, and the fleeing fugitive attest the fact that Kentucky is still the "dark and bloody ground" of the west. Morgan, the guerrilla chief, with a large force has taken Lebanon, a town about 45 miles from Louisville, burnt government property, captured Colonel Johnson and a company of federal soldiers, levied contributions on Union citizens, robbed the bank, committed murder, and dashed on with his band to other towns where similar scenes will be enacted. The rebels have destroyed Perryville, and, unless prevented by a force sent from Cincinnati, have doubtless sacked the city of Lexington. The greatest excitement prevails in Kentucky and is spreading to counties of adjacent states bordering on the Ohio...."

"*Mein Gott*, our families will think we were in that attack if they know we are in Lebanon. They will be worried sick," Johann said.

The other men nodded.

"I am going to write a letter to Rabert tonight to tell people we are all right, that we got here after Morgan attacked." Johann added.

Pleisch, folding the newspaper, said, "And I am going to write to *The Reporter*."

Life in Helvetia moved at a much slower pace, but was very much affected by the reports and rumors of Morgan's raids in Kentucky. The mail packets moving down from Louisville and up from Evansville or Paducah brought news several times each week. No sooner had a boat churned up to the wharf boat when news began to sweep up and down the streets.

Rabert distilled the war news from the newspapers and passed it on through *Die Zeitung*. He rode over to Coaltown several days each week because there was so much activity there. In spite of the undercurrent of southern sentiment and the virulent anti-abolitionist editorial sentiments of the Coaltown *Reporter*, Rabert did not feel the isolation from the rest of the country he felt in Helvetia.

There was a lot of army activity in Coaltown. Ships leased by the army to carry supplies to Grant's forces on the Mississippi stopped regularly for coal. General Love positioned a rifled ten pound Dahlgren cannon on the river bluff in the event of a Confederate raid.

Rumors constantly circulated about bands of southern sympathizers in Hainesville, just across the river. It was known that a number of men from that community were in the Confederate army. Their families would be supporters of any raiders who appeared on the scene. Access to many small boats along the river in the hands of southern sympathizers would enable a small force of raiders to establish a position on the north bank of the Ohio.

As had been the case at the beginning of the war, a portion of the court house was used to store cases of muskets and a good deal of ammunition. Two companies of Union Cavalry arrived in Coaltown in December on the steamer *Atlantic* and camped just outside the town as a mobile force to repel any crossing of Morgan or other raiders anywhere along that stretch of the river.

As was being done all along the Indiana side of the Ohio River, Captain Tobin's company of the Legion, the Indiana Home Guard, kept watch night and day along the river. Once, responding to information that guerrillas were about to attack Cloverport, Tobin embarked with four boatloads of his men to reinforce the Union sympathizers there.

Sometimes these precautions seemed hysterical to Rabert. At other times he thought that invasion from Kentucky was a serious possibility. The military situation there was so fluid. Union forces held a long string of strong points and garrisoned the larger towns, but sizable Confederate forces and their sympathizers from the local population could move with relative impunity from place to place.

The mail packets brought rumors that a force of 1500 Confederates under General Lyon had occupied Henderson or Owensville, stirring the citizens of Helvetia and Coaltown to call for more defenses. The Louisville newspapers reported on movements of a southern army that was coming out of eastern Tennessee to threaten Kentucky. Rabert concluded and published in *Die Zeitung* that the threats needed to be taken seriously but that there was no need for panic or over-reaction. He refused to be drawn into the hysterical warnings that kept spouting from *The Reporter*.

In the little house on Twelfth Street Marta kept busy tending her vegetable garden, which produced a lot during the summer. She worked a few hours every day, while the children played quietly on the little porch. One day was very like all the others, except Sunday when she put on her best dress, dressed the children and went to church. She always trembled when the pastor prayed for the safety and health of the men from the town who were away in the army. Fear constantly wrapped its cold hands around her heart. She missed Johann so much. She felt so alone, in spite of the almost daily visits with Matti. Every few months she wrote a short letter to her family and to Johann's brothers. There was little that she could say about Johann. His letters told only a little about what he was doing each day. He did talk about the other men from town. He described the town where they were camped. He talked about the awful food. The Weber brothers would not be very interested in that.

Getting enough money to live was always a problem. She still had two dollars of the $25 Johann had left with her when he enlisted. Every month she received a bank draft which was most of Johann's army pay. The government had made an arrangement where honest men in each state were appointed by the governor to work with a bank. Bank drafts would be made out by commanding officers for men in their units who wanted to send money home. These drafts were sent to a bank in the soldier's home state and then sent to their families. Johann was sending to Marta twelve dollars of the fifteen he was paid each month. It did not leave him much to spend at the company's suttler's wagon. He could not buy as much tobacco as many of the other men. When the men purchased some extra food from the suttler for their cook pot, he could put in a few coins.. To send his letters home he bought writing paper and a stamp. Marta knew he was sending most of his pay to her, and she was grateful.

Matti was well aware that money was tight for Marta. She often brought a few eggs or a loaf of bread when she visited. She sometimes spent a couple of hours helping Marta in her garden.

"I get so tired," Marta said. "Between the garden, cooking and taking care of the girls, I hardly have time to sit down."

"You are so little and thin. I worry about you," Matti answered smoothing her apron over her ample body.

"I don't eat much. I am just not very hungry most of the time. I did have one of those eggs you brought last night for supper. It tasted real good."

"The girls seem to be doing well. They are filling out."

"They like their milk. I go over to Goss's on the next street and get a little pail full of milk every day. Their son is in Company A, too. I offer to pay for the milk, but they just wave me off and say, 'We are glad to help the family of one of our brave soldiers.'"

"You are the brave one, I think," Matti smiled, looking right into Marta's eyes. "I am not sure I could do it alone, like you."

"It is not easy. You know, sometimes when I think of Johann, I am so proud of what he is doing. He is so good to send most of his pay home because he wants us to have enough. But, if I am honest, and I can say this only to you, I am simply furious a lot of the time that he went off and left us like this. How could he do that?" Tears ran down Marta's cheeks.

Matti put her arm around Marta's thin shoulders. *"Ja, es ist schwer.* I can see how you feel. I know he told Paulus that it was something he had to do, but it doesn't seem fair to leave you like this."

Marta sobbed as if a dam had broken. "I have never told anyone this, but I must tell you as a 'sister.'" She looked hard at Matti. "I often think that he went because he wishes he were free of me."

"Why do you say that? He always seems like a good husband. He works to take care of you."

"I have never been sure that he wanted to marry me. I was having a baby and we had to get married. He never seemed happy about it. And when Karl was born, it seemed as if he did not care for the baby. He never wanted to get close. He didn't mind leaving little Karl with my family when we came to America. Even now when I talk about him, Johann doesn't say much. I live for the day when little Karl can come over with somebody from our town, but Johann never wants to talk about that."

"You poor dear. That is awfully hard on you," Matti responded, hugging Marta.

"He is not a bad man. In fact, he is a good man. But I just live every day with this pain. Even when I take the draft to the bank to get the money he sends home, I have the feeling that he is paying to be away from me because I keep talking about bringing Karl over."

"I am so sorry. You just talk to me about it whenever you want to."

"Please do not ever tell anyone. Even my own family does not know that I have these fears. I am trusting you. I don't want you even to tell Paulus. Promise me?" Marta said, wiping her tears.

The Raberts were having supper in the house they had built on Ninth Street with help from Gretchen's parents, after living above the newspaper office for nearly a year. Gretchen reached across the table for her husband's hand.

"Charles, I was visiting some of the wives of the soldiers to take them some things from the Patriotic Society." She pressed her husband's hand. "It makes me feel guilty to have you so close when they are so lonely and needy."

"I know that a lot of them are having a hard time. Today I got a letter from the Courthouse in Coaltown asking me to put a notice in the paper. I have it in my coat pocket." Rabert went to the hall tree and retrieved the paper.

He read: "To those who desire to aid the suffering families of Perry County's brave volunteers: The Board of Commissioners of Perry County, being desirous of aiding the destitute families of the soldiers who are in the Army of the United States, have determined to give the patriotic citizens of Perry County opportunity to exhibit their devotion to the cause of their country and humanity, and to that purpose order that the Auditor of Perry County be and is hereby authorized to receive loans to the amount of five hundred dollars, and issue his certificate therefor, bearing six per cent interest, for which a special tax will be levied in June 1862 to meet the payment of the same. The money raised is to be applied to the relief of destitute families of volunteers who entered the Army of the United States from Perry County."

Rabert went on thoughtfully, "The County has the right idea, but they move so slowly on anything positive. Blow a bugle and tell them some southern raiders are coming and they will spend hundreds of dollars. But tell them that families are eating less than they should or having a hard time paying their bills because their men are in the army, and they say that they are working on a plan to help."

"Most of the families here in Helvetia have been sharing what they can," Gretchen answered. "We collect a hundred dollars or so every month. Some people give us good used clothes or extra blankets or bags of flour and sugar. We try to give it to those who seem to need it most. But there is never enough to go around. We have more than fifty families we are looking after."

"I'll try writing another editorial. I will try to put pressure on the county commissioners to be more generous. The trouble is that they know that a lot of people here in Helvetia cannot vote until they get citizenship. No pressure there. They have plenty voters in Coaltown but the editor of *The Reporter* is more interested in lambasting the abolitionists than in trying to get more support for soldiers' families."

"I wish he could talk to some of these women. They are so brave. I took some things to Marta Weber today. There she is, growing vegetables for her table now; turnips and potatoes for next winter. She has to take care of her three little girls. She was so thankful for the three dollars I could give her. She just held on to my hand."

"I do not often see her in town."

"How could you? She has her hands so full at home that I doubt if she gets downtown more than once a month, except to see if there is a letter at the Post Office. She cannot afford to buy anything except food. She said that Johann sends twelve dollars of his pay every month. But with the price of flour doubling she has to stretch those dollars to the breaking point."

"Johann is a good man. In our conversations he more and more saw the importance of keeping the country together. Here is a man, not a well-educated man, but very intelligent, who came to this country full of hope. He has had one disappointment after another. He arrived in Iowa and could not find decent work. He heard about Helvetia and brought his little family here to be part of a city that was being born. He used his small inheritance to build a house. He worked in the furniture factory, but they were only able to make ends meet, not get ahead. He dreams of having his own business, but the times run against him."

"But why did he have to volunteer for the army and leave his family?"

"I think it was two things. He wanted to help save the country, so that there could be prosperity and progress, a chance for his dream to come true. He really felt that he was becoming an American, in spite of his frustrations. But he also knew that after the war he might have a chance to make a new start. Don't forget, we all thought the war would last less than a year. Nobody thought that a three year enlistment would actually last for three years."

"But it is not fair. His poor wife is paying an awful price."

"I know. I know. All of these women are paying a heavy cost."

"You have to use the paper to let people know just how desperate some of these situations are becoming."

"I will try to do that, but it has to be carefully done. Most of them do not want pity, or charity. They are stronger than we realize. But we do have to make clear that we respond to their need because we are proud and grateful for the sacrifices they are making."

"You are a good man, Charles Rabert, to think of that. I just see their need and want to help so much that I forget how it must sometimes make them feel to have to look to others for help."

Paulus Frantz paid one of his frequent evening visits to the newspaper office, where the lamp-lit window indicated that Rabert was working late on the next edition.

"Busy? I don't want to cut off the news," he joked as he poked his head through the doorway.

"Come in; have a chair. I always have time to talk to our school teacher," Rabert waved expansively. "There is some cold coffee in that pot over there. I brought it from supper."

"I wanted to look at some of the last few papers you have gotten from Louisville and Cincinnati. Somebody told me that there was a fight somewhere in Indiana about the draft. The story was pretty confused and I would like to find out the facts."

"You are welcome to look through the papers. I do know that Governor Morton asked for some troops to break up a couple nasty situations in New Albany and some other place where crowds gathered because they were upset with this latest draft call for 300,000 more men."

Franz shuffled through the papers, looking for the stories. "Why would there be angry crowds. Indiana has always filled its quota with volunteers. There is never a need for a draft here. We are not like some of those states in the east where they have riots whenever Lincoln asks for more men."

"Do not forget that southern Indiana is a lot like a border state. We have a lot of old-time Democrats who have it in for Lincoln and the war. They would rather make compromise after compromise."

"These are the fellows they call Butternuts?"

"This is not a *Kerl* who sits around in the saloon talking about 'how this war to save the niggers is all wrong.' These are business men and politicians who have opposed the war from the start and who want it stopped. They make speeches and use their influence to oppose the moves that Lincoln makes to win the war as soon as possible."

"How do they get away with it. That sounds like treason to me."

"It borders on treason. Some of them have been arrested, even a few judges, but if it cannot be proved that they actually did something to help the enemy, not a whole lot can be done to them."

"I would lock them up."

"Yes, but do not forget that one of the reasons many of us came here is that there are guarantees of freedom here.. We remember '48 in Heidelberg."

"But these fellows are trying to upset the government that has gone to war to hold the country together."

"I guess my problem is that they claim their freedom at the same time that they have absolutely no wish to free the slaves in the south."

"No wonder you do not get along with the editor of *The Reporter* over in Coaltown. Every time I see one of his papers he is frothing at the mouth over the abolitionists and the Republicans in Congress. He keeps whipping up the folks over there to catch and send back across the river any poor slaves who make it to Indiana. He even had an article by some parson who wanted to hang all the abolitionists."

Rabert smiled, "I have little in common with my colleague except the capacity to spell. He sounds like he would be more at home in Alabama that in Indiana, except that he wants to save the Union, even if half of the country is slaveholding. Look at the way he went after Congressman Julian for proposing a bill that would repeal the fugitive slave law."

"He has quite a following in Coaltown. Plenty of those folks take everything he says as gospel truth."

"He may not be a Butternut, but he surely feeds them every week."

On their first assignment Johann and his squad marched through the streets of Lebanon and down the dusty country road toward Bradfordsville. At a crossroads a couple of miles from town they found a rude guard post that had been constructed by the troops they were replacing. There was a shack knocked together from scrap wood for protection against rain. Shallow earth works to defend the cross roads had apparently been dug weeks ago because weeds and grass covered the embankment which gave cover to the guards.

It was obvious that this was not really a fortified position. Their job was to sound the alarm if ever Confederate troops appeared, not to fight them off. If confronted by an advancing brigade or a large troop of mounted raiders, twenty men could not put up much of a fight. The squad put their knapsacks and rations in the shack and lounged about the earth works;

only half of the shallow rifle pits were shaded by an old maple tree. A farmhouse and barn could be seen just over a small rise in the land. Just behind the earthworks on the road from Lebanon an arched stone bridge spanned a small shallow creek gurgling over the rocky bottom. A path ran down to the creek, where many guards posted here before them had gone to get drinking water.

Johann was determined to follow the orders from Captain Pleisch. In spite of the peaceful rural scene of which they had become a part, they were to be vigilant.

Stocker had already sat down against the base of the maple and was taking off his shoes. "If I got to be here twelve hours, I'm goin' to get comfortable."

"Not so fast," Johann cautioned. "The captain said we had to have three men on look-out at all times. Stocker, you take five other men with your muskets. Each pair of you go down one of these roads in front of us. Find a high spot where you can watch the road. You probably will see where the others stood guard. I'll send replacements in four hours. We're going to take turns, four hours at a time."

Stocker, grumbling that he could not stay under his tree for the moment, picked up his musket and pointed to five other men, "You fellows come along with me. We are going on this dangerous guard duty. We have to protect the whole damned Union army from a couple rabbits and a squirrel."

Bauer laughed, "As soon as any Rebs hear that you are ready to attack 'em, they'll throw down their guns and run for home."

Geyer joined the sport, "I feel so honored to be serving with the man who won the war. Now we can all go home."

"You can laugh at me," Stocker protested, massaging his musket, "but I am goin' to fight hard. You'll see." He marched off toward the rifle pits on the top of a low hill.

The troops were allowed to go to Lebanon from their camp when they were off-duty to buy things in the shops. At first they were very shy about talking with the people they met in the stores. Although everyone was patient with their halting English. A few Germans in the town could be called on in a pinch.

Johann and Geyer walked down into the town one evening just to look around. Seeing several soldiers going into a saloon on Railroad Street, they took courage for their first venture into civilian society. Standing at the bar their blue Union uniforms lined up with men in working clothes. Others were playing cards at two tables in the back. Johann and Geyer smiled at the civilian voices, speaking in a strange nasal twang.

The barkeep mopped the bar in front of them. "*Zwei Biere...*," Geyer said with a smile, holding up two fingers.

Johann put some coins on the bar and they began to sip the foam from the top of their glasses.

"*Das schmeckt gut*," Johann wiped the foam from his moustache. "It tastes like the beer Reller makes in Helvetia."

"That reminds me. I got a letter from Margareta today. She said that *Die Zeitung* told about something that happened in Owensboro. The captain of the mail packet told Rabert that they had a near riot there. One of the boats, bringing wounded up the river from battles down along the Tennessee, docked in Owensboro. They had some southern wounded, I suppose on their way to the hospital in New Albany. One of those fellows died, and they put his body off at Owensboro. Some of the people there who side with the South, decided to take up a collection to bury him. They had a big funeral and a parade to the cemetery. It made a lot of the folks who are in favor of the Union mad, so they took up a collection of almost five hundred dollars and gave it to the military hospital they are setting up in Jeffersonville."

"I suppose it would be the same here in Lebanon. When we march down the street to the Bradfordsville road, I look at the people watching us. I keep asking myself, is this one a friend? Is this one an enemy? Some people smile, some people just stare, some people look the other way. I never know what it means," Johann said.

"I heard that somebody took a shot at the camp when the last soldiers were here."

"It would sure be easy to hide in the woods and shoot at us."

"You would think that people would be glad that we are here to protect them from more raids. But I guess there are plenty of folk who were happy when Morgan came over the hills," Geyer responded.

"I suppose there are saloons here in Lebanon where we would be treated like enemies."

"I do not feel that here. I suppose that is why we did not come in until we saw some other soldiers going in."

"We have to play everything safe. The danger out on Bradfordsville Road is not from southern soldiers. They are many miles away. If we have trouble, if someone tries to blow up that bridge, it will be from people in

Lebanon or some of those farmers who want to fight for the South and make trouble for us."

Geyer motioned the barkeeper for another glass of beer. "It bothers me that we cannot trust anybody. I do not like living like that. What kind of life is it when you wonder if every person you see is an enemy."

"I don't like it either. As soon as we finish our beer, we better get back to camp. We can tell the boys about this place."

The colonel ordered that whenever a detachment moved through the town, they were to march in formation. He explained that he wanted the people of the town to see that the soldiers were disciplined and business-like. He also wanted to remind the southern sympathizers in the community that this was a strong military force.

Johann's squad marched smartly through the center of Lebanon as the sun was lowering in the western sky. They looked straight ahead, muskets on their shoulders. Their packs and blanket rolls were on their backs. There was no talking in the ranks until they passed the edge of town.

Having relieved the daytime guards, the squad took their familiar positions along the roads which converged at the guard post. Four men were posted along each road, sitting on the nearest high ground to watch the road. The others rested near the shanty along the creek, ready to change the guard after four hours.

Darkness fell shortly after their arrival. The men built a small fire in a circle of stones along the creek bank. They unrolled their blankets on the smooth ground near the shack. Soon most of them were asleep. Johann had to stay awake during the first half of the night to change the guard. Only then could he sleep. He pulled his blanket around him and leaned back against the crude shelter. Occasionally he walked around to stay awake, put a little more wood on the small fire, looked at his watch.

His mind turned back the years, remembering how this watch had been given to him by his brother Gustav at the time of his marriage to Marta. Gustav was the soldier in the family, the one who came home in uniform, the one who was a musketeer for the King of Prussia, although in peacetime. Now here was Johann, who was so glad that he never was called into the Prussian army, across the ocean, in uniform, standing guard along a country creek, in the middle of a war that raged miles away. Johann murmured, "What would you say to me, Gustav, if you could see me now?"

Geyer and Bauer and two other men were at the guard post a quarter mile down the road toward Bradfordsville. The quiet countryside unrolled ahead of them. They talked in low voices.

Bauer mentioned the most recent edition of *Die Zeitung* which had reached them in camp. "Did you see what Rabert wrote about a southern army comin' from Tennessee into Kentucky?"

"*Ja.*, but that's a long way south of here. We'll never see them. I bet that our army is coming from Nashville to chase them back south."

"I can see why they would want to come to Kentucky. The people here who side with the South will probably join up with them to drive back our Union army."

Geyer thought for a moment. "I don't think that will happen. The ones who want to fight for the South have already gone to join their armies."

"Maybe you're right. I hope so."

The men fell silent. They paced back and forth atop their little hill to stay awake. Another boring night!

"What was that? I thought I saw a light," Bauer said softly.

"Where? I didn't see anything."

"It was just for a little....Over there, just about on the horizon to the right of that barn. It was dim, like a lantern. Help me look for it."

Geyer peered into the darkness, joined by their companions. One of the men kicked their little fire apart so that they could see better in the darkness. They strained to look where Bauer was pointing.

"There it is again. Didn't you see it? It was just for a moment."

"I am not sure, but I think I saw..."

"There it is again. You must have seen that!" Bauer said.

"You are right. There is someone out there with a lantern," Geyer agreed.

"Should we send back for the sergeant?" one of the men asked.

"*Nein.* I don't want to seem foolish. You fellows stay here. I am goin' to walk out in that direction a way and try to get a closer look," Bauer said.

"All right. Just be careful coming back so we know it's you. And don't let the men on the other roads see you. They're liable to take a shot at you."

"I'll be back in half an hour. I'll walk right down the middle of the road so you can see me and know who it is." Bauer took his musket and began walking toward where the light had been.

Bauer had only been gone for ten minutes when one of the men said, "Listen. I hear something. It sounds like horses galloping. Listen!"

379

"Right. I hear it too. It is a bunch of horses, not just one rider."

Geyer said, "You go back and get the sergeant! We'll stay here and watch. Something funny is going on out there."

"Keep your eyes open for Bauer. He'll come right back if he heard those horses."

"Any bunch of people riding around like that in the middle of the night are up to no good. We better get into our rifle pits and be ready to fire if riders come down that road. If there are many of them, we can't stop them, but maybe they'll be scared off if we shoot at them."

"Here comes Bauer, running right down the middle of the road. He heard them too."

"I see Bauer but I do not see any horses. I can still hear them. Do you?"

Bauer came running up. "There are a lot of...horses down the road," he said, catching his breath. "I didn't see anything..., but I could hear a lot of horses pounding along. We should tell Johann."

"We already sent Hans back to tell him."

"Here he comes now."

Johann ran up to the outpost and looked out over the road and the farm ahead of them.

"Do you hear those horses?" Bauer asked. "We saw a light out there a little while ago. Something is going on."

Johann took charge. "Go back to the guard post," he ordered one of the men. "Leave two men there and bring the rest up here with their guns. Send somebody to the other outposts and bring back two of the men. Spread out on both sides of the road and keep down. If you can find a ditch or a fence to give you some cover, that's good. Make sure you have a handful of cartridges with you."

The men followed orders and covered the road with their muskets. Johann called Geyer. "Albrecht, I want you to go back to camp and report this to the captain. Those are our orders. If we see anyone, we will fire a volley or two. If it is a big force, we will fall back across the creek and try to keep them from coming across the bridge. That would give time for the company to get between us and Lebanon. Move right along, Albrecht."

A few minutes after Geyer left, a shot rang out from behind them at the guard post. "All of you, except Bauer and Stocker, stay here and watch the road. Fritz, you and Jake come with me. Keep low," Johann said, running back toward the shack.

Another shot broke the stillness of the night. "Those *verdammten* fools are shooting at us," Stocker puffed.

"No. They must see something along the creek."

The voice of one of the men at the shack called, "Over that way," pointing to the north. "I hit one of them. I saw him fall."

Johann took charge. He ordered his four men, "Keep your muskets loaded. There may be more of them."

"I saw at least two men coming toward the bridge along the creek bank, just at the edge of the water," the soldier named Braun blurted excitedly. "When I called '*Halt!*' they started to run. That is when I shot. One fell and the other climbed the bank and ran. Peter shot at him, but it was too hard to see."

"Keep alert," Johann commanded. "There might be more of them out there. Fritz, come with me. You men be careful not to shoot at us. I want to see what we have out there."

Johann and Bauer, keeping their muskets at the ready, crouched low and ran along the creek bank toward the dark shape barely visible in the darkness. It was a man, still, draped over the edge of the creek bank, his arm trailing in the gurgling water. Approaching him warily, they poked at his body with the muzzles of their muskets. They could make out a dark stain which spread across the entire back of his coat.

Bauer said, "*Er ist tot!*" With his boot he turned the body over. "He is dead all right. The shot went right through his chest."

"Just leave him there until the captain comes," Johann said. As he spoke his foot touched an object on the ground. "What is this? It feels like a powder barrel."

"Sure enough. They were going to put this under the bridge and blow it up."

"We will just let everything alone until the captain gets here with more men. The important thing for us is to be ready for others to attack. We know there are horsemen out there. Get back to the bridge!"

Bauer stood very still, listening. "From here I do not hear those horses, but they were sure riding hard when we heard them out on the road."

Johann said, "I wonder if they were planning to attack us from the other side of that ridge so that we would all go rushing over there and let these fellows sneak in and blow up the bridge."

Bauer leaned against the stone side of the bridge. "That fellow out there did not look like he had a uniform on. He was dressed like the farmers around here."

"Well, we know that there are more of them out there. So all we can do is keep careful watch until the captain comes and it gets light. You stay here with these two and guard the bridge. I am going up the road to the other men to tell them what happened. We will just keep a few out there to watch. I'll send most of the fellows back to help you with the bridge. Spread yourselves out around the bridge. Use some of those rifle pits. We know the bridge is what they were after, so we need to be sure they do not make another try."

Within an hour Captain Pleisch and a detachment of about fifty men arrived and spread out across the area. Putting his hand on Johann's shoulder he said, "Good work, Sergeant. As soon as it gets light we will move a force down the road and see what was going on over that hill."

"What about that body by the creek?" Johann asked.

"The Colonel is going to ride out at sunrise. He can decide then what to do. We need to look around as soon as we can see."

"We have not heard the horsemen for at least half an hour. My guess is that they have pulled back."

"You say that the fellow by the creek is not wearing a uniform. It must just be a bunch of the rebel farmers trying to make trouble. We know that Morgan is raiding again a hundred miles to the south, but we have not heard of him up this way."

Colonel Owen and several of his officers rode in as the sun came up over the peaceful farmland. Johann and the captain quickly filled him in on the details of last night's action. They walked over to the dead man. In the dawn's light they could see that he had been carrying a small keg of powder and a length of fuse.

"It is clear enough," the Colonel said, "that they were going to blow up that bridge. Send a man back to town to get a wagon. We will haul this body back to town after everybody is up and around. I want people to see that someone was killed trying to make mischief and that we resist these kinds of attacks. Then we will let his family, whoever they are, claim his body for burial. I want his body treated with respect. We will wrap it in a blanket and not put it on display. See if there is an undertaker in town and let him handle it

"Sergeant, now that the other squad has come to relieve you, I want you to take this detachment and your squad. March down that road past the farm. When you are over the hill, fan out across the fields on either side and see what you can of where those horsemen were."

They marched off and within a short while had come across a small dirt lane, crossing the Bradfordsville Road. The roadside was coated with heavy dust and the dirt road was churned with hoof prints. A dusty hat was in the ditch and a jug with a corncob stopper.

"This is where they were," Captain Pleisch said to Johann. The hoof prints ran about a quarter of a mile in each direction. "It looks to me like they just galloped back and forth on this road. A dozen horses pounding along this lane could sound like a whole troop of cavalry coming over the hill."

They went back to report to the Colonel who was waiting beside the crude guard shanty.

"Well done, Pleisch! Sergeant, I think you were right; they were trying to get you to chase them to let these fellows try to get in behind you and blow up the bridge. I want the names of those two men who were guarding the bridge. This is the first enemy action we have had in the regiment and I want to give them a good word."

Captain Pleisch ordered Johann, "You take your men back to the camp and get some sleep. You have had a busy night."

The squad was the center of attention back at camp. The whole company gathered around to hear about the attack. Stocker became the self-appointed main spokesman. "I knew we were in for it when I heard all them horses. There must have been a hundred of 'em right down the road from us. I was sure we were goin' to see the elephant. That southern cavalry is all over the place. My guess is it was Morgan!" Stocker paused to take a big chew of tobacco, looking around the circle of faces. "We got in those rifle pits. I laid out my cartridges. We HAD to be able to slow down a force that big. They musta known we were out there because they pulled back and never come over the hill to face us. A couple of dozen of them rebels came up in back of us. They all had powder in barrels and would have blown that bridge sky-high if Braun didn't hit one of them. Course, he just fired at the crowd, but he got one. The rest ran away as fast as they could. I tell you, men, it was pretty rough out there for a while."

Geyer pulled Johann to one side. "Too bad he could not shoot off his mouth instead of a musket. He would have killed that whole regiment. What a windbag!"

"I hate to spoil his fun. The other fellows will figure out pretty soon that it was not the battle Stocker says it was."

The soldiers in Lebanon began to fit the little touch of the war on the Bradfordsville Road into the larger picture of what was going on in central Kentucky. The newspapers from home that circulated through the camp reported a Confederate advance into northern Tennessee and then into Kentucky well to the east of Lebanon.

After the Union victories at Shiloh and Corinth, General Buell and his Union army of 40,000 men had moved slowly across northern Alabama toward Chattanooga. The strategy was to divide southern armies by keeping pressure on a number of centers many miles apart. Because Buell refused to let his army live off the land, seizing supplies from civilians and looting farms and stores, he had to be supplied from his base in Nashville, many miles to his north.

The war in Tennessee and Kentucky did not have a front line stretching continuously for miles. The civilian population, particularly in eastern Tennessee and northern Kentucky, was a mixture of northern and southern sympathizers. Armies and smaller detachments moved from strong point to strong point, without really occupying all the territory in between. Both Union and Confederate forces fought to protect their own supply lines and to disrupt those of the enemy.

The two greatest threats posed by the southern forces were the cavalry raiders of Nathan Bedford Forrest and John Hunt Morgan. These highly mobile detachments of a thousand or more horsemen could strike against lightly garrisoned towns, like Morgan had done at Lebanon, destroying railroads and bridges, cutting supply lines and moving on. Even *Die Zeitung* and the Coaltown *Reporter* which had been sent to the 60th Indiana, had pointed with alarm to the possibility that these raiders might well attack through Kentucky and across the Ohio River into the coal fields of southern Indiana. The Helvetia Foresters and Home Guards all along the river were kept on constant alert against such attack.

The real concern of the Union army focused on protecting the major supply base in Nashville and its rail links to the north. A second concern was the rail lines south from Nashville that were necessary to supply Buell's army inching toward Chattanooga. In mid-July Forrest captured Murfreesboro, taking prisoner two Union generals and the garrison with all their supplies. He paroled the troops, sending them south toward Buell. In this swift raid Forrest effectively cut Buell off from Nashville for weeks.

Far away in Virginia McClellan was mounting huge offensives against Lee and Jackson without gaining victories. In the west Grant was opening up the Mississippi with a series of victories capturing or outflanking Confederate strongholds on islands or on the banks of the river in Missouri and western Kentucky. In between, Halleck's Army of the Tennessee sought to stabilize Buell's offensive to split the Confederacy into two weakened halves.

Although there were conversations about newspaper accounts of these movements of armies, for the men of the 60th Indiana the war was really in Lebanon and its surrounding countryside. In spite of the increased vigilance after the attack on the Bradfordsville Road bridge, camp life was deadly routine. In the heat of August the little peaked two-man tents in the shadeless field outside Lebanon never cooled. The blue woolen uniforms scratched perspiring skin.

Johann and his squad were cooking dinner in front of their tents. Two chickens bought from a farmer's wife along the road roasted over their small fire pit, spitting fatty fireballs in all directions. Some ears of corn, their husks turning brown, roasted at the edge of the fire. The men sat on a few old boxes and empty casks watching Geyer poke at the chickens with his bayonet. He had been chosen their cook after several disastrous other elections,

"Those chickens about done?" asked the insatiable Stocker.

Buhl answered, "Give it a little more time. This is going to be the first g-g-good meal we had in a while..."

"Seeing that woman and buying the chickens is a real switch from that swill the quartermaster gives us. So enjoy it while you can...Besides, we have stuff from the box that my wife sent," Geyer said.

Stocker proposed, "There are enough chicken yards 'round here that we could have chicken ever' day if we wanted to. We are helpin' these people. They owe us a few hens. You back me up, and I'll see that we have chicken regular."

Buhl reminded him, "The C-C-Colonel would give you hell. He had that fellow sitting on a barrel under the flagpole for a week with that sign around his neck telling everybody he was a thief."

Every few weeks, wives and families sent small boxes to their men. There would be socks and underwear for the recipient. After a few angry quarrels the men had agreed that food items would be shared with their mess mates.

385

Geyer said, "Margareta put a nice *Stollen* in the box and a loaf of bread. That is what will taste the best to me."

"It will be better than the last box of stuff we got from the Ladies Patriotic Aid Society in Coaltown. By the time that got to us it was nothing but a pile of crumbs mixed in with all those socks."

"Your Margareta is a good cook," Stocker added. "I hope when I get home I can find a cook like that to marry me."

"Any woman who had to cook for you would work herself to d-d-death in a year's time," Buhl laughed, poking at Stocker's bulk on the box beside his.

"Don't laugh," Stocker answered. "I know what good food is. My mother runs the best boardin' house in Helvetia. No wonder I have high standards when it comes to eatin'."

Buhl kept up the joke. "Geyer's cooking puts meat on your bones, and Johann here marches it off back and forth to B-B-Bradfordsville Road."

Johann joined the fun. "If you have a slab of Margareta's *Stollen*, we will have to make you march double time to the bridge. Otherwise you are going to want to take a nap when we get there.... All right, let's eat our supper and get ready to march."

CHAPTER 18

A week or so later Col. Owen assembled the garrison in the pasture below the tent field. "We have received a telegraph warning that Morgan and a big force of horsemen are riding through southern Kentucky and might be heading this way again. We do not know just where they are. We are ordered to be prepared for him to strike in this direction. We have Lebanon in good shape to defend, but we are going to strengthen our position. We are going to move the small guard posts about five miles further down each of the roads on the highest ground we can find so they can give us more warning time if he heads this way. From now on we will have a horseman with each guard squad, who can get word back to us fast if Morgan is sighted. We are going to put a force of fifty men at each of the old guard posts as skirmishers if he comes along. If we can show that we are prepared for an attack, he might well not try it.

"This may be the first time we are really challenged by more than a few farmers. We could face a major Confederate force. It is our job to drive him off if he heads this way. Are you ready to fight? *Sind sie bereit zu kämpfen?*"

The men yelled a resounding *"Ja,"* waving their caps and thumped each other on the backs.

Gathered around the cooking fire, where Geyer was stirring a stewpot of army beef, potatoes and cabbage, the men soberly talked over the colonel's orders.

"How could we ever stand off a thousand horsemen? They would ride right over us. It wouldn't even be a f-f-fight," Buhl said.

Even Stocker put aside his usual bluster. "We couldn't hardly slow him down."

Geyer continued stirring his pot. "I think the colonel was saying that if we show we are really ready in strong positions, Morgan might look for another plum to pick in some other town where there aren't as many federal soldiers."

Johann broke in, "We know what we have to do. Morgan cannot be allowed to get up to the river. He would cross into Indiana for sure and do a lot of damage."

"I'll fight like a tiger to keep him away from that river," Geyer said.

Johann added, "I was thinking last night about some of the talks we had in Helvetia when the war began. Some people said we had to fight to keep the Union together. Some people wanted to fight against slavery. I keep remembering how the men from the Colonization Society were looking for a place, they would not go anywhere there was slavery."

Geyer agreed. "Slavery is an awful thing. Rabert in *Die Zeitung* keeps talking about this being a fight for freedom." He dipped in his ladle and tasted the stew, after blowing on it.

"*Ja*! But some of the fellows from Coaltown tell me that *The Reporter* says that the editor there wants to hang all those easterners who want to do away with slavery. He said they just make things worse." Johann said.

Stocker in a rare thoughtful mood spoke. "When I was a boy in Switzerland, our teachers always told us that to be free was the most important thing in life. That's what the story of Wilhelm Tell was all about. But we didn't know nothin' about black slaves."

"Even around Lebanon here you see a few farms where they have slaves. You see *die Schwartze* working out in the fields and the little shacks they live in. The farmers buy and sell them like cows. That doesn't seem right to me," Geyer argued, poking his bayonet at the chunk of beef in the stewpot.

Johann said, "One of the sergeants from Company B told me that he heard about a fight they had in Gen. Mitchell's Division...somewhere south of here. Slaves were running away from their farms and coming to the Union army. Orders said that the army had to send them back home. A bunch of officers from Illinois regiments said that they would not do that. They said that this war was to end slavery. General Mitchell said that they were disobeying orders and that he would have them shot in front of the whole division. They had to back down."

"I can see how they felt," Geyer responded. "If we had some runaway slaves coming into our camp, I would sure hate to send them back.

I think I would tell them which way the river was and let them get into a free state."

"You'd be going against orders," Stocker spat into the dust.

Buhl got into the conversation. "You don't have to worry about that happening. I haven't seen any s-s-slaves coming into camp here."

Stocker addressed Geyer, "Come on, let's eat. That beef must be chewable by now."

"Don't count on it! Get your pans and I'll ladle some out for you," Geyer responded. "I did the best I could with that meat. When it came out of the barrel, it was starting to turn green. I tried to wash it in the pond before I cut it up to put in the pot."

"I'll try anything. Ladle me out a chunk," Stocker grunted.

The men held out their plates to Geyer and received their portion of the tallowy stew.

"Sergeant, how about you?" Geyer asked.

"I am not hungry. I will just dip some bread in the juice," Johann said.

"You haven't been eating much lately. As the cook, *es tut mir leid*," Geyer laughed.

"*Nein*, you are a good enough cook. I am just not hungry..."

Stocker broke in, "Has all this talk about Morgan got you that worried, Sergeant?"

"No. I just have been having a lot of belly aches lately. I do not feel much like eating."

"*Mein Gott*, I hope I never feel like not eating," Stocker joked.

Johann did not say that he had vomited often in the past few weeks. He assumed that his indigestion could be traced to the poor food they ate most of the time. Tough salted army beef and hardtack did not go down easily. He longed for some of his mother's creamy milk soup and homemade dark bread.

About the same time as rumors of Morgan's raids, the newspapers told of efforts to bring more men into the army. Heavy casualties in a growing number of battles, together with the evolving strategy of fighting on various fronts from Virginia to Alabama to Arkansas spread Union forces thinner than the commanders demanded. Men were leaving the ranks as one year enlistments expired.

Geyer put *Die Zeitung* aside as he sat with Johann and Buhl in the shanty at the guard post. "Rabert writes that Lincoln is calling for 300,000 more three year volunteers. That is a lot of men. They must be expecting this fight to go on for a while."

"I wonder how many have to come from Perry C-C-County? Buhl asked. "They don't seem to have trouble filling their quota. They never will have a draft there if men keep signing up."

Johann added, "I guess some places do not get enough men to volunteer, so a lot of their people get drafted--just like *Preuszen*. I thought we were getting away from that stuff."

"You sound like you had to come to this army. You volunteered, d-d-didn't you?" Buhl asked with a touch of irony.

"*Ja, das ist richtig.* The more I thought about it, the more I was worried about the United States breaking up into little pieces," Johann said. "It would be like it was in Europe, all little kingdoms and duchys. That did not get us anywhere in a thousand years. This is a big, strong country and I don't want to see it weakened. I still believe that these hard times will pass and we all will have our chance to get ahead."

"Well," Buhl joined in, "I guess I am one of the few who is here because I really am against slavery. We Swiss always believe people should be free. It really bothers me to think that people are owned like cows and sheep."

Geyer responded, "You better not talk too loud about all that. A lot of the men don't give a damn about slavery. You ask one of the fellows who reads the Coaltown *Reporter*. They'll give you an earful."

"I hear that they are trying to get more men to enlist by offering more money on top of the $100 the government is paying," Johann added. "Some of the fellows were talking to some soldiers from Illinois and they said some counties there are giving volunteers an extra hundred or two when they sign up. That will be a lot more than the Patriotic Aid Society is giving to help support our families."

Johann thought of how hard Marta was trying to get along on the pay he had sent home and the few dollars from the Helvetia Patriotic Society. It didn't seem fair that new volunteers were getting three times as much as he and his men were getting. I am not going to say anything, he thought, and get the other men stirred up. There is nothing we can do about it anyway.

Buhl spoke up. "*Die Zeitung* said that men who get drafted are allowed to buy a substitute for $300, or they can just pay $300 and they will never get drafted. That is a year's pay for m-m-most of us."

"That is bound to make trouble," the sensible Geyer said. "The army will be made up of poor men. The newspaper said that most of the substitutes are people who have just come to the country from Europe, fellows like we were a few years ago."

Buhl spoke up. "When you get here and cannot find a job, $300 would be good pay for three years. How do you think they got all us Swiss and G-G-Germans to make a whole regiment?"

"The captain said to me yesterday," Johann reported, "that we are still getting good men in the army. The officers agreed that the volunteers are hard-working, honest men, good soldiers."

"They sure got good men from Helvetia. Even Stocker, for all his big talk, does his duty. It probably will use up all the government's money to feed him, but he pulls his weight most of the time," Geyer laughed.

Letters from Helvetia arrived regularly. Marta wrote to Johann:

> The girls are standing right here beside me in the kitchen. Emma is telling me to say that she misses you. Anna just shakes her head "yes" to say that she misses you too. We all do. But we are getting along all right. Matti gave me a couple of nice dresses that fit Anna. Jenny is starting to take a few steps. I have to watch her so she does not hurt herself by falling against the table or the stove. She is a good baby and hardly ever cries. Some of the ladies in Coaltown sent a box of women's and children's clothes to Helvetia for the soldiers' families. Some of the stuff was pretty shabby, but some was quite nice. We put it all out on a table at the *Turnhalle* and everyone took turns picking out a dress or shirt. I got a nice warm dress that will be good when winter comes. Most of the things were way too big for me. I got a dress for Emma too. We are getting some good things from the little garden I have behind the house. Matti helped me plant it. Emma goes with me to hold the basket when I go out to pick the beans or cabbages. In a few more weeks we will be able to start digging the potatoes. I planted as many as I could. But there are still so many tree roots that the ground is hard to dig. We are all worried because we keep hearing about a southern army that is marching north and about that man Morgan who burned the town where you are. The Helvetia *Förster* are keeping watch at the river day and night. Last week a few soldiers came and set up a camp on the hill south of town where they can look both ways at the bend of the river. In Coaltown they have been sent a big cannon to protect the town from attack. The home guard there practices shooting at a little

boat they have tied out in the river. One of their shots carried all the way over the river into Kentucky. Herr Rabert told me that they had some horse soldiers from our army at Coaltown to help guard against an army coming across the river. He said that 200 of them with their horses came by steamer and are camped just outside of town. The people of Coaltown are so glad to have them guarding them that they have one party after another to keep the soldiers happy. He said that now they are being moved to Kentucky, so they must be somewhere around you. If they have soldiers in Coaltown and Helvetia, why can't they have the men from here guard their own homes. It does not make any sense to have you somewhere off in Kentucky and to bring men from some place else to camp here and guard us. I don't know where you are. Your letter said Lebanon, but I do not know where that is. I hope it is not near the fighting. If you hear that the southerners are coming, I hope you just run into the woods and hide. They ought not expect a man with a wife and four children to risk his life in the army. We left our home and came all the way across the ocean to get away from that kind of business. Do the people in Lebanon have parties for you? They should be grateful that you are guarding them. I wish you were guarding Helvetia. Herr Rabert has a paper in the window of the newspaper office, whenever he hears that somebody has been wounded. They have been men who were part of Frey's regiment which left Helvetia before you did. They had three men die of sickness. One of them was the Roth boy. I have to push myself to look at the list because I am always afraid I will see somebody from the 60th. Emma and Anna want to draw kisses at the bottom of the letter. I will put them down for Jenny and from me.

    Ich liebe dich. X X X X

    Marta

By late summer rumors of the approach of the Confederate Army swept back and forth across Lebanon and the soldiers' camp southwest of town. Col. Owen and his officers huddled over their maps and the latest telegraph messages from headquarters in Louisville.

It had become clear in the past few weeks that this was a serious campaign. The Confederates were moving north across eastern Tennessee. Buell's advance on Chattanooga came to a halt because raiders were constantly cutting the railroad which supplied him. Most of these raids meant that it would take several days to rebuild the track or put up a temporary trestle. But in early August Morgan put an end to Buell's campaign by cutting a major rail line near Gallatin. His cavalrymen rolled a captured box car, packed with powder, into a tunnel and blew it up. It would take weeks to rebuild the tunnel.

Buell was weakened and had to begin marching north to be closer to his base in Nashville. The Confederates led by Kirby Smith crossed into Kentucky and captured Barbourville and seemed to be heading toward Lexington.

Col. Owen pointed to the towns where there were reliable reports of the southern advance. "It looks to me that they are staying to the east of us here. With possibilities like Lexington and Frankfurt, they will pass us by. To take those places would put them in a position to attack either Louisville or Cincinnati. I do not think they will bother with Lebanon."

"If they did, we would be put out of action in an hour," Browning said.

"It is more likely that we would be joined up with other regiments and sent back to defend Louisville," Col. Owen suggested.

"I would think that we are going to be in this fight one way or another. Should we tell the men?"

"I do not see any need to keep it from them. We have had virtually no desertions, but we will have to watch out for fellows who head for the hills if they think action is coming. I am going to get us out of the garrison mode we've been in and get the men drilling regularly. I will talk to them tomorrow. After it gets dark tonight I want to see all our officers and their sergeants in the farmhouse."

Johann joined his men sitting in front of their tents. They had spent the day on the Bradfordsville Road, returning in time for their supper, now sitting with their cigars in the dark. Johann had been called to headquarters before he had touched his plate of greasy stew.

"What is the word, Sergeant?" Stocker asked. "We going to head for home before we even see a reb?" Stocker shot a stream of tobacco juice into the darkness.

"Not so," Johann responded slowly. "You may get your wish. The Colonel says that the Confederates have a big army to the east of us. He doesn't think they will come to Lebanon, but we may go to them."

Stocker waved his kepi, "Hoorah. We're goin' to get into the fight. Now we'll see who the real men are. You still got them dollars, Sergeant. I'm going to win that bet. I ain't goin' to run when we see the elephant-- you'll see; you'll all see."

"You will do all right, Stocker," Johann reassured him. "Now, men, we are going to get into some serious drilling. There will be close order drill every day while we are here in the camp. While we are out at the guard post, we are supposed to be repairing our equipment and cleaning our muskets. They want us to be ready to move out on very short notice. So get your rest."

After the men had gone to their tents, Johann walked to the edge of the woods near the top of the low knob they called Corley's Hill. Stepping behind a low bush, he vomited. Because he had not eaten supper, there was little food to give up. He retched again and again. The burning in his belly was worse than it had been in the last week. Wiping his face he walked slowly back down the hill toward the tents.

The next day, sitting in the shed at the guard post, Johann pulled a dog-eared sheet of paper from his pack and sharpened his pencil with his bayonet.

> *Lieber* Marta,
>
> I do not have time to write a long letter. We are at our guard post out in the country, a few miles from Lebanon. I do not know how much longer we will be here. There is talk that a big southern army is coming this way and that we have to keep them from capturing Louisville. I do not know what that means for me. Until now there has been no reason for me to worry because I have always been many miles from an enemy army. I think that may change. I do not want to worry you by writing this way, but it would be wrong for me not to tell you what things are like here. I want you to know, and I want you to tell the girls when they are older, that their papa loves them. I wish that I could have provided better for you all. I have always tried to work hard, but I never have been able to find the kind of job that would make us comfortable. That is the great pain of my life. Sometimes I think I was selfish in wanting to bring you to the new country. Maybe I should have tried harder to find my fortune in the homeland. I might have walked away too soon. I know that it was hard for you to leave. I should not have asked you to do that, Marta.
>
> When I come home, I am going to work so hard for all of you. I will work night and day so you can have a good life. I have not lost my dream, but right now it seems so far away. You may not hear from me for a while because we may be on

the move. I will write when I can. You are in my thoughts more than you could know. I know that you did not want me to go into the army. It has been very hard for you, I know. But, Marta, I had to go. This is our country now and I do not want to see it become weak and poor. Our dream depends on living in a strong, free country where everyone has a chance to have a good life. I will do everything in my power to be a good soldier and to come home safely so that we can enjoy the dream together.

    Your husband,

    Johann

Every day Col. Owen would gather his troops on the parade ground in the hot August sun to report the latest word on movement of the Confederates. Most of the men only had a vague idea of the location of the towns he was talking about. They did realize that there was not much opposition to the advancing southern army. Apart from concentrations at Nashville and Bowling Green, the Union forces were so scattered that they could not mount a strong defense until they could all come together.

At least once a day a train would pull into Lebanon and unload supplies. Dozens of wagons would almost immediately load the food, blankets, muskets, ammunition, and a few cannon to supply the garrisons in towns still in Union hands across eastern Kentucky.

The colonel also reported on movements of the Union army in Tennessee and Kentucky. Holding their bases in Nashville and Bowling Green would be possible only if the railroad lines could be kept open between Louisville and Nashville. But the movement of the Confederate army in the eastern part of the state could flank the railroad and attack Louisville from the east. The colonel warned, "This would put at risk the entire campaign of our army. If Smith and Bragg succeed, we lose Tennessee and Kentucky. We would have to pull back across the Ohio. So we have to do our part to keep this from happening."

Stocker said out of the corner of his mouth to Bauer, next to him in the ranks, "*Scheiß!* Stuck off here in this side-track town, we ain't going to do much to keep nothing from happenin'."

"I think he's telling us that we are going to move out soon," Bauer whispered.

The conversation continued when they were dismissed by Col. Browning.

Johann said, "I heard you fellows talking in the ranks. That is looking for trouble, you know."

"Well, was I right?" Bauer asked. "Are we going to move out and fight that southern army?"

"Nobody knows for sure. The colonel is waiting orders. He wants us to be ready if the order comes."

"Sergeant, you don't look good.. You are getting so thin and, like my mother used to say, your color isn't good."

"I'll be all right. It is just that the food does not agree with me. I have a bellyache most of the time. I am going to eat bread and milk for a few days and let all that greasy stuff go."

As they walked past the haystack, Bauer whispered, "Don't look now but there is somebody hiding under that hay. Let's have a look."

Johann and Stocker turned quickly and ran to the stack. After a few pokes at the hay with his musket, Stocker said in a low voice, "Damn! There is somebody in the hay all right."

As he spoke a black arm emerged from the hay. The hay was brushed aside and the three soldiers saw a young black man, shaking with fright.

"Don' shoot me; don' shoot," he said, holding out his hands in front of him.

Stocker motioned with his musket for the man to come forward. "Now what do we do?" he asked.

"I don't know, but he is scared to death. He must be one of those run-aways. What do we do, Johann? You are the sergeant." Bauer said.

"The orders are that we are supposed to turn him in so he can be sent back to his owner," Johann replied with very little authority in his voice.

Stocker, without his customary bluster, looked hard at Johann, saying, "If we call the officers, you know that he gets sent back. I am a *Schweitzer* and I believe that men are free. I'm for letting him go. Hell, give him a chance!"

The run-away continued to quiver, looking pleadingly at the soldiers. He had no idea what they were saying, what language they were talking. Stocker moved his musket aside and put his hand firmly but gently on the man's arm.

Bauer smiled at him to show that he meant no harm. "Let's help him get away, Sergeant. I don't want to be part of making him a slave again. I couldn't live with myself."

"I have not disobeyed an order since I was in the army, but I don't like this. If anybody sees us with this fellow, we are in trouble. What do you want to do with him?"

Bauer answered, "Let's just put him back in the haystack. He will know that we are not going to hurt him. Maybe when it gets dark we could get him up to the woods and let him go."

"I don't know why he picked a place like this to hide, right in the middle of an army camp," Stocker said.

Johann replied, "I suppose he thought that since the Union army was fighting against the slave states, he would be safe with the men in blue."

"He ought to be. I am not goin' to turn him in," Stocker insisted. "I'll come down here tonight and take him to the woods."

"Try to tell the poor devil to get back under the hay. I don't know how you will tell him your plan to take him to the woods," Johann said.

Bauer stood watch to see that no one saw what was going on. Before Stocker motioned the man to get back under the hay, he looked right into his face and said as carefully as he could in halting English, "Night....I come....go woods." He pointed to the trees at the top of Corley's Hill. The man nodded and crawled under the haystack while Bauer and Stocker made sure that he was well covered.

The three men walked slowly to their tents. Johann ordered, "You are to tell no one! Good luck tonight, Stocker.... You can have my coat for him to wear until you get him to the woods tonight. He is about my size."

Johann did not inquire further into the adventure. The next morning, when Stocker returned his coat, he winked at his sergeant.

In the sleepy county-seat town of Munfordville, several dozen miles southwest of Lebanon, Col. John Wilder commanded a small union garrison ordered to guard the huge Louisville and Nashville Railroad bridge over the Green River. Wilder set up his headquarters in the courthouse in the center of the town. Most of the two hundred inhabitants just went about their daily business. A few who were unionists welcomed the regiment, and southern sympathizers in the town and surrounding farmside just ignored the occupying force.

Unless cut temporarily by marauding irregulars, Wilder was in contact by telegraph with Union Headquarters in Louisville and in Bowling Green.. He received regular, although fragmentary, reports on the movement of southern armies pushing north from Tennessee. There would be word of an attack on a town in eastern Kentucky, then a few days later report of another attack fifty miles further north.

Wilder knew that Buell was moving a large force from Nashville to Bowling Green to avoid being outflanked by Smith and Bragg. At first Wilder felt no concern because the action was many miles away, but when orders began coming through moving up reinforcements, it appeared that there was increasing possibility of enemy action drawing closer. Wilder was encouraged by Louisville's assurances that his force would be strengthened to protect the vital railroad bridge. The bridge was the largest between Louisville and Nashville. It was 1800 feet long and in the center was 115 feet above the river. Three tall cut-stone piers supported the long spans of iron trusses. The bridge was so big that if it were destroyed by the enemy it would cut off rail supplies for the entire Union army in Tennessee and southern Kentucky for months. This was the most vulnerable point on the entire line between Louisville and Nashville.

But Wilder's concern grew when Buell's plan to bring his army further north toward Munfordville was thwarted by Confederate cavalry temporarily cutting rail and telegraph lines to slow the Union movement. Finally Wilder realized that any help he received was not going to come from Buell. If he was going to be reinforced, it would have to come from the north.

A few days later in Lebanon Colonel Owen again addressed his troops on the parade ground.

"Men of the 60th Indiana, I am going to be very honest with you. We now have word that there are two Confederate armies moving north through Kentucky. Smith has captured Lexington and is moving on the capital, Frankfurt. That will put him between us and the Ohio River. Some of our forces are moving down from Louisville to meet him.

"But we now know that General Bragg with a sizable force is moving up from the south between us and the troops in Nashville and Bowling Green. He will be trying to get to Louisville from the south. So we are being moved to join other regiments and form a sizable force to keep Bragg away from the Louisville and Nashville Railroad. We will leave Company B here in Lebanon, but the rest of you are to get ready to move tonight.

"Take the tents you have been using with you because we'll be camping with the rest of the army. Be sure you take all the ammunition you have with you. The quartermaster will bring all our supplies with us. After sundown we assemble with your full packs, ready to move to the railroad. A train will be waiting for us. Now get a good meal and pack up your gear. Things are not going to be as quiet and easy-going as they were in Lebanon."

The heavily loaded train moved out of Lebanon on the bumpy track toward the Junction as darkness fell. It was jammed with men and equipment. There were only two coaches, and the rest of the train was made up of freight cars and one flat car on which a squad crouched behind burlap bags filled with dirt, their muskets loaded for action. Although to the best of their intelligence, Bragg's army was still miles to the south, there was always the danger of cavalry raiders or groups of local southern bushwackers ambushing the train as they had done at New Hope Station.

Unlike their earlier train rides, Johann's squad was somewhat subdued, as they looked out over the hilly countryside in the moonlight. It had been full moon just a night before. The wheels screeched as the train lurched through the switches at Lebanon Junction and turned southward on the main line of the L & N. At every railroad bridge, a couple of dozen blue coats stood guard, lounging by their rifle pits, just as Company A had done on the Bradfordsville Road. They waved as the troop train passed.

A few miles further along, just after crossing a creek, the train stopped to take on water for the boiler and fill the tender with cordwood. Recognizing that the stopped train was particularly vulnerable, the officers awakened the troops and ordered the men out of the train with their muskets. They formed on both side of the train, ready for action. Once the locomotive had taken on water, a short whistle signaled the men back on to the train.

As they were nearing the town of Munfordville, trouble struck. The third and fourth cars of the slow-moving train lurched as their wheels left the tracks. One of them turned on its side next to the track. The other perched across the tracks.

"Everyone out," officers shouted all along the train. "Form a picket line. Company A, you go on that side. Company C, you get over here. Be wide awake. This is a favorite trick of these rebs. They loosen the rails and send the train off the track; then they attack. Captain, send ten of your men to fan out toward the east and see if anyone is out there. Lieutenant, you send ten of your best out to the west and do the same thing. If you spot any rebs, fire away and we'll come running."

One squad was ordered to the overturned freight car to help the soldiers out through the door on the topside. It was quickly reported that no one was seriously injured. A few cuts were bandaged by lantern light. The packs and weapons were retrieved from the derailed cars.

The pickets returned and reported no sighting. The colonel consulted with the engineer. It would be some hours before the train would be able to move. The damaged cars would have to be pulled to one side and the tracks repaired. A messenger was sent ahead to the town to dispatch a telegraph message summoning a repair crew.

Gathering his officers, the colonel said, "The engineer tells me that there is a road into Munfordville just a short way over here to the east. Form up your men with all their gear. We are going to march the rest of the way. It is only two or three miles. We should be there by sun-up. I want to be marching in 15 minutes, so get them moving. We will get some wagons from the town to come back for the rest of the supplies. Company C will stay here to guard the train and our supplies until we can get them into the town. Now, get those men formed up."

Johann and his men marched under their heavy packs, blanket rolls across their left shoulders, muskets sloped on their other shoulder. The sky above the eastern horizon began to show the first flicker of dawn. Coming up the road toward them were half a dozen wagons. Women and small children sat on stacks of household belongings piled high on the wagons, while on the side of the road men and older children walked. They pulled off the road to let the marching column pass. Johann watched their faces with their look of fear and anger. Some of the little ones whimpered and cried. Johann thought of his little family in Helvetia and felt deep pity for these terrorized families, trying mightily to get out of the way of a battle that was coming as sure as the sunrise.

Cresting a low hill they saw a town, a square church tower, a cluster of houses. Quite a few of the houses were large brick homes with wide porches, others were much more modest log houses. A large two-storey red brick church stood on the south side of the main street. The number of houses suggested that the town could not have more than 200 inhabitants. But now it was largely deserted.

The column halted in front of the brick court house in the center square of the town. A flag indicated that this was the headquarters. Officers emerged and talked with the colonel. He went to the front of the column and ordered his staff to begin the march again. They continued to the southeast and crossed a rickety pontoon bridge, barely wide enough for a wagon, over the Green River. A dozen wooden houses huddled around a building with a sign: Woodsonville General Store. Beyond the little settlement stood a church, its clapboard walls badly in need of paint.

Not far from the church a large earthwork was being constructed. It was a star-shaped fort with high earthen banks being dug by what must have been at least two companies. It had not rained in weeks and the ground was so dry that the men had to dig with picks. Their sweaty faces and backs were coated with dust. The fort was surrounded by a deep ditch from which the earth for the walls had been excavated. From the outside the walls were more than 10 feet high. Johann had never seen anything like it. There were platforms for several cannons built into the mounds of earth that formed the walls.

Half a mile further along the dusty road they saw blue coats everywhere, hanging on shrubs and stacks of muskets, as the men had stripped to their union suits for hard labor. The fresh troops were joining the main force across the river from Munfordville. Men were digging a wide trench and throwing the earth in a pile in the front of the trench. They waved and shouted at the new troops marching by. Johann and his men did not understand what they were saying but they waved back. Col. Owen at the front of the column pointed his sword at a grove of trees and passed back the word that this is where they were to move into the line.

Captain Pleisch came back to Company A. "We are supposed to dig a trench between that little lane and those rocks over there. The colonel said that if the ground is too rocky to dig, gather rocks as big as you can handle and build a wall in front of you."

Johann asked, "What is going on here? Can you tell us?"

"Our main job is to defend that big railroad bridge you can see over there through the trees. The Confederates are reported to have a big force moving this way," he said as he pointed to the southwest. "They told me that soon we will have 4000 men here, but the rebs may have a good many more. So we have to have a strong position. There is a good chance that they will attack sometime today."

All day long the men along the whole line sweated on their earthwork. They cut down the trees in front of their fortification to clear a field of fire, dragging the logs with horses from nearby farms to strengthen their earthen wall, piling a long mound of the tops of the tall trees at the far edge of the cleared area to make it difficult for an army to charge their position. There were some large rock formations just to the right of Johann's men. They piled cabbage-sized boulders into the openings between the rocks, making a small fort.

Standing on top of the big rocks, Johann could see the line of trenches and rifle pits that ran from the little town of Woodsonville, through which they had marched, where the large earthwork they called Fort Craig was being thrown up. The trenches ran as far as he could see to another fort, a two-storey log blockhouse, beyond the southern end of the bridge. Officers who came by to inspect their work referred to this fortification as the Stockade. It had a stout wall of foot thick logs embedded in the earth. The line of trenches ran in a broad semi-circle for about three-quarters of a mile. Back across the broad Green River, he could see the roofs, the church, the courthouse in Munfordville. He imagined the feverish activity in this sleepy Kentucky town as troops concentrated there. What a different day this must be than the customary Saturday when farmers and their wagons would come into town with their families. Many of the families had already fled to the countryside.

Early that afternoon the Union commander, Col. Wilder, had ridden down the line on his big brown mare, stopping every few minutes to sweep the hills to the south of their position with his telescope. He was a handsome man in his early 30's, tall, with a black beard. He paused at the positions of the 60th Indiana. "Tell your men, Owen, our job is to keep them away from that bridge. If they capture it, it cuts our supply line to Nashville. If they blow it up, it would shut down this railroad for a long time with disastrous results. I have been told that the Confederates tried to blow it up last year when our troops drove them out of Munfordville. They only damaged one of the piers. We can't let them have another try. You've got your work cut out for you, if they come."

Later that afternoon the men heard what sounded like three or four explosions to their north. They thought little of it, since that was not the direction from which the enemy was coming.

What the men on the south side of the river did not know was that a force of Louisiana cavalry under brash, ambitious Col. John Scott had been sent by General Smith in Frankfurt to ride south and try to make contact with Bragg's advance. If they could link up the two armies, Louisville could be captured. Scouts had ridden past the train wreck north of Munfordville. Realizing that the line was disrupted Scott ordered his men to ride forward. Then he looked over Munfordville from the north. Farmers along the road told him that there were fewer than a thousand men, green troops, most of them foreigners. Scott believed that if he could capture Munfordville and the L & N bridge, he would surely land a promotion. Filled with bravado, he sent two of his captains under a flag of truce into the town to demand the surrender of the garrison.

They rode under their white flag slowly up to the courthouse, looking straight ahead, but aware of the dozens of blue uniforms all along the streets. Giving their reins to the flag bearer, they marched smartly past the sentries, up the steps and into the courthouse. As soon as he read Col. Scott's document, Colonel Wilder rejected the demand and told Scott's emissaries that he and his large force would defend the town and the bridge. The Union and Confederate officers in the room saluted each other. The gray uniformed officers turned on their heels, walked out of the courthouse, mounted, and, following their flag-bearer, rode back out of town, looking neither to the right or the left.

Wilder immediately telegraphed headquarters in Louisville and described the situation. He proudly announced that he had rejected the demand for surrender. He asked that reinforcements be sent to help stop or deflect Bragg's advance from Glasgow, as well as to deal with those pesky cavalry raiders who scurried around somewhere to his north.

Scott was disappointed that his swashbuckling offer was refused. He ordered a light artillery battery attached to his cavalry unit to lob a few shells from their mountain howitzer into the fields around Munfordville to the north of the river and rode north and east to make camp for the night.

His men stopped some horsemen on the road and learned from them that a Confederate advance guard of Bragg's army was in Cave City, just a dozen miles to the south. Scott immediately sent a rider to inform their commander of the situation in Munfordville. If each attacked, one from the north and one from the south, they could easily capture the place.

General Chalmers, wakened in his headquarters in Cave City, immediately recognized the opportunity. True, his orders from General Bragg were to hold at Cave City to block Buell's march toward Louisville, giving Bragg a chance to make his planned fast advance north to join forces with General Smith. But if he moved to attack Munfordville, he would still straddle the railroad between Buell and Louisville.

Buglers woke his sleeping troops before midnight and soon the whole Mississippi brigade was formed on the road and began marching east and north to position themselves by early Sunday morning at Rowlett's Station a mile in front of the Union fortifications at the southern end of the bridge.

Behind the marching regiments the cannons of the brigade were drawn by huge farm horses and wagonloads of supplies taken from Cave City.

Relieved that the attack had not come that Saturday afternoon, Johann and his men, exhausted from their digging, rested in a little shady cemetery just behind their line. Leaning against a few of the simple tombstones, they ate their field rations of hardtack, together with some peaches and early apples they had picked from a few trees nearby.

They could see, glinting in the setting sun, the long railroad bridge they were defending with its three tall stone piers holding up the iron girders. As the sun began to set, Johann walked from one rifle pit to another on the hill overlooking Munfordville across the river. He could see the small campfires that marked the wide arc in which the Union Army was spread for a couple of miles on both sides of the river to the south and west of the town. Night fell.

Off to the side of their position was the little country church with its stubby square belfry, on the other side of the overgrown graveyard, whitened in the brief periods of moonlight. Down the road a few yards was an old bleached farmhouse, abandoned long before the local farmers fled the neighborhood yesterday, when word began to spread that a battle might be coming.

The amber light of a lantern shown through the broken windows of the house. Captain Studer and Captain Pleisch had told their lieutenants and sergeants to report to them there at nine o'clock. Some of them had already arrived. Two horses were tied to the porch post. Johann felt a little out of place because his English was the slimmest of all the men. He understood a good bit of what they were talking about and comprehended all the orders, but when he spoke, it was always in very broken English. He was much more comfortable among his own men where he could speak German.

The house was decrepit. One had to be careful walking around the three rooms because the wooden floors were missing some planks. Lieutenant Schmidt joked, "We ought to trick the reb army into coming through here; they'd all break their legs."

Captain Studer knocked the ash from his cigar. "You'd better hope they don't come through here. If they get this far, we've been flanked.... Well, find something to sit on and we'll go over the plans."

A couple of the men found boxes. One used a piece of stovewood to prop up a three legged chair which he found in the kitchen. Johann looked around for a place to sit. Finally he took a drawer from the rickety bureau in the bedroom, stood it against the wall and eased his weight down.

"Good thing you're a little guy, Weber," Schmidt said. "That drawer'll just about hold you." When they all laughed, the three legged chair gave way, dumping Schreiber to the floor.

"*Mein Gott,*" Johann howled, "I t'ought dey shot you."

The captain spread a crude map on the floor in front of him. "Can you see in this light?...Look here....This is Munfordville, behind us on the other side of the river. We've got two batteries here, on that little hill just west of town. We've got a battery at the Stockade and another one right over here in Fort Craig by Woodsonville. We've got most of our men on this side of the river, dug in on both sides of the railroad tracks. If the rebs come through, they'll have to come up the valley along the tracks. They can't get across the river. We'll be ready for 'em right here. We got breastworks and rifle pits on all the high ground. We've cut down the trees in front of the breastworks so there is no place for them to hide if they get that close to us. We've got that huge, long wall of brush to keep them from charging down the valley. We've got a regiment of skirmishers in rifle pits out beyond that wall of brush to give us plenty of warning if they bring up a force. We've got all the advantage. They'll have to walk right into the muzzles of our guns. I want you to tell that to all the men. This will be the first fight for most of these men. They need to know that we're in a very strong position. It'll take their whole army to dig us out."

Lieutenant Graf said with a bit of hesitation, "I'm a little worried because none of us have ever seen any fighting. It wouldn't be the first time that green troops turned and ran at first sight of the enemy. What do we do then?"

Captain Studer looked hard into every face in the room, seeing the fear in their eyes, in spite of trying to look courageous. "I'm counting on you to see that that doesn't happen. General Buell is depending on us to hold this bridge. If they cut this line, we'll have a hell of a time supplying our army in Bowling Green and Nashville. We're strung out all over two states, all the way down to Alabama. We think that Bragg's main army is way over to the east of us. But you better believe that if the division coming our way breaks through us here, he'll be force-marching the whole army this way. We can't let that happen."

The assembled officers murmured their support of that resolve, uneasily looking around the dim room.

The captain smiled confidently and said, "Let's drink to that. I got a jug tied to my saddle that I just happened across in an empty farmhouse on the other side of the river. Is there anything around here to drink out of?"

Schmidt took the lantern and reconnoitered the musty kitchen. There was a clatter and he was back with an assortment of dishes balanced in his arms. "I got four coffee cups, two saucers, and a couple soup bowls....Not very fancy, but they'll all hold whiskey."

Pulling his bandana from around his neck, he wiped off the dishes as best he could. "Couldn't find no water bucket...not sure there's even a well. The whiskey'll wash the dust off 'em quick enough."

He passed the cups to the captain and the lieutenants. "Schreiber and I'll take the bowls. Weber, you and Schultz get the saucers. Since they aren't very big, you get two fills."

"Then you'd better get back to your men. I want to keep them on their toes all night. The pickets out front have orders to shoot if anything moves up ahead on that track."

They headed back to their positions. After walking up and down his portion of the lines to reassure the men, Johann smiled as he talked to one of the young soldiers in his pit, holding a little brown dog wrapped in a tattered plaid blanket. "I found her down the road when we marched over here. She just got left behind. She followed me for a while and when we dug in here, she just crawled in the hole with me. Tomorrow I'm going to teach her to dig rifle pits. Might as well get some work out of her." He laughed nervously, trying to mask his fear.

Several of the men were gathered around a small fire in the shelter of a dark outcropping of rock. They were all down on their hands and knees, laughing and poking each other. Johann moved closer to see what was going on. In the light of their little fire they had cleared a small flat area. They had drawn a circle in the dirt and had four cockroaches under a cup in the center. When they lifted the cup, the roaches would scurry. The first to cross the line was declared the winner. Although Johann couldn't imagine how they identified each bug, each man apparently claimed one of the "racers," as wagers were made and paid off after each race.

Every few minutes the waning moon would briefly show itself through a gap between clouds. Johann's men crouched in their shallow holes or behind the huge black boulders, pointing their muskets down the railroad track which came from the south toward the L & N bridge.

Johann thought of his soldiers, all Germans and Swiss from Perry County. In the year since their enlistment they had never seen a Confederate fighting man, just disarmed prisoners. They had never fired their guns, apart from the three or four shots fired on the Bradfordsville Road. They'd only read about battles in the newspaper.

"Keep your eye on those woods down there along the track, *meine Knaben*," Johann said to his men, trying to sound like a leader. The anxiety he was feeling threatened to make his voice crack. "If the rebs are going to try to take that bridge, they'll come that way."

"*Ja, wohl*," came back the response from tense men in the pits.

Walking back toward his rifle pit Johann knew that the men were all covering up their nervousness. He thought of Marta in their little house in Helvetia. What if he were killed here in Munfordville? What if he had to go home without an arm or a leg? His gut churned with such thoughts. He got the familiar funny hollow feeling at the base of his tongue. He stepped behind a bush and vomited. In a momentary glow of moonlight through the leaves,, he saw that his vomit was once again bloody.

Johann sat against a large oak, pulled his blanket around him, pushing his kepi down over his eyes. He woke with a start when some distant pickets began to fire. A Union cannon thumped from across the river and a shell burst along the tracks a couple of hundred yards ahead of their position. A constellation of sparks flew skyward. "Here they come," he shouted to his men. He held his watch close to the embers of their campfire; it was not yet five o'clock.

In the first dim daylight and through the heavy ground fog they could catch occasional glimpses of the Confederate troops marching toward them in squads all along the line. There was sporadic popping as a few of the Union soldiers fired along the picket line beyond the piles of brush.

Col. Owen came along the line, "Hold your fire, men! No use wasting ammunition when they are half a mile away. Let them come to us."

The firing erupted from several hundred yards in front of the Union lines. The skirmishers from the 74th Indiana who had been sent out to harass the approaching enemy came under fire from a detachment of Confederate sharpshooters, who climbed trees and maintained a deadly fusillade. The pickets, unable to fight back, tried to work their way back to the lines through a narrow opening in the high wall of brush in front of the federal entrenchments. Watching through his telescope, the Confederate

General Chalmers, unable to see the fortifications through the fog, assumed that the running skirmishers were a general Union retreat.

The distant Confederate line moved closer. Their artillery began to fire at the Stockade and Fort Craig. After a short pause the front ranks began to run toward the Union entrenchment, yelling at the top of their lungs. The officers and a few of the soldiers had gray uniforms, but the majority of the men wore nondescript work clothes.

"Fire," shouted Col. Owen.

Stocker was the first to fire and then began the complicated process of reloading. He had never before tried to load while crouched in a trench-- Bite off the end of cartridge, pour powder down the barrel, put in ball and paper from cartridge and tamp it all down with the ramrod. Put percussion cap on nipple.

The whole line was firing now. Clouds of acrid powder smoke, mingling with the early morning fog, swirled in front of them. Union cannons from the north side of the river joined those in the Stockade and Fort Craig, firing completely over the battleground to the Confederate lines beyond.

"I can't see them in all this damn smoke," Stocker yelled. He fired in the direction of the enemy without aiming. Johann ran out of the trench and crouched behind a large tree, vomiting again. More blood. Then he went back to his place in the line.

Occasional breaks in the smoky cloud showed the Confederates still advancing, in spite of the rain of bullets falling on them. Here and there a man fell. Then with a yell the front rank began to charge toward them. The brush piled at the far edge of the clearing in front of the earthworks did its job. The southerners could not run through that thicket of branches. Those who tried made easy targets. For more than an hour repeated attempts were made to breech this line, first down near the Stockade and then a half hour later nearer the Woodsonville end of the trenches.

Several cannon boomed off to the left, beyond Woodsonville and the shells burst in front of Fort Craig, just ahead of the attacking southerners. Through a break in the smoke Johann could glimpse several large formations of Confederates veer off from their charge and move to the north from where the cannon fire came. Assuming that another Union battery had gone into action, no one on either side of the battle line realized that this brief barrage had come from the light howitzers of Scott's Louisiana cavalry, trying to support the Confederate advance of Chalmers' division from the left flank.

This diversion blunted the Confederate attack for nearly an hour, but then a series of successive charges were attempted. Men were falling all along the line as the deadly fire poured from the trenches. The brush line held again and again.

Johann looked up and down the few yards of the line that he could see through the smoke. He saw only one Union soldier lying still in the trench. A few others were binding up wounds, but their earthworks and stone walls kept them from becoming easy targets.

Through the clouds of smoke Johann could see a long column of blue coats coming from the pontoon bridge. Led by a few officers on horses, some of them marched into Fort Craig. The rest marched along behind the entrenchments and took positions near the railroad.

Johann said to Geyer, "Look at that. There are hundreds of fresh troops. These must be the men they said were coming from Louisville."

Just then another assault was launched against Fort Craig and the whole line began to fire. Captain Pleisch ran up.

"I need three men," he yelled. "The officers in the fort are afraid that sharpshooters will get up in that church belfry and shoot into the Fort. So they want the church burned. You three, come with me! *Mach' schnell!*"

In only a few minutes smoke began pouring from the windows of the church. Soon the whole building was ablaze, thickening the blanket of smoke that covered that end of the battleground. As Johann watched the flames, he thought of old man Scharf's tale of the church in Endigen during the battle between the Prussians and Austrians. He thought wistfully: a couple of bullet holes in the weathercock are certainly better than burning the church to the ground.

Pockets of intense gunfire seemed to move up and down the line: to the Stockade, then off to the left toward the star-shaped Woodsonville earthwork. The only break in the fighting came in mid- morning. The Union troops nearest the tracks saw a white flag waving from behind the brush piles. The officers commanded a cease fire in response to the flag of truce. When the rattle of musket fire fell into an eerie stillness, three graycoated horsemen moved down the track under their white flag. When they reached the lines they were immediately blindfolded and taken to Col. Wilder at the court house. Word passed up and down the line like wildfire: The rebels want to surrender. The fight is over!

But in the court house it was another story. The officers had brought a letter from General Chalmers demanding surrender of the Union forces at Munfordville. He pointed out that he had a force of 10,000 and could easily destroy the couple thousand Union defenders. Col. Wilder knew that this vaunted Confederate force had thrown itself against his fortifications on the other side of the Green River and had not gained a foot beyond the brush piles. He knew that, with the arrival of the train from Louisville with Colonel Dunham and his regiments, he now had double the couple thousand troops Chalmers assumed. He had good reason to assume that more reinforcements were on the way. Taking a sheet of paper from his field desk, he wrote a courteous note to General Chalmers stating that his forces were well able to withstand attack and that he would not surrender. He asked the Confederate officers to take this note to their commander with his respects.

The gray clad colonel replied, "If you do not wish to surrender, General Chalmers requests that you grant a truce of four hours to permit both sides to remove their wounded from the field?"

Colonel Wilder nodded and said, "By all means." Turning to one of his aides he said crisply, looking at his watch, "Send orders to all officers that there is to be a cease fire until four o'clock this afternoon. Have our men push one of those flat cars on the siding between the town and the bridge onto the main track. Push it over the bridge and through our lines as far as the brush piles. The Colonel's forces can take it from there to remove their wounded to the rear. Is that agreeable, sir?"

"Thank you, Colonel. It will be much better for the wounded than to be carried in wagons over these country roads. We will work as quickly as possible. We have a number of dead to bury and we do not have many tools to dig the graves."

Wilder said to his aide, "Put some picks and shovels on that flat car, Lieutenant."

The Mississippi officer held out his hand. "You are more than generous. My compliments, sir," he said saluting smartly. He turned to his escort to be blindfolded for his ride back through the defenses.

When they were out of earshot, the Colonel turned to his staff. "Tell the men to hold their fire for now but to expect more attacks. The Confederates want that bridge badly and will try to find ways to force our line. We are going to have plenty more attacks, you can be sure of that. So keep the men vigilant and ready to fight. But give them until four to evacuate their wounded, unless they start firing at us."

The last group of reenforcements to arrive in Munfordville in late morning, the 50th Indiana, was commanded by Cyrus Dunham. Colonel Dunham outranked Wilder and made it clear that his orders were to assume command of the Union forces at Munfordville as soon as the present phase of the attack ended. Wilder took the change in command with good graces. He acknowledged himself to be a business man with limited military experience. He had done his best and felt adequate to the task when the garrison was only a thousand men and their task simply to guard a long, high bridge. In a way he was very glad to be relieved of the tactical responsibility that was obviously becoming much heavier with each passing hour.

The lull on the battlefield continued even after four o'clock. There was no more gunfire, no waves of charging Mississippians, no sniping by the sharpshooters.

Monday morning brought no more large attacks against the Union line. There was sporadic firing and an occasional artillery shell fired from both sides. It was as if the strength of the Union fortification had completely frustrated the Confederate advance. The heavy casualties of the first day of the fight produced caution on the part of the Confederate generals. They felt no great urgency for another frontal assault because they knew that Bragg's entire army was coming up behind them. Soon they would have enormous superiority over the defenders of the bridge. They would have more than enough artillery to level the fortifications and the town. They would have to fight for it, but the outcome was now assured

In the Confederate headquarters at Rowlett's Station General Simon Bolivar Buckner went to the farmhouse where General Chalmers was quartered. This was the same Buckner who had been captured the previous winter when he had to surrender Fort Donelson. He had been confined for a time in Indianapolis and then in Fort Warren in Boston Harbor. He had only recently been exchanged and returned to duty.

Saluting Chalmers, he said, "Sir, we are attacking the town where I grew up. Our family home is just a few miles up the river. I went to school in Munfordville. I know this country like the back of my hand. May I be permitted to draw out a battle plan that I think should enable us to take the town, and the bridge, with ease. May I show you on the map?"

Gen. Chalmers moved the oil lamp closer to the map. "Show me what you have in mind."

411

"The Union forces are almost totally south and east of the river defending the southern approaches of the bridge. Here," Buckner pointed to the map. "They also have a pretty strong battery of heavy artillery on a low hill south of the town, on the far side of the river. They probably have a small force of infantry supporting that battery. To the best of our knowledge they have committed almost all their forces to this side of the river. We know how strongly fortified their position at the bridge is. We paid a heavy price trying to force that position from the front. Because both ends of their line are anchored at the river, there is no way of flanking them."

Chalmers nodded and pulled the lamp closer. "I know how many we lost today in that attack. We might be able to take them if we throw our whole force at that line, but I am not sure that a bridge and a thousand Yankees are worth the price we would have to pay."

"Let me show you another way," Buckner said, smoothing out the map. "It does not show on your map and I wager it is not on the Union maps, but just about nine or ten miles up the river there is a shallow area where the river can be forded easily when the water level is not high. If you were to agree, I could take my brigade and as many others as you can spare and cross over to the other side of river and come at Munfordville from the north. There is that Louisiana cavalry unit already over there somewhere. The river bottom at that shallow area is rocky enough that we could easily move some heavy batteries through. I know shortcuts through the back lanes, so we can stay away from the main roads.

"Well north of that Union battery, there is high ground west of the town right at the edge of the woods, which could command the town and the Union fortifications on this end of the bridge. We know they have most of their men over on this side of the river. I doubt if they have more than a headquarter's company in Munfordville. They would have no way to attack my forces without abandoning their fortifications at the bridge. We know they will not do that. So we would have them in a trap. Wilder would have to surrender."

Chalmers saw immediately the potential success of this strategy. "Brilliant, simply brilliant, Buckner. What a stroke of luck to have a home-town boy on our side."

"I think that if we can surprise them with this move, we can win without much of a fight. I guess I am somewhat selfish in wanting to find a way to keep Munfordville from destruction. The people who own those houses and stores are my friends."

"Take your brigade and Polk's. Take half of those Mississippi batteries. Start as quickly as you can. You'll know the way. As soon as you are in position on the other side of Munfordville, begin firing on that battery west of town. When we hear your fire, we will know that you are there. We will keep pressure on the Union lines on this side of the river."

"I can probably be in position by day-break, certainly by mid-day tomorrow. With your permission, I will get the troops moving as soon as possible."

General Chalmers began issuing orders to his aides. "Get word to Forrest and tell him what we have planned. I want him to move further up the river, cross wherever he can with his cavalry and be ready to attack the enemy if they try to retreat from Munfordville and move north toward Louisville. As long as we have Wilder boxed in so nicely, we don't want him to escape."

Turning to another aide, Chalmers began dictating orders for General Hardee to move his regiments as close as he could to the Union lines on the south side of the river without attacking. He wanted to show that he had sufficient force to keep pressure on the entire Union defensive position. Let them think he was massing for another attack tomorrow.

"This sitting in this here ditch is gettin' harder than all the shooting yesterday," Stocker said. "Them chiggers is eatin' me alive," he scratched at his legs. "Geyer, you got any of that salt pork. Give me a little hunk to rub on my ankles and keep these damned bugs off."

Johann looked hard at Stocker and said, "It looks to me that you are going to have a chance to do some more shooting. Look how many cooking fires they have over there. It looks like fireflies, there are so many."

Buhl chipped in, "The waiting is what is hard. They are going to c-c-come at us again. Their cannons are going to start throwing more shells at us. All we can do is wait. I don't like that."

"Me neither," Stocker said.

"You are unusually quiet, Albrecht. What are you thinking?" Buhl asked quietly.

Shifting his body in the trench, Geyer ran his hand over his face. "I have been doing a lot of thinking. I am pretty sure I killed one of those rebs yesterday. I shot just as he was trying to climb over the brush. He just hung on some of those big branches. He never moved for a long time after that until they came along and carried him off."

"Good for you," Stocker said, scratching his backside against one of the boulders. "One less to shoot at us."

"It is not that easy," Geyer answered, "One minute he was alive, and the next he was dead. He was somebody's son, maybe somebody's husband and papa. I changed all that." He ran his hands over his face again.

"Don't be so hard on yourself," Buhl offered as comfort. "You don't know that you k-k-killed him."

"He never moved again. He was just still, for a couple of hours."

"If I was you, I'd be cutting a notch in my rifle stock, " Stocker grunted.

Bauer looked Stocker right in the eye. "Why don't you shut that big mouth of yours! Can't you see that it really bothers Albrecht...If one of those fellows over there shot me, I would rather think of him feelin' bad about it than carving a notch in his gun. I don't see how anybody can take pleasure in this--hundreds of men trying to kill each other."

"This is war, man. That is what it's all about," Stocker continued to argue, spitting tobacco juice across the trench.

Johann said with unfamiliar sternness, "*Halt*! *Genug*! That is enough! We are here because we volunteered to fight in the army to save the country we call home. It is not one man against another. It is two armies, standing for two different things: union or separation. I try not to think of men out there, but I can't get it out of my mind either, Albrecht."

"Maybe they will pull back and we won't have another attack," Geyer said wistfully.

"That would be my hope too, but I am afraid we could both be wrong," Johann replied.

That night and the following morning, Tuesday, was fairly quiet. Occasionally a few shots would ring out somewhere down the line. Here and there a company of southerners would move out of their line and fire a few volleys at the Union entrenchments. The batteries to the west of Rowlett's Station fired every half-hour or so at the Stockade and Fort Craig.

Several new Union regiments in uniforms that were not powdered with dust came into the ranks. They were assigned sections in the line of trenches, strengthening the Union position even more. Wagons went along the line with new supplies of cartridges and rations.

When it appeared that there would be no massive charge that morning, a few cooking fires were lit in the shelter of some large rocks and coffee was boiled and strips of bacon or salt pork were roasted on ramrods over the fire. Once in a while a Confederate sharpshooter perched high in a tree across the lines shot at an exposed Union trooper, cautioning everyone that danger was still very present.

At mid-morning the main body of Braxton Bragg's army began marching in from the south: regiment after regiment, battery after battery, a long line of creaking supply wagons. Bragg had hoped for a much larger force. As soon as he had entered Kentucky a week before, he had distributed a lengthy and florid proclamation to the people of Kentucky. He urged the men, loyal to their state, to join his ranks and throw out the northern invader. So confident was Bragg that his proclamation would stir a flood of Kentucky recruits that his wagon train had 15,000 muskets to arm them for the victory. But the recruits did not come in any significant numbers, and he had to march on with his weary force.

Arriving at the lines facing the Union defenders of the bridge at Munfordville, the units began spreading across the fields around Rowlett's, behind the ranks of the Mississippi regiments who were firing sporadically at the Union lines..

"Come in, General," Chalmers said when Bragg rode up to the front porch of the farmhouse, which was his headquarters. There was no warm greeting in return from Bragg.

"Take me inside so that I can have a look at your map and see the whole situation, Chalmers," the commanding general ordered. "The rest of you can come in in a little while."

Once in the parlor, Bragg drew off his dusty gauntlets and glared at Chalmers. "I have a bone to pick with you, General. We might as well get it out of the way right now and clear the air. Then I will say no more of it. I was most upset when I learned that you had left Cave City, where you had been ordered and came up here on your own against this Union garrison. That was not my plan. I want to move north as fast as possible with the whole army to join up with Smith; as early as possible, sir..." Bragg paused to let his rebuke sink in..."I intended to by-pass every garrison and avoid every skirmish to keep moving north. Smith is at Frankfurt, and together we could have Louisville in two or three days, if we move fast. Buell is still down in Bowling Green, behind us. We can easily beat him to Louisville. But your misguided adventure has put that whole plan in jeopardy. Instead of forced marching toward Louisville, we are stuck here until we can capture this garrison. This could take days--precious days. It could throw away our whole opportunity to stay ahead of Buell. I do not need a big engagement! Understood?"

Chalmers stood before his commander. "I am sorry if I made trouble for your plans. I did not mean to disobey orders. I saw what looked like an excellent opportunity to gain an advantage. That is not a large force over there, but they are so strongly fortified in that little bridgehead that it has proved more difficult than I had imagined."

"Well, what is done is done. Now you know how I look at it. I will say no more of it."

"Sir, I do not wish to sound like I am trying to excuse myself for disrupting your plan. But the situation is better than it appears. There is every reason to believe that we will take Munfordville this very day." He then proceeded to explain Buckner's maneuver, which was well under way.

"Very good," Bragg replied. "I want this concluded as quickly as possible. We still might be able to save the plan, if we are not held up further. This is the best chance we have had in the mid-west since the beginning of the war and we cannot afford to lose it. Now show me on your map what the situation is."

Musket fire began to sweep in a wave along the Confederate lines. There were no charges of the brush pile; just a steady volley of gunfire. Bullets whistled by and splattered against some of the rocks around the 60th Indiana.

"Keep down. Our orders are not to do a lot of shooting back as long as they are not moving toward us. Once in a while you can take a shot to let them know we are still here, but there is no use wasting all our ammunition," Johann ordered.

"They are getting ready to do something. The whole place is heating up,"Buhl said, coughing as the wave of acrid smoke began to drift across from the Confederate lines.

This same pattern continued through the morning. Confederate sharpshooters occasionally picked off some careless soldier who dared to stand up in his rifle pit and stretch or who tried to peer over the breastworks. Several times Johann could see far down the line bodies of the dead or wounded being pulled back from the trenches.

For most of the morning the crouching armies kept up their sporadic fire, chewing bits of hardtack after loading for the next fusillade.

Stocker could not contain himself any longer. "Why don't those stupid officers of ours let us charge them. We beat 'em so bad Sunday; if they saw us coming, they'd turn tail and run."

"How are you going to get through that brush pile?" Geyer asked. "You would have the same trouble they had."

"*Scheiß*! I'd go straight down them railroad tracks, where there ain't no brush pile. The only reason the rebs couldn't try to come through there yesterday was the cannons in the Stockade. They'd have been shredded like kraut. But those cannons won't be shooting at us. Run a couple of regiments through that gap by the tracks and then fan out and the rebs would have to run."

"We would be fools to come out of these strong fortifications. Out in the open, they could pick us off from all directions," Geyer answered barely concealing his disdain for the boisterous Stocker.

However, this attack which Stocker had wanted actually did materialize. Around three o'clock there was a lull in the firing. Col. Dunham ordered a reconnaissance to see if the Confederate forces had pulled back.

Capt. Pleisch called his sergeants together behind the pile of boulders. "Well, men, we're going to get into the fight. We are ordered to go out in front of Fort Craig and set up a picket line on that little ridge." He pointed to a rise a couple of hundred yards beyond the fort. Our job is to keep the enemy from circling around Woodsonville. Get your men together. They should take all the ammunition they can get in their cartridge boxes. Leave everything else behind these rocks. We are to meet on the north side of Fort Craig in ten minutes."

Johann gathered his men and got them ready to move. They advanced cautiously. According to plan the cannons in Fort Craig were shooting far over the ridge they were to occupy. About a hundred men ran forward. Spreading out on the low ridge, they took shelter behind rocks and logs.

"Keep low and watch for them to come across that field," Johann told his men.

They heard Pleisch's voice. "I can see them in that line of trees. Send a man back to the fort to tell them to fire into that woods."

"I am going to try a shot," Stocker announced. He aimed at the woods and fired.

A small group of Confederate soldiers emerged from a little gully on their right. Firing swept along the picket line. Enemy balls whistled over their heads from the muskets that poked over the bank of the gully. One man down the line screamed, grabbed his shoulder and fell. His mates pulled him behind a boulder. After a while he began to crawl back to the earthwork fort.

"That squad cannot get out of the gully. Keep your eyes open for other men coming from another direction," Johann warned.

For an hour they fired at every Confederate head that poked over the edge of the trough. Occasional artillery shells from Fort Craig discouraged any other forward movements. There was very little firing from the Confederate side. Then they heard volleys being fired down the line on their right.

A company of the 50th Indiana was ordered through the gap at the track to see if the Confederates were pulling back. No sooner had they advanced a few hundred yards when they came under heavy fire. The men dropped to the ground and sought to fire back. But the Confederate fire was so heavy that they were pinned to the earth. Only then did the rest of the regiment charge through the gap, formed a skirmish line and fired volley after volley at the southerners, suppressing their fire so that the advance company was able to crawl back to the lines, leaving a few of their number in the field.

Suddenly in late afternoon there were several loud explosions as shells rained from nowhere on the Union batteries on the north side of the river.

"That don't sound like our cannons, and no shells went over our heads into the reb lines. What the hell's goin' on?" Stocker tried to look back across the river.

Johann tried to keep his voice calm. "Don't worry about that. Just keep you eyes on those fellows out there. If they start to rush us, we want to be ready."

Consternation and confusion reigned in the courthouse in Munfordville "What in hell was that?" Colonel Dunham said, rushing to the window. A lieutenant rushed up the walk to the courthouse and breathlessly announced, "They are behind us, to the north. They have artillery up in the woods shooting at our batteries between the town and the river."

On the little hill west of town the frantic Union gunners tried to turn some of their cannon around to counterfire, but they also had to respond to the increasing crescendo of fire from the fortifications on the other side of the bridge. Only steady artillery fire would discourage the Confederates from another frontal assault all along the line. The need to fire on two fronts, in the face of shells exploding around them as the Confederate artillerymen found their range, was a massive challenge. When one of their cannons sustained a direct hit, killing its crew, they had to retreat into their trenches and give up any attempt to return fire.

At about half past four the guns fell silent: first the cannons booming north of town, and then the musketry from south of the river. Word was passed down the Union lines, "Stay where you are. Keep down." The strategy was obviously to wait to see what would happen next.

As the shadows lengthened several Confederate officers with a flag of truce rode up the railroad track from Rowlett's Station. They stopped at the Stockade and asked again to be taken to the Union headquarters.

They were blindfolded and taken to the courthouse. Colonel Francis Peavy of the 10th Mississippi dismounted and was led with his companion into the building where Colonel Dunham waited. Peavy saluted and took a letter from the front of his tunic. "General Bragg's compliments, Sir," he said, extending the letter to Dunham.

The letter read:

> Sir, surrounded by an overwhelming force, your successful resistance or escape is impossible. You are therefore offered an opportunity by capitulation of avoiding the terrible consequences of an assault. Braxton Bragg, General, Army of the Mississippi

Dunham read the short message again. He knew he was in a tight situation. If he could play for time, Buell's forces which he had every reason to believe were coming up fast from Bowling Green might be able to threaten Bragg from the rear.

Addressing Peavy, Dunham said, "Sir, my compliments to General Bragg. I very much appreciate his letter but I would like a few hours to think it through. My officers are scattered across the field and I would like to consult with them before taking such a momentous step. I would request General Bragg's patience until nine o'clock this evening. I will have consulted my officers and will have an answer for him then. Please convey this response to your General."

When Peavy made his report to Bragg, the General was irate. "That blind fool. Does he not realize that his situation is hopeless. I must outnumber him six to one. I have ten times the artillery he has. Well, let him talk with his people. It will not change anything. He is in a noose and cannot get out. It is getting too dark to think of mounting an attack. We will finish him off in the morning. So let him talk until nine o'clock."

In town Dunham immediately telegraphed his plight to Louisville. He needed assurances from Louisville that reinforcements were on the way. Without help, he could not hold out and would have to surrender.

Dunham had not fully described his situation because he did not actually know how tightly he was encircled. Before the flag of truce arrived he had not had time to send out skirmishers to learn the strength of the force that had appeared in his rear. For all he knew it was that smart-aleck Louisiana colonel who had demanded surrender from Wilder a few days past.

Dunham's telegram brought anger from the headquarters staff. "That windbag is always exaggerating the seriousness of his situation. Bragg is just bluffing. Dunham has a strong defensive position. He can tie Bragg down for a couple of days and give Buell a chance to get between Munfordville and Louisville to block Bragg's advance."

General Gilbert, who was in command, said, "I want Dunham out of there. He is going to blunder into defeat. Order him to turn over command to Wilder. Wilder fought them off on Sunday and he can do it again. Telegraph that off right away."

The message reached Munfordville and was handed to Colonel Dunham. He turned pale, then red. He snatched a pen from his desk and wrote a very brief message, "Send this right back to Louisville!" he fumed.

In Louisville headquarters the telegrapher took the brief message immediately to General Gilbert, who read, "I refuse to serve under a man who is my junior, especially in a time of grave crisis. I ask that you reconsider."

"Reconsider?" sputtered the Gilbert. "Who does he think he is? Order Dunham to report to Wilder under arrest. I do not want him interfering any further. "

Dunham had summoned his officers to a council of war. They must talk through their situation to see if there was a way to resist a serious attack from two sides. Gathered in the court room, the conversation was just beginning when the second telegram from Louisville was brought in. Dunham looked at it and said, "Colonel Wilder, I must talk with you. Come into the hall."

He showed the two telegrams to Wilder. "I am at your disposal, Sir. You are directed to take command."

The two men walked back into the room. Dunham said loudly, "Colonel Wilder has been ordered by Louisville to take command."

Wilder cleared his throat and spoke as calmly as he could. "Men, this is an overwhelming responsibility. I did not seek it, but since it is thrust upon me, I will do my duty." He paused. "Now let's see what our situation is."

"How do we know Bragg is not just bluffing?" Captain Burrell asked.

"We do not know," Wilder replied. "We do know that he has brought up some units into the lines facing Fort Craig. We know that he has gotten some artillery into the woods north of town, but we have no idea whether it is just a battery and a handful of bushwackers, or if he was able to move a sizable force in behind us."

"I do not think Bragg would commit his whole army to fighting us. He must know that Buell is coming north from Bowling Green. Bragg has to keep the bulk of his forces south of here to engage Buell," Burrell added.

"How are we going to find out?" one of the lieutenants inquired.

Wilder paced the room. "Until we know what we are facing, I do not see how we can decide whether or not to give in to Bragg's demand that we surrender."

"Bragg says he has overwhelming force."

Speaking resolutely, Wilder said, "I am going to ask that we be shown. If they will not permit several competent officers to observe their strength, they will have to demonstrate it by force of arms."

At first the men looked puzzled, then nodded their consent. Wilder stated, "I take it that is unanimous. Captain Burrell, you come with me. Pick one of your sergeants to carry the flag of truce and we'll go to talk with Bragg."

Just after 8 o'clock the three men rode with their white flag across the railroad bridge, past the Stockade, toward Rowlett's Station.

In the Confederate headquarters Braxton Bragg was talking with Buckner, who had ridden around from his position north of Munfordville.

"If we do not hear from Dunham in another half hour, we will know that they decided against our request for surrender. I want to get clear with you how we can bring this adventure to a speedy conclusion," Bragg smoothed his full black beard, tapping his foot impatiently on the farmhouse's rag carpet.

"Polk's division is in the woods," Buckner reported. "We have the batteries right at the edge of the woods. We already demonstrated that we can reach that Union battery south of the town. I am sure that our Parrots can reach the fortifications at the south end of the bridge. We can hit their

421

two forts and the earthworks in between. We are on higher ground. They have no place to go."

"We will just maintain our fire. With your guns doing the work, there is no purpose in wasting our men on a charge of their position. But I want this finished quickly. We have wasted valuable time already and I do not want to spend days reducing this barrier halting our advance."

"We are ready to do whatever you think best."

"If we have to fight, let it begin at sunrise. Ride back to your position and be ready to ...."

There was a commotion on the front porch. A young captain rushed in. "Flag of truce, sir. Three Union officers."

"There's our answer, Buckner." To the captain, "Bring them in."

Wilder and Burrell saluted as they came through the door. "I am Colonel John Wilder, now commanding the Union forces in Munfordville. This is Captain Burrell."

Bragg gestured at two of the parlor chairs. "This is General Buckner who holds the position in your rear. Be seated, gentlemen." He looked hard at his adversaries, seeking some indication of their response.

Wilder cleared his throat several times. "The officers of our force have met to consider your letter. We believe that before acceding to your demand for surrender, we need to be convinced of your assertion that your overwhelming force makes our position indefensible. Two days ago General Chalmers made the same assertion, which we rejected, and successfully repulsed his repeated attacks. You can understand, sir, our reluctance to surrender without knowing that we truly are in an impossible situation."

Bragg's famous temper flared. Jumping to his feet, he sputtered, "You doubt my word, sir! You think I would not tell you the truth?"

Wilder was taken aback by the outburst. He responded very calmly, "I am not saying that you are tricking me, sir. But I know that two sides in a conflict can see it quite differently. We feel that we somehow need to assure ourselves that our situation is as hopeless as you say."

"What kind of answer is that? You and your officers are fools if you risk a fight. I demand that you surrender unconditionally. I give you one hour to make up your minds," Bragg retorted.

Buckner asked, "Sir, may I be permitted to talk with Colonel Wilder?"

"I do not see much good in it. But if you want to waste your time, I will not stand in your way."

"Colonel, come out on the porch with me," Buckner proposed.

Wilder exchanged looks with Burrell and rose to walk outside. "I would appreciate a conversation, General."

They sat in two rocking chairs. Wilder spoke first, "General Buckner, do you understand our request for verification? I have been in the army for a little more than a year. I am a business man. I own a foundry in Indiana. I am used to making decisions based on knowing the facts. I am not trying to be troublesome. I hope you believe that. I merely need to know what our situation is, what the facts truly are."

"General Bragg and I are military men, with years of experience in the army, before and during the war. I was a friend of your General Grant for many years. Our way of thinking is to see your request as a way of gaining time in hope of being reinforced. That, of course, we cannot let happen. You understand?"

"I do, sir. I just do not know what is right for me to do. So I try to reach the right decision in the way that is most familiar and useful to me, and to those with whom I deal."

"Let me talk with General Bragg and try to explain this request, which I am sure you realize appears to him to be duplicitous and foolish. Wait here."

In a few minutes Buckner emerged from the front door. "I think I have persuaded him, although he maintains that it is against his better judgment. He proposes that I take you through our position here, south of the river. Colonel Peavy, whom you met in Munfordville, will take your Captain Burrell to General Polk's position on the other side of Munfordville. They can easily be back here in three hours if they go directly through your lines. Then you will have to decide. Is that agreeable?"

Wilder answered, "You are very kind, General. I am deeply appreciative. I thank you for your understanding. Send Colonel Peavy and Captain Burrell with our flag bearer back to our headquarters to tell them the arrangement and then on to your position. If I may have paper I will write a brief letter of explanation which will assure safe conduct for Col. Peavy and let my officers know that our request is being granted."

"Very good, Colonel. I will be ready to leave when you are," Buckner turned back into the farmhouse, Wilder following.

It was after 2:00 a.m. when Peavy and Burrell returned. Buckner and Wilder awaited them in the farmhouse parlor.

"Gentlemen, you wanted to see our overwhelming forces. Have you seen enough to convince you that your situation is indeed untenable?" Buckner asked.

Wilder looked first at Burrell, then at Buckner and Peavy. "While I can only guess how many thousand troops you have on this side of the river, I do know that I saw 46 field guns."

"And I saw at least a division and 26 pieces of artillery to the north of Munfordville," Burrell reported.

"General Buckner," Wilder slouched in his chair, "I must agree that your forces are indeed overwhelming. We have but ten guns and no promise of new supplies of ammunition from Louisville. I trust you will not be offended by my need to get the facts."

"No, Colonel, I respect your need to know," Buckner said quietly. "Now, as you promised, you must decide."

"That is right. You have convinced me that you indeed have the means to destroy or capture our force. That is not deniable."

Buckner nodded.

"As I told you and General Bragg, I am not a soldier. You have satisfied me, as a rational man, that it would be prudent for me to surrender. Now I must ask you a strange question, 'As a professional military man, what is the proper, the honorable thing for a soldier to do in these circumstances?' I do not want to bring dishonor on our forces by doing a cowardly or improper thing."

Buckner paused, clearing his throat before speaking. "This is most unusual."

"I know, but I must turn to someone who knows proper military procedure. I perceive you to be an honorable and honest man," Wilder went on. "I am not thinking of my own reputation, I do not want my response to be seen as cowardice on the part of our forces, or for our cause to be dishonored by our giving up."

Memories of the wintry Cumberland River flashed across Buckner's mind. "I do not know if you are aware of it, but less than two years ago I faced a very similar situation. I had to surrender Fort Donelson to your General Grant's superior force. I was not seen as a coward, although I had to take that step with massive regret."

"How does one decide what is the honorable decision? Must I fight or must I surrender?" Wilder reached for a bandanna from the inner pocket of his blue tunic.

"There is no hard and fast rule." Buckner looked hard into Wilder's face. "If you have information that would induce you to think, that the sacrificing of every man at this place would give your army an advantage elsewhere, it is your duty to do it."

Wilder put his head in his hands, thought for several long minutes. Then he looked up at Buckner. Clearing his throat, he said, "I believe I will surrender."

Buckner nodded and said, "Let me talk with General Bragg."

Remembering Bragg's somewhat surly attitude earlier in the night, Wilder winced. Bragg would insist on unconditional surrender. He was a tough soldier, without the gentler understanding Buckner had shown. He sat, wordless, looking at Captain Burrell, whose face gave no hint of his sentiments. Muted voices issued through the window of the parlor. Wilder could catch only snatches of Buckner's words. "Honorable man....." "Reasonable...." "Not a soldier but a good man...." "Willing to surrender honorably...."

Bragg must have been facing away from the window because Wilder could only hear his deep voice but could understand no words coming from the Confederate commander.

A few minutes later Buckner emerged. "I have talked with General Bragg and explained your situation. He welcomes your offer of surrender, believing that it will spare many lives on both sides. He has authorized me to negotiate the terms of surrender with you."

Terms of surrender, Wilder thought. That means he is no longer asking unconditional surrender.

Buckner went on, "In light of the courageous defense your men made of their position and our sensitivity to the struggle this situation has brought to you, I am prepared to offer terms. We propose that you and your force will be permitted to surrender with the honors of war."

"Honors of war? I do not understand," Wilder stammered.

"You and your entire force will march tomorrow morning at six o'clock to Rowlett's Station," Buckner said. "You may parade from your positions. You may fly your colors and your band, if you have one, may play. At the Station you will surrender to General Bragg, Your men will stack their muskets, and your cannon will be delivered, unspiked. You will be given rations. You may keep your colors. You will be paroled according to the rules. You and your men are to march south along the track, where you may join General Buell's force. But under parole, you are not permitted to fight. You will be returned to a parole camp in the north until you are exchanged. Is that understood?"

"Yes, General. You are generous."

"I honor your struggle, Colonel," Buckner said, saluting. "You may return to your lines."

Returning the salute, Wilder said, "I thank you for your courtesy, General, and I will fully inform our people when I return to Union headquarters."

Orders moved through the Union ranks at Munfordville during the pre-dawn hours. Johann and his men tried to understand what was happening.

"Surrender? *Scheiß*!" Stocker demanded. "We beat 'em back two days. They lost a lota men out there and we lost only a handful along the line."

"Col. Owen and Pleisch say that Col. Wilder was taken to the Confederate lines last night and shown that they have many times the men we have, that they have nearly eighty cannons on both side of the river. It is hopeless to fight back," Johann reported.

"That coward...," Stocker grumbled.

Geyer tried to calm him. "Listen, he was just trying to keep us from getting killed. Can you imagine what eighty cannons would do to this line? I am thankful for his good sense. It takes a brave man to know when he is helpless."

"What will become of us? We will be prisoners, like those southerners were at C-C-Camp Morton," Buhl added.

"We will see in the morning. Capt. Pleisch says that we are all to march out tomorrow after sunrise. We take only our muskets, bayonets and knapsacks with our own stuff. Leave everything else right here. The orders are to march like we are on parade," Johann directed.

"I am going to fill my sack with hardtack and apples," Stocker mumbled. "We ain't goin' to see our supply wagons again, don't forget."

Johann said, "It will be sunrise before long. Get a little rest if you can." He walked away from the men to the little grove by the cemetery. Crouching behind a tree he retched again and again. He did not want the men to see how sick he was. Talking to himself, he said softly, "*Ach*, Marta. Now what will happen to me? Will I ever get back to Helvetia, or are we going to be farther and farther away. I wish I could be back with you and the girls in our little house. I am not cut out to be a soldier. I am no fighter. This makes no sense. For two days many men died or were wounded and now we give up what we were defending. We could have given them the bridge at the beginning and saved all the suffering." He wiped the bloody vomit from his mouth.

It was a little after six o'clock when the soldiers in the trenches heard the music of their little band coming from Munfordville. Soon a procession began across the bridge. The color bearers carried their flags in the lead, followed by the ten men of the band, four drummers and four trumpeters and two trombones. Colonel Wilder and several other officers were on horseback. Just behind them was a single horsedrawn cannon, with gunners riding on the caisson. The companies from north of the river marched behind them in ordered ranks. The men from the Stockade formed their ranks and joined the march. Then the units in the trenches and from Fort Craig at Woodsonville fell in behind them.

The column, marching as if on parade, stretched from the bridge to Rowlett's Station. There a number of Confederate companies were drawn up in their ragged butternut clothes, many of them bare footed.. General Bragg and General Buckner waited in front of the farmhouse headquarters. Bragg stayed on the porch, frowning. Buckner stepped down as Wilder dismounted and saluted.

Buckner, returning the salute, said, "General Bragg has appointed me to receive your surrender."

Wilder drew his sword and handed it to Buckner, who said, "I receive your surrender, but wish to return your sword as a measure of my respect for your judgment in avoiding further conflict."

Wilder blinked back his tears, returned his sword to its scabbard and saluted again.

"One moment," Buckner said. "I understand that Col. Owen and the 60th Indiana are among your troops."

"That is correct," Wilder responded.

"I wish to speak with him."

The word was passed back through the ranks and Col. Owen came forward.

General Buckner returned Owen's salute. "Sir, I know of your service at Camp Morton where many of my men from Fort Donelson were imprisoned before they were exchanged. You are known for your courtesy and kindness. I wish to thank you and your men for their humane treatment of my men."

"Thank you, sir." Owen answered. "I will tell my men."

Buckner said in a fairly loud voice, so that the front ranks of the officers and troops could hear. "General Bragg has issued the following instruction: Your men are to march past Rowlett's Station and place their weapons where our officers will indicate. Officers may keep their personal sidearms without ammunition. Wagons await you to give each man who wants it three days' rations. You are all to sign the oath of parole. Then, as non-combatants you are to march south to join General Buell's force, which we are told is moving toward us from Bowling Green. He will eventually send you north where you will be in a parole camp until you are exchanged by the Commission."

Buckner did not add that Bragg was intentionally sending this sizable force to Buell because they would be a burden to his advance. Four thousand more mouths, who were honor bound not to fight, to feed and four thousand bodies to shelter. Far better with Buell than heading north for Louisville ahead of Bragg's army.

"Thank you, General. Permit me to instruct my officers of the procedures to be followed," Wilder responded.

Only those soldiers in the first few companies in line could see the drama as it unfolded. The whole long column of the Union garrison was ordered to stand at parade rest. The color guard carefully removed their flags from their standards and put them in their knapsacks. The officers moved to their regiments and companies in the line of march.

The whole morning was devoted to company after company marching forward to deposit their Springfield and Enfield muskets in the growing stacks of weapons beside the dusty road. Then each company swore the oath of parole and signed the parole rosters: they would not fight again until officially exchanged for captured southern soldiers. Everyone knew that this was a matter of personal and national honor.

Wagons on either side of the road offered each soldier a number of pieces of hardtack, a little chunk of dried meat, and a handful of peanuts, scooped from large burlap bags. As the men moved past the wagons, they held out their knapsacks into which these meager rations were dropped.

Stocker pointed to the U.S.A. printed on the bags and murmured to his comrades, "This is our own stuff they're givin' us."

Just before noon the whole garrison had completed the process. On orders from their officers they formed ranks again and began marching down the road toward Cave City, as the southern officers had directed. The word passed back through the ranks: "Hold up your heads; march smartly. You are still Union soldiers."

Col. Peavy saluted General Bragg. "By our best count we captured 155 officers and 3,921 men signed the parole roll. We have counted about 10 cannons. There are wagonloads of ammunition and a couple of barns full of food over in town. They destroyed their paper work at headquarters, as one might expect."

"Well done, Colonel," Bragg's face was creased with one his rare smiles. "Well done."

Turning to Buckner, "You did very well, sir, getting us into position to encircle him. And I appreciate the way you persuaded Wilder to surrender. I guess he merited the honors of war. It was an honorable surrender...but he took a lot of persuading."

Buckner smiled, "Do not forget that he knew very little about soldiering, but he was man enough to admit it."

So the long parade moved out of sight over the horizon toward the south and Buell.

CHAPTER 19

It was a very long day. The late summer sun beat down on the blue coated column. The men wiped perspiration, opened their blouses, tied bandannas around their necks. By noon they had passed Cave City. Wilder's aides rode ahead looking for the advance elements of Buell's army which was supposed to be marching north from Bowling Green. In mid-afternoon they made their first contact. Wilder ordered his men off the road and into a tree edged field. The men crowded together in whatever shade they could find.

Wilder and two of his aides talked briefly with the commanding officers of the advancing regiments. Then they rode south, passing by the marching troops.

Johann sat with his back against a tree.

"You don't look so good," Geyer said.

"I will be all right after a little rest...just feeling very tired," Johann responded.

Stocker stretched out on the grass along the fence. "*Mein Gott*, marching makes me hungry. I already ate all that *Dreck* they gave us this morning."

"That was supposed to last you three days. You are going to just waste away, while the rest of us break our teeth on that hardtack. Too bad for you," Geyer joked.

"I'll save you," Johann joined the game. "You can have some of mine."

"You mean it? What are you goin' to eat?" Stocker shook his head, pondering what was for him unthinkable.

"What I would like is a big cup of milk, nice cool milk. Or I would not mind a bowl of good milk soup with soft bread and butter floating on the top," Johann patted his stomach.

"Baby food! What I would like is a nice big chicken. You don't think we could find one when they let us stop for the night?" Stocker asked with a smile, knowing that his hope was in vain.

"Listen, *du Fresser*," Geyer shook his finger. "This army marching along here is going north as fast as it can to fight that bunch that beat us. They are not going to be worried about feeding you. You are not allowed to fight any more, so you are dead weight."

"He's w-w-weight all right," Buhl joined in,.

Stocker stood up. "I'm goin' to walk back to the little creek we just passed and see if I can fill my water can. I will be right back."

When he returned, he said with a broad smile, "You know, I just remembered. Back when we was leaving Camp Morton, Bauer, you bet me a dollar that I would run when we saw the elephant. Well, we got in our battle and I did not run. So I win, *richtig*? We each gave the sergeant our dollar. Still got my money, Johann? I am ready to be paid."

Johann pulled out of his blouse the little sack he wore around his neck. "Here are the same dollars you two gave me in Indianapolis." He laughed, "I figured that you would forget all about it and I was going to use them to start my own business when we get home. Here you are, Jakob. You earned it."

Bauer held out his hand. "You won. Too bad you could not have gotten to their supply wagons. You would have starved them into surrendering all by yourself."

Stocker stretched out again on the grass, pulled his kepi over his eyes and smiled. "Wake me up for supper."

The sun was lowering when Colonel Wilder rode back beside the long line of marching troops. Calling his officers together, he reported, "I found General Dumont and explained our situation. Naturally, we need to keep out of the way. They are moving toward Louisville as fast as they can, to get there before Bragg. Since we cannot fight, we are a hindrance. Our orders are to stay right here until the army has moved past. Then we are to follow them to Louisville. We are to stay half a mile behind the army. They will give us a few wagonloads of food. Once they get beyond where the rail line has been cut, trains will be there to move as many as they can to Louisville. They may have to fight Bragg, if he is still holding Munfordville. But it is marching for us. Keep your units together. We'll just wait. We have nothing to make camp, so just get the men as comfortable as you can and have them eat their rations until we get our supply wagons."

Johann could not think of eating. He did not want to concern his men so he nibbled at a piece of his hardtack. Like the other men drifting into the underbrush to relieve themselves, he would walk into the woods to vomit bright blood once again. He thought, if I can only hold out until we get to wherever they are sending us. Marching sixty miles over several days was not a pleasant prospect.

When Buell and his army reached Louisville, he deployed them almost immediately to the southeast. He located good defensive positions and set his troops to resist the advance he assumed Bragg and Smith would make once their forces joined. Soon Buell had his army of 77,000 men well enough organized to go on the attack against Bragg and Smith.

After the surrender. Bragg had quickly moved out of Munfordville and to the north to join Smith, marching toward Louisville. He had called Buckner before leaving Munfordville and laid out his plan.

"We cannot afford the time it would take to bring that whole bridge down. It would take a massive effort to blow up those piers."

Buckner answered, "I know that all too well. When we got pushed out of Munfordville last December, I tried to demolish the pier on the far end. We used all the black powder we had and couldn't get it down."

Bragg ordered, "Put some men to work burning the wooden deck. The ties and the tracks will collapse into the river. It won't be any good to Buell for a while. Besides, if Smith and I can take Louisville, we're going to have to depend on this rail line for our supplies. So I don't want the whole bridge destroyed."

Bragg's main force moved north and occupied Bardstown, poised to attack. Still believing that he could salvage the border state Kentucky for the Confederacy, Bragg left most of his army in Bardstown and went to join Smith at Frankfurt, the state capital, on a political mission.

The previous year, shortly before the movement of Union forces into western Kentucky against Fort Henry and Fort Donelson, southern sympathizers had organized a state convention at Russellville and had elected a slate of officials for a Kentucky independent of the Union. They applied for admission to the Confederacy, and when accepted, they elected representatives to the Confederate Congress. They also elected a provisional state government, which had been forced into exile when Union armies took over most of the state.

Now that he was in possession of the state capital, Bragg decided to inaugurate the provisional Lieutenant Governor, Richard Hawes. Leaving General Polk in command of the sizable force in Bardstown, he moved a small detachment of his army to Frankfurt, joining Smith for the inauguration. Bragg was convinced that by formalizing the Confederate state government, the people of the state would overwhelmingly support the southern cause, and Kentucky would no longer be a border state..

Meanwhile, in Louisville Buell faced a personal crisis. There was great dissatisfaction in Washington with his performance: his plodding progress in the movement to attack Chattanooga, his failure to fight aggressively in Tennessee, his slow movement north to counter Bragg's incursion into Kentucky. President Lincoln and the commanding General Halleck had sent a courier by rail to Louisville with dispatches removing Buell from command. But the instructions were that the orders were not to be given if Buell was preparing an attack or engaging the enemy. In spite of his movements against Bragg, the dispatches were delivered and Buell prepared to turn over command. His successor, General George Thomas, interceded and telegraphed Washington, asking that Buell be retained in command at least until the operations he had planned were carried out. So Buell was permitted to continue in command.

Buell sent about a third of his army to attack Frankfurt and two of his three corps to drive out the southern forces at Bardstown. This was the first attack Buell had planned in four months. The division moving against Frankfurt quickly got close enough to bring the capital under artillery fire. The shelling brought a rude interruption to the Confederate inauguration ceremonies.

The Munfordville garrison reached Louisville two days after Buell had arrived. All around they saw the feverish preparations for supporting the attack against Bragg. Trains were being unloaded and long columns of wagons moved out of the city to the southeast.

Wilder's men could not participate in any way as parolees. They became sensitive to the angry glares of soldiers and civilian workers. Four thousand blue coated soldiers standing idly about in the midst of all the activity attracted cat calls and shouts of "slackers." A few of the men were ready to wade into their tormentors.

Soon orders came that the weaponless troops were to board some of the trains returning north after unloading. Col. Wilder instructed his officers to have the men march smartly. "We are not in disgrace. We put up a good fight. We have nothing of which to be ashamed. March with your heads up, as good soldiers."

They were to be taken to Indianapolis over-night. So they were crowded into empty box cars and began the last leg of their retreat. Without enough room in the cars to lie down, they sat back to back, rather tightly packed, dozing, as the train rocked on its northward journey.

In the first light of day they were met in Indianapolis by an officer of the Provost Marshal. He conferred with Col. Wilder and orders were issued for the men to form ranks and march through the slowly awakening city to a camp on the edge of town.

"Don't tell me that we are headed back to Camp Morton," Geyer said.

"No, it is some different place. I don't know what it is called," Johann answered.

But Johann was wrong. He had no way of knowing that two battles in Kentucky, Richmond and Munfordville, had produced thousands of captured and parolled Indiana soldiers. At first Washington directed all these men to be sent to Camp Chase in Columbus, Ohio. Governor Morton protested. He wanted his men closer to home until they were exchanged. He had heard stories of the terrible overcrowding and low morale at Camp Chase.

Morton had faced real opposition from Secretary of War Stanton. Stanton did not like the whole parole system. He strategized that it would slow the Confederate advance if they had to guard and feed and house thousands of prisoners rather than sending them north. But the cartel had been appointed and the parole and exchange plan had been in effect since mid-July. Then Stanton allied with Governor Tod of Ohio, who proposed that paroled regiments be sent to Minnesota to resist a serious Indian uprising there. Morton argued that this violated the oath of parole, while Tod insisted that parolees were only disqualified from fighting in the civil war not Indian wars.

Finally, the sheer problem of trying to deal with almost ten thousand parolees, more than half of whom were from Indiana, caused Washington to yield to Morton's demand that his men be sent to Indianapolis. Camp Morton had been nearly emptied by large exchanges during the summer.

The few remaining prisoners could be sent to other camps. Camp Morton would become Indiana's primary parole camp.

Marching from the railroad yards down the same streets through which they had marched away from Camp Morton in February was a strange experience. Soon the high walls came into view beside the Turnpike and the column turned into the main gate. Two regiments had arrived before them and were busy raking and sweeping, cleaning up from the prisoners who had left a month earlier.

The 60th Ohio was assigned to barracks along the northern edge of the encampment. Each company had two barracks. The walls were lined with four-tiers of bunks. Long tables were arranged in the center for eating.

Once they were settled in their barracks the regiment was assembled on the parade ground. Colonel Owen spoke to his men. "I want to explain our situation. We are still a military unit and under military discipline, so camp life will be pretty much what it was before we went into the field. I remind you that each of us is under the parole oath. We are not allowed to do any military duty. But we can continue daily drills, because before many weeks we will be exchanged and returned to our duties. You will get new uniforms and equipment in due time. As you can see, there is a lot of work to be done to fix the camp up. We will start on our own barracks.

"You can leave the camp with a pass from your Captain when you are not on duty and go into the city, but you must be back by sundown. Any one who does not return when required will be regarded as a deserter and punished accordingly. I remind you that you are on your honor, and our country's honor, to abide by the rules of parole.

"You have been good soldiers, and you fought bravely at Munfordville, so I am expecting you to continue as good soldiers. Dismissed!"

They had barely gotten into the routine of the camp when one of the men ran in with the German newspaper from Louisville. He shouted, "They whipped Bragg...Big battle...The Rebs are retreating back to Tennessee."

Johann and all the other men crowded around to hear someone read the article from the paper. It recounted the battle at a place called Perryville, which Johann's men recognized was not far from Lebanon.

"It says that we had 4000 killed or wounded and Bragg lost more than 3000. He turned and headed back south. Buell figured he was so badly whipped that he didn't even bother to chase him."

"Well, that got even for Munfordville," Stocker growled, raising his fist into the air.

Buhl added quietly, "If we hadn't been c-c-captured, we would have been in that battle. Four thousand......!"

"I had enough battle for a while," Geyer pushed back his cap. "I didn't care much for those rebs bouncing bullets off the rocks all around me."

Johann responded, "I wonder how many our side captured. They will exchange them as soon as they can. Then we'll be out of here."

"Yes, and b-b-back where all the shooting is."

Stocker vented his anger. "At least it is not as boring as just sitting around waiting."

"I would rather be bored than d-dead."

Geyer waited until the other men had left the table. Then he turned to Johann. " I am worried about you. You are getting so thin. I have been watching you. You don't eat anything. You spend a lot of time in the latrine. Why don't you report for sick call?"

"My gut is all tied in knots. It hurts all the time. As sergeant I had to keep going. I have been vomiting blood since we were in Lebanon," Johann confided in his good friend.

"Go let that doctor have a look at you."

A small field hospital was attached to the camp to care for the wounded and the sick. Johann joined the line of men waiting to be seen by the doctor. He had heard the jokes about sick call, the men who went again and again in the vain hope that the doctor would excuse them from duty. He hated to be seen in the company of these fakers.

Dr. Bray looked over the tops of his spectacles at the slight, pale man in the ill-fitting sergeant's uniform. He did not know what this fellow was talking about: *Magen, Blut, kotzen, Schmerz.* "

"Walters," he called to an aide, "come over here and tell me what this man is saying."

"He says that his stomach hurts and that he has been vomiting blood."

"Ask him how long this has been going on."

"He says since summer, when he was in Lebanon."

"Why did he wait all this time to come?"

"He says that he did not want to let his men down. He just ate less. But it has gotten a lot worse. He has not been able to keep anything down for a week."

Dr. Bray poked around on Johann's abdomen, noting the wince. "Let's keep him here for a couple of days. Get him a bed and see to it that he gets soft food. I'll look at him again tomorrow.

Johann turned even more pale when Walters told him that he going to be in the hospital. Although his company had not had many men in the little hospital in Lebanon, Johann had heard other men talking about them as if they had a death sentence. They talked about men going to the hospital and dying of the diseases that swept through them.

The hospital was much less crowded than the other barracks. Low iron beds stood in long rows. The walls were rough unpainted boards. There were five windows on each side. Someone, perhaps some of the women of Indianapolis who were walking about the hospital with long white aprons over their dresses, had tried to decorate it with some flags and bows of colored ribbons tied around branches of evergreen.

Walters took Johann to a bed in the middle of a row, talking to him in German. "You can stay dressed but take off your boots when you get on the bed. Hang your uniform on the hook by the bed. Here is a night shirt for you tonight. The privy is over there in the corner, through that door."

Only two of the other patients in the room spoke German, and they very quickly came over, sat on the edge of the bed, and began to talk.

Time passed very slowly for Johann. Looking out the window, he could see the companies drilling, soldiers walking slowly up and down the paths between the barracks.

Johann wrote a long letter to Marta telling her about moving from Lebanon to Munfordville. Since it was in the past, he wrote in detail about the battle, and about the surrender and coming to the parole camp. He really did not understand enough about parole to tell Marta just what was involved. He did not tell her about his stomach trouble and being in the hospital. It would only worry her to know that he was sick. One of the aproned women, who spoke a little German, said she would post the letter for him.

In spite of the soft bread and milk they gave him, there were still trips to the latrine to vomit. After several days, when Dr. Bray and Walters came, the doctor said, "You are not going to do this army any good. These men will soon be exchanged and go back to duty. You could not possibly go with them in this shape. I am going to write a discharge for you and send you home."

When Walters told Johann what the doctor had said, tears came into Johann's eyes. The thought of being back in Helvetia made him very happy.

"Get your stuff together," Walters instructed. "Then go to the surgeon's office and I will have your papers ready for you. Then you can go back to your barracks. You can leave tomorrow morning."

The men of Johann's squad gathered around him when he came through the door of the barracks, slapping him on the back.

"L-l-look who's here!" Buhl shouted.

"You're still pretty skinny. I don't think they did a very good job," Stocker put his hamlike hand on Johann's shoulder.

Geyer was much more composed. "What is the story, Johann?"

Johann did not know how to tell them of his discharge. It did not seem right that he should go home to Helvetia while they had to go back to fight. He cleared his throat several times before he could say, "They are sending me home as disabled."

Geyer broke the long pause. "What did they say was wrong with you?"

"Walters said the doctor called it 'stomach hemorrhage.' It will take a long time to get well, so they want me to get out of the army and go home."

Geyer shook Johann's hand, "I am glad for you. You will be better off there." He smiled at Johann.

"Pretty soft, I'd say," Stocker laughed, ignoring Geyer's glare. "When do you go?"

"Tomorrow morning, they said. I can ride on one of those trains to Louisville. I suppose I can get on the mail boat to Helvetia. I have to go talk with Capt. Pleisch. I'll be back in a little while." Johann turned and left the barracks.

The next morning Johann packed his few belongings into his knapsack and was ready to leave. He had drawn a few dollars from his pay to buy his tickets back to Helvetia. They told him that the railroad would only charge him half fare. He looked around for his men, but no one was in the barracks. *They are probably getting breakfast.*

As he stepped out of the barracks, he saw that Geyer had the men drawn up at attention. Their uniforms were neater than they had been in weeks; their line was straighter than it had ever been. They snapped a salute, smiling broadly.

Johann solemnly shook hands with each one and exchanged a few words. Most of the men gave him letters to take to their families in Helvetia.

Stocker grinned, "I told mama to take one of her pies around to your house. I know you don't eat much, but it'll be just what the doctor ordered."

"You have told us so much about her cooking that I am looking forward to it. Thanks, Jakob," Johann thumped Stocker on the back.

"And you, Buhl, take care of yourself," Johann said.

"*Ja.* I will. I d-d-don't have anybody in Helvetia to write to any more, but I will be thinking of all you folks there," Buhl replied in his customary quiet way.

"*Ach,* Albrecht," Johann held on to Geyer's hand. "You have been a good friend. I will be waiting for you when you come back to Helvetia. I will tell Margareta that you are a good soldier and that she should be proud of you."

"*Auf wiedersehen,* my friend."

Johann picked up his knapsack and walked toward the gate. He turned once more and waved.

The *Star Gray Eagle* was puffing from Coaltown to Helvetia through the early morning mist. Johann watched the shoreline, where the trees were turning color. The small side-wheeler came around the bend in the Ohio, and Johann could just make out the wharf boat. Two men stood on the wharf in the dim light. A wagon and its team were backed up to the dock ready to load half a dozen crates onto the deck.

Johann strained to see a familiar face. It was almost a year since they had all marched to the steamer at this very landing on their way to the army. The street was lined with people; a band was playing. How quiet it was now, except for the wheezing steam engine of the boat.

They docked. Johann walked down the gangway and across the wharf boat. He could see a few people moving along the street. He had had no way to let Marta know that he was coming. She may not even have yet received the letter he wrote from parole camp. He wanted to run up the streets, but found himself walking slowly, deep in thought.

What was this homecoming going to be like? The little girls would find him a stranger. Marta might find him a stranger. Would he be able to find a decent job and begin supporting his family the way he wanted to?

How had being in the war changed him? Would he be able to eat again without being sick?

As he walked up Humbolt Street, crossed Ninth Street, he saw a familiar figure limping across the street ahead of him. It was Paulus on his way to the schoolhouse. He stopped in his tracks and waved.

"Johann, good to see you," he grinned, pounding Johann on the back. "I wondered who that soldier could be. Are you just arriving?"

"*Ja*. I came on the boat just now. Marta does not know I am coming. I do not want to frighten her, coming early in the morning."

"Listen, she will be so glad to see you that she will not care what time of day it is. You look pretty thin. Have you been sick."

"*Ja*. That is why they sent me home. My stomach is bleeding. I hope I get better soon, once I get away from army food. How is Matti?"

"Just fine. She spends a lot of time with your little wife. They have become very good friends."

"When Marta wrote letters to me, she always talked about Matti. I was so glad she had such a good friend." Johann took a few steps. "Well, I have only a few feet left in a long journey. I will tell Marta that I saw you."

There was the little house on Twelfth Street. In a few places the paint had worn away, but it looked so good. When Johann went around the house, he saw that the kitchen door was open a few inches. Smoke was coming out of the chimney from the stove. He could see Marta moving about in the kitchen and hear her talking. He stepped up on the little porch.

Marta heard his footstep and turned to the door. The sunlight was behind the figure, delaying her recognition for just a moment. Then she ran to the door. "*Kinder, Papa ist gekommen.*" She threw her arms around Johann, crying on his shoulder. "You are home!"

Holding her close, Johann whispered, "*Ja*, I am home."

"I am so happy. I never thought this day would come."

"I am home to stay."

"You will not have to go back?"

"No, I have been sick. I have something wrong with my stomach, and the doctor sent me home."

"You'll get better now that you are here." Marta pulled the two little girls from behind her skirts and picked up baby Jenny from the floor. "Here is Papa."

As he had suspected, the girls peaked around Marta shyly. "Sit down and let me look at you," Marta said to Johann. "You look so thin and tired."

"I am tired. I was riding on a train and then the steamboat for a day and a night. I was too excited to sleep last night."

Emma stepped out and smiled at Johann.

"Come, let Papa hold you. You are getting to be such a big girl."

Emma held up her five fingers and began playing with the buttons on his tunic.

"Five years old, what a big girl."

Anna sideling over, put her arms around Johann's leg.

For a few days, Johann just rested, alternating between staying in bed and sitting in a rocking chair in the kitchen. He told Marta he hated being limited to staying at home, but he just did not have the energy to go out of the house. "At least,' he said, "I am back in Helvetia."

On the second night after his arrival Paulus and Matti with their two children came with a big basket of food for supper.

Matti bustled about, helping Marta set the table. "We thought we had to do something special to celebrate the hero's homecoming."

Johann answered, "I am no hero, just a man glad to be home."

"We know about the battle you were in," Paulus said. "Rabert had a big write-up about it in the paper as soon as word came from Louisville. It must have been quite a fight."

"I don't want to hear about it," Marta protested. "I just wish this awful foolishness would be over. It makes no sense for men to be killing each other."

Matti added, "I think the leaders should sit down and settle this fight. The ones that are still standing will have to do that in the end anyway. Why not do it now and save a lot of lives?"

"I would wish for that too, but it is not going to happen," Paulus said. "What do you think, Johann. How is this going to end?"

Johann paused, closed his eyes for a moment. "I do not think it will end until one side cannot fight any more. That may take a long time. Once you have been in the fight, all you think is about your side winning. You have risked your life to win, and you are not going to give up. Our side had to surrender at Munfordville, but everybody knew that we would be fighting again before many months."

"Was it bad?" Marta asked softly.

"I was never so scared in my whole life. To be shooting at men and to have them shooting at you is awful. We were behind rocks and banks of earth and piles of brush. That was bad enough. But the southerners had to come at us right out in the open. I don't know if I would be strong enough to do that. That is what kept going through my mind all the time we were fighting: suppose they ordered us to charge; could I do it!"

Marta put her hand on his arm. "I am so glad you did not have to find out."

"That's enough. I would rather talk about something else—like Helvetia," Johann said, looking into the face of each one.

"Let's do that while we eat," Matti said, uncovering her basket. "Here is bread and some boiled potatoes. Good, they are still nice and hot. And here are some slices of ham. And I cooked the last cabbage we had in the garden. The frost will get them soon anyway." She gently pushed away the children who had crowded in to peer into the big basket.

"What a feast. You'll have to come home more often, Johann. We do not eat like this all the time," Paulus said.

"You all sit down. *Kinder*, you sit on the chairs. Matti and I can hold the little ones. Johann, you can pull up that box," Marta organized the crowd.

"I'd offer to sit on the box, but I would not fit. There is twice as much of me as there is of you, Johann," Paulus laughed. "So I am afraid you are on the box, even if you are the returning hero."

Matti took charge. "Our Anna is big enough to sit on the box. The rest of you take the chairs. There, now. Let's eat before it all gets cold. And there is an apple pie for later."

During the meal Johann hoped no one would notice that he was not eating much. It smelled so good. He took a few small mouthfuls and chewed and chewed to take up time. No one said anything.

While they were clearing the table, Matti said quietly to Marta, so that the men in the other room did not overhear. "Johann did not eat much. He is so thin. I thought good cooking after the army food would taste good."

"He has something wrong with his stomach. That is why they sent him home. He has a hard time keeping food down. His stomach bleeds. The only thing he really can keep is milk soup. He said the army food was awful and made him vomit all the time. He is going to see Dr. Rupp. I hope he can get some medicine to fix it. I don't say much because I don't want him to see how worried I am. Johann spends a lot of time in bed. He is so weak."

The doctor pulled at his full beard as he sat by Johann's bed. Johann had tried to recall in as much detail as possible the difficulties he had had with his stomach during the past year in the army.

'You are doing the right thing," Dr. Rupp said. "Keep that up until you are not vomiting up blood any longer."

Marta asked, "How can he get strong again, if that is all he eats?"

"Johann, you are going to have to take care of yourself for a long time. Just take it easy for a couple months. Let's see if we can get that bleeding stopped completely. That is what makes you so weak."

"You mean I am not going to be able to look for a job. I have to get back to work, to get some money to support my family."

"First you have to get your strength back. I do not see how you managed in the army. You could not possibly do a day's work while you are so weak. Working would keep you from getting well."

Johann looked at Marta. "You were better off when I was in the army. At least you got a little money from my pay. Now we are not going to have anything coming in."

Marta, her eyes filling, said, "Try not to worry. We will make it. There is that money you are supposed to get when your army enlistment is over. Maybe that will come."

Dr. Rupp pulled on his overcoat. "I know it is hard, but try not to push too hard. You are going to have to take things easy for a while. If we can get your stomach to stop bleeding, we can get you back on your feet. I will take another look at you next week."

He picked up his satchel and walked to the kitchen door. "*Ach*, it is starting to snow a little. *Auf wiedersehen.*"

"Run for the doctor. Little Karl is burning up with fever." Katerina Wiesner shook her sleeping husband.

"*Mein Gott, was ist los?* August, still half-asleep, mumbled.

"Get dressed and go get the doctor! I went in to see Karl. He was sitting up in bed, talking but not making any sense. When I put my hand on his forehead, he is so hot."

August struggled into his clothes. "Won't it wait until morning?"

"This child is sick. I've never felt anybody so hot. He is shaking all over. Get a move on!"

When the doctor saw the convulsing child, his face was grave. Taking charge, he told August, "Get me a pail of water, right from the well. Cold."

To Katerina he said, "Get a bed sheet. As soon as August brings the water, we'll wet the sheet and wrap it around this boy. Take his nightshirt off."

Once this was all done, he took a bottle from his satchel. "Here. Let's see if we can get a little of this in him."

Then began a vigil that lasted for three days. August and Katerina took turns sitting by the bed night and day. Karl, wrapped in the wet sheet, slept restlessly.

Doctor Schnader came twice a day. He sat by the bed in deep thought. "That medicine is all I have to give. It usually helps bring a fever down, but I don't know what else I can do. I could bleed him, but I don't like to do that with such a young child. We'll just have to hope and pray that the fever breaks soon."

Katerina put a cool wet washrag on Karl's head. "It's awful to have him so sick and so far from his momma and papa. They would be wild if they knew how sick he was. If he doesn't make it, how could we ever tell them? It would kill her."

"*Ja.* It's hard. You have done everything you could for the boy."

Katerina rose from the chair beside the bed and went to wake August. "I think something is changing. Sweat is just pouring out of Karl. I think the fever is breaking. *Gott sei ewig Lob und Dank.*"

As soon as it is light, get Doctor Schnader. He said to call him if there was change."

For the first time in the whole crisis a slight smile passed over the doctor's face. "He's better! The fever is going down! We can get rid of these wet sheets. Just wash him and let him sleep."

Karl's eyes moved around the room, without the wild stare that had been there during the last few days. He reached out to Katerina, who, uncharacteristically, threw her arms around him.

"You've got to write to Marta and tell her how sick Karl was," Katerina said to August a few days later. "At least we do not have to send bad news."

"*Ja,* I will write tonight. I hope that this will make them send for him. We do what we can, but we are not his momma and papa."

"You certainly do a lot for him. You take him fishing. You are always carving out some little toy for him. He's like your own son."

"He seems happy enough."

"I wish he would be happy when I ask him to do something. He just looks at me until I get firm with him."

"Once he has a few years of school, the teachers will show him how to mind."

"He knows I am not really his mama, so he doesn't think he has to do what I say."

"I'll talk to him about helping you more."

"I doubt if that will help. He knows you won't make him do anything."

"Well, I'm sorry for the little fellow. I guess I do go pretty easy on him, but he must miss his folks."

"Well, write your letter."

In early December as they were finishing supper, Johann heard someone come on to the back porch. When he opened the door, Margareta Geyer came in.

"I got a letter from Albrecht today, and he wanted me to bring it to you, so you could know where he was."

Marta quickly made a place at the table. "Can I give you coffee?"

"*Nein, danke,*" Margareta said, pushing her heavy shawl aside. "Here, You can read it."

Johann turned up the lamp and held the letter close to the light. "We always had to write with a pencil because there was no way to carry ink. It is not easy to read without good light."

He started to read aloud.

> I am writing this from a steamboat on the Mississippi River. Would you believe we went right past Helvetia in the middle of the night on Thursday. After we passed Coaltown some of us stood by the railing and watched for Helvetia. There was not much moonlight so we could not see much. All of our hearts were heavy because we were so close to the ones we love and could not even wave at them. I almost cried.
>
> They came to the parole camp on November 22 and told us that we had been exchanged by the commission. That meant that we would be back on regular army duty. There was not even time to send a letter to tell you that we were out of the camp. The next morning we were on a train to Louisville. Then we were all put on two steamboats and started down the river.

We did not make any stops until we got to a town called Cairo in Illinois. We stopped there to load food and coal. It only took a few hours. Then we started down the Mississippi River. We are now docked in a city called Memphis in Tennessee. There are thousands of soldiers here. We will only be here for a few days they told us. We got all new stuff: guns, knapsacks, shoes, blankets. I dread those new shoes. They hurt for a week until they get shaped to your feet. By the time you get this letter we will be somewhere down along the river. Every day many steamboats take some of the men from here and head south. We are being sent to General Grant who is fighting to capture a place called Vicksburg. I do not know when I will have another chance to write. I just wanted you to know that for a few minutes we were very close, dear one. If only we could have stopped in Helvetia for a few days. *Ich liebe dich*, Albrecht.

Take this letter to Johann so that he knows where his old *Genosse* are. We are all doing well. Stocker is ready to show General Grant what a hero he is. His stories about Munfordville get bigger and bigger. It is a wonder that we lost.

The winter months were hard. Fierce cold winds roared out of the north. There were two blizzards which piled drifting snow in all the streets. The cold seeped through the walls of the house. The kitchen stove glowed and Marta kept putting in sticks of wood from the pile in the corner of the porch. She kept the children in their coats, and Jenny in her crib near the stove. At night they piled on every available blanket and featherbed. Marta heated a brick on the stove, wrapped it in a towel and warmed the girls' bed before putting them in.

In the early morning light Marta, wrapped in Johann's heavy army coat which hung from her narrow shoulders and almost touched ground, with a muffler and cap she had knitted, trudged down Humboldt Street to Goss' house on Eleventh Street to get her bucket of milk, following a narrow path made by a horseman through the drifts.

When she got back home, Johann sitting by the stove said, "It makes my heart heavy to see you having to do all the work. You have to chop the wood for the stove, go after the milk, cook, take care of the children. I have never felt so useless in my life."

After she had unwrapped herself, Marta held her hands over the stove. "We will be all right." She sat down heavily at the table. "I am very tired, but we will be all right." Her face reflected the stubborn determination that had always been part of her disposition.

"Maybe I can help with the cooking."

Marta laughed, "Then we would all have sick stomachs. If you want to keep your eye on the little girls, it would help. Hold Jenny on your lap. Tell them some stories about Neuhaus and Endigen. Tell them about your brothers. Tell them about coming across the ocean."

"I think they are still afraid of me. I just sit here hour after hour, rocking, listening to my hair grow."

"Speaking of your hair, I am going to try giving you a haircut. No wonder the girls are afraid. It is getting awfully shaggy."

"I do all right shaving. Bauer used to cut our hair in the army. He bought some scissors and was the barber for a lot of men in the company for five cents a head. At first we looked pretty chopped off, but he got better."

"I made a lot of hats. I ought to be able to cut hair."

"What a Godsend," Marta said when Johann opened the envelope from the army and pulled out a bank draft.

"They told me in Indianapolis that they would pay what they owed me. When it didn't come right away, I just figured that it would get lost in a mountain of records and I'd never see it."

"How much did they send you?"

"It is for one hundred and seven dollars. That must be for the last months when I was not paid and some of the money I was supposed to get for enlisting."

"If we are careful, we can make that stretch out for a good while. Before too long we'll have the garden."

"It has to last until I can work again. I hope that won't be too long."

Just a few days later Marta told Johann when she came back from the grocery store with a bag of flour, "I stopped at the post office. We got a letter from Papa. Karl has been very sick."

"Is he better now?"

"*Ja*. He had a very high fever for days. He almost died.. Oh, Johann, just think how we would have felt if he had died…without ever seeing us again. I can't bear to think about it."

"But your father said he was better now."

"We've just got to find a way to bring him over before it is too late."

"Right now, he's better off there. Here we have a war, no job, no money."

"I just have to find a way."

"Be patient. Wait 'til we get back on our feet."

As the winter months passed and it started getting a little warmer in the daytime, Dr. Rupp encouraged Johann to take short walks. He even was able to walk downtown. One day he stopped at the office of *Die Zeitung* for a few minutes to see his old friend Rabert.

"Johann, my friend," Rabert greeted him, rising from his desk. "Come in; sit here by the stove."

"I can only stay for a minute. Marta will have supper ready."

"It is good to see you out of that rocking chair. You must be feeling better."

"My strength is coming back. I still cannot eat much regular food, but the bleeding in my stomach has stopped. Dr. Rupp said that by summer I should be much better. But he warned me it is going to be slow. I stopped by because I wanted to ask you something."

"Oh?"

"Could you help me to learn some English? I know I do not need it much around Helvetia, but in the army I went a lot of other places. I saw that if a person is going to get ahead, he has to be able to talk to the Americans. I would like to learn to understand and talk some English."

"You are absolutely right. I studied English hard when I got here in '49. I saw that if I only knew German, I would be cut off from much that is going on in the country. I know, I make my living with a German newspaper. I sometimes fear that I am standing in the way of more people in Helvetia learning English. Then I think that, if they learn English, *Die Zeitung* can help them keep their German too."

"What do I need to do?"

"Let me see if I can find the books I used when I got started. Gretchen got me a little dictionary in German and English. That helped a lot. I think we still have some simple storybooks in English. Let me look around for them. I would be glad to teach what I can."

"I would really appreciate that," Johann said.

"You know, Gretchen is a far better teacher than I am. Let me ask if she would be able to give you a few lessons. Your wife could learn too, if she wants."

"I will talk to her about it. Well, I better get home."

"I am happy you stopped. Paulus still comes over some evenings, and we have good talks. Come along with him. I want to hear about your experiences. Tell Marta hello from Gretchen and me."

Johann was glad to be able to sit with Rabert and Paulus around the stove in the newspaper office on cool spring evenings. One night their conversation was interrupted by the loud clanging sound of the iron wagon tire, hanging in the town park just down the street. They put on their coats quickly and ran into the street. Was this the dreaded alarm, the signal that raiders were crossing the river? Then they heard a voice crying, *"Feuer! Feuer!"* There was a red glow in the dark sky to the east.

They joined the crowd running toward the fire, but Johann could not keep up with his companions..

"Mein Gott, it is the schoolhouse," Paulus screamed, running as fast as he could with his bad leg.

By the time they reached Tenth Street a crowd encircled the blazing school. Smoke poured out of the windows. Paulus ran toward the door, thinking he might be able to pull out some of the books and desks.

There was the sound of breaking glass as flames began to push out of the windows. There was a scream from the crowd, "Get back!"

Paulus ran to Matti who was wrapped in a heavy shawl. He threw his arms around her and pulled her tear stained face to his shoulder.

"Why don't you people get your buckets?" she yelled in frustration.

"It is too late, *Liebchen,*" Paulus stroked her hair. The fire was breaking through the shingles on the roof. "It is gone, our school is gone. It is all gone." Tears streaked down his cheeks.

Johann felt so helpless as he stood with the crowd, his stomach knotting. He felt like running through the crowd to the dark street and vomiting. But he stayed, his eyes drawn to the cloud of sparks which swirled upward as the blazing roof collapsed. People from the houses across Tenth Street ran home to make sure their roofs did not catch fire from the sparks.

Rabert, standing nearby, said to Frantz, "Paulus, this will make more sense tomorrow, but I need to say it now. If I know the people of Helvetia, they will all pitch in to build a new school. I will use *Die Zeitung* to get everyone behind it. The people worked to get this schoolhouse, and we will work to get another."

"Ja, I know. But it will be summer before we can build." The bearded teacher wiped his eyes and shook his head sadly.

He turned to Johann, "Johann, will you take Matti home. She is getting too cold. Maybe you could ask Marta to stay with her until I get home."

Johann walked slowly with Matti the two short blocks to their house. He put a few sticks of wood on the embers in the kitchen stove and told Matti to warm herself there until Marta came.

He walked as fast as he could through the chilly night. Before going in the house he went around to the outhouse and retched again and again. It was the first time in several weeks that he had been ill. All the running and the excitement of the fire was just too much.

When he went in, Marta was standing by the kitchen window wrapped in a quilt, watching the dim glow in the sky. "What is burning?"

"It is the schoolhouse. There will be nothing left."

"Poor Paulus and Matti. Poor children."

During the rest of the spring, Paulus taught the children at makeshift desks in the *Turnhalle*. Rabert wrote to the editor of the German paper in Louisville and told him of the tragedy. A few weeks later the *Star Gray Eagle* dropped off a box of books, slates and chalk from a school in Louisville. Under Rabert's direction money was raised for the new school to add to the insurance they had received.

The conversations at the editor's office were full of Frantz's excitement about plans for the school, the buying of lumber and millwork, so that the carpenters could begin.

Gretchen Rabert stopped at Johann and Marta's house with a small packet of books. Twice a week she came for an hour or so to review their lessons.

Marta said, "This makes me feel like a little girl again. It has been so long since I even thought about lessons."

"You are doing very well. It is slow going, I know," Gretchen smiled.

Johann joined in, "It is slow reading the stories when we have to look up so many words in the dictionary. We try to go over the same story again and again until we know all the words."

"That is probably the best way," Gretchen answered.

Marta laughed, "Emma watches us working at the table after supper. She says she is ready to learn too."

"Well, Let her read along with you. In a year or two they will be learning English and German in the school," Gretchen said.

"That is not going to be easy. There are plenty of folks in Helvetia who want only German. Old man Kutz told me '*Im Himmel sprechen wir Deutsch.*'" Johann added. "If they ever got out of town, they would see that the whole country talks English. If we are going to do much business with the rest of the country we have to be able to talk with them. We have to be able to read American newspapers." He paused, embarrassed. "I don't mean that we would stop reading *Die Zeitung.*"

"Charles would be glad to hear that. A lot of what he puts in the paper comes from the American newspapers he reads. He told me that one day he wants to have a newspaper in English and one in German. But there will have to be more people like you and some of the good business people before that can happen."

Marta did not mention the lessons to Matti until she could say a few sentences in English. One day when Matti arrived at the kitchen door, Marta greeted her in English. "Good morning, Matti. Come in."

Matti gave one of her hearty laughs, "Listen to my little American friend."

Matti and Paulus had picked up a good bit of English during the three years they lived in Cincinnati. From that time each of her conversations with Marta had a few sentences in English.

At breakfast one morning in May, Johann said, "I am going down to the furniture factory this morning to see if they have any jobs. It is time for me to get back to work and have some money for my family."

"They would be glad to have you back again. But I do not want you to work too hard until you get your strength back."

"I will be all right. It will take time. I just have to be patient."

"If only you could eat better. You will not be able to do much work just on milk soup."

"At home we ate a lot of milk soup, believe me, and we all did a day's work. Everytime I eat it, I think of Mama cutting the big thick slices of brown bread to break into the milk."

"I would like to see you eating potatoes and eggs and some meat every now and then when we can afford it."

"*Schatzi,* think of how cheap it is to feed me. If we had our own milk cow, it would be even cheaper," Johann smiled. "Albrecht Geyer did a lot of our cooking in the army. He used to worry about me too. But that Stocker boy ate enough for both of us. He kept saying how much he missed his mother's boarding house down near the chair factory. How that man could eat. We had a good time laughing at the way he shoveled in the food."

"I'd like to hear you laugh again," Marta said.

"Things are going to get better, even better than they were before I went to the army. You will see."

He had been welcomed back at the factory. They even gave him his old job as a varnisher. He was glad for that, because it did not involve a lot of lifting and carrying. He knew he did not have the strength for that.

Life began to settle back into a routine. Several times when a steamboat brought back the body of a soldier from Helvetia who had been killed on a far away battlefield or who had died in a camp hospital, Johann was asked to put on his uniform and march with a few other men who had been in the army. After a funeral in one of the Helvetia churches, usually on a Sunday afternoon, they would march to the cemetery on the hill east of town.

As it became warmer, the men in the furniture factory would sit outside to eat their lunches. Max Blum, who worked in the planing mill, said to Johann, "We need more men in the *Förster*...Most fellows back from the army joined us. Told 'em I'd ask you. Hear you were a sergeant... We could use leaders."

"I got sent home from the army," Johann said, "because I have a bad stomach. I am not very strong because I cannot eat much. I am not sure I would do you much good. I cannot do long marches any more."

"Don't do much marching, just a little drilling once a week. Most time we just watch the river at night in case some of those raiders try to attack the towns on this side."

Johann remembered seeing the aftermath of Morgan's raid at Lebanon. He certainly would fight, even if he did not have much strength, if Helvetia was threatened by raiders. "If I can help, I will. But the men have to understand that I am not lazy, I just am not well enough for a lot of drilling and heavy work."

"We need good eyes and your army experience. You know Gus Schultz...He come back with only one arm. He takes his turns watching the river"

"All right, I will join the *Förster*."

"Something new since last summer. Town council voted that every man in the *Förster* will get 40 cents off his town taxes. Come to the drill on Sunday afternoon...Pick the night you want to watch the river...Only have to do it couple of times a month."

"Marta is not going to like this. She even gets upset when I put on my uniform for a funeral."

"You'll be out of her bed only couple of nights a month," Blum laughed, poking Johann in the ribs with his elbow, "Not too much to give for your country, *nicht wahr?*."

One spring evening, Rabert was more animated than usual. "You men will not believe the story I heard in Coaltown when I rode over there today. The whole town is stirred up. They tell me a couple of saloons had fist fights.

"It seems a family named Schneider had a young colored girl cooking for them. A bunch of fellows got the idea that she was an escaped slave. One night last week after supper they went to the kitchen door. When she came to the door, they snatched her, threw a blanket over her head and took her down to the river. They put her in a boat and rowed her over to Hainesville. They took her to the jail and told the jailor that she was an escaped slave and that it was the law she had to be sent back. When they got back to Coaltown, they were bragging about it in a saloon. Some soldiers who man that battery on the riverfront heard them. They got in a boat and rowed right over to Hainesville and demanded that the jailor give the girl back to them. He got stubborn so they held a gun to his head and brought her back to Coaltown. Schneider did not think it was safe for her to be in their house, so he sent her to some of his relatives. The soldiers took the fellows that dragged her to Kentucky and had them put in jail for kidnapping."

Paulus said, "I thought that the law said that escaped slaves had to be sent back. I certainly do not agree with that, but it is the law."

Johann told them, "We found a slave hiding in a haystack in Lebanon. He was scared to death. We knew we were supposed to turn him over, but we could not do it. So at night Stocker helped him move on toward the river."

Paulus nodded his assent. "We should be proud of you doing the right thing." He poured more coffee into their cups.

Rabert went on, "Coaltown is all in an uproar. The town is really divided. And my colleague at *The Reporter* keeps it stirred up. He thinks that the whole war was brought on by what he calls 'those radical abolitionists.'"

"You know," Johann mused, "when the soldiers talked to each other, especially when there was fighting, nobody mentioned slavery or the Union. All you could think about was not getting killed. Once you are face to face with the enemy, ideas just do not seem that important. All that matters is staying alive."

"*Ja*." Rabert said, pacing back and forth. "I can see that. I was never in the army but when I was in student demonstrations in '48, our 'brave' Prussian army fired on us, unarmed men. I have heard the bullets whistle and splat on the walls. But when the shooting stops, even though there is still danger, the ideas are powerful. They stir me now and shape the way I look at things, even after 15 years."

"I would not be a teacher if I did not think that ideas are important. I have to teach these children that freedom is a treasure, that all people have the right to be free."

"I try to do the same in *Die Zeitung.* "

Johann asked, "Why is it that people like us who came to America because we knew what it is like to be controlled by a king and even the church, will not stand up for freedom here in the new country?"

"I think that people become afraid of freedom," Paulus said. "All of a sudden they realize that they have to make their own decisions. But it is even more frightening to give other people the right to decide for themselves. We are afraid that things will get out of control."

Rabert poured more coffee. "This is what defeated us in '48. People wanted freedom. But then they got cold feet and backed away from those who were working to get them freedom. Better to have order, even oppression, than risk things getting out of control."

"You think this is why so many people do not go along with freeing the slaves?" Johann wondered.

"Partly," Rabert said. "Some of them think that black slaves are somewhere between human beings and animals. Since they are not really human, they could not handle freedom."

"There were some free blacks I knew when we lived in Cincinnati," Paulus said. "Nobody can tell me that they are less than human."

"I met a Negro on the ship, while we were docked in Southhampton. He was the first black man I ever saw. You know, he spoke German, had worked for some sort of diplomat. But he was nothing like the black slaves I saw on some of the farms in Kentucky."

Rabert commented, "That is the other reason people are not for freeing the slaves. Millions of them know nothing but hard labor. They cannot read or write. That is what people are afraid of getting out of control. What can these people do if they are no longer slaves?"

"*Ja*, but couldn't they keep on working on the farms, but be paid and be free to go other places to work?" Johann asked.

Paulus shook his head sadly, "That is the problem. Suppose millions decided that they did not want to pick cotton any more. They do not know how to do anything else. Where could they work? Who would feed them? It is a terrible problem."

Rabert was quick to answer. "Education is the only answer. If we win this war and free the slaves, we have to be ready to put up schools, with good teachers, on every plantation, in every village, to teach them; not just the children but the grown-ups as well. It will be a difficult task."

"Much as I would like to see that, I do not think it can happen. It would take hundreds of thousands of dollars," Paulus said. "Look how we have to struggle to get enough money to pay for our school here, and it is our own children we are thinking of."

"In the prison camp a lot of southern soldiers could not read or write. And they were white men. They had a lot less schooling than in the north."

Rabert stood up. "We are not going to solve that tonight, and we all have to work tomorrow, so we had better blow out the lamp."

Johann and Marta were relieved when he started being able to bring home eight dollars a week. Wages had gone up due to the war. Before going into the army Johann had been paid a dollar a day, six dollars a week.

Marta reported after a trip to Goffnet's store. "It is good you are getting more money from the furniture factory. Prices in the store keep going up and up. Flour has nearly doubled in the last year."

"You do a good job making our money stretch."

"Do you think you could build a little chicken coop out by the shed. We could get some chicks from one of the farmers. Then we would have our own eggs and even a chicken to eat once in a while."

"That's a good idea. There is enough scrap wood around to build a little coop. I don't know why we didn't think of that before."

In mid-June, southern Indiana, including Helvetia, was thrown into anxious turmoil by reports of a series of raids by elements of Morgan's cavalry at a number of points along the Ohio River in Kentucky. The *Förster* increased their watchmen along the river. They had daily rather than weekly drills in the park along Eighth Street. They were encouraged by word that several companies of the state home guard were coming from Indianapolis. The Perry County Legion had been mobilized and had been sent to larger towns along the river.

One company was sent to a place a few miles up-river from Coaltown. Their task was to protect a large federal ram, the *Monarch*, which was grounded on a sandbar at Flint Island, near Derby. It could not get off until the level of the river rose. That would require some heavy rains. Fearing that it would be a tempting target for the raiders to capture and defend it until it could get off the bar, the Legion placed an artillery battery and an small encampment of the Legion on the Indiana shore, fifty yards from the stricken steamboat.

All along the river, the towns were on alert. Johann stood his watch in the crude wood tower which had been built on a point just upstream from Helvetia. Another tower was being built about midway between Coaltown and Helvetia. Guard duty was boring. The nights seemed to last forever. The men were ordered not to talk, so that they could hear any sounds from the river than indicated a raid. They listened for voices or creaking oars. They watched as best they could for activity on the Kentucky river bank. There was just farmland and woods across the river from their tower.

When he returned to his house at daybreak, Johann would tell Marta that absolutely nothing had happened during the night.

"Then why waste your time sitting up there all night. You need your sleep."

"No, it is important to watch. I know how fast raiders can move. They can attack a town without warning, destroy what they can, and move on in a few hours. I saw what Morgan did in Lebanon just hours before we got there. There were fires, shooting, taking money from the bank, causing all the people to run out of town to hide in the woods. It was very bad. It would be terrible here in Helvetia, or in Coaltown. If watching the river at night will keep that from happening, I'll give up a little sleep."

Just a few nights later a detachment of 62 men crossed the Ohio at Robert's Landing between Coaltown and Rome. They were a part of Morgan's larger force which was again raiding up through central Kentucky. Captain Thomas Hines, with the cooperation of southern sympathizers in Breckenridge County on the northern edge of Kentucky, gathered a number of boats, including a large keelboat. They rowed quietly across the river toward the sparsely populated farmland on the Indiana shore near Rome. Once they had secured a landing place without being detected, the keelboat made several trips across with their horses.

Hines told his men when they were finally assembled north of the river, "Men, we have two major objectives. We want men and we want horses. Our intelligence tells us that there are people here who will be happy to join up with us and be part of our company. We also know how much General Morgan needs horses. Keep your eyes open for good riding stock."

"Which way do we ride?"

"We are going to head north a piece, as far as Paoli. We have to move fast. There are probably not any federal forces of any size in this area. Ask any men you see if they want to join us. If they do, tell them to get their guns and horses and come with us. For those who are not on our side, check every pasture and barn for good horses. Here are some vouchers captured in Kentucky, drawn on the Union Quartermaster in Indianapolis, which General Morgan signed. For every horse you take, give them one of these vouchers made out for forty dollars."

One of the men asked, "How far is this Paoli?"

"On the map I have it looks like about 50 miles. We may not get all the way there. We have to be back here at the river by midnight day after tomorrow. The boats will be waiting for us. They cannot wait there long, so we can't be late. Let's ride."

The alarm sounded in Helvetia, someone pounding on the iron wagon tire hanging in the park. A rider had galloped in from Coaltown. Breathlessly he shouted that a horseman had come in from upriver with word that a company of raiders were crossing the Ohio in the open country about 18 or 20 miles up-stream from Coaltown, up beyond where the *Monarch* was stuck in the mud. The report was that four to five hundred of Morgan's raiders were attacking across the river.

He said, when he had caught his breath, "Col. Fournier has sent fifty horsemen ahead to reinforce the men guarding the *Monarch*. They should be there before midnight. That may be what the Confederates are heading for. The colonel is gathering the rest of the Legion regiment to march northeast to try to catch up to the raiders, if they head north. He wants any men we can send him to get to Coaltown and wait for orders to join him. If you have wagons or buggies, use those. We have to move fast. He orders all home guard units along the river to watch for other crossings. He thinks Morgan may try to cross at several points, so you need to watch carefully. Get all the men you can to be ready and armed to meet an attack if it comes here."

The members of the Legion moved quickly to get their muskets and packs, to locate wagons and buggies. The *Förster* gathered at the park. They got their supply of muskets and cartridges from the store room at the *Turnhalle* and marched to their lookout tower.

Several of the men suggested, "Johann, you were a sergeant. You tell us where to go."

Putting aside his customary reticence, Johann began to take charge.

"Hans, you take six men and go about half a mile up the river toward Coaltown. Find some high ground along the river and keep watch. Max, you take six men and do the same thing downstream, about half way between Helvetia and Troy. Georg, you take six men back to Helvetia and get up on the roof of the wharfboat. The rest of us will stay here by the tower. Be as quiet as you can, so you can hear if anybody is trying to cross. If we hear shots, we will know somebody is trying to cross. If that happens, everyone stay at his post and keep watching. The extra men here at the tower will go to where the shots are coming from."

"I wish we had a cannon, like Coaltown," Hans Schmidt said. "If there are a lot of them, we will never stop them with a few dozen muskets."

"Don't forget that we have an advantage," Johann said. "If they come, they will be out in the open. We can take cover on the land. I know from experience that if you have cover, you can hold off a much larger force. All right, get to your posts!"

Riding as fast as his horse could gallop toward the *Monarch*, Col. Fournier questioned every person they saw to learn which way the raiders were heading. When two farmers told them that they had heard horsemen heading north, Fournier sent part of his men to the *Monarch* and turned the rest north toward the town of English. Fearing that his horsemen were badly outnumbered, he told them just to scout to locate the raiders, but not to engage them.

"The rest of our men will be coming up pretty soon. Unless we have the advantage, we will not attack. Try to stay out of sight. If they are going north, they will eventually have to come back to the river. If we stay between them and the river, we can pick the spot to stop them."

Later that day, some of the Legion troops found a farmer whose horses had been taken by the raiders. For the first time they learned the size of the raiding party. It was not the hundreds that had been reported, but only about 50 or 60. That word was passed back to Fournier. He also learned that the Confederates were still heading north and east. He kept most of his Legion regiment near the river and was content with a number of scouting parties watching for the raiders to come back toward the river.

On the second day Fournier got reports that the raiders were retracing their way back to the Ohio. They had gotten nearly to Paoli, had taken a number of horses from farms along the way. The home guard had been gathered in Paoli, and Hines and his men decided not to press an attack.

Hines' troopers had spotted some of the mounted men from the Legion. Suspecting that a larger federal force was behind them, Hines realized that it might be difficult to get back to the place where the boats were to pick up his men. Besides, the boats were not due until tomorrow night. He turned his men to the east, riding parallel to the river some twenty miles to the south. He realized that most towns would now have their home guards. He could not afford to get into a skirmish at each town. So he moved cross-country.

Fournier was worried that his plan might not work. Cavalry could move very fast, and the main body of his troops might not be able to move fast enough to stay between them and the river.

Late in the afternoon a young boy on a huge plow horse rode into the camp.

"My daddy, he's Brant Breeden, sent me. Some of your soldiers, they come to our farm just after them rebs rode away. My daddy said to tell you that them rebs are heading for Blue River Island." The boy stopped to catch his breath. "They asked my daddy where was a good place to cross on their horses. He tol' 'em that they could ride out to Blue River Island, because it is shallow this time of year. Daddy tol' 'em how to git there. He tol' 'em that the channel on the Kentucky side of the island was deeper but it was pretty narrow and they could get across."

Thanking the boy, Fournier started his troops moving toward the island. He revised his plan to get between the raiders and the river. He would let them get to the island and then attack. He would have them cut off and could capture the whole lot.

When Fournier got within sight of the island, the Confederate force was already splashing out to the flat, low spit of land in the middle of the river. Mounted men of the home guards who had been pursuing the raiders followed close behind. The Legion and the home guards took cover behind trees and gullies along the bank and began to fire at the hapless raiders and their horses gathered on the side of the island facing Kentucky. Only a few scrub trees and bushes sprouted up from the island. A few of the men were jumping into the river and swimming toward the Kentucky side. Most just milled around on their horses. Realizing their difficult position, most of them made no effort to fire back. It was clear that they were trapped on the island. Just then a small, shallow-draft paddlewheeler, the *Izetta*, with a cannon blocked on its deck, came around the bend in the river, tipping the scale completely against them.

Several white flags were waved from the island. Fournier and his mounted men rode out, up to their stirrups in water. Some of the Legion, holding their muskets and cartridge boxes high over their heads, waded out and took control of the island.

After the raiders were disarmed, Fournier questioned a few of the cavalrymen. He learned that their commander, Col. Hines, and several of his men had swum to the Kentucky shore and escaped the trap. They also reported that they had seen several of their comrades go under before reaching the far shore and presumed that they had drowned. Five men had been wounded on the island.

Once back on the Indiana shore, Fournier's men counted 57 prisoners and 70 horses. He sent them under guard to Derby, instructing his men to get them to the army in Jeffersonville or Louisville on the first steamboat available. Then they could come back to Coaltown on the mail packet.

When the Legion troops got back to Coaltown and Helvetia, as well as a few other smaller towns, the townspeople realized that the raids, which were so often rumored, could actually happen. The war could come to them.

It was only a few weeks later that another alarm went out. Morgan and a large force of 2500 cavalry were crossing the Ohio, further upstream from Hines' crossing. They captured two small steamers near Brandenburg and spent most of a day ferrying the entire force to the Indiana shore where they burned the paddlewheelers. As they started northward toward Corydon, home guard riders spread out in all directions to sound the alarm. Alerted by telegraph, Governor Morton was told that 10,000 Confederates were invading Indiana. By telegraph and couriers, he immediately mobilized every available fighting man through the state, assuming that Indianapolis was Morgan's target. Nearly 60,000 were called out. Many of them began converging on the state capital to repel Morgan's raiders.

Morgan had another strategy. He had gone to General Bragg and argued that sending a strong cavalry force into Union held territory in Kentucky and crossing into Indiana and Ohio would force the federal commanders to turn their armies northward from Tennessee, relieving the pressure around Chattanooga. When he proposed this expedition to General Bragg, the commander agreed only to the diversionary attack into northern Kentucky, the same territory Morgan had raided the previous year. Morgan argued that there were plenty of southern sympathizers in southern Indiana and Ohio, men who would willingly join his forces. Bragg remembered all too well that he had invaded Kentucky with exactly the same plan the year before, and it had not worked. Bragg specifically ordered Morgan not to cross the Ohio. Just raiding towns in central and eastern Kentucky would be enough to draw the Union forces back from Tennessee.

As soon as Morgan was moving through northern Kentucky, capturing one town after another, he quickly got beyond Bragg's reach. He assumed that once Bragg saw his successful raid into the north, he would forgive the breach of orders. Morgan knew that the Army of Northern Virginia was poised to move north into Pennsylvania. He would mount a similar attack in the mid-west. His plan was to ride in force through Indiana and Ohio, never getting far from the Ohio River, so he could return south if necessary. But he would hurt northern morale by demonstrating their vulnerability to attack, he would destroy and disrupt what he could in his long ride through the Union heartland. He would keep riding east until he could join up with Lee, who was beginning the invasion of Pennsylvania. Symbolically he would link the western armies of the Confederacy with the Army of Virginia, showing the world the dominance of southern forces. This gallant invasion would require the Union to divert large forces to chase him, weakening Union positions on other fields.

After a skirmish to capture Corydon, Morgan paused to have lunch at a hotel. There the owner's daughter told him of Lee's defeat at Gettysburg. So the grand strategy was no longer relevant. He would continue his eastern path of invasion, going around the major cities of Louisville and Cincinnati, burning bridges, cutting rail lines, destroying all the supply depots he could find. Day after day passed in this game of cat and mouse. Morgan did not want to risk pitched battles, giving Union troops a chance to mass against him. He had to keep moving to make his strategy work.

One of Morgan's possible avenues for returning to Kentucky was a series of locations near Buffington, Ohio, where in summer the Ohio was fordable. What Morgan did not know was that the river was swollen by heavy rains upstream. When he got to the fords, he found not only that they were impassable but a force of several hundred Union soldiers with two cannons were guarding the fords. As the new day came a Union gunboat, able to sail up from Cincinnati on the swollen river, came around a bend and opened fire on Morgan. Then a large force of Union cavalry attacked his rear. Morgan drove his men out of the trap, galloping eastward.

After seven more days of feverish riding and skirmishing, Morgan was cornered at Salineville, Ohio and forced to surrender with his remaining 364 men. For thirty days they had invaded southern Indiana and Ohio.

After the initial alarm in Helvetia and the gathering of Fournier's regiment of the Legion, the alerting of the *Förster* to defend Helvetia, word came that Morgan was moving eastward, away from them. Every few days one of the steamboats brought newspapers from Louisville and Cincinnati. With their telegraphs they could trace Morgan's movements day by day for the entire month. In Helvetia, even though the news was several days old, there was great interest in the progress of the raid. When word of Morgan's capture reached them, they rang the church bells, even though the surrender had been three days earlier.

The following week the newspaper told how Morgan and his men had been taken first to Cincinnati where General Burnside refused to parole them. He sent them to Columbus where they were put into the Ohio State Penitentiary and treated as common convicts. This created an outrage in the south.

"Served 'em right, if you ask me," Max Blum said to the men in the watch tower.

Fritz Rauscher yawned. "At least we don't have to worry about no raiders comin' across. I don't know why we have to keep comin' out here."

"Don't be too sure. Morgan wasn't the only raider they have. There's nothing to keep a handful of Kentucky lads from rowing over here and burning a few barns or houses," Johann cautioned

Blum went through the motions of sighting along his musket toward the river. "At least old Morgan is a jailbird now. Throw away the key. Serves him right."

Johann spoke up, remembering Camp Morton, "It seems to me that he is a war prisoner, not a convict."

"After all the damage he did, sounds like a criminal to me. That Burnside must have really been furious to refuse to treat him like a prisoner," Blum spat.

"Well, at Munfordville last year we fought off the southerners for a couple of days, killed and wounded a lot of them when they tried to charge our lines. But when we had to surrender the next day, they treated us like men, even said we put up a good fight."

Rauscher put in, "I say raiders is skunks. Good riddance. Treat 'em rough, I say, and they'll think about sending more of those bastards up here. I hope they rot in that jail."

"*Ja*, I know a little about raiders," Johann said quietly. "I saw what Morgan did in Lebanon. We got there just a day after he raided that town. He did a lot of damage, scared a lot of people, burned up a lot of army supplies. But that is war. Both armies are trying to destroy their enemy. Both sides shoot, they burn, they charge. I tell you it is an odd feeling to know that somebody is shooting at you, trying to kill you. But you know that they feel exactly the same way because you are shooting at them. I just know that when we marched out of Munfordville after two days of trying to shoot the Confederates, they were not mean to us. I can't say they were friendly, but they did not hurt us--and they could have. They did not treat us like convicts."

"I say raiders is different. They made us sit out here in this damned tower night after night," Rauscher complained.

Johann said calmly, "Well, things have settled down a lot. We still have to watch, but we don't have any raiders coming at Helvetia."

CHAPTER 20

It was about this time that one of the infrequent letters arrived from Endigen. Julius' letter had news of the family.

> Dear Johann and Marta,
>
> We hope that things go well for you in *Amerika*.. We got your letter about the war and Johann being in the army. Every suppertime in our family prayers Karl prays for his safety and for all of you. Because I do not know how to send him a letter in the army, I will send this to Helvetia and you, Marta, can pass on the news to Johann. Karl and Emily have made a few improvements to the family home. It needed a new roof and Karl had two small rooms built on the back. One opens off the kitchen. It is supposed to be for a girl Karl wants to hire to help Emily with the cooking and housekeeping. The other room, which opens off the parlor is for *Mutti*. She has trouble going up the steps, so she now has a nice little bedroom. During the days she spends a lot of time sitting in the kitchen. I have the whole attic to myself. I have my desk and two nice chairs. Emily got a nice carpet for the end where I have my chairs and desk. She put up some curtains. It certainly looks a lot nicer than when all us boys lived up there. Gustav is doing very well in Nikolai. Last year he invented a process for making green straw paper in his mill. He can do it cheaper than other mills, so he is getting a lot of business. This year he is building a new paper mill in Nikolai. He has built a big house for his family. Right now paper is a lot better business than linen. Karl and I still run the business, but we buy most of the goods from a factory that uses steam looms. We still have a few of our old

weavers who do very fine goods for us, but most of the folks
who used to weave have given up. The machines could weave so
much cheaper and faster. Quite a few of the young people have
moved to Breslau and some of the smaller cities and found work
there. The older folks scratch out a living on their small farms.
We have had quite a few funerals lately, mostly old people.
Our old neighbor Sharf died last winter. *Doktor* Felsman had
a bad fall and cannot go around to visit his patients any more.
Some still come to his house and he takes care of them there.
Teacher Radecke also died. The church was packed for his
funeral. So many of his pupils who still live around here came.
It has been hard to find a new teacher and they may have to
close the school. Because so many young families have moved
away, there are not as many children. We talk about you both
often, and your little girls. We pray that the war will soon end
and Johann can come home from the army. God be with you,
and praises be to Him.

Brother Julius

"We have to write to tell them that you are home from the army. We
just did not think to do that," Marta reminded Johann.

"You are right. I thought of it a couple of times, but then forgot to
do it."

"I did write once after you were gone to the army, but after that there
was so little to tell. I hate to write just about troubles."

"I guess that is how I got out of the habit. At first we wrote several
times a year. But then, when work was so hard to find and our dreams were
not coming true, I just did not have the heart to write."

"I write to Papa and Katerina. Mainly I want to know how little Karl
is getting along. They never write long letters, but they do tell me how Karl
is growing. They were worried, too, when you went to the army. I worry
about them. Katerina has been sick. She has to walk with a stick."

"I am sorry to hear that."

"You know, Johann, I think that taking care of Karl may be too hard for
her. We have to bring him over here, so she doesn't have so much work."

"A growing boy would not fit into our little house. We do not have
enough room."

"He is going to have to come before long. We have to figure out how
to get a bigger house."

"You are talking like a crazy woman. How could we afford a bigger
house?"

"We have to find a way, even if we have to borrow money to get another place."

"Without being able to do steady work, who would be foolish enough to lend us money?"

"We still have that hundred dollars in the bank that we have promised to keep for an emergency. Maybe this is an emergency."

They both knew that "emergency" meant money for the trip back to Silesia, in case they had to abandon their effort to live in America. Like their other arguments about bringing Karl to America, the conversation gradually petered out.

In Matti's kitchen, Marta sat across the table from her good friend making small talk. Suddenly she gave a huge sigh and began to cry quietly.

"What's the matter, *Liebchen*?" Matti reached out to pat Marta's hand.

"I do not know what has gone wrong," Marta sobbed. "Something bad is happening. I don't know...."

"Don't cry. Tell me."

"It's Johann. I don't know what is wrong."

"You mean his stomach trouble?"

"No. It is more than that. I don't know...."

"What do you mean?"

"Don't say anything to anybody, not even Paulus. Promise?"

"All right. I don't like to see you so unhappy. Tell me what is wrong."

"Well. Something, I don't know what, stands between me and Johann. Ever since he came home from the war, at night...in our bed...he is so far away."

"This is since he came home?"

"*Ja*. He always liked to hold me in his arms. Well, we had four babies.... But now...now he just turns toward the wall. He has touched me only once since right after he came home. If I try to reach out to him, he just says that he doesn't feel good, or that he is worn out. I don't understand what is wrong," Marta sobbed.

Matti held Marta's hand tightly. "I would find it hard to believe...but do you think he goes to some other woman?"

"I don't think he would do that. I sometimes think that something must have happened to change him while he was in the army. He does not say much. He did tell me that he was in one bad battle and was almost sure he would be killed. But that is all he has said."

"Do you think it has anything to do with his stomach sickness?"

"I know he worries about that. He is not very strong, not like he was before. He always says he is so tired."

Matti nodded.

Marta wiped her eyes, "I don't know if he is worried about having more babies because he can't work steady, or if he has no love for me. He has changed so much."

"I can see how he might worry over more babies."

"He did say that he worries about never being healthy again. He told me that he worries if I would be able to take care of the family if the sickness got so bad that he couldn't go on."

"I can understand that...."

"Matti, you are the best friend I ever had. I just had to tell somebody. I am so worried and so unhappy. Don't forget, you promised not to tell Paulus or anyone."

Matti hugged Marta, enfolding her slight figure. "You can count on me...any time."

One of the things Johann noticed was the web of rumors that was woven from one end of Helvetia to the other. On the street, in the saloons, at the factory, people were always telling something that they had just heard. There were rumors about battles that were being won or lost, of new draft calls, of people who were secretly helping the southern cause. Johann said to Rabert that it seemed that every time somebody came back from a visit to Coaltown, a flood of rumors swept across Helvetia.

He said, "Coaltown is like a big funnel. They pour in the wild stories about what is going on in the country, and it runs right down into Helvetia."

"You are right," Rabert replied. "I try to give the real news in *Die Zeitung*. But I get it from the newspapers that come to me on the *Star Gray Eagle*. Even that news can be twisted by the editors of those papers. I try to make a judgment about what seems to be true, before I put it in my paper. Sometimes I have a hard time knowing what is true."

"But like you have said many times, newspaper men put in their own opinions."

"Just look at the difference between *The Reporter* and *Die Zeitung*. I am a Republican and favor President Lincoln. The Coaltown editor is a Democrat who wants to keep the Union, but wants the war to end by making a compromise on slavery with the south."

"*Ja.* Your wife helped us to try to read a few articles in the *Indianapolis Journal* and in *The Reporter* she brought to the house. Even though we had to work a lot to understand many of the words, she helped us see what they were talking about"

Rabert smiled, "Gretchen is a good teacher."

"We could see that they were very different. Of course, I know for myself that there is a lot of difference between Indianapolis and Coaltown."

"In Coaltown, and probably in Indianapolis too, there are people who are against the war. They are called Copperheads,..sometimes Butternuts. I read in the *Indianapolis Journal* that there is a group called the Sons of Liberty. They seem to be mostly in southern Indiana."

"You mean they come right out against the war."

"At first they were not very open, because they did not want to be accused of being southern sympathizers, or even traitors."

"*Ja*, there was that story last year when Gruber came back from Coaltown. He told us there was a lot of excitement over there because they said spies in the post office were opening some people's mail; they suspected them of being for the south."

"I remember that," Rabert said. "I also remember that meeting they had in Coaltown on New Year's Day, just before the war. They drew up those six resolutions. One of them even proposed that the border between the north and the south be further up in Indiana, not along the Ohio River, so we would be part of the south. That one did not pass, but it did show that a good many men there were with the south. That left a real bitter taste in a lot of mouths."

"That would make us like Kentucky, wouldn't it?"

"*Ja*. There was a big fuss a few months later when Major Key, who was always well thought of in Coaltown, was forced to give up his commission, because he was the one who had proposed that a committee be formed to draw up the resolutions. He did not even support that resolution, but they made him resign anyway."

"I never heard anything like that going on here in Helvetia."

"I doubt very much if we have any Copperheads here. Practically everyone in town comes from Switzerland or Germany. We do not have any family ties in the south. We have never approved of slavery."

"*Ja*, I have never heard anybody here who sides with the south. If they do, they keep their mouths shut."

"You will not hear much of that in some of the other towns either. Most of those who are against the war are speaking out in political terms. They are Democrats and are thinking about how they can vote Lincoln out of office and end the war. The election comes up this year."

"It seems so strange that people can speak out against the government like they do. At home you would have been in real trouble."

Rabert nodded thoughtfully, "I know that all too well..." He paused then went on, "Governor Morton has been making strong speeches accusing the Democrats of being unpatriotic because they are not supporting the war. He even called the Copperheads traitors. I support Morton, but I sometimes think this is more politics than principle. He does not hesitate to call anybody who opposes him a Copperhead."

"How does the editor of *The Reporter* get away with it? Is he a Copperhead?" Johann asked.

"Even though I do not agree with him on most things, I would not want to hang that name on him. He can write as he does every week because you notice he always starts by making a strong case for preserving the Union. I give him credit for believing that. He really blames everybody on both sides who is fanning the fires of the war. He hates those northerners who speak out so strongly against slavery. He also has nothing good to say about the southerners he calls firebrands, who started the war and keep it going. He'd like to hang them all."

"That is pretty strong talk. Would he hang the president too?"

"He has never suggested that, but he would like to get rid of him by voting in a Democrat president in the election. He believes that that would settle the war and go back to the way things were before the secession and the war."

"I cannot see that happening after all the fighting and dying."

"Well, the war will have to end someday. The two political parties just have different visions of how it will end for the best." Rabert began shuffling through papers in his desk drawer. Finally he pulled out a piece of newspaper.

"I saved this piece that he wrote in *The Reporter* a little while ago. I think it pretty much shows how his thinking goes. Let me read it with you. Some of his English is pretty fancy.

'The *Indianapolis Journal*, and other dirty abolitionist sheets, make charges that there are in existence, in Indiana, treasonable associations, to resist the payment of taxes, preventing the enlistment of soldiers and other damnably treasonable purposes--These charges against the citizens of Indiana, whose devotion to the best interest of the country is the theme of honest laudation in every portion of the loyal states, are caught up and rehashed by the *Louisville Journal*.

Since the first publication of these charges time sufficient has elapsed for somebody to be caught, at least the locality where meetings are held could be determined and some good men be set to watch for the miscreants; but this has not been done. We get vague rumors, suspicion, and charges. We will contribute our mite in exposing such persons and associations and in bringing the offenders to justice; but we do not believe there are such associations, and have never believed it; it is only one of the brood of pestilent falsehoods fabricated to aid the sinking cause of the party in power in the coming contest in Indiana.'"

Rabert returned the paper to his desk drawer, "So you see, he is loyal to the Union, but he is strongly opposed politically to the president. He does not seem to believe that there really are Copperheads in the state."

"What do you think?"

"There certainly are people in the north who oppose the war. A few of them really want the south to win and become an independent country. But it is my belief that a larger group are simply Democrats who have always believed that the way to preserve the Union is to let the south keep its slaves. They oppose the secession, but they do not oppose slavery for the south."

"How will it end?"

"The election will tell us. The people will vote for the approach they think is best, just as they did four years ago. We will see."

Marta looked up from the garden where she was on her knees picking beans. Coming around the corner of the house was Max Blum. Johann was leaning heavily on his co-worker.

"Johann got sick at the factory...asked me to bring him home... vomited a lot of blood and fainted."

"Bring him inside. Let's put him here in the rocker in the kitchen." She went on, "Johann, how do you feel?" She stroked his hair.

"I feel weak and dizzy. Max almost had to carry me along the street."

"...you be all right, Marta?" Max panted.

"I can manage."

"Then I...get back to the factory. Rest, Johann. *'wiederseh'n*." Blum shook Johann's hand and walked quickly away.

Johann put his head in his hands, "I am so sorry. I thought I was better. I have not felt good for a couple of days."

"I will go get that new doctor. We haven't needed anyone since Dr. Rupp died...What is this new man's name?"

"Brucker, I think Rabert said."

"Will you be all right if I leave you here with the girls. I could send Emma to get Matti."

"Now that I am sitting down, I am not dizzy. I will be all right."

It was suppertime when they heard the doctor's step on the porch. He was tall and straight, with gray hair and a short beard. He put down his hat and his satchel on the kitchen table and pulled up a chair beside Johann.

"Let's have a look at you. Your wife tells me you were a sergeant. I was surgeon for the 23rd Indiana for two years. So we are brothers," he laughed. "Now what happened before you came home from work."

"This morning was nothing different. I just varnished one chair after another on my table and sandpapered the ones I did yesterday. I do not have heavy work, nothing more to lift than a chair. All of a sudden I got this awful pain in my stomach. I had to vomit. I got as far as the fire bucket by the door. I just kept retching up blood again and again. Then I fainted."

"You have done this before?"

"*Ja*, but this is the first time I fainted. I vomited many times in the last couple of months I was in the army and then for about six months after I got sent home. Then I got so I didn't feel sick all the time and I didn't have to vomit. I was feeling good enough to work. All this excitement with the raiders, I guess, got me stirred up. I do watch duty with the *Förster*."

"What did Dr. Rupp advise?"

Marta said, "He just let Johann eat milk soup for several months. That seemed to help."

"Let's go back to that. If it helped before, it should do it again."

"How soon can I go back to work?" Johann asked, looking to see Marta's expression. "I have to work."

"We have to see. You better not think about working for a week or two. Let's get your strength back." The doctor made no move to leave, but leaned back in the chair.

"I think I have heard my friend, Charles Rabert, talk about you. You spend some evenings down at his office."

"*Ja*, we know Frau Rabert too. She is helping us learn to read a little English.," Marta said.

"Good for you. I knew Charles at Heidelberg. I am another Forty-eighter. We both got in trouble with politics when we were students. And we both came to America. I first went to Troy to practice medicine. That was about a year before you started to build Helvetia here. I did not know Charles was in Helvetia until I got a copy of *Die Zeitung* and saw that he was the editor. I rode down to his office and surprised him. He almost fell off his chair when I walked through the door."

"He is a good man, a very smart man."

"That he is. I have always respected him as a good thinker. He has the best newspaper around here. He is so reasonable. He does not rant and rave like some others."

"I have learned so much from him." Johann said. "I would not know anything at all about America if it were not for him and our school teacher, Paulus Frantz. They are so much better educated than me, so I keep my ears open and my mouth closed."

Marta added, "And Frau Rabert is so kind. She never laughs when we make awful mistakes trying to read the newspaper in English. She says she is proud of us wanting to learn some English."

"If you are to become real Americans you will have to be able to talk to all the different people in the country. It is all right to talk to a *Landsman auf Deutsch* here in Helvetia and to read *Die Zeitung*. But you will know more about the country if you can read the big city newspapers and talk to the people from other places."

Marta went on, "Frau Rabert says that it is important that the children learn English in school, not only German."

Johann added, "And us too. If you never put a foot outside Helvetia, you might think you do not really need English. But even over in Coaltown there are many people who do not speak German. In the army our regiment was all German and Swiss. Even our colonel, even though he was English American, could talk to us in pretty good German. But when we were with other regiments, it was hard to know what to do. And in the cities... well, we saw how that was when we traveled across the country from New York. We always had to look around for somebody who could talk German before we could do anything."

The doctor said, "I learned that same lesson. After I had to get out of Heidelberg, I went to Italy for a year. I had to learn Italian before I could really get along. Then I came to America in 1851. I knew some English from being with an English student at Heidelberg. I learned to read English, but talking it was something very different. Once I got to Troy I had patients who could only speak German and patients who could only speak English. I was the only doctor around, so I had to be able to understand them all. I read and read, until it was no longer a problem."

"We do the best we can."

"Keep at it. It is worth your time. Well, I must be on my way. I will stop again next week and see how you are feeling. Just take it easy."

"What do we owe you for coming?" Johann asked.

"Let us say for this first visit it is one old soldier helping another old soldier. You can pay me for the next time I come," he laughed.

Rabert stopped at the house the next evening, having heard of Johann's illness. When Johann mentioned his new doctor, Rabert smiled. "He is a fine man and a good doctor. Did he tell you that we knew each other at Heidelberg? We were quite a team in forty-eight. He rounded up the other students to meet and discuss ways to make the country more democratic, and I made the speeches. When the government started cracking down, throwing people in jail, threatening to close the University, a lot of us packed up over night and went home. Our parents realized right away that we were going to have trouble in our own cities, so they helped us get out of the country. I got the first ship I could to America. Imagine how surprised I was years later when he came to the newspaper office and I learned that he was the doctor in the next town a few miles down the river. We had quite a reunion."

"You are lucky to find somebody you knew in the old country."

"He is still a good friend. Did he tell you he was in the army?"

"*Ja*, he said we were old soldiers."

"After he was in Troy for several years, he was elected to the Indiana legislature. When the war started, he resigned and became an army surgeon. His ideals from forty-eight would not let him stay out of the struggle. He got back from the army just about the time that Dr. Rupp died. So Magnus moved, with his wife and son, over here to Helvetia to take over. He still sees some of his patients from Troy."

Marta said, "It is good to have a doctor in town. He got over here just a few hours after Johann was brought home from the factory."

"He will get you back on your feet. Does he think you are going to be laid up for long, Johann?" Rabert asked.

"He did say I could not work for a while. That was not good news; I need to work."

"I know. But, maybe, while you have to rest at home, you would like some more English newspapers to practice on. Gretchen will stop by with a few."

As they were struggling to read a copy of the *Louisville Journal*, Marta protested, "I don't understand all this talk about 'draft.' What is that?"

Johann answered, "It means *Wehrpflicht.* "

"I thought that was why all the Prussians came to this country. They didn't want to be drafted into the Kaiser's army."

"It says in the paper that President Lincoln has called for 500,000 more men. It says it is the third call this year. He has asked for more than a million men this year."

"All those men! All those children and wives! I hate that."

"The army needs the men if we are going to win."

"Win! Win?" Marta said, "Who wins? Some poor woman with her children?"

"But men are being lost in battles. Men are being sent home with wounds or sickness. Somebody has to take their place. Somebody had to take my place so I could come back to Helvetia."

The mounting calls for more men were a constant topic of conversation in the streets and saloons, the office of *Die Zeitung* and the factories, the kitchens and bedrooms of Helvetia. Sitting at the kitchen table one August evening, Marta and Matti could hear Paulus and Johann talking on the porch.

"I heard that our Troy Township has a quota of 176 men," Paulus said. "That is a lot of men."

"It said in *Die Zeitung* that Perry County is one of the few counties that has always filled its quota with volunteers. Nobody ever had to be drafted from here."

"It is going to get harder and harder. Most of the young fellows have already volunteered."

Johann said proudly, "We have been reading some things in *The Reporter* from Coaltown. The paper said that one of their men, a fellow named Schneider, just got back from Jeffersonville on the packet. He said that they had the names from Troy Township on the wheel for the draft, but that he persuaded them not to make the draw because we always got volunteers. They said they would wait ten days."

"I heard that too. Some of the men might need the bounty. Now the army is paying $100 for each year of enlistment. The County Board has voted to add another $50. Now Col. Mason, who I think lives in Coaltown, is trying to get people to give to a fund to add to the bounty for Troy Township."

"I know how hard it was for Marta when I was in the army. I sure was wishing I had some extra money to help her. I sent as much home from my pay as I could, but it was never enough."

"This bounty is getting to be a regular business. Some places, where they are not getting volunteers, have started paying big amounts. There was a fellow came through on the *Star Gray Eagle* a few days ago. He was sent out from someplace in Ohio. He was offering $300 in bounty in addition to what the army was paying."

"If that keeps up, Troy Township won't have enough volunteers to meet the quota. But you can't blame the men who need the money."

"In these latest drafts, the government put in a new system. If you are on the list to be drafted, you can pay what they call a commutation fee of $300 to the government, and they take your name off the list. That is where they are getting the money to pay the $300 for volunteering. They say that out in the east thousands of men are paying that fee. Some bosses are paying the fee for their good workers, to keep them on the job."

"The paper said something about buying substitutes. What is that?"

"The law said you could pay somebody to take your place if you were drafted. At first they did not pay a whole lot, but the price kept going up and up. They say that is the reason they set the commutation fee at $300. If you could get excused from the draft for $300, you would not pay more than that for a substitute."

"It sounds like if you have money, you don't have to go to the army. There are enough poor people around who need the money."

Paulus nodded, "That seems unfair to me, too. It makes it a 'poor man's war.'"

"It must be working. They get enough volunteers to fill the quotas."

"I read somewhere that of all the millions of men in the army only about 10,000 have actually been drafted. The rest are volunteers and bounty men."

After supper, when the girls were in their bed, Marta turned to Johann, "I had an idea. Matti and I were talking today. She told me that that Frau Heinzl, who died, was a seamstress. She had a sewing machine. Her

475

husband would be willing to sell it for eight dollars. I would like to buy it. I could do some sewing for people, the ones Frau Heinzl sewed for. That would help us with some money. It would pay for itself in no time."

"Bless your heart," Johann smiled. "I am feeling some better. Soon I will be able to go back to the factory."

"But even then, I could help. I like to sew. I suppose this machine is not too much different from the one I used to run at Fraulein's in Neuhaus."

"Well, you could make clothes for the girls."

"I can do more than that. There are only a few machines in Helvetia. People need a lot of things sewed. *Was denkst?*"

"If you want to. But you already have so much to do."

Marta seemed to have new energy after she had brought home the sewing machine. Paulus had loaded it on to his wheel barrow and brought it to the house. Johann helped bring the machine into the kitchen.

"I made room for it over here by the window. Put it here," Marta directed.

"It is pretty crowded in here," Johann suggested.

"Move the wood box out on the porch. It will mean a few extra steps, but it will give room for the machine."

Later Marta said, "I have my first order. Frau Schreiber wants me to make her a dress. She will pay me a dollar and a half for making it. She has the material. That will get me started."

"Are you sure it won't be too much work for you?"

"I like to sew. If the girls don't keep hanging on to my skirt, I can get a dress finished in a couple of days. If I would have too many people wanting things, I would just have to tell them that I can't do it right away."

A week later, Coaltown and Helvetia were thrown into near panic by a man who had rowed from Hainesville, across the river from Coaltown. He reported that a group of armed horsemen had ridden into the town. Rumors immediately spread that another raid like Morgan's was underway. A rider was sent to Helvetia to warn that the Hainesville had been occupied.

There had been a Union gunboat, *Springfield*, tied up at Coaltown since Morgan had invaded Indiana. It was an old stern-wheeler which had been crudely converted into an ironclad. It mounted one large Parrott gun on its foredeck.

Hearing of the raiders in Hainesville, the officer in command of the gunboat, quickly got up steam, pulled out into mid-river and made ready to fire. The grocer from Hainesville who had carried the alarm across the river went along on the *Springfield*.

He clutched at the captain's sleeve. "You can't bombard our town. You'll do more damage than the raiders."

Captain Edmund Morgan tried to reassure him. "Don't worry. I'll do the aiming myself. We can shoot over the rooftops and scare them off. They will know that we can hit them if we want to."

The man pled, "Be very careful. Please, be careful."

"Just trust me."

They could see the people of Hainesville running into the stone church for protection. Others were running toward the edge of town.

"They'll get in some of the mineshafts out there," the grocer said.

The captain sighted down the long barrel of the cannon. "That will do it. Fire!"

There was a mighty roar, a burst of smoke and the scream of the shell arching toward Hainesville. There followed an explosion on the hill just beyond the town.

The crew reloaded. The captain aimed again and fired.

"Please be careful. My family is over there. Those are the houses of my friends."

"Trust me,' the captain insisted. "I just want those raiders to know that if they keep the town we can destroy them."

"You can't do that," the grocer argued.

"My friend, we will not have to. They are not going to argue with this big gun. I am so sure that I promise you on my word, that if there is any damage from our gunfire, I will personally pay for it."

This did not fully restore the merchant's confidence. "I beg you, aim carefully."

One of the officers of the *Springield* was scanning the far shore with his telescope. "They are riding out. See, over there, beyond the last white house..."

The captain carefully reaimed the cannon. "Now that they're out of town let's give them a shot to speed them on their way. This one will not be high. Fire!"

As summer wore on *Die Zeitung* and the English papers Gretchen brought to them were full of accounts of the Union attacks on Atlanta. Some of the papers had maps that showed in battle after battle the progress of Sherman's army.

Johann pointed to the map in the *Louisville Journal*, "See how all the railroads come together in Atlanta. If Sherman gets that, he can cut off most of the supplies to the southern army."

"After all those battles you would think that they would be so tired of fighting that they would just give up," Marta answered.

A few days later, late in the afternoon the *Star Gray Eagle* brought the news that Atlanta had been captured. The bells in the two churches began to ring, spreading the good news. The *Förster* gathered and began a spontaneous celebration. Men gathered driftwood from along the riverbank and from nearby woodland. A huge pile was made near the boat landing. As soon as it got dark the whole town gathered and lit the bonfire. The *Förster* shot their muskets into the air and fired their little cannon several times out over the river. Most of the members of the town band brought their instruments and began an impromptu concert. The brewery wagon brought kegs of beer and crates of glasses.

Johann and Marta walked toward the excitement on the riverfront. Johann carried Jenny and Marta held the hands of the other girls. Every time there was shooting Jenny began to shriek, burying her face in Johann's shoulder. Couples were dancing on the wharf boat, stomping and whirling to the tunes the band played.

"It has been a long time since we saw people having a good time like this," Marta said with a smile.

"It almost makes me want to dance too," Johann laughed.

"You have to learn how first," Marta joked. "I always wanted to dance with you at the fair in Neuhaus, but you always said they didn't teach you to dance in the country."

"They didn't," Johann protested.

"I don't believe you. You just did not want to learn. I know they dance a lot out in the country. I could teach you."

Johann just shook his head.

Marta pressed on. "Look at Matti and Paulus. Even with his bad leg, they are dancing."

"We can't. We have the girls to look after in this crowd."

"Oh, all right," Marta pouted. "But I am going to ask Matti to teach you, since you won't let me."

"It will make my stomach worse," Johann groaned, turning his head so Marta would not see his smile.

"You scoundrel," she laughed, nudging him in the ribs. "I have a good mind to ask Paulus to dance with me. Here, you hold the baby!"

"You wouldn't!" Johann protested.

"I will. I have not danced since I was a girl in Neuhaus. It is about time."

Just then Matti and Paulus came walking from the wharf boat. Matti pushed her damp hair from her face. "Quite a celebration. It made me feel like a girl again. Here, I'll look after the children. You and Johann dance a while."

Marta laughed, "The rascal says he doesn't know how. Come on, Johann, this is our chance. I'll show you in a minute."

"Go on, Johann," Paulus urged. "If I can do it, you can." He gave Johann a push toward the wharf.

Marta took his arm and pulled him along. "Come on. Let's try it."

Once out on the wharf boat, Marta gave quick instructions. "Put your arms like this. Now two quick steps this way, turn. Just keep doing that. There is such a crowd, no one will be watching us."

Johann followed instructions, and soon they were part of the swirling crowd in spite of Johann's awkwardness. Seeing the sparkle in Marta's eyes, which he had not seen for a long time, Johann said, "You do enjoy this, don't you?"

"I haven't felt like this in a long time. For a few minutes there is no work, no responsibilities, no worries, just *Genuss*, we need some enjoyment in our lives."

"Are you so unhappy?" Johann asked.

"I am not unhappy all the time. I have my girls; I have my home. But it is so nice to have just a few minutes when I am having fun, just having fun, nothing else. I know it can't be all the time, but a few minutes are wonderful."

"A little dancing means that much to you?"

"That is just part of it. It is everything put together. The whole town is celebrating. Everybody is happy. Listen to the laughing. When was the last time you heard so many people laughing at the same time in Helvetia?"

"*Richtig*. The whole town is happy tonight, even the families whose men are far away in the army."

"It is those who are far away who bring us sadness," Marta said slowly and looked away.

Within the next few days it was clear from the newspapers that the fall of Atlanta was just one victory. The war was going on in many places. Men were still fighting and dying.

A few days later another letter from Julius arrived. In it was a bank draft for 200 *Reichstaler*, which, he said, Mother wanted to send to Johann and Marta. Because she knew it was hard for him to work when he was sick, they needed the money more than she did. Her needs were taken care of and she wanted Johann to have this now. There would be a little more when the time came to divide her estate.

In the following days Marta kept up her steady argument for buying a larger house.

"We need more rooms. If we can bring Karl over, we will need a room for him. I have been asking at the store if they knew of anyone who was going to sell a house."

Johann said angrily, "Marta, you had no right to start talking about that. We have not decided to get a bigger house."

"You said that we did not have the money for a bigger house, but now you have the money from Julius. Why not sell this house and get one with the room we need."

"But we don't know if we will need the money just to live. You forget that I am not getting regular pay."

"I know that we need a bigger house," Marta said stubbornly. "I am going to keep asking around."

A few weeks later Marta brought up again the subject of a larger house. "At the store today Herr Gofinet told me that the Frau Schultz on Ninth Street in back of the Catholic Church is going to sell her house. She is going to live with her daughter in Troy. I walked past the house on my way home. I have never been inside but it looks bigger than this house. I think we should go to talk with her."

"You don't give up, do you?"

"I have always gone along with you without one word of complaint. Now I am asking you for this one thing," Marta argued quietly. "Just come with me to look at the house."

Johann answered grudgingly, "Oh, all right. We can go tomorrow."

The house on Ninth Street was indeed larger than the home they had built. Widow Schultz was anxious to sell it.

"I wanted to sell the house ever since Georg died last spring. He was sick—a couple of years. Right after we got the house built, his heart was bad. He could not lie down in bed and would just gasp. It was a mercy when he died."

"How much are you asking for the house?" Johann asked.

"My son says it is worth four hundred."

"Seems like a lot. I would have to paint it and fix it up some."

"We couldn't do anything to the house while Georg was so sick."

Marta put in, "We would take good care of the house. I like a nice clean place. So it would be in good hands. We just need more room."

Johann said, "I think I know your son. Wasn't he in the 60th Regiment?"

"*Ja*, he still is. They are in Louisiana. So you were in the 60th too."

"I was sent home because my stomach is bad."

"He still has a lot of stomach trouble," Marta added. "He can't work regularly, but we need a bigger house for our family."

Widow Schultz looked at them long and hard. "I really can't stay here much longer by myself."

Johann, thinking that she would probably not accept a lower price, said, "We could pay 350 dollars. I couldn't pay any more than that because there will have to be some work done."

"I need to talk to my daughter first. Let me send word to her. Come back next Monday and I'll have her answer." She smiled at Marta, "I like to think that somebody will have my house who will take good care of it."

"Oh, I would. I would."

The offer was accepted and Johann began to talk to friends from the furniture factory, to Rabert and Paulus, to see if he could find a buyer for the house he had built. A few days later Max Blum stopped on his way home from work.

"My brother and his wife are looking....They been renting one of those places that were thrown together by the Colonization Society right at the start. Pretty flimsy because they were in such a hurry to get them up. I told them you built this place yourself and that it was pretty nice."

"Bring them around to see it."

"How much you going to ask for it?"

"It is a good sturdy house. It should be worth $450 with the next door lot. I asked Fleischer, the carpenter who helped me put it up, and he thought that was a fair price."

Johann experienced an excitement he had not anticipated as he told Paulus about the houses he had bought and sold.

"It really was Marta's idea. She is right, I guess. We do need more room. But I grew up in a house where my brothers and I all lived in the loft. We got used to not having a lot of *Lebensraum*. "

"When are you moving?"

"As soon as I can get a farmer with a couple of strong sons to haul us over to Ninth Street."

"I suppose Marta is excited. She will want to show Matti the new place. They have a good time *klatschen*. Matti will be happy that Marta will not live any further away than you are now."

"Frau Schultz has gone to Troy, so I have a chance to go over the place and see what needs to be done before we move in. Fleischer is going to meet me there tonight and look around. I hope it isn't too much."

It took the carpenter several weeks to finish the repairs to the house on Ninth Street.

"Digging out the cellar under the kitchen was the biggest part of the job," Fleischer reported. "But now you will have a place to store your potatoes and turnips. I put in good solid stone walls."

"I used to work with a mason. You did a good job," Johann replied.

"This is the time to fix these things. It is a good house but, like lot of these places, some of the wood was too green when it was built. I had to replace a lot of the beams underneath. Your floors will be a lot straighter now and the plaster won't crack any more."

"When I looked at the house, it seemed in such good condition."

"Those crooked beams were the only real trouble I found. But now you have a lot nicer place. Your wife has a nice brick bake oven. You have a good little stable out in back, where you can keep a cow. Yes, sir, a nice little place."

"We were so crowded on Twelfth Street, but I will miss that house. I built most of it with my own hands with your help. Blum bought a good little place there."

Sitting at the kitchen table one evening after their move, Johann was writing in his *Tagebuch*.

"You know, I have not written in this book for years. I got out of the habit once we were in America. There was so much to do. But I think I'll put in it a list of the improvements we have made to this place and what it cost us."

Marta looked over his shoulder, "How much did you have to pay Fleischer?"

"A lot more than I thought it would be. With all the material, we paid $290."

"We paid Frau Schultz $350 for the house. So we almost spent more for fixing it up than to buy it."

"Yes, but we got $450 for the house on Twelfth Street. So we have to pay the rest from the money Julius sent. We will still have just a little money in the bank."

"I hope it was not foolish to spend so much on the house," Marta worried.

"Now don't complain! You kept saying that we needed a bigger house. Now we have got it!"

Marta nodded her response.

Johann continued, "I guess we should feel lucky. We were able to have enough money to come to America and make a home here because we had my inheritance from my father. Now the money from Mother is getting us a bigger house. If only I could work, things would get better."

"Yes, but try not to worry."

"I have been feeling a little better. I am going to try to go back to work."

The newspapers they tried to read and the conversations Johann had with Paulus and Rabert focused on the growing interest in the next election of the president. Rabert began writing articles to help people in Helvetia understand both the process of electing a president and the candidates and their issues. President Lincoln was seeking to be re-elected. Rabert explained that this was uncommon. For the past several decades presidents had served for only four years. *Die Zeitung* argued that Lincoln should be re-elected so he could win the war and restore the Union. The editor also pointed out that there were some other Republicans who wanted to be president, but that Lincoln was clearly the leader.

The paper explained that there was a struggle between the congress and the president over how the south would be handled after the war. Some in congress wanted the south to be severely punished for rebelling. They favored seizing the property of any man who fought for the south. The abolitionist wing of the party wanted slavery to be totally abolished in the reunited country and all the slaves set free. Most wanted the unconditional surrender of the Confederacy. There were long debates over who should control the reunification: congressional leaders who wanted radical changes or the President who wanted to try to heal the country. Rabert wrote that the Republican convention in June showed that the desire to heal was beginning to gain favor. A Union sympathizer from the Confederate state of Tennessee, Andrew Johnson, was nominated to be Lincoln's vice-president.

In Coaltown, *The Reporter* gave a very different picture. The editor's longstanding allegiance to the Democratic Party was complicated by the fact that the party was split in two. One half was called the Peace Democrats. The editor pointed out that while he shared their opposition to any emancipation and their desire to restore the Union to the way it had been before the war, he did not like the strong support they received from the Copperheads and Sons of Liberty, who were undermining the war effort of the north.

The editor's loyalty was much more with the segment of the party known as War Democrats, led by George McClellan, who had been the renowned Union general in the early years of the war, but had been relieved of his command by Lincoln. The War Democrats clearly wanted to win the war and then have a convention in which all the states would reestablish the Union on the basis of states rights, which implied that the southern states would still have the right to be slaveholders.

The Democratic controlled legislature in Indiana had voted against allowing soldiers to vote without coming back home, because they feared that these would be Republican votes. Union generals in the south were urged by the Republicans to grant furloughs to as many soldiers as they could spare, so that they could return home to vote in those states which did not permit soldiers to vote in the field.

The Democrats were confident that the respect many veterans and soldiers had for McClellan would sweep him to victory. To try to win votes away from the Peace Democrats, McClellan's vice-presidential candidate was George Pendleton, a close ally of the Copperhead leader Vallandigham.

The political campaign of 1864 was very spirited. Rabert asked Johann and Paulus if they wanted to go with him in his buggy to Coaltown for a political rally that was planned for Saturday night.

"You would be interested in this. You should see how the political parties work. You should hear the speeches and see the excitement. I know,

Johann, that you cannot vote yet, but Paulus and I will vote. You should see how people make up their minds about their vote."

"*Ja*, I will not be able to understand all of the speeches, but it would be good to see."

When they reached the courthouse square in Coaltown, huge pine torches were burning all around two wagons, covered with bunting, that had been drawn up on opposite sides of the courthouse. Nearby each of these speakers' platforms were smaller wagons and wheel barrows with barrels of beer and cups, making sure that the evening would be filled with enthusiasm. The small delegation from Helvetia first stood on the edge of the crowd gathered around the Democratic platform. A member of the Indiana legislature was the orator of the moment, shouting with leather lungs.

"We've got to get rid of that baboon in the White House. He is responsible for keeping this terrible war going. The South knows that it is beaten. I have it on good authority that already there have been messages saying that the South is willing to make peace and come back into the Union. All they want is a guarantee that they will not lose their states' rights. But, no. Lincoln isn't willing to sit down with them and work out a peace. That stubborn fool keeps insisting on freeing the slaves. The war goes on and on, our men are killed and wounded every day, all because Lincoln wants to do away with slavery. And if he gets his way, think what it will do to the country. There will be millions of ignorant black slaves roaming around the country looking for work, coming to our towns to take away our jobs, taking our women. I tell you, the whole fabric of America as we know it and love it will be destroyed.

"That must not happen. What we need is a solid leader, proven on the fields of battle, whose objective has never been to destroy the South, but to bring it back to the Union. General George McClellan will have the experience and the skill to negotiate with the Confederacy and to bring them back into the Union with honor. You can bring our men back home, you can bring peace and prosperity instead of this terrible conflict. Vote for the Democrats led by General McClellan!"

As they walked away a little, Paulus said, "It seems to me that they are saying that the whole war was a mistake, that it was fought for nothing."

Rabert turned to Johann, "Did you understand what he was saying?"

"I got the part about wanting the war to end. I do too."

485

"But he was arguing for the war to end in a particular way." Rabert then quickly filled in the details. "How would you, or the men you served with, feel about that?"

"I think everybody would be very glad for the war to end. But what he says would mean that all the sacrifices were useless. I have told you what I think: that on the battlefield men are not thinking a lot about ending slavery or bringing the south back into the country; all they think about it staying alive.. But that is very different from saying it was all useless, that the country should go back to the way it was before the war. I could not agree with that."

Both Paulus and Rabert nodded agreement.

Rabert said, "They are counting on people being so tired of the war that they will be willing to give up the cause just to end the war. They figure that all the calls for drafting more men will make people want to just give up. This is what the Copperheads have been saying all along."

"Let's see what the Republicans are saying," Paulus said, walking around the courthouse.

The crowd gathered to hear a well-known Coaltown lawyer was smaller. His empty coat sleeve suggested that he had returned from the war. He paced back and forth on the platform.

"Friends, we are close to winning this terrible war. Every day we hear reports of new victories. We know, oh, how many of us know, the high cost of this struggle to restore the Union.

"I listened to what the Democrats were saying. They want to go back to the way things were before the war, the old Union, divided between north and south. Our President, Abraham Lincoln, also wants the war to end, the Union to be restored. But, and mark these words carefully, it must be a new Union--not simply restoration of the old Union. You heard his call in the speech he gave at Gettysburg last fall--some of you read it in the newspapers from other cities that print the truth. Our President called for the making of a new nation, with a new birth of freedom. This is the cause for which so many men have died at Gettysburg and across the land. This long and bloody struggle must end with a nation, a Union, that is stronger, not weaker than it was before the war.

"Stand with Lincoln, my friends. Stand with him to bring this war to its victorious conclusion. Let all men be free to live and work in one united country. Honor our brave men who have died, that their deaths have not been in vain." A few in the crowd cheered. The rest clapped their hands a few times and turned to the wagon with the beer.

The buggy ride back to Helvetia was filled with animated conversation.

"It seemed to me that the crowd was more with the Democrat," Paulus observed.

"Maybe so. I am not surprised in Coaltown," Rabert answered. "*The Reporter* is a strong influence there. That opinion has not changed much since before the war: restore the Union but let the south go its own way, keep slavery."

"I really wish I could vote," Johann said.

"I think you could. You have been here long enough to become a citizen," Paulus answered.

"You are right. You told me it was five years after you got here. We have been here for six years. My mind has been so much on getting my health back and trying to work a little that I just lost track about being here for five years. I guess I felt so much like I was a citizen that it was not much on my mind. But tonight really showed how important it is to be able to vote."

Rabert said, "There may be enough time before this election; we should take you and some of the others to the courthouse and get your citizenship."

The following week's edition of *Die Zeitung* had a long article on the importance of becoming a citizen as soon as you were eligible.

"August," Katerina Wiesner said as he husband came into the kitchen, "You have to talk to Karl."

"What's the matter? I'm awfully tired tonight. I worked hard today; no rest at all."

"Well, I don't want to make things heavier for you, but you have to talk to that boy."

"What's he done now?" August put his coat and cap on the peg behind the kitchen door.

"He just won't mind. When I tell him to bring in some wood, or to get water from the well, he just looks at me. He defies me. Today he said back to me, "Grandpa never makes me work.'"

"I don't like to be hard on him."

"Maybe you should! If he lived with his folks, he'd have to do his share of the chores. You're just too soft on him."

"*Ja.* I suppose you are right. I do want him learn to do his share of the work. But I can't make him do it. "

"Why not? You're his grandfather. You have given him a home, food, clothes for years. You've got to make him obey."

"What do you want me to do? Give him a whipping?"

"If you don't get him straightened out, somebody else will do it later on. That will be harder on him, mark my words."

"I look at him and think: You poor little kid, you can't help it that you haven't seen your mama and papa for eight years."

Katerina shook her head. "You are a good man, August Wiesner, but you have to stand up to this boy before it is too late."

"I'll try talking to him."

"*Ja,* just like before."

A month before the election, there was great excitement when letters arrived from men in the 60th Indiana who had been fighting in Louisiana. Following a disastrous campaign along the Red River, they were moved back to Vickburg. The entire regiment was given a furlough, their first, and was being sent north by steamboat.

Helvetia prepared for the return of Company A, many of whom had not been home since their departure almost three years before. Bunting was hung on the wharf boat. When the side-wheeler *Comanche* came around the bend of the river at Troy, it gave long blasts on its deep-throated whistle. The town band began to play. As the boat came closer, the blue-coated men crowded the portside railing, perilously tilting the boat. Families were in the front ranks of the scores of townspeople who stood along the riverbank near the landing.

Johann strained to see familiar faces among the men as he and Marta stood in the crowd. Marta held Jenny and the two little girls complained that they could not see. Johann picked up Emma for a few minutes and then lifted Anna for her turn.

When the boat finally tied up and the gang-plank was lowered from the prow, men and their families embraced on the stone-covered embankment leading down to the wharf boat. Then the rest of the crowd surged forward, shaking hands, pounding backs.

Johann had a hard time seeing over the heads of people pressed in front of him.

"Let's go back up on the street. It is too crowded here," he said to Marta.

"Good. They will all come up that way."

"There's Jakob Stocker," Johann said, waving. "Stocker...Stocker. *Wie geht's?*"

Stocker had a broad smile as he gripped Johann's hand. "Hey, Sergeant. Johann, *Wie bist du?*" Stocker threw his arm around Johann's shoulder. "And here is your wife and girls. Good to see you, Marta. It is good to see everybody."

Then turning to his mother who was wiping tears from her round, red face, he said, "Let's go home, Mama. I am ready for some of your good cooking."

She clung to his arm and smiled through her tears. "You just wait 'till you see what I've been getting ready."

"Johann! Johann!"

"Albrecht," Johann saw his old friend, Geyer, coming in the crowd, holding his wife's and his daughter's hands.

One after another the men greeted each other.

A few days later Johann sat with Geyer, Bauer and Stocker under one of the trees in the park. Only Stocker wore his uniform; the other men were in their ordinary working clothes. After they had talked and joked for a while, Stocker said, "Come on, Fritz, us two bachelors need to help them get rid of some beer. Let's go over to Schlotzhauer's. I'll pay."

After they had wandered off, Geyer turned to Johann. "I can't tell you how good it is to be back in Helvetia, even if we have to go back to Louisiana in another week."

Johann answered, "I am sorry you are not finished with the army. When I heard you were coming I thought that since your three years are almost up, you were coming home to stay."

"No, they want us back," Geyer said sadly. "They said they wanted us home for the election. I don't think they knew that almost half of us can't vote."

"At least it got you here for a little time. It is so good to see you all again. I have missed you especially, Albrecht. Your Margareta brings your letters, when you can write. It is good to hear about my old friends."

"There was a lot I could not put in my letters, because I did not want to worry Margareta. We saw a lot of fighting...bad fighting."

"I have thought of that often. Here I sit in Helvetia and my friends are fighting battles. I only fought at your side those few days in Munfordville."

"After they sent us back down the Mississippi to Memphis, we were put on a fleet of boats going up the Arkansas River. There must have been 50 boats. We got put on the shore with thousands of other soldiers and attacked a place called Fort Hindman. It sure was different from Munfordville. We had a lot of gunboats and their big cannons. We did plenty of shooting too, but we had so many men and guns that the Confederates had to surrender. They just could not stand up to such a force. Then they loaded us all and our prisoners on the boats again and went back down to the Mississippi."

"Were any of our fellows hit?"

"I think that we had half a dozen wounded. One fellow, I think his name was Schweikert, from over around Coaltown was killed. I do not remember anybody from Company A getting hit. It's hard for me to keep the battles we were in separate."

"It must have been hard to keep going."

"We did not sit around like we did in Lebanon. We were on the move all the time and had one battle after another. We were part of the fight to take Vicksburg. It lasted a couple of months. General Grant had armies coming from all directions. We would move on boats to one place, then walk for miles through swamps where the mosquitos were worse than bullets. It would pour rain, and then the sun would come out to steam us, as we walked through the mud. We got so tired we could hardly put one foot in front of another. It was hard to find a place to make camp for the night, and everything was too wet to make a fire to cook. Stocker just about went crazy."

Johann laughed, "That boy needs his food. But he looks like he turned out to be a pretty good soldier."

"Stocker is all right. He even got over telling his stories about what a hero he was. Feed him and he'll fight."

"How did you do through all this, Albrecht?"

"It has not been easy. After all that marching they got us back across the Mississippi below Vickburg at a place called Bruinsburg. The steamers just kept going back and forth across the river all day and all night. They brought thousands of soldiers. Grant worked hard to get armies on all sides of Vicksburg. We went way around to the south of Vicksburg as part of the big noose Grant was laying. Once we all got across the river, there were three big Union armies. They told us we were under a General McClernand. The armies kept pushing ahead, about 5 or 10 miles apart. We had to fight for every town we came to."

"You must have been dead on your feet."

"Every river or creek we came to had the bridges burned or blown up, so we could rest for a couple of hours until they got a new bridge built. They would tear down the nearest barns and use the timbers for the bridge. Then it was march some more. We had so many men that the battles did not last long, but they were fierce if you were the first regiments to go in. We had that in a couple of places. We took some losses there. The Confederates would fall back to the next creek or river, they called them bayous, and put up a fight there. Our cannons would chase them back far enough that we could get across as soon as there was a bridge or we could wade holding our guns over our heads to keep them dry. Then we'd have to attack and drive them back some more. We had a couple of weeks of that."

"I don't think I would have had the strength to keep going like that."

"By then we were so used to it that we could almost march in our sleep. We never really made camp. At night we'd just wrap in our blanket in a ditch or under a tree. One good thing is that we had plenty of food. The farmers had all run away, so there were cows and pigs and chickens aplenty. We ate real good, when we could stop long enough to get cook fires going. We ate mostly after it got dark. We would cut strips of meat and hold them over the fire on our ramrods, if we had time. But on the days when we marched from sun-up till dark we just chomped on our hardtack."

"You know," Johann said, "it really makes me sad to hear how hard it was for you fellows. I should be with you, but I can't. I would not last a day. But you have had all that danger and I sit here safe in Helvetia. It is not that I liked being in the army, but I should be doing my duty. I should be at your side. When I came home, I promised myself that I would not enjoy pleasure while you men were still out there fighting. It just would not have been right."

"Forget it. You did not run away from the army. You were sick and they sent you home. Believe me, there have been plenty of times I wanted to be in Helvetia."

"*Ja*, but you will go back to the army when your time here is over. I'll just sit here until I am strong enough to go back to varnishing chairs."

"I hope that they send us back to some place where there is not so much fighting. I have really wished for some place like Lebanon. That all seems so peaceful now."

"It was not very hard, was it? At least not till Munfordville."

"Johann, I tell you there were times in the last couple of years when I thought I would never see Helvetia again. Don't say anything to Margareta or Marta, because I don't want her to worry. We were in an awful battle at a place called Champion Hill. The southerners were on top of a small line of hills. They had cannons up there and earthworks. There were some narrow gaps between the hills. We would charge up to the hill, try to get through one of those gaps; then they would counter-attack and drive us back again. Then we'd charge up another time. Schmidt and Rosenberger were killed and half a dozen of our fellows were wounded. I was terrified. The only way I could run forward was to think that it would be a disgrace if I turned and ran. So I charged with the rest and hoped I would not get hit. I tell you I was so scared I pissed in my pants."

"I don't know if I would have the courage to be in that kind of battle."

"You stood and fought at Munfordville, didn't you? You led us out in front of that fort."

"But we weren't charging right into their guns the way you had to....I remember when they brought Rosenberger's and Schmidt's bodies back. I marched in their funerals."

"We had five battles in three weeks after we crossed the river. Most of the time we would be in ranks, fire a volley, move ahead fifty yards, fire another volley, move ahead. We charged maybe five or six times during all those battles. But the worst of the charges was at Vicksburg. After we chased them out of Champion Hill, the southerners could only retreat back to Vicksburg, where they had forts and trenches in a big half circle around the city. They had a lot of cannons, too. It was real hilly, too, and they were always on the tops of the hills."

"Sounds impossible."

"It was. On two different days after we got there, they lined up the whole army to charge those fortifications. We were lucky not to be in the front line for that first charge. They just got wiped away. By the time our turn came, it was obvious that it was not going to work, and we got called back. But two days later..." Albrecht turned his head away so that Johann would not see the tears in his eyes.

"Two days later," he continued, "we were right behind the first ranks to charge up that hill. It was terrible. I never want to see anything like that again. The regiment ahead of us just got cut down like with a scythe. Every cannon on both sides was firing. The smoke was like fog, only it strangled you. I couldn't see anything. We were tripping over bodies and falling. Some of our men were shot. Gus Hess was killed we found out later.

There was no time to reload after you fired your musket. We just couldn't go any further. I couldn't get air. Finally I just stumbled and fell down. Then the next regiment came running up behind us and the same thing happened. It was just impossible. The southerns would roll cannon shells down the hill with their fuses lit. They would roll into the bodies which were stacked up and explode. Finally the bugles called us back down. I crawled back a way and then got up and ran down to our lines. I did not even notice that my arm had been grazed until Stocker saw the blood on my sleeve. I was lucky. It was just like a little cut, but I came that close to losing an arm, or worse."

"*Mein Gott*," Johann said. reaching out to his friend, who was wiping tears from his eyes. "That must have been terrible."

"I was so glad when they stopped charging those earthworks. I could not have gone again. I have always obeyed orders since I was in the army, but I am not sure I would have gone again. I still dream about that day. Margareta says I yell in my sleep."

"Were other fellows in the regiment hit too?"

"Three of the boys were killed and about ten, I think, wounded. The generals stopped the charges. They decided that they would starve them out. So as soon as we got rested up, they put us to work digging deep ditches all around the city. Our cannons just kept shooting, all day long, boom, boom, boom! Our boats in the river kept shooting from the other side. It must have been terrible in the city. That kept up for over a month.

"We just sat in those ditches. We hollowed out places in the hillside and put roofs over them. In some places our men dug tunnels from our trenches under the southern fortifications, filled them with gun powder and blew them up."

"That must have ended it."

"They held out for more than a month. We just sat there and would not let anything in or out of the city. They finally had no more food and had to give up. We saw some officers come out under a white flag. They got taken to headquarters somewhere. After a couple of hours, they went back again. Then a whole bunch of southern officers came out under a white flag, and there was a big meeting with our generals in the woods. We just sat in our ditches and waited. There was no more shooting. After more than a month of cannons going off every few minutes, it seemed so still. We could hear the southerns talking up in their fortifications."

"That was when they surrendered? We read about it in the newspapers."

"*Ja*, we saw the officers ride back into the city, and men yelled up and down the line, 'It is over! It is over!' We threw our hats up in the air and danced around in our ditch. I was never so glad to hear anything in my whole life.

"The next day one of our brigades marched into the city. There were white flags on all their forts. We just stayed in our ditches until they formed us up and marched us to line one of the roads coming out of Vicksburg. Then the southern army marched out between our lines. They did not have their guns, the way we did at Munfordville, but they marched out. A lot of them were carried out on litters or were lying in wagons. Our generals paroled them to go home. They looked terrible--just skin and bones, covered with ragged clothes. I'll never forget their eyes, sunken way back into their heads, glassy. They had been through a much worse time than us. I think they were as glad as we were that it was over."

"That all happened almost a year ago," Johann said. "After all that, it would seem fair to let you come home for rest."

"We stayed most of the summer at Vicksburg. Then they kept moving us around Mississippi and Louisiana. There was a lot more fighting. We lost more men. Our squad was spared. We didn't lose anybody, even though we were in some bad situations. I just can't think much about it all. This is the most I've said about it to anybody."

In his edition following the election on November 7 Rabert reported that Perry County had voted for Lincoln, who received 1112 votes. McClellan lost the county by only seventy votes. Following the newspapers in Cincinnati and Louisville, *Die Zeitung* said that the vote of the soldiers and veterans was important in Lincoln's victory in many states. They were angry about the involvement of the Copperheads in the Democratic Party.

"This war has hurt a lot of us," Geyer paused..."For the rest of our lives we are going to be marked by it. I wonder if it is worth all the suffering."

"The south is losing, so the country will come back together again."

Geyer thought for a moment. "I wonder if that can happen. Both sides have gotten so bitter. After trying to kill each other for three years, can we live in peace?"

"Things cannot be the same as they were before the war," Johann shook his head.

"Slavery will have to stop. I have wondered about that. You remember, we saw a few slaves when we were in Lebanon. But, I tell you, Johann, in

Louisiana and Mississippi there are thousands and thousands of slaves. There are way more black people than white. How will that work out when they are all free?"

Johann said, "It is not just down south. There was quite a fuss in Coaltown just before you got back. The Legion caught a boatload of raiders coming across. Col. Fournier put some of his men to guard them. He picked four Negroes, who were hiding in Coaltown after coming across the river a while back, and gave them muskets to guard the raiders. Some of the folks in Coaltown were so mad that they stormed up to Fournier and demanded that he take the guns away and put white men to guard the prisoners. The town marshall was yelling the loudest. They threatened to get rid of Fournier as head of the Legion in Coaltown. Fournier stood up to them and said he was in command. When they kept arguing, he had the marshall arrested and was going to send him to Louisville for trial. But they let him go after things calmed down. So even up here people do not trust the black men."

Geyer said, "People here do not realize how many black soldiers there are in the Union army. In some of the battles we fought there were regiments of black soldiers. Their officers were white men, but they were right in the thick of the fight. Col. Owen told us that some of them were from up north and some of them were slaves who had escaped. People should know that."

"The only thing I remember reading in the paper was about black soldiers who were shot after they surrendered," Johann added.

"I think that is why they fought so hard. They did not want to be captured....Well, Johann, we have to leave tomorrow. A steamer is supposed to pick us all up in the morning. Then we have the long ride back, I guess to New Orleans. I wonder where they will send us from there."

"Your three years will be up in a few months. Then you can be back in Helvetia to stay."

"I know. I hope our fighting is over. Surely the war can not last much longer. Well...*Auf wiedersehen..*" Geyer shook Johann's hand and slowly walked away.

Marta and Matti were sitting in the kitchen of the new house on Ninth Street, Marta was crying.

Matti tried to console her. "I know you miss your boy."

"I thought when we got the house and had more room, we could start making a way for Karl to come to us. I talk about it to Johann every few days, but he just keeps making excuses: we don't have enough money; wait until he can have steady work again."

"I am surprised he doesn't see how important this is for you."

"Johann is a kind man, but he just will not give an inch on this. He is good to the little girls, but I don't think he has any love for Karl. He never had much to do with Karl. He was just a baby, and Johann never had to take care of him. My stepmother took care of Karl while I was sick, and then, when I finally got my strength back, I took care of him. I don't think Johann held him more than a couple of times."

"Some men are like that," Matti answered, setting aside the pot of potatoes she had been peeling.

Marta nodded, "Johann takes care of the girls. He holds them on his lap, he tells them stories. If Karl came here, Johann could teach him how to do things. He would enjoy having a son."

Matti put her arm around Marta's shoulders. "I wish he could see that."

"I hate to say it, but I don't think Johann will ever bring Karl over. He won't say that, but he always has a string of reasons why Karl can't come now," Marta said, wiping tears from her cheeks.

"You'll just have to keep asking him, until he gives in."

"I thought that when we got this bigger house,.. Johann knew that I wanted it so Karl could live with us again. As soon as we got moved in, I kept asking when we could arrange for Karl to come. I can tell that it is making Johann angry. I don't know what to do."

"Do you think that if I explained the situation to Paulus, he could talk to Johann and change his mind?" Matti asked, anxious to help.

"I think it would just make him more angry to know that I had talked to somebody about it. I am just going to keep bringing it up every few weeks. When we were very young, I used to be able to get him to do what I wanted. I could coax him to do anything."

Johann came in the kitchen door as Marta was preparing supper. He was smiling broadly. "I just went down to the furniture factory and got my old job back. They said they were glad to have me."

Marta immediately responded, "Are you sure you are well enough to go to work?"

"I will never know unless I try. I have been feeling a lot better lately. I was able to help with the moving and fixing up the house. I didn't do heavy work, but I kept busy. So I decided if I could do that, I was ready to go back to work."

"Well, all right. But I don't want you doing more than you are able."

"I need to start feeling like a man again. I don't like being an invalid. There is too much to do."

"The girls will miss you around the house. They have gotten used to your stories."

"They have heard them all a couple of times. They want to know all about Endigen and Neuhaus."

"They ask me about some of the places you tell about, and some of the people." She paused. "They never ask about Karl. Is he ever in your stories?"

"I would not have much to tell about Karl. He was just a baby."

"Don't you think about him at all? I imagine what he looks like, what he doing, what he says. I often wonder what he thinks about us. I know that Papa reads him my letters. They can show him our picture, but he does not know us at all. Oh, that is so sad."

"I am sure he is happy in Neuhaus. He is well taken care of. It would be hard for him to get used to strange people and strange places."

"We wouldn't be strange for very long. He would know that he is loved here too."

"I am not sure it would be safe to come while the war is going on."

For months the war had seemed very far away. There was news of battles in Virginia; Sherman was marching across Georgia; a Confederate Army in central Tennessee was defeated at Franklin. Then suddenly Helvetia and Coaltown were alarmed again by enemy action nearby.

The wagon tire in the park clanged a warning. The *Förster* rushed to their tower. The Louisville and Henderson packet, the *Morning Star*, instead of stopping as scheduled at the wharf boat in Helvetia, had gone by, steaming as close to the Kentucky shore as possible. Armed men could be seen on the deck. There was no sign of the small number of Union soldiers who guarded every steamer on the river. No passengers were seen.

The afternoon quiet was broken by the rumble of the big Parrott gun in Coaltown. Four times, like distant thunder, the cannon was heard. It must be firing at the steamer.

By evening, reports reached Helvetia. The packet had docked in Hainesville, rather than its scheduled stop in Coaltown. Telescopes showed that a troop of men, assumed to be southern guerillas, had captured the boat at some landing downstream. Col. Fournier loaded the available men of the Legion onto the *Springfield* and prepared to cross the river to attack the marauders. He ordered the cannon to fire over the town several times and then to aim at the packet.

The armed men ran off the ship into the town. Citizens, both northern and southern sympathizers, terrified at the prospect of bombardment, screamed at the raiders to get out of town. The approach of the gunboat, fully loaded with armed men sped their retreat.

The panic-stricken passengers rushed from the cabin of the packet where they had been confined. They told Col. Fournier how a few of these men had boarded the packet at Lewisport landing, a dozen miles downstream. They shot the four soldiers guarding the boat, and threw a black steward overboard. Then the rest of the men had boarded and forced the captain to sail along the Kentucky shore to Hainesville. The raiders had forced all the passengers to hand over their money and watches and other jewelry.

"It sounds to me that this was more bunch of pirates than a military action," Paulus said when he spoke with Rabert that evening.

"Certainly there are not any regular Confederate forces within several hundred miles. But I was told that bands of southern sympathizers in some of the Kentucky towns organize to attack and create as much mischief as they can. I pity the poor folks over in Hainesville. This is the third time they have been raided."

Johann joined the conversation. "These scoundrels must know that they have lost the war. These raids do not help the South at all."

"I suspect that fellows like this are just ruffians who are taking advantage of the situation to do some robbing. They got away with a few hundred dollars from the passengers on the packet," Rabert added..

Paulus limped to the coffee pot, "I feel sorry for the men who were killed. That is such unnecessary waste of life."

Johann said with fervor, "The war must surely be over soon. Then this waste can stop."

CHAPTER 21

The feeling that the war was nearly over was tempered near the ending of 1864 by another call from the President for 300,000 men. Unless Troy Township furnished another 105 volunteers by February 15, 1865, there would be a draft. It was getting harder to find enough men in the township. Some young men were going elsewhere to enlist for the large bounties that were being offered in other counties, even other states. Bounty brokers arrived occasionally on the mail packet and went immediately to the nearest saloons to offer men hundreds of dollars to go to another community to enlist.

Max Blum talked about the latest offers while they were eating their lunch beside the big heating stove at the factory. "I was really tempted... Fellow said he was from someplace in Ohio. Offered a bounty of $640. Put that with the $100 a year the Army is giving, and you have a nice little nestegg. A man would have at least $740 for the first year, plus a hundred a year if the war drags on."

"That is a lot of money." Johann stretched his legs. "I thought I would get a $100 for the time I spent in the army, but because they sent me home after only a year, I got only $35." He snapped the lid on his lunch pail.

"Perry County'll have a hard time coming up with enough men. They are tight with bounties. They add a stingy $50 or $100. No wonder fellows go someplace else...What do they need with 300,000 more men?"

Johann recalled his talks with his friends from the 60th. "Well, take the 60th for instance. They enlisted for three years. They will be coming home very soon unless they re-enlist. The Army has to replace the fellows who are coming home."

Picking his teeth with a sliver of wood, Max said, "*Die Zeitung* says most of the fighting is over. The South is whipped...they just won't give up. Bet most soldiers are just doing guard duty."

"Let me tell you, guard duty can heat up into a battle in a hurry. But, you are probably right."

"I'm going to see what these traveling guys have to say. That kind of bounty—be a lot better than a year's wages in the factory."

"It is worth thinking about."

Matti and Marta were baking stollen together in Matti's kitchen while the children played in a corner.

Matti opened the oven door and poked her finger into the hot stollen. "You're awfully quiet today. What's wrong?"

"Johann and I had another of our arguments last night. I asked him again about bringing Karl over. He is usually such a quiet man, but he yelled, 'I do not want to hear that any more!' It really scared me. He was so upset."

"That doesn't sound like Johann," Matti shook her head.

"I have kept asking every few days. He just keeps saying that it wouldn't be good to bring him now. It is becoming a real wall between us."

Matti nodded as she took the stollen from the oven.

The words flooded out of Marta. "I don't see why we can't. We have a little money. Johann has been able to go back to the factory. It seems that his stomach sickness is better. He hasn't vomited lately and he is eating a little better. I don't see why we can't arrange for Karl to come over with somebody. I am sure that someone from Neuhaus is coming every few months. Johann says wait 'til the war is over. It is not fair!"

Matti put her arm around Marta. "It is hard on you, isn't it?"

Marta wiped her eyes. "I thought when Johann agreed to get a bigger house that he was planning for Karl to come. But he is as against it as he always was. For some reason, he just doesn't want Karl to be here. He used to just get quiet when I brought it up, but now it makes him angry. That makes me angry too. How can a man not want to be near his own son?"

"It does seem strange," Matti ventured.

"I just don't think he loves Karl the way he does the girls."

"Well, he has not seen Karl for, what is it, seven years?"

"I can't stop asking. I just don't know what to do."

A few weeks later Johann sat at the table after supper, obviously wanting to say something. Marta waited, hoping that maybe he had reconsidered his unwillingness to talk about bringing Karl over.

"Max Blum and I had a talk with a fellow from Ohio after we finished work. What would you think if I could make $750?" He wiped his plate with a crust of bread.

"750 dollars? They will put you in jail if you rob the bank," she joked.

"I would have to be gone for a while, probably only a year."

Marta stood up. "A year? How would we get along. We barely could make it when you were in the army."

"We would have money in the bank."

"Where would you be?"

"Back in the army. This fellow is offering $640 dollars to any man who will go to Ohio with him and go in the army. They pay that much for you to take the place of one of their men."

"You are not healthy enough to go back to the army," Marta said quietly, sitting again in her chair.

"I have been doing better. I have not had vomiting spells since last summer. I have been able to work at the factory. Beside, the army will not be too hard now. It will be like it was while we were in Lebanon, only there we had to worry about raiders. It might not be as much work as I have at the factory."

"I...I don't want you to go," Marta bit her quivering lip. She reached out to put a hand on his arm.

"I think it is worth it to be able to put some money in the bank. We have limped along with just a little in case of trouble. This would give us enough when the war is over to start a small business and get on our feet. Max is going to do it, and I think I should too."

"I don't want you to go, but I suppose, like the last time, you will go anyway," she said with a touch of bitterness in her voice.

"Last time I went because I wanted to help save the country. All I got from it was a bad stomach that has kept me from getting ahead for more than two years. This time I can get the money to give us a good start after the war."

"Stay with us at home. I promise I won't keep asking to bring Karl over. We need you here."

"I can do more good for everybody by enlisting for a year."

"The money isn't as important as keeping well. You'll just get sick again from that awful army food."

"I will know what to do this time. Believe me, I will take care of myself."

"Can't I say anything to make you change your mind?" Marta touched his arm again.

"This is the best thing to do. It is a chance to give us a fresh start. When I get home from the army, we'll have enough money in the bank. We won't have to worry about money any more."

Within a week, Max and Johann were on a steamboat for Cincinnati. The bounty broker, Gerhardt, had given them $20 of their bounty and directions for getting to Cincinnati. They were to go to an army encampment with the papers the broker had given them to be mustered into an Ohio regiment that was already forming there..

They sat by the stove in the deckhouse. The chill February weather kept them from the windswept deck. The boat was crowded with soldiers and a number of civilians, some with their families.

Johann told Max, "My guess is that in less than a year we are going to be back in Helvetia. I really wonder why they are willing to pay such a good bounty when the war will soon be over."

"*Ja*. Why doesn't a fellow just go in the army for a year...save paying the bounty?"

"Well, it gives us a chance to get ahead," Johann stood up and walked to the cabin window and looked out at the gray river.

Max joined him and wiped steam from the glass. "You had experience in the army...I don't know what to expect."

"Last time our whole company were men I knew from Helvetia. This time we'll be a couple of strangers. I suppose most of them will speak English. I hope somebody talks German. I've learned a little English, so I can probably figure out what they are talking about."

"I won't know what to do."

"Don't worry about that," Johann laughed. "You can be sure they will tell you what to do, and expect you to do it."

Following the directions Gerhardt had written out for them, Johann and Max walked from the steamer landing to a long brick building near the waterfront. A large flag flew over it, and men in uniform were going in and out. A line of men reached down the front steps. Johann soon learned that these were men who were enlisting, and they joined the line and recognized several men who had boarded their steamer in Louisville. Many of the men had a bag of personal belongings.

Once inside the building the line wound into a room where an army surgeon was examining each man. A clerk wrote down the name of the potential recruit. Then the doctor felt their pulse, looked at their throats, felt to see if they were feverish, stared into their eyes. After this very cursory physical examination, those who passed were directed to an adjacent room where a clerk took down more information. Johann told them his name, answered that he had been born in Prussia, gave his age as 34 years and 4 months, his occupation as a varnisher. The clerk wrote: Eyes hazel, Hair light, Complexion fair, Height 5 feet 2 inches. The clerk scratched out the "Three Year" term of enlistment and wrote in "One Year." Neither the clerk, who was making out one in a thousand such forms, nor Johann, who did not understand the fine print in English at the bottom of the form, paid any attention to the small print which indicated that the recruit affirmed that he had never been discharged for disability or by sentence of court martial. Johann signed the Declaration of Recruit, dated February 15, 1865, which was put in a stack for the surgeon and captain to sign at the end of the day. The paper also indicated that Johann's service was being credited to Johnson Township of Champaign County in the Fourth Congressional District of Ohio, which would pay a bounty of $620 upon enlistment. Johann asked that it be sent in a bank draft to Marta. She would see that it went into the bank.

Once finished with that process, the men were gathered in another large room, directed to a table where there were slices of bread, cheese and ham. Late in the afternoon an officer strode to a small platform at the end of the room. "I am Captain Ed Sanders. You are becoming Company C of the 188th Ohio Volunteers. We are going to take you to the top floor where you will be staying for a few days while we get you your uniforms and equipment. The rest of the regiment has been gathering at Camp Chase in Columbus. In a week or two they will join us here in Cincinnati."

After a few days the newly outfitted men were marched several times a day to a nearby park to drill. It was all too familiar to Johann. Blum struggled to learn the commands. Many of the men were rather lackadaisical in their drilling.

Talking to Blum as they took a walk after supper, Johann said, "It sure is different than the last time. We were just as green as these men, but our officers took it very seriously. They wanted us to be the finest regiment in the army. They kept telling us that some day our lives might depend on being able to carry out orders immediately. But nobody here believes that we will ever see a battle, so they don't drill very hard."

"Well, war's almost over. Captain said the southern army has been driven out of Kentucky and Tennessee...Fighting is all over there."

"I hope they are right."

"Hard to understand what the officers want. I guess if you don't understand—just watch what the other fellows are doing," Max said.

"*Ja*, the other time it was a German regiment, so everyone could talk German. But I only have heard a few other men speaking *auf Deutsch*. Last time the whole company was from Helvetia, so we knew each other. Here only you and I know each other."

"Some of them seem pretty friendly," Max stopped to light a cigar.

"We'll have plenty of time to get to know them." They leaned on a railing overlooking the river.

"Cincinnati seems like a nice city. Stopped here for a few days on way to Helvetia five years ago. Seems a lot bigger now. I see they stopped building a big bridge across the Ohio and just have a pontoon bridge for wagons and people.. I think they have the railroad tunnel under the river. Look at the size of that tower they have on this side. They were building that when I was here before, but I guess they stopped because of the war. Looks pretty much like it did then."

"It looks like a pretty good sized town on the other side too."

"Some people I was traveling with stayed here...Doubt if I could find anybody. Got to know some of them pretty good on the ship."

"It's funny how you become good friends and then never see people again. It was the same with us. I have never seen a soul we knew on the ship, since we said *"Auf wiedersehen"* in New York. We had a really nice family with us in steerage on our ship. It was so crowded you had to be friends," Johann chuckled.

Captain Sanders stood before his company. He was a short man with graying hair, trim in his uniform. He addressed the men after their supper. "Men, tomorrow, March 4, the rest of the regiment is coming on a train from Columbus. We and Company F, which has been training on the other side of the city, will join them. Pack up your things and be ready to march to the depot tomorrow afternoon. We may be on the trains for a couple of days, on our way to Tennessee where we will become part of the 1st Brigade.

"Because there is no railroad from Cincinnati to Nashville, we have to go first to Lexington. There we will change trains and go west to Louisville. Then we'll get on the L&N, which will take us to Nashville."

One of the sergeants came over to them. *"Ich bin Georg Schlee,* your sergeant. You fellows who talk German are going to be in my squad."

Max smiled broadly and said to Johann, "Good. Going to be a lot easier now."

It was a slow journey. The train with the regiment from Columbus arrived several hours late. It was nearly dark when they reached Lexington. The officers told them to get off the train and eat their rations. The men stretched out on the platform, in the depot, in the freight warehouses, pillowing their heads on their knapsacks and blanket rolls. Finally, after midnight a locomotive with a long line of cars, passenger and freight, puffed into the station and the sleepy regiment tumbled onto seats and boxes. The sun was just rising when they began the trip toward Frankfurt to Louisville.

Johann recognized the railroad yards in Louisville, through which he had passed several times a few years earlier. They were loaded onto another train. When they finally began to wind south around noon, Johann said to Blum, "We are going to see some of the places I was when I was in before."

They looked out the window as they passed through Lebanon Junction. Johann pointed out the line that had taken them to Lebanon. An hour or so later Johann said, "We must be getting near to Munfordville. Somewhere along here is where our train went off the tracks."

They watched as they approached the town. Soon they were on the bridge over the Green River, moving very slowly. Through the bare trees they could see the embankments of Fort Craig. Johann pointed, "That is where we fought. We were right over there. The southerners were trying to reach the bridge, but we fought them back for two whole days."

Max strained to see out the dirty window, finally raising it to see better, in spite of the cool March day. "...Must have been awful."

"It was much worse for the other side. We had rocks and ditches. They had to try to get to us."

"...Wouldn't like to have somebody trying to shoot me."

Johann looked out the open window. "Here is where we marched to surrender two days later. That was the end of the fighting for us." He pulled the window down.

It was very early morning of the next day when they reached Nashville. They were given an hour to stretch their legs, walking around the rail yards piled high with barrels and crates. Rows of cannons and wagons ringed the yards. When they heard the bugle, they went back to get their packs and muskets. The officers formed them into a column to march to the train that would take them on. Soldiers working on the mounds of supplies, laughed and jeered as they passed.

"You call that an army."

"Left, right, left, right. Come on, you yokels, get together."

"This your first day in the army?"

"God help the Union, with a rag-tag army like this."

The men of the 188th tried to ignore the hooting. A few made an effort to straighten their lines and to march in step. Most just trudged along as before.

In the depot there were newspapers for sale. Big letters on the front said "Lincoln Inaugurated." Some of the soldiers bought papers. From their conversations, Johann and Max could piece together that Lincoln was beginning his second term as president.

Sgt. Schlee looked at the paper. "It talks about the President's speech. He talks about finishing the war, ending slavery, and then binding up the nation's wounds."

Another soldier said, "That is a hell of a big order. We're going to win, that's for damn sure, but I don't see how the country is going to heal after four years of this kind of fighting."

Soon they were on a train heading southeast from Nashville. They were barely out of the city when they could see the marks of the fierce battle which had been fought there just three months before. Shattered trees marked the horizon and the foreground. The brown and muddy fields were scarred by shallow earthworks and craters from cannon shells. Small mounds of raw earth covered the dead who were buried on the battle field. Shattered wagons and cannons still lay about. Here and there a farmhouse was in ruins and a mound of charred timbers showed where a barn had stood. The chill of a March day with low-hanging gray clouds accented the desolation.

They had ridden only another two hours when they saw a second battlefield. The fighting here must have taken place a year or more before. Spring and summer had muted the marks of destruction, but it was still evident that heavy fighting had covered these fields. As they passed over creeks and small rivers there were piles of partly burned timbers along the track, the remains of trestles burned by the enemy. In one river was a rusting locomotive, turned on its side. These evidences of fighting sobered many of the men.

"It must have been awful around here."

"Looks like a lot of them didn't make it."

"I ain't never seen nothing like this."

One scruffy loudmouth said, "Damn! We got here too late. I missed my chance to be a hero for the girls at home to worship."

"Maybe you missed your chance to be in one of those graves out there," his companion replied.

The train pulled into a station and stopped. A crooked sign beside the depot said "Murfreesboro." Capt. Sanders ordered: "All out; form ranks on the road!"

The regiment marched to two large meadows at the edge of town, along a creek. Several wagons began unloading piles of tents. Sergeants drove stakes into the soft earth to show where the rows of tents should be pitched. Hayracks brought piles of straw that the men could put in their tents. Johann and Max pounded in their tent stakes and put up their pointed two-man tent. Johann took a shovel from the pile of tools at the end of their row.

"What you going to dig?" Max asked.

"I lived in these things before. When it rains, you will be glad we did our digging now," Johann said, starting to dig a small ditch all around their tent.

"Looks like you know what you are doing. I thought you looked like you were in the army before. Right?" said the fellow in the next tent.

"*Ja*. I was. " Johann held out the shovel, motioning for his neighbors to dig too.

"This is just like it was in Lebanon," Johann said to Max a few days later. "We did the same thing there. Lived in tents in a farmer's field, marched to a place and stood guard. There we guarded roads and bridges, here we guard railroad and bridges."

"Seems like wasted time...rebel armies are far away."

"Don't be too sure. In Lebanon we saw how that can change in a couple of days. A couple thousand raiders could ride in without any notice. I have seen what raiders can do. Besides there are plenty of people around here who are with the south and could burn a bridge just to hurt our side."

"...Sitting around on a railroad trestle is mighty boring." Max spat over the side of the trestle. "I kind of wish we were in that big earthwork north of town;...the one they call Fort Rosecrans. They've got all those cannons around them."

"What would be better about that?"

"I don't know. With lots of men around...guess you feel like you are doing something a little more important."

"Well, if you want to be doing something important, ask the captain to send you down to the depot. You could spend the whole day carrying boxes and rolling barrels around. If you got bored, they would let you move one of those big piles of stuff onto another pile on the other side of the tracks," Johann laughed.

"Oh, all right. I'll sit by my trestle and keep quiet."

After only a week in Murfreesboro Johann began again to have stomach pains. He did not mention it to anyone for several days. He tried to eat just bread, washed down with army coffee. He avoided the almost daily stew which his mess mates cooked up. He did not have to exert himself much. There was very little drilling. They would stand guard duty along the railroad for a day or a night. The rest of the time was free.

Long nights wrapped in his blanket in his tent were a torment. He kept turning over and over in his mind the return of his illness. Had he been foolish to enlist again? Would he be able to stick it out for a year? If he just took it easy, could he get over the pain in his belly?

Blum noticed that Johann was eating very little. "What's wrong? You haven't eaten a square meal in days."

"I'll be all right. It's just my old stomach troubles."

"Listen, I remember that time I took you home from the furniture factory 'cause you got so sick. Better tell the sergeant...go to sick call."

"I am going to wait a while to see if it passes. Don't you tell anybody!"

"All right, but don't let it get too bad."

"I heard the men talking about some of these fellows who go to sick call every few days. There is nothing wrong with them; they are just lazy bums. I don't want anybody to think I am one of that kind."

"Tell them that you had this trouble before. I'll tell them you aren't lazy."

"*Ja.* but then they will say I should not be in the army. I would have to give the money back. Just give me a few days. It will get better."

Blum said nothing more about it until a few days later, while they were on guard duty. He heard Johann retching from behind a clump of bushes where the men relieved themselves.

"You are sick, man...heard you vomiting."

Johann sat down against a tree, pillowed with his knapsack, "I've only done it a couple of times, and there is no blood."

"Still think you should go to sick call, before it gets worse."

"If I keep vomiting, I'll go on Saturday."

"Your wife won't forgive me if I let you get real sick," Blum argued.

"You are a good friend. I am grateful for that. If I am not better by Friday, I'll go."

The line for sick call reached to the street from inside the brick warehouse which was the army hospital in Murfreesboro. It was more than an hour before Johann reached the head of the line and tried to explain his illness in very broken English to the white aproned surgeon who sat at the table writing.

"Stomach hurts. Hard to eat; only *Brot*--bread. Last few days; vomited a number of times." Johann mimed some of his report.

"Any blood?"

"*Nein*; green."

'When did your unit get to Murfreesboro?"

"Two weeks."

"I'll give you some medicine. No reason you can't go back on duty." The doctor reached to another table in back of him and handed Johann a small bottle filled with brown liquid. "Take a spoonful of this before every meal." This miserable brew was so obnoxious that most of the malingerers either recovered quickly or developed a new complaint.

Before supper Johann pulled the cork from the bottle and sniffed the thick liquid. It reminded him of the stench of the flax that the weavers in Endigen soaked in water. He took a quick swig and gagged. Swallowing hard he managed to keep the foul stuff down. The taste would not leave his mouth. Even the bread he ate tasted terrible.

In spite of following the surgeon's orders, Johann's nausea continued. He still vomited several times a day.

Blum insisted. "You've got to go back to that doctor...not getting any better."

"He thinks I am just lazy. I could tell it from the way he talked to me."

"You are sick and he better know it."

Sick call the following morning was crowded as before. The surgeon, Dr. Whitaker, looked hard into Johann's face.

"Weren't you here before?"

"*Ja*, my stomach...still bad."

The surgeon poked Johann's abdomen, which caused him to wince.

"You said you vomit a lot? Blood?"

"When I eat...after...Blood...*einmal*, one time"

"What is your duty?"

"Guard...*Eisenbahn*," Johann pointed to the south.

"At least it is not heavy work. I'm going to put you in the hospital for a few days so you get some food that won't hurt you. Go over there and they will assign you to a bed."

A few days in the hospital extended into a week, two weeks. Johann was given light duties, mopping the floor, helping some of the bedfast patients. Most of the beds were full. A young lieutenant called Sinclair from the 188th was brought in with a raging fever. Dr. Whitaker assigned Johann to sit with him and to put wet towels on his forehead. The young officer was delirious most of the time, calling out for "Molly," thrashing about in his bed. Johann was with him the next day when he died.

His bed was soon filled. When Johann walked around the ward the next morning, in one bed only a mop of tousled hair showed above the top of the blanket. Later that morning this soldier threw back the covers, stood up beside the bed, scratching himself furiously, and surveyed his new surroundings. Johann saw a vaguely familiar face.

"Hey, don't I know you?" the scraggly young man slurred. "You was on the ship."

His memory triggered, Johann recognized Kurt Nauman. The skinny, slovenly boy, whom Johann had last seen pilfering from the dock in New York, still did not look like a man. His hair hung dirty and unkempt; his pimply face was framed with a thin, scraggly attempt at a beard; his crooked half-smile uncovered brownish, uneven teeth. His left hand was wrapped in a dirty bandage.

Johann said, "*Ja*, I remember you."

"What the hell you doin' here?"

"In the army, like you are."

"Where you livin'... before the army?

"Indiana."

Nauman sat on the edge of his bed. "I been all over. I stayed in New York for a while. Then I rode the freight trains all the way to Texas. I worked for a while there. For a year I was on a boat going back and forth to Mexico. I even went to California. I was in a wagon train that got attacked by Indians." His voice rose as he described his exploits.

Still the big talker, Johann thought. I'll bet not even half of it is true.

"I had a lot of sickness. I was in a hospital in New York for a couple of months. I didn't have no money. They finally put me out. I wrote to what is left of my family at home, but they wouldn't send me nuthin'. If Papa was still alive I would certainly not be here. My stepmother, that old bitch, wouldn't even answer my letter. I slobbered all over her telling her how much I loved her and missed her, but nuthin'! I told her I was bein' good; didn't drink 'r fight. I told her that I didn't have no money to get a room and was afraid of freezing to death on the streets. I even had the doctor write to them to get his money, I owed him fifty dollars, but nobody ever answered." Nauman scratched his tousled hair.

Johann felt a touch of sympathy for the unfortunate young man, remembering that he had been sent alone to America. "So now you are in the army."

Nauman leaned close and lowered his voice. "Hell, I been in the army four times. Ever since they started handin' out that bounty; it's good money. I enlist, get the money, and then as soon as I gets a chance, I just walks away. Nobody even bothers to chase me. I travel back north and find another place where they are handing out bounty. It's the easiest money I've ever made."

Johann tried to hold back his disapproval, "Doesn't it bother you that you are stealing that money?"

"I figured that I been here seven years and this country hasn't given me a damn thing. Until I started going into the army, I never had much more than I came with, which was empty pockets. So if they are going to hand out money, I'm goin' to take what I can. What else can I do?"

Nauman rambled on, "I wanted to go back to Germany and begged my family to send me money for a ticket, but they wouldn't do it. I was sick a lot. I got hurt on a couple jobs and had to quit. Since I been in the army I wrote and told them that I got promoted to *Kapitan* and had a couple of hundred men under me. I even told them about some big battles I was in and how I got a medal for bravery. Nobody even bothered to answer my letter. So now I figure I can get enough money from bounties that I can start a peddling business. What's wrong with that?"

"The wrong part is not taking the bounty; the stealing is running away and enlisting again. You never intend to keep your part of the deal. I call that wrong." Johann started to walk away.

"Listen, there are dozens of fellows who are in here on account of the bounty they collected. For all I know, you got bounty to enlist."

"Yes, but I promised to serve my year and I'll do it."

"Serve it in the hospital. That's pretty smart: warm food, soft cot."

Johann felt his temper rising, "The surgeon knows that I have a real sickness. As soon as my stomach is better, I'll be back on duty."

"Yeh, I'll bet. You ain't no dummy, Jonny. You may not jump your bounty, but you're gonna work out an easy year, that's damn sure."

Johann said nothing.

Nauman chattered on. "How's that little missus of yours? She was a pretty little thing. Miss her?"

"She is home with our three girls."

"Then what are you doin' here?"

"Doing my duty as a man."

"How much did they pay you to be a man, huh?"

"Nobody has to pay me to be a man," Johann growled at Nauman.

"What you gonna do with the money, Jonny?"

"None of your business."

"I'll bet you're gonna spend it on booze and cards and wild women. Have a high old time, huh, Jonny" Nauman mocked.

Johann clenched his fists

"You know," Nauman kept up his diatribe, "they take advantage of us guys from the old country, especially us Germans. Every outfit I been in has had a lot of *Ausländer*. You know that too."

Johann nodded. "*Ja, aber....*"

"Don't tell me, 'yes, but.' What has this country given you? Are you really better off than you were when you got off the ship with me in New York?"

"I have my own home without any debt."

"Had good jobs, have you?"

"Well, we got here in hard times. I admit that I thought it would be easier to find good jobs." Johann fidgeted as he talked.

"So good old honest Jonny worked for a dollar a day. Hell, I had days when I would make 25 dollars playing cards for a few hours. Never sweated, never had a blister, never had a boss yelling at me."

"When the war is over, times will get better. There will be plenty of good jobs."

"Sure," Nauman mocked, "I'll bet you that us foreigners will get all the good ones. They'll make all of us bosses right away. Ha."

"Don't you have any appreciation for this country? Don't you see how we have so much more freedom than in the old homeland? Don't you want to vote for your leaders?"

"So all your dreams for this great new world have come true, eh?," Nauman smirked. "Doesn't sound to me like you are a rich man. You haven't started your own business, have you? You got twenty men working for you—poor suckers you hired right off the boat?"

"Shut your *verdammten* mouth! They ought to send you out of here the way they threw you out of Germany," Johann's anger rose.

"I'm really gettin' under your skin, Jonny. You're fooling yourself that this is a great country. You just can't admit it's a lie," Nauman said with a wicked grin.

"I still have a dream. I fought for that dream in 1862 and I'll fight for it again, if I have to."

"You'll wake up one of these days. I never been a soft-in-the-head dreamer like you. Nobody ever gave me nothin', at least since my papa died. I learned the hard way that if I get anything, I have to take it. They offer me money to be a soldier and I take it. It's a pretty good deal. I stay in the army for a month or so, then I walk away, sell off my uniform to some guy who wants warm clothes. Then somebody else offers me money to be a soldier all over again. I figure it's the good job I was supposed to get over here."

"You disgust me. Rascals like you give us honest, hard-working Germans a bad name," Johann growled and walked away.

He avoided Nauman completely and was relieved when the scruffy bounty jumper was released from the hospital the next day.

Johann's strength returned as he ate the soup and bread and drank the milk that was given to all the patients. The surgeon was pleased that his vomiting had stopped. "We'll keep you here for another week before we send you back to the cooking fires. You are going to have to be careful what you eat."

In the evening of that day suddenly there were several loud explosions as some cannons on the outskirts of Murfreesboro fired. This was followed by a wave of erratic musketry.

"What's going on?" one of the patients yelled. "Is Forrest raiding Murfreesboro again?"

Dr. Whitaker rushed to the door of the hospital and shouted to the men running down the street, "What is happening?"

No one answered until a captain came along. "They got a telegraph at headquarters that Lee has surrendered in Virginia. Lee surrendered to Grant."

"The war is just about over," the surgeon told the men in the ward. Even the sickest began to cheer from their beds. Ambulatory patients rushed to the windows to watch the growing procession. Johann watched the men pounding each other on the back, exchanging great bear-hugs. Wide-eyed faces glistened with sweat or tears.

"*Gott sei ewig Lob und Dank*," was the prayer that came softly to Johann's lips. He closed his eyes and could visualize the *Star Gray Eagle* gliding into the wharf boat at Helvetia, walking to the house on Ninth Street, hugging Marta and the little girls, talking with Paulus and Rabert. The war would be over and he could make a new start. There would be plenty of jobs.

One of the ambulatory patients had run outside and taken down a flag that was tacked beside the entrance and was waving it from the window. Other patients were banging their tin cups on wash basins to join the celebration that was building up outside. The small regimental band began an impromptu parade through the streets. Most of the townspeople stayed in their houses with the shutters closed in contrast with the jubilation of the Union soldiers. Johann reached for his pencil and paper.

> *Liebe* Marta,
>
> The news has just reached us here in Murfreesboro that the southern general, Lee, has surrendered in Virginia. There is great happiness, even here in the hospital where many of the men are very sick. The end of the war must be near. There are other southern armies here and there, but surely they will soon give up and we can all go home. It has been a long hard war and many men have died--on both sides. I have been so lucky. My life was only in danger from bullets at Munfordville, but there is sickness everywhere in the army. In spite of my stomach sickness, I never caught any of the fevers that killed more men than bullets. I will try to let you know as soon as they tell us we can go home.
> *Immer,*
> Johann

A few days later Johann was visited by his comrade, Max, "Johann, am I ever glad to see you. How long they going to keep you cooped up in this hospital?...Have they made you well?"

"I feel a lot better. The vomiting has stopped and my strength is coming back slowly. I cannot eat much at a time, but I can keep the food down now. The surgeon says I will not be able to eat some of the things that come out of the cook's pot."

"Well, then you'll come back soon...Good to have my old friend to talk to once again. Suppose you have heard that we will be going home soon."

"It will not take me long to pack up," Johann joked.

A week later the mood changed abruptly from celebration to gloom. Word came from the telegraph and spread from end to the end of the camp in minutes: Lincoln has been shot! The President is dead!

Johann was doing his chores in the hospital when a sergeant ran in with the tragic news. A hush fell across the ward. A gaunt man in a bed in one corner turned his head to his pillow and sobbed. The patients looked at each other blankly as the words sank in.

A chill passed through Johann. What would this mean? The war was almost over, but people were looking to Lincoln to bring the country back together. Johann did not have the whole picture. He knew that Rabert admired Lincoln greatly. He was a common man, like all the rest, not somebody who put himself over everyone else like a king. Johann had agreed with Lincoln's unswerving desire to maintain the Union. That was why he had gone into the army. Now no one knew what would happen. Without the president, would the country stay divided?

A few days later a letter arrived from Marta.

> *Lieber* Johann,
>
> I am so excited I can hardly hold the pen. We got wonderful news today. I suppose you got it too in Tennesee. They say the war is over. Soon you will be coming home to your loving family. Oh, I am so relieved. I have never been so happy in my whole life. I had to send a letter to you at once, even though I know you will not read it for another week. In the middle of this afternoon the steamboat docked with its whistle screaming. It just kept on and on, like the world was coming to an end. You could hear it all over town. Folks ran to the wharf boat to see what was the matter. I gathered up the girls and walked as fast

as we could. People were running down the streets yelling, "The war is over!" The captain of the *Star Gray Eagle* had the news from Louisville that the southern army surrendered and their capital city was captured. You have never seen such celebration. The whole town went crazy. People didn't even go home for supper. The *Förster* kept shooting their cannon. A bunch of the men made a huge pile of wood and brush down near the river and set it on fire as soon as it got dark. It lit up the whole place. I was afraid that the cloud of sparks would fly onto roofs and set the shingles on fire. Some people waved flags. A lot of the men got too much beer and were not too steady on their feet. Everyone was just going around hugging and yelling. I just couldn't stop crying. I have been holding in my tears for so long and they all came pouring out. I was afraid I would frighten the girls. All I could do was tell them that the fighting was over and you would soon be back home. I have not been so happy since the first time you came home from the army. All the wives and mothers of the men in the army are shedding tears of joy. We have all been living with half of our world missing. Surely after the terrible war there will be plenty of jobs. All the men will be able to find work. The factories will be making lots of furniture; the boats will be hauling it all up and down the river. I think your dreams are finally going to come true. I hope you can come home soon. We will be here, waiting.

Ich liebe dich,
Marta

A few days later a second letter arrived.

Lieber Johann,

The joy and celebration I told you about in my last letter has disappeared. On Easter Sunday, just about the time we were coming home from church, the steamboat came and once again there were long blasts on the whistle. The captain told everybody that the President had been shot. I was sorry to hear that, but I didn't know much about him, so I did not get as excited as some of the folks. There wasn't a whole lot of crying but everyone went around with very sad faces. I saw Frau Rabert and she told me that they thought it was a terrible loss for the country, particularly now when the war is ending. I felt terrible sadness when she said that her husband was afraid that, without the President, it would be impossible to bring the country back together in peace.

I think it would be terrible if after all the suffering, all the men killed, all the children without fathers...what if it was all for nothing! I don't know where they got it, but people began draping black cloth on the fronts of all the buildings--the school, the churches, the factories, the stores. People gathered together in the park by the Catholic Church. The *Förster* were all standing in a row along the little band stand. *Unser Pfarrer* and the Catholic priest said long prayers. Herr Rabert stood up and talked about what a great man President Lincoln was and how the people of the country had to see to it that his work went on until there was really peace in the country. The band played some sad songs. That little fellow who always struts around with the *Förster* got up on the platform and made a speech and said that the southerners had shot Lincoln. He said that he would shoot down any southerner he found. He was all for getting boats and going over to Kentucky to kill some of the ones who sided with the south. He scared me; he was so full of hate. He just kept yelling "Revenge! Revenge." Herr Rabert finally stood up again and told the man that the dead President would be honored more by peace than by more hate and war. I was so thankful I was standing by Paulus and Matti. I thought fighting was going to start right there. Most of the people clapped for Herr Rabert. I hope that shooting the President does not mean that you will have to stay in the army much longer. That would bring me even deeper sadness.

Ich liebe dich,

Marta

Just a week later the surgeon said to Johann, "Time for you to get back to your company, Weber. I'll write your orders. We'll miss you around here. You have been a good helper."

"*Danke Schön, Herr Arzt,*" Johann stammered.

"See that you eat the same things we have been giving you in the hospital."

"I'll try, but it is not easy. We eat what the cook makes."

"You know that bread and milk always is good for you. You can always get your hands on that."

Max welcomed him back to the camp on the edge of town. "Nobody moved into the tent, so you can come right back. Glad for the company."

"Thank you for keeping my stuff. It is good to be breathing fresh air."

"No wonder they sent you back. The captain told us last night that we are moving. We are going to a place called Tullahoma. Don't know how far away it is. Won't be no different from here: just more guard duty."

"I don't mind. Now that the fighting is over, we just sit there anyway."

Tullahoma proved to be as boring as Murfreesboro had become. Most of the men became very impatient, seeing that they were no longer needed because the fighting had ended weeks before. To relieve some of the boredom Johann wrote to his brother Gustav.

> *Lieber* Gustav,
>
> I am still in the army, although you probably know that our terrible war is over. We are in a southern town as guards, but there is little reason for it since all the southern armies have stopped the fighting since last month. Southern soldiers are coming back home. Most of them look very thin and sad. Some of them turn their backs whenever they see us. Some of them are farmers and are trying to plant some late crops. Others just sit around in the town, because there are no jobs for them. The black people just wander around because they do not have any place to go. They are not slaves any more because the war has been won. A very few have been hired by the men who used to own them, but others roam around looking for places to work and earn a little money. You see whole families walking down the road in the daytime and sleeping in the open at night. I feel sorry for them, but I have it only a little better. I am miles from my home. I sleep in a tent. I sit around all day "guarding." I hope they send us home soon. I am looking forward to better times. We Germans can hold our heads high. Americans won't making fun of us anymore or won't fight to keep us from voting. They know that thousands of Germans joined the army to keep the country together. All the Germans and Swiss in Helvetia will get the place going strong. After four years of war the factories will be turning out the goods people have had to do without during the war. I'm looking forward to getting a real good job and making a place for my family in the town. You ought to think about coming over here. It is such a growing country, you would soon find a place to start making paper. Think about it! Karl and Julius would never

leave Endigen, but you have seen some of the outside world and would do very well over here. I will write to the family once I get home again. It should not be long now.

Immer,

Johann

One day in July Johann was called to the captain's tent. Captain Saunders was sitting at his camp table. Johann saluted.

"I have something here for you, Weber," the captain said, holding out a small piece of paper.

Johann looked at the paper and said haltingly in English, "I read only little English."

"Well, this is a paper excusing you from all drills, inspections and reviews because you have been chosen as the cleanest and most soldierly appearing man on Picket Guard," read the captain slowly with a smile.

Understanding some of what the captain was saying, Johann expressed his thanks.

"I know you have been sick, but the surgeon wrote on your orders that you were a good helper in the hospital. Good to have you back." He saluted.

Johann returned the salute and took the paper back to his tent.

He and Max labored over the words until they finally had it all figured out.

Max laughed, "Lucky rascal. First you spend a month in a soft bed in the hospital, then you are so clean that you don't have to drill for a month. Maybe if I cleaned up, they would send me home early."

Johann smiled as he thought: I wish this had happened before I wrote to Gustav. I don't think he ever had anything like that in the Prussian army.

It was only a month later that the regiment was loaded on the train and taken back to Nashville. No longer were large garrisons necessary, although some federal forces remained in most towns of any size on railroads.

Thousands of Union troops were gathered in tent camps that dotted the fields around the edge of the city. The officers tried to keep their men occupied. Except for the occasional token drills every afternoon the men sat and whittled and argued. They were not allowed into the city because some earlier regiments had gotten into drunken brawls. Every day a few regiments were ordered to the headquarters buildings in Nashville to be mustered out.

Max paced in front of their tent. "When is our turn? This is so stupid, sitting around day after day."

"Probably they are mustering out regiments who have been in the army for a couple of years. We've been in only seven months. So we're at the end of the line," Johann responded.

"*Ja,* some of these fellows look like they have seen a lot of fighting. I guess we are lucky."

"We haven't even fired our muskets. Nobody has been shot."

Blum nodded, "The captain said yesterday that we had 45 men die in the hospitals. That's a lot of men in seven months."

"I saw a few of them die of fever when I was in the hospital. It's as bad for them and their families as if they were in a battle."

"You were one of the lucky ones, They got you fixed up."

"*Ja,*' Johann said quietly, "but the surgeon told me that I am always going to have a bad stomach. I just want to be strong enough to get a good job in the furniture factory."

It as not until September 21 that the 188th Ohio Volunteer Regiment was ordered to headquarters. They left their tents standing for the next troops brought to Nashville. They were to take only their muskets and packs and their personal belongings.

Johann marched with the regiment through the streets of the city. These parades had become so common that most of the citizens simply went about their business. Knowing that their time in the army was now measured in hours, most of the soldiers already were mentally becoming civilians. The ranks in the line of march were crooked. Only some of the men bothered to march with the beating of the drum. Max smiled as he saw Johann draw himself to full height, even though most of the men were taller than he. He marched with such seriousness; eyes straight forward, musket slanted on his shoulder.

At the warehouse which had been converted into headquarters the men were taken inside by companies. For more than an hour Company C waited in line, shuffling forward as the line slowly moved ahead. The large hall was lined with flags. Long tables staffed by uniformed clerks made out papers for each man, as he reached the head of the line.

Johann's turn finally came. The clerk called down the line of tables, "Hey, Jake, I got some of your countrymen. Come on over here."

A heavy-set soldier ambled to the table.

"*Wie geht's, Landsmann*," he said jovially. "Let's see your pay card."

Johann dug the dogeared card out of his pocket.

"Well, Weber, let's make out the papers and send you home." He took an ornately printed document and wrote in Johann's name, unit numbers, dates. Then he said, "Well, it's been a while since the army gave you any money. Hmmm, last pay was June 30. The record says that you owe the army six dollars for weapons, but you've got your musket, so we don't have to charge you for that."

"I was in the hospital in Murfreesboro for a couple of months. When I got back, my musket was gone. I guess somebody took it out of the tent. The captain got me another one from somewhere. This is it."

"Well, I am not going to charge you for that. The army owes you $29.41 in back pay and you get the two thirds of your army bounty for nine month's service; that is $66.50 more. They pinch every penny." He scribbled the figures on a slip of paper.

"Take your musket over there to the Quartermasters. Then take this to the paymaster's when they tell you to and he'll give you your money. Have a good trip home. They are going to ship your regiment to Camp Chase just after noon. '*Wiederseh'n.*"

"*Guten Tag, Landsmann*," Johann said.

It was a week later when they were assembled at Camp Chase in Columbus. Each man was was given his pay and discharge certificate. Then they went to the depot to get trains for their homeward journeys.

It was already dark when Johann, Max and several hundred other soldiers got off the crowded train in Louisville.

"Now what?" Max asked as they pushed through the crowd of men in uniform.

"I guess we should find where the *Star Gray Eagle* docks. If we are lucky, one of the mail packets will be heading down river tomorrow. We should be back in Helvetia by tomorrow night."

"I can't wait. Home is going to look awfully good. Soft bed, good cooking, my brother's family."

"They won't know we are coming. That's the way it was the last time I went home from the army. I got into Helvetia and walked into the house like a ghost. I wish there were some way to let them know we are coming," Johann said.

"There is a saloon. Let's get a good glass of beer and eat our way down the length of the bar," Max rubbed his stomach.

"Maybe we should find the *Star Gray Eagle* first and see when it leaves. I would hate to miss the boat because we stopped to eat first."

"Guess I can hold out for a little...I'm really ready to get myself around something different from army food."

"I think I remember where the *Star Gray Eagle* docks. I am pretty sure it is down this way."

It was the following afternoon when the mail packet docked at Coaltown.

"Only another hour," Max said, overjoyed at the thought of seeing his old friends once again.

Johann was anxious to see Marta and the little girls, but he could not forget the secret unhappiness that had persuaded him to go back to the army. I hope Marta doesn't keep harping about bringing Karl over. I just don't want that. I can't tell Marta that I blame a ten year old child for building me a new trap. I was trapped in Endigen, and in the awful apprenticeship, and then with family responsibilities before I ever had a chance to live. Even since we came to America I've been trapped by not ever having a good job. Marta has been a good wife. She is a good mother. She is stronger than I am. Maybe now that the war is over and I am home again, things will change. We will start having some good luck. We can get on our feet and make the life here I have always dreamed of.

The blast of the paddle-wheeler's whistle broke the chain of his moody thoughts. Helvetia came into view around the bend of the river.

CHAPTER 22

Coming home from work on a late November evening, Johann walked to the stove and warmed his hands. "It is getting cold. I am sure glad I fixed that place on the roof last week."

"When I stopped at the Post Office," Marta said, "there was a letter from your brother Julius. Here....I did not want to open it until you came home. It is unusual to get two letters from him in the same year. I hope it is not bad news."

Johann broke the seal and unfolded the letter, his hands shaking. He began to read:

> *Lieber Bruder und Schwägerin,*
>
> I have sad news for you. *Mutter ist Tod.* She died peacefully in her sleep on the thirteenth of October. We are grateful to God that she had no suffering. She seemed to be tired all the time, but was not sick. Karl's serving girl found her dead in her bed when she looked in to tell her breakfast was ready. Now she sleeps in the church cemetery next to Papa. The whole village came to the funeral. Her old friends, the few who are still living, were there. The rest sleep beside her in the cemetery. Karl helped Mother invest the money she got from Father's estate and selling the house to him. Her needs were simple so Karl and I provided for her daily wants. In a few months we will be sending you your share of Mother's estate. It should be around four hundred *Reichstaler*, maybe more. We have had no word from Gotthelf for over three years. I will keep his share in the bank in Waldenburg in case he should ever write to tell us where he is. Gustav wrote to tell us that he had a letter from you and that you hoped to be out of the army soon. God be

praised that the terrible war has ended. I hope you are home to
get this letter. If not, Marta can send the sad news to you. We
think of you often, especially when the hearts of our family
are heavy.

With love,

Julius

Marta put her arm around Johann's shoulders. "I am sorry. I know
how much you loved your mother."

"She was a good woman. I wish I could have seen her once more before
she died. "

"That's what is hard about coming to America. We will never see our
families again. It makes me very sad too." She almost began to talk about
young Karl, but bit her lip, turning her head away.

"She was the only one who understood me. She knew how important
it was for me to be treated like a man, not a boy."

"I am sorry that I never had the chance to really get to know her. She
was kind to me when we made those few little visits to Endigen."

"She told me once that she was pleased that we were married. She
liked you."

The sun was bright in Neuhaus and the church bells were ringing,
calling the faithful to worship. Katerina Wiesner was brushing the new
suit Karl was wearing for his confirmation. "Hurry up, August, it's time
to go to church. We don't want to be late today."

August limped down the stairs, leaning on his cane. "Very nice. A
handsome young man," he said appreciatively. "You are getting as tall as I
am. You make your *Grossvater* look pretty shabby."

"Nonsense. You look just fine," Katerina said, putting on her hat.

August put his hand on Karl's shoulder. "I remember when your
mother was confirmed in that same church. I tell you, she was the prettiest
girl in the bunch."

Karl answered, "I guess I wouldn't know that. I have never seen her;
just that picture."

"*Ja,* I know. One day soon things will be right for you to go to America.
I know they want you to come."

"Then why don't they send for me. You say they want me to come."

Katerina interrupted, "There are so many reasons it hasn't worked out.
Your Papa has been sick a lot since he was in the war. He can only work
some of the time, so they do not have much money."

"The teacher says America is a rich country."

"I know your Mama wants you to come as soon as they can afford it."

"When is that going to be?"

"Soon. As soon as they can," Katerina tried to reassure him. "Now, let's get going, Confirmation Boy. There is the second bell."

Postwar Helvetia was for a time the bustling city its founders had envisioned. The three furniture factories were working at full capacity. Two saw mills were busy producing wood to be dried for furniture and new buildings. The planing mill turned out doors and windows by the hundreds. The breweries produced enough beer for local consumption and shipped barrels of their surplus to other towns along the river. Kimel and Zins Foundry was making dozens of iron bedsteads. Hermann Brothers turned out half a dozen wagons a week. Steamboats docked almost daily at the wharf boat to load the products that were pouring out of the businesses in Helvetia. The side-wheeler *Diana* took on $8000 worth of furniture, 8 new wagons, and a large consignment of shingles destined for Galveston, Texas. When the river was too low for navigation the products were shipped by barge to Evansville or Louisville to be sent on by railroad.

Johann had had no difficulty getting his old job back, varnishing and polishing rows of chairs each day. He came home every evening dead tired. He sat in the rocking chair by the kitchen stove and talked with Marta while she got their supper. Emma was now old enough to help with the two younger girls. Jenny sat on his lap and played with his watch chain.

"Supper is ready," Marta announced.

"Come on, girls. Get on your bench. Here, Jenny, I'll lift you into the high chair," Johann said.

"Our own family circle," Marta said as she sat down. "When we all sit around the table, and I look at all of you, I am so thankful to have all of you."

Johann waited a moment and then added, "I am thankful too." He thought back to the family home in Endigen; sitting around the long table; his father intoning the Bible every evening; his mother putting out the bowls of steaming potatoes and beets, the round loaves of dark brown bread, the *Stollen* at the end of supper. But he could not erase the image of his older brothers: Karl speaking as if he were God; Julius, the faithful disciple, saying Amen.

Later that night, bundled under the feather bed, Johann reached out for Marta.. "You know, I thought tonight that I was so lucky. I have a good wife, I have three nice little girls. That is good......Let's find what you used to call 'our haystack.'"

Marta smiled in the darkness and wiped the tears from her eyes.

Johann reflected on some of the other men who had gone to the army. They were so different now. The war had aged many of them prematurely. There were a few men in Helvetia who carried the war in their bodies. Fritz Schultz had only one leg. Peter Schmalz had deep scars all over his face, where a Minié ball had torn through his cheek. The sharp twinges in Johann's stomach reminded him daily of the war.

The women of Helvetia, too, bore the marks of the war. The months of caring for their families in virtual poverty added years to their faces. A few families broke up when the husband returned, a very different man than the one who had left. There were nearly a dozen widows struggling to keep their families going.

At the factories and in the saloons at first there were lots of stories about the war: marches, battles, camps, hospitals. After the initial camaraderie only a few men kept telling their stories, which got more extravagant with every telling.

"Listen to that crazy *Prahler* blowing off," Albrecht Geyer said as they ate their lunch in a corner of the factory. "Sometimes it makes me grind my teeth and sometimes I just laugh when I hear him tell his stories. You know that nine-tenths of them never happened."

Max Blum nodded, "*Ja*,..makes it sound like he won the war all by hisself."

Johann leaned back against the wall. "It's all in the past anyway. We need to think about what we can do to get back on our feet."

"I thought it would be hard to come back to work after those years of fighting. It sure is nice to work our day and then go back home to a wife, and a good supper, and a clean bed," Albrecht added, whittling a toothpick from a piece of scrap wood.

"It's good to have money coming in every week. Marta is so glad to have a little extra for food. They really had it hard while we were away. I feel bad about that."

"Bet she is so glad to have you home again that she forgets how hard it was," Max said.

"I just hope these good times keep up. We'll be able to save a little and get on our feet for the first time since we got to America. With all the chairs the factory is selling, we should have very steady work for a good while," Johann said, putting the lid back on his lunch bucket. "Time to get back to work."

Marta opened the letter from Neuhaus carefully. Was this bad news? Was there sickness at home? She began to read:

> Dear Marta and Johann,
>   We want to tell you about Karl's confirmation. It was a nice service. He stood with the other young people in the front of the church while *der Pfarrer* had them recite from the Catechism. Karl's voice was so deep and strong. Compared to him the other lads sounded like birds. You would have been very proud of him. We got him a new suit for the service. It was nothing fancy. We couldn't spend much money because he is growing so fast that it will not fit him a year from now. We tried to get it a little big so it might last for a while. You would be surprised at how tall he is getting. He is as big as I am. He does pretty good in school but the teacher thinks he should work harder. He is smart but he doesn't like to work very hard. I remember how you used to do your school work, always worked until you got it right. He tries once to work a problem, but if he doesn't get it right away, he just pushes his slate away. I keep telling him to work hard in school so that when he comes to America, he will get ahead like his papa. We are glad that Johann is home from the army. We worried about him, but we never told Karl because we didn't want him to get upset. We hope all of you have good health.
>   Love from your father and Katerina
>   August Wiesner

As the next summer came Johann began to experience serious stomach pain at work.

He said to Albrecht walking home from work, "I am afraid my old trouble is coming back. I have trouble to keep food on my stomach. I am just not hungry."

"I thought before that it was just that awful stuff I used to cook for us in the army. Now you've got a good cook at home, and you still can't eat," Geyer answered.

"I don't want to worry Marta, especially with the baby coming, but she knows something is wrong. Just when things were looking good, this has to happen. Without much food I feel so weak. I can still do my job, but it is harder every day."

"Maybe you should see Dr. Brucker."

"I am afraid he'll only tell me that I can't work. That would be a disaster. We need those wages. I can't put my family through hard times again. Soon we'll have another mouth to feed. Damn!!! Why can't I get well?" Johann kicked a hitching post at the side of Main Street.

The October moon was shining through the bedroom window when Marta shook Johann's shoulder.

"You better go get Frau Jehle. I think the baby will come soon. Take the lantern and go over to her house. I'll try to get things ready here. Be quiet so you don't wake the girls."

When he got back with the midwife, they found that Marta had started a fire in the cookstove under several of their largest kettles, full of water she had pumped. She had gone back to bed, after putting a small pile of bedsheets and towels on the chair next to the bed.

"How is it going, *Liebchen*," Frau Jehle brushed back Marta's hair. "Soon we have a fine new baby. I'll just sit here a while."

The sun was just coming up when Johann heard a baby cry in the bedroom. He had gone to get Matti and Paulus after returning with Frau Jehle. As soon as they arrived, Matti had gone to help the midwife while Paulus sat by the stove with Johann.

Matti called down from the bedroom, "It's a boy."

"Can I come up," Johann called.

"Wait a few minutes."

Paulus chuckled, "Well, now you've got a son. You'll have some company among all these women-folk." He filled his cup from the coffee pot on the stove.

Johann answered, "I have to go out back for a minute. If Matti calls, tell her I'll come up right away."

He ran out behind the privy, vomited and ran back to the house and up the stairs..

Marta smiled as he came into the room. "Come see your son. He looks just like Karl when he was born."

"How are you?" Johann asked.

"I am fine. It is easier every time," Marta said with a smile of pride, folding the blankets around the baby's head.

"She got along just fine," the midwife added. "It is good you called me when you did. We did not have much time to wait."

Matti asked, "What are you going to name the baby?"

Johann answered, "We said that if it was a boy, we would call him Friedrich."

During the next year Johann had periods of illness when he got so weak that he could not work for several weeks. Then his strength would slowly build up and he would go back to the factory for a few months. After a while, it would start all over again.

Sitting in the kitchen rocker during one of these times of illness, he reached out and pulled Marta to him. "It isn't fair for you. I just make more work for you, getting sick every few months. I am so sorry."

Marta pressed his hand. "We'll make it. The older girls are getting to be good help. They watch after the little ones, they help in the garden. Emma can set the table and help with the dishes."

"*Ja*, but I can't do my part. That's what bothers me."

"Your part is to get yourself well. That's your job. Get yourself strong again. We'll be all right."

In 1868 Helvetia was divided, not for the first time, by a great controversy over language. There had been little need for anything but the German language, the native tongue of almost every adult in Helvetia. A few of the better educated people could also speak English and could relate to the outside world to do business. Many of the men who had been in the army had picked up some English from contact with fellow soldiers and some of the civilians they dealt with while off duty. They also became very aware that most of the country surrounding the closely knit immigrant communities spoke English. If they were going to become part of the country fully, they, especially the young people, would have to learn English.

Editor Rabert wrote:

> Although I know that in time *Die Zeitung* would no longer
> be needed, I strongly favor learning to speak and read English.
> We live in America where English is the common language.
> It would be good for young and old alike to learn English in
> addition to the German they already know.

529

We need to teach in our schools in the English language. We need to keep our city records in English, because we have to use English when we send papers to the state government in Indianapolis.

If we want Helvetia to become a vigorous part of the country: selling our products and buying those things we require, we all need to be able to speak, read, and write English as well as German.

Almost at once voices were raised opposing this position. People knew that a number of German communities had persuaded the state legislature to sanction public schools teaching in German if the community wished. In the streets, over supper tables, in the churches and the *Turnverein*, in the saloons the debate raged.

"If we give up the language, we lose the most important tie with our homeland. Our children will have no way to keep in touch with family in the homeland."

"We won't be able to sing our hymns in church or read *Die Heilige Schrift.*

"We have to look forward, not back. We left Germany and Switzerland to come to America. Now that we are here we should learn to speak the language of the country."

"After I left Helvetia for the army I saw that I could not fit into the country until I knew some English. I spent three years in parts of the country where only English was spoken. I picked up as much as I could."

"I was in a German regiment and didn't have any problems because I did not know English."

Johann was part of that conversation. "I was in a German regiment. Our men and some of the officers spoke German but still we were lost when we were tied up with other regiments. We didn't understand half of what was going on. And then the second time I was in the army, there were only a few fellows in our company who didn't speak English. That was hard. I really wished I knew a lot more English."

"*Ja, aber* won't it break up families? Parents won't be able to talk with their children any more. You know what happens when children don't listen to their parents."

"Teach these young folks English and they are going to leave Helvetia and their families."

"If we don't teach them English, they never will be able to go anywhere but Helvetia to work."

"Who would want to leave Helvetia?"

Although the debate never ended, almost all the younger people and less than half of their elders began to learn and speak some English. The remainder resolutely persisted in using German for all their communication.

As Johann walked home from work, Charles Rabert called to him from the door of the newspaper office.

"Johann, I have something to show you. Come in for a minute."

"Pull up a chair and look at this paper I got from Indianapolis."

Johann began to read an article headed, "Colonel Owen Honored" He slowly read, occasionally asking Rabert to translate a word.

Colonel Owen Honored

Colonel Richard Owen, who commanded the 60th Indiana Volunteers, received a unique tribute on Sunday when a statue in his honor was dedicated at the site of Camp Morton on the north side of the city. Colonel Owen and the 60th regiment guarded prisoners of war at the camp in 1862.

The statue was given by former Confederate captives at Camp Morton with a plaque giving tribute to the Colonel for his just and humane administration. It will be recalled that during the period of his command there were no stories of cruelty, short rations, harsh discipline.

Colonel Owen is the only officer who commanded a prison camp who has had a monument raised for him by the southern prisoners after the war.

"I thought you would be interested in seeing that because I know you thought he was a good officer. I will put this in *Die Zeitung* next week so all the men of the 60th can see it. I am sure you all deserve the honor along with the colonel."

Johann responded, "You know, I had not thought of it for many years, but when we marched out to surrender at Munfordville, the southern general, Buckner, told Colonel Owen that his men from Fort Donelson reported, after they had been exchanged, that Colonel Owen had treated them so well. Later the colonel, who could talk to us in German, told us what Buckner had said. The Colonel said that he was proud to command men who were so well disciplined in following his orders. He was a good man."

"It hardly seems possible that was six years ago," Rabert said.

"That was the first duty we had in the army. I still remember how uncomfortable I was to see men who were prisoners. At the time they did not like us very much. You could see it in their eyes. I would be filled with anger and hate too if I was cooped up in four high wood walls. It is terrible to be a prisoner."

"How are you feeling? I haven't seen you for a while," the editor asked.

"I have good times and bad times. Lately my stomach has been bothering me a lot. Dr. Brucker gives me medicine but it does not help too much. I can work for a few months and then I have to stay home for a month or two. The factory is good to take me back when I can work."

"It is a shame. You always seemed healthy before you went to the army."

"Some men lost an arm or an eye. I guess I lost a healthy stomach."

"I was reading that they have a new government act to give relief to soldiers' families. Maybe you ought to look into that if you cannot work steadily. Next time I am in Coaltown, I will stop at the Court House to see what I can learn about that Act."

"That would be good. Marta tells me that another baby is on the way. I worry about not being able to work, when I have a growing family."

After the birth of another daughter, Louisa, Marta once again began to brood over Karl's absence. She resolved to try once again to persuade Johann to bring Karl over.

"I need your help, Paulus' too," Marta said to Matti.

"Oh? What do you need us to do?"

"I have decided to talk to Johann again about bringing Karl over. I haven't been able to mention it for several years. He gets so upset if I bring it up. I just stopped doing it."

"*Ja.*"

"The last letter I had from my father said that my step-mother, Katerina, has not been well. I could tell he was worried about her. Although he did not mention it directly, I think that having Karl is extra work for her: cooking, washing. He is thirteen years old now; so she has two men to look after."

"He could be a lot of help to her, or to you."

"That is what I was thinking. With Johann being sick so much of the time, it would be a lot of help to have a strong young man around."

"Wouldn't Johann agree, so you could have more help? Matti asked.

"*Ja, aber* he might feel bad that I need help because he can't take care of things. He feels bad enough about not being able to work much. Oh, I don't know...."

"What could we do?"

"Johann thinks a lot of Paulus. He might listen to him. I just can't talk to him about it."

"I'll ask Paulus."

A few days later, as he sometimes did, the schoolmaster casually asked Johann to go with him to Hoffmeister's saloon for a glass of beer. They sat at a table in the back corner of the saloon, far from the noisy card players who filled the room with cigar smoke.

After some small talk Paulus approached his commission gingerly.

"You're really getting quite a family, lovely children. Did you, or was it Marta, once say that you had another son who is still in Germany?"

"*Ja.* Karl."

"How old is he now?"

"He was born in 1856, the year before we came to America. So I guess he must be around 12 or 13."

"Who takes care of him?"

"The Wiesners, Marta's father and step-mother. I am sure they take good care of him."

"So you have not seen him for 12 years."

"No....Marta's people send us a letter once in a while and mention how Karl is."

"Do you plan to have him come over?"

"Marta does. But he is not old enough to make the trip by himself."

"Surely there are people from your town who could bring him along when they come to America."

"Maybe. We don't know anybody who is coming."

"It must be hard for you to have a child you have not seen since he was a baby."

"I guess it is hard for Marta. I just never think of him."

"You don't!"

"No....only when Marta starts arguing to bring him over."

Paulus was quiet for a while. Then he said, "I don't understand."

Johann leaned across the table. He spoke very quietly. "Paulus, I am going to tell you something I have not ever told anybody. I have a son who a total stranger to me. My only memory of him is as a little baby. He is very different than the children we have here. I see them growing up. Karl does not seem like a real child to me. Understand?"

"Not really..."

"I don't want you ever to say this to anybody--not even Matti. I am afraid I would not be able to treat Karl as a father should. You see, Marta and I were just friends. I was just an apprentice dyer. I wasn't ready to get married until I had a chance to make my own way. We used to take long walks in the country. I thought she was pretty and nice to be with. But one thing led to another and she was in a family way. I had to be a man and marry her. I thought a lot of her, but I was not ready to tie myself down with a wife and family. I had been tied down in our little village, always treated like a boy while my older brothers were the men. Then I was tied down as an apprentice. I lived in one trap after another. I wanted to be a man on my own before I thought of getting married...but that didn't happen. Here I was with a wife and baby, still tied down--more than ever."

Paulus nodded understanding.

Johann rushed on. "Every time I saw that baby he was reminding me that I was a prisoner. It was hard to feel any love, I didn't even feel much like a father. Now, it is different with the children here. But I tell you, Paulus, I have always been afraid that if Karl was here, all that anger and resentment would come out. I would not be able to give him the love I give to the other children. It would be very hard for him. So it is better that he stay with the Wiesners."

"Does Marta know that you feel that way."

"I doubt it. But I can't tell her, because it would be saying to her that twelve years of marriage were no good. I won't do that to her. She has been a good wife. I can't complain about that. But, Paulus, she trapped me; along with all the others, she trapped me. And the baby is the sign that tells me that. If he were here, I would be reminded of that every day. I cannot expect anybody else to understand, but that is what I think."

Paulus told Matti that Johann was resolute in his refusal to bring Karl to America. "I just don't think that it ought to be brought up. It just makes him upset. With his bad stomach he shouldn't have more burdens."

"What do I tell Marta? She wanted you to persuade Johann to send for Karl."

"I don't really know what you can tell her. I can only say that it will make trouble if she insists on talking about it."

"Couldn't you tell him that's wrong?" Matti said, raising her voice. "Oh, you men. Stubborn as mules."

"I am not saying I agree with Johann, but it is his life. I can't tell him what to do. He just gives a thousand reasons why it is not wise to bring the boy over here."

"He respects you. Couldn't you talk some sense into him. You could make him change his mind?"

"He is my friend. He has had a hard life in many ways. Now he is not at all well. I can't cause him more trouble. It would not be right."

"Well, so be it! I don't know what I will tell Marta."

The subject did not come up again. Johann's health deteriorated. He was able to work less and less at the furniture factory. He sat long hours in the kitchen of the house on Ninth Street.

One day Charles Steinauer came to the door.

"Weber, I come from the Town Council. We want you to stand for election as Town Treasurer next month."

Johann was completely flustered. "I am not sure I could do that."

"We talked it over. We know that you are an honest man, and smart. You could do the job just fine."

"But I haven't been able to work at the factory for weeks."

"We know that you haven't been well since the army. But you could do most of this job from your house. It is a matter of keeping the books, putting money in the Helvetia Bank when the taxes come in, and writing drafts to pay the bills. I doubt if it would take more than a few hours a week. You would come to the Town Council meetings every month to report."

"Well, I suppose I could do that. It wouldn't be like trying to work all day at the factory."

"Several of the men who served with you in the 60th said you would be a good man for this job. It pays $20 a month. That isn't much, but every little bit counts."

"If you all think I can do the job, I am willing to try."

"I want to take Karl to the photographer to have a picture to send to Marta and Johann. They have not seen him since he was a little child. They should know how he looks now; he is becoming a young man," August Wiesner said to Katerina.

"That is a good idea, but do we have money for something like that?"

"I don't think it costs a whole lot. I won't buy any *Tabak* for a few weeks."

August had persuaded Karl to go to the barber before they went to the photographer. Katerina insisted that he put on his best clothes, although they did not fit very well. She did not accompany them to the photographer's studio on the other side of Neuhaus.

"Here it is. Let's go in," August urged his sixteen year-old grandson.

The photographer, who called himself *Doktor Hals,* led them to his studio at the back of the house. Tall windows behind his camera let a good bit of daylight into the room. He had several large curtains picturing various scenes which could be arranged behind the subject. August watched as Karl chose a view with a columned corridor outlined in heavy drapes.

"Well, then, stand over here young man."

"My suit is too tight, can't you just take a picture of my face?"

"*Ja.* But I have another idea," Hals said. "Your grandpapa tells me that this is to go to your mama and papa in America. We want them to see what a fine man you are becoming. I have something that you might be interested in….One moment." He stepped into another room.

When he reappeared, he was carrying a uniform. "Here put this on. We'll make you look like a young prince."

Much of the reluctance Karl had been expressing melted away. He put on the uniform, with its silver buttons down the front of the tunic. Hals put a military cap on Karl's head and slung over his shoulders a great coat with silver epaulets. Then, stepping into the other room for a moment, he brought forth a gold handled sword with tassels. He began to pose his subject in front of the stately backdrop: standing tall and proud, his hands resting on the sword, which pointed on the floor in front of him.

"The light is good. Look over my shoulder…here. Now hold very still….very still."

Hals emerged from under the black hood at the back of his camera. Changing the plate holder, he said, "Now let's try one with a little smile. You looked awfully serious in the last one."

The session over, Hals said to August. I'll have the pictures ready by day after tomorrow. You can pick the one you want and I'll make the picture to send to America.

To Karl he said, "You are a good looking young fellow. Your folks will be very pleased. Your grandpapa told me that I took their picture just before they went to America."

"Is that so?" Karl, divested of his uniform, muttered.

After the town election Rabert said to Johann, "I am happy that you are our new treasurer. I know you'll do a good job."

"I am learning how to keep the books. My mother used to tell me that I was like her father, who was a teacher. I was good with figures. I am sorry she is not alive any longer, to know that I am a town official. She would be very proud."

The editor went on, "I wonder…I have a small desk in the back of the office that never gets used. Would you like to have it so you would have a place to do your bookkeeping? It wouldn't take up much space."

"That would be a big help. Marta would be so glad to get me off the kitchen table. I am always in her way."

"I'll have a couple of the fellows carry it over tomorrow. It isn't heavy."

"I am very proud to be an officer in the town. The only other time I had official responsibility was when they named me sergeant in our company. I was surprised both times. I never really thought of myself as a leader before."

"You are a bright fellow. You know how to get along with people."

"If I could just get my health back. I just don't have any strength. I walk to the bank or the post office and I have to rest for an hour."

"I am glad that you can be useful to the town without putting more strain on your health."

"I am really enjoying the work."

By the autumn of 1871 Johann's strength was slowly diminishing. It had been almost three years since he was able to work in the factory. Even his work as treasurer seemed to require more strength than he could muster.

"I am worried about you," Marta said. "You are getting so thin. Your legs are like sticks."

"I wish I could eat right. The food you put out for the children looks so good, but I just can't eat any more."

"I don't see where you get the strength to do what you do."

"I can't do that much any more. Even walking a few blocks is more than I can do."

"I'll go to the post office if it is too hard for you."

"I don't want that. If I can't go any more. I'll just resign as treasurer. I'll do it as long as I can."

"I could help. Even the few dollars they pay you helps buy food."

"I know that we're having a hard time. The money Julius sent after mother died is just about gone."

"I have tried to be very careful about spending."

"You do a good job managing the house on just a few dollars every month. We have the six dollars from the Soldier's Relief and twenty from the town salary. And your sewing brings in more."

"I have been thinking. I once was a good milliner. I could start making hats and bonnets right here. I'd need a little money to start buying some of the materials, but I think I could have a pretty good business."

"Is there anybody else in town making hats?"

"No. Everybody orders bonnets from a place in Evansville. I'm sure they would be glad to have a place right here where they could go to get their hats. I could get a couple of books like Fraulein had in Neuhaus. That would take care of the fancy hats. But mostly people will just want ordinary bonnets. I made so many of those, I could still make them in the sleep," Marta said with real enthusiasm.

Johann smiled, "You have enough energy for both of us. Bless your heart. Why don't you make a list of the materials you would need to start, and we'll see if we can order it from Evansville or Louisville."

"I'll just get a little at first, until we see if people will buy hats."

Before long Marta had a list of regular customers. Even pregnancies and birth of two more daughters did not interfere with her business. Emma was now old enough to watch over the younger children, while Marta worked at her hats. Johann spent a few hours each day keeping the town's books.

In the summer of 1874 Johann's health began to deteriorate rapidly. He ate very little, just drinking warm milk. Marta shared her worries with Matti.

"I don't know how he keeps going. He is becoming just skin and bones. If he tries to walk downtown, he has to turn back because he is so exhausted. He just sits in the kitchen and looks out the window."

"I'll admit, he doesn't look good. But I worry about you, too. Especially since you are carrying another baby. You look so tired."

"I worry about the baby. I really wasn't counting on another baby. It just happened. This is not the best time to be bringing another mouth to the table. Oh, Matti! What am I going to do? I always thought Johann would get over his sickness and we could get back to normal. But I think now that he is not going to make it. The last month has been bad for him. I'm so worried."

"*Liebchen*," Matti said, putting her arms around Marta, who began to sob. "I know it is hard. These have been terrible years for you."

"I feel so sorry for Johann. He just sits and looks out the window for hours. I know what he is thinking. He was always so sure that his dream of good times would come true, but things just keep getting worse."

"He would always talk about how a time would come soon when there would be plenty of good jobs."

"And when there were jobs, he was too sick to work. He always dreamed that we would be able to save enough to have our own business, like his brothers. He believed that if we came to America, he would be free to make his way. But things never worked. He used to be such a hard worker. It breaks my heart to see him so weak."

"Does he ever talk about it?"

"No. He just sits and looks out the window."

A few weeks later Johann did not get out of bed to start the fire in the cook stove, as he usually did.

"I am so tired. I think I'll just stay in bed for a while," he said.

"You rest. I'll get breakfast for the children. Once Emma and the older girls are off to school and I have the little ones settled, I'll come back and help you get up."

"That's all right. I'll just try to sleep a little longer. I am so tired."

"That will do you good."

When Marta came back to the bedroom an hour later, Johann was turned toward the wall. Only when she stood beside the bed, could she see the large bloodstain that covered the pillow. She touched him but his cold hand did not respond. Gathering the little children from the kitchen, she went as fast as she could to Matti's house.

Breathless, holding her prominent belly, she threw open Matti's kitchen door. The little children were crying, not understanding the obvious panic of their mother. Matti pushed her tousled hair out of her eyes.

"Come. Come to the house. Something has happened to Johann. I am so afraid."

Matti threw her shawl around her shoulders and picked up the two smallest girls.

"Should we send somebody for the doctor? I can call Maria from next door."

"I don't know who to call. You know, Dr. Brucker died last Friday. I heard that his son, Charles, has been seeing his patients for the last few weeks. He is awfully young and has been a doctor for only a year or two, but maybe he could come."

Matti dispatched her neighbor for the doctor and then hurried with Marta to her house.

The scene in the bedroom had not changed. It was obvious to her that Johann was dead. Matti put her arms around Marta, who was trying to embrace her children. Matti led them into the kitchen.

When they got back from the cemetery on the little hill just east of town, Matti and a group of neighbors gathered with Marta and her children in the house on Ninth Street. The Raberts were there and the Geyers, Max Blum and his wife, some friends from Co. A of the 60th Indiana. The women moved through the crowded rooms with cups of coffee and pieces of the pies they had brought. Marta sat in the parlor, surrounded by her children.

Charles Rabert stood and called for attention. "Friends, we are here because we have lost a man we loved and respected. Ever since the early days of Helvetia, I looked forward to the times he stopped at the office to talk. He was always interested in learning more--about America, about politics, about history.

"Some of you knew him well in the army. You saw him as a leader, choosing him as your sergeant. But, as I have heard a number of you say, you respected him because he always stood with you, not over you.

"We all came here at the end of a long voyage from our homeland. Now Johann is an immigrant beginning another new voyage. Many of us came to America...and to Helvetia, because we had a dream. Johann believed in that dream, even when things were not going well. He went to war because he wanted to keep the country strong so that the dream could come true. Even in the last years, when he was sick and increasingly weak, he held on the dream. That is something he leaves with us: the call to believe in the dream and to work to make it come true.

"Marta, we want you to know that you and Johann have good friends here in Helvetia. We will do everything we can to help you in a difficult time. Right, Gretchen? Right, Paulus and Matti? Right, Albrecht and Margareta? Right, Jakob Stocker? Right, Max Blum? All of us are here to stand by you."

"Thank you. I do thank you," was all Marta could say as she held her children close, her eyes filled with tears.

As Marta's time drew nearer, Matti stayed with her. The baby boy was born on the last day of the year, just two months after his father died.

"I am going to call him Johann," Marta said to her friend. "Even though he will never know his father, he can bear his name."

The trees were leafing out when Gretchen Rabert made her weekly visit to Marta, helping her with her reading and looking through the style books. She was one of Marta's best customers. Unlike most of the women in Helvetia, she had a sense of style. She had beautiful clothes, many sent to her from her parents in Cincinnati. She would come to Marta with a new suit or gown and go through the books of hats to find one suitable for the new clothes.

"I've been making plans to go for a visit back to Berlin. My grandfather wants me to come for a few months. Charles is willing for me to go. So I may need a new hat or two for the trip. I want to show them that we have some nice things over here too, even though they would have a hard time understanding life in Helvetia."

"You pick the one you want and I'll make you a masterpiece."

"I am so excited. Charles is already making the arrangements."

On Gretchen's next visit, after some serious hat planning, Marta swallowed hard several time and screwed up her courage to speak.

"I want to ask you something, but I'm afraid," she said haltingly.

"Go ahead. What is it you want to ask?"

"It is a favor...a huge favor."

"If I can do it, I'd be glad to."

"Well, I think I told you once how Johann and I left a son in *Schlesien* with my parents. I have wanted for years to bring him over to be with us. He is 20 years old now. Well, if we could arrange the details—would it be possible for him—to come back with you, so he doesn't have to make the trip alone? I have dreamed for years of him being with me again"

"That is a pretty big responsibility. I would really like to help. Let me talk to Charles."

"I think I have enough to pay for his way. I just want him to be with somebody good, who would see that he got here safely. I would be so grateful if you could help me get him here."

"I'll talk to Charles, and we'll see if we can work it out."

After Gretchen had left, Marta lit the lantern and went to the cellar. She stood on a box and reached up to a stone at the top of the foundation wall. She pulled the stone out and reached into the space behind it. Her small hand brought out a little bag holding five gold pieces.

She remembered how she had sewn the gold into Johann's trousers and into her petticoat before they left Europe. When they finally put the gold they had brought with them to Helvetia, converted into dollars, into the bank, she had secreted these five coins. Johann had never noticed, or if he had, never mentioned it. In their house on Twelfth Street and then on Ninth Street, she had found a safe hiding place for the coins.

There were times, particularly when Johann was in the army and she had such difficulty finding enough money to feed the family, when she was tempted to take the coins to buy food or clothes. But she always resisted. This was the money she had hidden for years, money with which to pay for Karl's voyage to America. If the money were ever spent for other purposes, she would have no hope of ever seeing him again. She put the coins back behind the stone, until it was time to give them to Gretchen to pay for Karl's ticket.

Gretchen Rabert left on the *Star Gray Eagle* on a bright spring morning. Marta and her children stood on the wharf boat with the editor as he said goodbye to his wife. Then Gretchen turned to Marta and held her close.

"Do not worry, little friend," Gretchen said, "I'll be back in July and I'll have your son with me."

"I count the days. You have my father's address? He will be waiting to hear from you, telling him when to bring Karl to Berlin for the trip to America. Dear Gretchen, you have made me a happy woman. I can never thank you enough."

"You take good care of your little brood, until I bring them their older brother. You watch out for her, Charles."

The steamer whistle signaled that it was time to cast off. Marta looked at Rabert with brimming eyes and said, "We will both be living for the day when we see the steamer coming back with Gretchen...and with Karl."

The days were filled with dreams for Marta. What would Karl look like? She had seen only the picture her father had sent a year ago. Karl stood erect and proud in a uniform of some sort. It was not an army uniform. He looked so elegant, so proud of himself.

She would be so happy to see him again after all those years. He looked strong. He would be such a help; a young man to help her with her eight other children. A young man would give the boys someone to look up to as they grew older. If he was handy like her father, he could do all those little jobs Johann used to do. Once he got rested up from his trip, he might even be able to get a job and help with the family expenses.

While the children were gathered around the supper table, Marta talked to them about their brother and how they would all be so happy to see him.

Every time Charles received a letter from his wife, he shared it with Marta. They both were happy to learn that she had gotten tickets to sail from Bremen on the second of July. It would take more than two weeks to land in New York and four or five more days on the train and steamboat to reach Helvetia. So they should be arriving before the end of July. Gretchen would send a message on the new telegraph when they arrived in Cincinnati, where they would get the next steamer down river.

Charles Rabert stood at the kitchen door with the telegram in his hand. "They are in Cincinnati. They will take a boat to Louisville and get the *Star Gray Eagle* to Helvetia. Gretchen thinks they should be here on Thursday."

"I can hardly wait. Two days more and I will see my son. I am so excited I can hardly breathe."

"We will both be happy to see the *Eagle* come around the bend. I will let you know if I hear any more."

No sooner had Rabert left when Matti came to the door.

Fanning her perspiring face Matti said, "I saw Rabert walking up here. I figured he had news about Karl's arrival."

"*Ja.* They come on Thursday. I am so excited that I haven't slept through the whole night for a week. The children are all excited too."

"I feel almost as excited as you do."

"Matti, what will he be like? He will not remember me at all. He will not know me. I haven't seen him since he was just a baby. It is going to be very strange."

"In a few days that will all go away. You'll feel like you have never been separated for all those years."

"I sure hope so. He won't even know what I look like. The only picture they had in Neuhaus was one we had taken just before we left for America. We never had a picture taken after that. I was twenty-three. Now I am a 42 year-old woman."

"He will soon know how much you have wanted him to be here for all these years. He will know how you sacrificed so that he could come over."

"I don't know how I can tell him that I wanted him to come and his father always argued against it. I do not want him to know that his father did not want him."

"He probably knows that you didn't have the money."

"But you know that in Germany they think everyone in America has lots of money. We didn't want to tell them how hard it was for us. Johann was a proud man."

"It may take a little time for Karl to get used to things here, but he will fit in very quickly. You'll see."

The dreamed-of reunion on the wharfboat was understandably a bit stiff and formal. As the paddle-wheeler tied up, Marta could see Gretchen with a young man beside her. She waved furiously. Then the gangplank came down and the stream of passengers came toward her. Rabert embraced his wife. Marta held out her arms to Karl. He came toward her very slowly and held out his hand to shake hers, bowing stiffly. Marta quickly introduced the older children whom she had brought to the dock, while Matti looked after the younger ones at home. As they walked off the dock and into the town, Marta somewhat tentatively put her arm around Karl's waist, and herded the other children ahead of them toward Humboldt Street. She looked up at him and said, "Wait until you see what we've cooked for you."

That evening over dinner Gretchen was talking with her husband about her visit with her grandparents and reporting on how things were in Berlin. She talked about the ocean voyages and compared it to their first coming to America.

Late in the evening she said, "You know, I am really worried about Marta's son. He is an odd young man. I thought at first it was just because I was a complete stranger to him, but he never did become friendly. In fact he was downright surly most of the time. I expected him to be interested in the trains and ships, the things we saw, the people we met on the ship.

"When we got to New York, we had a flare up. I made some innocent comments about how happy people were to get to America. He snapped back that this trip was not his idea, but that he had to come. I really was shocked. I know how Marta has spent everything she has to get him here. I bit my tongue and said that he would soon feel at home here. He hardly spoke to me for the rest of the trip. Poor Marta, if he treats her that way. It will kill her."

"She may be little, but she is strong."

"But she is so alone. There will be no strong man to stand up to this young fellow."

"I'll keep an eye on him. If he gets out of line, I'll talk some sense to him," he ran his finger down the dueling scar in his cheek. "Paulus has a lot of experience dealing with young people. He'll help too."

In the house on Ninth Street Marta served the chicken she had roasted, the first meat they had had in several months. She had shown Karl to the room that she had set aside for him. She helped him put his clothes in the dresser. Now in the circle around the table, she was trying to acquaint Karl with his new family. He talked with Emma, but ignored the younger children. He heaped his plate with chicken and potatoes and began to eat greedily. Marta tried to overlook that because he was the honored guest at this reunion, as she tried to pass out small portions to all the other children.

Marta and Emma got the younger children in their beds. She looked forward to a little time to talk with Karl. They sat at the kitchen table. It was so awkward to break the silence.

Finally Marta spoke. "I know I said it before, but I have looked forward to this day for so many years. Just to be able to see you. I am so happy."

Karl mouthed a large forkful of the pie Marta had set in front of him. "*Ja. Ja.*!" he said impatiently. "They told me that you always wrote about wanting me to come."

"I wanted so much to bring you along when we came all those years ago. But we were afraid that a baby could not stand the trip. I thought that we would be able to bring you in just a few years, but it never was possible until now." She reached out to touch his muscular arm. Tears filled her eyes. "But now you are finally here. You will like it. Helvetia is a nice city. You will get acquainted soon with some young men your age. My good friend, Paulus Frantz, the school teacher, knows all the young people and will help you get acquainted. You can get together with them at the *Turnhalle*. Oh, you will like it."

"We'll see," he mumbled.

"Tell me about my father and Katerina. How are they? I miss them too."

"They are all right, I guess....Just a couple of old people."

"They were so good to take care of you all these years. I am really thankful to them."

"They just sit around. I did not spend a whole lot of time at home."

Marta sensed that Karl didn't much want to talk. She thought: he is just tired and there is so much new to get used to. In a few days we can have better talks.

A few weeks later Paulus said to Matti, after a visit to Marta's, "I can't understand that young fellow. He is not interested in anything. I tried to introduce him to the Schreiber boy and to some of the young people down at the *Turnhalle*. He just says a few words to them, then walks away with his nose in the air."

"He is not very friendly. I tried to talk to him about his trip and he would just say a few words and close up. He just seems angry."

"What does he have to be angry about? Can't he understand how Marta sacrificed to get him over here?"

Matti shook her head and wiped her eyes. "She is crushed. She dreamed all these years of being reunited with her son, and now this."

"I feel like boxing his ears; that ingrate! Maybe I should have a straight talk with him, tell him what he is doing to Marta."

"Somebody is going to have to. It will have to be a man. It is obvious he wouldn't listen to a woman."

"If we could get him a job, it might help. The chair factory might be able to use him. They would probably give him work because he is Johann's son. Unless his attitude changes, he won't last long in any job."

After several conversations with Paulus and Matti Marta talked with Karl.

"Paulus talked with some of his friends who work at the chair factory. They said that they would have a job for you. It is the same place where your father worked."

Karl barely stirred in his kitchen chair. "I cannot do that kind of work in a factory. In Neuhaus. Grandfather never made me work. I wish I was back there."

"You can meet young fellows at the factory. You can do things with them."

"What do I have to talk about with these *Tölpel*? They are just a bunch of dumb farmers. They don't care a damn about what is going on in the homeland."

"Give them a chance! These are good people."

"I had good friends back in Neuhaus: Nicholas and Charles and Peter. But I had to leave them back there and come here where I don't know a soul."

Marta put her hand in his arm. "I want you to be happy here with us. We are your family. Would you do it for me?"

Karl stiffened visibly, "You aren't my family. A few letters a year from strangers did not make me part of a family."

Wiping tears from her cheeks, Marta looked hard at her son. "If only I could tell you how much I wanted you here, you wouldn't feel like a stranger. You have always been here—in my heart. Please don't make the pain I have felt for nineteen years worse. *Bitte! Bitte!*"

Karl made no gesture to comfort her. "Aww, I'll go to the chair factory to make you happy. But I am not a factory worker."

A few mornings later Karl set off for his first day of work, carrying his father's lunch pail. Max Blum saw him walking up to the factory and joined him.

He smiled as he said, "I knew your papa. We were in the army together. They told me you was comin' to work here."

"*Ja*," Karl responded. "I don't know anything about factories."

"I'll show you around. You'll get the hang of it real soon."

They walked into the paved yard at the side of the two storey brick factory. There were large stacks of lumber everywhere, carefully built up so air could circulate through the layers of boards.

Max said proudly, "Another month and all this wood will be chairs goin' down the river to make some little woman happy."

"*Ja*," Karl muttered.

"We eat our lunch out here when the weather is decent. You'll get to know some of the fellows. They are a good bunch to work with. Most of 'em knew your papa. He was a good man. Sometime I'll tell you about our time in the army."

"I know nothing about him. The last time he had anything to do with me I was a little baby in *Schlesien*."

"Here comes Greiner. He's the boss. He'll show you what he wants you to do…Hey, Otto, here's your new man. I'll see you at lunch time and introduce you to some of the fellows."

Karl trudged off to work every morning and trudged home every evening. Marta tried to encourage him with little success.

"They keep yelling at me to work faster," he grumbled. "I have to carry pieces of wood to the cabinet makers. 'Come on. More wood over here. *Mach' schnell!*' I am not going to run, just to make them happy. Nobody is going to order me around like that."

"Once you get on to it, it won't be so hard. Your father had good friends who worked with him there."

"It is so stupid. Any idiot can do what they have me doing. It doesn't take brains to carry boards around. I hate it!"

A few days later Marta was surprised to see Karl coming down the street in the early afternoon. He kicked a stone along Ninth Street.

"What are you doing here at this time of day? Are you sick?"

"I quit! Old man Greiner kept telling me to bring the boards faster. I wasn't going to carry them three at a time. I am no slave!"

"…Now what will you do? "

"Well, for today I am going fishing." Karl got his pole from the back porch and walked sullenly toward the river.

The next months were filled with many days fishing, interrupted occasionally by a few weeks at a new job: first at the Deckert's planing mill, then at Goffinet's store. Marta went to her old friend.

"Matti, I am at my wit's end. Karl has lost another job. He works a few weeks and then walks away from the job. Every time I think he'll stay with the job, bring home his pay. But, no. He comes home and goes fishing."

548

"I can't figure that young man out. He has everything to be thankful for, and yet he throws it all away. I hate to say it, Marta, he is lazy—a lazy *Kerl*."

"I try to understand. I suppose my father never made him work because he was sorry for the boy whose parents lived on the other side of the world. They gave him whatever they could and he got used to it. He expects everyone to do what pleases him."

"Well, he can't expect you to do that for him. You have your other children to care for. He is old enough to be helping you, not giving you pain."

"I hoped that he would earn money to help with the family. But, no, he can't work--or he won't work. He's rather sit alone by the river and wait for the fish to bite. Oh, Matti, what can I do?"

"Tell him to grow up and be a man, that's what I'd say."

Marta paced the kitchen floor, waiting for Karl. She heard the rattle of his fishing pole as he leaned it against the back of the house. When he put his foot on the back porch, she stood squarely in the middle of the kitchen doorway.

"I want to talk with you, *Junge!*" she said with all the authority she could command as a small woman. "Sit down there on the wood box!"

Karl slumped down on the box, pushing his hands into his pockets. He looked surprised because this was the first time since his arrival his mother had raised her voice to him.

Standing in front of him, her hands on her hips, she looked him hard in the eye, trying to keep the tremor from her voice. "I just don't know what to do," she began slowly. "Year after year, oh how I looked forward to the great happiness of having my son with me. But I don't see any happiness. You have no joy being here. You never smile. You just go off by yourself to the river or sit around the house doing nothing."

Karl looked at her from the wood box, barely lifting his face. "What's there for me to be happy about?"

"*Ach*, you don't try! If you stayed with a job for more than a week, if you got acquainted with some of the young fellows in the *Turnverein*, things would be happier for you. If you could just feel part of the family...."

"You say I spend too much time at the river. Well, it's one place I don't have kids running all over."

"You can't talk that way," Marta protested, eyes flashing. "They are your sisters and brothers....I had dreams of their older brother helping me take care of them, becoming the man of the family...."

Karl interrupted, "I was thinking the other day....You have that little stable out in back. If you could get it cleaned out and fixed up a little, I could live out there."

"I wish you would just stay here in the house."

"I hate the house!" He kicked the wood box.

Marta shook her head sadly. "I just don't have the money to do much to fix up that little barn. If you want to work at it, we'll try to make it fit to live in. We'd have to get a little stove for the winter. Maybe Paulus or one of your father's friends could help us."

"They will do what you ask."

Karl continued to sulk. "The sooner I can move out there, the better." He stood up to leave the porch.

"You stay right here, Karl. I have more to say to you." Marta said firmly. She was resolved to try to clear the air. "You are going to listen to the story of what happened after we left Neuhaus to come to America. Your father came to this country with a dream of a good life. He worked so hard and everything he did was to make his dream to come true. He believed that it would—almost to the very last. That kept him going. I wish I could tell you how many times things got very bad—no jobs, money running very low, hard times, the terrible war. In spite of all that, he hung on to his dream."

Karl did not respond.

Marta put her hand on his shoulder. "I wish you could have known him. He never gave up his dream. Even when things were very hard, he held on to that dream; no matter what, he held on to that dream."

Karl stood to look out into the growing darkness. He shrugged, "Well, that may be, but *Ich bin ein Einwanderer mit keinem Traum.* I am a immigrant without a dream." He walked slowly into the house to his bed..

EPILOGUE

It was past midnight. The fire in the cook stove had gone out. Marta pulled her shawl around her shoulders as she sat in the kitchen rocking chair. She had turned down the coal oil lamp, barely lighting the room. Deep in thought, she stared straight ahead, occasionally wiping her eyes with her apron.

Ach, Johann, if only I could talk with you, she thought... But I can only talk to myself:.. what am I going to do?.. My heart is breaking, and there is so little I can do about it... *Without a dream*, the boy said... How awful!.. What pain there must be in that young heart! Tears ran down her cheeks, and she did not bother to wipe them away... For a moment I hated him, my own son..... All the love for him that has been in my heart for all these years just drained away—but just for a minute. I had no right to hate him... It is not his fault

When I think of the ways dreams shape our lives!.. All those years at home, working for the Bauers, working for *Fraulein*, I had a dream... I would fall in love with a good man, I would be married, I would have a family... I would have an easier life... As I made hats I day-dreamed about what a wonderful life I would have... And then I met you, Johann, and the dream became stronger... It seemed more real... I had found the man to love and to make a new life with... I was never so happy in my whole life... I felt like a swallow soaring and swooping through the sky; I felt like a rosebud opening into a beautiful flower... My dream was coming true!

I know that you, Johann, had a strong dream too. You talked about your dream more than I did... You dreamed of becoming a strong grown man, making your own decisions, taking care of yourself,.. being free to guide your own life... That dream took you out of Endigen to work for

Wagner…and brought you to me… That dream took us across the ocean to America… That dream took us to Helvetia. You wanted to be in a country being shaped by big dreams… Saving that dream even took you to the war…Everyone who stepped off that boat with us was following a dream. Instead of walking the same road for generation after generation-people were making a new life… I can remember how excited you were telling me about Helvetia after your first trip… You could hardly wait to get to the place where a whole new town was rising up from the forest… There would be a house of our own, there would be good jobs… and a chance to save enough to start your own business… I did ask you once if you weren't afraid of waking up from your dream.

Life has a way of making us change our dreams…I loved you, Johann, and in time, I think, you came to love me…My girlish dreams had to grow up just like I did…Things don't always turn out the way we dreamed… *So geht's… So geht's,* she sighed…Now you are dead,.. but I have our children…*Ja…* my children…She gave out a long sigh.

She rocked for a while, closing her eyes for a few minutes. *Ach,* Johann, life does sometime make dreaming so hard…It's like walking through deep mud, like in the early days here in Helvetia…Your boots get heavier and heavier, until you can hardly keep walking,..but then you hit a solid place and it's easier…I feel like I've been walking in the mud for the last years… I'm ready for the solid place. I am so ready.

For so many years I dreamed of having Karl come to be with us in Helvetia…From the time we came to Helvetia, I kept asking you if it was not time to bring him over…You always had a reason why we could not bring him now…How different life might have been if he had come when we got the house built…He would have grown up with his family. He would have known that we loved him…Maybe I didn't try hard enough to make that dream come true…

But finally the time came and the dream could come true…From the time Frau Rabert talked about going back to visit Germany, the spark of my dream fanned into flame…As soon as we got plans made for him to come, I dreamed of him sitting with his family at the supper table. I suppose I dreamed that he would fill your empty chair, Johann…I don't mean that really, but I did dream of having a man to help me raise the children. I dreamed of being able to talk with him the way we used to talk. I dreamed of having some wages coming every week, so we wouldn't have to scratch so hard for everything.

I wept when Karl said he had no dream...For a minute I almost yelled that I didn't have a dream any more either...But that can't be true; it can't!...I doubt if I will ever be able to help him dream...It may be too late... But I must help our other children to dream.

One of the great sadnesses of my life was to know how much you dreamed of a good life, free, making your own way, and how little of that dream came true...You should be honored for the way you never gave up that dream, not until very near the end...You always kept the hope that things would get better.

It took real courage to hold on to that dream when everything got in your way: your disagreements with your brothers, the trouble finding jobs when we first got to America, the war, your bad health after the army... You never gave up,.. You just kept trying to make the dream come true... How hard you tried!...You'd drag yourself off to the chair factory when you were so weak, but you never complained.

Marta continued to rock and think as the lamp sputtered and went out...It was a great pain that your dream and my dream pulled against each other...I never really understood that...I felt I had to put your dream first because you were dreaming for both of us...My dream of having Karl with us would not have changed your dream that much...I always thought it would be part of your dream of a new life in a new land......

I am not just making excuses for Karl... No, we left him in Neuhaus with the seed of a dream for him to come to us,.. but for years we did not make that dream come true...Well, I tried,.. but not hard enough...She sighed. No wonder he doesn't believe in dreams. That boy was helpless to make the dream of coming to live with his mama and papa come true. Only we could have done that... We, you and I, worked to get to our dreams, but Karl could do absolutely nothing.

I never really understood why you didn't want Karl to come, Johann ...I guess you were waiting for your dream to come true—so your son would be proud of you..

Marta stopped her slow rocking and walked to the window, staring out into the black night. When our dreams do not work out, what can we do?..Give up? Get bitter and angry? Or help somebody else to dream?...She stood as tall as a small woman can.

ACKNOWLEDGEMENTS

Supplementing a small collection of family letters and journals, my understanding of the immigrant experience was broadened by *News from the Land of Freedom*, a collection of German immigrant correspondence, edited by Walter Kamphoefner, Wolfgang Helbich, and Ulrike Sommer, published by Cornell University in 1991.

I am grateful for the help of librarians at the Hart County Historical Society, Munfordville, KY, the Tell City Historical Society, Tell City, IN, and The United States Army Military History Institute, Carlisle, PA.

Also helpful were the following resources:

De La Hunt, Thomas, *Perry County: A History*. Indianapolis: W. K. Stewart, 1916.
History of Warwick, Spencer, and Perry Counties. Chicago: Goodspeed Brothers & Company, 1885.
Maurer, Wm., *A Historical Sketch of Tell City, Indiana, 1858-1917*.
Winslow, Hattie Lou and Moore, Joseph H., *Camp Morton 1861-1865, Indianapolis Prison Camp*. Indianapolis: Indiana Historical Society, 1940.

Paul Irion is Professor Emeritus of Pastoral Psychology at Lancaster Theological Seminary in Lancaster, PA. Priot to his retirement he published six professional books and textbooks. This novel is a retirement project growing out of his long-term avocational interest in history, genealogy, immigration and the Civil War. He lives with his wife Mary Jean in the Willow Valley Retirement Community near Lancaster.